I0607278

THE OUTLAWS

OR

EPPING FOREST.

Profusely Illustrated.

1873

London:

HOGARTH HOUSE, 32, BOUVERIE STREET, E.C.

HOGARTH HOUSE LIBRARY.

BOUVERIE STREET, FLEET STREET, E.C.

The following is a list of the REVISED EDITIONS of the Hogarth House Works, published in Volumes, bound in Illustrated Covers, also in Penny Weekly Numbers, all in print, and ready for immediate delivery:—

TOM WILDRAKE'S SCHOOLDAYS.

In Five Vols., price 1s. each; also complete in one Vol. as a Prize Edition, and handsomely bound in cloth and gold, price 5s. 6d.—This celebrated School Story was the first of its class ever issued in weekly numbers; and in the face of numerous imitators it still holds the foremost place. The story is a faithful narrative of the life of a high-spirited young Englishman at school—showing what he did and how he did it, and what he learnt and its influence on his after-life. The story is carried on through Tom Wildrake's adventurous career, down to the time when he felt himself entitled to rest on the laurels he had so nobly won by his many brave deeds during the heartrending Indian Mutiny and in Australia and elsewhere.

YOUNG TOM'S ADVENTURES

In Europe, Asia, Africa, and America.

Complete, price 1s. 6d.—This is a sequel to "Young Tom's Schooldays," and narrates his hair-breadth escapes and adventures both with wild men and animals in the four quarters of the globe.

THE BOYS OF BIRCHAM SCHOOL.

Complete, price 1s. 6d.—This story claims to be the first school story that ever appeared in a periodical solely devoted to boys. For dramatic incident and genuine fun it has never yet been equalled.

CHARLIE AND TIM AT SCARUM SCHOOL.

Complete, price 1s.—This story of the life of two boys, who are sworn chums, at school, has always been a popular one with our young friends; showing, as it does, how a sincere friendship may be formed at school which may have lasting effects on our boys' after lives. Every schoolboy should read it.

CHARITY JOE; or, from Street Boy to Lord Mayor.

Complete, price 1s.—This is the true story of an outcast, who, by his honesty and indomitable will, rose to be the Chief Magnate of the First City in the World. His adventures at school, and, accompanied by his dog Toby, with a travelling showman, should be read by every lad who wishes to know what an English boy can do, no matter how humble his first start in life, or how great his temptations.

OUT ON THE WORLD.

Complete, price 1s.—This history goes direct to the heart of the reader, being a story of real life, depicting the troubles and trials of two children who were stolen from their home by gipsies. Little Jack's brave defence of his fellow-prisoner, Lilly—He shoots at Tinker Tom—They escape and tramp to London—Their adventures en the way; they join a troupe of tumblers and become street-players—They are recognised by the gipsies—The fair—The booth on fire; and, after many narrow escapes, they are captured by Tinker Tom, who cruelly ill-uses them—They are traced by the players to Tinker Tom's den—They are followed and risk their lives to save the children from a horrible death—The children are restored to their parents through the skill of the detective police, and well reward those who assisted them in the days of their adversity. This work is very graphically illustrated with numerous Wood Engravings.

YOUNG TOM'S SCHOOLDAYS.

Complete, price 1s. 6d.—This is the story of the life of Tom Wildrake's son at school; and, although complete in itself, should be read by everyone who has read "Tom Wildrake," as all the readers' old friends reappear in its pages.

RAGS AND RICHES: A Story of Three Poor Boys.

Complete, price 1s.—The illustrations to this work are from the inimitable pencil of Phiz (H. K. Browne), who did so much towards rendering popular many of the works of Charles Dickens. So faithfully is the story of these poor boys told, and so realistic are the scenes described, that it has been pronounced by competent critics the best story of London life published since "Oliver Twist."

FRANK FEARLESS; Or, the Cruise of the Firebrand.

Complete, price 2s. 6d.—We doubt whether for fidelity of description and stirring incidents this magnificent sea story has been equalled since the days of Captain Marryat. The story of the misjudged hero's long and troubled conflict, not only with the pirates, but with his own mistaken countrymen, should be read by every true British boy who can lay its lessons to heart and profit by them.

MIDSHIPMAN TOM; Or, the Cruise of the War Cloud.

Complete, price 2s.—This is the faithful narrative of the life of a Midshipman on board a Man-of-War, and shows the trials, temptations, and prizes incident to the career of a boy who wears the uniform of our gracious Queen at sea. Though strikingly sensational, the element of fun is not omitted.

BLACK-EYED SUSAN; or Pirates Ashore.

Complete, price 1s.—The pathetic and stirring story of William and Susan is here told in a way which is bound to enlist the sympathies of all who are possessed with a true Briton's love of adventures at sea.

THE BRIGANDS OF THE SEA; Or, the Sailor Highwayman.

Complete, price 1s. 6d.—Money Marks, the hero of this most extraordinary romance of the sea, is no imaginary character, and nearly all the soul-stirring incidents herein described are founded on fact. The career of this world-famed highwayman of the sea is one of the most sensational narratives ever offered to the reading public. It is profusely illustrated by an eminent artist.

THE WAR CRUISE OF THE MOSCA; Or, the Six Fighting Mids.

Complete, price 1s.—In this Stirring Story of the Sea, the talented author takes a wide departure from his school and military stories, and shows us that though he is familiar with the cavalry sabre, he can give us a vigorous and truthful account of the life of those whose lot it is to wield the sailor's cutlass, and fight their country's battles on the boundless deep.

FOR HONOUR; or, the Young Privateer.

Complete, price 1s. 6d.—This powerfully written story of the life of a Privateer during one of the most stirring periods of England's Naval History, is a marvellous combination of the sensational and the humorous. No British boy can read the sayings and doings of Monkey Jack and Crikey without a laugh, and no British boy can read the heroic actions of the young Privateer without feeling a thrill of exultation that he also belongs to that glorious Empire on whose domains the sun never sets.

ADRIFT ON THE SPANISH MAIN.

Complete, price 1s.—This Story of the old Buccaneers carries us back to the glorious days of good Queen Bess—the days when England settled for all time her right to the title of "Empress of the Seas."

ALL'S WELL.

Complete, price 1s.—The story under the title of the above popular seaman's cry is full of pathos, sensation, and humour. In dramatic situations it is probably superior to any story of the sea ever written. With each copy is presented gratis a Magnificent Portrait of the greatest naval hero of modern days—Horatio, Lord Nelson.

SHEET-ANCHOR JACK.

Complete, price 1s.—A powerfully-written narrative of the life of a jolly jack tar "before the mast," and should be read by every true English boy.

THE PIRATE'S ISLE; Or, the Wonders of the Deep.

Complete, price 1s.—This is a story of adventure, both on sea and land. Full of sensation, pathos, and fun.

THE BRITISH BOY SAILOR.

Complete, price 2s.—A faithful narrative of the life of a poor boy on board a British Man-of-War, during the glorious days of Nelson, showing what a British boy's pluck can do to raise himself superior to circumstances.

WILLIE GRAY; Or, the Wreck of the Polar Star.

Complete, price 1s.—In this spirit-stirring story the entranced reader is carried into strange countries, and through strange perils by flood and field; but, from first to last, the interest is so well sustained that those who once take up the book are unable to lay it down until every line has been perused.

HOGARTH HOUSE, BOUVERIE ST., FLEET ST., LONDON, E.C.

CONTENTS.

CONTENTS.—*Continued.*

THE OUTLAWS
OF
EPPING FOREST.

"TOUCHING HIS HORSE GENTLY WITH HIS HEEL, BATSWING BOUNDED OVER A DITCH!"

CHAPTER I.
THE BET AT THE CLUB.

"SHE's the most beautiful girl in the world," cried Sir Arthur Bowring, "and as pure as she is beautiful."

"Nonsense, Sir Arthur; you are always mad when a woman is in the way."

"You may say what you like, but I am ready to back up my opinion with a heavy bet."

The speakers were a party of young men who had met together at a splendid club in Piccadilly, and were lazily sipping their wine and talking scandal.

Sir Arthur Bowring was a tall, slim young man, or about twenty-five, with a merry twinkle in his eye and a good open countenance. The rest of the company was composed of fashionably dressed young men, all of whom seemed to have taken as much wine as was good for them.

"Tut, man," cried another, "I don't believe that either women or horses are worth a farthing unless they have blood."

"Neither do I," laughed another, "for both creatures without blood would look remarkably ghostly."

"Laugh away, gentlemen, as much as you like," cried Sir Arthur, "but I will still maintain that the maid I mention is the most beautiful one in all England."

"Nonsense, Sir Arthur," cried one unhealthy youth in whose face dissipation had set her stamp; "you can't be serious to talk in this way of a common country girl."

"A poor farmer's daughter," cried another.

"Worse, a mere peasant," exclaimed a second.

"With rough, coarse hands from milking," laughed a third.

"'Fore Gad! Sir Arthur," exclaimed a fourth, "you are the most impossible fellow out; you've always got some Phillis in your eye. Love with you seems to be an incurable disease."

"Nay, there, my lord, you're wrong," said Sir Arthur. "I am not in love, I almost wish I were. Still I maintain that she is the finest damsel in all England, and here I drink a bumper to the Maid of Epping."

"Here's with you in that," cried one of the young men; "I'll drink to any woman so long as there's good wine to be had."

"Fore Gad! so will I," cried Lord Fitzboodle, jumping up.

"Well, then, gentlemen, fill your goblets up to the brim," cried Sir Arthur: "bumpers, gentlemen, bumpers; for she whose health we drink is worthy of them. There must be no heel taps in such a case. Now are you all charged, gentlemen?"

"All!" was shouted out as the young men sprang to their feet, goblets in hand.

"Then here's to the health of Mistress Alice Landon, the Maid of Epping!"

"The Maid of Epping!" chimed in the young men, clinking their glasses together, and then tossing off the wine.

"May I seek to know what is the cause of this enthusiasm?" asked a gentleman who had just entered the room.

"Ah! Redfern," exclaimed Lord Fitzboodle, "glad to see you; fore Gad! sit down and have some wine, old fellow."

Lord Redfern was a tall, square-built man, of about thirty or thirty-five, with long black hair, small sharp eyes that cast evil glances on every one. His nose was long and red, plainly showing its owner's predilection for the bottle. His hands and feet were large, and coarse blotches covered the former. His cheeks were puffy from intemperance, whilst the roundness of his stomach showed that he was not indifferent to the good things of this life.

"Need you ask what is the cause of this merriment when Sir Arthur Bowring gives the toast? 'Tis woman, lovely woman, to be sure."

"Is Sir Arthur such a gay Lothario that no woman can escape him?" demanded Redfern.

"Not I, my lord," said Sir Arthur, "but, had you seen the lass of whom I speak, I wager you would judge me right."

"What complexion is she?"

"White, with a roseate tint, as when the evening sun in winter reddens the hills of snow."

"Her hair?"

"Fine and soft, as a spider's thread, but spun in gold."

"Her eyes?"

"Blue as the heavens, and like them filled with truth."

"Her teeth?"

"Pearls; pearls set in those sweet ruby rows, her lips."

"Her voice?"

"Low and sweet as the summer wind when stealing over an Æolian harp. But, in one word, she is perfection. Words cannot paint her many beauties, man cannot dream her wondrous purity."

"Ah!" sighed Lord Fitzboodle, languidly, "she is an angel."

"Better!" cried Lord Redfern, sardonically, "she is a woman!"

"And how do you make that better?" asked Sir Arthur.

"Because she can be won."

"There you are wrong, Redfern; not ice itself is colder than is she."

"Perhaps so—to those who know not how to woo."

"What mean you by that?"

"Why, that had I met this fair maiden, I would have wooed and won her," said Redfern, biting his nails.

"Ha! ha! ha!" shouted the young men, looking at the speaker's ugly face, "Redfern for ever!"

"Laugh as you please, gentlemen, but I swear I would have done so. May I ask, Sir Arthur, how, and when, you met this damsel?"

"Decidedly: her father is a farmer, residing in a small farmhouse some two miles from Epping, just on the border of the forest, and her name is Alice."

"Alice what?"

"Alice Landon."

"A pretty name, truly; and, could we trust your description, a pretty girl."

"A marvel."

"Would that I could meet one like her," murmured a handsome young fellow in a languid manner. "I'd give a thousand pounds for such an one."

"Bah," exclaimed Sir Arthur, springing from his chair, "I cannot bear to hear you fellows speak of women thus. To me they are so holy, that to breathe their names in ought but reverence seems blasphemy."

"What!" cried Redfern, chuckling, "may we not descant upon the marvellous beauties of this wondrous girl?"

"You, of course, can do as you like, my lord, replied Sir Arthur, coldly; "of course, I cannot prevent you; but I can prevent my ears being insulted by listening to such talk."

"And how?" demanded Redfern.

"By leaving you. Gentlemen, I wish you good night."

Bowing to the company, and casting anything but a pleasant look on Redfern, he left the room.

"Sir Arthur is deeply bitter," said the handsome young man who had expressed his desire to possess such a beauty as Alice. "I wonder whether it is nice to be in love."

"Sir Arthur is a fool," growled Redfern, aside to the last speaker. "Look you, Lord Harry Leslie, he knows no more the way to win a woman than a boy of fifteen. Now you do understand these things. A thousand pounds would buy this jade with ease."

"Do you think so?" said the young man lazily. "If she's like what Bowring says, I'm sure I'd give it."

Lord Redfern looked down at his indolent pupil and smiled.

Lord Henry Leslie was immensely rich, and for that reason had been taken under the patronage of Lord Redfern, who was terribly poor.

Redfern had led his young friend into all sorts of dissipation, managing by these means to sap his mind and strength, and get him into his power at the same time.

Easily led, Leslie had dropped into the trap almost directly, and Redfern now lived on him constantly.

Of course he could not take the money without seeming either to do something for it, or appearing to win it at cards, dice, or by wagers.

The latter was the favourite way; for Lord Henry was too indolent to care for gambling to any extent. Wagers he did not object to, as they always were made so that the trouble should devolve on Redfern, and that the result in either case should be agreeable to Lord Henry.

"I would willingly bet you a thousand pounds that before a week is out the damsel is yours."

"Indeed, but it would be a load of trouble."

"Think of the triumph it would be over Sir Arthur Bowring."

"Yes, so it would—but then the trouble?"

"Pshaw, Leslie; you are too indolent. But I'll bet you two thousand pounds that the girl is yours without trouble. Now, is it agreed?"

"It is; the bet to be decided within the week."

"Done!"

"Done!" replied the other, with a grin.

"What's up now?" cried out one of the company. "Another bet, Leslie, eh? You are sure to lose. Redfern always wins."

"Not so sure this time," replied Leslie.

"What is the bet, then?"

"That I bring the beautiful Alice Landon to Leslie's house within a week," said Redfern.

"Capital!" cried the others. "Here is to your success."

"And my revenge!" muttered Redfern, as he emptied his glass.

CHAPTER II.
"£500 REWARD!"

On the morning after the events related in our last chapter, a red-haired youth dressed in the garb of an ostler might have been seen leaning against a horse-trough that stood opposite a wayside country public-house situated at the foot of Stamford Hill.

His vest—coat he had not any—was a bright red with gilt buttons; his cord breeches were much too loose for him, and his coarse blue stockings were filled with holes.

His shirt sleeves were rolled up as far as they would go, and a red handkerchief was twisted carelessly round his bull neck.

Jerry Blinker—such was this individual's name—did not look a prosperous person; still there was a merry look about him that showed that care sat lightly upon him.

With hands plunged deeply into his breeches pockets, whistling a doleful tune, Jerry Blinker, as we said before, leant against the horse-trough, and gazed at a bill which had just been stuck against the walls of the hostlery.

The bill he was reading ran as follows:—

£500 REWARD.

"Whereas a certain highwayman known by the name of Batswing, has, on numerous occasions, stopped, waylaid, robbed and maltreated many of his Majesty's subjects, and has aided and abetted a band of robbers, which it is believed now infest Epping Forest—in committing great depredations in the surrounding country, the above Reward will be given to any person, or persons, who shall deliver him safely to the custody of the Governor of one of his Majesty's prisons; the reward to be paid on the conviction of the aforesaid Batswing.

"A reward of £200 will be given to any one who will deliver the said Batswing up DEAD to the Governor of Newgate.   "By order, &c."

"A wery pretty bill, and wery well worded," said Jerry, "but I guess it will take them all their time to catch the Bat. Lord! what a feller he is! He's here and there and everywhere afore you can turn round. Still it can do no harm to give him warning of this. Likewise to let him know that Lord Clumbers' plate is being moved into London; he may do some business with it."

Whistling the same doleful ditty he walked up the road a little way, then turning down a lane came upon a blacksmith's shop, from which came the merry cling of the hammer, mingled with the still merrier sound of the smith's voice.

"He's 'ard at work," said Jerry. "I wonder what he's a singing now." He listened and heard the following song:—

"Oh Jerry Noakes he was so short,
    Just four foot and no bigger;
But yet he rode a fust rate horse,
    And nimbly pulled a trigger.
        Ri too ral loo ral loo ral loo,
            Ri too ral loo ral lay,
        He'd rob the people right and left,
            And then he'd cut away."

"Blest if he ain't always a singing," said Jerry; "there he goes again. I do believe he sings in his sleep."

Again the voice of the smith rang out rich and clear:—

"Full many a traveller he has stopped,
    And relieved them of their cash, sirs;
But Jack Ketch grabbed poor Jem at last,
    And pretty soon settled his hash, sirs.
        Ri too ral loo ral, &c., &c."

"That's a pretty song, too," said Jerry. "If he sings that to most of his customers, I should think it made them feel particularly comfortable."

"What are you a looking in that way for?"

The smith, who had heard the approach of Jerry, chose to resent this criticism of his singing, and only replied in another song:—

"I'd sooner be a soldier, a sailor, or a tinker,
    Than be that thieving rascal whom folks call Jerry
        Blinker."

"Thank you for nothing," said Jerry, "but I've news that will make you sing on the other side of your mouth."

"Why, is that you, Jerry?" cried the smith, as if he had not known the ostler was there. "Blest if you don't get uglier every day."

"Stash that," said Jerry. "You must let the Bat know that the hue and cry is out against him. Five hundred reward if he is taken alive, and two hundred if he is taken dead."

"Phew!" whistled the smith, "that's pretty strong. He must hear of that."

"Yes: and as he may need money you may as well tell him that old Lord Clumber is going to bring all his plate in his carriage by the north road."

"Who told you that?" demanded the smith.

"Why one of the grooms as was a riding on to town on business. I had a drop of beer with him, and tapped him at the same time."

"That's good news, but the t'other ain't. I can't make up my mind how the Captain's to get out o' this scrape."

"Some people aint got no minds to make up," said Jerry.

"Is that your case?" demanded the smith.

"Newgate will be your case in a precious little time," replied Jerry. "Come be off and don't stand curry-combing your 'air with your finger nails in that awful manner."

The smith took off his apron, and putting on a velveteen jacket and fur cap, winked at Jerry, and walked down the lane singing:

"O what for poverty should a man care,
    If saddled and bridled he has a good mare;
And of jolly horse pistols a nice-looking pair.
Whilst gentlefolks jewels on their persons will wear
    For his use or abuse and his dandified air."

"Sing away," said Jerry, "but if you don't tell the Captain in time I would not stand in your boots, although they were top boots. I must get back to the inn, or I shall get toko from that lovely but somewhat violent female, Mistress Wapshaw, landlady of the Birdcage."

Saying which he hurried back to the inn.

CHAPTER III.

THE ABDUCTION AND ASSASSINATION.

Lord Redfern lost no time in putting his scheme for carrying off Alice into execution.

In those days might was most frequently right. The opulent and lacivious noblemen gave way to their passions and committed crimes with impunity, escaping the punishment they deserved only through their wealth and power, whilst the poor man received the severest punishment for the lightest offences.

Procuring a worn-out old horse, Lord Redfern disguised himself as a well-to-do tradesman, and mounting the hack, rode off to Epping, and soon managed to discover old Landon's farm.

Having convinced himself that he was not mistaken in the place, he rode silently on until he had penetrated some way into the forest; here he pulled up, and, dismounting, drew a pistol from his pocket and deliberately shot his horse through the head.

He next drew his sword, and taking his hat from his head cut it through the crown with one blow. Afterwards he pierced his coat in all directions, and finally inflicted a slight wound in his own arm.

Bestowing a kick to the lifeless body of the poor horse, Lord Redfern walked slowly away until he reached the skirts of the forest, then breaking into a run, until he reached Landon's farm, where screaming loudly for help he fell exhausted by the door.

"Why, what's the matter with the man?" said an old greyheaded man who opened the door.

"Oh, help! help! help! I am murdered," cried Redfern in heartrending accents.

"Merciful heaven!" exclaimed a sweet female voice, "who could have done this?"

Redfern took one hasty glance at the speaker, and knew at once that she was the beautiful Maid of Epping.

"Oh, for the love of heaven," groaned the deceiver, "take me in and succour me, I have been set upon by highwaymen, who shot my horse, and maltreated me because I defended myself. See! see!" he cried, "I bleed to death, I bleed to death."

"Nay," replied the honest farmer, "the wound is but a scratch. But come in and rest yourself. A tankard of ale will soon set you to-rights, or my name is not Landon."

Lord Redfern needed no further invitation, but getting to his feet as if with the greatest difficulty, staggered into the cottage, where he fell into a chair and groaned piteously.

"Come, come," said the old farmer as he placed a foaming tankard of ale upon the table, "there is the draught that will cure all ailments. Drink, and then let us know how all this happened."

Redfern took a deep draught of the liquor, and then commenced. "I am but a poor dealer in cloth goods, and this morning was on my way from Sawbridgeworth, where I had taken money, to London."

"Have you lost your money?" inquired the farmer.

"No, good sir; by the help of Heaven and my own courage I saved that. However, when I arrived at this horrid forest I put my tired steed to a quick trot, for I like not such places. But before I had ridden far, four highwaymen pounced upon me demanding my money or my life."

"Was the leader a man dressed in black with a long cloak?"

"Aye, that he was—a tall, gaunt-looking fellow."

"It was Batswing I'll be bound," cried old Landon.

"It may have been. But to return to my story. I drew my pistol and fired at one"—here he produced the pistol he had discharged—"then one fired at me, and as you see, the bullet passed through my coat; then another shot my horse through the head, and of course I fell with my poor steed to the ground."

"The murdering villains!" cried the farmer. "How did you escape?"

"Aye! that they were. Drawing my sword I fought my way through them, though, as you perceive, my hat is nearly cut in twain, and my clothes are pierced in divers places. At length I reached the open country, and cried aloud for help; on this the robbers fled, and I ran to this place for shelter."

"You did well," replied the farmer, "for I will protect any honest man against such ruffians, though it cost me my life. You're safe now under Robert Landon's roof."

"Landon!" said Redfern, starting, "Landon! I surely have heard that name before."

"I doubt that," replied the farmer, laughing, "for I am but a poor farmer. But come, Alice, 'tis past our dinner hour. Prepare the meal; doubtless our friend will join us."

Of course Redfern was only too pleased, and after the dinner was finished he declared that his bones ached so that he could not move; so the kind old farmer pressed him to stay all night. Time passed on: Redfern amusing the old man with different tales about London, until after supper the farmer fell asleep.

Placidly the old man slept: such a sleep as only the good and pure know. A smile played on his lips whilst his head sank gently on his bosom.

Cautiously Alice crept about the room as she removed the supper things; careful to make no noise lest she should disturb her father. When all was done she took a seat by the old man's side.

"Mistress Alice," whispered Redfern, "one word with you. Think me not too bold if I ask you if you are the damsel known as the maid of Epping?"

"Some foolish folks call me so," replied Alice, blushing.

"Then in one thing at least I have been fortunate to-day," said Redfern, "for fate has brought me to this farm."

"I do not understand you."

"A customer of mine asked me to give you this ring, and to deliver a message to you in secret."

As he spoke he gave Alice a splendid diamond ring.

"You mistake me, sir," said Alice; "take back the ring. I know no one who would send me so valuable a present."

"Am I mistaken then?" said Redfern, as if amazed; "do you not know a gentleman called Arthur Bowring?"

Alice hung down her head, but made no answer.

"Oh! I see, I am not mistaken; he loves you and will make you his wife."

"His wife!" exclaimed Alice, clasping her hands.

"Aye, his wife: you shall be a court lady; dress in fine clothes. But, hush! your father is awaking. Meet me here in an hour alone, and I will deliver the message."

At that moment old Landon gave a tremendous yawn, and stretching out his arms and legs exclaimed,—

"Come, Alice, come, 'tis time you were in bed. And you, my honest friend, must be tired; so let us be off. Good night, friend, and may you sleep well."

"Good night," said Redfern; "may you sleep the better for the hospitality you have shown me."

He shook hands with the old farmer, and then, as he passed Alice, whispered, "Remember, here in an hour's time."

Alice made a sign of acquiescence, and Redfern entered his sleeping apartment.

"She is indeed beautiful," he muttered. "Oh, Sir Arthur, this will be a glorious revenge for all your taunts and jeers. To see her another's mistress, and perhaps one day in my power. Oh, it will be glorious."

Overcome with his thoughts of revenge, Lord Redfern threw himself upon the bed, and positively rolled about with delight.

Suddenly he was aroused from these pleasant reflections by hearing the clock in the kitchen strike ten.

He arose from his couch, and drawing the window curtains on one side gazed out into the night.

It was a glorious one. The moon had just risen in her full, and bathed the surrounding country in a flood of silver.

The stars glimmered like diamonds in the blue vault of the heavens, and a soft wind gently stirred the branches of the trees, whose leaves kept up a soft and pleasant murmur.

Straining his eyes to see down the lane as far as possible he discerned a close carriage standing in a shaded part.

"That is well," he said. "Williams is a trusty fellow. Now nothing is wanted but the girl."

Opening the door of his room carefully, he crept down stairs into the kitchen, where he found Alice waiting for him.

"I feel I have done wrong," she exclaimed as he approached her, "very wrong in meeting you, therefore give me your message and retire."

"My fair lady," cried Redfern in a smothered voice, "my message cannot be said so quickly. You love Sir Arthur?"

"Would I had never seen him!" cried the poor girl.

"And why?"

"He is too high ever to love me as his wife."

"No, no. I bear his proposals with me to-day; the ring I gave thee was one of betrothal."

"It cannot be true," murmured the delighted girl.

"It is. I have but to ask you one favour; it is his only condition."

"And that is—"

"That you fly with me to him to-night."

"Never!" cried Alice.

"It is his wish. Things you do not understand prevented his coming, and—"

"Silence!" said Alice in a loud voice.

"Hush!" cried Lord Redfern, "you will disturb your father, and all will be discovered."

"Begone!" cried Alice, "I see through you now. All that you have said is false. Heaven alone knows why you should have told these falsehoods. I cannot tell. But I warn you to begone, or I will summon my father and have you whipped from the door."

"Silence! you jade, or I'll strangle you," cried Redfern, seizing her by the arm. "Silence! D——n you, be still."

"What would you do?" cried Alice, startled into submission by her captor's violence.

"Listen! I have sworn to carry you off to-day, and by heaven I will. Come quietly, and your fortune is made. Resist me, and I will use such violence that may spoil your beauty for ever."

With a sudden effort Alice wrenched herself from his grasp, and rushed across the room crying loudly for help.

In a moment Lord Redfern had seized her again, and had thrown a heavy cloak over her head.

Stifled by the cloak, and overcome by fear, she fell fainting into his arms, and he was about carrying her off when he was seized by old Landon.

"Villain!" cried the farmer, "is it thus you repay my hospitality?"

"Unhand me, old dotard," cried Lord Redfern, placing Alice on a chair, and turning round so as to face the farmer.

"I'll not let you go," cried the courageous old man, "until I know who and what you are."

"Be warned, I say, and let me go," cried the other.

"Not till the constable has you," cried the sturdy old farmer, redoubling his efforts to throw Redfern to the ground.

"Then your blood be upon your own head," said Redfern between his teeth.

For a moment all was still; neither man spoke another word. Fast locked in each other's grasp, they swayed backwards and forwards, but neither fell or moved a foot.

No sound was to be heard in the room but the heavy panting of the combatants as they drew their breath.

The veins on their foreheads swelled out like whipcords, and their muscles were knotted and hard as iron.

Suddenly Lord Redfern withdrew his hand from the old man's throat, and seized the wrist of the hand by which Landon was grasping his, as if he would release himself.

Encouraged by this sign of weakness, Landon redoubled his efforts, and forced his antagonist on one knee.

Quick as lightning, Redfern slipped his hand from his throat to his breast, and drawing forth a knife, plunged it into the farmer's heart.

With one deep moan and a heavy sigh Farmer Landon rolled over on to the floor a corpse.

A heavy silence succeeded the turmoil caused by the struggle—it was the stillness of death. The very air seemed to be filled with awe at this monstrous crime—this terrible murder.

Redfern, whose character for ferocity and cruelty partook much of the nature of the tiger, no sooner saw his antagonist fall than he sprang upon the lifeless body in glee. He had tasted blood and longed for more.

"So," he shrieked in the dead man's ear, "you would dare to stop a nobleman in his pleasures, vile serf! But your daughter is in my power. She is mine! mine! mine!"

"You can't answer," he exclaimed. "Ah! he is dead; it is a pity he died so soon. I should have liked to torment him, but as he is dead, all is over. So now to business."

Lifting Alice's senseless form in his arms he passed down the lane. But the night air refreshed her.

At first she merely uttered a deep sigh, but gradually her senses returned to her, and she struggled to release herself from the cloak.

"Be still," said Lord Redfern as he clasped Alice tighter in his embrace; "there is no hope of escape now. You are mine."

As he spoke he reached the carriage, and with the assistance of his groom placed Alice inside; then springing in himself, directed his man to drive as fast as possible to London.

In the short time she had been alone Alice had made haste and removed the cloak from her head, and was again calling loudly for help.

"Silence!" cried Redfern, placing his hand over her mouth, "silence, or I will strangle you."

Alice sank back exhausted, and the next moment the carriage was rattling fast in the direction of London.

CHAPTER IV.
"HURRAH! FOR THE ROAD."

Between Edmonton and Waltham, in the days when this, our story, happened, there was scarcely a house to be seen. Tall hedges ran on each side of the road, over which might be seen broad meadows, deep, rocky dells, and dark lanes, made gloomy by over hanging trees.

The moon, as we have said, shone brightly down on these broad pasture lands, giving them a wondrous air of quietness, making every object visible, save where the gloomy shadow of some tall tree fell upon the fields.

From one of the dark dreary lanes a horseman suddenly emerged. He was dressed entirely in black. A large black hat was pulled over his brow so as to conceal his face: a useless prevention, for that was covered with a black mask. A long black cloak was thrown carelessly over his shoulders, falling loosely over the flanks of his horse.

The horse was a fine spirited animal, black as jet. Its well-formed neck and small head showed that it had Arabian blood, whilst its deep chest and powerful limbs proved that it also partook of the good old English stock.

Notwithstanding the fire and spirit of this superb animal, it was evidently under the perfect control of its master, who seemed to guide it more by his own will than by the rein.

They were a ghostly-looking pair. An air of mystery seemed to hang about them, making them appear supernatural.

With one bound the horse cleared the road, and with another the high hedge on the other side, and then *flitted* across the moon-lit fields.

We say "flitted," for the movement of the horse was peculiar. Now it would dash forward in a straight line, anon it would turn off at sharp angles, then fly off in a tangent; and all this *without making any noise*.

As the rider and the horse flew swiftly on, the long cloak spread out behind them, and at each turn of the horse it fell, then rose with a strange flicking motion which could be compared alone to the movement of a bat's wing.

It was, in fact, no other than the terrible outlaw, for whose arrest five hundred pounds was offered.

For some moments he kept up this peculiar flight, and then suddenly paused.

"By my faith," he muttered, "the smith was right. There is a coach coming down the road, and at a devil of a rate too. Well, now for Lord Clumber's plate without asking him by your leave, but rather *with his service*."

Touching his horse lightly with his heel, he cantered across the field, lept the hedge, and once more stood out in the road, and took up his position under the shade of a tree.

Drawing forth a pair of horse pistols, he examined them carefully to see that they were properly loaded, and then, replacing them, he loosened his sword in its sheath.

This done he waited, anxiously listening to the sound of the wheels as they approached.

"They have no lights," he muttered as the vehicle came in sight.

"I suppose they think there is less danger. By Jove, at what a rate they are travelling! And only one coachman—that is strange. Hark, what is that?"

At that moment a shrill cry for help sounded from the carriage; then followed scream after scream of the most agonising character.

"By heavens, it is a woman in distress," cried Batswing, drawing a pistol. "I will save her though I loose my own life in the attempt."

Putting spurs to his horse, he dashed up to the carriage, and, presenting his pistol at the coachman, ordered him to stop.

The coachman dropped the reins instantly, and sat shivering with fear on the box, praying for mercy.

"Dare to attempt to move, and I'll blow your brains out," thundered the outlaw; then, riding up to the carriage, he smashed in the glass with the muzzle of his pistol, and, presenting it at Lord Redfern, ordered him to alight.

"Curse you, what do you want?" growled Lord Redfern.

"Your gold and jewels."

"There, take what I have," said Redfern, at the same time placing all the gold he had in the highwayman's hand. "And now be off."

"A little more politeness if you please," said Batswing. opening the carriage door." "I must trouble you to alight."

"You have all that I possess," said Lord Redfern, "What more do you want? My life?"

"No, I only care for valuables; please step out."

As Lord Redfern saw the pistol pointed straight at his head, he found there was no help for it but to comply.

"D——n you," he muttered, "I'll be revenged."

"Now, madam," said the highwayman, bowing politely to Alice, "I heard you call for help, please tell me if I can be of any service to you."

"Oh save me, save me from that horrid man."

"So, sir!" exclaimed the outlaw, "this is what you call, I suppose, the conduct of a gentleman, an honourable man. Bad as my calling may be I would sooner follow it than stoop to be such a wretched coward as you are. Come madam, I will take you wherever you wish. What is your name?"

"Alice Landon," replied the maiden.

"Alice Landon," cried Batswing. "Can it be possible. Alight, madam. Leave this fellow's carriage, and trust yourself to one who never yet injured a woman."

With the greatest kindness Batswing helped the maiden to alight; but as he did so Lord Redfern drew forth a pistol and shot at the outlaw.

Luckily he missed his aim.

Throwing away his weapon Lord Redfern dashed up the road, and narrowly missed being shot by a pistol Batswing fired after him.

At that moment the sound of horses hoofs were heard coming quickly along the road, and then a loud hullo!

"Confusion!" muttered Batswing. "It is the troopers, I know their cry too well. I cannot leave this girl here. She must be saved."

Quickly swinging her into the saddle before him, he gave his horse the rein, and, clearing the hedge, dashed across the country.

CHAPTER V.

THE FLIGHT FOR LIFE.

When Lord Redfern had run up the road for some little way, he was delighted and astonished to see a party of dragoons making rapidly towards him.

"Help! help!" he cried, "or she will be murdered."

"What is the meaning of this?" cried the officer in command, dashing up to him.

"I have been attacked and robbed by highwaymen, and my daughter, my only daughter, carried off."

"What is to be done?" said the first officer in command to the second officer.

"What sort of fellow was this highwayman?" asked the second.

"A tall fellow dressed all in black, on a black horse with a black cloak."

"By heavens, it's Batswing," cried the younger officer; "there is five hundred pounds offered for his arrest. Let us leave four of the men to take charge of this plate and pursue him."

"Will it be safe?" asked the senior officer.

"Perfectly," replied the other. "Remember the *old man's daughter* is in the power of these ruffians. You take the command here, and I will lead the pursuit. You have nothing to fear, since Batswing is in full flight."

"Fear," replied the other officer proudly, "I have no fear were I to meet Batswing alone; take your men, take all but three, and trust me you will find the treasure safe on your return."

The word was no sooner given than the young officer. followed by some four or five dragoons, dashed off in eager pursuit of Batswing, who could just be seen crossing the fields.

After taking one glance at the pursuit, the officer sighed, for he longed to be with them, then slowly turned and rode back to the carriage, over which he had to keep guard.

Taking advantage of this Lord Redfern hurried back to his carriage, where he found his coachman but scarcely recovered from his fear.

"Get up, you lazy scoundrel," exclaimed his lordship; "mount the box, and drive as fast as possible to London."

"But the highwaymen, my lord?

"Drive on!" cried his lordship, "or by heaven I'll blow your brains out."

Springing into the carriage Lord Redfern lowered down the front window, and no sooner had the unfortunate coachman mounted the box, than he threatened him with instant death if he did not drive on at full speed.

Thus encouraged the coachman seized the reins, and whipping the horses as fast as he could made them gallop down the road at full speed.

Whilst this was going on the pursuit of Batswing was kept up with unflagging interest.

Over hedges and ditches, across meadows and fields on went the chase. Now and then Batswing would, with one of those wondrous evolutions which had gained him his name, turn sharp round as if riding at his pursuers, then when within a few feet of the foremost one he would discharge his pistol at the horse, bringing both rider and horse to the ground. Then he would flit rapidly away, shooting off at right angles, quickly distancing his followers.

Still the men with undiminished courage spurred on their horses, the young officer cheering them on by voice and gesture.

Carbine after carbine was discharged after the fugitive, who seemed to escape wounding only by a miracle.

"Curse them!" he muttered, "will they never give in? I dare not go straight to the cave: they might discover my retreat; then all would be up. Would that the clouds would cover the moon!"

Casting a hasty glance at the heavens, he saw with delight that his wish was about to be realised, for heavy clouds were rapidly coming up from the south.

"I must breathe my horse," he said, "I can do it—they can't." Checking the rein he let his horse drop into a gentle canter, so as to rest it for a few minutes; for the poor animal was carrying a double burden.

No sooner did the foremost trooper see this than he urged his horse on at full speed, at the same time calling on Batswing to surrender.

With a laugh of defiance Batswing discharged his pistol at the man, who rolled off his horse, a pistol-bullet having entered his side.

Touching his horse gently with his heel Batswing bounded over a ditch down a bosky dell, cleared a deep wide rivulet that ran at the bottom, dashed up the other side, and once more reached the open country.

One rapid glance showed him that only three men were now following him, the foremost of these being the young officer, who was cheering his men on with difficulty.

"They are nearly blown," muttered Batswing; "so the game is mine."

With a sudden twist of the rein he turned as if making towards Hatfield. No sooner did his pursuers see this, than they made for the high road, thinking that Batswing's horse being tired he would not take any more leaps; and, therefore, the first in the road would have the advantage.

Over went the troopers in gallant style; but no sooner had they done so than the highwayman turned his horse's head, doubled, and made straight towards Epping Forest. This ruse was soon discovered, but not before Batswing had gained some considerable ground.

The pursuers galloped swiftly after Batswing, whom they could now scarcely see, for the rain was falling fast, and the clouds completely covered the moon.

Thicker and thicker grew the trees, as they flew past them: they had entered Epping Forest.

The young officer, like most Englishmen, was an ardent lover of the chase, and had become so enwrapt with this man-hunting, that he forgot to see if his companions were following him. Guided by Alice's white dress he still rushed madly on; but, suddenly, to his horror, the gleam of white disappeared, and no sound but the fall of his own horse's feet could be heard.

"Can it be possible that this Batswing, as he is called, is some terrible, supernatural being," thought the young officer. "Whatever he is I will try to find him."

In those days, when the belief in ghosts and supernatural agencies was firmly fixed in the human mind, it required no little courage to come to this determination. But the young officer did not hesitate for a moment.

He urged his steed rapidly forward, but all was still; there was no sound of any one near.

Utterly disgusted at his non-success, he turned his weary horse to retrace his steps, and then discovered that he had lost his way.

Lost in darkness he took what seemed to be a path, but was really only a small cutting in the wood. His horse stumbled over a tree, and the next moment rider and horse fell heavily to the ground.

CHAPTER VI.

WHAT BEFELL FROM A HORSE CASTING ITS SHOE.

Sad and wearily did the convoy plod along the dark and dreary road, keeping guard upon the carriage which contained Lord Clumber's family plate.

Down came the rain, drenching the troops through to their skin, and making the roads several inches deep in slippery mud, so that the poor horses, already greatly fatigued, could scarcely keep up a trot.

They had just passed through Tottenham when the officer discovered that his horse had cast a shoe.

"Confound it!" he muttered, "what is to be done now? What a fool I've been to let those men go galloping helter-skelter over the country after that highwayman. What do I care about his arrest? If I lose this plate all the blame will be put on me. I must have this shoe put on, else the horse will go lame. I wonder where there can be a smith hereabouts."

At that moment a dismal whistling struck upon his ear, and peering into the darkness he beheld a youth saunter idly out of a lane into the main road.

"Hillo! my lad," he cried, "do you know a smith's about here?"

"'A course I do," rejoined the lad; "every fool knows the merry smith of Stamford."

"The more reason you should know him and the less that I should," replied the officer. "If you will lead me to him I will give you a crown, for my horse has cast a shoe."

"Phew!" thought Jerry, for the lad, as no doubt the reader has already guessed, was that worthy individual. "Phew! here's a pretty go, they're soldiers, sha'nt I catch it from the smith, that's all?"

"Why don't you answer?" demanded the officer sharply.

"I know his smithy," said the lad, scratching his head, "but I don't think he stops there up to this time o' night."

"Where is his cottage, then?"

"About three mile or more from here across the lanes."

"Any way, you must lead me to the smithy. I must take the liberty of using the smith's tools, and seeing what can be done myself."

"It's all up," thought Jerry; "there's Purplenosed Bill, Jack the Fondling, and two others up there a blowing their bacca, and none of them likes soldiers."

Suddenly a brilliant idea struck him, and advancing to the officer he said,

"I'll tell yer what will be the best plan, Captain. I'll run up the lane to see if there is a light in his place. I shall soon hear if he's there, for he's always at work and singing; that's why we call him the Merry Smith."

"Do so, my lad, and you shall be well rewarded."

Jerry Blinker needed no further encouragement, but dashed away.

The officer waited impatiently for Jerry's return, for the night was anything but a cheerful one, as the rain was falling in torrents. But he had not long to wait, for Jerry returned very soon, and, panting for breath, announced the complete success of his errand.

"He's there, yer honour, a singing and a 'ammering away like a good'un," said Jerry.

"All right, my lad; lead on," said the Captain.

They marched slowly on, the carriage dragging heavily behind the tired horses, now and then the wheels sinking into deep ruts and brushing against the hedges; for, to the officer's annoyance, he found the lane became narrower and narrower as they proceeded.

"Hang it all, my good lad," cried the officer, "why did you not tell me that the lane was so narrow? It will be impossible to turn the carriage round."

"I didn't know that you wanted to bring the carriage up here," said Jerry in an idiotic manner; "and I didn't know you wanted to turn it round."

"Curse you for a fool," growled the officer, "there, go on; perhaps the smith will be able to tell us how we are to manage."

They soon approached the smithy, for not only could they see the ruddy gleam of the fire, but they could also hear the smith as he sang out lustily, keeping time to the tune with his hammer—

"Oh, merry indeed is a blacksmith's life,
That is if he happen to have no wife
With a scolding tongue as sharp as a knife,
To fret and worry him with her strife.

With a cling and a clang, a clang and a cling,
Merrily now the sledge hammers ring,
With a cling and a clang, a clang and a cling.
The blacksmith is happier far than a King."

"What, ho! master blacksmith," called out the officer, "stop your merriment awhile and attend to work."

"I' faith, not I," shouted back the blacksmith, "he works but badly who has not a merry heart."

"Cease your jests, good fellow," cried the officer, dismounting from his horse and leading it into the forge; "there is a time for all things."

"True, most noble sir, and this is the time to give up work."

"Not so fast. My horse has cast a shoe, and I must have it replaced."

"Well, then, if I must I must; so place the poor animal here. Woa! woa! Good faith, you have had a heavy drive."

"Yes, we have come a long way to-day."

"And won't those gentlemen come in and warm themselves?"

"They may come in one at a time," said the officer, "but the others must stay to guard the plate—that is," he added, suddenly remembering himself, "the ammunition."

"Ammunition," thought the smith, "they don't carry ammunition about in carriages generally. Plate, he said at first. It must be Lord Clumber's then."

As the officer seemed disinclined to continue the conversation, the merry smith, whilst heating the iron, continued his song—

"Yet a blacksmith's a man whom maids love well,
For he kisses them all, yet they never tell,
Though the kissing rings out like a silver bell;
They like it so much they never rebel.

With a cling and a clang, a clang and a cling,
Merrily now the sledge-hammers ring;
With a cling and a clang, a clang and a cling,
A blacksmith is happier far than a king."

"Do you know, your worship," said the blacksmith, "when I first saw you at the door I took you for a highwayman!"

"A pretty compliment, truly," laughed the officer; "have you many pass this way?"

"Well, I have had customers who did not seem wishful to talk too much about their business. But I'm not curious."

"A want of curiosity is a good failing," replied the officer drily.

"Do you know, sir, whether it be true that there is an order out offering a reward of five hundred pounds for the arrest of that terrible fellow, or fiend, Batswing?" inquired the smith.

"There is such a reward offered I believe," said the officer.

"I should like to get it," sighed the smith.

"That at least is hopeless," laughed the officer, "for by this time Batswing is either arrested or dead."

"Why, how is that?" asked the smith eagerly.

The officer related what had happened whilst the smith fixed the shoe on the horse's foot.

"Then you did not see him arrested or shot?"

"No; but he was too near us to escape."

"I don't know that, he's a rum animal. Well, sir, there's your horse shod; and now I think I'll close my shop."

"Thanks, my good friend," said the officer, throwing a guinea on the forge; "keep that for your trouble. And now, will you tell me how I am to get this carriage back into the main road?"

"That I can't. Why, what on earth made you bring it up here?"

"I could not leave it behind."

"It is the treasure," thought the smith, taking a hasty glance at the number of the party.

"Well, my man, can you not devise some remedy?"

"That I can't—unless—"

"Unless what?"

"You go on up this lane. It makes a circumbendibus like a half hoop. You know what I mean."

"Yes, a half circle——."

"Ah! that's it; and then it comes out in the north road again."

"Do we lose much by it?"

"About a couple of miles."

"Well, it can't be helped," said the officer as he mounted his horse.

"I suppose not," said the smith vacantly.

"Now then, Sergeant Jones," cried the officer, "take one of the men and ride a little behind the coach; the other will ride on with me in the front."

"Is the road good up here?" asked the coachman disconsolately.

"Pretty fair; that is, if the rain aint softened it."

"Bah! you're a fool," was the polite reply.

"Good night, captain," shouted the smith as the cavalcade drove off.

"Good night," replied the officer.

"Glad to serve you at any time, Captain, that you're passing this way," shouted the smith; "good journey to you all."

"Thanks, my good fellow, thanks," was the reply; and the next moment they disappeared in the darkness.

Bob Blow the Bellows, as the smith was called by his friends, stood watching and listening out in the road for some minutes, and then rushing into the smithy, he locked and barred the door.

This being done he removed some boards that had been placed against the further end of the room, and which had hidden four stout brawny men.

"Have they gone?" demanded one.

"Gone! Yes. Up, lads all. There is work in hand that will repay us all. Not a moment is to be lost. They say our Captain Batswing is taken; I don't believe it; but should it be so, at least, we'll avenge him"

The men with a cheer lept to their feet.

"We're all ready, Bob. What's the plant?"

£500!!!
REWARD
BATSWING
!!!DEAD!!!
OR
ALIVE

THE BIRD
CAGE INN

JERRY BLINKER.

"Patience, my lad," said the smith, "patience, and you will see."

CHAPTER VII.

THE HIGHWAYMAN'S HOME.

When Batswing had suddenly disappeared from the young officer's gaze, there was, as the reader may guess, nothing supernatural about it. On the contrary, it was done in the simplest manner in the world.

The night, as we have already said, was very dark, and, consequently, as they went deeper into the forest the darkness increased, until the young officer could only be guided as to Batswing's whereabouts by Alice's white dress.

At first the highwayman was astonished at the young man's perseverance, began wondering how he could follow him, and happening to cast his eyes downwards, at once perceived that Alice's white dress was the guide.

Quickly drawing his black cloak down, he wrapped it round the still insensible girl, and drawing into a recess in the wood, soon had the satisfaction of hearing the young officer dash past him.

In this manner Batswing managed to escape.

"Fool!" muttered Batswing, as he heard the young fellow dash past him, "how little do you know that it is by my mercy alone you owe your life."

He looked down at the girl, and bending his ear close to her mouth, listened intently.

"Poor girl!" he murmured, "she still is insensible. I must procure assistance, or she will die."

Turning his horse's head down a narrow path, until he came to a thick clump of underwood, skirting this for a little way, he found a small opening through which he passed, and cantering over an open space, he reached the mouth of a cave.

A low whistle soon brought forth two rough-looking men, to whom Batswing consigned his horse, and then bore the still fainting maiden into the cavern.

It was a large vaulted place, running a great distance underground, ending, or apparently ending, in a large chamber.

In this chamber a number of men were seated round a huge fire, the smoke of which escaped, or rather partially escaped, through a hole in the roof.

A large cauldron was slung over this fire, and evidently contained some good viands, for the aroma it gave forth was most appetising.

The men, who were waiting for their suppers, were amusing themselves in the meantime by drinking and joking.

"Hail to our Captain!" they exclaimed, as Batswing entered.

"Hush!" he exclaimed. "Make no noise ; where is Madge?"

"Here am I," replied a stout, fussy little woman hurrying up. "What's in the wind now? Why I'm blest if it aint a gal."

"Yes, Madge, it is the only prize I have carried home to-day," said Batswing, laughing, "and had it not been for my bonny mare, I don't think I should have managed that."

"What, has the treasure escaped?" cried one of the men.

"Yes, it was guarded by soldiers, who gave me a nice chase. One of them, a young officer, is still here in the forest. I left him close by the Devil's Dell ; two of you go and seize him ; but mind, no unnecessary violence."

Two of the men sprang to their feet, and hurried away to do their Captain's bidding.

"Here, Madge, take this girl, and see that she is well tended to. She has gone through enough to-day to have killed two women of stronger courage than she appears to have."

The old woman took Alice in her arms as if she were a child, and removing a board which was so plastered with clay that none would have guessed that it was not part of the cave, disappeared down a secret passage.

Throwing his cloak on one side, the Bat, as we shall call him, that being the name he was known by amongst his followers,—his horse being called the Bat's *wing*—threw himself down by the fire and burst into a loud laugh.

"Why, what is the matter, Captain?" said a rough fellow the others called Hugh.

"Matter!" cried the Bat, "matter enough, I think. Here have I been out half the night trying to capture a treasure, and have only brought home a weak girl, that I don't know what to do with."

"Slit her weazand," suggested Hugh.

"I advise none of you to attempt it," said the Bat sternly. "The first one to lay a finger on that girl will be my enemy."

"Why, you aint agoing to fall in love, are you, Captain?" said Hugh.

"Not I, Hugh ; you may rest assured of that. But there is too little virtue in this world to send any out of it."

"I'm not so sure of that," replied Hugh, doubtfully.

"I am, and that's enough," said the Bat sharply. "But, gentlemen, I have not yet told you of the honour that has been paid your Captain by his Majesty's grateful Government."

"What's up now?" cried the men.

"They have offered five hundred pounds reward for the arrest of your humble servant."

"No?"

"It's a fact, I can assure you; and two hundred pounds reward for his dead carcase."

"Shameful!" cried the men.

"Not at all," replied the Bat ; "I think it's remarkably attentive of them. One thing is evident, that is, that they value me more than I do them."

A hoarse laugh was the answer to this sally.

"But, Captain, this is serious."

"Oh! not at all ; no one will betray me."

"I don't know that. What shall we do?"

"Do? Oh, I've made up my mind what to do."

"What?"

"Get both the rewards."

"Impossible!"

"Not at all : the two hundred pound one will be mine in a week, the five hundred one will be mine in a month."

"Nonsense!"

"It is perfectly true, I assure you ; and what's more, when I have the money we will have a merry carouse in this cave or in the Mint with the money, and laugh at the Government."

"What, after you're dead?"

"There, we have had enough of that," said the Bat, "let us change the subject. Has any one seen anything of our friend the Merry Smith?"

"No! but, hark! here come our men back with the young officer."

"'Tis well he has not escaped," said the Bat ; "he might have led the troops upon us."

At that moment the young officer was led in, his arms bound tightly behind him.

Rising from the ground the Bat stood before the young man, and questioned him sternly.

"What is your name?" he demanded.

"By what right do you ask?" retorted the other.

"By the right of might," retorted the Bat. "Your life is in my hands."

"Then keep it," replied the officer ; "it is not worth my having since it has been so contaminated."

"You are over bold."

"Not so ; no man is that. The truest boldness is to do one's duty, the greatest cowardice is to fail in so doing."

"Do you value your life?" demanded Batswing.

"As a gentleman, yes ; but were I in your place I would shoot myself, and save the hangman the trouble of a journey to Tyburn."

"Dare you defy me?"

"Why ask me if I dare when you see I do it? My actions are my answers."

"Enough, sir," replied the Bat, "so bold a man cannot fear to die. Lead him forward to execution."

The men led him forward and placed him before the Bat.

"My men," cried the Bat, "you see this man; he has discovered our retreat and will betray us. What is to be his doom?"

"Death!" cried the men solemnly.

"You have heard your fate," said the Bat ; "prepare to meet it."

"I have but one regret at losing it," replied the young officer. "I would have wished to die by honest hands."

With a contemptuous shrug of the shoulders, the Bat drew a pistol and levelled it at the prisoner; but before he could pull the trigger a piercing shriek sounded from the back of the cave, and Alice, rushing in, threw herself on the breast of the young officer.

"Spare him! spare him!" cried Alice.

"Alice!" exclaimed the young man, "you here! Unfortunate girl, are you in league with these wretches?"

"How is this," said the Bat, "you seem to know this maiden."

"Perfectly well, it seems," put in Hugh with a coarse laugh.

"I thought I knew her," replied the young officer

proudly, "but since I have met her here I find I have been deceived. So do your worst. I am prepared to die."

"Stay," said Batswing, "I would not have you die wronging a virtuous girl. Alice Landon knows nothing of us. To-night I rescued her from the clutches of a villain who was carrying her off by force."

"Is this true, Alice?" asked the young man.

"It is, indeed," cried Alice; "the man declared he came from you, and gave me this ring."

"The monster!" cried Sir Arthur, for he was the officer; "this is Lord Redfern's ring. Oh! he shall pay dearly for this."

"Stop, stop, my good sir," cried the Bat; "you seem to forget that you are a prisoner."

"For the first time," cried the young man, "I plead for my life. Let me but have time to avenge this outraged girl, and I will return here instantly."

"That is impossible."

"I implore you to let me have but two days."

"It is impossible," replied the Bat, "unless"—

"Unless what?"

"Unless you become one of us."

"One of you!" cried Sir Arthur, starting back.

"Yes, one of us."

"But I am a King's officer."

"The more reason we should kill you; you would us if we were in your power."

"But I have taken an oath."

"And so have we. If you would save your life you must join us. We do not ask you to become what we are; but merely to swear never to betray, but always shield us from harm."

"Oh! Arthur, Arthur, for my sake, swear it," cried Alice.

"I cannot!" replied Sir Arthur.

"Then die!" said the Bat, levelling the pistol.

Before he could bring it to bear, Alice threw herself at his feet, and implored, in piteous accents, for her lover's life.

"You see, Sir Arthur, how I am placed," said the Bat. "I dare not let you go, for you know the place of our retreat. Resign your commission, and then you will not be forced to pursue us. Take the oath we require, and you shall not only be free, but shall have our aid to crush this girl's enemies, and, trust me, they are powerful ones. She, too, must take the same oath. On these conditions alone can I spare your life."

"My life I would willingly give up sooner than join you," replied Sir Arthur, "but I feel that if I die Alice will be lost."

"Then you consent?"

"I do."

"'Tis well. Undo his arms, and blindfold him and the girl."

This order was quickly obeyed. Then two of the highwaymen took Sir Arthur and Alice by the arms and led them down the secret passage at the end of the cave.

CHAPTER VIII.
THE OATH—JONATHAN WILD.

Slowly, and with a funereal tread the prisoners were led along. Sir Arthur, by putting out one hand, knew he was being led through a subterraneous passage. But the men, noticing that he was feeling the walls, quickly placed his hand down, so that he should make no mark to retrace his steps.

Now turning to the right and now to the left, it seemed to the captives that they must have marched at least a mile, when suddenly they could tell, by the sound of their footsteps, that they had reached some large apartment, although the air was still close and musty.

Alice trembled in every limb, but a kind voice whispered in her ear:

"Be not afraid, fear nothing that you may hear or see. No harm shall befal you or your lover."

For a moment all was still, then a deep voice demanded:

"Whom have we here?'

"Poor wanderers, who would seek for rest in the bosom of our brotherhood."

"Are they willing to take the oaths?"

"They are."

"Let them see the light."

In a moment the bandages that had been placed over their eyes were removed.

They looked round, and Alice nearly sank to the earth with terror at the sight she saw.

They were in a large crypt, or vault, which had evidently been at one time used as a receptacle for the dead.

Broken coffins, from which bones protruded were scattered everywhere about. Here and there might be seen a grinning skull, whose eyeless sockets seemed glaring at the unfortunate prisoners.

The whole of this gloomy scene was lit up by two immense flambeaus, which were burning on a rude altar that stood in the centre of the vault.

On this altar were a huge human skull and two thigh bones, the latter crossed so as to form that emblem of death "the skull and crossbones."

Behind the altar stood Batswing, dressed in his sable habiliments.

"Children, step to the altar; and repeat this oath after me."

With trembling limbs Alice advanced; indeed, had it not been for her companion's assistance she would have fallen to the ground.

Sir Arthur advanced boldly, and gazing fully at the Bat, exclaimed,—

"Be quick over this ceremony, or else the lady will faint. I think the word of a gentleman should suffice without this mummery."

"Place your hands upon this skull, and repeat after me," said the Bat.

They did as they were desired, and then in solemn accents the Bat propounded the oath to them, which Alice repeated in trembling tones, and Sir Arthur in a loud, dauntless voice.

Scarcely had they pronounced the last words, when a hoarse laugh sounded at the back of the vault. They turned round, and beheld a man standing on a flight of stone steps leading to a trap-door.

The new-comer was a man about thirty, dressed in a brown coat, three-cornered hat trimmed with gold lace, and huge riding boots that reached to his thighs. Round his waist was a belt, in which he carried two enormous horse pistols; a huge cutlass dangled at his side, and in his large brawny right hand he clutched a stout cudgel.

There was something so particularly villanous in this man's countenance that people naturally shrank from him.

His forehead was flat, sloping down to his small cunning eyes, which were placed one on each side of his head like an animal's. His nose was long and sharp; his mouth a huge gash which, when he attempted to smile, drew back all wrinkled to his ears, like the mouth of a snarling wolf, displaying a row of exquisitely white but irregular, sharp-pointed teeth. He was strongly built, but too angular in his proportions to be reckoned well made, whilst his peculiar half-swagger, half-creeping gait took away all claims to grace or ease.

"Ha! ha! ha! ho! ho! ho!" laughed, or rather snarled this man.

"By my soul, this is good. Our profession is looking up. Who would think that Sir Arthur Bowring would turn highwayman, or dubsman. Eh, ha! ha! ha!"

"Wretch!" exclaimed Sir Arthur. "If you dare apply such epithets to me—"

"How dare I? Why I have heard and seen you take

the oath. Henceforth you are in *my* power, and so is the fair Alice Landon."

With a cry of rage Sir Arthur was about to rush on the man, but the Bat held him back.

"Hold! for your life," he whispered; "that man, or devil, is not to be met by blows, but by cunning."

"Who is he?" demanded Sir Arthur.

"Ask no questions," whispered the Bat, who under the cover of a struggle with Sir Arthur managed to carry on this conversation unperceived by the stranger. "Ask no questions, do not fear this man; I have sworn to bring him to the gallows, and believe me I will."

"Away with this folly," cried Sir Arthur. "I have had enough of this child's play. I am no boy to be treated in this manner. Who is this snarling hound?"

"Did you address yourself to me, Sir Arthur," said the man, raising his hat politely.

"What is your name?"

"JONATHAN WILD!" thundered the man.

Sir Arthur staggered back, overcome with a sickening disgust at being in the presence of the most diabolical fiend that ever existed in human shape.

With a coarse laugh Jonathan strode down the steps, and walking up to Batswing, said,—

"There's been some queer games on the road to-night, Bat, and if I'm not mistaken I can recognise your handiwork in it."

"And if there be, what's that to you?"

"Only I thought some business might be done, that is all."

"There is no business."

"Hum! Lord Clumber's plate was on the road."

"It has escaped."

"Death and the Devil!" exclaimed Wild, losing his temper. "What fool's game is this?"

"The plate," replied the Bat, "was well guarded by soldiers, and therefore impossible to touch."

"You are a fool; the plate was worth daring anything," replied Jonathan Wild, stamping with rage.

"Then why did you not attempt it yourself, Master Jonathan," cried Batswing, confronting his antagonist. "And hark ye this, you Devil's Spawn: I have no man speak to me in the way you do, and if you presume to do it again, I'll wring that bull neck, thick as it is. Don't scowl at me—frown you can't for want of eyebrows. Remember I know too much for you, Master Jonathan, and if I swing, you go to."

"What nonsense is this!" cried Jonathan, trying to smile; "am I not your old friend, eh?"

"Yes, you have been my friend, as much as you have been any man's. Hark ye, Sir Arthur, beware of this fellow. I need not say do not fear him—such a nature as yours never could fear so vile a thing—but beware of him. Never trust him in the slightest way. Look to yourself, and rely on me to assist you."

"A friendly speech," sneered Jonathan.

"A well-meant one," replied the other.

"And as such I take it," replied Jonathan, meaningly.

"You are now one of us," whispered the Bat to Sir Arthur. "I will see no harm comes to you or yours. You must remain here to-night. Alice must remain longer; but, fear not, Madge shall take care of her. To-morrow you can go to London."

"To-morrow," thought Jonathan, who had overheard the last speech; "to-morrow I will commence spinning a web to catch you both, and then I'll suck your blood."

CHAPTER IX.
THE MERRY SMITH TRIES AN EXPERIMENT.

No sooner had the smith called his comrades than they, one and all, sprang to their feet, ready for action.

"What's in the wind now?" demanded one whom the rest called Growling Teddy.

"I've an idea that will make all our fortunes?"

"You've always some idea to make our fortunes, but blest if I ever see any of it."

"You've always something to grumble at."

"Well, and ain't I got good cause, old Blow the Bellows?" cried Growling Teddy; "do you want to argue?"

"Not now; I haven't got time for it."

"When yer have, come to me; I'll serve yer cheap."

Whilst this conversation was going on, Bob Blow the Bellows had collected two strong pieces of rope, each piece being about thirty feet in length. These he coiled up into two coils, and gave them to his companions to carry.

"Now, then, my lads," he cried, opening a trap, and bringing out some pistols; "choose your own barkers, and look well to the loading and priming, and have your swords ready."

"Why, what on earth are you going to do?" demanded the Growler.

"Carry off Lord Clumber's plate," replied the smith, resolutely.

"Carry off the plate?" cried the other, "why it's guarded by them there cussed soldiers."

"What of that?"

"What of that? why all of that, I think. Do you want us to get our brains blown out?"

"I don't think that there is much fear of that in your case; all I can say is that I want the plate, and the plate I mean to have, come what may."

"I wish you may get it," said Teddy.

"Thank you for your wishes," replied the smith, hurriedly slipping off his apron and putting on a tight-fitting coat, and then fixing a mask over his face.

"If you're all going, I suppose I may as well go too," said the Growler.

"You know you need not come unless you like," said the smith.

"I know that as well as you do," replied the Growler; "but I will come. if I want to come no one will prevent me."

"No one wants to prevent you, do they?" said the smith, smiling.

"I don't know that," grumbled the other, taking up his pistols, examining them carefully, and fixing them in his belt. "I don't know how it is, I never say a thing unless some one contradicts me."

"Serve you right," said the smith.

"If we're going we had better go," said another.

"Are you all ready?" asked the smith.

"All," was the reply.

"Barking irons in order?"

"Perfectly."

"And your swords loose in their sheaths?"

"Yes."

Turning round, the smith heaped some small coal on to the furnace so as to hide the blaze, and then extinguished the light. After this he dropped on his hands and knees, and, opening a small hutch at the back of the hut, just large enough to admit the body of a man, he crawled through and was quickly followed by the rest. Teddy the Growler, being the last, naturally had to close the trap, for which extra trouble he grumbled dreadfully.

"Now, my lads," said the smith, "if we keep straight across this field we shall arrive at the lane before the soldiers do; so come along."

Starting off at full speed they dashed across the field.

The night was still dark and gloomy; the rain falling in heavy showers, cutting the face, and nearly blinding the men as it was driven against them by the wind.

The soft turf of the field had been converted into thick mud, which clung to their heavy boots, and greatly impeded their progress.

Still they kept on, not caring one iota for wind, rain, or mud, their whole attention being directed to the plunder before them.

When they had crossed the field they arrived at a high hedge, over which they soon clambered, and then came into a deep lane, on each side of which grew some fine old trees.

Selecting two of these trees—one on each side of the lane—the smith took one of the ropes and put one end round each tree, so that the middle laid slack across the road.

He then proceeded about twenty yards further down the lane, where he selected two more trees, round which he placed the second rope in the same manner as he had done the first.

He then made each of his four followers take one of the ends of the ropes, giving them strict instructions at the same time to pull lustily when he gave them a certain signal, so that the ropes should be tightened. Having done this, he ordered them to crouch down close to the bank, so as to hide themselves.

They had not long to wait.

Crashing and splashing along they could hear the troopers riding their jaded horses, urging them on at their full speed, and cursing at the weather.

Amidst all this confusion they could hear the heavy lumbering coach as it jolted over the bad road.

"Now, lads, keep still," whispered Bob Blow the Bellows.

Onward went the officer with the trooper and crossed the first line without noticing it; so also did the carriage, for they were going at a quick trot.

No sooner had they passed than the smith drew a pistol, and, firing at the coachman, brought him off the box.

No sooner did the highwaymen hear the signal than they tightened the ropes.

The troopers could not stop their horses, which, startled by the sudden explosion of the pistol, galloped forward at a tremendous rate. The tightened ropes took the soldiers across the chests and hurled them to the ground.

In a minute there was a highwayman kneeling on each trooper's chest and holding a pistol in unpleasant proximity to the poor fellow's head, whilst the merry smith, taking the reins from the horses in the carriage, cut them up, and first tied the coachman to a tree, after which he safely fastened the rest of the soldiers.

"I am really sorry, gentlemen," said Bob, "to have had to treat you in this dreadfully rude manner; to unhorse you in such a way on such a road is, really, not polite. But I could not help it."

"What is it you want?" demanded the officer. "Remember I am in the King's service."

"Trust me I shall not forget it," replied the smith, "although I hope we may never become better acquainted."

"What do you want, rascal?" cried the officer.

"Not politeness, or I should not come to you; but I will take what is far more valuable to me, and of which I am sure you possess most."

"What do you mean?"

"Firstly I will take your purse. Thank you," said the smith, as he emptied the officer's pockets.

"Now I will have your watch."

In vain the officer swore: the smith continued robbing him until he had taken everything of value that he could find.

"I am sorry you don't wear rings," he said coolly; "they are always pretty and sometimes valuable. Let me advise you to do so in future, for my sake."

"Tormenting devil!" cried the officer, stamping with rage. "I will see that you soon have a ring round your ankles."

"Thank you kindly for the promise," said the smith; "in the meantime I will just take a peep at my Lord Clumber's plate."

"Help! help! help!" shouted the officer.

"Silence! or I'll blow your brains out," cried the smith, putting a pistol close to the officer's ear.

"If I could only get my hands free," growled the captain between his teeth.

"But you can't," was the cool reply of the other, "and that being the case don't try. It is only throwing away your strength."

But as the officer did not seem to see the force of this argument the smith called Teddy the Growler to him.

"Mr. Growler," said the smith blandly, "would you have the kindness to take care of this gentleman? Don't be rough with him, if you can possibly help it; but, at the same time, we must have no noise, no disturbance, it's so very rude."

"You rascals!" growled the officer.

"Come, I say; none o' that," said Teddy, "I ain't used to that there sort o' language. I want quietness, I does, and I means to have it too. I'm a guardian of the peace now—ho! ho! ho!"

This idea seemed to please Teddy so much that he positively shook with delight, much to the captain's horror, for it is far from pleasant to have a loaded pistol pointed at your head at any time; but it becomes far worse when the gentleman who holds the pistol is trembling and shaking with laughter.

"For heaven's sake, man, take care," cried the captain.

"Oh, don't mind me," said Teddy. "I never had a haccident yet. All the men I ever shot I intended for to do; there was no accident about it at all. They never complained about it neither: I hates cruelty, I never only wounds a man."

This interesting conversation was suddenly brought to a close by a cry of astonishment which the smith gave as he looked into the carriage.

"Why, what's up now?" cried the men.

"The treasure; the plate!" gasped Bob.

"Well, what of that?" demanded the Growler.

"It is gone!" shouted the smith.

"Gone!" echoed soldiers and highwaymen together.

"Impossible!" cried the officer.

"You've been playing some trick with us?" cried Teddy, shaking his pistol in the officer's face; "and I'll be revenged."

"Stop!" cried the smith, seizing Teddy's hand just in time to save the officer's life.

"Why should I stop?" commenced the grumbler. "It's just like you; when I'm just going to work you come and stop me."

"Do you know anything about this robbery?" demanded the smith of the officer.

"On my honour not a word," replied the other.

"When did you last see the chest safe?" demanded the smith.

"Just after I had sent a detachment after the highwayman Batswing. I know it was safe then."

"It has gone now," replied the smith impatiently, "that is evident; so we have nothing else to do but to go also."

"Oughtn't we to quiet these here soldiers?" asked Teddy.

"No," cried the smith, "touch one at your peril."

"I'm blest if I ever did see such a ill-tempered creature," growled Teddy.

"Gentlemen," said the smith, "I have no wish to injure you, or inconvenience you more than is actually necessary; therefore, if you will give me your words not to call for assistance until a quarter of an hour has passed, I shall be most happy to permit you to remain as you are without gagging. If you refuse me, I shall be forced to have recourse to that most unpleasant operation."

"We are in your power, sir," replied the officer; "therefore you can do as you like. But since the plate has gone, and as I can bear witness that you have not stolen it, I am willing to give you my word not to cry for help until the time you state has elapsed."

"Spoken like a sensible man," cried the smith. "It is no good crying over spilt milk, as the proverb says;

and I can assure you that I am as sorry the plate has been stolen as you are."

"What's to be done now?" demanded Teddy.

"Mount these horses," whispered the smith; "there are four of them, so that you will have one apiece. Gallop off to Epping with all we've taken to-night; and give it into the charge of the captain to divide amongst us. The horses will be useful for the boys. Don't lose a minute."

"The men did as they were bade, and the smith accompanied them down the road until he came to a small gap in the hedge.

Wishing them good bye he sprang through this, and made his way homewards.

CHAPTER X.

JONATHAN WILD SWEARS VENGEANCE.

When Jonathan Wild left the vault and returned to the cave, he found the robbers still carousing round the fire.

"Drunken fools!" he muttered to himself, "to think that so many fellows should let so great a treasure pass. I'll be equal with my friend the Bat. He is the only man that has dared to defy me, and by Heaven he shall swing at Tyburn yet."

At this moment he was interrupted by the appearance of the Bat and Sir Arthur, who were in deep conversation with each other.

Approaching towards the fire, the Bat made a sign for his men to keep silence, then throwing back his large black cloak addressed them as follows:—

"My men, here is a gentleman who has taken the oaths of brotherhood with us: not by choice, as we have done, but by compulsion. Still he is a man of honour, and has sworn to keep our secrets inviolate. I therefore command all the brotherhood to treat him with respect, and never to betray that he has become one of us. On his side, he will do all in his power to protect us from harm, so long as we keep faith with him."

A hearty cheer followed this announcement.

"Ha! ha! ha!" chuckled Jonathan to himself. "I am bound by no oath; and if I were, I'd break it, for a price. Either Sir Arthur must pay me or some one else must. Secrets are worth money, and I sell to the highest bidder."

After Sir Arthur had taken a cup of wine in proof of his friendship with the band, the Bat led him to the mouth of the cave, where they found the young soldier's horse ready saddled and bridled. The horse was quite fresh, having been well groomed and fed.

"If you follow this path," said the Bat, "it will lead you to Enfield, where I advise you to remain until daybreak. Should you meet any of our band use the words, 'The Bat flies by night,' and they will let you pass."

"Thanks!" cried Sir Arthur. "How shall I ever return you your kindness?"

"Fear not; one day I shall ask you to favour me."

"And trust me I shall be ready to do so."

"By the way, there is one thing I wish you would do."

"Name it, and it shall be done."

"In the gay world, you may meet a young man whom once I knew; his name is Percy Marvel—a gallant young fellow—rather given to boasting, and terribly fond of gaming."

"I have heard of him," replied Sir Arthur.

"If you meet him, treat him kindly."

"He shall be my friend."

"No," replied the Bat sternly. "I would not have it so."

"And why not?"

"I have my reasons," replied the other sadly. "Ask me no more. One day you may know all, at present my lips are sealed."

"If I am not to be this young man's friend, how am I to help him?"

"By recognising him when you meet in society. Don't gamble with him, above all don't quarrel with him."

"But if I meet and like him, may I not make him my friend?"

"Do as you like," replied the Bat; "but, if you will take my advice, you will merely know him as an acquaintance."

"What is to become of Alice?" demanded Sir Arthur.

"Fear not for her," replied the Bat. "She shall be well provided for by Madge until I can in safety return her to her father."

"Farewell, then," cried Sir Arthur. "We shall meet again."

"Yes," replied the other.

"When?"

"That I know not, but be assured of this, if you require help, I will not fail you."

"Thanks, but there is but small chance of that, I think."

"I hope so, but fear danger is nearer to you than you think."

"How so?"

"Who was it attempted to carry off the girl I rescued?"

"It must have been Lord Redfern, but in his disguise I knew him not."

"Beware of him, and———."

"Well?" demanded the young man, impatiently.

"Above all, beware of Jonathan Wild."

"What! that contemptible bloodhound; that wretched thief-taker?"

"Be not foolish," said the Bat, "he is no contemptible foe. Money and power are both in his hands. There is an old saying 'that there is a skeleton in every house.' Jonathan lives by raking out these old musty bones, and terrifying the owners of them into submission by rattling them in their ears."

"Well, thank Heaven I have no skeleton," laughed Sir Arthur.

"Be not too sure of that," replied the Bat; "you may not as yet have discovered the secret cupboard that contains it; but when you do, trust me, you will dread it all the more because it has been concealed."

"It may be so, and now, good night—would that I could say my *honest* friend!"

"You may say so, with quite as much truth as you say it to the gentlemen of the Court. We rob men of their gold; the gallants of the Court rob men of their estates, their honour, but *they* are gentlemen. Honesty by courtesy is like hereditary titles, and may be claimed by thickheaded thieves and fools; therefore, by courtesy, *I* will have none of it."

"As you will," replied Sir Arthur. "I have discovered many things to-night."

"And what are they?"

"That honesty, philosophy, and mercy may be found in a———well, I don't know what to say."

"You mean a rascals' cave. Believe me, many years after this, when the science of thieving advances, as it will do with all other sciences—you will see that the thieve's work will be turned into a business, and to a certain extent be considered honourable; but then, the idea of demanding money will be dropped, and that of swindling people out of it will be taken up."

"It may be so," said Sir Arthur. "And now, farewell, and trust me you shall not find that I have forgotten your kindness, should you ever require my services."

"Farewell," cried the Bat, and entered the cave.

"So," cried Jonathan Wild, "you have sent off your gallant at last. You have made a good day's work, my friend."

"I do not understand you," replied the Bat.

"But, 'tut! man. Don't be a fool; you know well enough what I mean. Sir Arthur is a rich man, and will be much richer in a little while."

"And what of that?"

"Why, when *we* threaten him with exposure he *must* pay."

"And do you dare tell me that you intend betraying this man?"

"Of course, why not?"

"Have you no honour?"

"None!"

"Miserable cur!" cried the Bat, "take warning by what I now tell you. If you dare to interfere with this gentleman, by Heaven I'll have your life."

"You!" thundered Jonathan, "why you are in my power. I have but to raise my hand and in a week you will swing at Tyburn."

Scarcely had the words passed his lips than a well-directed blow from Batswing stretched him on the ground.

It was some minutes before he recovered himself, then rising slowly he wiped the blood from his mouth and said:

"I give you four years longer; at the end of that time your blood shall answer for that blow—I swear it by Heaven."

With a fierce scowl at the Bat he turned slowly on his heel and strode away.

CHAPTER XI.

WHAT BECAME OF LORD CLUMBER'S PLATE.

When Bob Blow the Bellows arrived home, he was surprised to find that some one had been in the smithy, for some of his tools had evidently been moved. The furnace had been stirred up to make a blaze, and some sheet iron had been placed round it in such a way that the light should not show outside the door.

"Damnation!" cried the smith, "who could have been here?"

He searched about the place in every direction, but could not find a single thing to give him a clue to guess who had been his strange visitor.

"It's no good," muttered the smith, "that some one has been here is evident, but who the devil it is I don't know. I must change my clothes and face it out any way."

Quickly stripping off his mask and coat he hid them away, then drawing off his boots, which were thickly covered with mud, he concealed them under some rods of iron, and then slipping on his leather apron, he seized hold of an iron bar which had been left in the fire, and placing it on the anvil commenced hammering away like mad, at the same time singing:—

"The moon is rising up aloft,
    The bright stars gleam on high,
When I in accents kind and soft
    Must bid my love good bye.

The tears come rolling down her cheek,
    And sobs her bosom heave;
The parting words she cannot speak,
    In silence I must leave.

But dash the tear-drops from your eye,—
    They don't become a man;
Stick to your work—your fortune try,
    And do the best you can.

"I don't hear anyone about," said Bob, as he left off humming and singing; "well, here goes for another stave—

"Mincing Moll was a lady fair,
    A lady of high degree;
But she left her father's lordly halls
    For to roam along with me.

"For she was a lass as liked a glass,
    Likewise her liberty;
So she mounted her horse, as a matter of course,
    And bolted away with me. D'ye see?
    And bolted away with me."

"And bolted away with me! d'ye see? And bolted away with me!" echoed a shrill voice outside the door, on which, at the same time, some sharp kicks were delivered.

"Blessed if there ain't that cursed little imp, Jerry Blinker. What can he want here at this time o' the night?"

The smith unbolted the door and admitted our young friend, who capered into the room whistling, and, hopping up to the forge, commenced warming his hands.

"Well!" said the smith, "what is it you want now?"

"Civility!" cried Jerry; "that there costs nothing; whilst rudeness does."

"You'll find that familiarity costs more than either, you young imp of Satan," said the smith angrily.

"Ho! ho! ho!" laughed Jerry, holding his sides and capering about like one possessed; "ho! ho! ho! now lively the merry smith is to-night; it's quite a treat to see him."

"Curse you, keep quiet," growled the smith, "or I'll split your skull with this sledge-hammer."

"Come, come," cried Jerry, "don't let your good fortune make you proud, Bob Blow the Bellows. How much is the plate worth? Is it enough for all on us to become honest upon, eh? Shall we retire to some suburban retreat, take a willa, wed a wife, and wisit the wealthy?"

"What has the plate got to do with you?" demanded the smith.

"What has it got to do with me? Why a great deal, to be sure. Didn't I bring the sodgers up here to your shop? and didn't I put you up to the rig? And are yer going to round on a chap in this manner? Now, look here, Bob Blow the Bellows, none o' yer larks. I've done a lot o' things for you, and we've been sworn pals, and if you're a going to cry out 'offs,' I'm not; and so I give you warning I won't be done, not by nobody."

"Don't be too sure of that," said the smith; "who are you, I should like to know, that you should not be done as well as your betters, eh?"

"Betters, indeed," replied Jerry Blinker, indignantly, "and who are my betters?"

"Why, I'm your better, ain't I?" roared the smith.

"No, you're not!" shouted Jerry; "and I'll prove it afore long."

"You, you little imp! You prove yourself my better? Why, I could crush you with a blow!"

"Hold, hold, good Master smith," cried Jerry, shrinking away from the huge menacing fist which Bob shook at him; "surely it is not by strength alone you would prove who is the best? That must be done by cunning. Now, I am willing to wager you five pounds that I am a better schemer and, therefore, a more able man than you are."

"You, manniken, bet five pounds! Why where would you get it?"

"From the first person I met who happened to possess that amount."

"And do you think any person in their senses would lend you such an amount?"

"I should not take the trouble to ask them," replied Jerry.

The smith looked at the lad for a few moments, and gradually his features commenced to relax, and at last he broke into a merry laugh.

"Curse me, if ever I saw such a young brute!" he cried at last.

"That's neither here nor there," replied Jerry. "Do you take the bet?"

"Just to punish you, I will," cried the smith; "now prove yourself the best man of the two!"

"Done!" cried Jerry. "Now, to commence with: Who brought the soldiers round here, and gave you the tip about the plate?"

"Why you did, to be sure."

"And how did you act?"

"For the best," growled the smith. "But, with all your sharpness, my young buck, you were out in your reckoning."

"How so?"

"Why, there wasn't any plate or jewels at all in the coach."

"No!" exclaimed Jerry, in deep amazement.

"No; not a thing," cried the smith. "So much for your sharpness, Mr. Perky."

"So much for my sharpness, indeed!" sighed Jerry, gloomily; "where do you think it could have gone?"

"How should I know?" said the smith. "Perhaps you can tell me, Mr. Cunning?"

"Perhaps I can," crowed Jerry.

"You!"

"Yes, me!" shouted Jerry. "Who's the best man now?"

"Where is it?" demanded the smith incredulously.

"Here!" replied Jerry, writhing on the ground in delight; "here, in this very smithy; all safely stowed away under the false forge, yonder. Ho! ho! ho! How I did grin when I saw you and the rest running over the fields after an empty coach. I couldn't call you back for laughing."

"But how did you manage to prig it?" asked the smith, grinning with delight.

"Why, when you were a hammering on the forge all the soldiers got as near to the fire as they could, and consequently were almost deafened by the clang of your hammer. So I crawled under the coach, and with a spring saw which I always carry with me, I cut out the pannel underneath the seat of the carriage. That done, in I crawled. I found that there were three cases inside, all of them able to pass under the seat; so I shoved them out on to the soft mud in the road, where they fell without making any noise. Soon after the carriage rolled away, leaving the plate behind. When they had gone I dragged the boxes into the ditch, and then came here to get some tools to break them open; and then I saw you fellows making off to steal what wasn't to be found. I broke open the boxes, carried the plate in here through the trap. Then I dragged the empty boxes to the pond, filled them with stones, and sank them. Afterwards I took the piece of wood I cut from the carriage and, breaking it up, burnt it in your furnace. And now I'll trouble you for five pounds."

"Well, I'm blest if you ain't a trump," cried the smith, "and if I—"

At this moment they both started to their feet in alarm.

"Hush! what was that?" whispered the smith.

"Someone crying for help," replied Jerry, "I'll be off and reconnoitre. If there's danger you shall hear the cry, if not I shall return to the inn, creep into the loft, and have a good sleep. You'd better pretend to be asleep also."

Acting on the hint, the smith threw off his apron, and coiled himself on some rough blankets; whilst Jerry crept through the secret hutch behind the smithy.

CHAPTER XII.
THE BENIGHTED TRAVELLERS.

The smith listened anxiously for some time, and was then startled by the hooting of a screech owl close by his smithy.

He listened to hear if it were repeated, but it came not. Again the shouts for help were heard, and shortly afterwards the tramp of men's feet followed by some heavy blows at the door.

"Who's there?" demanded the smith in sleepy tones, "Can't a fellow have a moment's rest?"

"Open the door, in the King's name," cried a stern voice.

Carefully drawing off his boots, the smith stole across the room to where some pistols were hidden, and seizing two of them advanced to the door.

"Before I open this door," he exclaimed, "I must first know who and what you are. This is no time for honest men to be out."

"We are the soldiers who passed here but a little while ago, in charge of a carriage."

"If that be the case," demanded the smith, "what has brought you back, and on foot too?"

"We have been robbed of everything; horses and money."

"Come, come; this trick will not serve," cried the smith. "The gallant captain whom I saw here—having had the honour of shoeing his horse—was not a man to be robbed or played with."

"That is true," replied the voice, "as you will find out if you do not open the door immediately. I am in no mood for parleying out in the wet."

"Well, as there is nothing in my abode for men to rob," said the smith, "I will let you in."

As he spoke the smith threw open the door and admitted the captain and the three soldiers.

They indeed made a miserable appearance; their clothes, torn and covered with mud from the rough usage they had received, were dripping with wet, whilst their faces were blue with cold.

It was with the greatest difficulty that the smith could contain his merriment at the wretched figure which they made; but prudence overcame his inclination to laughter; and holding up his hands he exclaimed,

"Goodness gracious, my masters! what have you been doing?"

"Doing!" exclaimed the officer, "nothing. Would that we had been doing something, instead of being treated in this ignominious manner."

After some further inquiries the captain related how the soldiers had been unhorsed, much to the amusement of the smith, who, however, received the history with many exclamations of surprise and alarm.

"Who do you think the thieves were?" demanded the smith.

"How should I know?" replied the officer, "unless it be some of the band of that notorious highwayman, Batswing."

"It is he, you may depend upon it," cried the smith; "he is the terror of the surrounding neighbourhood."

"It strikes me, friend, that he and his rascals must have some good friends in the peasantry round about to help them."

"Nay, I think not that," said the smith, "for they all fear him so."

"How could he have followed us so well, unless he had been informed of our movements?"

"Doubtless some of his scouts have followed you; and while you rested here for your horse to be shoed gave him the signal."

"It may be so," said the captain, "but he shall pay dearly for this freak."

The smith never answered this, for at that moment the distant but distinct cry of the screech owl sounded in his ears.

"Curse it, what can be up now?" he muttered to himself, "there is mischief abroad. I wish I could get rid of my guests; it would be much safer. But I dare not hint at such a thing."

"Do you live here?" demanded the captain.

"No, my cottage is at Edmonton. I am seldom here after dark, but, to-night having work to do, and the weather being so bad, I determined to stay here."

"Have you no spirits that you can give us to refresh our weary frames? You shall be well paid for it. Not now, truly, for those wretched thieves have robbed us of every farthing, but I will send you the money."

"Nay, worshipful sir," replied the smith humbly, "I have a bottle of brandy which is at your service,

HOW THE GOVERNOR OF NEWGATE PAID THE REWARD.

but I require not payment for it. I am poor, but honest, and it shall never be said that I turned from giving hospitality as far as my poor means go to those who are in distress."

As he spoke he rose from his seat, and opening a cupboard placed some glasses and a bottle of brandy before the soldiers.

At that moment a loud "hallo" was heard outside the smithy.

All paused and listened.

"House a hoy!" shouted the voice, "What ho! there. Have you no pity, that you will let a fellow-creature die from cold on such a night?"

"Who is that?" demanded the officer sternly. "You seem to have very late visitors, master smith."

"Pardon me," replied the smith, "I never had them until you set the example. I know no more who this

No. 3.

is than you do. Some poor benighted traveller, I suppose."

"The voice does not sound so weak," replied the officer.

"Gentlemen, you are masters here." said the smith coolly; "therefore I will do as you like. If you bid me open the door I will do so; but if you are afraid, why then I will tell this fellow to go on down the lane until he comes to Stamford."

"Afraid!" said the officer; "we have no fear, and, as we have now as little to lose as you say you have, open the door as soon as you will."

The smith made no reply, but at once threw open the door.

It was some time before any one appeared, and then a strange figure presented itself to the wondering gaze of the spectators.

The figure was that of a young man of about twenty-five to thirty, tall, and well-made, with a bold, hand-some, though somewhat defiant countenance.

His features were large and regular; but the most striking part of his face was the immense eyes, which at times appeared mournful and at others twinkled with good mirth and comic humour.

His dress had been handsome, but was now torn in shreds and bespattered in mud. An empty sheath that had evidently once held a goodly sword, dangled at his side, but his belt was devoid of pistols.

A battered three-cornered hat was placed carelessly on his head, giving him, in spite of his wobegone state, a devil-may-carish air.

"What ho, my masters!" exclaimed the young fellow as he entered the open door. "You seem a goodly company, indeed, to let a poor devil, who has been completely robbed and half murdered, shout himself hoarse without making even a sign or sound that he is heard."

"How should I know that you have been robbed," grumbled the smith.

"Faith, I know not—if you had persisted in not admitting me," replied the stranger.

"It seems that every one has been robbed to-night," cried the smith ill-temperedly; "and that they will all stop in my poor smithy. I should have thought that gentlemen would have preferred going to the inn down yonder to such a dirty hole."

"Tush, man; when a fellow is in a plight like this a barn would be a paradise. But have these gentlemen, whom I see are soldiers, been robbed?"

"I' faith, sir, we have," said the captain, "and in a way that is most disgraceful."

"For my part I have certainly been robbed and badly treated; but I gave the fellows, although there were four of them, a good deal of trouble, therefore I hold the robbery no disgrace to myself."

"Four of them," cried the captain; "it must have been the same gang as robbed us."

"Probably it was."

"What sort of men were they?" demanded the officer.

"Oh! burly rough fellows, mounted on rather jaded hacks. Two of them, by the way, were leading a couple of horses that had undoubtedly been taken from a carriage. The leader was about the size and make of our friend here who has granted us shelter."

"By heavens! it is the same band," thundered the officer.

"Which way did they go?" asked the smith, pretending to be alarmed, and hastily barring the door.

"When first I met them they were going the way to Epping; but on the arrival of a fifth man—"

"A fifth man," demanded the captain.

"Yes, a tall, lithe fellow, dressed in black, with a long black cloak."

"That must have been Batswing," screamed the soldiers and the smith together.

"That it was not," replied the stranger coolly.

"How do you know, sir?" demanded the officer. "I hope you have no dealings with that wretched outlaw."

"It is evident that I have had with his band," replied the stranger, showing his torn clothes.

"This is no time for jesting," said the officer impatiently; "a large treasure has been stolen, and it behoves every one to give what information he can to aid in its recovery."

"My dear sir, have I ever refused to do so?" demanded the stranger.

"Perhaps not," replied the officer; "but I wish to know why you are so confident that the mysterious man in black whom you saw was not Batswing?"

"I am not only certain it was not, but I am also prepared to swear that this terrible Batswing had nothing whatever to do with the robbery you speak about."

"You will excuse me, sir, if I state that I think your information not only singular, but also very suspicious."

"But, my dear sir, do have reason. I am giving you

what you required—information; but you will not take it."

"Proceed, sir, proceed!" said the officer, stamping his foot impatiently.

"So I will, if you let me alone. As I was saying, the men were going towards Epping when first I met them by my misfortune. They cried, 'Stand and deliver.' I answered 'Go and be '——you know what. I drew my sword and fought; but at last was thrown from my horse and held on the ground, whilst my pockets were rifled."

"Well, well," cried the officer.

"Ah! I see; my robbery don't interest you at all; but to proceed. No sooner had they completed their task than one gentleman kindly suggested it would be as well to 'dash my brains out,' whereupon the leader of the band objected. An argument ensued of which my life was the pleasant subject, and to which I was anything but a disinterested spectator.

"Just at the moment when I thought my friend was getting the worst of the argument, this mysterious figure appeared, and instantly all the men clustered round him, taking care, however, to keep me a safe prisoner."

"It must have been Batswing," muttered the officer.

"If it must have been it must," said the stranger, "but as it could not have been it could not." The mysterious figure spoke a few hurried words to the men, the greater part of which I overheard.

"The game is up," he exclaimed.

"How so?" cried one.

"Batswing is shot."

"Impossible!" cried a third.

"Alas! it is too true," said the new comer, "a party of bloodthirsty dragoons pursued and shot him. He crawled into a country girl's hut, who now holds the body determined to claim the two hundred pounds reward."

"It cannot be," cried the men, who were all deeply affected.

"Alas! it is indeed true," answered the mysterious individual in black; "our noble captain is no more. His generous heart no longer beats; his balmy breath has fled, his gallant spirit departed."

"Tush!" cried the captain, "to use such terms to a thief."

"Why not?" demanded the stranger, "he is dead, and funeral sermons are proverbially untrue."

"May I ask how you escaped being killed? These men are scarcely kind knowing their chief killed?"

"Believe me, sir, you wrong them; their grief had softened their hearts, and they were merciful."

"What shall we do with this hound?" said one.

"Knock him on the head," said my rough friend.

"Let the poor beast go," said the mysterious individual, evidently not meaning my horse, for at that moment he mounted my steed, "Let the poor beast go, and we will make our best way to Barking, and from thence take ship to France."

"And so they left you?"

"And so they left me. I scrambled up, and having found this broken half of my sword wandered on, now and then shouting for help, until seeing the light of this forge I made to it."

"And right welcome you are, sir," cried the officer. "It is a great consolation to me to know that this arch fiend is shot. I will go and see his body to-morrow at Newgate."

"It will be there in the morning, depend on it," replied the stranger, "The lass won't care about keeping a dead man, and she will care about getting the two hundred pounds. I shall certainly go when I get back to town."

"Supposing we go together then," said the officer.

"With pleasure," replied the stranger.

"Your name?"

"Percy Marvel—and yours?"

"Captain Jennings, of his Majesty's Dragoons."

"I am delighted to make your acquaintance, captain," said Percy; "I wish we had something to pledge each other in, were it only to drink to better fortune."

"Here is some brandy," replied the captain, "come, let us have a bumper."

"With all my heart," replied Percy, filling his glass; "here's to our next merry meeting."

"With pleasure."

"But how are we to get back to town in this dreadful plight? We shall be laughed at by all the wretched little ragamuffins in London."

"Faith, I know not. How goes the night, smith?"

"The rain has ceased, and the moon is rising."

"Then," cried the captain, "I will start directly, and reach London under the cover of night. Will you march with us?"

"I feel too tired; so if our friends here will permit me, I'll take a rest by the fire until morning. Then I will proceed to town in a hired coach."

"As you will," said Captain Jennings, "we shall soon meet again.

Ah! yes, say to morrow at two for a little dinner at my house in St. James's Street; we can go from thence to Newgate."

"Agreed!" cried the captain, shaking Percy warmly by the hand, "farewell then until to-morrow. Now, men, follow closely."

The men placed themselves in order, and the next minute they were heard splashing through the muddy lane.

When they had gone some way the smith rushed into the house, and quickly closing and bolting the door seized Percy Marvel by the hand.

"What is the meaning of this, captain?" he cried in hurried tones, "why run this risk?"

"Risk, what risk? Who will know the Bat, the terrible Batswing, in this gay plumage."

"But have you had a fight?"

"No—I was pursued, but escaped. I met our little friend, Jerry Blinker. As I came alonghe told me all that has happened, and assisted me in froming this disguise."

"What is to be done with the plate?"

"It must remain here until we can ship it in safety."

"But how about your engagement to-morrow with the Captain?"

"I shall keep it," said Percy, or, as he was mostly called, "the Bat."

"What! visit Newgate?"

"And why not?"

"But Jonathan Wild hates you," cried the smith.

"Truly, but he little thinks that the gay, light-hearted Percy Marvel is one and the same with the gloomy and mysterious Batswing."

"If he discovers it you will lose your life."

"Nay, be not so sharp. I can only be condemned by a jury, and proofs may be wanting. Besides, prison bars can be cut and locks forced."

"But consider."

"I have considered, and am determined to go, come what may."

"May I not go with you?"

"No; Jerry Blinker will need you to carry out another scheme that I have formed. The boy is clever, and you, during my absence, must obey him. He has my orders, and will tell you what to do. Now let me sleep; but mind you wake me at dawn."

Wrapping himself up in a blanket, the Bat threw himself on the ground, and was soon in a deep sleep.

CHAPTER XIII.
JONATHAN WILD AND LORD REDFERN PLAN VENGEANCE.

Jonathan Wild's house in the Old Bailey was a dismal-looking building, standing some little distance back from the main road. A dingy paved courtyard ran up to the dirty door steps which led to a strong oaken door, lined with sheet iron and studded with huge headed nails.

In the middle of this prison-like door was a brass plate, on which was inscribed the odious name of "Jonathan Wild."

The windows of this gloomy dwelling were protected by strong iron bars, so closely placed together that they excluded the greater part of the light, whilst the solid character of the masonry in which they were embedded showed the immense strength of the building.

Dull and miserable as the external appearance of the house was, it was nothing to the indescribable feeling of terror with which the interior inspired one.

The stairs, the walls, and the floors were all of stone. Huge iron rings with chains to them showed that the rooms were often used as dungeons; whilst other rings on the floor showed where traps were to be found leading to secret passages, the terrible history of which we shall have to touch upon elsewhere.

One room in this house of horrors was termed "the office," and was used by Jonathan Wild as a place wherein to receive his clients.

The furniture in this room was simply a huge table, on which were writing materials, a large arm-chair for the thief-taker, and a smaller one for any visitor whom he might deem worthy of asking to be seated.

Round the walls were ranged terrible mementoes of criminals who had been executed, together with artfully wrought iron manacles to secure prisoners in such a way as at the same time to cause them terrible agony.

On the morning when this chapter commences Jonathan was seated at his table in anything but a pleasant mood.

His wolfish eyes glared with intense hatred, and his lips were drawn back so tightly that they showed his gleairng teeth.

Opposite him, wrapped in a large roquelaure, or riding cloak, stood Lord Redfern, looking almost as evilly disposed as Jonathan Wild.

"And so, my Lord," said Jonathan Wild quietly, "you are willing to pay five hundred pounds to me if I can bring this highwayman to the scaffold."

"Yes, willingly."

"May I ask what is the cause for such determined hatred, my lord, to one who, as far as I can see, has never done you harm?"

"What matter the cause of the hatred if it exists," cried Lord Redfern.

"True," replied Jonathan; "it is an old belief that hatreds which are without a cause are the most intense."

"Cause or no cause, my hatred is to the death."

"You have heard the news, my lord, that arrived this morning?"

"No; what was it?"

"Lord Clumber's jewels and plate, which were being conveyed to London under a convoy of soldiers, have been stolen."

"Stolen! impossible," exclaimed Lord Redfern; "they were safe at Enfield."

"Ah!" cried Jonathan, with a fiendish sneer, "how does your lordship know that?"

"At least I—that is—I heard so."

"I suppose your lordship was not on the road last night?"

"Why do you ask? The idea is too absurd."

"As to the idea being absurd, that I am not so sure about," said Jonathan, fixing his keen eyes on Lord Redfern; "the reason why I asked was this. If you had been on the road last night there would be little use in my telling you the rest of the news."

"I suppose more robbery."

"No," replied Jonathan.

"What then?"

"Murder!"

"Murder!" echoed Lord Redfern, shrinking back.

"Yes, murder, my lord. It appears an old farmer living near Epping was basely murdered last night. His name was Mark Landon. You may have heard it, my lord."

"I? no—no—never!" exclaimed Redfern.

"His daughter, a beautiful girl, disappeared: in fact, was carried off against her will yesterday."

"Against her will? How know you that?"

"Because the carriage bearing her towards London was stopped, and the girl rescued by Batswing."

"By Batswing!" faltered Lord Redfern; "how is that if he stole the plate?"

"He did not steal the plate; but he rescued the girl. The man who had carried her off gave the alarm to the soldiers who were conveying the jewels, and they pursued the highwayman."

"And the man who was carrying the girl off?"

"Said he was her father, but in the confusion escaped in his carriage."

"Who could the man be?" said Lord Redfern.

"Would your lordship like to know?" sneered Jonathan.

"Of course I should."

"And why?"

"To bring the villain to justice," cried Lord Redfern in a dramatic style. "Has he not slain the father; desecrated an honest hearth; torn away a fair and innocent maiden? Poor was the home, no doubt; but to me the poor man's hut is as sacred as the King's palace."

"Ho! ho! ho!" roared Jonathan; "so you would know this man?"

"I would! Who is he?"

"Yourself!" thundered Jonathan Wild, springing to his feet.

"Me!" faltered his lordship.

"You, my lord! It is useless to prevaricate with me. You slew the father in carrying off the daughter against her will. I know this. But fear not, your secret is safe with me."

Lord Redfern bit his lip, but did not answer.

"Of course you hate Batswing. Men hate to be foiled in their intentions, although those intentions be bad ones."

"Can you prove what you have said?" demanded Redfern in a firm voice.

"I can," was the stern answer.

"But you will not."

"No; if you are true to me."

"And Batswing?"

"Shall die!"

"When he is dead, the five hundred is yours," cried Lord Redfern.

"He shall not live long, my lord; rest assured of that. I, too, have a score to settle with him, and those whom Jonathan Wild hates seldom live long."

"And why do you hate him?"

"That is my secret," replied Jonathan with a grin.

"Can you not hunt him down, then, and have him tried and hanged at once?"

"No."

"Why not?"

"Such men as Batswing are difficult to manage. They are too powerful to be treated as ordinary men. Besides, my lord, I will be candid with you; if I were to betray Batswing in the open manner you wish I should have to betray some dozens of other rascals who are valuable to me. Mine is a peculiar business."

"It is, indeed," said Lord Redfern sardonically; "it strikes me that there is but little difference between the thief and thieftaker."

"Not much, I admit. You know the adage, 'Set a thief to catch a thief!'"

"And supposing I were to betray you to the authorities?" said Lord Redfern.

"They would pretend not to believe you," said Jonathan, with a smile; "they know my power and value it. Now, were I to take it into my head to discover the murderer of Farmer Landon—"

"Enough, enough," cried Lord Redfern; "speak no more of that, I pray you."

"I might find the right man; but if business was more profitable the other way, I should not find the right man. Still, I would, to satisfy the Government, the public, and justice, find and hang a man, if it were only to keep up my reputation."

Lord Redfern shuddered at this man who could so calmly tell his own villany.

Taking a pocket-book from his pocket, Lord Redfern drew therefrom a couple of one hundred pound notes and placed them before Jonathan.

"There is your silence money," he said: "is that enough?"

"For the present," said Wild, coolly pocketing the notes. "I see, my Lord, that we shall soon understand each other."

"I see we do," replied Redfern.

"When shall we say Batswing is to fall?"

"As soon as possible."

"Remember, five hundred pounds are mine upon his death. No matter how or where he dies, the five hundred is mine."

"On one condition."

"And that is—?"

"That he dies before six months is out."

"Agreed."

"If he is executed for the murder of Farmer Landon, an extra five pounds shall be yours."

"That is difficult," said Jonathan. "Any one executed as the murderer, will prevent the real murderer being tried."

"I will give five hundred pounds for the execution of Batswing as Farmer Landon's murderer, and two hundred for the execution of any one of his band for the same offence."

"Agreed!" said Wild; "the case shall soon be settled."

At this moment Lord Redfern was startled by a sharp knock at the door.

"Who is that?" he demanded.

"My porter, gaoler, or anything else you like to call him."

"What can he want now?"

"That I cannot tell," replied Jonathan; "the best way will be to question him, it is something important or he would not be here, that is certain."

As he spoke he unlocked the door and admitted a dark beetle-browed man.

If nature had tried to make a villain of as deep a dye as Jonathan Wild, but of a lower type, she could not have succeeded better than she had done in the case of Ralph Johnston, or Rough Ralph, as he was generally called.

The forehead was low and receding; his eyes small with drooping lids, that gave them the appearance of being half closed.

A small lump of loose flabby flesh formed his nose, which hung down so close to his mouth, that he seemed to have no upper lip at all. His mouth was large, with heavy thick lips that hung down like those of a negro.

The two most striking characteristics in this terrible countenance were the lower jaw and chin. The jaw fell in a straight line from the ear till it reached the level of the chin, to which it ran out, forming a complete right angle. No animal ever possessed a more powerful or massive jaw.

The chin was immensely long and flat, not even showing the least sign to a division.

This creature was a giant in size and strength, as he was a demon in cruelty. Unlike his master, there was one vice which he did not possess, and that one was cupidity. Rough Ralph would not do anything for money; he no more cared for gold than for water. Give him as much to eat and drink as he wanted, and he asked for no more.

This made him valuable to Jonathan, as he was unbribable; for Wild took care that Rough Ralph should be well fed and generally half drunk.

But, although Ralph would do nothing for money, there was nothing he would not do for the love of cruelty. To torture any one was his delight, his pleasure was to watch other people's agonies; and for this great quality Jonathan had made him his head gaoler.

"Well! what is the matter now?" demanded Jonathan, sharply.

"Batswing is taken," growled Rough Ralph.

"What!" cried Lord Redfern, "Batswing taken! where is he?"

"In Newgate."

"Good!" exclaimed Jonathan, "I'll take care he does not escape."

"That ain't at all possible," growled Rough Ralph.

"What is not possible?" demanded Jonathan sharply.

"That Batswing should escape," replied the other.

"And why not?" demanded Wild.

"Because he's dead."

"Dead!"

"Shot through and through," growled Rough Ralph.

"Can it be possible?" exclaimed Lord Redfern.

"Of course it can; the girl as brought him in, that is his body, got her two hundred pounds paid her by the Governor, for the body was recognised at once, and has gone back to Epping."

"The five hundred is mine," whispered Jonathan.

"I know it," replied Lord Redfern, "but let us make certain that this tale is true."

"That is soon done. Come with me and we will view the body. There can be no doubting that," said Wild.

"Agreed!" replied Redfern, "fear not; this once proved, and the money is yours."

Jonathan Wild paused only to throw a cloak over his shoulders, and seizing his bludgeon, he led the way from his own fearful prison to the little less dismal one of Newgate.

CHAPTER XIV.

HOW THE £200 REWARD WAS CLAIMED.—THE BODY RECOGNISED.

Early the morning after the robbery of Lord Clumber's plate, a covered country cart might have been seen driving slowly across Smithfield in the direction of Newgate.

The cart was driven by a country girl whom few people would have considered pretty, for her lank red hair seemed only restrained from breaking out from underneath her poke bonnet.

She was, however, neatly dressed in a blue gown just short enough to show a somewhat thick ankle and an undoubtedly large foot.

By her side was seated an old woman with a sharp nose, and a peculiar vicenish look that was anything but prepossessing; whilst a peculiar sniff accompanied by a convulsive twitching of her boney fingers was decidedly unpleasant.

Onward in silence the young maiden drove with her silent companion, both evidently being unused to the town; for they kept as far back under the cart cover as they possibly could, so as to avoid the gaze of the passers by.

At length they drew up at the large gate of Newgate, and the maiden springing out of the cart, boldly rang the bell.

"Well," exclaimed a burly gaoler, "what is it you want, eh?"

"Please, sir, I want to see the Governor," simpered the girl, making a bob curtsey.

"See the Guv'ner," cried the man, "well I'm blest if I ever 'eard tell of such a thing."

"Oh! but please, sir, I must," said the girl, earnestly.

"Oh! you must, must yer?" replied the man; then turning to some one inside the lodge, he called out—

"I say Zac, come here; here's a rum go. Blest if there ain't a bit of a gal come for to see the Guv'ner."

Zac, who was also stout and burly, rolled up to the wicket, and lolling at the opening with his hands in his breeches pockets, whistled softly and shook his head slowly.

"I should think not," said the first gaoler, who seemed perfectly to understand these movements; "I should rather think not."

"What do you mean?" asked the girl.

"Why, that it can't be done, my dear. Guv'ners don't come for the axing. That's so, isn't it, Zac?"

Zac, who still continued staring and whistling, nodded in assent.

"But I've something important to tell him—or rather, to give him."

"Give it me, then," said the first gaoler, winking; "won't I do as well?"

"No!" replied the maiden; "I'm sure you will not."

"Well, if you can't tell me what your business is, I can't disturb the Guv'ner for nothing, so you had better be off," said the first gaoler, about to shut the door.

"Oh! do stay a moment, sir," cried the girl, clasping her hands; "I will tell you if you will let me whisper to you. I don't want anyone to hear, or you'll have a crowd, and I can't abear a crowd."

"Well," said the mollified gaoler, "what is it all about."

The girl whispered something in his ear which made him open his eyes and mouth with astonishment.

"Wake up, Zac," he cried; "unbar the door and lead that there cart into the yard, whilst I go for the Guv'ner."

This command made the taciturn Mr. Zac open his eyes wider and whistle a little louder. But, although he did not say one word, he drew his hands from his pockets and commenced unbarring the door.

This done, he seized the horse's head and led the cart into the yard, closing the gates behind him. Having accomplished this piece of work, he leant against the wall, plunged his hands into his breeches pockets, whistled, and watched the girl.

They had not long to wait, for Mr. Pitt, the Governor of Newgate, came hurrying towards them, followed by a number of turnkeys.

"Which is the girl?" demanded Mr. Pitt.

"That's her, sir," said the first turnkey, pointing at the girl.

"Oh! you're the young woman, are you?" said the Governor.

"Yes, an' please your worship," said the girl, making a bob.

"Have you got it with you?"

"Yes, yer worship!"

"In this cart?"

"Yes, yer worship!"

"Some of you take it out and lay it on the table in the lodge," said the Governor to the turnkeys.

In a minute two men lifted a *something* wrapped up

in a sheet from the cart—a long peculiar bundle that made the men shudder.

It was a corpse.

They bore it into the room of the lodge, and slowly unwrapped it.

It was the body of a tall, well-made, but rather slim man; the face pale, with hollow cheeks. A deep pointed moustache covered the chin and upper lip, giving the countenance a somewhat fiendish appearance. This ghastly figure was dressed in a complete black suit, the only change of colour being round a hole just over the region of the heart. That was stained with blood.

For a little time the men gazed at the body in silence. At length Mr. Pitt broke into a low chuckle.

"So, so, the Devil has got his due at last! Won't Mr. Wild be in a rage when he hears this. The prince of highwaymen taken, and he no finger in the pie! He'll be Wild by name and wild by nature. Ha! ha! ha! ha!"

"He'll be hawfully to think that he'll have none of the reward," said a turnkey.

At this remark Mr. Pitt became silent and thoughtful; for, until that moment, he had never considered that he also would have no reward.

Mr. Pitt was celebrated for his dreadful meanness and love of gold. He could not bear to think that any one should gain money when he did not share in it. So far did his rapacity go that he bought from the authorities the pleasantest part of the prison—called the Press Yard—for five thousand pounds; this he let out to prisoners at premiums varying from twenty to some hundreds of pounds, by which means he amassed a large fortune at the expense of the poor prisoners who were thrust into the dismal dungeons in other parts of the prison only because they were unable to pay the premium for the Press Yard.

"Ah! the reward," he muttered, "I had forgotten that. Here, Jacobs, place the body in some other place, and you, my lass, follow me. Who is that old woman?"

"My mother, an' please your worship," said the girl, bobbing a curtsey.

"Well, she had better come too."

Mr. Pitt led the way to his private office, and, after telling the old woman and her daughter to be seated, shut the door.

"I suppose, my lass," said the Governor, "that you are anxious to get the reward, eh?"

"If you please sir," said the girl, snigging.

"What is your name?"

"Mary Jane Smike," replied the girl, modestly.

"Well, Mary Jane," said the Governor, tapping her on the cheek, "it will be a nice wedding portion for you. Won't it ma'am."

"She's deaf, sir; its no use speaking to her," said Mary Jane, pointing at the old woman.

"I wish she were blind, I know what I would do."

"What, sir?" asked the girl innocently.

"Kiss you," cried the amorous Governor.

"For shame, sir," cried the offended maiden, springing back just in time to avoid the kiss, and, at the same time, delivering a hearty smack on Mr. Pitt's cheek.

"Never mind, never mind," he cried, trying to smile, but rubbing his cheek at the same time. "But about this reward."

"Well, sir, I suppose you will give it to me."

"Me, my dear? I have nothing to do with it. Besides, the body has not yet been identified."

"But you know it is the man."

"Oh! undoubtedly."

"Then why don't you give me the money?"

"Because it ___ ___thing to do with me; the Government will have to pay you."

"Shure, sir! Sir, shall I have to take the body up to the King's palace before I gets paid?" cried the girl.

"No, no, no; it only wants one or two people to swear that that is the body and you will have the money—say in a week."

"And I shall have to come back all this way again?"

"There is one way I might manage it," said Mr. Pitt.

"Please tell me how," whined the girl, who seemed about to cry.

"You see I have'nt got enough money here. I have a hundred and fifty pounds, and that's all."

"Well, sir," said the girl, stupidly.

"Now, if you would hand me a receipt for the full amount, I would give you the hundred and fifty pounds, and save you all further trouble."

"But you would have fifty pounds for yourself."

"Of course I must have some pay for my trouble."

"But I must ask my mother first," said Mary Jane Smike, and, bustling up to the old woman, commenced bawling the proposition into her ear.

At first the old lady objected strongly; but Mr. Pitt spread out the hundred and fifty gold pieces on the table in such a tempting way that she could resist no longer, but, clutching them up, shuffled them into her bag, at the same time bidding her daughter sign.

"You are sure it is the man," demanded Mr. Pitt.

"Yes, sir; he told us so himself, and all about his being chased by soldiers; and he told us that we were to get the reward when he died, for the trouble we took with him."

Mr. Pitt sat at the table and quickly penned out a declaration to the effect that Miss Mary Jane Smike, of Holly Cottage, Epping, swore to the body being that of one Batswing, &c., and then proceeding to give a full account of how the highwayman had been shot, but had managed to reach the cottage where he died, &c., &c.

This document he made her sign, at the same time telling her that she must hold herself in readiness to appear when wanted to prove this declaration.

He then wrote out a receipt for two hundred pounds, which Mary Jane had to sign; which she did in a very bad style.

When once he had secured these documents he lost no time in showing the two women to the door, and hurrying them from the building, so that no one might question them.

In vain did the first gaoler, who imagined a young wife though plain with two hundred a-year would be no bad match, try to get a word with Miss Mary Jane.

That young lady bundled her mother most unceremoniously into the cart, and then sprang in after her, showing a great deal more leg than might be thought quite proper. Seizing the reins, Mary Jane flicked her whip unpleasantly close to the gaoler's legs, at the same time her left eye opened and shut with a motion that suspicious people might have called a wink.

"She's a rum 'un," growled the gaoler as he shut the door and entered the lodge. "Well she's sure to come again to get the brads, and if she does I'll see if I can't persuade her to become Mistress Gummidge."

Lost in these dreams of gold, if not of love, Mr. Gummidge was about to fall asleep when he was aroused by a sharp tinkling at the bell.

With a half-muttered curse he arose, and throwing open the wicket beheld two fashionably-dressed gentlemen standing at the door.

"Is Mr. Pitt in?" demanded the tallest.

"Yes, sir, I believe he is," replied the gaoler.

"Tell him that Captain Jennings desires to speak with him."

Overcome with the appearance of his visitors, Mr. Gummidge showed them into the lodge, and telling Zac to attend to the door, departed in search of Mr. Pitt, with which gentlemen he soon returned.

"Ah! Captain," cried Mr. Pitt, advancing and rubbing his hands, "I am glad to see you well. Hope you have not come on business. Ha! ha! ha! this is not a pleasant place for that sort of thing."

"In good earnest, no," replied the captain, "but my visit to-day is rather one of pleasure, for I understand that you have to-day received the body of the notorious highwayman, Batswing."

"They say 'ill news travels apace,' Captain," cried Mr. Pitt, "but this time it is good news that has flown so quickly."

"By that I am, I suppose, to understand that you *have* received the body."

"You may, Captain, you may."

"Then I must ask you to be kind enough to shew it to me."

"What, are you so interested in the case?"

"Unfortunately, yes," replied the Captain, "he or his band robbed me of a treasure I had in trust last night. It was one of my soldiers who gave the rascal his mortal wound."

"Oh! if that is the case I will show him to you. This way, gentlemen, this way."

But as they were leaving the lodge they were stopped by another violent ringing at the lodge bell.

"I suppose if the news goes about we shall have a busy time of it. Open the door, Gummidge, and if it is any one for me tell them that I am engaged just at present, and that they must wait."

"It's Mr. Wild, sir, and a gentleman," called out the gaoler.

At the mention of Jonathan Wild's name Mr. Pitt turned round, his face, beaming with smiles, and, walking up to the thief-taker, said in a jeering voice—

"So, Mr. Wild, you've heard the good news, eh? Ah! I thought so, I can see it by your face."

"Yes, I have heard the news," muttered Jonathan, "and I and this gentleman would see the body."

"A friend of yours, Mr. Wild? May I ask his name."

"No!" growled Jonathan, "people who come here dont't care generally about their names being known."

"Come, come, Mr. Wild, you need not be so cross because you have lost the reward; you must remember how lucky you generally are."

"What has the reward to do with either you or me?" demanded Jonathan, fiercely.

"With you perhaps not," said Mr. Pitt, blandly, 'but with me it has a great deal to do."

"How so?" demanded Wild sharply.

"Ah! that is a secret at present," said the Governor, "one day I may tell you, but not at present."

"Curse you!" exclaimed Wild, "what is the good of our standing here talking, let us see the body at once, it is not a pleasant sight."

"He! he! he!" giggled the Governor, as he led the way, at the same time whispering to Captain Jenning's as they walked along, "Jonathan will be so mad to think he has missed the reward. I am so glad to think how he has been done; its perfectly charming."

"I wonder whether Batswing is of your opinion," said the Captain.

"To be sure he is," said his friend.

"How so?" asked Mr. Pitt. "Batswing is dead."

"Just so; but although those who die should forgive their enemies, I don't think any man could possibly forgive Jonathan Wild."

"By Jove, you are right," grinned the Governor, "although I say it as should not, for Jonathan has made lots of money for me. But he is a fiend, and no mistake."

They now entered the darkened room where lay the dead man. All shrank back with the exception of Jonathan Wild, and he, with an exclamation of impatience, drew the sheet from the face.

For a moment he stood gazing at the ghastly face, then turned quickly round on Mr. Pitt.

"What is the meaning of this?" he cried.

"The meaning of what?" cried Mr. Pitt, in alarm.

"This," thundered Jonathan Wild at the top of his powerful voice; "this is not the man!"

"What!" shouted the governor, "not the man?"

"No!" returned Jonathan Wild.

No sooner were the words uttered than all the party advanced to the side of the corpse and gazed at it.

"You must be mistaken, Mr. Wild," cried Mr. Pitt; "you really must."

"I am not, I tell you," replied Jonathan. "That is no more Batswing than I am."

"Mr. Wild is right," said Captain Jennings; "that is not Batswing."

"Then who the devil is it?" demanded Lord Redfern.

"My sergeant, Jones, who pursued Batswing last night. Doubtless he was shot whilst following up Batswing, and that rascal has dressed him up to get the reward. They have altered the face as much as possible, but I can swear to it being my man."

"He will not get any reward," said Jonathan; "he will not venture to send to claim it."

"They have got the reward," groaned Mr. Pitt.

"Have got it!" cried Jonathan; "what do you mean?"

"They—they induced me to pay it them in advance," groaned the unhappy Governor.

The idea of the deceit and the spectacle of the unhappy gaoler writhing in agony, made the company shout with laughter, amongst which mirth Jonathan Wild's was the loudest.

"Ho! ho! ho! Mr. Pitt," he shouted; "you've overreached yourself, eh! I can assure you that I am very pleased that I had nothing to do with this reward. For once Batswing has been of service to me."

"Oh! you may laugh!" roared the unhappy Governor, who was now completely at bay. "You may laugh; but I'll not be swindled, for all this. I'll find out the women and make them confess who instigated this wretched, wicked swindle on a poor man; and when I've found the miscreant he shall be brought to justice, however powerful he be; be he thief or thieftaker, I don't care."

"You had better care," snarled Jonathan, spitefully. "But I forgive your ravings, for no doubt you are mad to think what a fool you have been."

"One thing I am certain about," cried the Governor; "and that is that you shall never touch a farthing of the reward; for I, and I alone, will take this man."

"You!" said Jonathan Wild contemptuously.

"Yes, I!" cried the Governor. "Do you think nobody can take thieves but yourself?"

"Some people take anything that is brought to them," roared Jonathan, pointing to the corpse; "and they meet their reward."

"Oh! you are very clever, I have no doubt," replied the Governor; "but I am willing to bet you two hundred pounds that I take Batswing before you do."

"Done!" shouted Jonathan, mad at being thus dared. "Shall we stake the money?"

As he spoke he drew forth a heavy pocket-book filled with bank notes and memoranda of different kinds.

"There is no occasion to stake the money, Mr. Wild," said the Governor, who could not bear the thoughts of parting with his money.

"As you will," replied Jonathan, replacing his pocket-book; "but the bet is still on.

"Oh, certainly," replied Mr. Pitt.

"That being concluded, we may as well leave," said Captain Jennings; "this place is very close. Mr.

Pitt, I will send down a guard for this body so that the poor fellow may have proper burial."

Slowly they turned and left the room, the Governor leading the way.

As they passed one of the doors Lord Redfern stumbled over the mat and fell against Jonathan, who by this means rolled against Captain Jennings' friend, Mr. Percy Marvel, who threw the thieftaker off in a very unceremonious and haughty manner; but the next moment he apologised, and they left the prison as friendly as could be.

Captain Jennings and Percy Marvel strolled leisurely away towards the Strand, whilst Jonathan and Lord Redfern paced on towards Smithfield.

"Who do you think did this trick?" demanded Lord Redfern.

"Batswing himself!"

"But he would not venture into Newgate."

"No; but his accomplices would. You do not know the power of these men: they have agents everywhere"

"So it seems."

"Where are you going now?"

"To set on some man to spy out this fellow."

"Let me see, a young girl and an old woman brought the body in a cart. Hum! inquiries must be made along the road. I'll leave a note at my house for Ralph, and then we will, if your lordship likes, have a drive over towards Edmonton to hear the news."

"I have no business there," growled Lord Redfern.

"It will be much better for you to come," replied Jonathan, coolly; "it will lull any suspicion that may arise."

"As you will," said Lord Redfern;" but let us haste."

They hurried back as fast as they could to Jonathan's house, pushing past the people, jostling and being jostled by everyone they met.

At last they reached Jonathan's dwelling, and were soon once more in his office.

"Ralph," cried Jonathan; "Mr. Pitt, the Governor of Newgate, has been deceived. They have not taken Batswing, so that you will have the pleasure of being his gaoler yet."

A fiendish grin lit up the monster's face.

"I have some notes to leave for you to attend to about our prisoners. You understand."

Rough Ralph grinned and nodded.

"Hell and furies!" cried Jonathan, as he felt in his pockets. "Where is my pocket-book?"

"You had it a short time ago," replied Lord Redfern. "I saw you with it in your hands."

"It has gone! gone!" cried Jonathan. "Five hundred pounds stolen, and from me; he dares even to rob me."

"Whom do I suspect?" roared Jonathan. "Why, there is but one man in all England who dares do such a thing."

"And that is ——"

"Batswing!" screamed Wild, shaking his fist in the air, "he and only he dared touch me or mine. He has defied my power, refused to pay me tribute; and I have sworn that he shall hang for it. But now there shall be a worse fate for him.'

"What do you mean?" asked Redfern, shrinking back in horror from Jonathan, who looked more like a fiend than a man.

"Mean! Never mind what I *mean;* you shall see, my lord, what I can do. Rough Ralph, prepare the vault by the well, and see that the irons are strongly made, and *rough*—you understand. We will keep this "Bat" caged for our amusement for some time before we deliver him up and claim the reward. I have a plan that will trap him before many days are over."

"Are you sure of that?" demanded Redfern.

"Positive," cried Jonathan; "before this day month Batswing shall be my prisoner: and once in my power, nothing in heaven or earth shall save him!"

CHAPTER XV.

MISS MARY JANE SMIKE AND HER MOTHER PROCEED HOMEWARDS.

When the cart drove away from Newgate both Mary Jane and her mother drew as far back from the gaze of the public as they had done on their way to the prison.

The little horse covered the ground beautifully; it trotted through Bishopsgate down to Shoreditch, and from thence on its way to Stamford.

"Now, then, do you go first or shall I?" demanded the mother.

"You go on first old 'un," was the unfilial answer.

The old lady, however, took no notice of this unflattering answer; but drawing herself as far back as she could, first removed a wig: then wetting the corner of a towel with some water out of a bottle, she removed much of the colour and many of the wrinkles out of her face.

She next commenced turning her dress inside out, which, strange to say, seemed to be really the right way of wearing it, the trimmings and all being of a much finer colour.

After having smoothed her hair, she placed a much smaller bonnet on her head, and then coming forward took the reins from Mary Jane, who unceremoniously dug her in the ribs, at the same exclaiming—

"Well, I'm blest if you ain't a good un. Why, nobody would know you now. You look so blessed honest. Ha! ha! ha!"

"Hold yer tongue, yer fool," cried the old lady, but with evidently a contented and flattered smile. "Go and get your duds slipped, in case the slops should grab us."

Being thus bidden by her mother, Miss Mary Jane crawled to the back of the van like her parent had done.

Shall we peep into the privacy of a maiden's dressing-room, though her boudoir is but a van with straw at the bottom?

Shall we violate that secrecy which hangs around a virgin?

No; we will take but a slight peep, and then pass on.

She, too, has removed her bonnet, and has replaced it with a jockey's cap, much the worse for wear, from under which her short, rough, red hair protrudes like a scarlet chimney-sweeping machine.

In a moment she has thrown off her petticoats—in fact, all her female attire—and stands up neither more nor less than our thieving friend, Jerry Blinker.

Quickly pulling on his top boots, which had been concealed under the straw, he did his female attire up into a bundle, and once more took the reins from Madge.

"Now, Madge, old lady," said the incorrigible young rascal, "tip us the whip, and when we get to a quiet part of the road you must slip down, and I'll go on to the 'Birdcage,' whilst you trudge on to the merry smith's, old Bob Blow the Bellows."

They soon reached a narrow lane, down which Jerry drove, and there, where no one could see them, the old woman alighted, taking the bundles with her.

Bidding Jerry make haste, the old woman took a footpath across the fields, whilst Blinker, who had fallen into his old habit of whistling, struck the canvas covering of the cart, and groomed his horse down with a wisp of straw.

After this proceeding, he carefully rubbed some dust on his face, so that he might have the appearance of having been hard at work.

He then turned the horse's head round, and drove back to the main road, where he let the pony amble along as he liked.

It was a bright day, and the weather being fine. had an oppressive effect upon Jerry Blinker.

JERRY OUTWITTED BY THE QUAKER.

Besides, the pony had no need of any guidance, and knew his way home perfectly well; therefore, why should Jerry not take a nap?

There was no reason why he should not—at least, so he thought—and therefore he determined to have one.

Letting the reins slip gradually from his grasp, he was soon wrapped in a gentle slumber, stretched full length at the bottom of the cart.

How long he had remained in this position he did not know, but he was aroused from his dreams by a rough shaking, and a voice thundering in his ear—

"Get up, you young hound; what are you doing here?"

No. 4.

Rubbing his eyes with the back of his hand, Jerry looked up and saw Jonathan Wild on horseback at the side of the cart.

He then took a glance at the other side of the road, where he beheld a man on horseback, muffled up in a black cloak, who evidently did not care about being recognised.

"Why don't you do what I tell you, you young rascal?" shouted Jonathan, holding up his whip as if about to strike.

"Boo-oo-oo," bellowed Jerry, acting the thick-headed lout to perfection; "Wha-wha-at have I done, zur."

"Hold your infernal noise," said Jonathan, "or I'll break every bone in your skin."

"Wot d'yer want," roared Jerry; "I ain't a' been and gone—and gone—and done nothing, have I?"

Jonathan's only reply was a rough shaking.

"Leave a feller alone, can't yer?" cried Jerry.

"Where did you come from?" demanded Jonathan.

"Lunnon, o' course."

"Where are you going?"

"To Stamford, to be sure. Don't go a sticking your knuckles into a fellow's windpipe like that. Why don't you hit one yer own size, eh?"

"If I can't shake any more wit into your numbskull," shouted Jonathan, at the same time shaking Jerry vigorously, "I'll shake the little you have in out."

"Wha-a-at are you after?" gasped Jerry.

"For heaven's sake," cried Lord Redfern, "leave the lout alone; he'll disturb the country for miles around."

Acting upon this advice, Jonathan Wild gave the lad one more shake, and then dropped him in the corner of the cart.

"Have you seen a cart pass this way?"

"Several on 'em," replied Jerry, wriggling his head and running his finger round his collar as though it were too tight for him.

"I mean a covered cart."

"Well, so do I."

"One something like this."

"This ain't a covered cart at all," said Jerry, scratching his head.

"In heaven's name, come on and leave this dolt," cried Lord Redfern, "we shall get no good from him."

"Look here, my lad," said Jonathan, "here is a guinea for you if you can answer me some questions. Will that brighten your wits?"

"Yees, zur," said Jerry, laughing.

"Well, then, have you seen a covered cart, something like this would be if it had a canvas over it? You know what I mean—a tilt."

"Oh, yes; I seed plenty of them at Hornsey Fair."

"Curse the boy, he's a perfect idiot," muttered Jonathan: and then added aloud, "I mean have you seen a cart like the one I describe, driven by two women, pass down this road."

"Noa! I seed a cart summut like this, but that there was driven only by one woman. There was a woman, an old 'un, seated by her, but she had nought to do with the driving on the 'orse."

"Of course I meant that."

"Well, why did'nt you say so?"

"Why did you not tell me before?"

"'Cause you didn't ask."

"Do you think these people are much ahead?"

"Much a what?" demanded Jerry.

"Much in advance of you?"

"I should'nt think so."

"How far should you think?"

"I should'nt think they were in front at all."

"Why not?"

"Because about half-an-hour agone I seed them take the turning up the lane more nor a mile and a-half back. The lane as leads over Muzzle 'ill. So I don't think as how they can be in advance."

Muttering a curse on the lad's idiotcy, Jonathan and Lord Redfern wheeled their horses round and dashed off in the way Jerry had indicated.

"So, so! Mr. Jonathan Wild," cried Jerry, when the horsemen were out of sight. "So, so! you're on the track, are yer? Then Batswing, Esquire, must look out, for as the merry Smith sings:—

'For there never was yet man, woman, or child,
    That was half such a fiend as Jonathan Wild;
At murders and torments he always has smil'd,
    Till maddened with envy the Devil's got riled,
To think he's outdone by Jonathan Wild.'"

"Ride away, you devil's own baby, and may you be always as successful as you will be in that lay, say I. But the Smith must know of this directly."

So saying he galloped up to the "Birdcage" and put up the trap.

Then, sauntering up to the bar, reported himself to Mrs. Wapshaw, the landlady.

Mrs. Wapshaw was a lady who could well fill that well-known description of "fat, fair, and forty." She was the first to the extreme, the second in moderation, and the last beyond a doubt, although she would not have admitted it to please anyone.

When Jerry entered the bar Mrs. Wapshaw was standing behind the bar serving some customers, with whom the merry widow was flirting and laughing in no small degree.

"Hilloa!" she cried, looking up sharply, "So you've come back at last, have you?"

"It looks like it," grumbled Jerry, who appeared as if he were sadly afraid of a blowing up.

"Looks like it, indeed! I suppose it does. Have you brought home those things I told you to purchase in London?"

"Yes ma'am."

"Well, where are they, then?"

"I took them into the kitchen the back way."

"And did you get those nails for the Smith."

"Yes; I suppose I'd better take them over to him?"

"Wait a little, I want you to do something for me. I should'nt wonder but that you are hungry?"

"Well, I am rather," replied Jerry.

"Well go into the kitchen, and I'll come and get you something; then I can see if you've brought those things right. Here, Meg!" screamed the widow, "Just take charge of the bar until I come back."

Pushing Jerry into the kitchen, the widow followed and closed the door after her.

"Well?" she demanded, holding out her hand.

"The gentleman sent you ten guineas for the use of the cart," said Jerry, laying that amount in the widow's hand.

"And where did you go, and what did you do?" demanded the window, half opening the other hand.

"He also sent you another ten guineas not to ask any questions," said Jerry, at the same time handing over that amount.

"There Jerry," said the widow, handing that gentleman over a couple of guineas, "there is something for your trouble; and, remember, silence is golden. And now eat your dinner."

"I must go to the Smith's first," said Jerry.

"Why? You know very well that you did not buy any nails."

"Perhaps I did; perhaps I didn't;" said Jerry; "all I know is that I must go there."

"But why?"

"Why? Jonathan Wild is on the look round on this road."

"Hem!" said Mrs. Wapshaw, meditatively; "I don't like highwaymen myself, although I must admit that they are gentlemen, and won't rob a poor widow. Still they do break the laws; yet I have often thought that one or two gentlemen who have called here look very much as if they followed that profession, and are always most free with their money, even if it is somebody else's. Do you think they are highwaymen?"

"I can't say," said Jerry with a leer; "I never ask any questions, and they never tells me no lies."

"What has Bob got to do with them?"

"Can't say; perhaps he shoes their horses, and finds it good for his trade, as other people do."

"Well, perhaps he does, Jerry; and as you've found it hard work I can spare you for an hour; so you may go if you like."

At that moment a merry voice was heard chanting in the stable-yard—

"Then ne'er let your spirits go down, my boys,
But quaff deeply the nut-brown ale;
Why should we fear whilst there's wealth in
the land,
And good pistols that will not fail?"

"I do wish Bob would blow his bellows in, any way, than singing those awful songs," said the landlady; "I don't know what people must think of him, I'm sure. Such a nice fellow, too; and ——"

Here the good landlady was interrupted by the entrance of Bob Blow the Bellows, who at once threw his arms round her anything but slender waist, and kissed her with such good will that the smacks sounded through the house.

CHAPTER XVI.

THE MERRY SMITH'S BIRTHDAY.—JONATHAN WILD AND LORD REDFERN ARE AGAIN PUT OFF THE TRACK.

"How goes it, widow?" cried the merry smith, giving that lady a slap over the shoulder that made her flesh quiver again, "by my word you grow lovelier and lovelier every day."

"Marry "—began the widow.

"Faith, that's what I want to do," replied the smith, "name the day, widow, and trust me the bridegroom shall not be wanting."

"Have done with your impudence, do," cried the widow, though evidently not displeased with the idea, "I never knew such a man as you."

"Long may you be of that opinion, widow. Come, landlady, let us have a glass and a song, for it's my birthday, and

"To quaff a bowl,
A song to troll,
Is meat and drink to a thirsty soul."

"Your birthday!" cried the landlady, "and how old are you to-day?"

"How old are you?" said the smith.

"Lor, 'sir, what a question," simpered the widow, "and yet I don't know why."

"I should mind telling you; I shall be thirty-one come Christmas."

The smith winked at Jerry, who returned the compliment by sticking his tongue in his mouth.

Suddenly clasping the stout landlady to his breast, the smith commenced singing:—

"I am but rude in ways,
I am but rough in tongue,
Or I would sing of lays
The sweetest that's been sung.

For all my theme should be,
Thy beauty passing rare,
Thy ways so bold and free,
Thy rippling sunlit hair.

Then turn not love away,
But cast one smile on me,
Thy love's translucent ray
Will make me happy be."

"For shame!" cried the landlady, pushing the merry smith away from her; "hark, I hear the customers calling, and must not tarry."

Again the awful smacking of lips was heard, and Mrs. Wapshaw, red as a peony, flounced out of the room.

No sooner had she gone than Jerry hastened to inform Bob Blow the Bellows of what had occurred.

The smith laughed loudly at the idea of Jerry having been one too many for Jonathan Wild, the cunning thief-taker.

"You may laugh," said Jerry, "but it bodes the captain no good."

"Well, what's to be done?" demanded the smith.

"The captain must know of it."

"The captain does know of it, my fine fellows," said a manly voice behind them.

Both turned round and saw a well-to-do farmer standing close behind them.

Jerry started back in horror, and the smith was about raising his hand to strike the intruder.

The farmer did not move, but putting out his hand guarded the blow with ease, and then bursting out in a loud laugh demanded, "Do you not know me, Bob Blow the Bellows; nor you, Jerry Blinker? Then my disguise must indeed be perfect."

"Blest if it ain't the captain!" cried Jerry, smacking his thigh, kicking out his leg, and screaming with laughter.

"And so it is," cried the smith, grasping Batswing's hand in his brawny fist and shaking it lustily; "why who would ever have known you in that disguise?"

"And why not?" demanded Batswing.

"Because you do look so respectable," said the smith.

"Thank you for nothing," replied Batswing. "But now to business. Jonathan Wild will call here before long, Master Jerry, so you're in for it."

Jerry turned rather pale at this intelligence, but did not move.

"Luckily for you, however, he did find a tilt cart that had been driven by two women up the lane; but as neither the women nor the cart answered the description, he found himself at fault, and will be here anon."

"What's to be done?" asked the smith.

"We must go into the bar and drink. Jerry had better make himself scarce when Jonathan comes in. You must ask me to pay you some amount for work done on my farm. I shall then leave you, and will send some one who will soon get rid of Wild. Be sure to shake hands with any one who comes in and calls you by name."

Having hit upon this plan they at once entered the bar, where they commenced smoking and talking.

They had not long to wait, for horses hoofs were soon heard coming at a rapid rate along the road, and a few minutes afterwards Jonathan entered the inn, followed by Lord Redfern.

"Good evening, my fine fellows," cried Jonathan, saluting the company, "have any of you been on the road from Tottenham lately?"

"I came down it about an hour ago," replied a man.

"Did you see a tilt cart driven by two women go along towards Epping?"

"No," replied the man, "I only saw one cart, and that was a dung cart."

At this moment the smith and Batswing commenced a loud dispute about money matters, until the latter, seemingly losing his temper, threw down a couple of guineas, and left the house in high dudgeon.

"Haven't I seen you before, friend?" asked Jonathan of the smith.

"Like enough, sir, if you live in the neighbourhood. I am pretty well known," replied the smith.

"I may want you one day, friend," replied Jonathan, meaningly.

"Always at your service, sir," replied the smith, "I'm a blacksmith, and am ready at any time to work for, or drink, or fight with you. For although I say it myself, as shouldn't, I can shoe a horse, drain a cup, sing a song, or wield a quarterstaff as well as any man in the country."

"You're obliging, certainly," sneered Lord Redfern.

"You look as if good old drink had coloured your nozzle well," said the smith; "if you can only wield the staff as well as you can the cup, you must be a clever fighter."

"Silence, fool," cried Jonathan, "this is a gentleman."

"They do say you may know a man by the company he keeps. Now, if you are true, the proverb's false."

Just as Jonathan was about to make a rough answer, a heavy countryman, in a slop frock and a billycock hat, slouched into the bar, and smacking the smith on the shoulder, exclaimed—

"What, Maister Blaw the Bellows, how bee'st thee? Tip us thy daddle. How go'st it, lad? We be main busy down our paarts, we be. Varmers says that there never woor such prices. They all on 'em prays for long life to the King, and a great bloody war to keep the price o' corn up."

"Lor' bless you, Giles; who would have thought to see you here?"

"Why nobody as I knows on," replied Giles. "I tuk it into my head to staart from Shadow Bush the day before yesterday and walk to London; so I don't expect that anybody will expect me much. But is it true what I hear tell about the highwayman and Jonathan Wild?"

"What about them?" inquired the smith in true astonishment, for he was amazed that Batswing, for he was the countryman, should dare to mention Wild's name when he was in such a perilous situation.

"No," he answered, at the same time signing that Jonathan Wild and his companion was listening.

"Why I think they folk at Epping be gane stark starin' mad, or they was a-trying to make a fool o' me. They said that Batswing, the highwayman, had been shot and taken to Newgate, but that his spirit came out o' his body and took another, and that he's riding about as gay as ever: and they wanted me to believe—ho! ho!; yas they did—they wanted me to believe that he picked Jonathan Wild's pocket in Smithfield, and they do say that he's left the empty pocket-book at the French Horn at Mill Hill for Jonathan to fetch away."

"Bah!" said the smith, "they knew you were green, Giles; such a thing ain't possible. Master Wild's too sharp for that."

"So I said; but they swore he had passed through Epping like a black shadow this morning, and that he has said that the man who murdered an old varmer near their town was a lord from Lunnun. I vorget the neam; its summat about a fern, too. I know that."

Jonathan was about to interrogate the countryman about the truthfulness of his news, when Lord Redfern seized him by the arm and dragged him by main force from the house.

"Curse you," cried Jonathan, "why did you not stay and hear what the bumpkin knew more?"

"I will not stay here any longer," said Lord Redfern, quivering with fear. "You did not commit the murder; I did. Let us go at once."

"Where?" asked Jonathan.

"To London."

"As you will, my lord," sneered Jonathan; "I will go with you to London, but it will only be to return here with my men a few hours later."

The horses were soon brought out, and Jonathan and his companion rode away.

Directly they were gone, Jerry, who had overheard the conversation, rushed into the bar and reported it secretly to Batswing.

"Fear not," replied the highwayman, "I shall be ready for him, never fear. And now that we have got rid of these fellows let us have a jollification in honour of the smith's birthday."

No sooner was the idea given than it was carried out.

In a snug little parlour far away from the public part of the house, bottles, glasses, pipes, and tobacco were placed on the table in quantities, and steaming bowls of punch were brewed and drunk. As time flew past the fun grew fast and furious; the widow became more and more amenable to the smith's atten-

tions; Jerry, who had been admitted to the company in honour of his recent exploits, drank and smoked like a man; whilst Batswing, entering into the fun of the whole thing, roared with laughter at Jerry and the lovers.

At length Batswing rose from the table, and, laying down his pipe, said in a serious tone—

"I must begone now."

"Nay, another bowl of punch, captain," cried the smith.

"Not so, my good fellow," replied Bat, "there is business in the way, and I never allow pleasure to interfere with business."

"Why, what business can there be to night, captain?" inquired Jerry.

"Why, a wealthy quaker, one Ephraim Ransom, will cross Highgate Hill at about ten to-night. I know he carries about five hundred pounds with him, and I intend to have it."

"Let me go, captain," cried Jerry, springing up. "I know the way to come over a Quaker."

"For shame, Jerry," cried Mrs. Wapshaw, "for shame; I won't have you talk of such things."

"Tut, tut, widow," cried the smith, who had now drank quite as much as was good for him. "Let the lad have his way; I like his spirit:

"'Oh! what for poverty need a man care,
If saddled and bridled he has a fine mare,
And of jolly horse pistols a good barking pair;
And gentle folks' jewels on their persons will wear,
For his use or abuse and his dandified air.'"

"Do let me go," cried Jerry, "you owe me something for the work I did this morning. Let me stop this old Quaker, and I will cry quits."

"And what will be your plan?" asked Batswing, smiling.

"Leave that unknown till I have got the money," cried Jerry; "that once safe, I'll make you scream with laughter by what I have to tell you. Oh! I will lead old 'Thee and Thou' such a life as never was."

"But you promise me that you will not lose the money?"

"That I will," cried Jerry, "trust me for that."

"Have you pistols and ammunition?"

"Lots," cried Jerry.

"Well then, off with you," cried Batswing, "but mind, if you lose the money you shall be made to pay for it."

"Never fear," cried Jerry. "I'll saddle the horse and be off in less than no time."

So saying Jerry dashed out of the room.

"Why, the boy must be mad," cried the widow.

"He'll—hic—he'll reach a-a-a elevated position in society," hiccuped the smith.

"Elevated position, indeed," said the widow, "the gallows you mean."

CHAPTER XVII.

JERRY'S FIRST ADVENTURE ON THE ROAD—HOW HE STOPPED THE QUAKER.

With heart elate and spirits eager for the fray, Jerry Blinker prepared him for his first attempt at highway robbery.

Jerry knew that if he allowed the Quaker the slightest chance of a struggle he would be lost; for although strong for his age he was no match for a full-grown man.

Quickly throwing off the upper part of his ostler's clothes, Jerry procured some of the garments that belonged to the barmaid and dressed himself up in them.

Having put on a long dark skirt, a thick cloth jacket trimmed with fur, and a bonnet with a thick veil, Jerry considered his disguise admirable.

He stopped for a minute or two to examine his appearance in a three-cornered bit of looking-glass which served him as a mirror, and, having come to the conclusion that he really made a very handsome young lady, a conclusion no one with less imagination and partiality than Jerry could ever have come to, he descended to the stable.

Selecting the best horse in the stable, Jerry put on a side saddle. He then took a couple of brace of pistols, and, mounting his horse, rode forth in search of adventure.

The night was a dismal one.

Heavy clouds scudded over the moon, who gave but fitful glances with her pale face to the earth.

The roads and lanes were deep in mud, and Jerry found that it was necessary to allow his horse to walk at a hand pace, in case he should require its utmost speed after he had waylaid the Quaker.

It was very cheerless when he came to the open common.

A low dismal wind howled over it; creeping through the low shrubs and making then rustle as though some one were crawling amongst them.

Now and then as the moon shone forth she caused such peculiar shadows to be cast by the bushes and trees on the ground that Jerry often started and mechanically placed his hands upon his pistols. But the clouds soon swept over "the orbed maiden," and left the plain wrapt in darkness.

Jerry began whistling for want of company, and commenced meditating that a highwaymen's life was not the best sort after all.

But he had given his word to Batswing, and he was determined to carry out his promise.

Suddenly he was startled by the sound of horses' hoofs approaching, and casting his eyes quickly round him he became aware of a very grave mistake he had made, through his inexperience.

He had advanced too far into the open country; there was neither hedge, tree, or embankment under whose shadow he could hide himsely so as to take the traveller by surprise.

Should he ride boldly on, and, meeting the Quaker face to face, boldly demand his money or his life?

That was a very good idea, but suppose the Quaker should be a very big man, things might be awkward for Jerry should he refuse to part with either his life or his money.

Should Jerry blow his brains out without speaking, and so avoid any unpleasant dispute? No, that might fail, the pistol might miss fire or Jerry his aim. What then should be done?

The traveller was now evidently approaching rapidly, and therefore Jerry was bound to make his mind up how to act.

Turning his horse away from whence the traveller was approaching, Jerry trotted slowly away.

He had not proceeded far, however, when he heard the Quaker close behind him, and a kindly voice called on him to stop.

"Whither art thou going, maiden?" demanded the Quaker in a mild voice, "Of a surety this is scarcely the time for so weak a vessel as thy dress bespeaks thee to be out riding alone."

"Oh, sir," cried Jerry, imitating a woman's voice, "oh, sir, I do beseech you not to hurt me, I am but a poor lass, that has been benighted on my road to Newington."

"Of a truth thou ridest late," replied the Quaker; "but fear not, I will not harm thee, but rather will keep thee company; and, as far as a man of peace may do so without violating his creed, I will protect thee should occasion offer."

"Many thanks," cried Jerry, seemingly overcome with gratitude, "many thanks for your kind offer, of which I freely avail myself."

For some time they rode on in silence, till at last the Quaker said, "May I ask the cause of thy travelling so late on this lonesome road?"

"I went to see my poor old grandfather," replied Jerry, pretending to sob.

"What, is thy grandfather so ill?" demanded the Quaker.

"He was ill, but he died this evening. I could not stay in the house, and so I rode home against the wishes of my friends."

"Thy friends had reason, for the roads here are far from safe. There is a vile fellow called Batswing, who haunts this place and commits most terrible atrocities."

"Oh please, don't speak in that way," cried Jerry, "or I shall faint. I have such a horror of highwaymen. I always had when I was poor, but now I'm rich I hate their very names."

"Rich!" said the Quaker, pricking up his ears. "Of a truth the names of these lawless men savour not well in the nostrils of the true and good. But, maiden, you said you were poor, but that you are now rich. How doth that come to pass?"

"My poor old grandfather has left me all his property; therefore, I shall be rich."

"Perchance I may have known thy grandfather. What was his name."

"Silas Green, but the neighbours used to know him as Miser Green."

"I have not heard of him," said the Quaker, "but did he really love the filthy lucre sufficiently to warrant people giving him that title?"

"He was rather stingy, but I don't complain, now that he has left me all."

"Has he left you much gold?"

"Over five hundred pounds," cried Jerry, clapping his hands, as if he could no longer repress his delight.

"Five hundred pounds," said the Quaker, "it is a strange coincidence, but that is the very same sum that I have gained by the sale of some land that I once held yonder. Five hundred pounds."

"It is a heap of money," cried Jerry.

"Verily it is a large sum," said the Quaker. "I suppose, maiden, that thou wilt now, after the giddy fashion of thy kind, turn thy thoughts to marriage."

"Oh, don't!" cried Jerry, giggling and wriggling shyly on his saddle, "you make me blush."

"Blushes become a virtuous girl," continued the Quaker, riding up close to Jerry. "If thou wilt take the advice of one who has seen much of the world, thou wilt not throw thyself away on a stripling who loves naught but vanity, but will chose a sober, quiet and religious helpmate, yea even like unto myself."

"Oh, sir!" cried the supposed damsel, "you quite frighten me with the suddenness of your proposition, indeed you do. La! sir, I never gave such a thing a thought. Not that I don't mean to say that I should not prefer being married, and having some one to protect me than to being single and having no one to take care of me."

"I see that thou art a discreet damsel," cried the quaker, getting his horse close up to Jerry's. "Now listen, I have a proposition to make to thee. If thou wilt become bone of my bone, and flesh of my flesh, I will protect thee faithfully through life. Art thou agreed?"

"But are you well off, sir?" inquired the weary Jerry.

"Yea, verily that I am," replied the Quaker, "I have the five hundred pounds I spoke of, which were paid me for my sale of land, now at my saddle bow. Besides this I have horses and a farm Now, maiden, shall we become one?"

"But will you protect me if I am in danger?"

"That will I."

"But I thought you never would fight, being a man of peace."

"**Nay maiden**, we will not fight under any provocation. We conquer by mental, not physical force."

"And if Batswing were here and demanded your money or your life, what would you do?"

"Give him the money after a little argument, and then think how best I could regain it."

As the Quaker spoke he drew close to Jerry, and placing his arm round the waist leant his head on the disguised ostler's shoulder.

"Wilt thou be mine maiden?" sighed the amorous Quaker.

"No!" thundered Jerry, at the same time placing the muzzle of a pistol so close to the Quaker's head that that gentleman nearly fell off his saddle in alarm.

"No, I won't take you, but I will your gold, for better or for worse, as the people say."

"Maiden!" exclaimed the Quaker, in alarm.

"I am no maiden," cried Jerry, swelling with pride; "I am Batswing, the outlaw of the forest."

At this announcement a strange convulsion seemed to pass over the Quaker's face, and he could only gasp out,

"You—Bats—wing, the dreadful outlaw!"

"The same," replied Jerry, boldly. "Now, hand over the swag. Come, no hesitation, but do as I bid you, or I fire. Mind, I am not to be trifled with, and, therefore, I would advise you to make haste. Bring out the five hundred yellow boys, Ephraim. I shall make better use of them than you will, I doubt not."

"I pray thee, Mr. Batswing, have mercy upon me. I did but jest, Mr. Highwayman, the gold is none of mine; it is only some that I have had in trust for my masters, Messrs. Whitney and Wooler, cloth merchants, of Bishopsgate Within. Therefore I pray thee, good gentleman, to let me keep the money."

"No nonsense, Ephraim, but out with the swag. My fingers itch to pull the trigger; so I think you had better make haste."

"But my masters will discharge me if I lose their gold without a struggle."

"But you know you must not fight, Ephraim," replied Jerry, laughing heartily at the poor Quaker's dilemma; "you conquer by mental, not physical force. Oh, thou unlucky Quaker, I fear me thou art in a bad case."

"But my masters are not of the Society of Friends. They are not men of peace, but more sons of Belial, using profane oaths and wicked phraseology. They are men of ungovernable temper, and will ruin me if I lose their money; they would sooner that I should lose my life than that they should lose their gold."

"They know which is the most valuable; so fire away, Ephraim, and hand over the canary birds, old drab and broad brim."

With a deep groan the Quaker undid his saddle-bags and handed them to Jerry; and then, taking hold of the latter's bridal, begged him to grant him one favour.

"What is it now, 'old yea and nae,'" cried Jerry, impatiently.

"You see, my good sir, should my masters know that I surrendered up the gold without a struggle, they will dismiss me, and I shall be ruined."

"And what is that to me?"

"Surely thou wouldst not hurt a poor fellow more than is necessary to carry out thy nefarious—I mean thy honest—calling Therefore, I pray thee that thou wilt oblige me by firing a bullet through my hat, so that I may show it, and swear that I have had a desperate encounter with five or six highwaymen; that I fought hard to keep the gold, but was at last overcome by numbers and forced to submit."

"What a jolly old liar you are, Ephraim," cried **Jerry.** "Blest if I ever seed such a downright old drab, double-dealing deceiver in all my life."

"Thou must consider the circumstances under which I am placed," pleaded Ephraim; "do, therefore, I beseech thee, fire at once."

"All right, Ephraim, here goes," cried Jerry.

"Pray be careful," roared the Quaker, holding his hat out at arm's length.

Bang went the pistol, and the bullet passed exactly through the centre of the crown, much to Jerry's delight, who not only liked the sport, but was proud of showing off his skill as a marksman.

"Now through this coat tail," exclaimed the Quaker, holding out his skirts, as if he were going to dance a minuet; "send it right through the middle."

Bang the bullet flew true to its aim, cutting a round piece out of the coat tail.

"Now through this skirt," cried the Quaker.

Jerry fired again; but either his aim was not so true or the Quaker winced, for the bullet flew wide of the mark.

"Why did you not stand still?" demanded Jerry.

"Nervousness, only nervousness," cried the Quaker; "try another shot,"

Jerry fired again, but again missed his mark.

"Do try again; do try once more," urged the Quaker.

"I would riddle you like a sieve," cried Jerry, "if I had some more powder, but I have not, therefore you must be content with what I have done."

"If that be the case, friend," replied the Quaker, suddenly producing a brace of pistols, and pointing them with unerring aim at Jerry, "if such be the case I must trouble you to give me back my gold."

"I say," cried Jerry, "what do you mean by this?"

"I am a man of peace, and would argue with thee, friend Batswing; thy calling is not an honest one; therefore I would advise thee to give it up. I have saved thee from one crime already, and it would almost be a mercy to kill thee to prevent thy further doing mischief. But I will not have blood upon my head, therefore dismount and depart in peace."

"You don't mean to say that you intend to leave me here without my horse!"

"Pardon me, my friend, such is my intention. Wilt thou dismount, or must I make thee?"

Poor Jerry could stand the unpleasant glitter of the pistol barrels no longer, and, with a sad heart, dismounted.

"Thou seest, friend," said the Quaker, "that we conquer by mental, and not physical, force. Good even to thee, friend. Mayst thou turn from thy wicked ways and live long; for if thou continuest in sin, I doubt not that thy life will finish at Tyburn."

So saying the Quaker slid the bridle of Jerry's horse over his arm and rode swiftly away.

"Curse me for a fool," cried Jerry. "What shall I say to the Captain and Bob Blow the Bellows? Aye! and what's worse, what will Mother Wapshaw say to me about her horse? It serves me right. I ought to have known that the devil himself is no match for a Quaker."

CHAPTER XVIII.
" JERRY TELLS HIS STORY.'

Slowly and wearily Jerry Blinker made his way across the heath, cursing the petticoats of which a little time before he was so proud.

At every step he sank over his ankles in the mud, and nearly left his boots behind him.

Bitterly he repented having ventured out on such an expedition by himself, for he knew that neither Batswing nor the Jolly Smith would ever let him hear the last of it.

To add to Jerry's discomfort, he caught his foot in the skirt of his dress, stumbled, and fell full length into a ditch.

"Well, I'm blest," he cried, in a passion; "I'm blest if this 'ere is at all comfortable. I've made a good thing of it to-day, I have; I've been done by a Quaker, have lost a horse, and am covered all over with mud in the bargain. I don't know what Mrs. Wapshaw will say, but I do know what the Captain and old Blow the Bellows will. They'll chaff my life out."

He sat for some time meditating what he should do until he became painfully aware that the ditch in which he reclined was anything but a dry one.

"Well, I'm bound to spoil my clothes, that is, somebody else's. I wonder what the barmaid will say about it? 'It never rains but it pours,' as the blind man said when he took shelter underneath a gutter to get out of a storm. I suppose I must go to the Bird Cage. Bird Cage! it will become a pretty trap for me. Only to think that I should do Jonathan Wild, the old cove at Newgate, and be sucked in myself. Well, I've 'eard some queer things said about fate, but if this is fate, I should like to hit her in the eye, that's what I should like to do."

Pulling himself out of the ditch, Jerry stumbled on his way, madly swearing at the wonderful difficulties with which he met, tearing the skirts of his dress as he forced his way through the hedges, until at last he found himself on the north road, and quickly made his way to the rear of the Bird Cage Inn.

His first idea was that he would slip into the hay loft; but, to his astonishment, he perceived that there was a light in the widow's room, and sounds of voices and laughter proceeding therefrom.

Poor Jerry was in such a state of misery and cold that he looked anxiously at the rays of warm light streaming through the chinks in the shutters, and cursed his stupidity again and again for having ventured on such an errand.

He turned sadly away towards the loft, his teeth chattering with cold, and hunger gnawing at his chest.

As he reached the stable door he heard the merry voice of Bob Blow the Bellows chanting the following song:—

"Let poets rave of women fair,
    Their beauty so divine;
But not a maiden can compare
    With laughter-breeding wine.
A maiden's love is sweet and dear,
    Each one has felt its sway,
But it may die in trembling fear
    Or slowly melt away.
But wine is true, so to her praise
    Cheerily will we shout,
And as our merry voices raise
    Hark how the corks pop out."

"Chorus!" roared the smith, and directly half-a-dozen voices sang the chorus so vehemently that the windows rattled again—

"Merrily, merrily drink away,
    Merrily, merrily shout;
Pop! pop! pop! drinking night and day,
    Hark how the corks pop out."

Poor Jerry did listen to the popping of the corks, and devoutly wished that he was one of the merry party.

He had during the song crept back to the window, and now stood close by it, listening to Bob Blow the Bellows singing the second verse:—

"Yet as the wine goes circling round
    A secret I will tell:
I freely own by love I'm bound
    To Hetty, Kate, and Nell.
And Sally, too, has such sweet eyes,
    Yet Annie's teeth are white;
Her raven locks dear Carry dyes,
    And makes them sunny bright.

My maidens fair, I love you well,
    Ah! could you all be mine;
But as you can't, why fare-thee-well,
    I'll stick to rosy wine.
So merrily, merrily drink away,
    Merrily, merrily shout,
Pop! pop! pop! drink night and day,
    Hark how the corks fly out."

A hearty round of applause followed the song, and then the Widow Wapshaw was heard expostulating with Bob.

"A pretty song indeed," cried the widow; "I wonder you're not ashamed to sing such a thing before a respectable female."

"Hoity, toity, widow," replied the smith; "why, what's the matter with the song, that it displeases you?"

"Displeases me, indeed! who says it displeases me? You'd better sing it to your Nellys and your Kates, with their teeth and eyes."

"Surely, widow, you would not have them without eyes?"

"Eyes, indeed! I'd scratch them out if I had them here!"

This announcement was received with loud shouts of laughter, in which—forgetting his deplorable situation—Master Jerry joined heartily.

In a moment he remembered that he must have discovered his presence, and knowing that if he attempted to fly a bullet would most likely be his fate, he marched boldly up to the door, which he heard the men unbarring.

No sooner was the door opened than Jerry was seized and hurried into the little parlour.

At first his appearance only caused exclamations of astonishment, but these were soon followed by roars of laughter.

He was, indeed, in a deplorable condition.

His clothes were torn and bespattered with mud, whilst his petticoats were wringing wet through.

His bonnet was crushed into all sorts of shapes save the right one; and was so covered with mud that it almost appeared made of the substance.

Hands and face had come in for a good share of the dirt, and helped to give Jerry a miserably comic appearance.

Jerry looked round the room and found that the company had considerably increased since he had been away; amongst these he recognised Teddy the Growler and several others of the band.

At the end of the table sat Batswing, calmly smoking.

"I'm blessed if it ain't Jerry!" roared the smith.

"Jerry," exclaimed Mrs. Wapshaw; "why, how did you come in that state?"

"Turn him out!" growled Teddy; "he ain't in a fit state to be in gentlemen's society. He'll get us sold, he's so precious damp."

"What is the meaning of this?" demanded Batswing sternly.

"It means I've been into the mud," said Jerry.

This rather self-evident fact, although said in a somewhat injured voice, illicited nothing but laughter.

"How about the expedition I sent you on?" demanded Batswing.

"If you'll give me something to drink I'll tell you all about it," said Jerry doggedly; "I can't speak without something to wet my whistle."

At an order from Batswing a bumper of wine was handed to the would-be highwayman.

Jerry tossed it off in no time; and then, having divested himself of the greater part of his female attire, he lit a long clay pipe and declared himself ready to answer all questions.

"In the first place," said Batswing; "did you meet the Quaker?"

"Which I did," said Jerry, shaking his head slowly.

"Did you succeed in taking the money from him?"

"Which I did!" repeated Jerry Blinker.

"And where is it!"

"Which I don't know!"

"Don't know!" cried Batswing; "what do you mean by that?"

"What I mean by that's this," said Jerry Blinker, puffing furiously at his pipe, and frowning in what he considered a dignified manner on the assembled company; "what I mean by that's this: I've 'ad an adventure would have made all you fellows turn green with fear. What do you think o' that?"

"Indeed!" cried the men; "what was it?"

"Now this here's what it was," replied Jerry; "I rode out, as you know, to meet that cursed Quaker."

"Yes, yes!" replied the men.

"Well, as you know, it wasn't a pleasant night; but that didn't matter to me. I took the best horse out of the stable."

"What! my favourite roan?" cried the widow.

"That's the one," replied Jerry, coolly.

"If any harm has come to it, I'll murder you," said the widow.

"No harm's come to it," replied Jerry; "the harm has come to me."

"Well, well!" said Batswing, impatiently; "how did you meet the Quaker?"

"The clouds had just closed over the moon, and all was so dark that you could not see your hand before your face, when I beheld the Quaker coming along at a rapid pace down the road, some hundred and fifty yards from me."

"How did you know it was the Quaker?" demanded Bob.

"Because of his broad-brimmed hat," replied Jerry, confidently.

"Hem!" coughed the smith; "you knew him by his broad-brimmed hat a hundred and fifty yards off, when the night was so dark that you could not see your hand before you?"

Scorning to notice the base insinuation as to the truth of his story, Jerry Blinker took a pull at his tumbler and proceeded:—

"Pulling my horse on one side I let him come up to me; and then asked him if he could tell me my quickest way across the heath. He appeared smitten with my charms at once, and proposed to see me across the heath in safety.

"Of course I told him that I had money; and so led the old boy on until he proposed marriage to me; at the same time stating that he had five hundred pounds at his saddle-bow. In a minute I presented my pistols and demanded his money.

"But the Quaker was no coward; dashing my pistol on one side he clasped me by the throat; and a desperate struggle ensued, which finished by my throwing him to the ground."

"Bravo, Jerry," said the smith.

"I, of course, had managed to keep my saddle all through," said Jerry.

"Which accounts for the state of your costume," sneered Teddy.

"But, no sooner had I thrown him to the ground than I alighted to seize the booty; but the Quaker was up again, and a terrible fight ensued. Over and over we both rolled into the mud, until with a heavy blow I managed to settle his hash."

"What! killed him," cried the men.

"No, I only stunned him," said Jerry. "Well, I had only just got the money all safe, and was about mounting my horse when the Quaker drew a pistol, and let fly at me."

"I thought he was stunned?" said Teddy.

"So he was, but he came to, don't you see. Well, this cowardly action so annoyed me that I determined to give Ephraim something to remember me by; and

so I walked over to him. As I approached he again let fly at me, but missed again."

"He must have been a bad shot," growled Teddy.

"Perhaps he was in such a state of fear he could not take aim," said Bob Blow the Bellows.

"That's more like it," replied Jerry, "but though he was a coward, he was no fool. The report of the second pistol was answered by a terrific shout, and to my astonishment I saw a company of Dragoons galloping over the field next to the one I was in."

"We've caught you, have we," screamed the Quaker; "you did not know that the Dragoons were close behind us, did you? Ho! ho! ho! I am a man of peace, but Ill come to see thee swing at Tyburn."

"Hastily relieving him with a blow over the head with the butt end of my pistol, I mounted my horse and galloped away, but not before the troopers had got sight of me, and were in full chase.

"It *was* a chase too: over hedges and ditches, across fields and down lanes. I never saw anything like it."

"At last I came to jump over a deep ditch and a hedge at the other side. It was a nasty place, but at it I went, and should have taken it in fine style, only unfortunately the night being so dark I had not noticed that a branch of a tree spread over the road. It caught me in the chest, threw me backwards into the ditch: the next moment I heard the roan galloping away down the road."

"What did you do then?" asked Bob.

"Do! why I remained quiet in the mud. Then I heard the thud, thud of the Dragoons' horses' feet as they came up, and flew one after the other over my head, and heard them halloaing as they darted down the road after my horse, for they still thought me on her."

"What a lucky set of men they must have been to miss the branch that knocked you over," said Bob.

For a moment Jerry seemed rather puzzled how to answer this observation, but he soon made up his mind what to do.

"Why the force I went against the branch broke it short off, and it fell with me into the ditch of course, leaving an open place for the soldiers. It's all very fine for you fellows to be grinning here, but had you been with me you would have laughed at the other side of your mouth, it's my opinion."

"May be we should, Jerry; may be we should," said the Smith.

"May be we should have managed things better," said Teddy.

"Ah!" replied Jerry, "it's all very fine for you to boast when you've been seated here drinking and smoking; but, if you could only show some of your courage when there's occasion, and talk less about it when there's no occasion, it would be better."

"I'll tell you what I'll do," growled Teddy; "I'll take the first occasion to wring your neck, you young cocksparrow."

"Hush, Teddy, hush," said the smith, "let Jerry finish his adventures."

"Come now," said Jerry, who pretended to feel indignant with the growler, "supposing as how that you were in a ditch as I was, what would you have done then, eh?"

"Crawled out of it," growled Teddy.

"And what would you have done then?—run home, or here, I suppose?"

"Perhaps I should. I suppose you did the same, didn't you?"

"No, I didn't," said Jerry indignanily, "I wasn't such a coward."

"Why what did you do?" exclaimed Batswing, with a look of surprise. "You did not follow and capture the dragoons, I suppose?"

"No, a course not; what I did was merely to crawl

THE ABDUCTION IN THE CHURCHYARD.

out of the ditch and creep back the way that I had come, in hopes that in the confusion the Quaker might have forgotten his money bags."

"And had he done so?"

"Not he, trust a Quaker for that. Quaker, bag and horse, had all gone."

"But how did you know the exact spot, eh?"

"Because of the big hole that was made by the struggle."

"Ah! I see," growled Teddy, "a reg'lar young earthquake, that's what you are. Ho! ho! ho!"

"We've had enough of this nonsense," said Batswing, sternly. "You, Master Jerry, have lost us over five hundred pounds by your stupidity. It was partly my fault, in having trusted such a task to you. But it will be the last time I shall do so. In future you must confine yourself to your stables."

No. 5.

"That will he not, indeed," cried Widow Wapshaw. "A nice keeper of stables indeed to let the horses be lost in this manner. No, no, Master Jerry; you had better seek some other place."

"And my dress, too," said Dolly, "my beautiful new bonnet with the cherry-coloured ribbons."

Here the disconsolate barmaid held up the muddy bonnet, which was so ludicrously out of shape that all laughed, and even Jerry could not repress a smile, unhappy as he was.

"Never mind that," said Batswing, "I will give you a new bonnet; and you, widow, shall have either the value of your roan or as good a horse in his place. As Jerry says the Dragoons are about I shall make myself scarce. Teddy and you fellows had better do the same. You, Bob Blow the Bellows and Jerry must wait here, so that if these soldiers do turn up you may mislead them."

The men quickly sprang to their feet and prepared to follow their captain, whilst Jerry, having begun to make himself more comfortable with the warm punch, was evidently pondering what more marvellous adventures he could concoct to amuse the merry smith.

"Good night," said Batswing, and a moment afterwards he and his party had left the inn by the back door leading on to the fields.

For some time Jerry and the smith remained silently smoking, whilst Mrs. Wapshaw was brewing a "night cap," as she called it, which was no less than a huge tumbler of hot grog.

"Why, Bob, how dull you are," said the buxom landlady, playfully tapping the smith's bronzed cheek, "Can't you give us another song?"

"Not to-night, my dear," said Bob; "somehow or other I feel as if mischief would happen to the captain. I don't like these troopers staying about here, as they have been doing lately. That Jonathan Wild has sworn to have revenge, and he'll do it, too."

"Bah!" said Jerry, "what's to fear? Why I sold Jonathan once to-day, and can do it as often as I like. You take my advice, Bob, don't go making yourself nervous in this manner. Do as I do, put a bold face upon all things, and you'll be as jolly as a sand boy."

"Ah! you're a hero, you are," said Bob.

"Well, I must own I'm getting on that way," said Jerry. "Lord, Bob, you should have seen me lead them troopers a dance. Soldiers! why I care no more for them than I do for——"

Jerry left off suddenly, started violently, and turned pale, for at that moment a heavy blow was heard at the back-door of the inn.

"Gracious goodness! what's that?" cried Mrs. Wapshaw.

"It's all up with us, I fear," said the smith.

"Why?" stammered Jerry.

"That blow was given with the hilt of a sword," said Bob.

"What of that?" cried Jerry, turning paler and paler.

"They are the Dragoons," whispered the smith.

"What's to be done?" whispered the landlady.

"You must let them in," groaned the smith. "Jerry is so brave, he will answer them; he'll meet 'em alone."

"If I do I'll be damned," said Jerry, with much energy.

"The door must be opened at all events," said the smith, "and we must take our chance."

Jerry and Bob Blow the Bellows listened attentively as the widow proceeded to the door.

"Who is there?" demanded the widow in a shaky voice.

"Open in the name of the King," was the reply.

At the sound Jerry nearly collapsed.

"What do you want at this time of night?" demanded the widow.

"A highwayman, whom we have reason to believe is now in your house. Open instantly, or we will burst the door."

"It's all over with us, Bob," sighed Jerry.

"All over with you, rather," replied Bob. "I am an honest smith, who gets his living by the sweat of his brow. Everybody knows honest Bob Blow the Bellows. Hold up, Jerry; if they see you in this state they'll know you are in the swim. Hold up, can't you?"

Dragging Jerry back into the parlour, Bob placed him on a sofa, and, thrusting a pipe in his mouth, bade him to be jolly.

After this, he threw himself into a chair, seized a glass of punch, and commenced singing—

"Oh! the blacksmith delights to hear glasses clink,
And right merry he grows with good old strong drink,

With a glass in his hand by side of his forge,
The blacksmith is happier far than King George.
With a cling and a clang, a clang and a cling,
Merrily now the sledge hammers ring.
With a cling and a clang, a clang and a cling,
A blacksmith is happier far than a King."

Taking courage from the merry smith's manner, Jerry seized a glass of punch, and commenced bawling out the chorus; but he had not proceeded further than the second line when his voice failed him, his eyes opened as wide as possible, his jaw dropped, and he remained as if petrified, staring towards the door.

"Why, what's the matter, Jerry?" demanded the smith, who was seated opposite to his friend, and, therefore, could not see what had caused this alarm.

"What is the matter?" continued the smith.

Jerry made no reply, but merely shuddered.

Bob Blow the Bellows glanced over his shoulder, and, with a most theatrical start, sprang to his feet.

There in the doorway stood a man dressed in a broad-brimmed hat and drab suit. The collar of his coat stood up, something in the military fashion, and the front was without lappels. His waistcoat was of the same solemn hue, as were also his kneebreeches and stockings, whilst his shoes were buckled with iron buckles of the plainest sort.

It was a Quaker, and Bob Blow the Bellows felt convinced, from Jerry's appearance, that it was not only a Quaker but the very identical one whom Jerry had tried to rob that very night.

The Quaker held two pistols in his hand, pointing one at Jerry and the other at Bob.

CHAPTER XIX.

THE QUAKER ARRESTS JERRY BLINKER.

"Friends," said the Quaker quietly; "it is my painful duty to arrest thee. The task is an unpleasant one to a man of peace like unto myself. But it has pleased Heaven to make me the humble instrument of its wrath against thee; and, therefore, I do advise that thou should'st at once come with me in quietness to meet thy fate."

"Why, what's the meaning of this, master Quaker?" demanded Bob Blow the Bellows; "you're a nice man of peace, I don't think, to come bouncing in here with your barkers full cock, presenting them at people's heads as though there wasn't such a thing as brains in the world."

"Friend," replied the Quaker; "I must confess that I knew thee not, and that thou may'st be honest; but the company in which I find thee maketh me inclined to doubt the fact; therefore, of necessity I must invite thee to accompany me."

"Look here, master Quaker," said the smith; "I don't know what you are aiming at. Blow me if I do. My name is Robert Stevens, commonly known as Bob Blow the Bellows, my occupation being that of a smith. I'm pretty well known to all the country round, and nobody has a word to say against the merry smith, so don't begin it now."

"Friend Robert," replied the Quaker; "since thou art so proud of thy good name, it would be well if thou were to pay more respect to thy company; seeing that it is likely to bring thy good name into discredit. I do not wish to harm thee, seeing that thou hast never harmed me; therefore, if thou wilt help bind this youth, thou mayest depart in peace."

"What has the lad done?" demanded the smith.

"Nothing."

"Then why would you take him into custody?"

"Because he would have done much harm if he could."

"How so?" demanded the smith.

The Quaker in very quiet tones then related how

he had been stopped by Jerry Blinker on the heath, and also the result of that encounter.

For a moment the smith looked at Jerry in surprise, and then asked in a solemn voice—

"Jerry, is this true?"

"No!" growled Jerry.

"Dost thou mean to say that thou didst not meet me on the heath, disguised like a woman, and try to rob me?"

"No," replied Jerry, "never."

"Didst thou not hear the troopers coming up to the rescue? and didst thou not turn and fly in terror?"

It was now Jerry's turn to look astonished.

He had never heard the sound of horse's feet, although he had been the last to leave the spot.

How, then, could the Quaker have heard them?

"Come," said the Quaker; "let our young friend be bound."

"You can't take him along the road to-night," said Bob.

"Hast thou a place where we can keep him in safety until the morning?" demanded the Quaker.

"Of a surety," replied the smith; "come, Jerry, you must be bound."

"What! you turn against me, Bob?" cried Jerry, in wonder.

"Needs must when the Devil drives," growled Bob, under his breath.

"So you do know each other," said the Quaker, suspiciously.

For a moment Jerry seemed on the point of betraying the smith, but his better nature triumphed.

"I have always known him to be good and kind till now," he said, sullenly; "I never knew him do any harm; and always loved him."

With an agility that might have been very suspicious, Bob Blow the Bellows trussed master Jerry up as tight as possible; but in doing so he managed to get his mouth close by the lad's ear, and whispered—

"Cheer up, my hearty! I'll see you out of this scrape, if only for those words. You see if I don't."

These words seemed to give Jerry fresh life; and he returned them with a sharp little wink that was the very slightest glimmer of an eyelid—nothing more.

By the Quaker's orders Jerry was carried up stairs and locked in a dark room; neither fire nor candle being allowed him.

How long Jerry remained in this place he could not tell; but the time appeared to him to pass so slowly that he begun to fear either that the merry smith had forgotten him, or that he could not find the means to procure the escape.

At last he heard footsteps creeping along the passage, and presently the door of the room was opened.

A low voice called him gently by his name—

"Jerry! Jerry! are you there?"

"Yes! is that you, Bob?"

"Yes! don't speak so loud."

"Is all ready for my escape?"

"Everything; I have made old broad-brim drunk. He is snoring away down stairs in the parlour."

"Undo these cords then; they hurt."

The nimble fingers of the smith soon had Jerry out of bondage.

The lad sprang to his feet and shook himself with delight at having gained his freedom.

"What's to be done now?" he asked.

"Creep downstairs and escape out of the back door to my smithy."

"Can't we give the old Quaker one for himself first?"

"No; take my advice and leave Quakers alone for the future. Those very religious coves are always one too many for us. I suppose it is their knowing sin so well makes them able to avoid it.

"At all events, let us avoid him," said Jerry, with whom the remembrance of the sly old Quaker seemed to have anything but a pleasing effect; "let us get out of here, this sort of game don't suit me."

"Come along, then," said Bob; "mind you don't make a noise, or old knee-breeches will be after you as sure as eggs is eggs."

Cautiously they crept down stairs and opened the back gate, out of which they stole, and made their way to the smithy.

A grey streak of light hung in the east, showing the approach of dawn.

A cold wind slid through the trees and mourned as if bewailing the departure of night and the coming of day.

All else in the world seemed still. Not a thing moved; the cattle were sleeping under the hedges; and the birds, with their heads tucked under their wings, were slumbering in the brake.

They soon reached the smithy, and on opening the door were glad to see a good fire burning, round which sat Batswing and his men.

"So," said Batswing; "I thought you would find the inn too warm for you, master Jerry. What's up now?"

"That infernal Quaker has turned up again," said Jerry.

"What? have you caught him at last?"

"No, he caught me," was the rueful answer.

Jerry then entered into a long account of what had happened at the Bird Cage Inn. Describing how the soldiers—some twenty at the least—forced their way into the parlour—headed by the blood-thirsty Quaker.

He then gave a description of his arrest, glossing over his terror, and dwelling with much pride on his refusal to compromise the smith, and winding up with a glowing account of the escape, and how he had wished to go back to destroy the Quaker, but was only restrained out of consideration for the smith, who entreated him to forego this deed of daring.

Scarcely had he finished this thrilling account than the whole of the company there assembled burst out into a loud roar of laughter.

In astonishment Jerry turned from one to the other, seeking for an explanation, but in vain.

Every one, the smith included, was too convulsed with mirth to answer his inquiring looks.

"Well, I'm blest if ever I seed such rum coons," said Jerry, in disgust; "why, what's up with you, Bob Blow the Bellows? You laughed at the other side of your mouth when the old Quaker was in the room. It wasn't laughter that made you shake then."

This sally only provoked more merriment.

"Oh, laugh away, gentlemen, laugh away," said Jerry, who was rapidly losing his temper; "it's all very well to laugh at others when you're on the safe side of the hedge; but had you been there you would have told a very different tale."

"We were there, Jerry," cried Batswing.

"And we can tell a very different tale," cried the smith.

"Hillo! why what's up now?" demanded Jerry, in utter astonishment.

Another burst of laughter was his only response, and certainly his looks quite warranted their merriment.

With eyes wide open, staring at one after the other as he slowly moved his head from one side to the other, as if it were balanced on a pivot, Jerry looked the very picture of amazement.

His lank jaw had sank upon his breast, and his respiration seemed almost to have ceased.

"Why, this is up, Master Jerry," said Batswing;

"the whole of the story you told me was entirely false; you never had a struggle with the Quaker at all."

"How do you know that?" demanded Jerry.

"How do I know that?" thundered Batswing, "why because I was there, you young rascal."

"You were?" gasped Jerry.

"Yes. You never struggled with the Quaker at all; but he robbed you of your horse, and left you to scramble home as quickly as you could."

"Why, where were you?" demanded Jerry. "I never saw you."

"Perhaps not, but I did you," replied Batswing, "and I shan't easily forget it."

"I'd have given something to have been there," said the smith.

"How is Silas Green, Jerry?" demanded Batswing, assuming the nasal tones of the Quaker. "Perchance, maiden, I may know thy grandfather, eh, Jerry. I suppose, maiden, that thou wilt now, after the giddy fashion of thy kind, turn thy thoughts to marriage."

"Ho! ho! ho!" roared the men.

"I'm blest if I didn't think it was you somehow," cried Jerry.

"Jerry," said Batswing, controlling his mirth at this unwarrantable statement; "Jerry, there is a very bad habit known as lying, one that often brings people into danger and trouble. It is one to which, putting it in the mildest form, you are very much addicted. Curb it while there is still time."

Jerry looked down sullenly.

"Don't think I am angry with you," continued Batswing; "I am far from that. You have performed wonders to-day; but you were getting too proud of your exploits, and, therefore, it became necessary that you should receive a lesson."

"Yes, but this is rather a hard one, though," grumbled Jerry.

"All the better: as most likely you will never need another. I wished to show you that your successes were not so much due to your own sharpness as to the cowardice and dullness of other people. Never be too reliant on yourself. Remember you may meet people as sharp and brave as yourself; and, therefore, above all things, reserve your fire. Never waste powder and ball, as you cannot tell when you may want them."

"I see I've been in the wrong," said Jerry; "only now I've learnt the lesson, don't let all the fellows chaff me about this affair. Remember, if I was robbed, the Quaker was Batswing."

"And Jerry the *quaker*," put in the smith.

The cold grey light of morning came stealing over the sky as Batswing arose and declared his intention of departing at once for Epping.

"I have to perform a disagreeable duty there," he said, "the most disagreeable one that ever fell in my way."

"And what may that be, Captain?" asked the smith.

"To inform Alice Landon of her father's murder. He will be buried this afternoon."

"That was a strange affair."

"It was indeed," said Batswing, "one that shall be revenged, too."

"Well, Captain, take a bowl before you leave us," cried the smith. "Remember what the old song says—

"When sorrow has siezed upon the mind,
    And moved us beyond control,
To drive away the blue devil'd sprites,
    One must have recourse to the bowl.
               The bowl,
One must have recourse to the bowl.

There's Madge, who is my own buxom wife—
    There ne'er was a jolier soul;
Why, every night she gets quite tight,
    Drowning her cares in the bowl.
               The bowl,
Drowning her cares in the bowl.

Take up the cup and drain its contents,
    But mind you quaff off the whole;
For headaches and care, with deep despair,
    Lurk in a half-emptied bowl.
               A bowl,
Lurk in a half-emptied bowl.

As he sang the song the smith poured out a good-sized bowl of wine, which he handed over to Batswing, who, in compliance with the request made in the last verse, drained it; and then, wishing his followers farewell, departed for Epping.

CHAPTER XX.

ALICE LANDON—THE ANONYMOUS LETTER.

Making his way across the fields, so as to avoid the main road, Batswing pushed on as rapidly as he could towards Epping.

Once or twice he saw detachments of armed men riding backwards and forwards, evidently in search of something or some one, and he had little doubt that they were the officers—known at that period as "Robins"—on the look-out for himself, or any discovery they could make as to the whereabouts of Lord Clumber's plate chest.

As he had very particular reasons for not wishing to meet these gentlemen, it became necessary for him to hide as often as he came near one of these parties, and to remain in concealment until they had disappeared.

In this manner he was hindered greatly, so that he did not arrive at the cave in Epping Forest until past one at noon.

No sooner had he entered the cave than he summoned Madge, and at once cross-questioned her about Alice Landon.

"She sleeps a little now; but after she received that letter she raved most awfully."

"That letter!" exclaimed Batswing, "what letter?"

"Nay, that I know not," said Madge, shrugging her shoulders.

"But who brought it?" demanded Batswing.

"That I can't say," replied the stolid old woman. "All I know it was found pinned to the wall close by her sleeping apartment, and was addressed to the beauteous Mistress Alice Landon."

"And what did it contain?"

"That I can't say. It spoke about her father's murder and a few such other trifles."

"Enough!" cried Batswing. "I must see Mistress Alice instantly. I fear I know too well the hand that penned this letter."

Following the old housekeeper, Batswing passed down the secret cave until he came to a small apartment, fitted up in a quiet but elegant style.

The rough walls were covered with hangings, and a Persian carpet was stretched on the floor. A large lamp which swung from the ceiling cast its mellow rays over the room, shedding a soft pleasant light on all parts.

On a low couch at the further end of this mysterious but not inelegant apartment was seated Alice Landon.

She was dressed in deep mourning, which had been provided for her by Batswing's special order. Her beautiful bosom, which rose and fell with deep sobs caused by her grief, was covered by a lace 'kerchief. Her hair was unbraided, and fell in massive tresses round her ivory neck, glimmering in the lamp-light like threads of fairy gold.

Her face was covered with a handkerchief which

she held to her eyes, and the low heart-rending moans which she uttered told the bitterness of her anguish.

Batswing stood for some moments watching this beautiful form, not liking to disturb such holy grief.

But so deep was Alice's affliction that she had not heard the approach of the outlaw, and fancied herself still alone with her sorrow.

"Madam," said Batswing at last, "pardon my trespassing on your privacy, but I have business that permits of no delay."

Alice started at the sound of his voice, and made a movement as if she would rush towards him, but checked herself.

"Why crave pardon of me, sir," she said, in sorrowful tones. "Am I not your prisoner?"

"Prisoner!" exclaimed Batswing, "No! What I have done was to protect you from harm. Did I not rescue you from the clutches of that scoundrel?"

"Oh! pardon me if I have wronged you," sobbed the girl, throwing herself at the highwayman's feet; "but all seems against me now. My heart is crushed."

"Rise, maiden, rise," cried Batswing, lifting her gently from the ground. "Heaven can bear witness that I am your friend and would die to serve you."

"Why was my father's cruel murder kept from me?" cried Alice, "why was I detained here?"

"Your father's unfortunate fate was kept from you, so that you would be more willing to remain where you are. Your returning home would have placed all our lives in danger. Had my own life been the only stake, I would not have deceived you one moment, but I could not play with my band; his men should always be a captain's first consideration."

"I see, I see," murmured Alice.

"I am told that you have received a letter denouncing your father's murderer. May I see it?

"It is here," said Alice, and taking a letter from the table she placed it in the hands of Batswing.

It ran as follows:—

"Mistress Alice Landon.—Avoid the scandal your present conduct is bringing on you. It is reported, and will soon be known as a fact, that you are now with the notorious Batswing, the outlaw. Give up this man to justice, and you shall be well rewarded. It is your duty to do so, for he is your *father's murderer!* To-morrow night, if you can escape from him, proceed along the forest path that leads to Waltham. An armed escort shall be waiting there for you, who will conduct you in safety. Remember, it is your duty to revenge your father's blood.—A FRIEND."

"Do you believe this?" asked Batswing.

"Believe it!" exclaimed Alice, "do I not know that it is false. The man who murdered my father was the one who carried me away; the one from whom you rescued me."

"Of that there can be but little doubt," said Batswing.

"Who could have written this letter, then?" demanded Alice.

"*That* I can answer," replied Batswing, with a bitter laugh. "This is the work of Jonathan Wild. No other but he would attempt such an open piece of knavery. Well, well, Jonathan and I know how fondly we love each other, and, therefore, I will not blame him."

"But when can I leave this place?" asked Alice, anxiously.

"Is it, then, so disagreeable that you wish to leave it?" asked Batswing, sadly.

"No. Oh, no, you have been very kind to me, but I fain would see my father before they ——"

A flood of tears prevented her finishing the last sentence. Nevertheless Batswing knew that she meant the funeral, and could scarcely answer her for his own grief.

"Alas! my dear child," he said, sorrowfully, "you are already too late; he will be buried to-day."

With a scream of agony Alice threw herself on the sofa and gave way to a fresh outburst of grief, which Batswing in vain attempted to alleviate.

At length she recovered her composure, and rising from the sofa she said in a calm, firm voice,

"Pardon me for my folly, sir; I know that my grief is unavailing, nay worse, for it hinders me from doing my duty."

"Your duty!" said Batswing, in astonishment.

"Yes," she replied firmly; "is it not my duty to follow my father to the grave? Do not deny me that last sad consolation, for I am determined that nothing but force shall prevent my carrying it out."

"Heaven forbid that I should ever be unkind to a lady," said Batswing; "therefore, madam, you need not fear that I will try to prevent you. I will not endeavour to conceal from you that there is great danger in this undertaking, but I pray the worthiness of the purpose may be our safeguard."

Raising her hands to his lips he withdrew before she could return him her thanks.

"Madge," said Batswing, "has any of the men turned up?"

"Yes," replied the old woman, "there's Teddy grumbling cause there ain't any dinner cooked."

"Send him to me, and then attend to Mistress Alice. And see that the veil she wears is thick enough to hide her face."

"Is she going out?" demanded Madge; "it strikes me she won't come back here again if she does."

"Begone!" said Batswing, "I have no time to answer questions."

No sooner had Madge departed, than Batswing, who was an adept at disguises, to which he owed much of his great success, took off the clothes he had on and exchanged them for a loose suit that hung about him in such creases as to give his limbs the appearance of being shrunken.

He then placed a long white wig over his own black hair, whitened his eyelashes and eyebrows, drew a few lines with a fine pencil at the corners of his mouth and eyes, and, taking a stick, tottered across the room the very picture of an old man of some eighty winters.

At this moment Growling Teddy entered the room and stared with astonishment at the figure before him.

"Why, who the devil are you?" asked Teddy, roughly.

"Your captain!" replied Batswing, straightening himself proudly.

"May I be cursed if I should have known you," grumbled Teddy. "Blow me if you ain't always a taking some one in. I never seed such a man. When you can't get travellers to try your hands on, why you sets to work on your own pals. I don't like it; I'm blowed if I do."

"Never mind, Teddy," said Bat; "but tell me what did you see as you came along?"

"More 'Robins' nor I care about," replied Teddy. "Curse me if I know what good them fellows are. They're always spoiling somebody's little game."

"Which way were they going?"

"Drawing back to London."

"Could you not learn what they were after?"

"Now what's the use of asking that question? Wasn't they Robins; and ain't it a Robin's nature never to be after anything but mischief?"

"True," laughed the Bat.

"Then what did you ask for? I hate to be asked foolish questions."

"Were there many people making their way towards Epping?"

"Whole 'eaps on 'em."

For what purpose?"

There's another question! To see the funeral, to be sure. Warn't the farmer murdered, and ain't murdered farmers curiosities—more's the pity—and don't all fools run gaping after curiosities, and ain't most people fools? Well, then, of course it must be to see the funeral."

"I suppose you are right," said Batswing; "you can go now."

"Are you going to the funeral with the girl?" demanded Teddy.

"I am."

"Ugh! another fool."

With this polite speech Teddy the Growler marched away, whilst the Bat went to escort Alice to her father's funeral.

CHAPTER XXI.

THE FUNERAL.—THE ARREST, ABDUCTION, AND ESCAPE.

It was late in the afternoon when Batswing, disguised as an old man, led Alice Landon through the forest on the sad errand which her affectionate heart had compelled her to undertake.

Alice was draped all in black, with a heavy veil drawn close over her face, so as to entirely conceal her features.

Batswing, wearing the dress we have already described, leant on Alice's arm, and tottered slowly along the pathway as if he had the greatest difficulty in walking.

In this manner they reached the border of the forest and gazed upon the open country.

The whole space was covered with people pressing eagerly on towards the little church, the bell of which sent forth the solemn toll for the dead.

"Be careful to keep up the appearance that I told you," said Batswing to his companion; "for much I dread that there is some danger near. I like not this crowd of persons."

"But my father was so loved," sobbed Alice.

"True," replied Batswing, and then added under his breath—"and so is his fair daughter."

"If you fear," said Alice, "I will go on alone."

"Fear!" exclaimed Batswing, "that is a feeling I never experienced, and as to letting you proceed alone, that can never be."

"And why not?" demanded Alice. "No one will hurt me."

"Why not? Have you forgotten the oath I gave Sir Arthur Bowring? Did I not swear to protect you from all harm as far as I possibly can? And as to no one hurting you, fair Alice, you must see that neither your beauty nor your purity can protect you against such villains."

Alice shuddered as she thought of the truth of these remarks; but she still continued her way, determined to carry out her filial intention.

As they approached the church they came across groups of people, a few of whom turned their heads to gaze at the tottering old man, as they thought, and his graceful daughter.

It was a great relief to Batswing to notice that these men, after a glance or two, or, perhaps, a kindly salutation, passed on their way without seeming to care who or what he was.

As they crossed an open meadow, a rough-looking farmer came up to them, and, after a slight glance at Batswing and his companion, commenced a conversation.

"Marnin', Gaffer," said the man; "the weather be changeable."

"It is indeed, sir," said Batswing, in a querulous voice.

"I 'spose you be going to see the funeral of the old farmer, loike other folks. Ah! it was a main cruel murder."

"Ah! that it was," said Batswing, squeezing Alice's arm as a warning that she should not betray too much emotion.

"Aye!" continued the farmer, meditatively; "it was a main cruel murder; such an unnatural one, too."

"So it was, so it was," said Batswing; then, turning to Alice, he said—"Hold up, Maggy dear. You must not let other's sorrows trouble you so. She is so sensitive."

"Daughter, Gaffer?" asked the man.

"No; my grandchild," replied Bat.

"Ah!" returned the man, "he's most blessed who has no children at all. Look at old Landon, how fond he was of his gal, and only to think that she should turn round and help murder the old man, so that she might run away with her lover."

It took Batswing all his strength to support Alice, who nearly fainted upon hearing this most cruel accusation.

"Hush, hush, good sir; you should not say that," said Batswing; "you have no proof that she is guilty of this foul deed."

"Proofs!" said the man with a brutal laugh. "I think the proofs are in the girl's disappearance: they do say that she ran off with that villain Batswing, who committed the murder. It was a good dodge of his putting the soldiers off their guard by having an accomplice in a carriage to meet them, and play old Landon's character."

"An accomplice!" said Batswing; "what proof have you he was so?"

"Proof!" exclaimed the man; "why, in the hurried way he made himself scarce when he had misled the soldiers. And if there be any more proofs wanted of the girl and highwayman's guilt, I should think it would be found in the coffin which I see over yonder."

As he spoke he pointed across a field in the direction of the church, and showed them the small funeral train wending towards the churchyard.

Poor Alice could scarcely repress a scream of horror at the man's brutal accusation and the sight of that awful long black chest wherein her father's murdered form lay cold and stiff.

But Batswing, with ready wit, came to the rescue, and supporting her as well as he could, declared that he was so tired that he must rest a short time.

"Shall I take your granddaughter on, Gaffer," said the man, stretching forth his hand; but noticing that Alice shrank shudderingly back, he gave her a scowl that was anything but agreeable.

"She can go if she likes," said Batswing, "but I must have a rest."

"There, lass," said the man, "you hear what the Gaffer says, so come along: it would be a pity to lose so pretty a sight as the funeral of a murdered father."

"Leave me," cried Alice, cowering down by the side of Batswing.

"Nay, Maggy: it is only the gentleman's kindness that makes him offer you this, I am sure," replied Batswing in quick tones, although his blood boiled so at the stranger's brutal impudence, that it was with difficulty he could resist the temptation to knock him down.

"You must excuse her, sir," he continued, glancing up to the stranger.

"She is very nervous and sensitive."

"Oh! very well," said the man, with a rough laugh; "she can do just what she pleases; but I'm not going to lose the show for any one: I can tell you that. So good morning, Gaffer; we may meet again.

"Pray heaven we do not," muttered Batswing, as the man hurried down the path.

"Who is that dreadful man?" said Alice.

"That I know not," replied Batswing—"all I know is, that I hate him. What a strange thing it is that there are some people that inspire you with detestation directly you behold them; whilst others make you love them at the first glance."

For a moment both were silent.

Suddenly the sound of the death-bell called Alice to her senses, and springing to her feet, she exclaimed,

"Let us go, I *must* be there."

"I fear much, Alice, that you will be in great danger. I do not like the looks of that fellow."

"Had he been an enemy, would he not have stayed by us?" asked Alice.

"Perhaps, and perhaps not," replied Batswing. "Whatever he is, I know he suspects that we are not what we wish ourselves to appear. Are you still determined to go on?"

"I am," replied Alice.

"As you will it, so must it be. But should any harm come of this, you must not blame me."

As he spoke, he arose from the bank whereon he had been seated, and taking Alice's arm proceeded towards the church.

Of all the beautiful services employed in our different churches, there is none more beautiful than that used for the dead. Grand in its solemnity, rich in its trust and hope, it touches the heart of the callous spectator; while it bears consolation to the true mourners.

In death all are equal—rich and poor, prince and peasant, mingle together in the grave. What though one has a fine mausoleum, built of sculptured marble, and the other a common mound of earth. Both have to kneel at the same judgment-seat. Monuments do not bring men nearer unto heaven; it is "only the good deeds of the just smell sweet and blossom in the dust."

The service in the church was over, and the coffin borne to the grave.

The sun was sinking fast behind the horizon as they stood bareheaded by the side of the grave. The last words were said by the parson, and sorrowfully all turned away.

Batswing was so moved by Alice's grief that he forgot to play his part as well as he otherwise might have done.

They had passed the church gate, and had entered a lane, when suddenly a party of men surrounded them.

A strong hand was placed upon Batswing's shoulder; and a sharp grating voice, which he knew too well, thundered,

"You are my prisoner: I arrest you for robbery."

Turning quickly round, Batswing beheld Jonathan Wild standing by his side, grinning with devilish delight as he beheld his victim's confusion.

With one blow Batswing struck Jonathan Wild to the ground, and then raising his oaken staff as a single-stick he charged the thief-taker's followers.

In the scuffle Alice was forced from his side, so that he was unable to protect her.

As she stood horror-stricken at this fearful attack, a thick cloak was thrown over her head.

Strong arms lifted her from the ground, and in a few seconds she was placed in a carriage, which drove rapidly away.

Batswing turned just in time to behold the abduction, and perceiving at a glance that no possible good could arise from his following the carriage; indeed such a proceeding would have caused his certain arrest, he turned, leapt the hedge, and in a few moments was dashing across the fields.

"Seize him!" cried Jonathan Wild, springing to his feet, and hastily wiping the blood from his face. "Perdition! have you let him escape? Pursue him at once. Five hundred pounds reward to any one who arrests him!"

The reward was no sooner uttered than all the countrymen, as well as the thief-taker's followers, joined in the chase.

"Stop thief! stop thief!" echoed all through the pleasant lanes, as Batswing bounded ahead of his pursuers.

One of the men perceiving that the highwayman gained on them drew a pistol—levelled it and fired.

Batswing stumbled forward and fell.

The bullet had struck him in the shoulder.

CHAPTER XXII.

JONATHAN WILD REGAINS HIS POCKET-BOOK—THE DOUBLE CHALLENGE.

When Jonathan Wild and Lord Redfern rode away from the Bird Cage Inn, Jonathan was in anything but a good temper.

Jonathan, a perfect savage animal, hating, detesting all virtue, and glorying in anything cruel and bad, always had the sincerest contempt for a ruffian who had not courage.

Perhaps if Wild could be said to admire anything it was courage, but even that never made any impression on him, beyond thinking how far he could make the owner of it subservient to his wishes and purposes.

After they had ridden a little way Jonathan suddenly checked his horse, and turning round to Lord Redfern, said :—

"I am a student of human nature, my lord, and must, therefore, crave pardon you. If the remark which I am about to make should seem somewhat impertinent, will you excuse me?"

"You can proceed," replied his lordship, "although I must confess, I should have thought Master Jonathan Wild the last man to have considered his fellow-creature at all."

"Now there you wrong me," said Jonathan with a chuckle. "It is by the study of my fellow-creatures that I have thriven in life. There is no use in knowing only one side of the thing, we must look on both. Man is like a coin—stamped on one side with vice, on the other side with virtue. The former side is left alone by pious people as too dreadful to mention: hence the impression remains very often as fresh as it was at first, until the coin is worn out. But your virtue side is rubbed and polished by your schoolmasters, legislators, and divines to such a degree that they always blunt the impress, if they do not obliterate it altogether."

"A pretty moral truly: how your virtue must have shined at one time," sneered Lord Redfern; "but what is the question you were about to ask me?"

"It is this—I should like to know how it is a man who is a coward can have the courage to commit a murder?"

Lord Redfern glanced keenly at Jonathan Wild, and then asked—

"Are all men cowards who are murderers?"

"Why do you ask me?"

"Because I know you have an extensive acquaintance with such people."

"I have," retorted Jonathan Wild, "from your lordship downwards."

"Dare you insinuate?"

"Tut, tut, my lord," said Jonathan; "you forget you are speaking to a man who dares do anything. I know you murdered old Landon: you have almost confessed the crime to me; therefore it is more than useless to deny it now. Had it not been for you I should have stayed and listened to what that country bumpkin had to say, and perhaps have discovered Alice Landon's whereabouts, and also how to arrest Batswing. I promised him four year's reprieve; but this last offence shall shorten the period."

"I fear that you will have more trouble to catch

this Batswing than you think. He treats you with contempt."

"Contempt!" exclaimed Jonathan, "how so?"

"Why, has he not robbed you of your valuable pocket-book, taken in the governor of Newgate, and actually sent you a message?"

"Ah! the message," said Jonathan, "yes, that must be attended to. Which way do you ride, my lord?"

"Why, back to London. Do not you do the same?"

"Of a surity, I do not: I ride to the French Horn at Mill-hill, and see if what the countryman said is true."

"How far is it from here?" demanded Lord Redfern.

"About seven to eight miles. Will you come?"

With a heavy groan Lord Redfern consented, and putting spurs to their horses, dashed away.

They soon arrived at the French Horn, the landlord of which wayside hostelry was a secret friend of Batswing's, who, indeed, had agents all over that part of the country.

After calling for a glass of brandy, Jonathan asked if it were true that Batswing, the celebrated highwayman, had been there and left a pocket-book for him.

"Are you Master Jonathan Wild?" demanded the landlord.

"I am."

"Then I suppose what that there chap said was true then. Was it?"

"How should I know, unless you tell me what he did say?" demanded Jonathan, petulantly.

"Very true, sir, very true," replied the landlord. "Well, sir, a fellow with a large black moustache, black hair, black boots and coat, rode up to the inn on a black horse."

"Yes, that is the man," said Wild.

"Well, he came stamping and swaggering into the place as if the house were his own. 'Give me a bottle of brandy,' says he. I did so, and he put it to his lips, and drank it clean off at a draught. Well, I stared at that, as any man would; so he laughs, and he says, says he: 'Oh'! you stare to see me drink like that, do you; but I've only just come to life again. I've been dead, and taken to Newgate; received two hundred pounds reward from Mr. Pitt, the governor, and afterwards stole the pocket-book of that infernal rascal, Jonathan Wild, the thief-taker in Smithfield."

"Curse him," groaned Jonathan; "I knew it was him."

"Well, I couldn't speak for staring in surprise at the fellow's impudence, although, after seeing him drink the brandy, I could almost have believed anything he said or did. So he threw a pocket-book down on the table, and he says, 'There is the thief-taker's book. I have taken out of it all that I want, you can return it to him now, and get the reward. Here's a guinea for you, one for the brandy, and another to deliver my message faithfully. Tell him, also, that I shall be glad to have the pleasure of Mr. Pitt's company to a little dinner in a week or two.' Then he jumped on his horse, gave a hollow laugh, and out flew his black cloak, and he flitted away."

"That is he," groaned Jonathan. "He must have been one of the people who took the dead soldier to Newgate, and robbed the governor of the reward."

"But they were women," said Lord Redfern.

"Who knows what they were?" replied Jonathan; "this Batswing can take any shape he pleases."

"Do you believe that he is supernatural then?"

"No, I mean he disguises himself so admirably that no one can discover the cheat."

"They do say he is very clever," said the landlord.

"Clever as he is, he shall not escape me," growled

Jonathan. "I bide my time; but when it comes I show no mercy. Where is the pocket-book?"

"There it is," said the landlord, throwing it on the table. "Now where is the reward I was promised?"

"Reward!" exclaimed Jonathan, "think yourself lucky that I do not arrest you for trafficking with thieves. Come, my lord; we have no time to waste upon this fellow."

So saying, Wild left the house, closely followed by Lord Redfern. They mounted their horses, and galloped away towards London.

"Curses go with you," growled the landlord, as he watched them go down the road. "It is such men as you that make men dishonest. Why, Batswing has more sense in his little finger than you have in the whole of your body. Only to think what beautiful lies he does make up, and how greedily these gabies swallow them. He thinks the Bat really *was* caged in Newgate. Bah! it will take a stronger cage than that to hold such night-birds as either the Bat or Jack Sheppard. Well, well, there's an old proverb about 'set a thief to catch a thief,' and who knows but that Jonathan Wild may prove too good a match for them yet, for he is the biggest thief unhung?"

Meanwile, Jonathan and Lord Redfern galloped swiftly to London, never uttering a word until they arrived at Jonathan Wild's house in the Old Bailey.

Here they dismounted, and entering it at once, went to Jonathan's office.

"What is to be done now?" demanded Lord Redfern.

"Done!" growled Wild, between his teeth, "done! why Batswing must be arrested, at all cost and hazards. He has taken everything of value and consequence out of this pocket-book."

"It is all very well to talk about his being taken; but the question is, how is it to be done? Our journey to-day has been useless. All that time has been lost to us, and gain to him."

Without deigning to answer this question, Wild touched a bell, and his trusty henchman, Rough Ralph, entered the room.

"Any news?" demanded Jonathan, sharply.

"Yes."

"What?"

"They have returned from Epping, and spread the report that Batswing committed the murder of the old 'un."

"And the girl?"

"Nobody knows nothing about her," growled Ralph.

"Capital; now go."

With a savage grunt Hugh left the room.

"Now, my lord," cried Jonathan Wild, rubbing his hands, and chuckling with delight, "has the day been wasted? are we no further on? have I been idle?"

"Perhaps not; but I must confess that I do not see how much we have gained by your actions. Neither Batswing or the girl is in our power as yet."

"No; but they soon will be, or if not both, at least one. Alice's sudden disappearance is suspicious. She escapes with Batswing. Your sudden disappearance, caused by cow—hem, we'll call it prudence—has given rise to the report that you were in league with this outlaw. These reports I will take care shall be carried to Alice, if she is still with Batswing, and she shall be tempted to escape and betray this man."

"She will never do *that*. Alice is too pure to stoop to such an action."

"Bah! she is a woman; all our best men have been betrayed by their girls."

"A pleasant theory, certainly."

"A true one, and therefore distasteful; true things generally are. Should this fail, or rather in case this might fail, I have another idea. We, with my men

THE STRUGGLE ON THE HOUSETOP.

all disguised, will go to old Landon's funeral. Alice is sure to be there, and most likely that fellow Batswing, for nothing ever frightens him. We will arrest them as the murderers, bring Batswing here, and you can take the girl anywhere you like. Now go; but remember to be here early in the morning."

"I wish the morning was here now," muttered Lord Redfern between his teeth. "Heaven only knows how I shall pass the time until I can grasp revenge. My blood boils for vengeance."

"Be calm, my lord," said Wild, with a malicious smile. "Remember that the most deadly things in this world are cold-blooded, such as the cobra. As for passing your time, go to your club, and see what is passing there."

"But there is that infernal wager; I could not pay it yet."

No. 6.

"The time is not up yet. Besides, the girl has disappeared. Who knows that you have not carried off the girl, eh? Hint at this, don't say you have; more danger is done to a person by hints than by plain speaking, whilst one may be proved a mistake, the other a lie. And now, good night. I am busy."

Seating himself at his table, Jonathan Wild commenced writing, and Lord Redfern slowly took his departure.

His lordship first wandered homeward, where he changed his soiled habiliments for the most gaudy he could find, in hopes that they might make him look fresh and charming—for, ugly as he was, he believed greatly in his own personal attractions. But, do what he would, he still looked worn and haggard.

He reached his club, and found nearly the same

party assembled as on the evening he had made the bet.

"Oh!" cried Lord Fitzboodle. "Fore Gad! here is Redfern; now we shall have some good news. Now, who is the man that has carried off this Alice Landon? Ha! ha! ha! the subject of the bet, you know, between yourself and Leslie."

Lord Redfern shot one hasty glance at the drowsy lord just mentioned, then shrugged his shoulders, and stepping up behind the couch whereon Lord Leslie was reclining, he leant over him and whispered in his ear—

"Really, my lord, you should not be so indiscreet as to mention these bets."

"The fellows bothered me to know," yawned Lord Leslie.

"Come, Redfern," cried another, "we've been trying to pump Sir Arthur Bowring, but he is as silent and surly as a mouse. Who carried her off?"

"Now, really, gentlemen, I cannot say," simpered Lord Redfern, shyly.

"Are you too modest?" asked another young gentleman, with a laugh.

"Modest!" cried another. "Modesty and Redfern shook hands and parted when he first drew breath."

"Thank you, my lord," said Redfern, "for the compliment to my mother. I wish I could return it."

A titter ran round the room at the expense of the young lord, whose mother was generally believed to have shown more love for the King than either her husband—submissive as he was—or her country required or particularly cared for.

"But about the girl," cried another man; "tell us about her."

"That is one of the few subjects I must not speak upon," replied Lord Redfern.

"Or *cannot*," said Sir Arthur, severely.

"Well, cannot, if you wish," replied Lord Redfern; "anything to oblige; but not that; no, not that. On that subject my lips are sealed."

"Fore Gad, I see it all," cried Fitzboodle. "Redfern is the man; he did the plant by putting on that outlaw fellow, the one they say is as good in the country as Jack Sheppard is in the city. He carried her off."

"And who murdered her father?" demanded Sir Arthur Bowring, sternly.

"Oh! bother. Ah! well, that *is* rather an awkward question," said Lord Leslie, yawning. "Perhaps, Redfern, you can answer that question?"

If Lord Leslie could have seen the glance his friend and toady gave him, he might have thought it worth his while for once in his life to wake up a little and endeavour to get rid of his dangerous companions.

"Of that I know nothing," said Lord Redfern; "perhaps he killed himself."

"Lord Redfern, you know that to be false," cried Sir Arthur; "you know that to carry out a diabolical wager you or your agents caused this fearful crime, and may Heaven bring you to your punishment."

"Sir Arthur Bowring," cried Lord Redfern, turning pale with rage, "you surely must be mad to make so grave a charge without any means of proving it. Many men would resent such an insult; but under the painful circumstances, having been one of the party who lost Lord Clumber's plate—pardon me, I know you only took the office as a friend, and well you performed it; may his lordship be thankful for your kind services, for, of course, you are not answerable, under the circumstances, for the loss; still, it must be annoying. Then, as a disappointed lover—I will not say a jilted one," here Lord Redfern simpered again, "I feel that you may be excused."

"Fore Gad, Redfern, you are a better fellow than I thought you," cried Lord Fitzboodle, who, as was his wont, had already taken too much wine: "you are,

upon my soul, and I'll drink to the pretty Alice's health, wherever she may be."

"I suppose I must drink that, eh, Redfern?" demanded Lord Leslie, in a somniferous tone; "though, 'pon my soul, it's a bore. I wish a fellow might drink in a recumbent position, like the old Romans."

"Drink it, my lord!" cried Redfern, pointedly; "if you do not drink it, I know not the man who should. If you lose one way, you gain another."

"Stop, gentlemen," cried Sir Arthur, springing up; "I forbid this. That lady's father now lies cruelly murdered; she herself persecuted by brutes in human shape. Oh! you may stare, my Lord Redfern, I mean you and that young gentleman by your side, whose drowsiness seems to have sent his honour to sleep. Your foul wager has become known, and amongst honest men both the master and his obsequious servant can find nothing but contempt."

The first drew back, overcome with a sense of shame; but Lord Leslie, who, indolent as he was, knew not what cowardice meant, stepped forward, and placing himself before Sir Arthur, replied,

"Sir Arthur Bowring, although I feel that your remarks are somewhat just, still I cannot forgive the way in which they have been put. Your insult has been quite enough for me to challenge you, and I do so at once. We fight to-morrow."

"As you will, my lord. I shall be ready to meet you at any time or place."

"Somebody will act for my second," said Lord Leslie, again dropping back into his sleepy mood; "only don't make it too early in the morning, it is such a bore to get up. Besides, the mornings are chilly just now. You'll stand for me, Fitzboodle? Thank you; see all the what-you-may-call-thems arranged; I hate trouble."

Having completed this speech his lordship sunk back on the sofa, quite exhausted, and soon slumbered again.

"Have you nothing to say, Lord Redfern?" demanded Sir Arthur.

"I have. I shall be most happy to meet you and prove at the sword's point that what you have just stated is false, as you were to your trust. I will meet you any time you please, except to-morrow."

"Make it to-morrow," drawled Lord Leslie, half waking up; "the sooner it's over the better, you know. I'll fight to-morrow, Fitzboodle. Remember that."

"Come, come, Lord Redfern," said Fitzboodle, "make it to-morrow."

"Pardon me, my lord, I really cannot," replied the other, firmly.

"And why not? If you have another little affair on, we can make our meeting at the same place, and so accommodate all parties."

"I have another little matter to settle," replied Lord Redfern; "but one where even *your* society would be one too many, my dear Lord Fitzboodle."

"Oh! I see; it is with a lady, I suppose," said a young fellow, laughing.

"You are right," replied Lord Redfern; "it is with a lady. *One* whom I would not disappoint for the world. The day after, I am quite at Sir Arthur's service. Before then I cannot be."

So the matter was soon arranged. Sir Arthur was to meet Lord Leslie the next morning, and, if he survived the encounter, Lord Redfern the morning afterwards.

CHAPTER XXIII.
THE PURSUIT.

With a savage cry of delight Jonathan Wild sprang forward to sieze our hero; but Batswing had recovered his feet and darted off as swiftly as a stag.

On came the wild crowd, halleoing and shouting,

leaping hedges and ditches, flourishing stakes and sticks, as they dashed after the fugitive.

Now and then Jonathan or one of his followers would discharge a pistol at him, but Batswing avoided them all.

Two dogs, who joined the chase, came so unpleasantly near that Batswing had to turn and settle them. This he did by the aid of his oaken staff, leaving the unfortunate brutes dead on the field. Still the men came nearer and nearer; fresh ones had taken up the pursuit, and were hurrying fast on his heels.

Suddenly he heard the tramp of horses' feet coming swiftly along the road, and his hand naturally sought for his pistols, but, unluckily, he found that in the hurry of exchanging his disguises he had forgotten to bring them with him.

Nearer and nearer they came; till, growing desparate, Batswing leaped a hedge and stood at bay.

Scarcely had he done so than the horse cleared the hawthorn row, and Batswing beheld that the rider was no other than Jonathan Wild.

"Yield, yield!" cried Jonathan, flourishing his huge cutlass over his head, "you are my prisoner."

Fortunately for Batswing the horse stumbled forward at the moment, and both it and the rider fell to the ground.

In a moment Batswing dealt Wild a terrific blow over the head, then quickly seizing his pistols, mounted the horse, who had already regained its legs, and dashed quickly away in the direction of Mill Hill.

The horse of which he had deprived Jonathan Wild was far from a good one, as Batswing soon found out, for she nearly fell at every jump and soon became blown.

"Oh! if I had my own old Batswing," he said to himself. "Well, I must not be ungrateful, for this poor old brute has given me a good rest. Curse the fellows, they have got torches, and are still pursuing. They will arouse all the country side for miles round; then I shall never escape."

They were now close upon Mill Hill, and the night being dark, Batswing could only tell the distance his pursuers were from him by the lights they carried and the constant noise they made by their shouts.

Finding that he had gained some distance upon them, he determined to play some trick that should lead them off the track.

Putting spurs to his horse, he galloped towards a hedge, leaped it, and, directly he was on the other side, pulled up.

Instantly dismounting, he quickly unsaddled and bridled the horse, letting it trot quietly away to browse in the field, a permission of which the tired animal quickly availed itself.

He then took the saddle and bridle in his arms, and crept along the hedge in the ditch, until he came to a tall tree, up which he climbed, seating himself on the thickest of the branches.

From this elevated position he could behold the pursuers as they came tearing over the fields. Horsemen, constables, countrymen, and boys all came dashing along, yelping and howling like a pack of hounds seeking for their prey.

The torches that they carried shed a red glare on the crowd, and helped them to see the obstacles and inequalities of the ground, but were rather a hindrance to their seeing far before or up above, for the flaring light made the darkness beyond its immediate circle appear darker, whilst the thick smoke came in such dense clouds that it got into the eyes of the pursuers and nearly blinded them.

"There they go," muttered Batswing, as he saw them break through the hedge some fifty yards higher up than the tree on which he sat. "I hope they won't discover the old horse; the sweat she is in would discover me."

"As I live!" he exclaimed, as a horseman dashed up and cleared the hedge, nearly running over some of the people on foot; "as I live, there goes Jonathan Wild! Will nothing kill that man? Surely he cannot be human. But then all the people round Epping seem to think that I am in league with the Devil, if I am not that old gentleman himself."

At that moment he was startled by hearing Jonathan shout as loudly as he could to the people who were leading the pursuit.

"To the French Horn at Mill Hill. I know he goes there."

"Right you are," thought Batswing, "and very glad I am, too, that you have given me that hint, for after it I shall go in the opposite direction."

Away dashed the crowd as swiftly as it could, Jonathan Wild's tall figure showing out above the rest like the leader of a troop of fiends.

No sooner had they disappeared than Batswing slipped down the tree, and struck across the fields in the direction of London.

Coming to a pond, he took off his grey wig, and, filling it with stones, sank it. He then washed the paint off his face and eyebrows so as to change his appearance as much as possible. For the same reason he turned up the collar of his coat, wrapped a coloured pocket handkerchief round his neck, and threw away his oaken staff—the latter he knew many of the crowd had had too many reasons to know—then struck off towards Highgate, which he reached in safety.

All was quiet in the village, and Batswing considered whether he should stop there. But on second thoughts he determined to push on to London, as he feared that Jonathan might send his emissaries through the different villages on their way back to London, and thus trace out where he had hidden. A long walk down a country road towards London is not pleasant at the present time, although we have a good firm road to walk on, and "the many lamps of London" light us to our destiny like a cloud of fire. But at the time of our story the roads were badly made, and were always in a bad condition. Deep ruts were formed by the heavy waggons or wains, many of which have been superseded by the quicker and cheaper transport of the railways. Added to this, London was at that period so badly lighted that it gave but very little reflection to the sky.

Footsore and weary, but not at all disheartened, Batswing turned down Drury-lane, and going down a stable yard, knocked at the back door of a hostelry that had for a sign that fabulous animal a "Blue Boar."

After repeating the summons once or twice he heard a shuffling down the stone passage, and a thick wheezy voice demanded? "Who's there?"

"It's all right, Toby Crick," whispered Batswing; "I bring news from Epping."

In an instant the door was opened, and Toby Crick stood ready to welcome the wanderer to his cheery hearth.

"Bless my soul alive, if it ain't the captain himself," wheezed Toby. "Well, now, who would have thought it? I should not. Come this way, come along."

"Wait a moment, Toby; have you any strangers here?"

"Bless my soul alive, no. There are a few fellows in the tap-room, but not a soul in my own private room. Why, how wet and cold you are."

"So I should think," said Batswing, as he entered the landlord's little snuggery. "If you had come as far through the country as I have I fancy you might have been in much such a state as I am now." "Ah! this is something like," he continued, as he warmed his hands at a good blazing fire. "Now Toby, first of all a good glass of brandy, and then a change of clothes as soon as you can."

44 THE OUTLAWS OF EPPING FOREST.

The brandy was easily enough found, but the change of garments was quite a different affair. However, a long riding-cloak buttoned close to the chin, a lace cravat, and pair of light top-boots, were found at last, together with a rather battered three-cornered hat, and, with the aid of these, Batswing looked quite a different character.

"Well, now, what has been the matter?" said the landlord, wheezing as usual.

"Not a word until I have had something to eat," said Batswing, "for I am as hollow as a drum and as ravenous as a wolf."

A good steak pie was soon put before Batswing, who applied himself with such gusto to it that the landlord—himself a great eater, as his fullness showed—who stood smoking his pipe in front of the fire, felt quite envious of his appetite.

Toby Crick was a most peculiar-looking little man. He stood about five feet four, and measured about the same round the waist—that is, where his waist ought to have been. His head was as round as a Dutch cheese, and would have been as bare of hair had it not been for a frizzy wig, commonly known as a "Brown George," which, owing to the polished surface on which it was placed, was constantly slipping over the eyes of the wearer, or on to the nape of his neck.

His face was what is vulgarly called "baggy." There were bags under his eyes; his cheeks hung in bags, and his double chin was formed of two huge bags. His nose and eyes had much difficulty in preventing themselves from being buried by his round cheeks, which were in rebellion against these highly useful organs. As to his mouth, it was something like the hole formed by shoving a knife into a new loaf.

This head was supported on a body—neck he had none—almost as round as itself. This was clothed in a striped waistcoat—coat he had none—and a small white tapster's apron, which hung down to his fat knees; beyond these showed a pair of fat podgy legs, encased in blue stockings, terminating in a pair of large broad shoes, garnished with huge buckles.

Such was Toby Crick, a heavy, sleepy, goodnatured individual, much given to eating, drinking, and sleeping; a man of few words, yet one who would lengthen his sentences by always adding his favourite exclamation of "Bless my soul alive!"

"There," said Batswing, throwing down his knife and fork, and pushing his chair back, "now that is over I will relate my adventures."

This he did amidst many exclamations of surprise from the landlord, who smoked his pipe and wondered how any man could be found to go through such trials and difficulties.

When the narration was over, Batswing leant his head upon his hand, and fell into a deep reverie.

"Bless my soul alive!" said Toby, "I could not do it to save my life. Run a number of miles, then ride a good many more, climb a tree, get down it again, and walk all the way here; why I know I could not do it."

Batswing could not repress a smile when he thought of the landlord's podgy little figure going through these different difficulties.

"What makes you so dull?" continued Toby.

"I was thinking of the poor girl," said Batswing, sorrowfully. "What will become of her? Heaven protect her, for she is surrounded by enemies in the guise of friends—deep-plotting villains, who have ruined many a strong man; and how should she, young and innocent, escape?"

"Bless my soul alive!" cried the landlord, "what can that noise in the streets be? It ain't a fight, it ain't, no it can't be."

"It is though," cried Batswing.

"Bless my soul alive! What?" said Toby taking his pipe out of his mouth, and staring at his companion in amaze.

"The hue and cry!!" cried Batswing, springing to his feet. "That blood-hound Jonathan has found me out."

"Bless my soul alive; it can't be," cried the honest landlord, quivering all over.

"But I tell you it is, though," said Batswing. "I know the sound but too well. Come what may, come what may, I'll sell my life dearly."

As he spoke he drew forth the pistols he had taken from Jonathan, and cocked them, first examining the priming and loading with great care.

"Not in my house, not in my house," cried the landlord, trembling in alarm. "I can't abear the sight of blood, it makes me sick. Ugh! it's so nasty."

"Curse your house!" cried Batswing. "Do you think I am going to stop here to be quietly hurled off to prison, without striking a blow for my liberty? At least one of the hounds shall answer for this; and if I have luck it shall be Jonathan Wild."

"Bless my soul alive!" screamed the now almost frantic Toby Crick. "Jonathan Wild coming to my house! Oh, we shall all of us be hanged for a certainty. Oh! if I'd never taken to this.

"Silence!" cried Batswing, "let us listen a little."

They did so, and could hear that the noise had rather augmented than decreased. In fact, judging from the tremendous hubbub, the crowd must have been terrific.

"They are searching the White Horse first," said Batswing. "Jonathan knows that I go there as a rule when I am in town."

"Hush!" cried Toby, "they are coming down the street; they are coming here. Quick! there is not a moment to be lost. Rush up stairs; if you get out of the top window you will find an iron bar protruding from the roof. Pull yourself up by this, and you can get upon the parapet. Make your escape any way, but don't be found in this house, for heaven's sake. Go now, never mind paying now, another time will do, only go. Don't, if you love me, be found in my house."

Overcome with fear and this unusually long speech, Toby Crick sunk back in his chair and gasped like a fish out of water.

For a moment Batswing reflected, and hearing the noise come closer and closer he determined to follow Toby's advice.

He sprung to the door in an instant, and dashed up the stairs to the top of the house, then paused to listen.

He had only taken Toby's warning in time, for he could now hear the heavy tramp of men as they ran down the passage.

Gently lowering the top part of the window, he crept out. Then holding on by the bottom sash he managed to pull up the top until he had nearly closed it, so that his escape that way should not be suspected. He then caught the iron bar and swung himself up into the parapet, where he paused for a moment to take breath and think what would be the best thing to do next.

CHAPTER XXIV.
ALICE LANDON FINDS HERSELF A PRISONER.

When Alice was torn away from her protector, as we have already described, she was hurried into a carriage, a man dressed like a farmer, but masked, sprang in beside her, the door was closed, and the carrage drove quickly away.

Alice endeavoured to remove the thick cloak that had been thrown over her head, but strong hands seized her arms, and with a leather strap pinioned them behind her.

The next minute a cord was tied round her throat, so that the cloak became fixed over her head in such a manner that her struggles could not move it.

"There," said a fiendish voice by her ear, "now my pretty Alice is mine. No, darling, don't struggle; you can't escape, and it is much better to say yes with a grace than to have to say it whether you like it or no."

To Alice's horror an arm stole round her waist, and the defenceless girl felt herself pressed to her persecutor's breast.

"Nay, do not be so modest, little one," said the man, as Alice when released shrunk from his touch as far as she could to the corner of the carriage; "we must tame the little bird; and when it is good it shall have gay plumage, and shall fly about; but until then it must be kept closely shut up in its cage."

Poor Alice in vain tried to close her ears to this diabolical talk, formed half of cruel triumph and half of false love and fulsome compliment. At last insensibility came to her aid, and she sunk back in a dead faint.

But notwithstanding her illness the carriage never stopped, but tore down the road at a rapid rate.

"We shall have no interruption from Batswing this time, at all events," said Lord Redfern, for as the reader must have guessed the villain who had captured Alice was no other. "I dare say that gentleman is pretty well torn to pieces by the crowd, and what remains of him is on its way to Newgate, to prepare to become one of the precious fruits of Tyburn tree."

Night came on, and still the heavy coach rolled swifty along the road, bumping over ruts and loose stones.

Lord Redfern, as the darkness drew around, evidently did not feel quite at his ease in spite of boastful language, for he drew forth his pistols, and after looking well to the priming, placed them on the seat before him, so as to be ready for instant use should occasion require.

Entering London by Bishopsgate they drove through the City, and turning down Ludgate proceeded up Fleet-street and the Strand, through Pall-mall, and turning up George-street, entered St. James's-square, where they pulled up close by the houses once occupied by Madame Churchill, mistress of the Duke of York, and Moll Davis, who held the same honourable relation to the Duke's brother, Charles the Second.

It was at that time a gloomy-looking square, with dark dreary houses, the sides of whose doors were ornamented with large iron trumpet-looking things which served for flambeau to extinguish the torches carried by the footmen, who marched by the side of the sedan chairs in which the lords and ladies returned home from their routes.

The house before which the carriage pulled up was a most gloomy one. The brick front was dark and dirty, the door was painted a deep green, and both windows and door-steps had evidently not been cleaned for an age.

The casements were tall and narrow, with no blinds or curtains to cheer them, but their grimy panes were made more gloomy by the heavy shutters that were closed inside, so as to exclude all light.

Any one passing by the house, or pausing to look at its grim exterior, would have imagined that it was empty, whilst the absence of any sign of its being "to let" might lead one to suppose that it was in the possession of spirits, or that other great evil power—Chancery.

No sooner had the carriage stopped than the door of the house opened silently, and Lord Redfern with his fair captive in his arms alighted from the carriage and bore her into the house.

No sooner had he entered the passage than the door closed as suddenly and silently as it had opened, discovering an old woman had been hidden behind it.

The passage, which was lit by one gloomy oil lamp, was paved with stone that, like the door-step, seemed never to have been cleaned; cobwebs hung from the ceiling and filled the corners of the place; whilst a close musty smell seemed to pervade the atmosphere.

The old woman, who stood mowing and mouthing at Lord Redfern, was certainly the most terrible-looking object in this dreary place.

She had evidently once been tall, but age had bowed her nearly double, but by bending back her neck she still managed to keep her face presented forwards, as if to spite mankind, for surely few faces were half so terrible.

The forehead, over which a few stray hairs, escaping from the cambric border of her close cap, straggled, was flat, narrow, and low, terminating at the eyebrows by two large projecting bones. Her eyes had once been blue, but were now a pale slate colour, bleared and watery, divided by a long, thin, hooked nose, which leant over the long pale livid slit—surrounded with wrinkles—that formed her mouth. Almost straight from this aperture shot out a chin made much in the shape of a shoe-horn.

Added to these hideous features, her cheek-bones were immensely high, and her skin resembled shrivelled old parchment more than anything else.

As if she were not satisfied at nature having made her so frightful, she seemed to take a strange delight in grinning.

She sucked her hollow cheeks in between her toothless gums, and then puffed them out again with a motion much resembling the palpitation of a toad's throat; whilst her long thin tongue shot out and quivered between her livid lips like an adder's sting.

This horrible piece of human nature was dressed in a rich satin gown, with a fine lace kerchief folded over her lean bosom.

Her hands—more properly speaking, claws—were encased in long mittons, which extended up her scraggy arms as far as the elbows.

Tabitha Osselton—or, as Lord Redfern politely called her, "Hecate"—was as vicious as she was ugly. She had known Redfern for many years, and had aided and abetted him in many deeds of profligacy that at the present time would have been deemed impossible.

"Has anyone been?" demanded Lord Redfern.

"Not a soul," croaked the dame.

"Not Leslie?"

"No."

"Is the room prepared?"

"Quite."

"Then lead on."

Shambling along, Tabitha led the way to a large apartment, furnished in the most luxurious manner.

The walls were draped with heavy plum-coloured velvet curtains, that hung from a magnificent gilt cornice, which ran round the ceiling.

These curtains were looped up with cords and tassels of heavy bullion, so as to show handsome mirrors.

Ottomans, couches, sofas, and settees, all covered with the same rich-coloured velvet, were placed about the room. The floor was carpeted with a rich Persian carpet of brilliant hues, and as thick and soft that the heaviest footstep on it would be inaudible.

The strangest thing in this beautiful apartment was the total absence of windows, the only light being given by a lamp which swung from the centre of the ceiling.

The door was also a singular contrivance, being formed by a sliding panel behind one of the heavy curtains, so that a person might enter without being seen by the occupant of the room.

Lord Redfern placed the still insensible Alice on one of the sofas, and then drew back to admire her beauty.

"She's a rare creature," said the beldam.

"She is, indeed," said Redfern.

"One of your obstinate sort, I suppose?"

Redfern nodded.

"Ah!" croaked the whole hag; "I like them best; they're always the worst when once they do give in."

"She is reviving," said Redfern; "give her the drink."

Hastily running to a side table, Tabitha poured out a small glass of wine, into which she poured a small quantity of red fluid from a little vial she took from her pocket.

She had scarcely done so than Alice heaved a deep sigh and half opened her eyes.

Lord Redfern drew back whilst Tabitha running up to her placed the glass to her lips.

With the natural thirst caused by the excitement and faintness, Alice drank it off, and the next moment fell into a profound slumber.

"She's off now," crowed the hag, with a diabolical leer. "What's to be done now?"

"Have you got the clothes ready?"

"They're all prepared."

"Then see that she be dressed in them before she awakes, so that my country maiden may find herself decked out like a Court lady when she awakes."

"Anything more?"

"Yes; let a handsome repast be placed ready for her. And be careful that she catches no glimpse of you at present."

Giving a meaning nod to the beldam, Lord Redfern left the room.

Hurrying to an ottoman, Tabitha threw up the top and discovered therein a most magnificent suit of ladies' apparel. These she drew forth and arranged by the side of the couch whereon Alice still slept, unconscious of all that was passing around her.

With nimble fingers and a marvellous dexterity, which showed that it was not the first time she had performed the office, Tabitha removed Alice's neat but somewhat coarse clothes, and replaced them by those she had taken from the ottoman. She then placed those which she had removed from Alice in the ottoman, which she closed and carefully locked.

She then took from a beautiful casket a magnificent set of diamonds and pearls, with which she decked Alice's fair person.

It was a wondrous sight to see the change made by the difference of dress.

The simple country girl, so blooming and retiring, had become, by the combined art of the milliner and jeweller, as handsome and dignified as a queen.

Tabitha disappeared for a moment, but quickly returned with a cold repast, which she placed upon a table close by the sleeping girl, together with some fine wines in costly decanters.

Having done this, she sat down watching intently for the moment when the girl would awake.

"Ah!" she mumbled, "young and beautiful, young and beautiful. So was I once; aye, and loved too. It was gay then to be sought after—to see the gallants following, and to treat them with disdain. But they had their turn as I grew older. They treated me with disdain; I was neglected for younger favourites. They would have thrown me on one side had I been foolish; but I said they were right to pass me by, and helped them so old Tabitha Ossleton still has fine clothes and jewels, and the gallants all do her behests. Ha! ha! ha!"

The croaking laugh seemed to have a tremendous effect upon Alice, for her pale eyelids quivered, and she heaved a deep sigh.

Perceiving that the moment of her awaking was fast approaching — for the drug which had been administered was quick in its effect but brief in the duration of its power—Tabitha arose hastily and left the room, to give due notice to Lord Redfern, who in the meantime had taken the precaution to change his quiet apparel for the most magnificent one he possessed.

No sooner did he receive the intelligence than he placed himself behind one of the curtains in such a position that he could behold Alice without being seen.

At first she merely sighed heavily; her sweet cherry lip trembling like that of a pretty child who had wept itself to sleep. Her throat and bosom heaved, making the diamond necklet and brooch sparkle in the light.

Slowly her trembling eyelids opened; and throwing one of her beautifully-rounded arms over her head, she turned uneasily on her couch, like one awaking from an unpleasant dream.

For some moments she gazed in wonder at the beauty of the apartments, and fancied that she was still in Batswing's cave, or else that she was dreaming.

Slowly she arose, and for the first time beheld the change that had been made in her dress.

She started back from the glass, at first imagining that she was in the presence of some great lady, but seeing the reflection do the same, she glanced at her garments and at once perceived the change.

Then all that had occurred rushed upon her brain with terrific force.

She knew that she had been carried away; and had but little doubt that it was by the same person who had torn her from her father's home.

At first she sunk upon the sofa, and covering her face with her hands wept bitterly. But she was no coward; and springing to her feet she tore the jewels from her neck and dashed them to the ground and trampled upon them. Then, overcome with emotion, she sunk back upon the couch.

"Do not these jewels suit you, fair lady?" said Lord Redfern, stepping quietly from his hiding-place.

With a start Alice looked up, dreading she knew not what.

Her cheeks became deadly white, and the colour forsook her lips. Was she dreaming or awake? She shrunk back in horror, for, despite his gold-braided clothes, she recognised in Lord Redfern the murderer of her father.

"If they are not costly enough," continued Redfern, "we will have others made to please you taste. A taste as delicate as your form. But where can I find jewels worthy of you? The finest diamonds could not equal the sparkling of your eyes, your hair outrivals the gold of India, pearls are your teeth, and rubies pale before your lips, whilst tinted velvet were coarse to your damask cheeks."

"Away!" cried Alice, springing from the couch, and facing Lord Redfern as he approached her. "Away, I say, base, cowardly murderer!"

Lord Redfern recoiled before the angry looks of the maiden. Her eyes flashed fire, and her bosom heaved in such a manner that he could not possibly realize the fact that in this imperious woman he beheld the same quiet, simple, country girl whom he had torn from her father's arms.

"Murderer!" he stammered, "I know not what you mean."

"Add not to your crime by lying," cried Alice. "Think you that I am so blind that I cannot recognise the wolf in the sheep's clothing? I know you too well. Would that I had not listened to your lying tongue; then had my poor father have been still alive to protect me."

"You mistake, lady," replied Lord Redfern, "I never saw your father. If I have done wrong it is for love of you. Your fame has reached the Court, and amongst our many toasts there is not one that is received with such enthusiasm as that of the beauteous Maid of Epping."

"My fame reach the Court?" said Alice, incredulously.

"It is indeed true, lady," cried Lord Redfern. "Fain would I have you for my own fair bride; but there is one who loves you dearly, and one whom I must not thwart. You must be his; but may not such love as mine receive some reward?"

"Begone!" cried Alice; "your speech is as foul as your heart."

Lord Redfern gnawed his lip with rage, and dared not trust himself to speak, so great was his passion.

At length, with great difficulty, he overcame his temper, and seating himself at a good distance from Alice, commenced in a calm voice,

"Madam, I do perceive that to argue with you in the present state of your mind would be almost useless. I will therefore content myself with a few simple statements over which I think you would do well to ponder, giving them due consideration. May I speak?"

"Can I stay you?"

Lord Redfern merely shrugged his shoulders, and then proceeded to speak.

"In the first place, madam, you have been kind enough to fix the blame of your father's death on to my shoulders, for what reason I cannot say. Not that I blame you for so doing, as I feel certain that had you not some good reason, one so pure would never venture such a statement."

"In mercy spare me these avowals," cried Alice.

"Let me protest my innocence," said Redfern, with an injured air. "I had seen you, and to see you was to love, but one greater, richer, and more powerful than I loves you also. I dare not press my claim before him. Still, as a true lover, I can save my mistress. I heard that it was reported that you loved this monster Batswing, the highwayman; and that in order to fly with him, you had been accessory to your father's murder."

Alice met this charge with a look of defiance which clearly proved her innocence, but, unabashed, Lord Redfern continued,

"Of course I could not, and would not, believe that such was the case; but love, which is always jealous, forced me to make inquiries, and I discovered that Jonathan Wild had a warrant for your arrest upon this charge."

"Impossible!" exclaimed Alice.

"Pardon me; it was not only possible, but true. For some reason, that most redoubtable rascal Jonathan Wild had such a string of evidence against you, that not only would you have been tried for the murder, but I greatly fear would have been condemned."

Alice shuddered, but made no reply.

"Like a true lover," continued Lord Redfern, "no sooner did I hear this than I determined to save you. Jonathan Wild thought you would attend your father's funeral, and determined to arrest you there. By whom he was foiled, you know."

"Think you, had I committed the deed you mention, that I should have dared be present at that awful ceremony."

"I do not," replied Lord Redfern; "but all who know Jonathan Wild know that if he have a reason for wishing to prove an innocent person guilty, he will do it, in spite of judge, council, or jury. I must confess your being by that notorious highwayman must have strengthened the prejudice the whole country now feels against you."

Alice made no reply, but calmly and quietly kept her eyes fixed upon Lord Redfern, who, consummate villain as he was, felt uncomfortable under that steady glance.

"You cannot deceive me," said Alice, in a clear, calm voice; "that is impossible. You may have cheated the poor country people into the belief that I aided in this foul action, for it would ruin you had I been free to tell the truth. I bid you now leave me, or I will summon the people of the house and denounce you as a murderer."

"By heavens, this is too much!" cried Redfern, who could no longer control his passion. "Hark ye, mistress, I would have you to know that you are in my power, and past experience might teach you that I am not a man to be crossed in my wishes. Scream, if you like; these walls are of such a thickness that no one could hear your cries; or, should a faint echo reach my servants, they would but laugh at you as a fool. What I have done is for our good. I no longer wish to deceive you. By carrying you off I have made a large sum of money; in other words, I have taken the liberty of treating you like they do slaves in Turkey, and have sold you. But before I present you to your future master I must curb that violent temper a little; we must be friends, for through you I mean to touch his pockets. Come, now, let us join hands; forget that little affair about your father, and you shall be rich and happy. Who knows? one day you may become a titled lady in reality. Lord Harry can be persuaded to anything, and—"

"Stand back," cried Alice, seizing a knife from the table and presenting it at Redfern's breast, who was advancing to her; "back! or by heavens I will kill you."

"So, so," sneered Redfern, as he stepped backwards, "you will not be friends? As you like; but I will tame you yet. If gentle means fail, there are others. You are not the first young girl I've tamed, and when I have brought you down, you shall kneel at my feet and sue for mercy."

"Kneel at your feet!" cried Alice, indignantly. "I would die first."

"Die! Now, mark; if, in a week from to-day, I do not find you ready to do my bidding, I shall hand you over to Jonathan Wild, who, I have no doubt, will take care you do not escape again. I did kill your father to gain you. I have won; and, therefore, will not draw back at the last moment. Think of what I have said, and be wise."

As he spoke Lord Redfern stepped behind the curtain.

For a moment Alice stood stupefied by the man's audacity, and then rushing to the curtain behind which he had disappeared, she tore it on one side in hopes of discovering a door.

No door was to be seen, but Lord Redfern had disappeared.

CHAPTER XXV.
THE DUEL.

It was a cold, bleak morning; the early grey dawn crept slowly up the eastern sky, bringing with it thin, drizzling mists, which clung to the trees and grass.

No birds whistled welcome to the dawn; indeed all seemed leaden and dull.

A heavy mist rose in ghostly clouds and rolled up the hills or hung round the ponds and rivers until a sharp gust of wind would blow it about, making it assume all kinds of ghost-like shapes.

On such a dreary morning as this two gentlemen galloped up to the fields which surrounded Chalk Farm, and, leaping their horses over the hedge, rode to a clump of trees, where they dismounted.

The first thing they did was to tie their horses to one of the trees, then wrapping their cloaks tightly round them they climbed a small eminence from which they could scan the surrounding country.

"I don't see them coming, Arthur," said one of the gentlemen; "I trust they are not going to disappoint us."

"Never fear, O'Neil," said Sir Arthur Bowring,

laughing; "Lord Henry Leslie is not the man to draw back at the last moment."

"Faith, then! an' he'd be no gentleman if he did," cried Captain O'Neil, in a strong Irish brogue. "Its a moighty cold mornin' to be afther paradin' over these fields, which are as damp as an ould Irish bog. Its a pretty little piece of sword play that would warm us up now. Supposing we have a few passes to kape the blood warm?"

"Nay, Captain," replied Sir Arthur, laughing; "I fear your blood is too warm already; and those same passes might end in a pass through my body, that might chill my blood for ever; and then you would disappoint Lord Leslie."

"Well's that's thrue, anyhow; but thin I should be here to take your place if he would not recave my apology. An' sure a betther apology could not be made than that you had already been killed like a gentleman, and could not be killed again by anybody."

"But his Lordship might argue the right of priority," laughed Sir Arthur.

"Bedad, but the laws of honour can't compel a man to be killed afther he's dead. Sure, its enough to be killed once in your lifetime for anyone, or anything."

"Of that I have not the slightest doubt," replied Sir Arthur; "but here come our men to interrupt our conversation, and call us to business."

As he spoke he pointed in the direction of the London road, down which two gentlemen were seen hastily galloping.

These cavaliers leaped their horses over the hedge in much the same manner as the former ones had done, and rode to the tree, tied their horses up, and then advanced towards Sir Arthur and his companions, raising their hats, a salutation which the others returned with the greatest politeness.

"A cold morning, gentlemen," said Captain O'Neil, politely; "an' bedad its not talking that suits it. The tongue's a good weapon by the fireside, but it won't do in the cold at all, at all."

"You are right, Captain," yawned Lord Henry Leslie. "Its an awful nuisance to have to get up so early, is it not?"

"What! an awful nuisance to get up for such pretty sport as this? Faith, and where is the pheasant shooting like it? It's the most exciting and amusing sport that's ever been invented for gentlemen, since Eve was given to Adam for the sake of introducing flirtation and intrigue."

"Yes," drawled Lord Henry; "I dare say you are right; only I should prefer it after dinner; that is all I mean."

"Gentlemen," said Lord Henry's second, stepping up to the group; "is there not some way to prevent this affair going any further? I am sure from what I know of both parties engaged that the matter might be arranged. In Heaven's name, Captain O'Neil, do help me in trying to stop this affair."

"By me faith not I," said O'Neil; "why should I prevent the boys having a little piece of sport?"

"Sport!" cried the other gentleman; "it may be sport to you, but it may be death to them, as the old fable says."

"Thin, sir, as your so moighty anxious to be paceable, will your man apologise?" demanded Captain O'Neil, fiercely.

"Decidedly not," drawled Lord Leslie. "For Heaven's sake, Fitzboodle, don't delay any longer; I shall get an asthma if I stay here much longer."

"Sir Arthur Bowring, let me appeal to you," cried Lord Fitzboodle; "as far as I can see this quarrel is a ridiculous one. Indeed, I may say that it was caused by another person, who ought to have been here now. Come, Sir Arthur, do be reasonable."

"Had I not intended what I said, my Lord," replied Sir Arthur, "I am willing to forego this meeting if Lord Henry Leslie will promise to repudiate the disgraceful wager he made with Lord Redfern, and also pledge his word as a gentleman to do all in his power to protect the lady who has been persecuted through his folly."

"I am not in the habit of being dictated to," replied Lord Henry Leslie, in a haughty tone.

"Sure, and your right in that anyway," said O'Neil.

"Then you refuse?"

"I do."

"Then the fighting is to go on afther all?" said O'Neil.

"Of course."

"Sure, you're a lad afther my own heart," cried the Irishman.

"As you will, gentlemen," sighed Lord Fitzboodle, who, for once in his life, was perfectly sober; "I would willingly have prevented this, for I cannot help feeling that we are all to blame."

"Enough of this," cried Sir Arthur; "if we do not make haste we shall be interrupted."

The seconds then stepped up to their principals and commenced preparing them for the encounter.

The long cloaks were removed, and each gentleman stood dressed in the richest costume.

The hats were thrown on the cloaks, then their coats were removed, leaving the opponents standing in shoes, silk stockings, and cambric shirts.

They next removed the lace fall or cravat and undid the shirts at the colar, so that there should be no tightness about the throat.

After this they rolled back the shirt sleeves far above the elbow, and then proceeded to place their men.

"Why, here is a splendid spot, as if made for the purpose," cried O'Neil; "sure, and we can't do betther than take this."

"Yes, that will do, it is even enough," replied Lord Fitzboodle.

"Place your man, then," said O'Neil, quickly turning Sir Arthur round to face his opponent.

"But, O'Neil," said Sir Arthur, "this is not right."

"Whisht now, be aisy," said O'Neil, in an undertone. "We've got the best of them anyhow."

"But it is not fair," persisted Sir Arthur.

"Hould your whisht, do," growled O'Neil.

But Sir Arthur would not be brooked in his determination, and, turning round to Lord Fitzboodle, he said,

"My Lord, you will excuse my interfering in your arrangements, but do you not perceive that unwittingly you have given me a considerable advantage over Lord Leslie? I have my back towards where the sun will rise, he will have its rays full in his eyes."

"Thank you, Sir Arthur," said Lord Fitzboodle, "it really escaped me. I will take another position."

"What a bother," said Lord Henry Leslie, petulantly. "I hate walking."

"Oh! the Homadod," growled O'Neil, under his breath. "If Sir Arthur don't make you dance quicker than you walk, by the powers I will. And Sir Arthur, too, when I had done as pretty a piece of finesse as ever was done by a gentleman, to give it up in that way."

The combatants were now ready, and, after the usual salutations, each fell into position, and the thin glistening rapiers crossed with a cold death-like clink. At that moment the pale watery sun broke through the clouds and cast a weird light upon the scene, making the swords glitter as the combatants slightly moved each wrist.

Firmly balanced on the left leg, the right one thrown forward, the body inclined backwards, the right hand level with the breast, holding the rapier's point pointed

THE OLD FLEET DITCH,

at the antagonist s eye, whilst the left arm was held in a graceful curve behind the head, each faced the other.

For a few moments—they seemed almost an hour—the two men remained perfectly motionless.

Their eyes were fixed firmly on each other with an eager watchfulness that was painful to behold.

Suddenly Lord Henry, by a movement of his wrist dropped the point of his rapier beneath that of his antagonist, but, quick as lightning Sir Arthur had guarded it, and then followed several rapid passes, each of which was successfully parried, until the two men fell back into the same position as that which they had first taken.

Both were evidently good swordsmen, and of equal strength. The seconds drew together and watched with eagerness the struggle, now and then exchanging a few words under their breath.

For some time the duel proceeded as coolly as if the performers had merely been trying their skill in a fencing school with buttoned foils. But after a time both men became more eager, and, consequently, less cautious.

Quicker and quicker were the passes, and more vehement and rapid the parries. The two men breathed heavily, and the muscles in their throats and wrists were swollen like cords.

Suddenly Lord Henry made a violent lunge, which Sir Arthur parried by a slight tap of the forte of his blade; then having forced his adversary's sword out of the guard, he lunged at his breast.

There was a sudden check as if the foil would not pierce the flesh, then a quick trembling of the blade, and the sword passed through Lord Henry's body.

Throwing up his arms, the wounded man tottered back, and fell heavily to the ground.

"Bedad, and he's got it," cried the Irishman, "but it's a consolation to think that it was a beautiful thrust."

No. 7.

"Take care," cried Sir Arthur, "we must stop this bleeding. Gentlemen, lend me your cravats and pocket handkerchiefs,"

In a moment they had formed a bandage, which they strapped round Lord Henry's breast.

"Bedad! and he always was fond of sleep," said the Irishman, "and I think its a long nap he'll be after taking now. You've given him his quietus at all events."

"For heaven sake be quiet, O'Neil," cried Sir Arthur. "Mount your horse, and get a coach so as we can carry the poor fellow to a surgeon."

The good-natured Irishman had no sooner found that he could be of use than he mounted his horse and was off in a moment.

Presently Lord Leslie drew a long breath and opened his eyes.

"I think," he gasped, "I think, Sir Arthur, you have cured me, I shall not do any more mischief."

"Oh nonsense, the wound is not deep."

"It is deep enough."

"You must not give way."

"Why? My life has been a useless one."

"But by living you may do good."

"I fear it is not in me."

"We none of us know what we can do till we try."

"I—" A sudden gurgling in the throat seized him, and passing his handkerchief over his mouth he removed it saturated with blood.

"I—I—," he commenced, struggling against the internal hemorrhage.

"I—must—speak."

"Indeed you must not, my lord," said Sir Arthur kindly, "in a day or two you will be better, and then can speak, but to do so now is dangerous."

"But—it will—be too late," gasped the man.

"Now don't worry at such a time," cried Lord Fitzboodle.

"Alice—," cried the wounded nobleman, seizing Sir Arthur's hand, " Alice—save—Redfern—villian—oh God!"

With a deep groan he fell back in a swoon.

"What is to be done now?" asked Lord Fitzboodle.

Sir Arthur made no answer, for his mind was too much fixed upon the terrible meaning which Lord Henry's words had conveyed to him.

Could it be possible that Lord Redfern had indeed succeeded in carrying off Alice Landon from Batswing? Were all the taunts thrown out by Redfern, the slanderous hints, true?

His brain reeled as he thought of the terrible possibility of the thing, and he cursed his hot temper, which had made him lose all chance of saving her.

"Look, Sir Arthur," cried Lord Fitzboodle, "he is dying."

Sir Arthur gazed at the wounded man, and tried to gather his scattered senses.

If she had been carried off, he argued, Batswing, or one of his people would be sure to have let me know, she must be safe.

"Sir Arthur," cried the young nobleman, "I cannot hear him breathe."

Sir Arthur leant over Lord Leslie and listened attentively.

"Do not be alarmed," he said quietly, "he still lives."

"Will he recover?"

"That I cannot say, I am no surgeon. I hope he may."

"Look here, Sir Arthur," said the young Lord, "I have been very bad, I know, but this has changed me. I'll never drink or be wicked any more."

"When the Devil was sick, the Devil a saint would be;

"When the Devil got well, the Devil a saint was he,"

laughed O'Neil, who had approached them unobserved. "Sure an' this little affair is nothing when you are used to it. Thank heaven it's no worse as the man said when the Devil ran away with him. Why, it might have been your own purty body lying stretched out on the grass. An' that would have been serious to you if not to your family."

"Hush, hush, O'Neil," said Sir Arthur. "Never try to kill good intentions."

"Sure and that's true enough; it's just waste of time, for they always die out of themselves. They're like early buds, always bursting out in unpropitious seasons, and getting nipped off before they have grown to respectable size."

"While we are talking here Lord Leslie may bleed to death," cried Sir Arthur.

"By the Holy Poker, that's true anyhow. So let us carry him to the coach."

With the greatest care they wrapped the wounded man up in a cloak and bore him across the fields to a lane where a coach was waiting. Lord Fitzboodle entered the carriage, and Sir Arthur and O'Neil mounted their horses and galloped back to London.

CHAPTER XXVI.

THE STRUGGLE ON THE HOUSE-TOP. BATSWING GAINS A NEW FRIEND.

When Batswing found himself on the top of the house he paused for a moment to listen if his pursuers were following him.

Yes: there could be no doubt of it. The noise of voices grew louder and louder as the men forced their way upstairs.

At first Batswing made his way to the front of the house, and stooping below the parapet, peeped over into the streets, but quickly retired, for the place was full of people.

"Damnation" he muttered as he crept slowly back to the rear of the building, "what pleasure can these men feel in hunting a poor devil to death? I never hurt such as these, but rather help them. I rob only the rich, whilst to the poor I am as liberal as a lord."

Slowly Batswing crept along the gutters.

It was a most difficult operation, for the tiles on the roof were loose and in many places the parapet was completely broken away: so that by one false slip he might be precipitated into the streets.

Batswing had just passed one of these dangerous holes, when he was checked in his progress by what at first seemed an insurmountable obstacle.

It was a row of spikes which protruded from a stack of chimneys down to the parapet and some two feet over it. These spikes were made in a fan shape, the interstices between the bars being boarded up.

How was the obstacle to be passed?

Batswing paused for a few moments to consider his position.

The noise in the houses and streets seemed growing louder and louder, there seemed no chance of escape save by overcoming the barrier.

He seized the bars in his hand and shook them violently, but, although they were old and rusty, they resisted all his efforts.

"I may as well be killed by falling off the roof of the house as off Tyburn Tree," he muttered, "at all events I will try it."

Seizing the top spikes firmly, he placed his foot on the bottom one.

He then poised himself for a moment in the air, resting entirely on the foot that was placed upon the sipke, then with a sudden spring he threw himself round.

The plan succeeded, and the next minute he was landed safely in the adjoining parapet.

With a feeling of exultation Batswing was about to creep along the parapet, when he was suddenly seized by the throat by a man who sprung out from the shadow of a stack of chimneys.

"If you attempt to move, or utter a sound, you are a dead man."

The speaker was a young fellow of about twenty-three, short, slim, and active.

His complexion was of a deep olive: his features well cut and regular: his eyes large and black as a gipsy's. His hair was clipped excessively short, showing the compactness of his head whose greatest fault was its great roundness.

The whole face spoke wonderful energy: whilst the somewhat too heavy and sensual lower jaw, showed that the man had allowed his passions to obtain a complete mastery over him.

"Silence I say," continued the man, thrusting a pistol close to Batswing's head, "submit at once and quietly, or I fire."

With a quick movement of the body our hero twisted round, at the same time dashing the pistol from the man's hand.

This movement caused his antagonist's arm to come over Batswing's shoulder.

Seizing his hand tightly in his grasp, our hero endeavoured to throw his assailant: but the other clung to him like a cat, until at last both were worn out and fell heavily on the sloping roof still clutching one another.

For a moment they remained locked in each others embrace, as if dead. But they quickly recovered their breath and recommenced the struggle.

They each endeavoured their hardest to get above the other, and at last Batswing succeeded in this manœuvre, he being much more powerful than his assailant.

But his victory was of short duration, for his supple antagonist, by a quick movement escaped from under him. Still Batswing retained his grasp, and the two rolled slowly down the sloping roof until they struck violenty against the parapet.

It was a moment of intense agony to both men, for they could hear the rotten old parapet crack, and then large flakes of the plaster falling heavily down in the stone-paved yard far below.

Piece after piece of the decayed wall crumbled down and fell with a dull heavy thud that made the men shudder.

Both remained still as death, neither daring to struggle, for they felt that the slightest movement might hurl them from the parapet into the yard beneath.

With straining eyes they glared at each other, but neither moved, all was still, save the heavy beating of their hearts.

"Look here," said the man to Batswing, "do you want to die?"

"Why do you ask?" demanded Batswing.

"Because I think there is every chance that you will," replied the other coolly, "and that before long too."

"If I do, you shall go with me," replied Batswing sternly.

"There seems to be but little doubt of that," replied the other.

"Don't you think you had better give in?" demanded Batswing.

"What would be the good of that?" replied the other, "I should only escape being smashed to be hanged; and I think of the two I prefer dying in company than alone. I always was sociable."

"What?" cried Batswing, "you will be hanged if you're taken?"

"I don't think there would be the slightest chance of escape," returned the other; "I don't believe a bit in the tender feelings of an enlightened British jury: and therefore must decline to grant them an interview. So come along."

As he spoke the man again grappled Batswing.

"Stay!" cried Batswing, "surely there is some mistake here. If you fear the 'Robins,' you are evidently trying to escape."

"Of course I am," said the other.

"Your name?" asked Batswing.

"Stow that rot," replied the other, "you know it well enough."

"I dare say I might," replied Batswing, "if I heard it. But I don't know you."

"What?"

"I tell you I don't know you," replied Batswing, "all I can say is I was escaping from the Robins the same as you appeared to be."

"Is that true?"

"On my honor."

"Then what is your name?"

"Batswing!"

"What! Batswing the highwayman?"

"The same."

"I can't ask you to embrace me, for you are doing that already in a most uncomfortable manner," laughed the young fellow.

"But who the devil are you?" enquired Batswing, in surprise.

"Jack Sheppard."

"Jack Sheppard the noted Cracksman?"

"No more and no less."

"Then let us be friends."

"To all eternity."

"Then let us get out of this, or we shall roll over. This cursed old parapet is cracking to pieces."

They soon scrambled to their feet, and stood for a moment looking at one another.

"Well, now we're up, who are you;" demanded the stranger.

"We have no time for explanations." said Batswing, "if I mistake not, I can hear the tramp of men coming over the roofs towards this place."

"But where are we to go?"

"That I don't know; but if we stop here we shall be taken. There is no chance of our escaping unless we try."

"That's true enough, so let us commence."

Stooping down, they crept along the gutter until they came to a window.

"Its no good waiting out here," said Batswing, "we must get in here and hide if we can. At all events, we can't be worse off than we are now."

"That's true," replied the other, "so lead on and I'll follow you."

Pushing open the window, Batswing and his companion sprang into the room, but they had no sooner done so, than their arrival was greeted by some dolorous screams which proceeded from a small tent bedstead, placed in one corner of the room.

Turning round they beheld two women sitting up in bed screaming.

"Silence!" said the younger man, "this is no time for hesitating; silence, or I will kill you."

"Wait a moment," said Batswing, "we'll see what persuasion will do first."

Advancing to the bed, he bowed politely to the ladies and commenced, "Ladies, you see before you two unfortunate fellows, who having had some slight disagreement with the law, are now hunted down by the constables with an energy really worthy of a better cause."

"Oh, go away," was the only answer the ladies, who were, to say the least, far from plain, made them.

"So we would, if we could," replied Batswing. "Nothing would give us greater delight, but we can't."

"What can we do for you?" demanded one of the girls' having partially got over her fright.

"Protect us from our pursuers."

"But how?"

"I am afraid I must trouble you for the loan of your night-caps."

"Mercy on us what do you mean?"

"No harm I can assure you. But there is no time to be lost I really must trouble you to rise."

"Look the other way then," said the girls.

Batswing and his companion did as they were desired, and in a few minutes the two girls told them they might look round.

They did so and found that the girls had slipped on their dresses.

"Now ladies," said Batswing in a whisper, for he heard noises in the house that aroused his suspicions; "I must trouble you to hide behind your tent-bed—the curtains will cover you. I am very sorry, but necessity compels me to take this very unpleasant mode of proceeding."

The two girls who had now overcome their fright, and seemed rather to enjoy the fun of the thing, hid behind the bed-curtains which completely concealed them, at the same time promising not to betray the men.

"Now then," said Batswing, "slip on the night-caps and jump into bed. Mind you are very modest and hide your faces."

They quickly donned the frilled night-caps and jumped into bed, but were only just in time; for they had scarcely covered their faces when they heard sounds of dispute on the stairs leading to the room they were in.

"My good woman will you stand on one side," said a stern voice. "I tell yer I 've the king's warrant to search arter this feller, and I will do it; come what may."

"Oh, you brute," screamed a shrill female voice. "Coming and breaking into peoples' houses in this sort of manner. I tell you that there's only my two daughters, Jane and Mary, in that room."

"Well we don't want to hurt your daughters, do we?" growled the man.

"I don't know what such a brute as you might do," screamed the woman.

"Look here, mother," replied the man, "hard words breaks no bones, but fists do. I'm going into that there room."

"Let me tell the girls to dress first then," cried the woman.

"They can keep all right in bed," replied the man.

"Thank goodness for that!" exclaimed Batswing, "had they made us get up we should have been lost."

He had scarcely finished, when they heard a short struggle proceeding on the landing, evidently between the old woman and the constable.

Setting up a piercing scream, Batswing dragged his companion underneath the bed clothes, and then commenced crying out in a falsetto voice, "Oh! the man, the man."

In a minute the constables rushed into the room, followed by the old woman, who, hurrying up to the bed, held down the clothes in such a manner as to completely conceal and nearly suffocate her supposed daughters.

"Oh, the man, the man, the man," continued Batswing.

"What man," cried the constable.

"The man that was getting into the window," cried Batswing, holding down the bed clothes.

"Where is he?" replied the constable.

"Gone, good sir, gone!" cried Batswing, "he came in at the window and stood listening, and when he heard your voices he sprang out again, and we heard him running along the parapet, and then we heard such a terrible crash I could not tell what was the matter, and so I shrieked—Oh! the man, the man, the man."

"By jingo, he must have fallen over," said one.

"Let us go and see; here Bill, just get outside and look," said the chief constable, and very stout, so consequently not anxious to trust himself on so slippery a path.

But Bill, although thin, did not seem more inclined than his superior officer to face the dangers of the parapet.

"He's not fallen off," growled Bill, "them fellows creep over the roof of houses like cats, and wait behind the chimberlies to pounce upon you like a hundred of coals."

"Somethings gone over," said another constable, looking out of the window, "for I can see some of the parapet broken away."

In a moment everybody's head was thrust out of the window and gazing in the direction indicated by the last speaker.

There could be no doubt as to the fact of the parapet being destroyed, and naturally everyone jumped to the conclusion that the fugitive had tumbled over.

"Let's see, it's the second house from this on the left hand," said the constable. "He must have broken both his legs at the very least, so we have him all safe at any rate this time. Follow me my lads, the reward's ours at all events.

Dashing down stairs pell mell, helter skelter, the constables rushed away, all anxious to seize their supposed victim."

When Batswing heard them nearly at the bottom of the house, he commenced struggling to release himself from the bed clothes, which the old lady still held pertinaciously tight down over her supposed daughters.

"Don't be alarmed my dears," cried the old woman, the monsters have gone now, they shan't hurt you, that they shan't. I'll protect you from them; don't you fear, the horrid rude creatures. Hugh!"

"I don't fear them," said Batswing, "what I fear is being choked."

With a scream of horror the old woman retired from the bed, from which Batswing and his companion sprang, panting for want of breath.

"Who—who—are you," gasped the old woman.

"Fugitives from the law," replied Batswing.

"Where are my daughters," cried the old woman.

"Behind the bed, and perfectly safe, I can assure you?"

The young ladies at an invitation from Batswing came blushingly forward, and in a few words related to the old woman the whole truth of the circumstance.

"And so huzzies!" cried the old woman, "you have dared to conceal highwaymen and housebreakers, have you?"

"Pardon me" replied Batswing, "it was you who concealed us."

"Yes, thinking you were my daughters."

"Now do I look like your daughter?" demanded Batswing.

The old woman could not repress a smile at this: and Jack Sheppard, seeing that the old woman was not bad tempered, struck in to help his companion.

"I wish we were like your daughters, for then we should be as pure as they are beautiful,"

"Oh its no use trying to flatter me," said the old woman, taking the compliment in some mysterious way to herself. "I know you gentlemen of the road are sad fellows."

"Aye; but rich ones," said Jack slipping a few guineas into the old woman's hands.

"Lord thank you gentlemen," said the old lady, "I don't *ask* for any reward; though some people *offer* it."

"Not only must you be rewarded but also these fair ladies," said Batswing, drawing off a couple of rings and placing them on the fingers of the two smiling girls."

"This is but a slight return he continued for your great services, but if you will let me know your names I will at some future time do you better justice."

"Mine is Maria Jackson," said the elder.

"And mine Louisa Jackson," said the other.

"Both pretty names," said Jack gallantly.

"And your good mother shall receive a good reward, if you assist us to get free from this house."

"That will be difficult," said the old woman.

"It must be done," said Jack.

"The constables and people throng the streets."

"Can you not lend us a disguise?"

"Well I have some coats and cloaks belonging to my late husband."

"We must venture it," said Jack.

"Undoubtedly," replied Batswing: "we may get through the crowd, and at all events we shall have a run for it."

"Then wait here gentlemen and I will fetch the garments."

With trembling steps the old woman left the room and proceeded slowly downstairs.

No sooner were they alone than Louisa seized Batswing by the arm, and in trembling accents exclaimed,

"You are betrayed."

"What?"

"You are betrayed."

"By whom?

"That old woman."

"Your mother?"

"She is not our mother."

"She has now gone to betray you."

"By heavens, I'll have revenge," cried Jack.

"Stay" said Maria "there is still a way to escape."

"How."

"Follow me."

"Can we trust you"

"If you doubt, stay here and you will be betrayed."

"That decides us," cried Batswing, "Come along Jack, look well to your barkers, and if we are taken dont let it be without a struggle."

Silently they followed the girl down stairs until they came to the second floor.

Opening a door which led into a long room at the back of the house, Maria whispered to them to be careful not to make a noise.

It was a long, low, miserable looking room, across which benches were placed as if it were a school.

Carefully avoiding these forms Maria led them to a window which opened on to the roofs of some outhouses.

"If you creep over these roofs," she said, in an under tone, "you will come at last to a lane, just broad enough for one to walk through. This will lead you to Lincoln's Inn Fields. Now farewell, more I cannot do to help you."

"Thanks Maria, "said Batswing," but cannot I do anything to help you."

"You might: but alas I know not how to communicate with you."

"Cannot you write?"

"Yes but the old woman you saw, will not let us leave the house."

"Well if you can write we may still manage it."

"How!"

"This day week put a letter out side your window telling me how I can serve you, trust me I shall get it safely, and that I will do all in my power to help you."

"Hush! Fly quickly I hear the constables coming."

Quickly closing the window Maria hurried away.

Jack Sheppard and Batswing paused for one moment and listened so as to be certain whether they were betrayed—there could be no doubt of it.

The noise of men rushing up the stairs could be plainly heard.

"There's no doubt of the old hag's treachery; come Jack let us be off."

They crawled along the roofs of the houses and at last dropped over in the lane. down which they hurried and soon arrived at Lincoln's Inn Fields.

"Where are you going!" asked Batswing.

"To the old house in the Fleet;" replied Jack. "Do you know it?"

"No, can I come with you?"

"Yes! and as day is dawning we had better not lose time, our present muddy state would call attention to us, and although we both may like politeness we can dispense with too much attention at the present time."

With a hearty laugh Batswing took his companion's arm and they both hurried away towards the old house in the Fleet, taking great care to avoid the large throughfares; although at that period there were but few people to be found in the streets of London so early in the morning, whilst the watchmen were generally fast asleep in their boxes; doubtlessly arresting thieves by the score in their dreams; but unfortunately for the honest inhabitants of the city, it was only in their dreams that they ever did so; for these elderly guardians of the peace kept it by running away from any disturbance they might hear.

CHAPTER XXVII.

A NIGHT AT THE OLD HOUSE BY THE FLEET DITCH. FARMER CROFT. BATSWING MAKES A DISCOVERY.

THE Fleet Ditch, at the time in which our story happened, flowed along where Farringdon-street now stands, across the foot of Fleet-street, from thence growing broader until it poured its black turgid waters into the Thames, sullying the waters of that river, which was then reckoned one of the cleanest and brightest in the world.

Of late years the neighbourhood extending from Farringdon-street back to Smithfield has been greatly improved; yet it is anything but a good one, many of the streets bearing a very indifferent, not to say bad character. For all that, no one traversing even the worst lanes and courts in this locality could imagine the fearful state of vice and filth that reigned there. Although not boasting the same privileges as the Mint did a little before this period, or that Alsatia (Whitefriars) had possessed for so many centuries, this neighbourhood had long been a rendezvous of most of the worst characters in London. It is true that, unlike the places we have just mentioned, the boarders of the Fleet were not defended against the attacks of the constables and turned into a city of refuge; but the inhabitants had so managed the construction of the houses that they committed the most horrible crimes without the slightest fear of detection. Trap-doors, secret passages, concealed prisons, underground vaults, and subterranean passages leading out to Fleet Ditch, were common enough; and many were the terrible crimes and narrow escapes managed by these means.

Day after day dead bodies were found floating out by the Nore, beating about in the tide as it ebbed and flowed. "Whence come the ghastly sights?" was the question which the trembling boatmen asked of each other; but no one could answer. The bodies were not dressed like sailors; most of them having the appearance of men who had been rather above than below the middle class. Had they come from the sea or the river? No one could answer for certain; they did not look like seafaring men, still they were found just where the tide from the sea met the tide from the river, and who could tell which had brought those terrible, mute witnesses of crime where they were found.

Some of the bodies were recognised as belonging to London. Friends had seen and known these men well and hearty only a few days before their swollen remains were discovered lapped by the hungry waters. Of course the Bow-street Runners were set to work to trace out who had committed these murders; but they nearly always failed. They shook their heads and looked at each other as they gravely muttered, "That's another piece of work from the Ditch; there's no mistaking the bites of them there Fleet rats." But, although they all knew where these murders were committed, no one could tell how or by whom they were perpetrated.

Towards this wretched den of crime Jack Sheppard led his companion. They crossed the Fleet by a rotten wooden bridge, so full of holes that Batswing could look down and see the dark, foul waters as they rushed over the thick, black slime and fœtid mud which oozed through the broken stones which served to form a sort of embankment to the unwholesome stream.

Big rats shot out now and then from holes and crannies, splashing into the water and running away as if business of the greatest importance had called them somewhere, whilst a cluster of them that kept dodging about and swimming round a strange object that was floating down the stream seawards, made Batswing's heart grow sick; for he felt that the object on which the rats were so eagerly feeding was a corpse.

"What a terrible place this is," said Batswing.

"It is not a pleasant one, truly," replied Jack, "but it is safe; and in our profession, you know, that is the chief thing."

"Perhaps," said Batswing; then pointing to the object on the stream, he asked shudderingly, "Do you see *that*?"

"Yes," replied Sheppard, cooly; "I don't mind those sort of things now. I did at first, but I have got used to them. Why the waters of the old Fleet abound with such fish as that. If they would only put a grating over the mouth of the Ditch they would catch some dozens a week, and save the fishermen at the Nore a good deal of trouble. Not only that—they would save burials as well, for the rats would make short work of them soon enough, I trow, leaving nothing for the undertaker to do; for the appetites of these vermin are as sharp as their teeth."

Batswing made no reply, but quickened his pace, as if anxious to leave the precincts of the accursed river.

"This way, this way," cried Jack, touching his companion on the arm. "We are close by the old house now. Once in there, Jonathan Wild and all his crew may try their hardest to discover us for what I care."

"Is your place of refuge so safe, then," asked Batswing?

"None safer, I can assure you. It is not a pleasant one, I confess; still, when once inside, it is not so unpleasant, after all. I know that you knights of the road go in for doing the gentleman, which we poor cracksmen can't do; still, we manage to make ourselves jolly enough, and stick to each other through thick and thin. Now, there's a fellow here that would give his life to save mine, I know; he loves me as if I were his son. He is a rough, uncouth fellow, it is true; but he loves me, and that is all I want."

"We knights of the road, as you call us," said Batswing quietly, "are not always so much to blame as people suppose. Some of us *are* gentlemen by birth and education, and have been driven to this life by receiving injustice from others. Not that I give this as an excuse for the lives we lead."

"Bah!" cried Jack Sheppard, "our lives need no excuse; at least, I don't want to find one for mine. I do what I like, and must take the consequences of it if I am nabbed. My father, Tom Sheppard, was a craksman before me, and swung at Tyburn."

"So I have heard," said Batswing; "he was helped there by Jonathan Wild."

For a moment Sheppard looked down and bit his lip. Then, with a quick, sharp, bitter laugh, he exclaimed—

"Yes, I believe Jonathan did do him that kind service; and, what is more, it is my belief that he intends to do the same office for me one of these fine days."

"And do you not intend to try and overthrow him first"?

"Overthrow Jonathan Wild! You might as well talk about trying to overthrow the monument as overthrow Jonathan. He is too well in with the Robins for that. Why, even old Pitt, the governor of Newgate, knuckles under to him.

"Still he can be overthrown," said Batswing.

"Perhaps so," replied Jack; "I wish I knew the man who would and could do it. I'd do to him what I never yet did to any other man."

"Indeed!" cried Batswing, "and what may that be?"

"Why I would acknowledge him my superior, choose him as my leader, and obey him to the death."

"I know not whether I *can* overthrow this fiend," said Batswing, "but I will try; I have taken an oath to do so, and by heaven I will, or perish in the attempt."

"Bravely said," cried Jack, "and, by Jove, you look the fellow to do it too."

"I will!" exclaimed Batswing, with emphasis.

"Then I will be your follower, if you will only grant me one favour."

"Name it," said Batswing.

"It is that you tell me how you came to take to the road?"

"That is a long story," said Batswing, sorrowfully, "part of which I must not tell; but that which I may reveal I will relate to you after we have partaken of some refreshment."

"Agreed," said Jack; "and, remember, I am at your command whenever you want me. This is our place. You had better let me, for the present, lead the way, for it is necessary that you should know the men that they may trust you."

As he spoke he turned down a narrow lane, through the centre of which ran a deep gutter, into which the refuse of vegetables and the offal of animals had been thrown, stopping up the drain and causing the water to flow out here and there into deep puddles.

On one side of the lane was a dead wall, whilst on the other was a row of large, dismal, broken-down houses.

What struck Batswing as most peculiar in these houses was the scarcity of windows. The few that were to be seen were narrow, and placed at a great distance from the ground, whilst the panes were so grimed with dirt that a fondness the inhabitants seemed to possess of closing the shutters appeared perfectly absurd and unnecessary.

Jack Sheppard glanced quickly up and down the lane to see if any one was approaching, and, perceiving that the place was quite deserted, knocked gently at the door.

"Who's dare?" demanded a thick voice, which evidently belonged to a member of the Hebrew persuasion.

"It's all right, Moses," said Jack.

"But you're not alone."

"No, I've a pal with me; it's all square."

Grumbling something to himself, Moses commenced unbarring the gate, much to Batswing's surprise, for he thought the old man would never leave off taking down bars, undoing chains and locks, and shooting back bolts.

At length the door swung upon its hinges, and Jack, followed by his comrade, entered the mysterious dwelling.

It was a gloomy place, with a close, prison-like odour clinging about it. The walls were blistered and discoloured with damp, the stairs were rotten and broken, whilst the balustrades had entirely disappeared.

"Vich vay will you go?" demanded Moses, who was a little red-haired old Jew, dressed in a greasy flannel nightgown and slippers. A dirty worsted cap, from under which his red elf-locks straggled, was placed upon his head.

His eyes were pink, and gleamed in the light with a strange fiendish fire that would have made a less bold man than our hero draw back in horror; whilst the dirt which begrimed the face and bony hands of Moses was enough to fill any one with disgust.

The old Jew held a candle in one of his claw-like hands, and shaded the other in such a manner that the rays fell straight upon Batswing, whom he eyed with a mixed glance of curiosity and malevolence. "Vich vay vill yer go, Captain Sheppard? Dare's a large barty of roisterers down in the kitchen dat vill be glad to see you and de shentleman."

"You'd better come down," whispered Sheppard to Batswing; "I'll answer for all the fellows being trustworthy—that is with anything but your purse—and they might be useful. They will do anything for me."

"Ish the shentleman strange to good company like ours?" demanded the Jew sharply, at the same time eyeing Batswing suspiciously. "Ve don't 'ave many strangers here."

"No, no," said Sheppard quickly; "but we are tired and want refreshment."

"I understand, Captain," replied the Jew, with an awful leer and a grin; "you vants a private room for a little vhile, eh?"

As he spoke he moved quickly towards the broken stairs, up which he was about to clamber, when Jack Sheppard stopped him.

"Come here, you old Judas Iscariot," he cried passionately; "did I not tell you that this was my friend? Besides, did you ever know Jack Sheppard lend himself to any of your cowardly ways? I tell you that this gentleman is one of us. Now lead the way to the kitchen."

The old Jew was so shaken by the violence Jack had used that he was taken with such a terrible fit of coughing that he could scarcely crawl down the stairs.

At length they reached the cellar—for such in truth the kitchen was, and Batswing was much struck by the confusion of voices that forced its way through the thick door which guarded the room.

Having paused one moment to recover his breath, Moses threw open the door and announced Captain Sheppard and his friend.

A hearty shout greeted the announcement; but the place was so full of tobacco smoke that Batswing was some time before he could see the company. Presently a man, of herculean proportions and very dark complexion, forced his way up to Sheppard and, seizing him by the hands, exclaimed—

"Hurrah, Cappen! so you ain't nabbed arter all? I heard the hue and cry out, and fell in with the crowd to see what was up, determined to go in for a rescue if you were nabbed; but as you were not to be seen I made sure that you had escaped clean off, or that Jonathan had set his hand on you at some other place, and that you had dropped into the net. But now I see you again, I'm as happy as a lord."

"I'm all right, Blueskin," said Jack. "Never fear for me; Jonathan don't want me just yet. By the way, you see this gentleman?"

"Yes," growled Blueskin. "What of him?"

"He is a particular friend of mine."

"Oh!" replied the other, in a tone of voice that denoted anything but pleasure at the announcement.

"It is my wish that you obey him when and wherever you meet him."

"Obey him!" demanded Blueskin, "and why?"

"Because I wish it," replied Jack, firmly. "Now go and tell the company that I have business with my friend here, and therefore do not wish to be disturbed. Tell them to go on with their mirth; that will not annoy, but will draw off notice from us."

With a low grunt the man sauntered away round the table, now and then stooping to whisper to the men as he passed, who, in their turn, glanced rapidly at Jack and his companion, and then turned their heads away as if desirous to show that they were not watching the new-comers.

Whilst Jack was ordering some refreshments, Batswing took a stool, and seating himself by the fire began to examine the room and the company.

It was nothing more than a low vaulted cellar. The walls were white-washed, and in one corner a rough funnel shaped chimney had been built, under which a wood fire blazed cheerily, giving forth not only a large quantity of heat, which was necessary to dry the humid atmosphere, but a large quantity of smoke which was totally unnecessary, the chamber and its occupants being quite dirty enough without the addition of soot.

Down the centre of this apartment ran a long deal table, covered with mugs, pots, and bottles of all descriptions. Round this table were seated some thirty or forty men, dressed mostly like mechanics, though some had a flashy style about them which showed they did not belong to that respectable body.

At the head of the table, seated on a chair much higher than the others was a huge burly man of about forty-five or fifty. His face was free, open and good humoured, his eyes sparkling with fun, and his wide mouth always smiling. His complexion was clear and ruddy, showing that he had been used to pass the greater part of his life in the open air.

Prepossessing as this man's appearance was, there seemed something about him that displeased Batswing. He could not tell whether it was the nervous twitching of the man's fingures, giving him the appearance of grasping at money, or whether it was the low chuckling, secret laugh. Whichever it was, Batswing took an indescribable dislike to this man.

The man was better dressed than any one else in the room, being clothed in the garb of a wealthy farmer or well-to-do country gentleman. Indeed, from his general appearance, Batswing put him down as a yeoman; a conviction he was confirmed in by hearing the men call the man "farmer," and also by his way of talking of cattle, and country produce.

The rest of the company did not possess any distinctive feature sufficient to make our hero notice them. All were drinking deeply and smoking fiercely, until the oil lamp that hung from the ceiling became dimmed with the fumes.

At this moment Jack returned, followed by Moses, who bore a goodly steaming bowl of punch, which he placed on a settle between the two friends, who at once commenced to partake of the generous beverage.

"You have a strange company here," whispered Batswing.

"Yes," replied Sheppard, coolly, "and rather a dangerous one. They won't hurt you now they see you are one of us; but had you followed that wretched old Moses up-stairs, you would most likely have been following that object which displeased you so much in the Fleet Ditch. No doubt it would have been more pleasant for the rats, but not for you. When we have finished this bowl, we can retire to a private apartment in safety, and there you can tell me your history, or at least such as you care about relating." At that moment Jack's voice was drowned by a violent noise, caused by the company beating their pots on the table.

"What is the matter now?" asked Batswing, who was trying to enjoy this strange wild scene of dissipation.

"Oh, nothing particular, only Farmer Croft is about to sing a song. He sings well, therefore we may as well listen."

As they refilled their glasses and prepared to hear the song, the farmer rose to his feet, and lifting his goblet high in the air said:—

"Gentlemen of the gentle craft, cracksmen all! I cannot express the gratification I feel in having been allowed to preside over you this evening. To me it is an honor that I shall never forget. I know that in many circles the profession which you have adopted is looked down upon; but so have many other noble professions before yours. Are we not told that we must help ourselves if we would be helped! what more do we do? Are we not told that riches are temptation? What nobler act could we perform than to remove temptation from our fellowman's path? Thus you see that we are but agents—poor and humble ones it may be—but still agents in a great work to benefit humanity, and therefore if you will permit me, I will sing a new song in honor of this genial, and, I may say, philanthropic society."

A roar of applause followed this speech, and Farmer Croft, after taking one or two puffs at his pipe so as to keep it alight, commenced the song of—

The Old Fleet Ditch.

You cracksmen and footpads who want a good treat,
Why just pad your hoofs and be off to the Fleet:
There's 'baccy and spirits, and lots of good beer,
And never a dubsman or robin to fear.
The rats of the Fleet are a brave jolly set,
Who kindness or hatred will never forget—
If short of the rhino, you never need care,
For generous pals you are sure to meet there.
    And no murmur of river was ever so rich
      As the deep gurgling rush of the dear Old Fleet
      Ditch.

If strangers or dubsmen should dare to intrude,
We quickly convince them such conduct is rude;
We show them that all their endeavours are vain,
And yet of our treatment they never complain.
They slip down a passage and make a retreat,
And sail to the Thames by the way of the Fleet,
But ere they depart in the way I've defined,
They thoughtfully leave all their purses behind.
    So no murmur of river is half so rich
      As the deep gurgling sound of the Old Fleet
      Ditch.

Then fill up your tankards till they overflow:
Leave not in the cup space for sorrow or woe;
The dear old Fleet Ditch is to us source of wealth,
So who will refuse to drink it's good health.
May it ever roll on so gallant and free,
To carry *dumb witnesses* down to the sea;
For no stream in the world could ever compete,
With that friend of our craft, the swift rolling Fleet.
    No murmur of river to us is so rich
      As the deep, sweet, swift sound of the Old Fleet
      Ditch.

A burst of applause followed this song, enough to have deafened one. Men thumped upon the table with their fists until the pots and mugs jumped again, at the same time shouting out the chorus, with the profoundest contempt for the air—in the loudest tone they could.

"Who is that man?" asked Batswing, in a low voice of his companion.

"I scarcely know," replied Jack, "he turned up here suddenly. I believe he came from Yorkshire; I think his line is cattle or horse stealing. Anyway he seems to make money fast, and has by some means got a tremendous hold on the men. Some how I don't think he like's Jonathan Wild."

"Who could?" said Batswing.

At this point the door opened a few inches, and a thin, short lad of about fourteen, riggled himself through the aperture into the apartment, unnoticed by all the company, except Jack and the Bat; the former of whom beckoned the lad to approach them.

The appearance of this youth could scarcely be considered prepossessing, either as to his personal beauty or his garments.

His head was inordinately large, and was covered over with a thick roofing of matted black hair, which, twisted in snake locks over his sallow forehead. His eyes, like his head, were unusually large and round, and filled with indescribable expressions. Now they would look sad and pensive, as if filled with deep and saddening thoughts; then, they would sparkle with wit and humour, and anon they became bright and twinkling with the excess of cunning. His nose was short and snubby; his upper lip short and full; his chin long, flat, and pointed. His hollow cheeks, the deep blue rings that circled his eyes, added to the extreme sallowness of his complexion, showed the lad was far from well; a fact that was made beyond a doubt by the constant low hacking cough, which he so vainly endeavoured to smother.

As for his garments, who could describe them. Patched they certainly were not, nor had they ever been. They were rags, and nothing but rags. How they clung to the lad's poor, thin body, no one could tell. Festoons of them clung to his arms, rows of them encircled his body, whilst two long strips of tatters, much resembling the "ornaments for your fire stoves," cried about by the women in the streets at the present day, encased his legs.

Shoes and stockings he had none, his feet being covered with cuts and bruises from walking over the sharp stones and exposure to the weather. He shuffled along with a peculiar eel like wriggle; keeping his hands constantly clasped over his chest, and stooping as if in pain.

"Who is this poor lad?" asked Batswing.

"Well, that's a question not easily answered," replied Jack, "no one knows who he is, or where he comes from. He was found one day on the banks of the Fleet Ditch. A mere baby of some days old. There's no doubt but that his mother preferred his room to his company, and took the shortest way to get rid of him."

"What do you call him?"

"You see he gets his living by running about with a link, so the fellows here have christened him Jack-o'-Lantern."

"It must be a poor life to lead."

"Yes, but the fellows are very kind to him," said Jack Sheppard, "a'int they Jack-o'-Lantern."

"Werry," was the laconic reply.

"You seem cold," said Batswing, kindly, "take a glass of this."

The boy seized the proffered glass, and drank it off at one gulp, then smacking his lips, and rubbing his stomach, he placed the glass down, his eyes twinkling with delight.

"My heyes, but that there is stunning," he cried, "its like swallowing a liquid blanket, that's what it is. It wraps round your innards and keeps 'em all on a glow. Blest if I should'nt mind a counterpane of the same material."

Batswing laughed as he poured out another glass, which Jack-o'-Lantern immediately dispatched after the other one.

"If ever you want to know anything about the Fleet," said Jack Sheppard, "Jack-o'-Lantern can tell you all about it. He knows all the secret places and ins and outs of the alleys and lanes in this neighbourhood."

"I should rather think I do," cried the lad, whose tongue seemed strangely freed by the effects of the punch, "I should rather think I do. Vy I've been born'd and bred amongst the rats o' the Fleet. I've slept amongst them o' nights, but they never 'urt me, never. Sometimes they comes and sits round me, and talks to me 'alf the night. I know what they say, and they knows what I say. They shows me the secret holes, they do, and tells me what they've seen done in 'em, until they makes my blood freeze again. But they enjoys it, they does; they sits up and purrs and wipes their long whiskers on their paws with delight."

THE GOVERNOR OF NEWGATE'S DOUBLE MISTAKE.

"You must indeed see some strange sights," said Batswing.

"Yes, but it ain't only down in the Fleet, I sees strange sights, I sees 'em all over London. Why, only last-night I seed a queer go, up west; a reg'lar queer caper that was and no mistake."

"Indeed, what was that?"

"Vy, I was standing in St. James' Square, thinking vot I should do, for my link had gone out, when up rolls a carriage to a large house that seemed quite empty. Vell, I was about to rush up to see if I could get a mag or two, when the door of the 'ouse opens vithout anyone a knocking at the door or ringing at the bell. Then open flies the carriage door, and out gets a man dressed like Farmer Croft, carrying a girl wrapped up in a big black cloak. He goes into the house, the door closes, and away goes the carriage. Now ain't that a

No. 8.

rum go? Lord! I stood for a 'our or more vatching that there 'ouse a vondering vot vas a going on inside. It looked so quiet and peaceful like, that I knew there vos williany underneath."

"By heavens," cried Batswing, "it must have been Alice."

"Hush!" said Jack Sheppard, catching his friend by the wrist, so as to prevent him springing to his feet, "you forget that we are watched here."

"I cannot help it," said Batswing, "besides we are amongst friends, and therefore there can be no danger."

"I am not so sure of that," replied Jack Sheppard, "from your exclamation, and Jack-o'-Lantern's news, I think it is probable that the man who carried the girl into that house may have some friends here. At all events it is best to be cautious."

"How was the lady dressed?" asked Batswing.

"As far as I could see, all in black,' said Jack-o-

Lantern, who seemed to become more and more interested in the affair.

"And the carriage?"

"A black one, close of course, with two horses—bloods I should think."

"There can be no doubt it is the man," said Batswing, "you must show me the house my lad."

Jack-o'-Lantern hesitated.

"You need not fear," continued Batswing, "you shall be well rewarded, and I will protect you from all harm. Come, will you show me the house now."

"This is all nonsense," said Jack Sheppard, "you must not leave here yet. If you want to help this girl, and I suppose that is the truth of the case, you must take things quietly. Remember it is more than probable that you are being carefully watched for at the present time, and to show yourself would only be to raise the hue and cry and cause your arrest. Be guided by me. We will stay here another hour, so as to throw off suspicion, for I see that we are being watched now. You see no one knows you here. Jack-o'-Lantern will come to us when this party has broken up, and then we will see what can be done."

"Sorry to interrupt your conversation gentlemen," shouted Farmer Croft from the end of the table; "but wont you join the company and tip us a stave."

"With pleasure," cried Batswing who saw that Jack was right, "we will join you for a short time and have another bowl, and then, if you will allow me, I will retire for I've ridden far to-day."

"Do you belong to the road sir?" demanded one man, as our friends drew up to the table,

"I have that honour," replied Batswing.

"Then give us a song of the right sort."

Seeing that it would be no use to refuse, Batswing cleared his throat and began the following song.

Drink Away Lads.

Come saddle my horse for my heart it is gay;
I'll just crush one cup and then I'll away,
For nought in the world can give me such delight
As a ride on my mare on a dark starless night—
The ring of her hoofs as she dashes along,
Keeps time to the tune of some old drinking song;
And never for trouble or wealth will I care,
While I'm quaffing a cup or riding my mare.
　　Then drink away lads, drink well and drink deep,
　　This life is too short for us mortals to weep,
　　Mount a mare, thorough bred, that outstrips the
　　　　wind—
　　I warrant you'll soon leave all troubles behind.

There's sweetness I own in a dear woman's smile,
But still I confess they are apt to beguile,
Temptation is only withstood by the few,
And what man can swear that his mistress is true!
A girl for some gewgaw to make her look gay,
Her man to the robins may chance to betray:
But my mare, like the wind before them will fly,
She'll save me from prison or else she will die.
　　Then drink away lads, drink well and drink deep,
　　This life is too short for us mortals to weep,
　　Mount a mare, thorough bred, that outstrips the
　　　　wind—
　　I'll warrant you'll soon leave all troubles behind.

Scarcely was the song finished than Batswing reeled back and would doubtlessly have fallen, had it not been for the prompt help of Jack Sheppard who caught him just in time.

"Great Heavens," cried Jack. "what is the matter."

"Nothing, a mere nothing," replied Batswing, "I received a slight wound in the shoulder the other day; a pistol shot, I fear the blood has burst forth again."

"It has indeed," said Jack, "here Moses, help me up-stairs with this gentleman, and mind," he whispered in the Jew's ear, "I sleep with him in the same apartment, so let me have no tricks. Do you understand?"

The Jew shrugged his shoulders, and muttering something about folly, lead the way up-stairs.

No sooner had they departed than Farmer Croft beckoned to a man who had formed one of the company, and whispered in his ear.

"Did you see him?"

The man nodded.

"You cannot be mistaken? It must be the man."

"Certain on it."

"How are you certain?"

"Why I seed Mr. Wild put the bullet into his shoulder,"

"Good: then be off at once, and give Mr. Wild notice."

"But Moses?" urged the man,

"Will be silenced by me."

"And the rest of the fellows?"

"Will not be here when you return."

"And Captain Sheppard?"

"Will also be out of the way. Now go and don't worry me any more. Remember time is precious."

The man slinked away; and shortly afterwards the Farmer took the opportunity to break up the meeting.

CHAPTER XXVIII.

BATSWING RELATES HIS HISTORY.

When Jack Sheppard had taken Batswing to his own room he slipped off his coat and examined the wound.

It was a very slight one, the ball having passed through, or rather grazed the fleshy part of the shoulder. Indeed, the hurt was so little that Batswing had forgotten all about it until the bleeding caused by the excitement he had gone through had produced the sudden weakness.

"I can assure you it is nothing," said Batswing, smiling at his new friend's anxiety.

"That is all very true," replied Jack, "but as far as I can see you want all your strength at the present time."

"That I freely admit."

"Well then let me bind it up carefully, for who knows how soon we may have to start from here. While I am attending to you, you can tell me what is this affair about the lady."

Batswing in a very few words related Alice's history, to which Jack listened most intently, and when it was over paced up and down the room.

"There can be no doubt that the poor girl is in the hands of this Lord Redfern," he said after a short pause, "but what we can do in the matter just now I cannot see. Redfern has money and Wild to back him, and with those, a man who is not troubled with conscience can do almost anything."

"That is true," replied Batswing, "but yet I feel that I shall not only save this girl, but overthrow this monster, who lives and thrives on the ruin and disgrace of others."

"Heaven send that you may," said Jack, "but now that we have a few moments to spare, I would fain know what caused you to take to the road. Judging from your appearance and manner, I should have guessed that by birth and station you were far above all that have ever followed that daring and dangerous profession."

"You would have guessed rightly," said Batswing, "and I will now perform my promise and tell you, as far as I can my history."

For a moment both were silent, Jack waiting with all attention for his companion to proceed, and Batswing gazing vacantly on the floor, as if trying to collect his thoughts."

"My father was a man of high family, holding a good position in the Court of James II., of whom he was a staunch follower. But for all his love for his King, my father could not close his eyes to the fact that the country was ruled badly; indeed he foresaw the terrible ruin that would fall on the house of Stuart, a ruin so terrible that that noble house would never survive it.

"Over and over again he advised his majesty to use gentle methods, to show more mercy, and above all to deal equal justice to both Roman Catholics and Protestants. This he did until he made himself obnoxious to the priests, who seemed anxious to revive the terrible day, of Bloody Mary.

"Although a firm Roman Catholic, my father's advice made him so many enemies that he found that his presence at Court was not only useless but distasteful to the King, and therefore at once retired to his country seat, where he remained in close seclusion.

"Most of the noble families whose estates surrounded those of my father were protestant, and therefore would hold no intercourse with our family, so that the only companion my father had was a steward who had served him for many years.

"Time rolled on, and at last my father heard that his predictions were about to be fulfilled. He at once hastened to the Court to offer his services once more to the King; but, through the agency of the priests, they were refused.

"My father returned again to the country, determining to devote the whole of his time to the cultivation and improvement of his estate. Soon after that, news came that the King had fled the country and that William of Orange and Mary were proclaimed King and Queen of England.

"About this time my father married a lady professing the Romish Faith, to whom he had been engaged for some time. This lady, my mother, was entirely ruled by the priests, and at once turned the Hall into a place where Jacobitish plots were hatched and planned.

"In vain my father protested against this, and pointed out to my mother the terrible danger she was drawing round her. She would not give way, declaring that her soul was dearer than her life, and she would venture all for the true religion.

"For some years popish priests were constantly coming and going about the Hall; and my father only escaped by a miracle from being impeached for treasonable practices. He became careless about the matter for he was the last of his race, I at that time not being born.

"Things went on the same way for some years. Then I was born; but by that time my father had caught the terrible infection of plotting, and could not leave it off. Besides King James, who was then in exile, was only too pleased to have my father amongst his adherents. He wrote autograph letters to him, which so pleased my parent that he swore that King James should return.

"Deeper and deeper grew the shadow over our house, but though the clouds lowered the storm did not burst, till the year 1700, and then the thunderbolt fell upon our family.

"My mother had six weeks before the fatal night given birth to a little girl, and the house was full of joy and thanksgiving for her recovery. I remember my dear father bestowing his hospitality on all comers; my mother, pale and delicate, was smiling on all around her, and listening to the smooth speeches of two Jesuit priests who were leaning over her chair.

"Suddenly a peasant rushed into the room and gasped out.

"'Fly my lord; you are betrayed. King William's troopers are nearly at the gate.'

"In a moment all was confusion, the servants were mostly stricken with a panic and turned and fled.

"Drawing his sword, my father turned to the few faithful ones who remained, and cried in a loud voice—

"'Draw for God and King James.'

"However enthusiastic my father and the servants might have been for the 'good cause' as they called it, the Reverend Fathers evidently did not think it worth risking their holy bodies, for, snatching me up, they touched a secret spring, a panel flew open disclosing a secret passage down which they rushed, only pausing to close the pannel.

"In their haste the Reverend gentlemen managed to strike my head with great violence against the wall, so that I became insensible, and must have remained so for some long time, as the first thing I noticed on my returning to conciousness was that I was at sea in a small sailing craft,

"After a rough voyage we made Boulogne on the French coast, and from thence I was taken by the two priests to St. Omer and placed at the Jesuit's college of that town.

"After I had been there some time I found the priests who had at first been most kind, had changed towards me. Their looks were colder and sterner than usual, and instead of treating me with respect, I was slighted if not treated with contempt.

"This went on until I reached the age of sixteen. I had made inquiries about my parents, but had always met with a stern rebuke for doing so, and a warning that I must no more think of the world, but devote myself unto heaven.

"One day I was summoned to attend upon the principal, and then for the first time I heard the truth of what had happened to my parents.

"When the soldiers had entered the room, my father and his few followers had attacked them at the point of the sword. The conflict was but a short one, my father was slain by his favourite and confidant—his steward—who had betrayed his master to the King.

"My mother was found dead in her chair: the fright and excitement in her delicate state of health having proved too much for her, but her child—my little sister— was gone.

"Proofs of my fathers treason were found in abundance, his property was confiscated and sold to the steward whom my father had enriched.

"'Now,' said the reverend father, 'you know the history of your unhappy parents. Your family no longer exists in England: your large estates have been given to the heretics, and you are powerless and penniless. In consideration of your father's services, we have determined to make you a priest of our order, so that you may still help in bringing stray sheep to the pale of the true church.'

"With that he dismissed me.

"No sooner had I heard this, than I became determined not to enter the church, which I looked upon as the chief cause of all my misery. But how was I to escape from the college, and even should I succeed in effecting that, how was a penniless youth to get back to England, where I proposed going in order to avenge my father.

"I knew it would be of no use trying to escape at night, as the gates were always closed and guarded with great care; therefore I determined to try it in open daylight.

"For this purpose, I one evening entered the gardener's lodge, and stole therefrom a ragged old suit of clothes, which belonged to the gardener's son. These I hid away until the next morning, and then at break of day I arose and dressed myself in the miserable rags; after which I descended to the garden, where I concealed myself until the gates were opened, when I advanced boldly to them, whistling as I went.

"The old porter wished me good morning as I passed out, observing that I was up betimes. My heart beat fast as I answered the old man, and my temples ached with the blood throbbing in the veins. Luckily for me the old man was very short sighted, so by pulling my cap down over my eyes, and imitating the voice of the gardener's lad, I managed to pass out.

"When once in the open air, I made my way as quickly as I could out of the town, in the direction of Boulogne.

"After walking some way, I began to fear I might be pursued, and therefore hid myself in a small plantation by the roadside.

"It was as well that I took these precautions, for I had not been concealed long, before I heard a trampling of horses hoofs, and presently the riders, who ever they were, pulled up at the wood.

"'Sapristi,' I heard one exclaim, 'this is a likely spot for the young brute to hide in: we must dismount, Pierre, and examine this closely.'

"'Bah!' replied the other, surlily, 'he won't have stopped here, he is off to one of the villages on a spree, that is all. For my part I cannot tell why Father Gringoire is so anxious about the cub. He will, doubtless, come back when he finds how difficult it is to live outside the college.'

"'You are an ass, Pierre,' was the polite reply, 'do you think that Father Gringoire cares one pin about the lad! No; he only cares for the money that is forwarded regularly from England, so that the boy shall not turn up where he is not wanted.'

"'He has friends then?' asked Pierre.

"'Friends! Ventrebleu! may I never have such,' cried the first speaker, 'No, no, Pierre, he has that which pays the reverend Father much better, *enemies*; see you that, Pierre, rich, powerful enemies.'

"'Why don't they have the lad put out of the way then altogether, if that be the case?' growled Pierre.

"'Parbleu! that is what they wish, I have no doubt; but Father Gringoire is not fool enough to kill the goose with the golden eggs. Come along, Pierre, we must search the plantation.'

"The two men alighted, and after they had tied up their horses, I heard them beating the underwood with their heavy whips, at the same time commanding me to come out, as if they were perfectly certain that I was there.

"At one time I nearly gave up all hopes of escape, for they approached me so closely, that I cannot tell to this day how they missed seeing me; however, fortune favoured me, and I soon heard them going farther and farther away from me.

"At length I ventured to peep through the bushes—there was no one near, but I could hear the men's shouts as they moved away in the distance.

"Suddenly a good idea struck me; I crept from my hiding place to the road, where I found the horses still tethered.

"Choosing the best one, I mounted him and galloped off, leading the other horse by the bridle. I took great care to choose the most grassy sides of the wood, so that the horses might not make much noise, and thus, the men being so far distant, I was not pursued.

"Turning down a pretty lane, I made my way as fast as I could towards what I thought was the direction of the sea coast. This lane led me out by a little village called Le Wast, a few miles distant from Colomberee. Having found some money in the saddle bags of the horses, I boldly entered the village, and pulling up at a little Auberge ordered some wine, and enquired my way to Boulogne, at the same time carelessly stating that I had to meet my master there with the horses, which he was about to sell.

"The landlady gave me the necessary instructions, so that, after refreshing myself I set out again on my journey, but instead of making my way to Bolougne, turned towards Ambleteuse, a small sea port, to the north of Boulogne.

"As I rode along, I noticed that my ragged clothes and the two horses caused me to attract more attention amongst the farm labourers than I liked. But how was I to get rid of either the one or the other.

"To avoid remark as much as possible, I rode down a small bridle path, leading through a large wood. The path narrowed and the trees grew closer as I proceeded, until the path seemed to disappear, and I had the comforting knowledge that I had lost myself.

"The first thing that I did was to secure all the money and pistols I found in the saddle bags and to conceal them about myself; then throwing my reins on the horses' necks, allowed the creatures to lead me where they would.

"By that strange instinct so remarkable in these noble animals, they seemed to divine my purpose, and turning sharp off to the left forced their way down a narrow path that I had not perceived, and which led out to an open space, where a man was engaged charcoal-burning.

"I must confess that I would willingly have passed the man, but could not; for no sooner did he hear the tramp of horses, than he left his work and advanced to meet me.

"Never in the course of my life have I ever seen a more villanous object than this charcoal-burner. His features were hideous in the extreme, whilst the soot caused by his occupation made him look as though he had come from the infernal regions.

"Placing himself right in my path, so as to prevent my proceeding on my way, he eyed me at first with a bitter scowl, and afterwards with a demoniacle smile of grim satisfaction.

"'So, ho, my young master,' he began, 'parbleu, horse flesh must be cheap for a lad like you to need two.'

"The horses are not mine, I replied, they belong to my master, whom I have to meet at Ambleteuse.

"'And where have you come from?' demanded the fellow.

"Colomberee.

"'And who may Monsieur your master be? Sapristi! I know Colomberee well, may be he is an acquaintance of mine.'

"Don't ask impertinent questions friend, I replied, for I saw that the man was not only suspicious, but certain that I had run away with the horses.

"'A thousand pardons my young master,' said the fellow, grinning, 'I would not offend you for the world. Come, to prove there is no ill-feeling, dismount, enter my hut and have a crust of bread and a cup of wine with me.'

"My first thought was to draw one of my pistols and blow the fellow's brains out; but on consideration, I concluded it would be wiser to do what he requested; therefore, throwing him the reins, I carelessly dismounted, and after assisting him to tether the horses, I entered his miserable den, which was as smoky and disagreeable as its owner.

"He produced a bottle of wine and some coarse black bread, of which I partook heartily, for my appetite was good.

"During my meal he continued asking me many questions, some of which I replied to, others I lied to, and the rest I refused to answer at all.

"At length the man rose quietly from the block of wood whereon he had been sitting, and going to the door, closed and fastened it.

"In a moment I sprang to my feet, and grasping the butt of one of the pistols I had in my pocket, demanded in as haughty a tone as I could assume, what he had closed and fastened the door for.

"'All in good time my little master,' the ruffian replied, as he picked up a huge oaken staff, 'all in good time, I wish to have a quiet talk with you before you proceed on your journey, and I mean to be answered, and what's more you must speak the truth or—' here he shook the staff in such a manner that to complete the sentence was quite unnecessary.

"'Keep your distance, said I coolly, and I will answer your questions.'

"'First then, you told me you were a stable boy.'

"'I did,' I replied.

"'You are not.'

"'I am not.'

"'You are one of those people who oppress the poor.'

"'I am not; do I look like it? I am poor myself.'

"'Your hands are white and soft. You have never worked.'

"'Perhaps not as you have; still I have worked.'

"'Yes; and I know how.'

"'How?'

"'As a *thief*. Those horses are stolen; I know it.'

"'And you wish to steal them from me,' I replied.

"'I!' cried the man, taken aback by my coolness.

"'Yes, you; do you think that I am so blind that I cannot see what you are? Charcoal burning don't purchase such wine as *that*. Come let us be honest—at least to each other. You want the horses: I want money, what will you give me for them? Name your own price: I shall not complain.'

"With an oath the man, raised his bludgeon, but I was too quick for him, and in an instant I produced, cocked, and presented my pistol point blank at his breast, making him recoil.

"'Come,' said I, 'let me have no more of this nonsense: your life is in my hands, and trust me I will not spare it should I have reason for taking it.'

"'What do you mean by attacking an honest man in his own house?' demanded the man who was evidently a coward.

"'As to your honesty my friend,' said I, 'the less you speak about that the better. Where is your money? Do not fear, I won't rob you. I shall only take a little and leave you in exchange the two horses and all the harness.'

"The fellow after some grumbling produced some half-dozen Louis d'or, half of which I took and returned him the other on condition he would bring out some more wine and drink with me. This he willingly did, as he was very pleased with his bargain. Of course I drank as little as possible, whilst I plied my host well with the liquor.

"It soon had an effect on him, and he commenced making me a confidant of all the crimes he had committed; all of which made so deep an impression on me that I shall never forget them However, to my joy, he at length fell fast asleep, and I managed to make my escape from the hut.

"Pushing my way through the wood, I at length came to a broad path which led me to the road, and in two hours time I was on the outskirts of Ambleteuse.

"It was dark when I entered the town, so I made my way to a shop and purchased a sailor's suit. These I tied up in a bundle, and going out of the town walked along the cliffs until dark, when being quite certain that no one could see me, I took off my old clothes which I threw into the sea, and put on my new garments. I then strolled still farther from the town, determining not to enter it until late, when I should most likely escape notice. But on a lonesome part of the cliff I came suddenly on an old house that had doubtlessly at one time belonged to some wealthy man, but was now a sort of country inn; part farm, and part Auberge.

"This struck me as being the best place for me to put up. Accordingly I went in and ordered some supper and a bed. The landlord, a rough seafaring man, demanded payment in advance: this I gave him, but sillily showed him the other Louis d'ors that I had.

"My supper was soon finished: and feeling thoroughly tired I went to my bed-room, which was a large, dark, old-fashioned room, with a fixed bedstead in an alcove.

"I was so disturbed with the thought that I might be pursued and discovered, that I could not rest in comfort, and therefore determined not to undress, and also to examine what means I had to escape by.

"The door had large bolts on the inside, which I carefully fastened and then proceeded to the window. This was made in the usual French style, opening down the middle and fastening with a catch. I opened it and looked out. The night was stormy and dark: the wind making a melancholy rustling amongst the ivy that covered the house, whilst the roaring of the stormy sea was terrible.

"Closing the window, I was preparing to go to bed, when I was struck by noticing that the back wall in the alcove which contained my bed, sounded very hollow. I had gone through too much not to be suspicious, and although I had no particular reason for being so, became more and more restless, till at last I took a blanket from the bed and laid upon the floor.

"After a while I fell into a light sleep, but had not slept long before I was disturbed by hearing a slight noise as if on the bed.

"In a moment I sprang to my feet, taking care however not to make any noise.

"There could be no mistake now that what I had considered my groundless suspicions were correct—the panel *did* move for I could plainly see a light round it.

"What should I do? If I fired a pistol the whole house would be disturbed, and then my capture, if not my death, would be certain.

"Uncocking one of my pistols, I grasped it tightly by the barrel, and placing myself behind the curtains of the bed, waited to see what would happen.

"Slowly the panel slid on one side and the hotel-keeper holding a large knife in his hand appeared in the aperture.

"He lean't over the bed and raised the knife, as if to strike, but before he could discover that the bed was empty, I struck him a violent blow on the back of his head, which either killed or made him senseless at once for he fell forward without uttering a groan.

"I flew to the window, opened it, and with the aid of the ivy clambered down the wall to the ground; which I no sooner reached, than I ran as fast as I could in the direction of the town, but in the dark I mistook my way, and after running a considerable distance found myself on the sea shore.

"This last adventure had made me so suspicious that I determined to walk by the sea the rest of the night, and for that purpose I strolled back the way I had come, only being careful to avoid the path leading to the top of the cliffs, and which would have of course taken me back to the Auberge.

"I had not proceeded far when I was alarmed by hearing the voices of men shouting and then the clash of swords mingled with the reports of firearms.

"'These' thought I, 'cannot be my pursuers, for they would not be fighting.' I hurried towards the spot from whence the noise proceeded; taking care to keep close to the cliff.

"Turning a sharp point in the cliff, I came suddenly on the combatants, whom I found to be a party of French soldiers and English sailors. The French were undoubtedly getting the best of it, for they had nearly twice the number of men: Nevertheless the sailors were fighting with great determination, retreating slowly towards a boat that was pulled up on the beach; at the same time preventing the Frenchmen from outflanking them so as to get possession of the craft.

"At last growing desperate the French captain, who was a giant in stature, sprang upon the sailor who was commanding the English, and by main force dragged him away from his companions, whom the rest of the soldiers charged with redoubled force, so as to prevent them assisting their leader. Seeing how unequal the struggle was between the two commanders, for the Englishman was as small as the other was big, I drew a pistol and fired at the Frenchman, who leaped into the air and then fell on the sands grasping them with his hands and biting them with his teeth.

"'Well done my lad who ever you are' said the captain.

"'I am an Englishman' I cried, 'take me with you to England.'

"'All right my lad,' cried the man as he picked up the Frenchman's sabre, 'we've no time for spinning yarns, but must work. If you want to sail with me you must fight your way to that boat or you'll be left behind as sure as anything. Now then: Roast beef and Old England, down with the Johnny Crapauds.'

"With this strange war-cry we charged the Frenchmen in the rear, the captain using his sabre and I my pistols with such good effect that the enemy, finding themselves attacked in the front and rear, fled, and I had the satisfaction, in less than half-an-hour, of standing on the deck of an English schooner.

"Of course I had to tell my history to the captain, who, in return, told me that he was half-smuggler half-privateer; or, in fact, ready for any daring thing that was likely to prove profitable.

"He had taken a fancy to me, and, in return for my having saved his life, taught me seamanship and treated me as his child.

"I sailed with this man for a few years, during which I had some strange adventures, which I will relate to you some other time. At last, I became captain of the ship, although but little more than a lad, and led her into some of the most difficult actions, for danger was the only thing that could give me relief. In one of these my ship was so cut about that she was forced to go into dock, and I was necessarily obliged to be idle; so, to fill up my time, I determined to re-visit my father's hall and discover the truth of what Father Gringoire had told me. It was late in the evening when I arrived there, so I turned into a small wayside inn to procure some refreshments, and to learn what news I could about the old place.

"I soon discovered that what I had heard was true. The steward who had betrayed my father was now master of the old hall and estates. I also learned that he was universally hated by the tenants, for he was a cruel, hard landlord.

"I was determined, come what might, to see this man and charge him with his perfidy: and, for that reason walked up to the hall and sent in a false name: taking care to set a title to it.

"I found this fellow—who received me with all courtesy, thinking that I was a great lord—seated in judgment upon a poor half-starved peasant who had killed a hare to feed his starving family. I will not shock your ears with all the barbarity with which this wretch treated the poor prisoner; suffice it to say, that after repeatedly striking the poor creature with a whip for daring to speak in his own defence, he sentenced him to the severest punishment the law will allow for such crimes.

"Putting aside the just indignation any man would have felt at such brutality, I was doubly enraged, as I recognised in the miserable peasant a man who had served my father faithfully.

"Springing to my feet, I spoke loudly against this injustice, and, in the heat of the moment, accused him of having betrayed my father.

"Pale with mingled rage and fear, he ordered his servants to seize me; but, as I drew my sword and stood on the defensive, they drew back.

"'In the devil's name, who are you?' he exclaimed, gnashing his teeth with rage; 'what have you to do in this place? You have no right here.'

"'No right here!' I cried; 'I am the master here. I am the son of the man who raised you to fortune, and whom you ruined and betrayed.'

"'Seize him!' he yelled; 'he is a rebel, a traitor, a Catholic spy.'

"'It is false,' I cried, turning to the astonished servants. 'I am the son of your kind old master; I have lost both title and estates through this man's treachery; but those who love me will follow me where, at all events, they will be free from such tyranny as yonder trembling coward has shown. I have been robbed, cast out of society, outlawed—for what? Nothing but difference of opinion and hatred to oppression. From this moment I devote myself to revenge on society the wrongs it has inflicted on me. Those who love me will follow me.'

"Seizing a blazing billet of wood from the hearth I struck the false steward with all my might across the face, at the same time crying—

"'I give thee this to remember me; and, at the same time, to mark thee in such a manner that I may always know thy face, disguise it as thou wilt.'

"Perceiving the violence inflicted on their master, the servants sprung forward to arrest me; but I eluded their grasp, and, rushing down the stairs, escaped, still carrying the burning brand with me.

"As I passed the granary I perceived that the door was open, and hurled the flaming fagot amidst the golden corn.

"The next minute all was in a blaze.

"The whole attention of the servants was directed towards extinguishing the fire, so that I escaped with ease. Nay, more; I waited on a high hill and beheld my father's hall, the home of my ancestors, reduced to ruins—to ruins—and by *my hands!*'"

For a moment Batswing seemed overcome by his recollection; but quickly recovering himself, he passed his hand over his eyes and continued—

"Perhaps it is better so, much better so, than that it should have been held by my father's murderer. From that moment I forsook the sea, and formed the band in the forest, amongst which are many of my father's old servants."

"Yours has indeed been an eventful life," said Jack.

"It has, indeed."

"And what are your plans?"

"To avenge my father's murder."

"And then to discover the fate of your sister?"

"Yes, and to place her in the position she ought to hold."

"If I can help you in any of these things I will," cried Jack Sheppard.

"But, hark!" suddenly said Batswing. "What noise is that on the stairs?"

Both men sprang to their feet and listened intently.

They had not long to wait, for a slight tapping was heard at the door. Jack Sheppard opened it, and Jack-o'-Lantern crept stealthily into the room. Then, closing the door, he asked in a low voice—

"Which on you's Batswing?"

"Why how did you know that either of us had that name?"

"Oh, it ain't you, Capin Sheppard, I don't believe; only you coves do change your names about so, that one can't tell who's who."

"I am Batswing, my boy," said the Bat: "but why did you ask?"

"'Cause the gaff's blown; that's what's the matter."

"Who has done this?" cried Jack, angrily.

"I never tells on nobody," replied Jack-o'-Lantern—"I don't like peaching; if I did, many a queer tale I could tell about them there things in the water which the rats like; but I keeps silent, I does; I don't like to see others blown on, that's a fact."

"You mean to say that we are betrayed?"

The boy nodded.

"To whom? Surely you can tell us that."

"To Jonathan Wild," said the boy.

"And will you not tell us by whom?" asked Batswing.

"No, I won't," replied the boy; "I'm blow'd if I'll peach for any one.

"I'd better ask Moses what is to be done," said Jack Sheppard.

"You'd better trust to me," replied Jack-o'-Lantern.

"The boy is right," said Batswing. "Hark! I hear a noise in the street."

"Don't look out of that window," cried Jack-o'-Lantern, pulling Batswing back, as he was advancing to the casement; they know which room you're in, and if once you're seen its all up with you."

"All right; but what are we to do, Lantern?" said Jack Sheppard; "you know the way about here better than any one, so you must lead the way."

The lad gave a knowing wink, and stepping to the chimney beckoned them to follow.

It was an old-fashioned fire-place, big enough to hold half-a-dozen of our modern ones. It had no grate, being merely a plane hearth, with a couple of iron bars (called dogs) laid across it transversely.

"Give us a leg up," said Jack-o'-Lantern, and the two men did as they were desired.

After searching a moment, the boy touched a spring, and, to the amazement of Batswing and Jack Sheppard, a large iron trap in the chimney swung open, leaving an aperture big enough for them to pass through.

CHAPTER XXIX.

THE GOVERNOR OF NEWGATE MAKES AN ARREST AND—A FOOL OF HIMSELF.

"And what's to be done now Arthur, darlin'?" enquired Captain O'Neil, as he rode with Sir Arthur from Chalk Farm on the morning of the duel.

"I scarcely know," replied Sir Arthur absently, "I shall go straight home."

"To be sure you will," replied the Irishman, "Faith! you went straight *home* this morning anyway. I don't think Lord Harry Leslie will trouble you any more."

"You don't mean to say that he won't recover?" asked Sir Arthur anxiously.

"One can't be positive about these little affairs," said the Irishman, "but I think his lordship stands a chance of visiting—

'That undiscovered country from whose bourne
No traveller returns.'"

"Do not jest on such a subject O'Neil," cried Sir Arthur, "it is too serious."

"Too serious? Bedad! that's the very reason you should jest at it. There is an old proverb which says that 'there is no use crying over spilt milk' and I think it is about as useless to cry over spilt blood. Besides, Lord Harry will have died like a gentleman, and therefore his death is better than his life; only there is one thing inconvenient about it."

"And what may be the inconvenience you seem to anticipate?" asked Sir Arthur.

"Why you see, my jewel, that Lord Henry Leslie was not only wealthy himself but he belonged to a very rich and powerful family. Besides he had, or has, many friends: some of them most unscrupulous, such for instance as Lord Redfern and his friends. Well now, if you had had the fortune to kill a plain gentleman like myself, no one would have cared a pin about it, and you might have stopped in your rooms until the matter blew over. But in this case it is very different. The news of this 'duel in high life' will spread like wildfire through town, and large rewards will be offered for your

arrest; and for mine too, for that matter. Won't Jonathan Wild be on our track: and Lord Redfern will seize the opportunity of getting you into prison so as to avoid having the satisfaction of meeting you as promised. Bedad, he did not like the idea at first, but when he hears this, he will tremble like a jelly."

"What are we to do then?" demanded Arthur.

"Make ourselves scarce in less than no time. Take a trip on the continent until our friends here can get our pardon. They'll soon manage that when we are once abroad and can't be touched, but they won't succeed whilst we are here and in their clutches. It seems a terrible thing that two gentlemen cannot have a bit of amusement without being interfered with."

"I do not think so," replied Sir Arthur; "this morning has stopped me seeing any justice in the sword. Death is too terrible a punishment for any crime."

"Bedad, but the law does not; why, under his most Gracious Majesty," here Captain O'Neil raised his hat, "they hang for everything and anything: a yard of calico or murder, it's all the same: the prisoner swings."*

"But the law is not always right."

"No; but it nearly always has might; and so I shall make myself scarce, not wishing to reside at Newgate under Mr. Pitt's care, or even to swing at Tyburn."

"You are right, O'Neil; and therefore I wish you a prosperous journey."

"But sure and it's yourself that will come with me," cried O'Neil.

"No, O'Neil; I must remain in London."

"In London! why you must be mad."

"That I am not."

"Well then it's love, and sure that's the same thing. Who is the lady?"

"One who is in great danger and trouble through the machinations of villains."

"Oh! sure then it's the same one who caused this pretty little affair."

"The same."

"And where is she now?"

"That I cannot say: but I fear the worst. Lord Henry Leslie, in the few last words he spoke, warned me of danger. I must see him directly."

"And what good will that be? Trust me he is as stiff as possible by this time. He won't get over this little bout. It was too good a lunge for that."

"Heaven knows I did not mean to kill him," groaned Sir Arthur.

"Nevertheless you have succeeded in doing so as well as if you had the very best intentions. So as your seeing him can be of no good now, you had better make up your mind to save your own precious neck and come with me."

"No, O'Neil, whether Lord Harry be dead or not, I cannot and will not leave England until I am satisfied that Alice is safe."

"And I shall not be satisfied until perfectly certain of my own safety," said O'Neil, "so good-bye Sir Arthur, since you are determined to adventure all to gain nothing. What good can you possibly do by staying? If you could show me that you could be of any service to the lady, I would stay and help you: but as you can't, I say again that your stopping here is only madness and nothing else."

"To you, as to most people, it may seem madness," replied Sir Arthur, "but I cannot leave this spot until I am convinced Alice is safe, or at least know her fate. I thank you greatly for your offer of service, but I have friends whom, I think, will probably be able to help me in finding her, or at least in giving me a safe retreat

*This is perfectly true: a woman, whose husband had been pressed into the army, thereby leaving her and her children penniless—stole a yard of calico, for which crime she was hanged by the special order of that homely, good, farmer King, George III.

from the officers of justice, should such an event become necessary."

"Well, if you will, you will, and all argument is but waste of time," said the honest Irishman, "so I'll wish you farewell and all success until we shall meet again. Don't be rash, my jewel, and go up to see after Lord Harry. Redfern is sure to be there to have you arrested, and what can you do then for the colleen. It's true Lord Harry would not wish harm to you, but if he's alive he will be delirious or speechless, and that comes to the same thing, and if he be dead, why then he could not protect you. So don't go near him, but wait and see what may turn up, and don't expose yourself to danger more than you can help. So good-bye, and heaven bless you."

Cordially returning the Irishman's good wishes, Sir Arthur wished him farewell and then rode to his own house, where he quickly changed his dress for a much plainer but stronger one.

He then ordered a fresh horse to be saddled, and having taken care to see that his holsters were fitted with pistols, all loaded and ready for action, he mounted his horse and dashed away towards Epping.

As he galloped along the road his dread as to Alice's safety seemed to grow less and less.

"How," he argued, "can she be in danger? Did I not leave her safe with Batswing at the cave? surely he would not betray her. No, that is impossible. If he were so treacherous as that, why should he have saved her from Lord Redfern, and why should he have so generously spared my life?"

As these thoughts passed through his brain he slackened his pace so that his horse fell into a quiet walk, unnoticed by its master who was deep in meditation, reflecting painfully over the occurrence of the morning.

From these painful thoughts he was aroused by his horse springing aside to avoid two horsemen who dashed suddenly from a side lane into the main road.

The two men were dressed entirely in black, with long black riding cloaks, the collars of which were turned up in such a way as to entirely hide the lower part of their faces, whilst the peaks of their hats were pulled down so as to conceal the upper part.

An angry curse proceeded from both men, but they dashed on, neither apologizing to Sir Arthur, or waiting for an explanation from him.

Sir Arthur's first impulse was to dash after them, and clapping his spurs to his horse's side he attempted to do so. His horse leapt a pace forward and then staggered back on its haunches nearly falling.

"Confound it," cried Sir Arthur, "what is the meaning of this. The horse cannot be hurt; it must be fear."

Again he tried to urge the horse forward, but the poor animal was unable to move.

Quickly dismounting, he commenced examining the mare to ascertain the cause of her strange behaviour, which he was not long in doing. The poor animal in starting on one side had in some way sprained its pastern and consequently was unable to move beyond a slow, limping, walk. Bitterly cursing his luck, and the careless riding of the other two horsemen, Sir Arthur took hold of the bridle and led the lamed animal down the road, encouraging her, as he walked by her side. by patting her neck.

Suddenly he became aware that he was followed by some half-dozen men who seemed led on by a tall thin man with a peaked anxious face. By the dress of the men any one might have taken them to be citizens of middle-class station; whilst their leader looked far above them. Yet for all this a quick eye could perceive something peculiar in their movements. They walked as if they had been partly drilled, or at least used to walk in bodies, whilst the quick, sharp, glances they cast

around them showed that they had been trained to watchfulness.

Quickening his pace, for he guessed they were constables, Sir Arthur pushed on as quickly as possible, but the condition of his horse prevented him making much haste.

At last he reached a small way-side inn which he entered, and calling for some wine asked for the stable-boy or ostler, and in a minute no less a person entered the room than our young friend Jerry Blinker.

Jerry took off his cap, pulled his forelock, and kicked his right leg out behind.

He then stood with his face puckered up as if about to whistle whilst waiting for the gentleman's orders.

"My mare has lamed herself on the road," said Sir Arthur, "therefore I must leave her here, whilst she is ill. See that she is well attended to and you shall be well rewarded. But in the mean time you must supply me with another horse."

"And when will yer lordship require the other 'oss?" asked Jerry.

"Immediately."

"Werry sorry sir, but it can't be done," replied Jerry, shaking his head.

"And why not?" demanded Sir Arthur sharply.

"For the simple reason that we ain't got one in the stable at present."

"Confound it, what is to be done?" said Sir Arthur impatiently as he paced up and down the room, "I must get on my way."

"I'm werry sorry sir," replied Jerry, "but the only 'oss we have in the 'ouse at the present time is a clothes 'oss and won't help you much."

"I suppose I must push on by foot," said Sir Arthur without heeding Jerry's impudent reply. "Be kind to my horse my lad and I will see that you are well recompensed. Here is a guinea as earnest."

"Thank'ee sir, what name shall I put the feed o' the 'oss down to?"

Sir Arthur paused as he was about to give his own name, wondering whether it would be safe so to do. Might he not be pursued because of the duel: or even should that not be the case, he would most likely be followed by some of Lord Redfern's myrmidons?

No! he would not give his own name, for whilst doing so could do no good, it very possibly might create danger.

Short as the time was that Sir Arthur took to form this determination, it did not pass unobserved by Jerry Blinker; who scrutinized Sir Arthur even more carefully than before, being certain there was some mystery in the case and determining to discover, if possible, what it might be.

"Blest if I don't think he's a highwayman out o' luck," thought Jerry, "anyway he seems a good sort, and a man may be a gentleman without being a highwayman. There's no law agin that as I knows on."

"You may put my name down as Stanmore," said Sir Arthur, "I may either call myself for the horse or send my servant. Which is the nearest way to Waltham?"

"Do you want the Abbey or the forest?" asked Jerry with a sly wink.

For a moment Sir Arthur stood and stared at his questioner in amazement, at last he said—

"I want the forest."

"I thought so" cried Jerry, slapping his thigh and winking, "blest if I didn't think you were"—

"Our prisoner!!" screamed a chorus of voices as the door was burst open, and the men whom Sir Arthur had seen on the road hurried in and seized the baronet before he could make the slightest resistance.

"Ha, ha, ha!" shouted the meagre man, "I've caught you at last, have I, you bloodthirsty villain. So your horse foundered on the road did it, eh? I guess you

THE APPROACH OF THE TORTURER.

won't have another ride until you go backwards to Tyburn."

"What do you mean?" demanded Sir Arthur sternly.

"What do I mean? oh, that's a good one too. What do I mean? why that I have got you safe and sound, and won't let you go until I hand you over to the hangman, that's what I mean. Ha! ha! ha! how surprised you look."

For a moment Sir Arthur was so overcome with astonishment that he could not speak. In the confusion the allusion to his being treated as a common felon quite escaped him, and when he recovered himself his attention, even in the midst of all his danger, was attracted by the change in Jerry Blinker's usually cheerful though somewhat impudent countenance.

Suddenly that interesting youth seemed seized with an ague; he became pale, his knees trembled, and his teeth chattered fearfully.

With eyes fixed and glassy, he watched the meagre man as a rabbit does a snake which has charmed and is about to devour it.

"This folly is too much," said Sir Arthur to the thin man; "you have either made some very gross mistake, or you have committed an impertinence for which, believe me, you shall answer dearly."

"Ha, ha, ha!" roared all the men, pointing at Sir Arthur jeeringly.

"'Pon my word he does it beautifully; no wonder he has baffled us all by his wonderful disguises; who can be surprised at his even taking me in?"

"Taking you in!" exclaimed Sir Arthur, wrathfully; "who the devil are you?"

"Who am I? As if you did not know who I was. Come, I like that, 'pon my word I do. It's charming, 'pon my word it is. I suppose you have forgotten doing me out of the reward, eh? If you have I have not, and I intend to be equal with you, that I do. Nay, more;

I mean to make the best of the bargain. You made one hundred and fifty pounds out of me; I mean to make *five hundred* out of you. Ho, ho, ho, ho! it will be a merry day for me when I see you tasting the bowl of St. Giles's. Ho, ho, ho, ho!"

Here the thin man screamed with laughter, and actually danced with delight.

"You have evidently mistaken your man, sir," said Sir Arthur, coolly; "I am a gentleman."

"A gentleman! a pretty gentleman, indeed! A 'gentleman of the road,' eh?"

"I can assure you I am no such thing," said Sir Arthur, with difficulty suppressing his temper. "This may be very interesting to you, but I can assure you that it is far from pleasant to me. Will you be good enough to answer me one or two questions? It may save both of us much trouble."

"Well," said the thin man, "of all the cool cards I ever saw, I think you are the most so. But I'll humour you a little to see how far you will go."

"In the first place, may I ask for what crime you have dared to arrest me?"

"What crime! You may well ask that, for you have committed so many that it would be difficult to tell which one was the worst, and therefore we have arrested you on all and each of them. Will that satisfy you?"

Sir Arthur shrugged his shoulders, and then continued—

"In the second place, I should much like to know who and what you are?"

"Who I am? Good again; don't know me, eh? We shall have the pleasure of sleeping in the same building to-night any way. Perhaps you'll be quite as comfortable as I shall be; but circumstances alter cases, you know. Do you understand me now; eh?"

"I am sorry to say your wit outstrips my understanding," said Sir Arthur.

"Then, to favour your humour, I will inform you that I am no less a personage than Mr. Pitt, and that I hold the position of governor of Newgate."

At this announcement Jerry scarcely could conceal his terror. He would gladly have left the room; but he saw that any attempt on his part to do so would not only be instantly frustrated, but would call down attention on his head, which might lead to detection.

"And now may I ask for whom you take me? At least I hope he is a gentleman."

"This is too much," said Mr. Pitt; "I am not to be deceived this time; I *know* who you are. I thought I was on the right track when I saw Jonathan Wild and his men on the road. Won't he be vexed when he knows how I did him. You see it's no good, Batswing; its all up with you."

"I can assure you," laughed Sir Arthur," you have made a very terrible mistake. I am no more Batswing than you are. I am Sir Arthur Bowring, of Stavely Hall, Devonshire."

"Oh, indeed! that's your other alias is it. How many more have you?"

"That which I have said is true; you can ask this boy," exclaimed Sir Arthur, in his indignation quite forgetting the fact that he had given Jerry a false name. "I have given him orders about my horse."

Mr. Pitt turned and looked at Jerry, who, we need not say, trembled beneath his sharp gaze.

"And who may you be, sir?" demanded Mr. Pitt.

"Please, sir, I'm the ostler o' this here inn," replied Jerry, putting on a very sharp and "'ossy" tone, so as carefully to avoid any resemblance in voice and manner to Miss Mary Jane Smirk.

"And what do you mean, sir, by having dealings with highwaymen?"

"Me have dealings with highwaymen? cried Jerry, indignantly;" "I never did nothing of the sort. How should I know a 'ighwayman from any other sort of a feller, I should like to know? Look here, yer honour,

s'posing a chap like that one over there comes in here and says to me says he, 'Here, my lad, there's summut the matter with my 'oss; I sees you're a sharp chap, and I can trust him in your hands. Get me another 'oss to go on with until you've fettled that one up all right and proper.' With that he chucks me over a guinea like a gentleman. So, says I, 'All right yer honour, I'll see to the nag; but, as to the other 'oss we ain't got such a thing far or near. so what's to be done?' 'Well,' says he, 'if so be that there's the case I must go on to the next inn; but mind as 'ow you see to my 'oss.' 'But to whose name am I to put down the mare's fodder and med'cin', says I? 'Mine,' says he. 'And what may that be?' says I. 'Sir Harthor Bowering, Esq., of Stavely 'All, Devonshire,' says he, in just that there style; so, o' course, I puts him down as one of the regular tip-top harristocracy; that's wot I does. 'Ow am I to know that he's a thief? I don't mix with them so much as your honour does."

"What do you mean, sir?" demanded Mr. Pitt, sharply.

"Well, I ain't 'ad the practice or I ain't a got the penetration as you have."

"Hem!" said Mr. Pitt, still keeping his eyes fixed sternly on Jerry. "Have I not seen you somewhere before, my lad? I seem to know your face."

"May be you do, sir; if you've been to Stamford, I'm pretty well known about here; but I don't think the London folk know me, as a rule."

Again Mr. Pitt examined Jerry's face carefully, but failed to see the likeness to Miss Smirk for which he was seeking.

"May I ask if you are determined to take me into custody on this absurd mistake, Mr. Pitt?" demanded Sir Arthur.

"That indeed I do, my good fellow, so you must prepare to march."

"What!" cried Sir Arthur, "walk! this is indeed carrying matters too far. I certainly will not walk in any such company, let the consequences be what they may."

"Oh, you won't, won't you?" grinned Mr. Pitt; "but suppose we make you?"

How far Mr. Pitt might have proceeded with his threat it is hard to say, had not one of his men touched him on the arm and whispered—

"You'd better have a conveyance, sir; remember the cause there is for a rescue. We can keep him all snug in this here inn until one on us fetches a hackney coach. and we shall have him quite safe."

"True," muttered Mr. Pitt, "you're right; it would be much safer."

Turning to Sir Arthur he said, in the blandest of bland tones, "I regret very much that you should still be obstinate enough as to deny your identity. Such a proceeding can do you no good. Still, I am not willing to treat a man who, to say the least, can assume the manners of a gentleman so remarkably well, harshly. Therefore, if you would prefer riding, hand my man a couple of guineas and he shall go and procure a conveyance at the nearest place possible. The price is high, but consider the trouble to the man, and the convenience to yourself."

"I do not begrudge the money," said Sir Arthur, as he threw the sum demanded on the table.

"Ah!" sighed the governor of Newgate, "easy come, easy go."

"Bring me a bottle of your best wine, my boy," said Sir Arthur, not noticing Mr. Pitt.

Jerry no sooner heard the order than he vanished, glad of the opportunity of leaving such undesirable company.

Mr. Pitt sighed as he thought of the extravagant manner of this, as he believed, highwayman, but said nothing; merely contenting himself by placing a man on each side of Sir Arthur, and another in the front of him.

These he ordered strictly to watch the prisoner, each to have his pistol presented at him in case he should endeavour to escape, and to be certain to fire should the prisoner show the slightest inclination to do so.

Mr. Pitt then retired with the man who was to fetch the coach.

"Grummidge," he said, slipping a guinea into that gentleman's hand; Grummidge, you may fetch the coach. Demand it in the name of his Gracious Majesty the King, they dare not refuse you; the country will indemnify them, and you need not waste that guinea."

The man winked, laughed hoarsely, and left the inn.

Taking advantage of Mr. Pitt's absence, Jerry Blinker hastened in with the wine, which he placed before Sir Arthur, at the same time saying with a sharp glance—

"Do you still want that horse, sir? I think I know where I can get one down in the village; the smith has just passed with a good one."

"Ha, ha, ha, ha!" roared the men, "blest if that *ain't* a good one. Want that horse now? I should rather think he did. Wouldn't he like to be on it just now! Oh no, not at all."

Again the men burst out in loud shouts of laughter, in which Jerry joined; but as Sir Arthur cast an angry glance at him, there was a strange meaning that that gentleman could not mistake.

"I think, my lad," said Sir Arthur, "there is many a true word said in jest, and I may still want that horse. Therefore do me the service of hiring it, and keeping it ready saddled for me. Don't let any one take it until either I am removed by this gentleman from here or am free to use it. Any way, the expense shall be paid and you remembered."

With a sly look at Sir Arthur, Jerry withdrew from the room.

"Will you drink, gentlemen?" said Sir Arthur, offering to fill their glasses.

"No, thank you, sir," was the quick reply; we ain't young enough for that."

"What do you mean?"

"We've seen them sort of things before. When once you're lodged safely in Newgate we won't mind drinking your very good health, but until then we'd rather not. You'll have plenty of time to stand drink there."

Sir Arthur made no further attempt to converse with the men, but sat quietly sipping his wine until the shades of evening closed around. Deeper and deeper grew the darkness, until Sir Arthur almost began to long for the carriage to come.

Meanwhile Jerry thought it better to make himself as scarce as possible, and therefore obtained permission from Mrs. Wapshaw to visit Bob Blow-the-Bellows, whom he found hammering and singing away as usual.

"Well, my young Touch-and-Go," said the smith, "what's up now?"

"Plenty, and lots to spare," replied Jerry. "I've had the pleasure of a hinterview with the governor of Newgate."

"What of that?" retorted the smith: "it's not the first time, and it won't be the last, you see. All I'm surprised at is that he has let you come away."

"Oh! stop that," said Jerry, "there's a reg'lar go on at our place; the Bird Cage, you know. No end of a row. There's old Pitt been and collared a swell at the inn whom he takes for the Cap'pen. One as ain't a bit like him, too. But a reg'lar good chap for all that. Dashed if I shouldn't like to get him off."

Jerry then explained to Bob Blow-the-Bellows what had taken place at the inn, and was greatly surprised to see that his story made Bob not only take great interest, but also become most unusually serious.

"You are right, Jerry," said Bob, after a few moments' reflection, "this is no matter to laugh at. We must get this young fellow off, or we shall catch it."

"We shall catch it? I like that, certainly," said Jerry

"And why in the name of fortune should we satch it for him?"

"You are a very clever lad, Jerry, but, for all that, you don't know everything."

"Neither do you," retorted Jerry; "but you may know the cause of this man being of so much interest to us. If so, please inform yours obediently, for I freely confess that I don't."

"This Sir Arthur is a sworn friend of the Captain's, that's all."

Jerry whistled a low whistle of astonishment.

"That's all, and enough too, I consider," said Bob Blow-the-Bellows, "so just come with me, and we will see what can be done."

Bob led the way to a back shed, which contained a fine black mare, whose glossy coat shone in the light of the lantern like satin.

As the smith entered, the noble animal turned her small but well proportioned head towards him, and neighed with pleasure.

"Woa, mare, woa, my beauty," said Bob, as he stroked her arched neck. "It ain't with me that you will ride to-night, my charmer: you must have a better charge. Not that I think you will like it so well. It's a strange thing, Jerry, that animals with any sense don't care for titles or money a bit."

"Oh! don't they though!" replied Jerry. "Just look at women. Why, its all they care for, ain't it?"

"Ah! but I don't mean that class of animals. And mark you this, Jerry, you are very anxious to become a man. Now, don't say you ain't, for I know that you are doing all you can to cultivate a *mouse starch;* although, owing to the colour of your hair, and the smallness of the quantity of the down, it merely looks, at present, as if you had been sucking an orange, and not wiped your mouth. But, as I was saying, if you want to be a man, never speak against the ladies—heaven bless 'em!—for no true man ever does that."

"What! bless 'em?" said Jerry, slyly.

"No, you young varmint," said the smith; "speak agin them is what I mean.

" 'For women they have a wondrous way,
    All mankind to entrance ;
  They win their loves with a single smile;
    And kill them with a glance.'

So take warning, Jerry, and never speak against women. And now follow me."

Whilst this conversation had been going on, the smith, with Jerry's assistance, had rubbed down the horse, and placed a loose halter round its neck. Taking the end of the halter the smith commenced walking down the lane towards the "Bird Cage Inn."

"Where are you going?" demanded Jerry, in a great fright.

"Why, to the inn, to be sure."

"But don't I tell you that Mr. Pitt's there? It's no good running into danger."

"*I* don't intend running into danger," answered the smith. "You must take the mare into the stable, and get it saddled and bridled. Do you hear?"

"Me!" gasped Jerry.

"Yes, you. All I have to do is to get Sir Arthur out of the place, and that's enough, I think. I suppose the officers did not seize the saddle and trappings of Sir Arthur's own horse?"

"No. I took that into the coach-house."

"Right. Well, just you harness this mare, and see that Sir Arthur's pistols are all rightly charged—that is, if he has any; if not, get him some. When this is done, lead the horse up to the side door, and stay there until either I or Sir Arthur comes to you."

Giving Jerry the end of the halter, Bob Blow-the-Bellows walked quickly on to the inn, which he entered humming a tune, in his usual careless manner.

"Good evening, Mrs. Wapshaw," he cried, saluting

the buxom widow. "This is queer news that I hear down in the village."

"And what news may that be?" demanded the widow, smiling on her admirer.

"Why, then, it can't be true, or you must have known all about it."

"About what?" demanded the widow.

"Why, it's going all through the village that that awful creature Batswing has been arrested in your house. I said it couldn't be true. But mother Green, she who keeps the general shop up above here, declared it was. So as I have been robbed by the fellow, I thought I'd just come over and see him."

"Eh! What's that?" demanded Mr. Pitt, who was standing by the bar. "Have you been one of the many victims of this terrible highwayman?"

"Indeed I have, sir," sighed Bob. "He's a regular bad one."

"Ah! that he is," said Mr. Pitt, drawing out his note-book slyly. "Have you any objection to tell me how this happened?"

"Oh! none in the least, sir, only talking is dry work."

"Very true, very true," groaned Mr. Pitt, who saw he would have to stand something to the smith. "Very true indeed; but drinking is a bad habit."

"So it is; but we all have our faults," replied the smith.

With a groan Mr. Pitt asked the smith into Mrs. Wapshaw's little back parlour, and then, having ordered a tankard of ale for the smith, listened patiently to that truthful gentleman's narrative, which ran as follows:—

"You see, sir, I was just coming down one of the Green Lanes, Tottenham, at about ten at night, for I had been up to Farmer Kittlebury's to receive some money for curing his cattle, which had been very bad, and as I had received a largish sum from the farmer, I stood treat to him and some other fellows at the ale-house."

"Money wasted! money wasted!" groaned Mr. Pitt.

"Very true, sir. Well, as I was saying, I had had a little drop too much to drink, and as I was acoming down the lane, whiz, whiz, something went across my path, so quick that I could not tell what it was, but as it went it looked for all the world like a *monstrous bat*. Well, I need not say I was a bit staggered, not to say scared; but the vision had a good effect on me, for it made me as sober as a judge. Putting my spurs to my horse, I dashed along the road at a fearful rate. When suddenly I felt myself seized by the collar, and the cold muzzle of a pistol placed close to my ear.

"'Money or your life' cried a stern voice.

"What was I to do? I knew that if I moved I should be shot, in an instant. All I was able to do was to get a full view of my antagonist, for at that moment the moon came out quite clear from behind a cloud. There he was, with his long black cloak and boots, scowling at me."

"Had he not a mask?" demanded Mr. Pitt.

"Devil a bit," replied the smith, "his face was as *plain* as your own."

"Then you could recognise him with ease?"

"Certainly."

"Well, what did you do?"

"What did I do? what could I do? I simply gave up my money.

"'Thanks' he cried, then shouted 'ho, ho, ho,' and then 'whiz' he had gone again."

"Ah!" said Mr. Pitt, shutting up his book in which he had been taking notes of what the smith had told him, "you will make a capital witness."

"Me sir?"

"Yes, you; for I've got the Bat safe and sound."

"The deuce you have! where is he?"

"Here in this very place. If you come with me I will show him to you. You recognise him instantly."

"Ay, that I shall, and gladly too. Do you think there is any chance of my getting back any of my money sir?" demanded Bob.

"Sure to," replied Mr. Pitt, inwardly chuckling at the falsehood he was telling, for he made certain that this temptation would make the smith recognise the prisoner at once.

"Well I shall be pleased," cried Bob, "I'll recognise him never fear."

Grinning with delight Mr. Pitt led the way to the room where Sir Arthur sat.

"There!" cried Mr. Pitt, holding the candle close to Sir Arthur's face, "there he is."

The Smith gazed at Sir Arthur intently, and then looked absently at Mr. Pitt.

"Well!" cried that gentleman, "what have you got to say now?"

"Why he ain't the man!"

"Not the man?" cried the infuriated Governor, "then who the devil is he?"

"I don't know," replied the smith scratching his head, "but I have seen him somewhere before."

Sir Arthur looked surprised at this, and Mr. Pitt pricked up his ears.

"Come, come," he whispered, "remember your money, think for a moment,—now where *have* you seen him before? you *must* remember. Don't consider his dress; these fellows have as many disguises as there are days in the year."

"His dress!" cried the smith slapping his thigh, "his dress, that's it."

"Ah! I thought that would bring it to mind," said Mr. Pitt in exultation, "come now, where have you seen him?"

"Why he's one of the officers as passed through Waltham in charge of Lord Clumber's plate. I couldn't tell who he was at first seeing him out of uniform."

"Its false," cried Mr. Pitt.

"It is true, and proves what I said was correct. I am Sir Arthur Bowring, Captain of His Majesty's Dragoon Guards," said Sir Arthur.

"This is a plot for the prisoner to escape," cried the Governor, "I see through it plain enough. The whole thing has been planned."

"I say, hold hard," cried the smith, "I'm only a poor man, but dash me if I'll be insulted by anyone. You ask me who this gentleman is, and I tell you. What more do you want? If you don't look out you may get more than you want, or care for presently."

"I'll have you all arrested" shouted Mr. Pitt, "you are all accomplices with the Epping robbers. I know you all, and you shall pay me for this."

How far Mr. Pitt's anger would have carried him it is hard to say, had it not been stopped by the sudden entrance of Mr. Grummidge, who throwing the door wide open, dashed into the room startling everyone therein by his paleness and agitation.

"What's the matter you idiot?" screamed Mr. Pitt.

"Oh sir" panted Grummidge, "you, that is to say, *we*, have made such a mistake."

"Mistake!" roared Mr. Pitt, "what do you mean."

"This is not Batswing at all. Whilst we have been keeping this man shut up here, the real Batswing has been pursued from Epping to Hendon by Jonathan Wild and his hounds."

"Can this be true?" groaned Mr. Pitt as he sunk back in his chair.

"That indeed it is sir, for I met some of Mr. Wild's men who had been knocked up by the chase and were coming across to this road to prevent Batswing getting back to the forest—That is if he has the good luck to escape."

"Escape!" cried Mr. Pitt, a faint gleam of hope lighting up his face, "he may have escaped eh? *Then* he may be here in disguise."

"Not yet sir at all events, for when these men left,

Mr. Wild was close upon the Bat's heels and had wounded him once with a pistol shot. Besides sir, they were in full chase over an hour ago, and we have had this gentleman in custody for more than three hours at the least."

Taking advantage of the confusion, Bob Blow-the-Bellows whispered to Sir Arthur,

"The boy Jerry waits at the side gate with a horse, give it the spur and turn its head towards Epping, and she'll carry you all right. Mind the word 'The Bat flies by night'—I'll see you before many hours are over."

The only answer Sir Arthur made to this speech was a quick significant look, then rising slowly he said in a haughty tone to Mr. Pitt—

"I presume sir, that even your incredulity and folly can go no further, and therefore I am at liberty to go."

"Go," cried Mr. Pitt in such a passion he could scarcely speak, "go, you may go to the Devil sir."

"Stop!" cried Sir Arthur, "I have borne your impertinence already too long, I demand an immediate apology for what you have just said; and unless I receive an ample and full one for the inconvenience I have suffered through your gross ignorance of your proper duty, I shall report your conduct to the proper authorities."

Mr. Pitt looked up with astonishment and began to splutter out some words of excuse, when Sir Arthur stopped him.

"Not another word sir; either you apoligise on your knees directly, or I will horsewhip you where you now stand; report you for your misconduct, and enter an action for damages for false imprisonment."

At the thought of losing his money Mr. Pitt fell down on his knees and apologised in the most humble manner.

No sooner had he finished than Sir Arthur left the house and proceeded at once to the side door where he found Jerry and the smith waiting with the horse.

"Not a word Sir Arthur," said Bob, "the mare will take you all right to the cave. I must wait here and see what I can learn of the cap'pen. Remember the words 'The Bat flies by night'."

Not waiting to give any reply, but merely pressing Bob Blow-the-Bellows' hand, Sir Arthur put spurs to his horse and galloped away at a tremendous rate.

The smith watched him down the road as far as he could on such a dark night, then turning into the inn went into the room, where he found Mr. Pitt still raving about everyone's dishonesty.

"It's no use crying over it now Sir," said the smith respectfully, "I told you that he wasn't the man. We all of us have our misfortunes, I have had mine, and you have had yours. You stood a glass to me, and if you are not too proud I'll stand one to you. You know when you want a fellow to indentify Batswing I'm your man."

Mr. Pitt groaned as he thought of the needless expense he had incurred; but as he felt faint and dry after his disappointment and passion, he accepted Bob's offer, looking upon it as at least something saved out of the fire.

Bob, in a generous manner, offered Mr. Grummidge and his companions something hot, which they willingly accepted, and by these means he managed to draw out a good deal of what the reader already knows concerning the abduction in the churchyard, and the pursuit.

Of the latter he learned enough to make him very uneasy; for our hero's escape seemed to him more than doubtful, for not only had Jonathan Wild been close upon him, but he had planted detachments of men to arrest him on all the roads to Epping.

He was just thinking that it would be desirable for him to return to his smithy, and from thence, if necessary, to the cave, when a voice at the bar made them all start.

It was Jonathan Wild's.

The smith at once bade the company good night, but, passing out at the back door, placed himself in such a position by the window of the room where Mr. Pitt was, that he could see and overhear all that passed.

When Jonathan entered the room his eyes and mouth looked, if possible, more cruel and fierce than usual.

Advancing to Mr. Pitt, he exclaimed—

"So you have the game, I understand, on your side this time."

"I!" groaned Mr. Pitt.

"Yes; have you not taken Batswing?"

"No."

"No!" how is that?" sneered Jonathan.

"I thought I had; but only found out, about half-an-hour ago, that I had arrested the wrong man."

"Ho, ho, ho!" laughed Jonathan, showing his tiger-like teeth in his delight.

"I could not help it," cried Mr. Pitt snappishly. You have not taken him yet."

"No, he has escaped me this time; but I know where he is, and will have him before twenty-four hours are over; I am now after another bird."

"What for?"

"Oh, nothing; a young spark murdered a nobleman out of jealousy, then bolted. So the friends of the murdered man have offered a cool three hundred pounds for the assassin's arrest."

"Indeed!" cried Mr. Pitt; "who is he, Mr. Wild?"

"One Sir Arthur Bowring."

"Yah!" screamed Mr. Pitt; "he was the man I arrested for Batswing."

"D——n!" thundered Jonathan; "where is he?"

"Gone—rode off—fled directly I released him."

"Which way did he go?"

"On the bye-road to London," cried Jerry, who had been listening to all that had passed; "I got him a 'oss and seed him start, thinking him a perfect gentleman."

Muttering imprecations loud and deep, Jonathan Wild dashed out of the inn, and, mounting his jaded horse, rode off in the direction of London, where he was soon followed by the disconsolate Mr. Pitt and his myrmidons; while the merry smith hastened off to the smithy, accompanied by Jerry Blinker.

CHAPTER XXX.

THE SUBTERRANEAN COMBAT. THE ADVENTURE IN THE DUNGEON.

No sooner had the trap in the back of the chimney opened than Jack-o'-Lantern crept through it, and was quickly followed by Batswing and Jack Sheppard.

The room which they found themselves in was exactly like the one they had just left, low, dirty, and miserable.

"I don't see that we have made much by this move," said Jack Sheppard, as Jack-o'-Lantern secured the trap.

"I don't know that," replied Batswing, "at all events we are out of that wretched old Jew's house."

"No we are not," grinned Jack-o'-Lantern, "both these here houses belongs to Moses."

"Hush, what was that!"

They listened attentively at the trap and could hear the sound of men in the other room, amongst the voices of whom they recognised those of Jonathan Wild and Moses.

"Confusion," cried Jonathan, "there is no one here. Have you allowed the fellow to escape?"

"Me, Mishter Vild? s'elp me, he vas here a few minutes ago, for I heard him speaking to Mr. Sheppard."

"How then could he have escaped?"

"That I can't say. Ah! yes, I have it. They have found out the trap in the chimney."

The next moment they heard the men forcing open the trap.

"Look to your weapons," said Batswing, "if we are

taken, at all events let us have the comfort of knowing that we killed Jonathan Wild."

"Follow me," said Jack-o'-Lantern, "they have not got the best of us yet."

Quickly opening the door, Jack-o'-Lantern rushed down the creaking stairs, closely followed by Batswing and his companion, but as they reached the ground floor a side door opened, and Jonathan Wild, followed by some half-dozen constables, dashed out to meet them.

"Yield," cried Jonathan, presenting a pistol at Batswing.

"Never," replied the Bat, striking the pistol up and closing with Jonathan.

"If you and t'other feller can get through this 'ere," whispered Jack-o'-Lantern to Sheppard, "bolt down into the cellar and I'll be there."

No sooner had he said the words, than twisting himself over the bannisters, he allowed himself to drop down into the basement.

Meanwhile Batswing and Jonathan Wild were struggling together violently. The pistol which Jonathan held had gone off in the struggle, lodging the contents in one of the constables, thereby rendering Batswing and Jack good service.

Batswing had now seized the pistol by the muzzle, and wrenched it round with all his force, thereby breaking Jonathan Wild's index finger with the trigger guard.

So great was the agony that Jonathan was obliged to leave go.

In a moment, Batswing, using the pistol as one would a dagger, struck his antagonist in the face, felling him to the ground.

Whilst this had been going on, Jack Sheppard had been anything but idle.

Drawing his sword, he had rushed on the constables, driving them down the narrow passage, and, mindful of the words of Jack-o'-Lantern, keeping the head of the stairs leading to the basement clear, so that when Batswing had freed himself of his antagonist, they might rush to the cellars as they had been directed.

No sooner had Wild fallen by the terrible blow, than Jack Sheppard called out,

"Now is our time, follow me."

Before the constables, who had thought Jack and the Bat were fighting to reach the street door, could recover from their astonishment, the two men rushed down stairs into the cellars.

The place was in complete darkness, still the men rushed on through a labyrinth of passages, now and then stumbling over things that crumbled beneath their feet, making them shudder, for sickening instinct told them that they were bones.

"I can go no further," said Batswing, stopping.

"But we are pursued," cried Jack Sheppard.

"I cannot help that, this place is a charnel-house."

"Still that is no reason why we should form part of its mouldy population."

"No, but I believe that boy has betrayed us."

"What, Jack-o'-Lantern? you do not know him as well as I do; he would die sooner than do such a thing."

"Where is he then?"

"Depend upon it he is somewhere waiting for us. In this cursed place a man may easily lose himself."

"True."

"Do you hear the constables? Hush, there is Wild's voice again."

Plainly enough rang Jonathan's deep-toned voice through the vaults.

"A hundred pounds to the man who takes Batswing, dead or alive."

"We had better prepare to meet them boldly," said Batswing.

"Look, what is that in the distance?"

"It is a light—a light from a torch or link."

"Follow it," cried Sheppard, "it is Jack-o'-Lantern, I knew he would not desert us."

The two men rushed forward in the direction of the light, which they saw glimmering in the distance.

Onward they went, until they saw Jack-o'-Lantern's ragged figure and pale face by the red light of the link which he held up aloft.

"Both of yer all safe," cried the lad, gleefully, "that's all right."

"Yes, Jack, but we are hotly pursued."

"What, have they come as far as here. I should have thought that Moses wouldn't have stood that."

"Why?"

"Look!" said the lad.

Holding the link in such a manner that the red light should fall in one corner of the vault, Jack-o'-Lantern pointed to a heap of human bones which had been stacked there, and which had been polished by the rats.

"Moses knows all about that," said Jack-o'-Lantern, "he knows more nor he would like me to tell. But then Mr. Wild is as bad as the Jew, they're all in the same game."

"What are we to do now?" cried Batswing.

"We must go along with the rats," replied Jack-o'-Lantern.

"With the rats?"

"Yes, down the sewers."

Whilst this rapid communication was passing, the voices of the constables became louder and the lights of their torches shed a lurid glare throughout the vaults.

"Yield!" screamed Jonathan foaming with rage, "you have no chance of escape,. You have reached the end of the vaults and can fly no farther"

"Don't fire," cried Jack-o'-Lantern to Batswing who was about to discharge a pistol at Jonathan, "don't fire, but follow me."

Quick as lightning Jack-o'-Lantern rushed into a deep recess in which there seemed to be a well. Seizing the rope, the boy, still grasping the link, allowed himself to slide into the pit, at the same time calling to Batswing and his comrade to follow.

Without pausing to think the two men slid down the rope.

"Cut the rope so that they may fall into the water," cried one of the constables.

"Hold, fool!" shouted Jonathan, "there can be no water there, or they would not dare to have gone into the well. This is but some fresh secret passage. We must follow them."

The men all drew back, and looked irresolutely from one to the other.

"Cowards," thundered Jonathan, "do you fear to follow these men? Stand on one side and let me lead you."

Gnashing his teeth and foaming at the mouth with rage, Jonathan swung himself over the low parapet that surrounded the mouth of the well, and descended rapidly.

Ashamed at their own cowardice, the men quickly followed and soon reached the bottom of the shaft, which they found led into the sewers.

These sewers were formed of low brick arches, the sides of which were covered with a thick coating of slime and fungi. Down the middle of these tunnels ran a black, foul stream of water, in and out of which plunged huge water-rats, whilst strangely disgusting insects crawled round and about the cracks in the brick-work.

"There they are," cried Jonathan Wild drawing his sword and pointing towards the glimmering light thrown out by Jack-o'-Lantern's link, "remember they are to be taken dead or alive."

Forward rushed the men, but Batswing and Jack Sheppard had time to prepare themselves for the attack, and had intrenched themselves behind a buttress that projected a good way across the passage.

THE OUTLAWS OF EPPING FOREST.

71

Strong as their position was, Wild was not to be daunted by it, but shouting to encourage his men, he dashed forward in hopes of being able to make Batswing and Jack leave the stronghold.

But the two robbers were not to be so easily driven away: they waited until the men were only one or two paces from them and then discharged their pistols with such good effect that four of the constables fell, and amongst them the two that held links, so that Jonathan's party was left in darkness.

At first they fondly hoped that Jonathan was killed, as he was one of the first to fall; but such was not the case. His foot had struck against a loose stone over which, luckily for himself, he had fallen, thereby missing a bullet that otherwise would have blown his brains out.

With a yell of rage Jonathan sprang to his feet, and rushing forward again, would doubtlessly have cut down Batswing who was engaged in loading his pistols. But Jack-o'-Lantern, seeing the danger the highwayman was in, sprang quickly forward and dashed his link in Jonathan's face, blinding him with the flames and smoke, and searing his face with the hot pitch.

With a scream of agony Jonathan sprang back, but in doing so, he dashed the link from the lad's hand, so that it was extinguished in the water, and the combatants were left in utter darkness.

"Quick, follow me," said Jack-o'-Lantern, and seizing his comrades by the sleeves, he led them rapidly down the tunnels, stumbling and falling about in the darkness.

At length they all three paused, quite out of breath, and listened.

"What are we to do now?" demanded Jack.

"Do?" replied Batswing, "get out of this terrible place as soon as we can."

"Yes, but how? I don't know which way to turn."

"Neither do I."

"First let us listen if we are pursued."

They remained quiet for some time and listened attentively, but not a sound was to be heard but the rush of the waters and the drip, drip, drip, of the damp from the roof of the tunnel.

"No, they have turned back," said Jack Sheppard with a sigh of relief.

"They are lucky in knowing which way to turn," said Batswing, "cannot we get a light so that we may be able to find our way out of this wretched place?"

"There's not much chance of that," replied Jack-o'-Lantern, "everything in this 'ere place is as wet as wet can be."

"Cannot you find your way in the dark," demanded Jack Sheppard.

"Not if I don't know exactly where I am."

"You're a pretty rat, to lose your way," said Sheppard contemptuously.

"Perhaps I am," grumbled the boy, "but it strikes me if you were to confuse a rat as I have been confused, and then drop him down suddenly in a part o' these here passages, not telling him whereabouts it is, or he is: it strikes me that it would take him a plaguey long time to find his hole."

"True my lad," said Batswing. "Well the best thing we can do is to push on. The thought of being lost in this place is horrible. There is only one thing to my mind that is worse."

"And that is?" demanded Jack Sheppard.

"To be taken by Jonathan Wild."

"I agree with you there," laughed Sheppard; "but it would indeed be fearful to perish here—to lie here and be destroyed by hunger."

"I don't think you would die of hunger," said Batswing. "This horrible gloom and fœtid atmosphere would soon wear your strength out, and if once you fell down exhausted, the rats would soon complete the business."

"Do you know if anyone has ever died down here?" asked Sheppard of Jack-o'-Lantern.

"Yes," replied the boy; "there was one old fellow used to be chained down by a wall here. I think he was mad, leastways, for the short time he was alive he was always a-jabbering, but he didn't last more nor two days. I brought him some food, but he would not eat it."

The two men shuddered at the boy's story, and quickened their steps, as if doubly anxious to leave this charnel-house.

Onward, onward they went, now striking against a wall, and having to turn down winding passages, that crossed and crossed each other like a maze, so that there seemed but little chance of their finding their way.

Suddenly Batswing burst out into a hearty laugh.

"Why, what's up now?" demanded Jack Sheppard, feeling much inclined to join in the merriment in spite of himself.

"Why, what fools we have been," laughed Batswing, "to be stumbling about here as if we were hopelessly lost, when the clue to the maze is in our possession."

"How so?" demanded his companion.

"How so? Why, if we follow the stream, we must come out at last, either in the Fleet Ditch or the Thames. Of course these tunnels are all so constructed that the water will drain off at some outlet."

"True," replied Sheppard; "but if I know anything of Jonathan Wild, all these outlets will be carefully guarded, so that directly we show our noses we shall be arrested."

"Not arrested, I hope," replied Batswing, proudly. "Believe me, it will take a better man than Jonathan Wild to take Batswing alive."

"That may be," replied Sheppard; "but, for my own part, I should prefer to live for a little longer time, if it were only to spite Mr. Wild."

"I agree with you there," said Batswing; "but, as I said before, I would much sooner die fighting, than in this miserable den, like a rat in a hole."

"So would I. Still, we are not exhausted yet, and therefore I vote we should push on a little further, and explore more of this passage."

"Very well then," replied the Bat, "only keep close, so that we shall not miss each other."

Again they struggled onwards, groping about in the dark, until Batswing's hand touched a chain, which seemed suspended from the ceiling.

"Hallo!" he cried, "what the deuce can this chain have been put here for?"

Jack-o'-Lantern, on hearing the exclamation, hurried forward, and passed his hand up and down the chain, and then along the walls at either side.

"I thought so," he exclaimed. "This is the spot where the old man was chained."

"How do you know that?" demanded Jack.

"Because here is the chain that he was fettered to," replied the lad. "Besides, I remember the other chain being here as well."

"Well, then, how far are we from an outlet?"

"We shall have to make our way back again," replied the lad. "We're now somewhere close by Newgate."

"That is a comfortable reflection," laughed Jack Sheppard. "It seems to me a case of 'out of the frying pan into the fire.'"

"But where does this chain lead to?" demanded Batswing.

"Well, that there I can't say," replied Jack-o'-Lantern, "but it goes up a sort of well place, like that we came down."

"Then the best thing we can do is to climb up this and see where it takes us. Jonathan Wild most likely does not know of this place, so we have a much better chance of escaping unperceived."

"You are the leader," replied Sheppard, "and I will follow you."

"Good," said Batswing. "Draw your sword, and hold it between your teeth, so as to be ready for immediate action, should anything occur to make us stand on the defensive. Now are you ready?"

"Perfectly. Lead on, and we will follow."

Seizing the chain in his grasp, Batswing—whom the reader will remember had been used to a seafaring life—soon clambered up it, till at last he reached a small dungeon-like place, into which he sprang, followed by Jack Sheppard and Jack-o'-Lantern.

It was a terribly gloomy place, but little better than the holes they had just left. Still they were not quite without light, for from a small grating, high up in the wall, a ray of cold grey light fell upon the oozy floor.

"Well," said Sheppard, "I don't think we have improved our situation much by this move. I think we had better have gone back, as Jack-o'-Lantern suggested."

"There must be some outlet to the place," said Batswing, looking hastily round.

"I suppose there must. See, here are some steps," said Jack.

They mounted the steps, and came to a massive door, thickly studded with iron clamps and plates. They also discovered, to their amazement, that the door was bolted on the *outside*.

By Jove, this is strange," said Jack. "Where can we be?"

"It looks to me very much as if we were in Newgate," replied Batswing.

"Impossible," replied Jack. "There would never be a place left so open as this in Newgate. Why, it would be one of the easiest things in the world to escape in that way."

"I know not where we are," replied Batswing, "but wherever it is, the place is evidently guarded like a prison."

"A prison!" exclaimed a hollow voice close by them. "This is no prison. This is hell. The fiends come here to torment you. They load you with chains, and scourge you with whips."

The two men sprang back in horror, and turning their gaze towards the place from whence the voice came, beheld a human creature grovelling on the ground.

"In Heaven's name, who are you?" demanded Batswing.

"Who am I?" exclaimed the figure, in shrill tones, that showed the speaker was a woman. "Who am I? How should I know who I am? I am mad!"

"Mad!" exclaimed the two men, recoiling in horror.

"Yes, mad. And who would not have been, who has gone through all that I have? For years and years have I been chained down in this miserable place, with no one to speak to but the fiends who come to scourge me. Daylight is almost unknown to me. Saving the small speck that falls close by the mouth of that pit, the glorious light of day has been unknown to me for years."

"Poor creature," said Batswing, gently. "Can you not tell us your name?"

"My name! I have no name. No one cares for me; no one knows me."

"Believe me, we are your friends," said Batswing.

"Friends!" exclaimed the poor wretch, hastily—"friends! I had friends once, but they all left me through him. No, I have no friends."

"I know not what you have done," said Batswing, "but I am certain that no crime you could possibly have committed could deserve so severe a punishment, and therefore I am determined to set you free."

"Free!" cried the woman, nearly springing up, but her chain pulled her down again. "Free! you set me free! No, no, you do but come to torment me like the rest. You would make me more miserable—try to make me weep. Weep! that is impossible. The fire of hatred that burns in my breast has long since dried up my tears. I live now only for hatred and revenge."

"I fear, poor creature, that she is indeed raving mad," whispered Jack Sheppard. "Most likely her friends have good cause to keep her here."

"Friends!" cried Batswing, contemptuously. "What friends would treat a poor creature in this way? No, no, her madness, if mad she be, is caused by cruelty—the cruelty is not caused by the madness. There is some mystery in this matter, which I am determined to clear up."

"If you clear up all the mysteries that happen in this neighbourhood, you will have plenty of work on hand. But I love romance, and so will go with you."

"My good creature," said Batswing, approaching the woman, tell me how and why you have been placed here, and believe me, I will do all in my power to assist you."

As he approached her the woman moved uneasily, and endeavoured to claw at him like a wild beast, at the same time uttering a peculiar snarling noise, that was terrible to hear come from human lips.

"I think you have met your match, Captain," said Sheppard, scarcely able to keep down a smile at the precipitate retreat Batswing was compelled to make.

"Our presence seems to make her more wild," replied Batswing.

"Stop, see there!" cried Sheppard, pointing in the direction of the woman. "Look at the boy."

To their amazement, Jack-o'-Lantern had dropped on his hands and knees, and crawling to the woman, had placed his arms round her neck. Then, carefully but boldly drawing her head down, he kissed her gently on the forehead. The effect of this kiss was magical. The woman first stared wildly around her, and then fell sobbing on the boy's neck.

"This is wonderful," exclaimed Jack.

"Poor creature," said Batswing, "doubtless that is the first kiss she has had for many years."

After a little while the poor creature became more pacified, and commenced singing to herself, and rocking to and fro.

"You are not afraid that we shall hurt you now?" demanded Batswing.

"No, oh, no," she replied. "You, I suppose, are good spirits."

"I don't think many people would call us good," whispered Jack to his companion. "Certainly the *best judges* in the land would not."

"Can you not tell me why you are shut up here?" demanded Batswing.

"No," replied the woman firmly, "that shall not be told until the hour of my revenge."

"Do you not know to whose house this dungeon belongs?"

"Know!" cried the woman, "of course I do. There is but one man in all the world who has a house like this. But, mark me, the day will come, when, disgusted with the brutal work of the vile wretch, the people will tear the house to pieces, and expose the terrible instruments of torture and fearful dungeons. In that day the strongest man will tremble and turn sick at beholding all this man's baseness and cruelty."

The men turned cold as they heard her words.

"Hush!" she cried, "here comes his chief torturer. Hide yourselves, or you will be lost."

Batswing, Sheppard, and Jack-o'-Lantern quickly withdrew to a corner, where they remained perfectly concealed, and anxiously waiting to see how this painful scene would end.

They could hear the sharp click as the lock was unfastened, followed by the shooting back of heavy bolts, the jar of massive bars, as they were removed, and the rattle and clang of chains, as they were cast on the floor.

"By Jove, I *do* believe we are in Newgate after all," said Jack Sheppard.

Slowly the door swung open, and a tall, burly-looking

JACK THREW THE ROPE WITH ASTONISHING DEXTERITY.

fellow, carrying a huge bunch of keys, and a lantern, descended the stairs.

"So you're there, are you, you cat?" said the man, as he placed the lantern on the ground, and looked at the woman. "You've been at your old tricks again, have you, ramping and raging about. You'll have to have the whip, as sure as my name is Ralph."

Whilst the man was speaking, Batswing and his companion were able to observe the woman's face by the aid of the lantern.

She was a tall woman, of about thirty to thirty-five, although her imprisonment certainly gave her the appearance of being much older. Worn and haggard as she was, she still had enough of good looks left to show that at one time she must have been superlatively beautiful.

Her long dark hair fell in massive ringlets over her

No. 10.

bare shoulders, that shone out white as snow above her ragged, dirty dress. Her eyes, owing to the emaciated condition she was in, seemed of a tremendous size, and glittered with that peculiar fire caused by an unsettled brain.

"You're a nice one, you are," said the fellow. "If I were master I'd soon settle you. I'm getting tired of this sort of game. It ain't half strong enough for me. There's your food. I wouldn't give you any, only I suppose the master has some game in hand with you."

As he spoke he threw a small loaf of coarse black bread to the woman.

"Now you've got all the comforts, food and lodging all for nothing, you're not grateful. You never even say thank you."

As he spoke, the man kicked the woman spitefully on the leg; but she neither showed marks of pain nor hatred.

"So nothing will break your spirit I see," said the man, savagely, "I haven't come without my whip though, so you must not flatter yourself. I've got it with me, and what's more, I'm going to use it."

With a fiendish laugh the man drew from his breast pocket a small whip, with some nine lashes, in each of which small spikes of metal had been cunningly inserted.

The woman drew her lips tightly together as she saw this dreadful implement of torture, and a slight moan escaped her as the man, twisting it round, made the thongs whistle through the air.

Baring his brawny arms, the man prepared to deliver the lash across the body of the shrinking woman, but at that moment Batswing dashed forward and felled him to the earth with one blow.

Quickly wrenching the whip from his grasp, Batswing delivered it with all his might and main over the broad shoulders of the scoundrel, who writhed with pain at his feet.

At length, worn out with his exertion, Batswing desisted, and ordered the fellow to rise.

"As I live," said Batswing, as he held the lamp close to the man's face, "as I live, it is Jonathan Wild's brute of a henchman and jailer."

"By heavens, so it is," exclaimed Jack Sheppard, "he shall not escape us now."

"Hold!" cried Batswing, catching Jack Sheppard's arm, as he was about to run his sword through Rough Ralph's body, "he must not die so honourable a death as that, besides, we must make him useful."

Turning to Rough Ralph he said quietly—

"If you refuse to do as I tell you, you are a dead man. In the first place, hand me those keys and all you have in your pockets."

With a low groan the man complied.

"Now," continued Batswing, "retire behind that buttress and undress. Mind, no loitering. Captain Sheppard will watch to see that you make haste, and in case you should not be quite as quick as we may require, he will take the whip to encourage you."

Rough Ralph hastened behind the buttress, and stripped as quickly as he could, but from the rapid way the whip fell, it was evident that his agility did not satisfy Jack Sheppard.

Quickly Batswing had found the keys that undid the locks confining the poor woman, who now rose to her feet.

"Quick, quick," cried Batswing, dress yourself in these clothes of your jailer's; they are far too large, but we must do the best we can."

In less time than it takes to tell, the woman was dressed in the man's clothes, and by Batswing's direction, mounted the stairs with Jack-o'-Lantern, so as to give an alarm should anyone approach.

"Now," said Batswing, "we will give you one chance for your miserable life: that is if you promise to make no resistance."

With chattering teeth Ralph gave the required promise.

"Very well then, Captain Sheppard please to bind that man."

The operation was performed with more dispatch than delicacy.

"Now blindfold him carefully," said Batswing.

Rough Ralph groaned as this was also done.

Suddenly he felt himself seized and lifted from the ground, and carried a little distance; then he was lowered cautiously down, until he seemed to be only held up by the wrist.

"I told you I would give you one chance for your life," said Batswing, in a solemn voice, "and I will keep my word, though never was there a villain who deserves death more than you do. The chance I have given you is this; grasp the stone on which I place your hands."

Rough Ralph felt himself lowered until his fingers were placed on the edge of a stone, on which he supported himself, vainly seeking for some ledge on which to rest his feet.

"I advise you not to struggle too much," said Batswing, "for you are now hanging on the edge of the well, and if you slip I would not answer for the consequences. Wishing you a very good day, we will leave you to your own meditations, which I am sure will be heartily pleasant if you reflect how you have helped to torture that poor woman whom I have just released.

In vain Rough Ralph sought to plead for mercy; his fear was so great that he could not utter a word.

In mute agony he heard the door closed, and the bolts and bars replaced. There he hung in the darkness, his fingers cracking with pain, yet unable to release them for one minute.

"Would any one come to release him?" was the thought that kept flashing across his brain, "or should he be dashed to pieces in the foul sewer below."

Whilst Ralph was enjoying those pleasant reflections, Batswing led his companions upstairs.

Door after door they had to unlock and lock again, until at last they found themselves in the main building.

"It is Jonathan Wild's house sure enough," said Batswing to Jack, "we must go to his office and see what disguises we can get."

Creeping cautiously along, they at length reached the place they sought, and Batswing at once entered.

"If I find him here," he whispered to Jack Sheppard, "he shall not escape, at least, not if I can help it."

"Nor if I can," muttered Jack.

But they had no cause for their fears, the room was quite empty.

"Now, Captain Sheppard," said Batswing, coolly, taking Jonathan Wild's usual seat, "if you will open and examine those trunks, I have no doubt you will find plenty of cloaks and hats that will do for disguises. In the mean time I will take a dip into Jonathan's private correspondence."

Whilst Sheppard clothed Jack-o'-Lantern, the woman and himself in long riding cloaks, Batswing quickly perused Wild's papers.

Many of them he destroyed, others he threw carelessly on one side, and the remainder he placed carefully in his pocket.

"Now we had better see to our arms," said Batswing at the same time taking down a splendidly mounted pair of horse pistols. "These will do for me, you had better choose what you like."

Sheppard and his companions quickly armed themselves, and the Bat noticed that a strange light seemed to burn in the woman's eyes as she clutched her pistols.

"Hush," said Batswing, "there is some one in the passage."

They waited patiently, but the footsteps passed the door and were lost in the distance.

"At all events we shall have a little money with us," laughed Batswing, as he took a heavy purse from a drawer, "but I cannot leave without leaving my acknowledgement with Jonathan."

Taking a piece of writing paper he wrote as follows—

"My dear Mr. Wild.—Driven by the vagaries of Fortune—assisted in her evil endeavours by yourself—I have been forced to take refuge for a short time in your house. Likewise, it has become necessary to borrow some riding cloaks, hats, pistols, money, &c., all of which I will return you when we have a little *friendly conversation*. I must say that your conduct—amusing as it has been of late—has not quite given me satisfaction. Still knowing you to be a greedy man, I have, to make up for the things I have borrowed, removed one of your prisoners from your care. Trusting you are well, have not lost your teeth, and that you will visit Ralph in his dungeon.—I remain, yours to command, THE BAT."

Carefully folding this note up, Batswing placed it on

the desk, then telling his companions to follow him, he left the room.

To his surprise he beheld two of Jonathan's myrmidoms standing in the hall.

Quickly placing his head inside the door he imitated Wild's voice so that the men might think Jonathan was in his office.

"Did you call, Mr. Wild?" he asked in a weak voice.

"Yes!" he replied in Jonathan's tones, "I did call you back to remind you to keep your word. Remember Batswing is to be in my house to-day or you forfeit your reward."

"He shall be here when you least expect it."

"Tell my men not to disturb me. If any one comes particularly for me they must send their message by Rough Ralph."

Closing the door carefully Batswing walked up to the jailers.

"Why how the devil did you get in here?" demanded the men with surprise.

"Why at the door to be sure," replied Batswing.

"Who let you in?" demanded the man suspiciously.

"Jonathan Wild, the great thief-taker himself," replied Batswing, "he is now busy in his office, and he told me to tell you that he would not be disturbed unless by Rough Ralph, and now open the door and let me begone, for I've business of importance to do before night."

"Ay that you have, if you carry out what you said just now," said the man with a grin.

"Oh! so you overheard what I was to do?" said Batswing as if in surprise.

"Of course I did. Mr. Jonathan don't speak like a woman."

"That's true at all events, and so good bye. You'll see me soon."

"And Batswing?" enquired the men.

"When you see me, you will see him," said Batswing, "I shall certainly not come without him. So look sharp out for me."

With a friendly nod and a pleasant laugh, Batswing took the woman by the arm, and waving his hand to the jailers hurried down the street, followed quickly by Jack Sheppard and Jack-o'-Lantern.

"He's a rumm'un he is," said one of the men, leaning up against the door post. "Well, Mr. Wild do get hold of some queer ones at all events."

"Only to think of the master creeping into the house and we not knowing it."

"He must have come in when Rough Ralph was in charge."

"I suppose he must. Lord how wild he is about this highwayman. I never saw him in such a fury. You see the fellow lets them all in. There's Mr. Pitt the governor of Newgate, see how he's been done and—"

"By jingo so have we," screamed the other man.

"What do you mean?" replied the other turning pale.

"Why, that Mr. Wild ain't at home at all; for there he is coming down the street with that red-nosed friend of his, and both seem in the devil's own temper. It strikes me we're in for it."

CHAPTER XXII.

JONATHAN WILD DISCOVERS HE HAS BEEN ROBBED.

THE two jailers stood horror-stricken as they beheld Jonathan Wild coming towards them, the more so as they could see that the thief-taker had evidently been badly wounded, his face being all the colours of the rainbow.

"What are you fools staring at?" cried Jonathan, passionately, as he saw the men's pale faces; "have you never seen a man who has received a blow in the face before?"

"I beg pardon, sir," stammered one of the men, "but something very strange has happened here; in fact I don't know exactly how to make it out."

"What do you mean," cried Jonathan, whose profession made him suspicious.

"Why, sir, I mean that there has been a queer game played here."

"Tell me what it is at once," shouted Jonathan, grasping the man by the throat, "or by heaven I'll murder you."

"Please sir it's not five minutes ago when we heard your voice in your office, and—"

"My voice in the office!" exclaimed Jonathan, "how could that be, when I have only just returned home?"

"That's just what astonished us, sir: and after that, sir, four people came out of the office, and we heard you—or that is—a voice like yours, command that they should keep their promise, and deliver up Batswing to-day, and then they all went away: the last one telling me that when he returned Batswing would be close at hand, and—"

"Fool, idiot, dolt," screamed Jonathan, "that must have been Batswing."

"But how could he possibly have got in here?" demanded Lord Redfern.

"How can I tell," replied Jonathan, sharply, "he seems able to go anywhere."

"I know he never came in by this door," said one of the jailers.

"Stop," cried Jonathan, "you say they were in my office?"

"I saw them come out, sir."

"Then there we shall find an explanation of this mystery."

"How so?"

"Batswing, if it should have been him—is not the man to let an adventure like this pass without claiming the authorship. Follow me my lord, I fear that you may be deeply interested in this."

With rapid strides he advanced up the passage and entered the office. No sooner did he perceive the confusion everything was in, than he uttered a deep groan and fell back into a chair.

"They have evidently been here," said Lord Redfern, "have they robbed you of any money?"

"Worse, far worse," roared Jonathan, "they have robbed me of papers that I cannot replace. They were secrets belonging to great families and were invaluable."

Lord Redfern could not help a smile of satisfaction passing over his face: for he was painfully aware that Jonathan held certain documents relating to him, and which he devoutly hoped had been destroyed with the rest.

"See!" exclaimed Lord Redfern, "here is a letter addressed to you."

Seizing the note, Jonathan Wild tore it open and read the contents, which we have already mentioned in our last chapter.

Crumpling the letter up in his hands, he paced up and down the room, foaming at the mouth like a wild animal.

"I do believe that this fellow is more than human," said Redfern.

To this statement Jonathan only replied by a contemptuous exclamation.

"I really am sorry for you Mr. Wild," continued Lord Redfern, "but I do not see that this great agitation can do any good. I think it would be far wiser to set about discovering how he came in here, and also how to counteract any ill effects that may arise from his having read your private papers."

"You take the matter very coolly," answered Jonathan.

"Why should I not? If I were you I would enquire into the trustworthiness of my men. They must have betrayed you."

"They are true enough, my lord: they would not deceive me, for I could bring either of them to the scaffold at any moment I like. You see I hold power over the highest and lowest people."

Jonathan said this in such a pointed manner, that Lord Redfern turned pale and bit his lip.

"You are too hot, Mr. Wild," he said, "it would be better if you would be calm."

"*You* may be calm," cried Jonathan, laughing savagely, "for you think that you are free from any evil caused by this man. Ho! ho! ho! how little do you know the danger that hangs over you. Ah! your lordship turns pale now and trembles: you don't seem quite as calm as you were just now, eh, my lord? Ho, ho, ho!"

"In heavens name, what do you mean?" cried Redfern, "how can I be injured by this affair?"

"Listen my lord," said Jonathan Wild, in bitter tones of hatred, "some years ago a certain gentleman became mixed up with a beautiful girl named Maud. How far this love affair was carried I need not state, but the beautiful Maud became a mother. Your lordship seems terribly agitated."

"Why do you tell me this?" demanded Lord Redfern, passionately.

"Because it suits my humour," replied Jonathan, "I like to see others suffer: you complained about my heat just now; don't you think that it would be better to be calm? I am calm. But to continue: Maud and her child became troublesome to a certain nobleman, over whom she seemed to have some immense power. So it became necessary she should be put out of the way."

"Fiend, devil," cried Redfern, "why do you torment me thus?"

"That I will tell you presently," said Jonathan, who seemed quite calm now, "a reward of one thousand pounds was offered for anyone who would remove the mother and child—that reward was accepted."

"Yes, by you," cried Redfern, "you murdered them, not I."

"Pardon me my lord, but I did no such thing."

"How so? you gave me your word—"

"My word, ho, ho, ho!" laughed the thief-taker, "why, lying is part of my profession. How do you think I should get so many men into my power, if it were not for swearing eternal friendship to them, while all the time I am planning their death. Bah! you are a fool, my lord."

"Then," faltered Lord Redfern, "she is *not* dead."

"She is not."

"Then you deceived me?"

"I did."

"And the baby?"

"That I believe is dead."

"Who killed it?"

"Maud."

"Maud! impossible."

"No one else did, if she did not."

"Why did she do so?"

"To save it from its father's cruelty. She became deranged."

"Then she *is* your prisoner?"

"She was."

"Was?"

"Yes: but Batswing has rescued her," said Jonathan.

"This must be seen to," cried Redfern, springing up and pacing up and down.

"You are too hot my lord," laughed Jonathan, "it would be better if you would be calm."

"You mocking devil!" exclaimed Redfern, "you shall answer for this."

"So should we both if it were tried at court," said Wild, "but you need not fear that. The only witness to appear against us is Batswing, and he dare not appear in court."

"Dare not! he seems to dare almost anything," groaned Redfern.

"Come," said Jonathan, "we must examine the vaults and remove anything that may create suspicion should a search be made."

Summoning his men, Jonathan led the way down into the grim vaults below the house.

Door after door he unlocked, and looked to see if the prisoners confined in the rooms were safe, at the same time expressing no little wonder and satisfaction at finding them all there.

At length they reached the dungeon where Batswing had discovered the poor woman, and Jonathan at once threw the rays of the lantern he carried towards the spot where she had been chained.

"She has gone, my lord, as I told you," he cried.

"And in this place she was confined," said Redfern, scarcely able to suppress the sickening sensation that crept over him.

"Yes, for some fourteen or fifteen years. It's a long time, my lord."

"And the child?"

"She threw down that well. At least it disappeared, and therefore she must have done so, that being the only way I can account for it."

This conversation had been carried on in a low tone, so that the jailers might not hear the substance of the conversation.

Turning to his attendants, Jonathan ordered them to remove the chains.

At that moment a weak voice was heard suing for mercy.

"Do, good, kind gentleman," exclaimed the voice, in tremulous accents, "take me from this dangerous position. My fingers cannot hold on much more, and I shall be dashed to pieces. I will betray Mr. Wild's secrets to you, if you will only release me. I am not fit to die."

With a quick glance Jonathan Wild took in the meaning of everything, and signing to the rest to be quiet, commenced cross-questioning the man.

"Do you promise to turn against Jonathan Wild, and tell all his secrets?"

"Yes, yes, if you will only release me from this position."

"Will you assist us to release all the prisoners confined in this house?"

"I will, I will."

"And will you give us keys, so that we can enter this house when we like, and, with your assistance, murder Wild?"

"I will, indeed I will," cried the man. "Only do release me."

"I *will* release you," cried Jonathan, drawing a pistol, and with the butt end of it smashing the fingers of the wretched creature, thereby compelling him to release his hold.

With a yell of agony, Rough Ralph left go of the stonework, but, to his astonishment, he fell unhurt on the floor of the dungeon.

A shout of laughter burst from the other men as Rough Ralph tore the bandage from his eyes, and gazed round him in wonder.

"You cowardly villain," exclaimed Jonathan, presenting the pistol at the frightened man, "if it were not that your malicious cruelty is useful to me, I would this instant blow out your brains."

"But how is it I am not in the well?" gasped Ralph.

"You never were in it," replied Jonathan. "They had merely placed you hanging to the side of the staircase, your feet being within two inches of the ground. They were more merciful to you than you would have been to them."

"Merciful!" growled Ralph. "I suffered the torments of the damned whilst hanging there. I'll never forget them."

"Them?" inquired Jonathan. "Who were they, then?"

"Batswing and Jack Sheppard."

"So," cried Jonathan, "these two have met together, have they? This must be stopped at once. My lord, you had better retire home, and remove a certain person out of London. Do you understand me?"

"Yes," whispered Redfern; "you mean Alice Landor."

"I do. At present we must keep quiet. This well must be covered in at once. You must see to that, Ralph."

"I! How am I to work with broken fingers?" growled the man.

"Your fingers would not have been broken if you had not been a coward."

"How was I to know where I was hanging?" cried Rough Ralph. "I was blindfolded. I felt them lower me down."

"Yes, from the top of the stairs."

"Yes, but I could not tell that. Get some one else to see to the closing of the well. I will have none of it. No work shall my hands do, save in the way of locking doors, chaining prisoners, or torturing, until I have had revenge—deep, deadly revenge."

Jonathan looked with delight at the evil countenance of his assistant, and grinned an approval of what he had said.

"You are right, Ralph," cried Jonathan. "Your crooked fingers will remind you of the injury you received. Seize Batswing, and you may tear him limb from limb, provided you leave enough of him to be recognized. Have revenge."

"I *will*," said Ralph, with a strange look at Jonathan.

CHAPTER XXXII.

HOW BATSWING OBTAINED TWO FRESH RECRUITS TO HIS BAND.

WHEN Batswing and his companions left Jonathan Wild's, they walked towards Smithfield, and then, turning quickly round to the left, crossed into Gray's Inn Lane, down which they made their way until they crossed Holborn; then, passing through Lincoln's Inn, they finally arrived at Drury Lane.

Not a word had been spoken. Batswing had led the woman by the arm, supporting her tottering steps, for her numbed limbs almost seemed to refuse to do their natural office.

Jack Sheppard and Jack-o'-Lantern followed at a little distance, so as not to attract more attention than they could possibly help.

Casting a glance back to see that his friends were following, Batswing led his companions down the narrow passage leading to the "Blue Boar," and tapped gently at the gate in the rear of that hostelry.

The door was soon opened, and once more the burly figure of Toby Crick, pipe in hand, stood in the entrance.

"Bless my soul alive! why, what's up now?" wheezed Toby. "Who in the name of fortune have we got here, and what do you want?"

"Shelter, Toby," said Batswing, raising his hat, so that the landlord might see his face. "Shelter for myself and friends."

"Bless my soul alive, you can't be in trouble again," said Toby.

"I am sorry to say that I not only can, but that I really am."

"I can't tell how you get through with it all," said Toby; "but follow me, and I'll do the best I can for you."

"There are no robins in the house, are there?" demanded Batswing.

"No; but I'd plenty of them last night," replied Toby, "but it wasn't you they were after. Still it was better that you had made yourself scarce, for they poked their noses into all sorts of places."

"Who were they after, then?" demanded Batswing.

"Why, Jack Sheppard. It appears he was at the "White Hart," some doors higher up than this. Well it got wind, and some constables were sent to arrest him, but he either wasn't there at all, or he escaped."

"He was as certainly there as he is here at the present moment," said Jack.

"Bless my soul alive, what do you mean?" demanded Toby Crick.

"Why, that I am Jack Sheppard."

"You?"

"Yes. Do you see anything particularly wonderful in that? I don't."

"But how did you escape?" demanded Toby.

"That you shall hear another time," said Batswing. "At present we must have a regular change of clothes. To be seen in these would secure our ruin."

Taking out the money he had stolen from Jonathan Wild's drawer, he directed Toby to proceed at once and buy clothes for all the party.

"But look here, Cap'pin," said Toby, "I can get you a good suit, and I have no doubt the other gentlemen can be fitted, but the lady?"

"Needs a disguise more than any of us," replied Batswing.

"But I don't understand women's fal-lals," pleaded Toby.

"I want no woman's dress," exclaimed Maud, suddenly looking up. "Give me a man's dress. I have a man's heart, my woman's nature is dead. I live now for one settled purpose, and have the courage and energy of a man to carry that purpose out."

They looked at her flashing eyes and tightly-pressed lips in wonder.

"And what may that purpose be?" demanded Batswing.

"You found me, and yet you ask me that!" cried Maud, fiercely.

"I guess what you mean. You would be revenged on Jonathan Wild."

"Ay, that would I, and on——" Here she paused suddenly.

"And who is the other person?" demanded Jack Sheppard.

"What is the use of telling you?" said the woman, passionately. Then, turning quickly to Batswing, she continued: "Do not think that I am ungrateful for the services you have rendered me. Far from that. I would serve you, follow you. From what I hear, I guess your profession to be——"

"That of the road," replied Batswing. "It is a dangerous life, but freedom is everything to me. Besides, I too have wrongs to redress."

"Will you let me follow your fortunes?" demanded the woman, eagerly.

"By Jove!" laughed Jack Sheppard, looking at the woman's handsome, but worn face, "this is a case of love at first sight."

"Silence!" said Batswing, sternly. Then, advancing to the woman, he took her kindly by the hand, and said to her,

"I fear you scarcely know the difficulty attending my granting what you ask. In the first place, my life is one of danger."

"Danger!" interrupted the woman. "I have borne too much ever to feel fear. What could give me more pain than I have already received?"

"That is true; but you now need ease and rest."

"Rest! ease!" cried the woman, with a short, scornful laugh. "What words are these to speak to me. I can have neither rest nor ease until my destiny is fulfilled. Let me follow you, and I will serve you faithfully to the last. Believe me, that during those long hours of darkness and solitude, I have had strange and awful visions. I knew you would come, and I knew you would grant me my request. Tell me, you will do so?"

Batswing paced up and down the room, not knowing what to do, when Jack Sheppard broke in,

"Look here, Captain," he said, "I have not the honour of knowing this lady's name. I say 'lady,' for there are two things that convince me she is so. In the first place, her speech and manners show it, and in the second, that fiend Jonathan would never have cared about keeping a poor person in such a place. No, had that lady been poor, she would have had a bath in the Fleet long before this."

"What you say is true," replied Batswing; "but how does that help me in coming to a determination of what to do in the matter?"

"Why, this much. If, as I suspect, this lady is valuable to Wild, he will do everything he can to recover possession of her, and I certainly think he will succeed, unless you grant her your protection."

"I fear you are right," said Batswing.

"Besides," whispered Jack Sheppard, "her imprisonment has evidently affected her brain, so that a change of air at Epping will do her a great deal of good. And again, she gives you a hold over Wild."

"Let it be so, then," said Batswing.

"You consent?" exclaimed the woman, joyfully.

"I do. Now go and change your garments. And, landlord, see that this lady has proper refreshment."

Toby Crick, who had returned with the clothes, bowed to Batswing, and led Maud from the room, handing her over to one of the maidservants, to see that she was properly attended to.

In a very short time they all re-assembled in Toby's little private room, and certainly it was wonderful to see the change that dress had made in the woman and Jack-o'-Lantern.

Toby's idea of dress was somewhat of a gorgeous kind, and therefore he had selected four of the handsomest suits he could find at a second-hand clothes shop.

The clothes, which were of velvet, were nearly new, and braided with gold and silver lace, so that the party had much more the appearance of the fops who strolled about in St. James's Park, than people who had only escaped by great daring from Jonathan Wild.

Maud had so arranged her hair that it was quite concealed under her hat, which she wore cocked somewhat defiantly, but altogether she made a very pretty cavalier.

Batswing's eyes wandered in admiration over Maud's make up, and then fell upon Jack-o'-Lantern, but no sooner did they do so, than the outlaw burst into an uncontrollable fit of laughter, in which he was joined by Sheppard.

Poor Jack-o'-Lantern looked anything but happy in his fine clothes. He held his hands carefully away from his sides, so that they might not touch his dress to soil it, whilst the uneasy way he twisted his neck about showed that he was not used to collars.

"What are yer a laughing at?" demanded Jack-o'-Lantern, sharply, and turning very red. "I don't want to be made game of, and I don't care about your clothes, that I don't. I didn't save you from Mr. Wild for what I could get. I did it because I 'ates peaching, that's what I did it for."

Maud placed her hand on the boy's shoulder, and drew him towards her. There seemed to have grown up a strange sympathy between these two, ever since Jack had crawled to her side and kissed her.

"Nay, I meant you no offence, my lad," said Batswing. "Indeed, we all owe you a debt of gratitude, which I shall only be too ready to try and repay. But you must be more at ease in these clothes, or you will be suspected directly. Swagger more, put your hands

in your coat pockets, and don't talk more than you can help."

Jack-o'-Lantern grinned, and walked across the room.

"That is better, much better. Now you must give me a full description of the house you saw the man carry the woman into yesterday."

Jack-o'-Lantern performed this task with an exactitude that made all mistakes impossible.

"Good," said Batswing. "Now, can you ride a horse?"

"I can hold one," said Jack-o'-Lantern.

"But can you hold on one?"

"I think I can," said Jack, scratching his head, and staring.

"Well at all events you must try; for you must accompany this lady to Epping. Toby Crick, see that two horses are made ready immediately—I trust madam that you will not be inconvenienced by having to ride on horseback; to travel any other way would be dangerous."

"I have no fear sir, as I am a good horsewoman."

"But now you must be a horseman," laughed Sheppard.

"And also you may have to use fire-arms," continued Batswing.

"I shall do my best Captain," replied Maud, "to deserve your esteem."

"Good, what name will you pass under?"

"Any; you choose: all are the same to me."

"Then take that of Malcolm, Captain Malcolm, you can say you have been in some of the foreign armies. Jack must travel as your servant."

"He had better have another name," said Sheppard, "Jack-o'-Lantern is too well known."

"You are right," replied Batswing, "what shall we call him?"

"You may call me what you like," replied the boy, "but there are only two names I'll answer to."

"And what may they be," asked Sheppard.

"The one I 'ave now, and the one the t'other link boys used to call me?"

"And what was the last."

"Old Flick and Flicker."

"I think we may dispense with the first name and also the adjective, and keep to the Flicker. So, Captain Malcolm your squire, Master Flicker, is at your service and I advise you to mount and be off. You must stop for half an hour at the Bird Cage Inn at Stamford Hill. Master Flicker must ask for one Jerry Blinker; show him this ring and he will take you to the merry smith's to whom you must give this note, and he will see you safely to Epping. And now mount and be off. I have looked at the pistols in your holsters, and they are all ready for service, so if occasion should call for action do not be afraid to use them. Remember that he who has first shot has the best chance."

Maud—or as we shall now call her, Captain Malcolm, sprang lightly into her saddle, and waving her hand to Batswing, rode away through the inn gate.

Jack-o'-Lantern—now known as Flicker—scrambled into his saddle and followed at a slow trot, his elbows and legs jerking about like those of a marionette.

"Well this is a strange adventure," said Jack Sheppard when they had seen their new friends off.

"It is indeed," replied Batswing, "an adventure that has not yet ended."

"I think she will turn out a rare woman," said Jack.

"Yes; and a bold one: she has learned the sad lesson of despair."

"And what are you about to do now?"

"Go to St. James's Square to rescue Alice Landon."

"Take my advice, do not go there till dark, or at least dusk. Then I will meet you, and if we cannot get in by the door it shall go hard if we do not get in by the window."

"Agreed; then at dark we meet in the Square, till then adieu."

CHAPTER XXXIII.

THE ATTACK ON THE HOUSE IN ST. JAMES'S. MURDER OF TABITHA OSSLETON. THE HOUSE ON FIRE. NEWS FROM THE CAVE.

Cold and chilly came on the dusk of the evening. A cold east wind came in heavy gusts round the corners of streets, freezing the people who were forced to be out and causing them to hurry quickly onward to their houses.

Cold and cheerless as the night was, two men, dressed in thick black riding cloaks, mounted their horses and rode slowly away from the Blue Boar Inn.

Passing out into the Strand, they travelled westward, pausing for a few moments by the Mall, where they met a closed carriage.

"Have you everything prepared James?" demanded the first horseman.

"Yes sir, everything," replied the man.

"And you know my directions. If a lady is placed in this carriage, never mind by whom, you will drive off at once to my house and see that she is well attended to."

"Very well, Mr. Marvel," replied the man.

Slightly returning the man's salutation, Batswing, or Percy Marvel, rode slowly away followed by his attendant.

"Well, I'm blest if this 'ere ain't a rum caper," said Growling Teddy.

"What are you grumbling about now?" demanded Batswing.

"I'm not agrowling," replied Teddy, "only it does rather knock a fellow over to know that you are a highwayman and yet you have carriages and swell horses."

"Perhaps it is because I am a highwayman that I do so."

"It may be, but I don't see the good of mixing one's self up in dangerous matters by coming to look after a woman. Why the best of them, at the best of times, are a source of annoyance and trouble. But to go housebreaking for one don't seem to me right at all. I don't like it."

"Never fear Teddy; you will run no risk," said Batswing.

"That's the very thing as puts me out. Why am I not to have anything to do with it?"

"Oh! you shall if you like," replied Batswing laughing.

"Well, and what am I to do?"

"You shall mind the horses whilst I and my friend go after this lady."

"Bah! there's a lot of pluck wanted for that certainly," growled Teddy.

"Pluck or not; there is a quantity of patience and attention required. See, there is Captain Sheppard waiting for us, so no more grumbling."

Batswing dismounted and Sheppard did the same. Both then gave their horses in charge to Growling Teddy and walked in the direction of the Square.

"I have everything prepared," said Jack, "and have already reconnoitred the house; there is a stiff bit of wall to get over first, then there is the lower part of the house, which is so defended that any attempt in that quarter would be useless, therefore we must climb nearly to the top, where there is an unguarded window."

"I leave everything to you," said Batswing, "I do not understand this sort of thing."

"Then my advice is not to go to the front as you proposed, but to the back, and break in. If we knock and alarm them they will be on their guard, and most likely we shall be arrested."

"But Lord Redfern has committed as great a crime as we have!"

"Greater; only he is a 'lord' and we are simply men which makes all the difference. Besides, we have no authority over the girl; and you know Wild is spreading all about that she helped you to murder her father, and afterwards eloped with you."

"But no one can believe in such a false hound as Wild."

"I don't know that; some people believe in the Devil, so why not believe in Wild. But here is the wall, be careful and follow me. Above all, be careful not to make any noise."

Taking a rope which he had concealed under his cloak. Jack Sheppard fixed an iron grapnel to one end of it, then throwing it with great dexterity, fixed it on the top of the wall.

Up this they both climbed, and then, by the aid of the rope and grapnel, they managed to reach the roof of the house.

"Now then," said Jack, "to do a little bit of housebreaking."

Taking a small steel crow-bar from his pocket, he applied it to a window, which in a few moments he managed to open so cleverly that not a sound was heard.

They both sprang in and then stopped to reconnoitre their position.

They found themselves on a narrow landing from which a spiral staircase descended.

"This is a queer place," whispered Jack, "what is to be done now?"

"There is but one thing to be done," replied Batswing, "and that is to descend."

Slowly and carefully they crept down the stairs, now and then pausing to listen.

Not a sound was to be heard. All seemed so quiet that Batswing began to fear that the house must be uninhabited.

They arrived at last at the bottom of the stairs, which seemed to terminate in a wall.

"Why, how is this," said Batswing, "the place seems to have been closed in?"

"There is some secret door here, you may depend," whispered Jack.

"Hush!" exclaimed Batswing, "someone is speaking on the other side of the wall."

Placing their ears close to the wall they listened attentively and heard people speaking, and Batswing recognised one of the speakers to be Lord Redfern. The other voice was evidently that of an old woman.

"I tell you, Tabitha, that your temper is getting beyond bounds; you seem to imagine that because you have assisted me in one or two plots, you are to do what you like," said Redfern, passionately. "Such is not the case I do assure you."

"But why did you have that beautiful creature removed to the Castle?" said the old woman, who was no other than Tabitha Ossleton, "surely she was safe enough with me."

"I tell you she was not: Sir Arthur Bowring loves her, and that unearthly thief, Batswing, watches over her, and for aught I know, they are now on the track."

"She has been removed then," whispered Jack.

"Hush!" replied the Bat, "we may find out where she has been taken to."

"I don't believe a word of what you say," screamed the old woman, "you have taken her away to annoy me. I know what it is, there is money in the case, and you begrudge me my share; I'll let all be known about you, how you came home disguised on the night of the assassination of the old farmer, whose pretty daughter is now concealed at the Castle. I'll—"

"Silence." shouted Redfern, "or I will murder you."

"Ay!" screamed the old woman, "as you did old farmer Landon."

With a terrible imprecation, Redfern flew at the old woman, and seized her by the throat.

"Great heavens, he is murdering some one," cried Batswing, "let us try to force this door open."

Retiring a few paces up the stairs, they rushed forward again, and throwing the whole of their weight against the door, burst it open and tumbled into the room.

At the moment they did so, Lord Redfern had thrown off old Tabitha Ossleton, and drawing a pistol discharged it in her face, blowing her head to pieces.

"Villain," cried Batswing, springing forward, "your time has come."

But Redfern was too quick for them; stepping behind one of the pillars, he touched a spring, and a secret door opened through which he rushed, instantly closing it behind him.

"Help! help! murder! thieves!! murder!!!" Batswing and Jack Sheppard could hear him cry as he rushed down the passage.

"The game is up," cried Jack, "we are caught in a nice trap."

"We must follow him, and—"

"Be taken up for the murder of this old hag: who by the way, richly deserved her fate; but for all that, I for one, don't feel inclined to swing for her. What can be done? hark how he is shouting. Trust me, this murder will certainly be placed to our accounts."

"I fear it will, but we must do all we can to prevent it," said Batswing, "to follow him would be useless. Stay; I have it, help me to take down these oil lamps."

"Why, what are you up to now?" demanded Jack Sheppard.

"Don't stay to talk, but do as I ask you," replied Batswing.

Quickly seizing the lamps they placed them on the floor. Then heaping up the furniture, Batswing broke the lamps over them so as to saturate them with oil. This done, he lit the heap, which blazed in a fearful manner, quickly catching the hangings on the walls, and setting fire to the highly polished panels.

"By Jove, the house will soon be one blaze," said Jack.

"So much the better," replied Batswing, "there will then be no proof that we broke into it."

"Good, but if we do not make haste we shall be found here, for I can hear that a crowd is assembling."

"Then follow me," cried Batswing.

They retraced their step up the winding staircase and reached the top of the house, from which they descended by the rope. The grapnel was then quickly jerked off by Jack Sheppard and fixed to the wall, so that they were enabled to reach the ground in safety.

"We must remove the grapnel again," said Batswing, "or they will see that we have been there."

The iron was quickly removed, the rope coiled up, and the two friends hurried to where they had left their horses.

As they approached the spot, they were startled to see that Growling Teddy was not alone.

Another horseman was close by his side, and had evidently taken charge of Batswing's horse.

"This looks queer," said Jack.

"It does, still we need not fear, for unless there are some more men concealed, we are three to one."

"May not your servant have turned traitor?" asked Jack.

"Not he, he would die first."

Hurrying up to the spot, Batswing demanded in a loud voice, "who goes there?"

"Thank heaven, you have come at last," cried the new comer, whose voice Batswing immediately recognised as that of the merry smith's, "I bring you bad news."

"Bad news!" exclaimed the Bat, "speak man, what is it?"

"Jonathan Wild is in Epping Forest."

"Well."

"He has a band of soldiers with him."

"Yes."

"And the cave is attacked."

Seizing his horse's bridle, Batswing flung himself into the saddle, and putting spurs to his horse dashed rapidly away, leaving the rest to follow as best they could.

CHAPTER XXXIV.

MAUD AND FLICKER ESCAPE TO THE CAVE AT EPPING.

JERRY Blinker was standing as usual outside the Bird Cage Inn, leaning against the horse-trough and whistling in his ordinary monotonous tone.

Since Mr. Pitt's visit to the Bird Cage, Jerry had not been as lively as he generally was; indeed, the constant appearance of the constables or 'robins,' as they were called, owing to their wearing red waiscoats, gave Mr. Blinker considerable uneasiness. Passing his hand slowly round his lower jaw, Jerry felt carefully in hopes of discovering whether there was any chance of his whiskers and beard growing, so that he might be better able to disguise his features.

"I don't like it," he burst out, suddenly, "I'm blest if I do—the way that that there old Pitt looked at me made me feel as if I had a rope necktie on, choke me if it didn't. He made my blood creep and my back open and shut, that he did; but only to think of a reward being out for anyone who could grab Sir Harther, and no one to know about it, so that old Pitt let him off; why, it is as good as a play, blow me if it ain't."

He had scarcely finished these reflections, when hearing horses hoofs in the distance, he sauntered out into the middle of the road, and sticking his hands deep into his pockets, commenced whistling again as he watched the travellers approaching.

The travellers, who were no other than the so-called Captain Malcolm and Flicker, rode round to the front of the Inn and dismounted before Jerry left the road.

"Well, they're a queer pair," said Jerry, "the eldest one seems quite the swell, but I can't make out the other. Blow me if he ain't got off the wrong side of his horse; from that, and the way he walks, I don't think he's been very much used to riding. I wonder if they have much swag with them. Well, I suppose I must go and do the per-lite to them, in 'opes of getting a tanner."

Sauntering carelessly up, Jerry took charge of the horses, whilst Captain Malcolm and her young squire entered the hostelry and ordered some refreshment.

Jerry groomed down the horses, admiring their various points, and speculating as to who or what the two equestrians were.

In the midst of this operation he was somewhat startled by the sudden appearance of Master Flicker, who crept into the stable in a mysteriously steathy manner.

"Hillo," my young twopenny-halfpenny," cried Jerry, "what are you up to now? this ain't the way to the drawing-room, my young buck."

"If it were, I shouldn't expect to meet you," replied Flicker.

"You're a healthy specimen of humanity, you are," said Jerry, leaning on one of the horses and staring at Flicker; "you'd be invaluable in a farm to keep the birds off the crops—that you would."

"Well, I should be useful at all events," said Flicker, "which you ain't, and I'm blest if you're ornamental."

"You're a helegant bit of hanhatomy you are," sneered Jerry.

"You're another," retorted Master Flicker, jerking his chin forward to give double emphasis to his words.

"If you call me names I'll punch your 'ead," cried Jerry, losing his temper.

"You'd better try it," replied Flicker, "it takes a man and not a monkey to do that."

Both the lads' tempers were now thoroughly aroused,

MAUD DEFENDS THE SECRET PASSAGE.

and in a few minutes they were rolling over and over on the ground, struggling about and pummelling each other with all their might.

They continued this highly interesting amusement until they were forced to pause for want of breath.

Sitting face to face on the floor of the stable, they wiped the prespiration from their faces and the blood from their noses.

"You're not a bad sort after all," said Jerry, "what were you coming into the stable for; eh?"

"I was coming in to see if you could tell me where to find a lad called Jerry Blinker."

"Jerry Blinker!" demanded Jerry, in surprise.

"Yes, Jerry Blinker. Do you know where I can find him?" said Flicker.

"Why, what on earth do you want with him?"

"What's that to you?" replied Flicker.

"A great deal," retorted the other, "who sent you here?"

"I shan't tell yer," replied Flicker. sulkily, "I want to see Jerry Blinker, and that's enough."

"Oh, that's it, is it; well cast your h'optics this way and gaze on me."

"Well, what of you—you ain't a beauty nohow."

"That may be, but for all that I am the very identicle, Mr. Jeremiah Blinker, Esq., after whom you've been inquiring."

"Why did you not tell me so at first?" grumbled Flicker.

"Because you did not ask," retorted Jerry, "never mind, I like your pluck, and so let us shake hands and be friends."

"Agreed," cried Flicker. "I suppose we are likely to see a good deal of each other now, so that we had better not quarrel."

Jerry Blinker shook hands warmly with his new-found friend, from whom he now learned that Captain Malcolm was a lady, how Batswing and Jack Sheppard had escaped from the Fleet, by his—Flicker's—assistance; how they had rescued Maud from Jonathan Wild, and robbed him.

"And where is the Cap'pin now?" asked Jerry.

"He's off on some other caper," replied Flicker. "I don't know what; but my master—that is, my mistress, you know—wants to be off at once, so you had better make haste and take us to the merry smith's, as you call him."

"So your mistress, or master, is in a hurry, is she—he—or it?" demanded Jerry. "Then all I can say is, that she has not been fortunate in her choice of a messenger. But follow me, and I'll take you there. Wait a moment, though. I've been in too many scrapes lately to be pleasant, so I think you'd better tell your master that he had better leave the inn as if proceeding on his journey, and I will be in the road whistling, and he can follow me."

This precautious movement was readily agreed to, and so speedily carried out, that in a few minutes the whole party were standing in the smithy.

"This is a bad job, Jerry," muttered Bob Blow-the-Bellows. "I don't like it."

"What don't you like?" demanded Jerry.

"Why, the Captain is getting into too many of these unprofitable capers. This last one explains a good deal to me, that's what it does."

"Does it? Then I wish you would explain a little of it to me," said Jerry, "for I'm blest if I understand you at all. Hang me if I do."

"It don't need much explanation," said the smith. "Haven't you noticed anything queer on the road to-day?"

"No."

"I've seen two or three companies of soldiers marching towards Epping by different roads. Depend upon it Jonathan Wild is determined to hunt us down."

"Phew!" whistled Jerry, "that's pleasant. What is to be done?"

"You must go back, and I must ride to the cave with this—this——"

"Lady," said Maud, "for so I mean to proclaim myself. My troubles have made me strong, and as what I shall do will be in revenge of my wrongs, I would have the whole world know who I am."

"That is as you like, mum, of course," replied Bob; "but I don't care about my name being known. So, with your kind permission, I'll just walk some dozen paces in advance, and you can follow as if you did not know me. As for you, Jerry, go back to the inn, and mind you keep your eyes and ears open."

"All right, Bob, old boy. I'm off, and I wish you a safe journey." So saying, he thrust his hands deep into his breeches pockets, and strolled leisurely away, whistling softly and meditatively as he went.

The smith was soon on the road, conducting Maud and her Squire towards Epping. On his shoulder he carried a basket of the implements used in his trade, so as to have the appearance of going somewhere on business, thereby hoping to allay suspicion.

He had just turned round the corner of a lane, when a loud voice in imperative tones called upon him to stop, and on looking up, he beheld a horseman standing in the road, with a pistol pointed with unpleasant accuracy at his—the smith's—head.

"In faith, good sir, I think it is I who should ask you to stop," laughed the smith, "for if your hand moves at all it seems likely I shall be minus my brains in an instant. Oblige me by lowering that pistol."

All this the smith said in as loud a tone as possible; so that his companions might hear in time to prevent their turning the corner.

"I am in no mood for jesting," the man replied in a rough voice, which Maud at once recognised as that of her old jailer. "A woman and a lad have escaped from custody: have you seen them on the road?"

"I must confess I have seen many women and lads," replied the smith, "indeed it is somewhat difficult to walk a few miles without seeing one or other, for these creatures are plentiful; nay rather too plentiful, for they are both somewhat troublesome; therefore if you do not describe them how can I know."

"Dolt! blockhead!" roared the man, "dare to trifle with me, and I will kill you. The woman is a lunatic, the lad a link-boy."

"Then I have not seen them. Such a pair one could not miss."

Muttering some deep oaths Rough Ralph bade the smith proceed on his way.

Here was a nice fix—He could not turn back, as Ralph would have become suspicious and followed him, thereby discovering Maud and Flicker, who had drawn their horses up close to the hedge, where they could hear the conversation without being seen. What could he do?

Trusting they would turn back to his smithy, Bob-Blow-the-Bellows bade Rough Ralph 'good day, and marched away singing with all his might—

Oh a bird had flown away from its cage
Where it had been kept for many an age;
But it scarcely had spread its wings to fly,
When a hawk came swooping through the sky—
Fly pretty birdie; I pray thee fly,
And trust me that help will come by and by.

Maud no longer doubted the danger she was in. In a moment her resolution was taken, and turning to Flicker she whispered a few words in his ear.

Quietly they drew and cocked their pistols, then putting spurs to their horses, dashed round the corner and seized Rough Ralph, who had turned round angrily towards the smith to bid him stop his croaking.

"Money or your life," shouted Maud, placing a pistol close to Ralph's right ear,

"Silence or I fire," said Flicker, clapping another one close to his left.

Rough Ralph stared hopelessly from one to another; and his jaw fell when he saw in whose custody he was.

"Mercy; mercy, I pray you?" cried Ralph in abject terror.

"Mercy!" said Maud, "what mercy did you ever show me."

"I did not do it by my own free will," faltered Ralph, "it was all Mr. Wild's doings, I swear it was. He is answerable for all."

"If you would save your life," replied Maud, "tell me the reason of the soldiers being on this road."

"They are going to attack a band of robbers at Epping," said Ralph.

"Under whose command are they to do this? Answer, or I fire."

"Jonathan Wild's," replied Rough Ralph.

The smith, who had turned round on hearing the noise, was overjoyed at seeing how matters stood, and crept slowly back to where Maud and Flicker were standing, begging them, in the most abject tones, not to hurt him, and cringing at every step as if he feared to feel a bullet pass through his body.

At first both Maud and the lad were astonished at this behaviour, but the woman quickly perceived the smith's purpose, and, keeping her pistol planted firmly against Ralph's head, she ordered Flicker to dismount and seize the smith.

This the lad did with the greatest alacrity, evidently enjoying the joke.

"Now remove the pistols from this fellow's belt," continued Maud.

With a quickness and dexterity that showed that it was not the first time his fingers had visited other people's pockets Flicker transferred the weapons from Rough Ralph's possession to his own.

"Now," said Maud, turning to the smith, "I have

no wish to hurt you: far from it. I only wage war with the rich, and such fiends as this man. But you must obey my commands, or I shall have to hurt you. Remember, I am fighting for liberty and life. Now will you obey?"

"But, noble sir," commenced the smith, "my duty to the laws"—

"Silence!" cried Maud, sternly, as she presented a pistol; "I am desperate, and have no time to spend parleying. Your answer, Yes or no."

"Yes, yes; I will do anything to please you, only take away that horrid pistol."

"Well, then, have you any rope with you?" demanded Maud.

"No, no, my noble sir," faltered the smith, in well-dissembled fear.

"You must have something to bind him with," returned Maud.

"I have my belt—I can do it with that; and I think I have some thick iron wire in my bag," replied Bob Blow-the-Bellows.

"Then see that you bind him hand and foot securely," said Maud.

The smith, with apparent reluctance, but secretly with the greatest delight, strapped Rough Ralph's arms behind him, and then, bending his elbows so that his hands came before him, he bound them so firmly with wire that Ralph groaned with the pain.

He then fastened his ankles together in the same manner, and afterwards gagged him so completely that he could not utter a sound.

"Now, roll him into the ditch," said Maud.

"But, sir, he has done nothing to me!" expostulated Bob, mournfully.

"Either do it directly, or I put a bullet through you first, and another through him afterwards. Will you do as I command?"

Without waiting for another order, Bob Blow-the-Bellows raised his mighty fist, and drove it full into Ralph's face, which it would assuredly have deprived of all beauty had it possessed any to start with.

Rough Ralph had, of course, no chance of keeping his feet, as his ankles were bound together, and therefore he fell with a heavy splash into a muddy ditch.

"Now," cried Maud, "mount this horse and guide me to Epping. No faltering, or you die."

Quickly the smith mounted Ralph's horse, and Maud, taking one of the bridles and Flicker the other, they galloped quickly away, seeming to have the smith in charge of them as a prisoner.

Slowly and with great difficulty Ralph managed to crawl, or rather wriggle out of the ditch.

He was in a terrible plight, all covered with mud and bruises.

Seating himself on the bank, he contented himself with groaning inwardly until he was released from his anything-but-pleasant situation by the arrival of a party of soldiers for whom he had been waiting.

To these men he related how he had been attacked by highwaymen, carefully suppressing the sex of his chief enemy, and the cause of her being so. He also related how they had carried off the smith as their prisoner, for so well had Bob Blow-the-Bellows played his part of coward, that Rough Ralph never thought that there had been any complicity.

"If that be the case," said the sergeant, "it is evident that the Bat is at the cave, and that the rest of his bold crew are with him. Never mind, they will have soldiers to deal with this time, not cowardly thief-takers."

"It's all very fine for you fellows to go on as you do," cried Ralph, "talking about us, but it's my idea you may all get the worst of it. For all that, I wish you luck. For my own part, I have had too much of these fellows already, and shall therefore go back to London."

Grumbling heartily and deeply, Rough Ralph hobbled away towards the Bird Cage Inn, where he related the way he had been treated, and also how the merry smith had been taken prisoner.

"What!" screamed Mrs. Wapshaw, "Mr. Stephens, our merry smith, as we call him, fallen into the hands of those horrible men at Epping; here, Peggy, Maria, come one of you or I shall faint. Oh! I can't speak."

The latter part of the widow's speech was undoubtedly true, for, covering her face with her pocket handkerchief, she was so convulsed with laughter that she really could not utter a word.

However, the maids ran to her assistance, and, after a proper quantity of slapping hands, burned feathers, and sipping of cordials, the widow thought she had sufficiently recovered her equanimity to face Rough Ralph and condole with him with a serious face.

Jerry Blinker howled furiously when he heard the news of the capture of his favourite smith, and proffered his assistance to Ralph in plastering up his face.

Brown paper, vinegar, and pepper—the hottest red sort—he declared was the only remedy to be used. At first the jailer objected to this treatment, but Jerry plied him with drink, and then applied his remedy in the following style:—

He procured a huge piece of brown paper, which he saturated thoroughly in white vinegar; he then smothered it with Cayenne pepper, and afterwards clapped it on Rough Ralph's face, regardless of the effect it had on that gentleman's eyes, nose, and mouth. He then led him to some dark and dismal lanes leading over Clapton Common, and, assuring him that he had only to walk straight on to reach home, left him to proceed as best he could, his eyes nearly blinded, his face smarting, and he nearly choked by the pepper.

No sooner had Jerry completed this than he repaired to the inn and privately assured Mrs. Wapshaw of his intention of going to see "the fun," as he called it, at Epping.

"Why, you silly little varmint, you'll be shot," cried the widow.

"Can't help that, as the hangman said to the man who complained that the rope tickled him. I shall go. Ain't the merry smith there—your angel, your beauty?'

"Hold your tongue, do, Jerry," cried the widow; "I hate such stupidity."

"Do you; then why turn red at the mention of his name?"

"I don't; if I turn red, it's the reflection of your carroty head."

"Well, don't cast reflections yourself, widow," replied Jerry, grinning. "But give me a letter to Mrs. Paddick at Epping, and no one will touch me; they don't know as I know the robbers."

"Well, if you must go, I suppose you must," said the widow, as she scrawled a hasty note; "bring me good news of the smith and I'll give you a guinea."

Jerry seized the note and was not long in preparing for his journey; in fact, his toilet seemed to consist of scratching his head, rubbing his face and hands on a dry towel, pulling the ends of his necktie and buttoning up the flaps of his trowsers pockets. Then sticking his hat on one side, he commenced in his usual way, whistling a melancholy air that was supposed by his friends to be a correct imitation of the wind blowing through a keyhole.

Having done all this he started on his way.

The widow was sitting mournfully listening to the labourers' talk about the soldiers being on the road, when Jerry rushed back again.

"Missus," he cried, "a guinea."

"What for?"

"Good news."

"What good news?"

"Bob Blow-the-Bellows is all right, he has just galloped past at a furious rate towards London."

CHAPTER XXXV.

THE PURSUIT.   SUCCESS OF BOB BLOW-THE-BELLOWS'

SCHEME.   THE CAVE REACHED.

Clever as the ruse was that Maud had played upon Rough Ralph, yet her having to take Bob Blow-the-Bellows with her as a seeming prisoner was the very thing to call forth suspicion, especially as they perceived by glimpses that the country around was dotted over with small detachments of soldiers, all of whom were moving in one direction, and that was Epping.

"By Jove! I think it is all up with us this time," said the merry smith—his rueful countenance anything but carrying out his mirthful sobriquet, "it seems the whole place is filled with red-coats. Let us get on that knoll and we shall have a better view.

They galloped quickly forward, and having reached the summit of the eminence the smith had pointed out, gazed round them.

Small detachments of soldiers were moving slowly and steadily from different points towards the forest; their heavy accoutrements and cautious advance showing that they were not only prepared for fighting, but for a desperate undertaking.

"This is very beautiful," said Maud gazing at the lovely scenery.

"It may be," muttered Bob, "but it is d——d disagreeable."

"What's to be done now?" inquired Flicker, "had'nt we better turn back."

"What would be the good?" said Bob, "we should be arrested for certain."

For a moment all remained silently watching the soldiers.

"This is that fiend Wild's doing," said Bob, "and the worst of it is Batswing is in London."

"Who takes the command when he is away."

"I or Grumbling Teddy," replied Bob Blow-the-Bellows, "but Teddy is in town also, and I feel that I shall not reach the cave."

"The captain must be fetched," cried Maud impetuously, "and that at once."

"Easy enough to say that," replied Bob, "but where is he?"

"We left him at the inn in Drury Lane," said Maud.

"Oh yes, that's all right enough, but that is no reason why he should be there now. Most likely he is up to some such prank as he was last night."

"That's true," said Flicker sharply, "he is up to another prank, but I know what it is."

"You!" cried Bob Blow-the-Bellows incredulously."

"Yes, I know," returned Flicker proudly, "why, I put him on the lay."

"By Heavens that is lucky," cried the smith, "tell me where I can find him."

"He's gone to break into Lord Redfern's house in St. James's Square."

"Why what on earth has he gone there for?" demanded Bob.

"To rescue a gal as Redfern carried off t'other night," replied Flicker.

"What! Alice Landon."

"I don't know nothing about that, said Flicker."

"You must instantly return to Drury Lane," cried Maud, "there most likely you will hear where you can soonest find the Bat."

"That is all very good," replied the smith, "but how about you? you won't know the cave. It's true that ring and the watchword will give you safety if you could find the cavern, but I don't see how you can do even that."

"We must risk it," cried Maud, "there is not a minute to be lost."

"That's very true, as is also the fact that we must risk something, but we must think which is the best way to act before we make the attempt. Now whilst we are here we may not attract attention so much; or rather we can escape notice. I know the way. It certainly is a dangerous experiment but one we must try, for it gives us a better chance of escape."

"Well, well, what is it?" demanded the others.

"How many pistols have you?" said Bob.

"I have four," said Maud, "two in my holsters and two in my belt."

"So have I, with those I took from the fellow we left in the ditch," said Flicker.

"Good," replied the smith, "I have the same number, reckoning those in the holsters of the horse I *borrowed*, and my own, without which I never travel."

"But what of that? had we twice the number we could not fight these troops."

"Patience, patience," said the smith, "I have no intention of fighting them."

Taking the pistols from his holsters, he carefully extracted the bullets therefrom, looked that the powder was well rammed down and the priming right.

"Now," he said, "each of you must take one of these pistols and place them where you can seize them on the moment, and mind you don't seize the wrong one by mistake, for you will kill me if you do, as I am to be the target for you to aim at." .

"I do not understand you."

"Probably not; but if you will listen patiently you soon may."

"Go on then and excuse my impatience."

"Well then, you take me along with you just as if I were your prisoner; but we make straight to Waltham Abbey. No doubt we shall be pursued and fired at, and I only hope we may escape being killed or even wounded, but for that we must trust to fortune."

"I fear there is not much chance of our escape," said Maud.

"If any soldiers come too near, you two must fire at them," continued the smith, "and mind you bring them down."

"Never fear me," said Flicker, "I'll have a pop at the sodgers."

"When we are some little distance from the Abbey, I'll point out a wide ruined doorway to you; you must gallop through that, go to where the altar used to stand and touch the exact centre of a cross that is painted on the panel that you will see there. The panel will fly back and you and your horses will be able to enter, but mind and close the panel after you. Give the band warning of the coming attack, and see that all is prepared to defend the cave."

"How will they know my authority?"

"By that ring and the watchword, 'The Bat flies at night.'"

"Good, and you? What will you do?"

"When we are close enough to the Abbey to see the door, I will turn and pretend to strike the lad; you must leave go of my horse and I will turn and fly. Whilst you, to keep up the deception of my having been a prisoner and led away much against my will, must fire after me, but mind you don't use the pistols that have bullets."

"Never fear, we owe you too much to be careless."

"Good; the soldiers seeing this will let me pass and pursue you, so that you will reach the cave and I shall be able to carry the news to the Captain. You will not forget my instructions."

"No, we will perform them to the letter," replied Maud.

"Then let us not lose a moment in carrying them out."

Maud and Flicker each seized hold of the bridle of Bob Blow-the-Bellows' horse, and putting spurs to their horses, galloped in the direction of the forest.

They had not proceeded far when some soldiers called

on them to halt; but of course they only pressed on the quicker.

"Save me! save me!" called out the smith, in tones of anguish. "Save me, or I am undone. They are taking me to Batswing."

"Halt, or we'll fire," cried out the officer in command of the party.

"Yah!" screamed the smith. "Help! murder! I shall be shot. Don't fire, good gentlemen, don't fire, for the sake of a poor honest blacksmith."

"What are we to do?" roared the officer to his soldiers, as they galloped after our friends. "The man is evidently a prisoner."

"Yes," replied the other. "Still, we can shoot at the others."

"But if we happen to kill the smith by mistake?" said the Captain.

"Then it will be his fault for being in such bad company, that is all."

"Scarcely a good excuse," laughed the other, "considering he was forced into it."

"Forced into it! Why, he is big enough to eat both of them."

"That may be; but they are armed, and he may not be."

"Well, we won't use fire arms if we can help it; but don't let them escape."

Whilst this was going on, the smith had been shouting out at the top of his strong voice for mercy, and imploring the soldiers not to fire.

Helter-skelter, pell-mell, over hedges and ditches, crossing streams, crashing through underwood, across meadows and ploughed fields, on dashed the smith and his companions.

A party of farm labourers had drawn themselves up in one part of the road in battle array, their arms being composed of pitchforks.

At first this obstacle appeared insurmountable, but Maud drew a pistol and discharged it at their leader who fell into a ditch, howling terribly, and clasping his right arm just above the elbow.

Seeing their leader thus placed *hors-de-combat*, the rest took to flight, and our friends dashed down the road at a rattling pace.

"I can't stand their escaping," cried one of the men, "so here goes."

Bang! went his gun, and the bullet flew crashing just above the smith's head.

"There, I told you so," said the officer, "you nearly killed the prisoner."

"I think we had better do that than let them escape," was the answer.

"Hear how the fellow howls," laughed one of the men; "he is a veritable coward."

On swept the pursued and pursuers over the beautiful country like a hunting party, making the air ring with their cries, and the turf fly from their horses' hoofs, bespattering their garments with mud.

The Abbey, a fine old ruin, soon appeared in view.

"See, there is the Abbey," cried Maud; "we shall beat them yet."

"Yes, that is the Abbey, sure enough," said the smith; "and only just in time, for these fellows are gaining on us. But a few more strides, and we shall see the door, or rather the doorway, for the door has long since vanished. Yes, there it is yonder—do you see it?"

"Yes," replied both Maud and Flicker, "we cannot miss it."

"You know all about the panel behind where the altar used to be?"

"Perfectly."

"Good; and there is no time to be lost. That fellow is coming too close to be pleasant. I must see what can be done with him."

"Shall I 'pot' him?" asked Flicker, in delight at the chance of getting a shot.

"No; but get the pistols without bullets ready. Have you them?"

"Yes."

"Well, then, be prepared to let me appear to wrench the bridle from your hand. I shall aim a blow at you, my lad, so be ready to wheel your horse round to avoid it. That will give me a chance of turning my nag round. When I have fairly bolted, mind that you both let fly at me—point blank, mind. You can't hurt me. When you have done that, put spurs to your horse, and gallop as hard as you can to the Abbey."

"We will do exactly as you command us to do," said Maud.

"Now, then, are you all ready?" asked the smith.

"Perfectly."

"Then here goes," cried Bob Blow-the-Bellows.

Quickly the horse's head was swung round.

Bob aimed a heavy blow at Flicker, which that gentleman quickly avoided, but nearly lost his seat in the saddle by so doing.

In a moment Maud and Flicker drew their pistols and fired.

Crouching low in the saddle, as if to avoid the bullets, Bob Blow-the-Bellows uttered an unearthly yell, and putting his spurs into his horse, managed so well, that in his furious retreat he charged and overturned the two nearest soldiers, thereby increasing the fugitives' chance of escape.

Dashing along, regardless of the soldiers' execrations, Bob Blow-the-Bellows was soon some distance from the scene.

Twice was he stopped and questioned, but gave his answers so clearly and described Rough Ralph's treatment so well, that they allowed him to pass, wishing him a safe journey, and laughing at his country looks.

Meanwhile Maud and Flicker entered the Abbey.

Not a minute behind them came the soldiers, but to their surprise neither riders nor horses were to be seen.

"They must have merely passed through the Abbey," shouted the officer. "Come, lads, let us follow them. They shall not escape us."

Without pausing a moment, the soldiers rode as fast as their jaded steeds would carry them out of the other side of the Abbey, but, though they galloped far and near, they could not find the fugitives.

How Maud and her companion entered the cave, and what happened to them therein, our next chapter will show.

CHAPTER XXXVI.

THE ATTACK UPON THE CAVE.—BATSWING TO THE RESCUE.—HOW FLICKER FELL.—MAUD TRIES A DESPERATE REMEDY.—THE EXPLOSION.—THE FOREST ON FIRE.—RETREAT OF THE TROOPS.—VICTORY!

WHEN Maud and her companion entered the Abbey, they lost no time in discovering the secret spring, and touching it, had the extreme satisfaction of seeing the panel fly back.

They were only just in time, for they had scarcely closed the panel when the soldiers entered the ruins, expecting to trap their prisoners.

The fugitives paused for a while to listen if any search was made in the ruins, fearful that by moving they might cause some noise, thereby discovering their whereabouts.

They were, however, soon relieved from all anxiety, by hearing the soldiers gallop through the ruined Abbey.

They then turned to examine what place they were in.

It was a low vaulted chamber about twelve feet square.

At the further end was a passage, large enough to admit a horse.

This passage gradually descended, and evidently led to some subterranean cavern, that seemed to be very deep beneath the earth.

Maud and her companion were enabled to discover this by the aid of a pale gray light that shone through some crevices in the old ruined wall.

"There is no time to hesitate," said Maud, "our way, evidently, is down that passage, so let us be moving at once."

Seizing her horse by the bridle she advanced boldly down the passage, closely followed by Flicker, who regretted he had no link with him, for the place was so dark and so filled with loose stone that they stumbled at almost every step they took, as also did their horses.

The passage grew deeper and darker as they advanced.

Now and then there were quick and sharp turnings, and the place was so dark that these were difficult to see, and consequently they had great trouble in avoiding dashing themselves and their horses against the rough stone walls.

At length they perceived a light, and hurrying towards it, entered a vault.

It was a terribly gloomy place, the nitches at the sides lay filled with coffins. The arched and groined roof was hidden in the dust of ages.

Huge cobwebs swung listlessly about in a cold air that came mysteriously in this vault, which seemed to have no outlet except that by which Maud came.

"Well!" cried Flicker, "I'm blest if this 'ere ain't as bad as the Fleet. I don't think we can have missed our way; besides, look at this lamp already lighted and placed ready for our use."

"I don't think it is placed for our use," said Maud, "but it certainly shows us that the place is inhabited, so that we cannot be wrong."

"That is so: but we surely can't be caught in a trap?"

"Nonsense, why should we be? What good could anyone gain by that?"

"I don't know: unless that smith fellow has betrayed us."

"But why should he turn traitor?" asked Maud, "he can have no reason to do so."

"He may know that Jonathan Wild would give a handsome reward for you."

"True."

"And he might also think it time to make friends with Wild."

"That might be so. Still he looked too honest to deceive."

"Don't trust to looks," said Flicker, "I ain't a beauty but I'd die for you."

"And why?"

"'Cause you are so precious plucky—that's why I likes yer I suppose."

Maud smiled and laid her hands gently on the lad's shoulder.

"Time was when I would have scorned this poor boy's admiration and love," she thought, "but now the affection of this poor ignorant creature is most precious to me, making me almost forget my troubles and wrongs."

For a moment they remained silent, lost in thought.

"Do you really love me?" demanded Maud, in gentle tones.

"I do, upon my honor," replied Flicker, resolutely. "I'll follow you wherever you go, you see if I don't, and let anyone speak against you that's all. Oh, yes—and I wont break his head, not at all—Oh, no, o'course not."

Having delivered himself of this powerful, though not very elegant speech, Flicker took Maud's hand in his and kissed it fervently.

"Hush," said Maud, "that was surely the tramp of a horse's hoofs on pavement."

They listened attentively, and soon were convinced that the sounds came from the further end of the chamber, where there appeared to be a stone wall.

"There is some secret door here of which the smith forgot to inform us," said Maud.

"Well, all we must do is to find it," replied Flicker.

"That is much easier said than done," replied Maud, "this place is doubtlessly well guarded against attacks. Still we must try our best."

They advanced to the wall and examined it carefully, but without success.

Just as they were about giving up the search, Flicker noticed that one of the horses had advanced to a certain part of the wall and was sniffing at it.

"This must be the place," he cried.

They renewed their search with double vigour, and this time with success. They were about despairing when Flicker, perceiving an iron ring in the floor, pulled it in hopes of raising a trap door.

No sooner had he done so, than a clanking sound was heard, as if he had set a load of levers to work, and in a few moments a panel formed of thin stone, so that it might look exactly like the solid masonry which composed the rest of the room, rolled slowly on one side, disclosing a large stable containing a fine stud of horses.

They quickly entered, and seeing a ring in the floor of the stable similar to the one in the vault, they pulled it and the panel instantly closed.

"Now then, to litter up and rub down our faithful horses," cried Flicker.

"You are right," said Maud, "that must be done, for the poor animals are dreadfully worn, and heaven knows that they deserve well at our hands."

A few bundles of straw were soon strewn on the floor, and some hay and corn placed in the rack and manger for the horses, after this a drink of water was procured from a well that they discovered.

Whilst Maud was busy doing this, Flicker had been hard at work scrubbing down the animals; hissing away between his teeth to keep the short hairs which flew off from the animals from entering his mouth.

As the two worked with a will the task was soon completed.

"Now we must again pursue our discoveries," said Maud, "but this time I believe we shall join the band without further difficulties."

They advanced along a passage until they entered the chamber which had been fitted up by Batswing for Alice Landon, during her stay at the cave.

In this room they found stacks of arms, all ready for use.

Two rough looking fellows were loading them as fast as they could.

"Friends," said Maud, in a clear voice, "I bring you news."

With an oath the two men turned round, and seeing Maud and her companion, at once presented the muskets they held at the new comers, at the same time bidding them in rough stern voices to halt.

"You may as well put down your guns," said Maud in firm but kindly tones, "I am a friend, and as I said before, bring news from your captain."

"What proof have you of this?" cried the men, still presenting their muskets.

"His ring and this letter," cried Maud producing both.

"But the watchword, the watchword?" demanded the men impatiently.

"The Bat flies by night."

The two men lowered their guns, but told Maud to

keep where she was until they had summoned their captain, or rather the one who had command of the band, during the absence of Batswing.

This was soon done, and Maud very quickly convinced him of the truth of her story, in proof of which she showed Batswing's ring.

"I am afraid, madam, you have come in a bad time for your own safety," said the man, "for we are now preparing to defend the cave against the attacks of some troops."

"So I believe," said Maud.

"Still, in the secret vault you will be safe."

"Safe!" cried Maud, "I am here to fight and protect not to be protected."

"But madam—"

"Listen sir; this morning your captain named me his lieutenant, and therefore I claim to have the right of being second in command to you."

"But really I—"

"Let us have no more words," said Maud firmly, "I am determined, so now sir let me see what preparations you have made for the defence."

As she spoke she took the man by the arm, and he led her through the passages up to the cave in the forest, stopping now and then to examine the way the arms and ammunition had been placed ready for use.

The mouth of the cave was barricaded just high enough to let the defenders crouch behind it in safety from the enemy's shot.

A number of men were already crouched behind this defence, ready for action.

"This door covered by plastered mud," said Maud, pointing to that at the back of the cave, "will not stay the soldiers one moment if they cross the barricade; it had better be left open so that we can retreat by it if necessary."

"I think you are right," said the man, "but should they once enter that passage the secrets of the vaults will all be discovered. What shall we do then?"

"And if we are all taken prisoners, what good would all the secrets of all the vaults in all this vast universe be to us then?"

"True; how then would you propose to defend this passage."

"With my life! If the soldiers enter this cave I do not think they will leave it soon."

"I do not understand you."

"Perhaps not now; but when the time comes you will. Grant me permission to give orders for the defence of this passage."

"Willingly, for I freely confess that I see no way of defending it but at the swords point, and considering the number of the troops advancing upon us, and that they are led by Jonathan Wild, whilst our brave leader is away, I cannot look upon the defence but as entirely hopeless."

"When a leader despairs, the battle is nearly lost," said Maud contemptuously.

"Will you take the command then and be responsible?" said the man bitterly.

"Ay! that will I with pleasure," cried Maud.

The man looked at her flushed cheek and sparkling eyes, and read therein a fierce determination and powerful will, before which his own trembled.

Without waiting for an answer, Maud turned round and calling the men to her, addressed them as follows.

"My men. This morning I was with your captain and he sent me down here as one of your band, in fact as his lieutenant. You all know the great danger that now surrounds you. We have nothing for it but to fight, and mark me, I will lead you to victory. The first man who dares to use the word 'surrender,' shall die by my hand. I swear it; and I never broke an oath. If you are true and brave we can beat these men back and remain true and free as ever. If on the other hand you surrender, what have you to look forward to? The

gallows Do you think you will be pardoned? Who ever knew His Gracious Majesty to pardon anyone he could hang? Therefore you see that, by proving yourselves cowards and surrendering, you make death certain, and that an ignominious one; whilst by fighting bravely you cannot be worse off, whilst your fate will be glorious. Added to this we have the chance of victory or escape. For my part I choose victory or death."

"Victory or death!" shouted the men.

"Quick then," cried Maud, "bring six of those barrels of gunpowder from the vaulted chamber and place them here; just by the entrance of the passage."

This was done, and Maud had the barrels pierced and a quick match placed so as to connect them all together.

Scarcely had this been completed, when a musket bullet whistled through the air and flattened itself against the wall of the cave.

"Ha, ha!" cried Maud, "the game has begun, quick men to your posts."

The men had only time to run behind the barricade, when the regular tramp of men advancing at double quick time could be heard.

"Reserve your fire till they are close upon us," said Maud in a low voice as she knelt amongst the men and deliberately pointed her musket.

Suddenly the soldiers halted and discharged a terrific volley of musketry into the cave, but owing to the barricade the volley was ineffectual.

With a hearty, ringing cheer, the soldiers charged, in hopes of taking the cave by storm, but when they were but a few yards from the entrance Maud gave in clear, shrill tones the word of command

"Fire!"

A quick volley followed, and the soldiers recoiled, leaving many a dead comrade on the field.

The robbers gave a hearty cheer in honour of their success and quickly loaded again.

Once more the soldiers returned to the charge, and again they were forced to retire, with immense loss, from the fire of the invisible defenders.

Flicker, who had possessed himself of a musket, was in high glee, evidently attributing the whole success to himself, as indeed in one way it was, for had not he saved Maud? and she by her courage and coolness, had made the men firm and determined.

A short painful silence followed the rattle of musketry. All was so still and quiet that the robbers became impatient for action and moved uneasily about as if restlessly anxious for the fight to recommence.

Laying down his musket, Flicker crawled on all fours on the barricade, and peering into the darkness, tried to make out what the troops were doing.

The detonation of the firing had caused the rain-clouds to assemble, and they now shed their liquid burthens in heavy drops upon the thick foliage of the trees. A fierce east wind, bearing the cold saltness of the sea over the flat marshes of Essex, came tearing through the trees, making them toss their mighty arms aloft, and groan as if in agony.

Nothing was to be seen, nothing was to be heard, save this mournful melody of the wild night.

"Victory! victory!" shouted Flicker, as he sprang on the barricade. "The soldiers have gone; we have beaten them; they have fled—hurrah!"

Scarcely had he uttered the words, when a bullet whizzed past his ear, causing him to fall headforemost back into the cave.

"Are you hurt?" demanded Maud, anxiously, her voice trembling for the first time.

"No, not at all," said the lad. "Only where have the soldiers gone?"

"They have not gone," said Maud. "This is only some ruse, so keep close, men, and look well to your guns and swords."

Again the troops were heard advancing, but this

time they came in open order, so as to avoid the galling volley from the robbers.

But this was not the only difference they made in their plan of attack.

As the troops advanced, a sharp fire, which told on the besieged, was kept up from the surrounding trees, in which some of the soldiers had been placed, in order that they might be able to fire over the barricade.

Gallantly the robbers, encouraged by Maud, kept up their fire, and many a brave soldier bit the dust; but their comrades advanced—under cover of the sharpshooters stationed in the trees—with that dogged perseverance that has often won England so many victories, in spite of bad generalship, and aristocratic selfishness.

Up the barricade the soldiers rushed in spite of the fire, so that the robbers had to throw down their muskets, and draw their cutlasses.

The cavern now rang with screams, groans, curses, and oaths fierce and deep. The clash of swords mingled with the report of pistols, whose quick flashes showed luridly through the smoky and sulphurous atmosphere.

It was indeed a most terrible and demoniacal scene.

Such a contest could not last long, however desperately the men might fight. Maud saw this, and was about to give the command for the men to retreat, when a soldier grasped her by the throat so tightly that she could not speak.

In vain she struggled to release herself, the man's hand seemed made of iron. Suddenly she heard a scream of rage, and Flicker, springing on the man's back, seized him by the hair, and dragging his head back, plunged a dagger in his breast. The next moment, with a heavy groan, the man fell dead on the floor; but before Flicker could release himself from his victim, in whose fall he had participated, a soldier struck him over the head with the butt of his musket.

Before he could repeat the blow Maud had sent a bullet through his head, and springing forward, she raised the lad in her arms, at the same time shouting to her followers to retreat to the passage.

This they soon did, Maud entering it last, still carrying the lad in her arms.

Quickly as the retreat had been executed, and although the robbers knew their way, and the soldiers did not do so, still the former had scarcely entered the narrow passage, than the soldiers were upon them.

Placing Flicker behind her, and telling one of the men to see him carried to a place of safety, Maud turned upon her assailants, and met them boldly. Pistol after pistol she discharged at the troops, having yet received no wound, for she apparently bore a charmed life.

Soldier after soldier fell, still others advanced boldly forward, until Maud had scarcely strength to draw a trigger.

Was all lost, then? Would the soldiers discover the secret of the passage, and the band be captured and destroyed?

No; Maud had one more remedy, and was about to apply it, when a clear, well-known voice was heard shouting a sentence that filled the hearts of the robbers with fresh courage and unbounded joy.

"*Batswing to the rescue! Batswing to the rescue!*"

High above the battle fray those welcome tones burst on the ears of the thieves, as the cheer of the lifeboat men on those of the shipwrecked mariner.

Then came the ring of hoofs, and then a crash amidst the besiegers. Batswing had leaped the barricade, and was now cutting down the soldiers in the rear, his bright sword doing terrible execution.

For a few moments he was seen on horseback, proudly giving his war-cry of "Batswing to the rescue," then his horse plunged suddenly forward, and the next moment, with a shrill neigh, rolled on the ground.

Was Batswing killed?

No; he is up again, fighting his way through towards his followers. Can he ever reach that passage, surrounded as he is by soldiery? Impossible!

Not so; for Maud has brought a band of trusty followers to his aid, who with redoubled energy charge the troops, and drive them back. One short, fierce combat, and Batswing is saved.

The passage is reached, but the troops quickly rally and follow fast, heedless of the volley that meets them.

"What is to be done?" cried Batswing. "If they reach this passage we must retreat on the Abbey. You, Maud, had better draw off most of the men, some half dozen of us can hold this passage until the rest have escaped. It is better that a few should die than the many."

"It may be so," replied Maud, "but I will not move until the last. Order all the men to retreat, and when I give the word, fly for your life, and I will fly with you."

"Strange woman," cried Batswing. "What do you mean?"

"To save us all. Do as I tell you—the soldiers are in a trap."

The order was quickly given, and the robbers retreated to the first vault, leaving Batswing and Maud alone to defend the entrance of the passage. Then Maud, calling to Batswing to fly, flashed a pistol on the quick match, saw it alight, and fled for life.

A terrific explosion followed, throwing both Batswing and his companion to the ground. The earth shook as though a violent earthquake had occurred, causing huge pieces of the rock in which the passage had been cut to become detached, and fall down.

For a long time the air of the passage was so foul that Batswing and Maud who had managed to creep to the vault, dared not advance down it, but at last it became pure enough, and accompanied by some men bearing links, they ventured to explore it and see what mischief had been done.

Huge boulders of stone lay in their path, but climbing over these they at length came near where the entrance of the passage had been. It was there no longer, the cave *had fallen in.*

Every soldier who had crossed the barricade had found a tomb; and not a man apparently remained near the fearful scene.

"At all events we are safe in this direction," said Batswing, "for even should they try to dig us out, it would take them an immense time. But doublessly they believe we have been killed; that we preferred death to being taken. But it is to you, Captain Malcolm, that we are indebted for this: how can I repay you?"

"Am I not still in your debt?" said Maud, "have you not given me liberty, life, everything? why then talk to me of repayment? I am now one of your band, willing to render up my life for you—but henceforth call me Maud. I wish those who know me, to know where I am. To feel that I am desperate, and that *I will have revenge.*"

"As you will, Maud," said Batswing, "but we must now see to the other entrance to our cave. There I have stationed Jack Sheppard and Teddy the Grumbler under the direction of the merry smith, so as to bring us news should that have been discovered."

Quickly traversing the way, Batswing carefully examined the different secret doors and passages in this subterranean abode.

All were quite safe. In the large vault where lay the wounded, who were being carefully attended to, Maud saw poor Flicker stretched; he was breathing heavily, and was still unconscious.

Kneeling over the wounded boy, this woman, who a few moments before had been fighting desparately, raised the lad's head and kissed him gently.

This done, she removed a cloak that hung from her

JERRY BLINKER COMES TO GRIEF.

shoulders and placed it on the ground as a pillow for the wounded boy.

Batswing reached the secret panel leading to the Abbey, and paused for a moment to listen intently.

No sound being heard, he gave a low cry like that of the owl.

This was instantly answered from without, so the panel flew back, and Batswing, followed only by Maud, slipped out into the open air.

"Well, Captain," cried the merry smith, who in company with Jack Sheppard and Grumbling Teddy hastened up to the place, "well, captain, how goes it, what has been done?"

"The soldiers have been beaten," said Batswing, "but the cave is destroyed."

"That I suppose was the terrific explosion we heard?" said Jack Sheppard.

"It was," said Batswing, sadly, "in that you heard the fate of many a gallant fellow."

No. 12.

"What a terrible night it is," said the smith, shuddering, "look at the lightning."

"Lightning," all exclaimed, "where?"

"Over yonder," replied the smith, pointing in the direction of where the mouth of the cave had been.

They all stood silently watching in the direction where the smith had pointed. Suddenly a bright light shot up into the sky.

"*That* is not lightning," cried Batswing, "*the forest at the mouth of the cave is on fire.*"

It was but too true. High flames rushed up into the air, dyeing the clouds with a deep red stain, as if the blood of the killed had bedewed the heavens.

Far, far, did the terrible glow spread, lighting up the surrounding country.

Millions of sparks rose and fell amidst the thick smoke as it rolled sullenly away. Herds of deer and young horses dashed across the forest, wounding and killing each other in their terror.

Flocks of birds whirled about over the flames, till they became suffocated by the smoke and fell into the burning mass. Others flew through the air screaming mournfully, as they winged their way.

"This is indeed a terrible sight," said Batswing.

"It is, indeed," said Sheppard, "I can't say that it gives me a relish for a country life. I have often heard of rural felicity, but if I am to take this as a specimen of it, I must say I don't like it at all."

"Hush! what was that?" said the merry smith, suddenly.

"Oh! only one of those wretched owls," said Teddy, "I can't abear them, they are always a-screaming about nothing. That's what they're after, for all the world like babies, and they're as mischievous too; that they are."

"That is *not* an owl's cry," said the smith, "it is the imitation of one, and if I mistake not, comes from Jerry Blinker."

"Still it may not," said Batswing, "therefore we will retire and watch."

They withdrew into the cave and listened, but their fears were soon put to rest by hearing Jerry's well known voice singing—

I bish I bas a Alderman.

I vish I vas a Alderman
　To be both rich and fat,
To wear a gold chain round my neck,
　And fur about my hat.

No king or queen in all the vorld,
　Should make my vorship stoop,
Vile I had venison for to eat,
　And likewise turtle soup.

I'd sit upon the bench so proud,
　The model of a beak,
And make the big-vigs * silent be,
　Ven 'ere I vished to speak.

I'd let the rich—if they would pay—
　Quite freely break the law—
But up I'd string each ragged cove,
　For daring to be poor.

"Stop!" cried Batswing, advancing from the cave, "have you so little feeling that on a night like this, when so many men have been killed, you can sing such a song?"

"And why not cappen?" demanded Jerry, "those who are dead can't hear me, and those who have escaped ought to be happy they have done so, and sing with delight."

"Ah!" said Batswing, anxiously, "but our troubles are not over yet. Who knows but that we may soon be attacked again, and conquered by overpowering numbers."

"Not this journey at all events," cried Jerry.

"How do you know that?" demanded Batswing.

"I've been with the sodgers, that's how I know, and haven't they got it hot? oh! no, not at all."

"But how did you get amongst them?" demanded the smith.

"Why as a honest citizen o' course; one as lives by the sweat of his brow, and not by picking and stealing like some folk as shall be nameless."

"Why you impudent young puppy," said Grumbling Teddy, "what do you mean by that? I'll break every bone in your skin; that I will."

"Enough of this," said Batswing. "I suppose presuming on your honest character, Jerry, you proceeded to the forest."

"That's just it cappen, but I found troops placed round so that no one could get near to the cave, and

* Barristers.

none could approach it. Well, I was forced to be contented; so I perched myself on a tree and wanted to hear what I could, for the night was too dark to see much."

"We do not wish to hear an account of the fight," said Batswing impatiently. "We know all about that. What has happened *since*."

"Well just as the forest caught fire, Jonathan Wild, all grimed with smoke, rode up to the tree in which I was concealed, with the captain, and such of the soldiers that had escaped the terrible explosion, and they holds a conversation.

"'What is to be done now?' demanded the captain haughtily, 'you have led us into a pretty mess. The cave was not so easily to be taken. I suppose you wished to get as many of His Majesty's troops killed as you could?'

"Then Jonathan swore a lot of oaths, and said something about a trap in the Abbey only it had been stopped up."

"He is right," said Batswing with a laugh, "I had that done."

"Then the soldier said, 'I have had enough of this dirty work; I have lost more men in this action than I should have done in a campaign. The poor devils of robbers are doubtlessly all dead, together with my poor fellows in the cave, and I only wish, Mr. Wild, that you were with them.'

"With that he turned away and gave directions for the trumpeter to sound the retreat: which he did, and I saw them all on their way to London followed by that arch-fiend Jonathan Wild."

"Then for the present we are safe," cried Batswing, "let us lose no time in informing our wounded comrades."

They descended into the vaults, and a large tankard of wine having been served out to each man, Batswing arose, and flagon in hand said

"Comrades, we may rest this night in peace, and recruit our strength by a jovial supper and cheering cup. The soldiers have been beaten. They are in full retreat towards London. We have conquered—VICTORY!!"

CHAPTER XXXVII.

HUGH FENTON DISMISSED THE BAND. BATSWING SENDS HIS FOLLOWERS ON VARIOUS EXPEDITIONS.

LONG and loud were the cheers that rang through the vaults as the men shouted victory. The wine cups clinked, and even the wounded smiled in grim delight as their friends leant over them, and told how bravely the fight had been lost and won.

No sooner had silence been restored, than Batswing, taking Maud by the hand, led her into the centre of the group of robbers, and raising his wine cup on high, thus addressed them.

"Comrades, the attack upon us was so sudden, that our emissaries were unable to bring us news about it, so that we might have had a proper notice. Consequently I was not able to arrive until the fight was nearly over. Therefore, I have to thank you all for the bravery with which you fought; driving back men drilled in warfare, and numbering twice as many as yourselves. But there is one that we all must thank; one whose noble deed saved us at the last moment. I mean this lady. Had it not been for her, the fight would have terminated in favour of our adversaries, and it is needless to say what would have been the fate of those who were taken prisoners, happier the ones who had fallen fighting."

A low murmur of approbation followed this remark, and Batswing continued.

"Like us, this lady has suffered deep wrongs—like us, she is anxious to avenge them. Her greatest enemy is Jonathan Wild. Is he not ours? In our band, deeds of courage never go unrewarded. What then should be the reward of the one who was saved us all? Can we repay such services with gold? Dross that we pick up in a night's ride, if we have luck, by the handful. No! we must show her our trust and our confidence in better ways than this. What say you lads, shall she not be our lieutenant? Is she not worthy of being the second in command?"

A hearty cheer rang through the vault, and the men tossed off their wine to the health of their new lieutenant.

One man alone remained silent, and that one was Hugh Fenton, the young man Maud had found in command of the cave.

"How now, Hugh Fenton," demanded Batswing, "have you aught to say against this proposition that you remain so silent and look so black?"

"I have not much to say, beyond this, that I for one refuse to obey a woman."

"And why, has she not gained the fight for us?"

"By accident, yes; but my idea is that no man should serve under petticoat government, and I for one refuse. Why should she, who has just joined the band be made lieutenant; whilst I, who have been here for years have no promotion."

"By heavens!" cried Batswing, springing forward, "dare but to utter another word and I will strike you to the earth."

"Hold!" exclaimed Maud, seizing Batswing's arm, "let me deal with this fellow."

Stepping forward, she stood with folded arms before the man, and in scornful tones commenced to question him.

"So you refuse to serve under a woman. You, whom I found trembling as with an ague at the approach of the soldiers."

"'Tis false," cried the man, turning pale with rage.

"It is true, you trembling coward," replied Maud, "did you not dare to talk of surrender? Did you not say that resistance was useless?"

The fellow remained silent for a few moments with his head bent down, unable to deny the accusation or to meet the eye of his accuser.

"Hugh," enquired Batswing, sorrowfully, "is this true?"

"And if it be, what then?" demanded the man, "I did not think it possible to keep the cave."

"You hear him my men," cried Batswing, "the trembling coward does not shame to own that he would have surrendered; what then is his fitting punishment? Answer all of you."

"Death!" was the unanimous and solemn reply.

"You have heard your sentence," said Batswing, "have you any reply to make?"

"None," was the answer, "but that I dispute your authority to treat me in this way. I indeed thought that there was no chance of saving the cave, but I did not mean to surrender it without making easy terms for all of us. Still I am in your hands, you have the power, and can do what you like."

The man was seized and pinioned. He was then blind-folded and placed with his back against the wall.

Some half dozen men were then told off, and ordered to load their muskets.

Slowly the words were given by Batswing.

"Make ready."

All was still, as the click of the locks were heard.

"Present."

Then followed the rattle, as the muskets were made to bear upon the unfortunate man.

Just as the word "Fire" was about to be pronounced, Flicker dashed forward, and throwing himself before the prisoner, exclaimed,

"No, no, no, don't fire; he shall not be killed. I won't have it. I won't have it done, I tell you. We have had enough blood already to-day."

"The boy is mad," said Bob Blow-the-Bellows.

"I am not mad," screamed Flicker. "I saved your life, Captain, when you were in the Fleet. Save this man's now."

"Enough," said Batswing. "His life shall be spared on one condition."

"Phew!" growled Grumbling Teddy, "I hate mercy. Why cant you slit his weazand, and have done with it at once? I hate doing things by halves."

"Silence!" said Batswing. "The condition is that you swear never to betray the secrets of this band. Do you swear that?"

"I swear it, on my soul," replied Hugh Fenton.

"You will also be expelled from our brotherhood, until such time as we may deem it fit to re-admit you. This will only be done when you shall have proved yourself faithful to our cause, and a true man."

"Fear not, Captain, but that you will find me a true man. Time will show who is in the right, and if I should discover that I have been in the wrong, I will freely own it, and beg for re-admission. But I doubt not but that I shall be able to make a name for myself, and form a band; but I pledge you my word that I will never do ought that can injure the whole or part of this fraternity."

"Good," replied Batswing; "and trust me, if you are in trouble, we shall not forget that you have been one of us. Now go."

Jerry Blinker led a horse to the entrance of the vault, and Hugh Fenton rode away, humming a lively tune.

"Good luck be with ye," cried Jerry; "and mind you show us how to behave ourselves on the road."

"Never fear, Jerry," replied Hugh. "This very night I will fill my pockets at somebody else's expense. You will soon hear of me."

"Yes, at Newgate," chuckled Jerry, as he returned to the vaults.

"I never did see such a man as you are," growled Teddy to Batswing. "Why did you let that cove go? We'd far better have knocked him on the head."

"And what good would that do?"

"I don't know," replied Teddy; "only I like to get things out of hand at once."

"It is better as it is," replied Batswing. "But, my lads, the greater part of our treasure lies buried beneath the ruins of our cave; therefore we must not waste time, but at once set to work and make gold."

"What plan do you propose?" said Maud.

"I," replied Batswing, "shall take the north road. You had better try the south, and take one or two fellows with you. The others I shall send out in different directions; and mind we all meet here in two days from the present time. Jerry Blinker will have to go to Drury Lane on a special mission, and Bob Blow-the-Bellows must take to travelling for a little while."

"What," cried the smith, "shut up my shop? Why, all Stamford and Tottenham will be in mourning. As to Widow Wapshaw, she will never recover the shock."

"Nevertheless it must be done. You must make your way towards Harwich. You had better travel as a tinker, and so avoid all suspicion. Your journey will take you some time, therefore you will not be able to be at the rendezvous I appointed for the rest. Still, I will take care that you shall be able to communicate with us."

"Well, if it must be, it must be. Sir Arthur went by that road—perhaps we shall meet."

"Sir Arthur Bowring!" exclaimed Batswing. "I had forgotten him. Why did he not remain at the cave?"

"Finding you were not here, he started for Tillingham Hall, as he was determined to find out Lord Redfern, and supposed that he might be there."

"It is well! you must watch for him. I will give you instructions how to act. In the meantime, let all take rest and refreshment, for to-morrow, at day-break, all must be up and away."

The men drew closer together, and many a jovial song was sung, and many tales were told, as the wine-cup circled freely round, so that it was late at night before the last of the party fell asleep, and the vaults ceased to resound with the echoes of merriment.

CHAPTER XXXVIII.

JERRY MAKES THE SMITH PROPOSE, BUT IN DOING SO MEETS WITH AN ACCIDENT.

THE first grey light of morning had just begun to streak the horizon as the merry smith stepped from his smithy, and, with a wallet swung at his back, and a good oaken staff in his hand, made his way towards the Bird Cage Inn.

He soon reached that hostelry, and passing round to the back of the house, found Jerry Blinker polishing some harness, and, as usual, whistling.

"You're at work early, Jerry," said the smith, as he sat down on an empty barrel.

Jerry nodded, and continued whistling as if no one was by.

"Is the widow up yet?" demanded the smith.

Jerry shook his head sorrowfully, but made no answer.

"Why, what's up now?" asked the smith; "have you lost your tongue?"

"No," said Jerry, "but walls have ears; so look out."

"What do you mean?"

"Why, that this 'ere house is full of soldiers, that's all."

"You don't mean to tell me that the widow is suspected?" said the smith, anxiously.

"Not she; she's too artful for that, Lord love yer. But they brought some of them as got wounded in the bit of a fight last night here and left them: that's all."

"Oh, that's all, is it?" said the smith.

"Yes, that's it."

"And the widow?"

"Is a-bed; having kept it up rather late last night. I say, Bob, them there soldiers are remarkably sprightly fellows, ain't they?"

"Yes; what of that?"

"They make their way wonderfully well with the women."

"I suppose so: it's the coat does it."

"It don't matter what does it, as long as it's done," said Jerry, mournfully; "it's astonishing how they do it, but they do. Still, nice fellows as they are, I shouldn't care about having a soldier for a master."

"For a master! what do you mean by that?"

"Only, the sergeant as is here has been paying the widow all sorts of compliments, and she seemed to like it, too. Least-ways, so I'm told. They say she swallowed them down as fast as if they was oysters, only there wasn't any vinegar and pepper to them. I can't tell what them soldiers do to make all the women folk like them so. Can you?"

Giving a sly glance at the smith to see what effect his story had, Jerry fell to polishing the harness and whistling as before.

Springing from his seat, Bob Blow-the-Bellows paced quickly up and down the yard, biting his nails and stamping as though he were in one of the most unpleasant of humours.

Jerry watched all this out of the corners of his eyes, but continued his whistling as if his thoughts were at least a hundred miles away.

At length the smith paused for a moment, and turning round faced Jerry.

"Jerry," he exclaimed, "is this the truth?"

"Is what the truth?" asked Jerry, in a puzzled voice.

"What you have been telling me about the widow?" said Bob Blow-the-Bellows.

"I am afraid so," replied Jerry; "I don't like the looks of it at all."

"You don't think she's serious?" urged the smith.

"I don't know so much about that," said Jerry; "I know if I were sweet upon her—which I ain't—I should not like it, I can tell you that."

"I don't like it," said the smith.

"Then, why don't you, go in and settle the business at once. She's just gone into the little back parlour there; you can get it over in a few minutes. I'd have it settled one way or the other. 'Yes or no,' that's what I would have, and no mistake. You're off on your travels; the sergeant has a bullet in his shoulder—he'll stop here a fortnight. Perhaps he won't go at all. Well, it's not my affair: only, when the sergeant's master, I won't stay, you see if I do."

The smith took one or two hasty strides up and down the yard; paused irresolutely for a few moments; then, striking his stick down firmly exclaimed, "I'll do it, by Jove!" and hurried into the house

No sooner had he done so than Jerry slapped his thigh, stuck his tongue into his cheek, closed one eye, and kicked out his leg violently.

He then proceeded to perform a wild dance, called the "Devil's Tattoo," which was far more noticeable for agility than grace, after which he seemed greatly relieved.

"I knew I'd make him do it," he chuckled; "Old Mother Wapshaw should stand me something for this. She's been trying to make him do it for ever so long a time, but couldn't. The soldier was a capital invention of mine, that it was; a capital one. But I must not miss the sport."

Climbing on to the top of an old water-butt, Jerry was able to see through the window into the room where Bob Blow-the-Bellows and the widow were. As the window was opened at the top, he could also hear what was being spoken.

At the moment when he had become the audience, the smith had his arm placed round the widow's waist, and was gazing into her eyes.

"So you are going away," said the widow in a low voice.

"I am, but only for a little time," replied Bob.

"Dear me, how dull the place will be without you," sighed the widow.

"All places will be dull without you," said Bob, tenderly.

"Good gracious, Mr. Robert, how you do look at one," simpered the widow. "I do declare you make one feel quite uncomfortable, that you do."

"I do not want to make you uncomfortable," said Bob, disconsolately.

Thereupon followed a long and rather an awkward pause.

"My eye, what a couple of old fools they look," grinned Jerry.

"I suppose you have come to have a stirrup-cup before your departure," said the widow.

"Yes—that is, no"—stammered Bob; "I came to see you—to—"

"What, Mr. Robert?" said the expectant widow, inwardly trembling lest Bob should break down and not 'pop the question.'

"Why, you see," stammered Bob, "I ain't good at speaking; at shoeing a horse I'm a first-rater, but I'm no hand at a palaver—so, so—to make a long matter short, I— I—I'll take a little brandy, Mrs. Wapshaw."

The widow could scarcely refrain from showing her disappointment at this failure. However, she procured the brandy bottle which she hoped would give her lover sufficient courage to plead his cause.

After drinking a couple of glasses full of the spirit in rapid succession, the smith coughed, squared his elbows and began again.

"It's a terrible thing, widow, when a man has to take to stimulants to keep up his spirits. I once thought I should never be dull, but now I'm as flat as stale beer."

"Dear me," cried the widow, "what has happened?"

"What has happened?" demanded Bob Blow-the-Bellows, with a deep sigh, and a lachrimous look, that nearly made Jerry burst into a loud roar of laughter, "what has happened? and can you ask me that?"

"Dear me, Mr. Robert, you make me feel quite nervous," said the widow.

"Nervous! what have you made me feel, Mrs. Wapshaw?"

"Happy, I trust," replied the widow, rubbing the back of one hand with the palm of the other, and looking on the ground, "I have always tried to make you feel at home."

"Happy: at home!" exclaimed the smith, "you have made me happy, yet you have made me miserable."

"I am very sorry," said Mrs. Wapshaw, "I never intended to do so I'm sure."

"Lovely widow," said the smith, pressing his hand to his heart, and looking out of the corners of his eyes, "lovely widow, I have a fire here that is consuming me; you, and you alone can squench it. Say you will be mine, do not leave me to pine in singleness. Say you will be the mistress of my heart and smithy. Speak, dearest, and give me hope."

"Really, Mr. Robert."

"Call me Bob," said the smith.

"Well, Robert: will that do?" said the widow, by way of compromise.

"For the present," said the smith.

"Well, Mr. Robert, I don't know what to say. When my dear, late lamented, Wapshaw died, I swore I would never marry again, that I did."

"But you didn't mean it?" said the smith.

"Oh, yes, I did," replied Mrs. Wapshaw, and then seeing the smith's disconsolate look, she added, "but—" and then stopped.

That "but" spoke worlds to Bob Blow-the-Bellows, it showed him that his chances were far from hopeless.

"But what?" he inquired.

"But before I knew Wapshaw I swore that I would never marry at all."

"Did you! and how did he prevail on you to consent?"

"He did not prevail on me to consent. He popped the question, and just when I was about to say 'no,' he caught me in his arms and stopped my mouth with kisses."

"Did he though?" said the smith.

"Yes, indeed he did," replied the blushing widow.

Bob Blow-the-Bellows, buttoned his coat, coughed, arranged his necktie, threw out his arms, drew in a long breath, and said—

"Mrs. Wapshaw, will you marry me?"

The widow shook her head, but before she could utter a word, Bob had caught her in his arms and stopped her mouth with kisses; much to the delight of Jerry Blinker, who was ready to die for laughter at the scene.

"There," said Bob, "that's finished."

"I'm sure Mr. Robert that—"

"Not another word, my dear," cried the smith, "I look upon the matter as settled. If Wapshaw did it that way, why should not I do the same? I must say that I most highly approve of Mr. Wapshaw's proceedings altogether, especially his death. It showed an amount of moderate retirement and delicate forethought, for which I shall never be able to thank him enough."

"Hush!" said the widow, "you really must not talk in that manner, and since you have forced me to consent to marry you, I must insist on your remembering the late lamented with respect."

"With all my heart, if you will promise to forget him. I'll do anything to please you; only, mind, you must get rid of all those soldiers."

"Soldiers!" exclaimed the widow, in astonishment.

"Yes," continued the smith, "and especially the sergeant."

"Especially the sergeant!" cried the widow, holding up her hand in surprise.

"Yes, no more love-making now, widow—that is—unless it be with me."

"Love-making," screamed the widow, "why, surely the man must be mad. What do you mean with your soldiers and love-making."

"Come, come, widow," said the smith, "of course what you did last night I have no right to say much about, but don't do it again."

"What in the name of fortune do you mean?" cried the widow, "I have not had any soldiers here, nor do I want any."

"Do you mean to say that there was not a number of wounded soldiers brought here, and that you were particularly sweet on the sergeant."

"Yah!" screamed the widow, springing from her chair in the excess of her amazement, "why, bless my soul alive, there hasn't been a soldier near the precious place for more than a week."

The comic looks of perplexity that the countenances of both the smith and the landlady now wore were too much for Jerry, who burst into such a tremendous shout of laughter, that both the lovers looked up, and at once perceived Jerry's fiery head.

Deep were the curses of the smith, and terrible were the vows of vengeance of Mrs. Wapshaw as they hurried out into the yard.

Poor Jerry saw that there was not a minute to lose, and at once endeavoured to effect his escape, in hopes that the storm would soon blow over. But, unfortunately for him, the lid of the water butt was insecurely fastened. He stepped on one side, the cover slipped, and the next moment Jerry was plunged feet first into the water.

In a moment the smith's anger was changed into mirth, and peal after peal of boisterous laughter shook his sides, which he had to hold for very pain.

Mrs. Wapshaw could scarcely repress her mirth, but she did so by a great effort, and shaking her fist at Jerry, she rated him soundly.

"Oh, you good for nothing, thieving, lying young varmint," she cried, "have you no respect for anybody or anything? I'm ashamed of you, that I am. After all that I've done for you, you ungrateful creature."

"Take me out! take me out!" cried Jerry shivering with cold.

"Not until you have confessed that all you told me this morning was a falsehood," cried Bob Blow-the-Bellows.

"I do confess it, I do confess it," gasped Jerry.

"And you promise not to repeat anything you saw until you have permission from us," added the widow.

"Indeed, indeed I won't," cried Jerry.

"Well give me your hand then," cried the smith, "I can't find it in my heart to be cross with you, although you deserve it. You should take care when you play practical jokes that they don't turn against yourself."

Giving Jerry his hand, he dragged him out of the butt and placed him in the middle of the stable-yard, where he stood looking much like a drowned rat; the water pouring off him in streams.

"And now widow I must leave you for a while," said the smith, "but we will have one cup before we go, in which our friend Jerry will join us; for I know that in spite of all his jokes he wishes us well."

"Well he shall have a glass," said the widow, "but he must stand in the yard to drink it. I won't have him come in the kitchen in that state."

"Why the kitchen is the proper place for *dripping* ain't it?" said Jerry.

"None of your impertinence," cried the widow, "or you shan't have the drink."

The drink was soon produced, and a good bumper passed round, in which they drank success to the smith's journey and his speedy return.

"Good bye, Jerry," said Bob Blow-the-Bellows, "and mind you don't bathe in your clothes another time."

"Oh! you need not talk," replied Jerry, "we both made a plunge together, only you have got into *hot* water and I into cold. But I shall get over mine the easiest."

The smith made no reply, but shouldering his bundle, marched gaily away singing—

"By the wayside wisdom grows,"
Says some learned thinker—
'Midst the hips and haws and sloes,
Oft' you'll see a tinker—
As he mends his pots and pans
'Midst his hammer's clinking,
Of mens' vast and varied plans,
Is that tinker thinking.
Sit ye down beneath the hips,
Gather wisdom from his lips.

"Well," said Jerry as he turned into the loft to change his wet garments. "it is true I got a ducking, but I had my way for all that. I had made up my mind that the smith should propose to-day, and he has. Poor fellow, he'll pay for this day's work, I warrant me."

With a sly grin and one of those peculiar winks for which he was famous, Jerry left off meditating and commenced whistling.

CHAPTER XXXIX.

JONATHAN WILD MEETS THE GOVERNOR OF NEWGATE MR. PITT'S LETTER AND PLOT. LORD REDFERN AND JONATHAN WILD START A PLOT TO GET RID OF LORD HENRY LESLIE.

ON the morning after the attack upon the cave, Jonathan Wild sat in his office gazing moodily at a letter he held before him.

"It is well he has removed her," said Wild speaking to himself, "this man or fiend seems to discover everything. Well. well, he *must* be dead now. That explosion must have shaken down the whole cave. It was that she-devil who did it. Desperation, and desperation alone, could have prompted so bold an act."

He rose hastily from his seat and paced up and down the room.

"Whilst *she* was in my power, I held him in my grasp, and now Batswing, if he lives—but no, he does not know the secret, and she is too proud to mention it.

"Besides if she do, *he* is proscribed by law and can do us no harm."

Again he paced backwards and forwards lost in deep thought, and then suddenly pausing, rang a bell.

The door opened slowly and a hideous face presented itself to his gaze.

So horrible was it, that even Jonathan Wild doubted if it could belong to one who still lived on this earth.

The nose and mouth seemed perfectly lost in a huge black and blue swelling, whilst on both cheeks there were terrible cuts and grazes as if the person had fallen on gravel with great violence. Clots of mud mingled with blood had dried upon his garments, whilst his heavy boots were thick with clay.

"Who in the devil's name are you?" roared Jonathan when he had recovered his surprise.

"Heugh! I thought you wouldn't know me," replied the man in a hollow voice, made sepulchral by the enormous swelling of his face.

"Know you! who would know you in that state? who are you?"

"I'm Rough Ralph," said the man.

For a moment Jonathan gazed at the man, and a fiendish look of delight passed over his face, for another's pain was always pleasant to him. But at present he thought it wiser to console his henchman rather than insult him. So in kindly tones he enquired into the cause of Ralph's troubles.

"So it was that wild cat;" he exclaimed, when Ralph had told him all, "it was indeed a bad day for us when we let her escape. She must be caught again Ralph; caught at once. That is if she exists, which I doubt."

"That is easier said than done," grumbled Ralph, "she fights like a devil."

"She does," replied Wild. "But hark! some one is enquiring for me; see who it is, and let no one enter unless their business is of importance."

Ralph soon disappeared, but quickly returned to announce Mr. Pitt, the governor of Newgate.

Mr. Pitt entered the room with a more than usually beaming face, and taking a seat opposite Jonathan, commenced the conversation in a very affable manner.

"Sad affair last night Mr. Wild, sad affair very," he began. "The King is in a desperate rage about the loss of his troops, he has doubled the reward for the arrest of Batswing, I suppose you have heard that?"

"What is the good of doubling the reward, for a man who is already dead—and buried," he added after a pause.

"That is very true," replied Mr. Pitt, "very true indeed. *if* he is dead and buried."

"What do you mean by that?" demanded Jonathan passionately, "I tell you I saw the cave fall in; the robbers must have been crushed to atoms."

"But I understand that there was *another* entrance to the cave," said Mr. Pitt.

Jonathan looked at his interrogator in surprise.

"Well I thought I would just call in and see how you were after last night's fatigue," said Mr. Pitt. "By the way, I heard you were robbed the other day. Is it true?"

Jonathan Wild turned livid with rage. How could this man, for whom he had such an immense contempt, know all about his secrets.

"Bah!" he said, "a mere nothing, a mere nothing; a a poor crazed body, a distant relation, of whom I had taken care of out of kindness, ran away, nothing more, nothing more, I can assure you."

"Well, I will not detain you," said Mr. Pitt crossing to the door, "especially as I saw a gentleman waiting down stairs to see you. If Batswing should be still alive, I suppose our bet stands good."

"Yes, yes," said Jonathan impatiently, "of course it does, good morning."

With a sly chuckle, the governor of Newgate walked away, and continued to rub his hands with delight until he reached his own room, where taking a letter from his pocket, he read as follows—

MR. PITT,—Honoured Sir—I have been one of the band at Epping forest, but that's all up now. The soldiers settled us; so I don't see why I should stick at selling the rest of them who remain. Batswing is wounded, and I know where to lay hands on him in Epping forest, as also I know where to take one or two others who are the leaders. If you will pay me one hundred pounds and let me go free, I will deliver them up to you to-night. If so be you agree to my terms, be at the cross roads this side Mare Street, with some half-dozen men—not more—as the clock strikes eleven, whistle three times and I will be with you. You may think this is another trick, but it is not. If you doubt me, ask Mr. Wild who was robbed last night by Batswing, to come with you. I can get you all the papers returned, and also the woman who was his prisoner.—Trusting I shall have the honour of seeing you, I am, your humble servant, LUKE LONGLEY."

"It must be all right," said Mr. Pitt in ecstacies, "if there was any deception he would not tell me to bring half-a-dozen men. I'll be there Mr. Longley, you need not fear, and when I have taken the others I may also require you my friend, Ha, ha, ha! these thieves always over-reach themselves at last."

Still chuckling over the 'cuteness he was showing, Mr. Pitt descended into the lodge and gave his private instructions to his favourite follower Grumidge to have all ready for the night's expedition, at the same time enjoining him to the strictest secrecy.

Whilst this was going on, Jonathan Wild had received another visitor, who was no less a person than Lord Redfern.

"Well!" said Redfern joyously, "the robbers are destroyed I hear—and Maud—"

"Lives!" replied Jonathan sternly, "Pitt has just been here, and from what he says I fear Batswing does also."

"What are we to do then?" cried Redfern turning pale.

"Bide our time? what has become of the girl?"

"She is now at my old ruined hall at Tillingham."

"And Lord Henry Leslie?"

"Is there also; I have persuaded him that Sir Arthur committed suicide on the field, and that it is believed that he was killed by him. As both seconds have flown the country, there are no witnesses to disprove the matter and therefore he cannot clear himself."

"But there is no truth in your statements?"

"Not the slightest, but shut up in that wretched old place Harry Leslie knows no better, and there he will remain until he has surmounted his scruples."

"Supposing he never becomes your tool again."

"Then he will become a corpse," replied Redfern coolly. "Between you and me Mr. Wild, there need be no secrets, in fact there cannot be any."

"Certainly not on your side," sneered Jonathan.

"Well, as you will," said Lord Redfern, "I mean to play my cards openly with you at all events."

"I presume then you require my assistance."

"I do; the fact is I do not intend Leslie to have Alice Landon."

"Do you love her yourself then?" demanded Jonathan.

"Love her!" sneered Redfern, "as well perhaps as I did anything in the world."

"Saving yourself," put in Wild, "so you intend making pretty Alice Landon, the daughter of the man you—well, silenced—your mistress."

"Hush! hush!" cried Redfern, "why do you remind me of that? I tell you I repent that act; truly repent it."

Jonathan looked first in surprise and then in contempt at the man before him. So changed were Redfern's tones that at first Wild felt inclined to believe him, but one glance at the cunning eyes, and brutal mouth, showed him that there was no remorse, but rather some new villainy at work.

"You repent, ho, ho, ho," roared Jonathan, "excuse my laughing my lord; ho, ho, ho, but I really cannot help it. It is so very funny."

"Funny," cried Redfern, "and why should it be so?"

"Faith I know not," replied Jonathan, "they say the bigger the rogue the better the priest; perhaps you will turn to religion. And so, to show your repentance for having caused the father's death, you make the daughter your mistress."

"I said not so; the fair Alice shall be my wife."

"Your wife?" gasped Jonathan Wild, now completely overcome with surprise.

"My wife—Lady Redfern; and why not? Is she not

young and beautiful. You are not surprised at Sir Arthur Bowring loving her; then why should you be that I do also."

"You two are very different men," said Jonathan dryly.

"But both are men, and therefore both may love."

"You may: but I don't think it is very likely. What property has this girl?"

"Property! none," cried Redfern, pretending astonishment.

"Hum! then it really is love?" asked Jonathan.

"Of the purest and most disinterested kind," replied Redfern.

"And what do you want me to do?"

"I want you to help me to get rid of Lord Harry."

"How?"

"We can get him shipped to the West Indies."

"But why? He does not love Alice Landon."

"No; but when he recovers from his wound, he has declared his intention of proving to the world that he did not kill Sir Arthur."

"Considering that the world never believed it, I see no difficulty in that."

"Just so; but then Sir Arthur returns—and all our plots will be disovered."

"Your plots, my lord, not mine."

"Well, as you will," replied Lord Redfern, petulantly. "At all events, he must be removed at once."

"It can be done for a certain sum," said Jonathan, thoughtfully.

"You know I always pay well," said Redfern.

"I know," replied Jonathan. "Well, then, the night after to-morrow a smuggler's vessel shall be ready off the coast close by Tillingham. I will go with you down to the Hall. You must persuade Lord Harry that his retreat has been discovered, and that he must fly. Should he resist we must force him on board. Once there, he will not return for some time."

"But should he absolutely refuse to go—what then?"

"Get him to walk down with you on the beach. I will see that there are some men ready who will speedily quiet his lordship. You know what I mean. Now go. Show yourself about, so that folk may not know of your absence from town. Above all, be secret."

"Farewell," said Lord Redfern. "The night after to-morrow we go to Tillingham. I will have all ready to start in the afternoon."

"You had better start in the forenoon, and see that there are relays of horses ready for us on the road. Remember, it is forty miles away."

"Fear not, I will be ready Till then, adieu."

"Adieu," said Jonathan, as he watched Lord Redfern down the passage, and then closed the door.

"So he would marry Alice Landon. What is the meaning of this? There is some secret he has found out of which I am ignorant. That must not be. He shall not marry her. At least, not yet. The fool, to tell me thus much; he ought to know that I will find out all his plans before I have done—ay, and ruin them, if they do not please me. I think the gentle Alice would make a good wife—if, as I suspect, there is property somewhere. Well, I will find this out sooner or later, but, until I am satisfied, no man shall marry the pretty Alice. Strange all men get interested in that girl; Sir Arthur, Lord Leslie, Lord Redfern, and even Batswing. Who knows, perhaps Jonathan Wild may become so too; and if that happens, farewell the hopes of all the others."

CHAPTER XL.

PARTY AT THE LOAD OF HAY.—THE CHALLENGE.—THE ATTACK ON THE ROAD.—THE ARREST.

THE Load of Hay was an old-fashioned wayside country inn, standing some little distance back from the road.

There was a snug, cosy look about it, which all our fine modern taverns can never equal. The quaint little doorway, whose well-worn step showed how well the house was frequented, flanked on each side by queer little bow windows, the one belonging to the parlour, and the other to the bar, teemed with comfort; the very horse-stone, for travellers to mount their horses, seemed familiar to one, whilst the ruddy light which shot out through the red curtains, piercing the darkness of the night, and stretching right across the road, told of a hearty welcome.

Jolly and comfortable as the outside of the house was, it was nothing to the inside. Lord bless you, there was nothing but jollity and good will there!

Look at the blushing landlady, as she stands in her well-polished bar, amongst her pewter and copper vessels, all of which seem to shine the brighter for her good-natured smiles. Why, she is contentment personified.

Then there is the landlord, indolent, easy, plethoric, and corpulent, as all good landlords should be. There he sits before the fire; his coat is off, the two first fingers of his right hand thrust between his third and fourth waistcoat buttons, whilst his left hand holds a long clay pipe, known as a "churchwarden," though why, it is hard to say; unless it was because they were very imposing, but of little value; the pipe is out, the bowl is turned downwards, scattering the white ash of the "Indian weed" over his short stumpy legs, that are stretched out towards the fire, at which the good man nods drowsily. Is not that a picture of contentment?

But let us turn to the left, as we enter the inn door, and pay a visit to the parlour.

It is a dear old snug place, panelled with oak. Heavy beams of the same material run across the ceiling, which is low. Round the room are pictures of the "North Coach," "The High Flyer," and several others, besides quaint old prints, mostly referring to hunting and shooting.

Down the middle of the room ran a long table, on which was a goodly show of glasses and bottles, whilst at each end was a teeming bowl of punch.

Around this social board were gathered some fourteen or fifteen men, drinking, smoking, and laughing in the merriest manner in the world. They were all dressed in riding coats and top-boots, the splashes on the latter plainly showing that they had ridden some distance that very evening.

The best dressed man in the meeting was the one who occupied the chair, or head of the table, and to him all paid the greatest respect.

A thick black beard covered the lower part of his face, and a huge patch shut out one eye. A heavy wig covered his head, and a heavily-braided three-cornered hat was placed jauntily on one side, so as to give its wearer a jaunty, devil-may-care look.

"I'm blest if I ever saw such a disguise," said one of the men in a low voice to the man sitting nearest to him. "Curse me, if any one of us would have known the Captain unless he had let us into the secret."

"It's quite true, Grumbling Teddy," replied the other, but there ain't another Batswing in all the world. He'd cheat the devil himself."

"He's done more than that," replied Teddy, "he's cheated Jonathan Wild."

The reader will perceive by this that the company assembled was a small part of Batswing's band, and that the man at the head of the table was no other than that redoubtable leader himself.

Raising his glass in his hand, Batswing looked across the table at a young man who sat somewhat gloomily at the end of the table.

"Hugh Fenton!" he cried, "I drink to your luck, my boy. Nay, man, never look so sad. Trust me that the day is not far distant when you will be one of us again; and believe me, I shall be as glad when the time arrives

as you will; so cheer up man, fill your goblet and pledge me."

"I pledge you Captain, with all my heart," replied Hugh, "but it seems hard that I should not be allowed to join in this expedition; nay, worse, not even to be permitted to know what it is."

"Hugh Fenton, you were dismissed our band until you could prove that you were to be trusted, and that your courage was firm, and your heart true. Had you behaved to some men as you did to us, you would have undoubtedly been shot; we have spared you, so be contented."

Hugh Fenton rested his head upon his hands in a discontented manner, but said no more.

"Come," cried Batswing, "it is nearly nine o'clock, and we shall soon have to start. Let us have some more punch and a song. What ho! Janet, more punch, I say."

"Dear me, dear me, what is all this fuss about?" said a smart girl, hurrying into the room, "one would think that you had not had a drop to drink all night, instead of having been all night drinking."

"Come, come, mistress Janet, a little less talk and a little more punch if you please, remember this old song," cried Batswing, and tossing off a glass of the steaming punch, he sang—

A Prating Woman's Tongue.

A prating woman has a tongue,
  That's like a bell that's lightly hung;
The clapper goes all night and day,
  Scaring friends and foes away.
    Maidens, pray, remember this,
    Thieves that come to steal a kiss,
    Still will fly thee, tho' thou'rt young,
    If thou hast a scolding tongue.

Now when a youth shall say "be mine!"
  Silent stand and hang thy head;
He'll know that thou dost mean "I'm thine,"
  Just as if the words were said.
    But if thou should'st prate—say "No,"
    He, perchance, may turn and go;
    Learn this proverb, or repent,
    "Silence 'tis that gives consent."

A roar of laughter followed this song; whilst Janet rewarded the singer with a look which she attempted to make fierce, but that melted into a smile of admiration.

In the midst of this merriment, Batswing sprang to his feet, and with a hasty gesture warned them all to be silent.

In a moment all was still, and many a hand sought a hidden pocket, wherein a pistol lay concealed, whilst every one turned their eyes upon their leader.

Presently the low sound of wheels was heard.

"It is a carriage coming down the road," cried Batswing, "run, Janet, and tell the ostler to have our horses all prepared."

"Surely you would not attack them so close to the house, Captain," said Janet.

"Not I, my girl," replied Batswing, "but we must be prepared against surprise."

The girl left the room, and the company remained silent, listening to the noise of the rapidly approaching wheels.

"This is not your game then, Captain?" said Hugh Fenton.

"It is not," said Batswing.

"Then will you leave it in my hands?" demanded Hugh.

"Certainly," replied Batswing, "only I would have you be cautious, this road has become so notorious, that I doubt much that any one will travel on it without plenty of arms and a strong escort. Therefore, be

WITH A WILD NEIGH OF AGONY THE HORSE DASHED DOWN THE ROAD.

careful, and do not spoil the matter so as to let our host be brought into it."

"Trust to me," replied Hugh, rising from his chair.

"Why, where are you going?" demanded Batswing, "you had better remain here until the coach arrives, most likely it will stop here, perhaps it may stay all night, and what then? at all events, if it passes the inn you will know that you are all safe, and can easily overtake it by cutting across country."

"You are right, Captain," said Hugh, turning rather red, "we have not all the judgment that you possess. If we had, no one would be able to travel."

The sound of the wheels came close up; the coach turned into the inn yard, and stopped at the inn door.

"There," said Batswing, "by the sound I should judge that it is a private carriage, and if so the owner will need a private room, so that you will have plenty of time to see what you will have to do, and what

resistance you are likely to receive from the traveller."

This arrangement was undoubtedly the best that could have been made, but unfortunately fate was against it, as was proved by a good manly voice in the bar, exclaiming—

"Nay, mine good host; I do not need a private room; I wish merely to give my horses a feed of corn, take a tankard of ale or a bowl of punch, and then proceed on my journey; therefore I will go into your parlour."

"But, my Lord," cried the landlady, "there are some gentlemen in there."

"So much the better; I love company."

"But, my Lord, they are a party of friends."

"Better still, I hate enemies, so if they don't object to my company I am sure I shall rejoice in theirs: therefore, lead the way."

No. 13.

"But I fear, my Lord, their rank in life—"

"Rank! fiddlesticks," replied the new comer. "I am no lord, besides, when a man travels he must not be particular. I doubt not, but that these gentlemen are honest bagmen or something of that sort."

"Ay, honest I'll swear," replied the landlady, "only not in your station of life, sir, but—"

"Away with all scruples, my honest dame," cried the man, "whilst I stand here talking I might have been drinking; therefore, I will waste time no longer, but go in at once. Bring me a huge bowl of punch, and if these gentlemen will not make friends with me over that, then they are churlish indeed."

The next moment the door flew open, and a tall handsome gentleman entered, whom Batswing at once recognised as no other than Captain Jennings, who had had charge of Lord Clumber's plate.

"Gentlemen, I have, with your kind permission come to crush a cup with you. I trust I do not intrude; if so, tell me, and I will retire at once."

"Intrude!" said Batswing, assuming a surly tone, "the room's a public one, and therefore as free to you as it is to me, or any of us."

"True, friend, but I do not like to thrust my company on any one."

"No need to make any excuses," said Batswing, roughly, but in a softer voice, "you are welcome as far as I am concerned, and that's enough."

Captain Jennings took his seat at the table and cast a rapid glance round.

"Hem!" he thought to himself, "I have fallen into a nice nest of highwaymen, and no mistake; well there is but one thing to be done, and that is to get out of it again. How— I must leave to providence and good luck."

There was a pause for a few moments, only disturbed by the noise made by the men as they puffed out their smoke.

"Travellers, I suppose?" enquired Captain Jennings of Teddy.

"Yes," replied Teddy, "on the road."

"Many a true word said in jest," thought the Captain; then added, aloud, "how is business?"

"It's been rather queer lately. Too much cutting down."

"He means the cave, I suppose," thought Captain Jennings, then again addressing the company, he said, "It's rather dangerous travelling hereabouts?"

"It is, very; I wonder you travel so late, sir. I suppose you stop here to-night?"

"Not I," replied the Captain. "I hope to be many miles north of this to-morrow."

"I hope you may," sighed Teddy, "but there's no knowing where you may be."

"Do you think it likely I shall be stopped on the road?" demanded Captain Jennings.

"I can't say, but I don't think it's impossible," replied Teddy.

"Bah! I have no fear," cried Captain Jennings, boastfully, "I'm a match for any highwayman that ever breathed."

"Perhaps you have a large guard?" demanded Hugh.

"No, only my old coachman, who never smelt any powder, save that which falls from his wig."

"You are well armed, I presume?"

"A couple of small pistols that are in the pockets of my carriage."

"Perhaps you travel without money?"

"I'faith not I, my purse is always well lined;" and as he spoke he drew forth a well filled purse and shook it gaily.

"And you do not fear being robbed?" demanded Hugh.

"Not a bit; I do not think half-a-dozen highwaymen could rob me."

"They mostly ride singly, I believe," said Teddy.

"Oh! as for that," said the Captain, contemptuously, "no single highwayman could ever rob me—I defy them all to try it. Why, we should only be man to man, and why should I not be as good as he is?"

"Ah! why not indeed?" demanded Batswing, "I never was stopped by a highwayman yet: and I should like to see the one who would do it. I don't think he would get off scot-free."

"That's right," cried Captain Jennings, "for my own part I am willing to lay a wager that no single highwayman, however brave he might be, could stop me, or even if he did attempt it, I am prepared to bet that he would bitterly repent it. No, no, they know me too well for that."

"Oh," said Batswing, pushing back his chair, and pretending to look suspiciously at the stranger, "they know you do they? I don't like folk who know highwaymen."

"You need not be alarmed, my friend," laughed the Captain, "I am not one of the fraternity. But, hark, I hear my carriage coming round, and so, gentlemen, I must wish you good night."

"Good night, and a safe journey," replied the men.

The Captain raised his hat politely and left the room, and a few minutes afterwards his carriage was heard rolling away in the distance.

"Now I'm off," cried Hugh Fenton, springing to his feet, "I can overtake him by the moor if I cut across the meadow to the bend in the road."

"I think you had better leave him alone, Hugh Fenton," said Batswing.

"And why? he is a regular braggart, without courage—and—"

"He is no braggart," said Batswing, "he is Captain Jennings, of His Majesty's Dragoons; I know him, and fear that he will do you a mischief."

"I fear not," cried the other, impatiently, "he has thrown down the challenge and I accept the gage, and you shall see how bitterly he shall repent his words, for I alone will empty his pockets and relieve him of his jewels."

"Well, as you will," said Batswing, "I have no control over you, so do as you like."

"Farewell," cried Hugh, "we shall meet again, and then I shall have proved myself worthy to be re-admitted into the band."

"I trust it may be so," replied Batswing, "but whatever happens, remember I am your friend, and will assist you, should trouble come upon you."

With a merry laugh Hugh left the inn, and springing lightly on his horse, dashed away.

It was a windy, chilly night. The trees bent and groaned as the sharp blast rushed through them.

Now and then heavy drops of rain fell, but they soon ceased.

The moon ever and anon shone out from between the dark masses of clouds that scudded along before the wind, and then again she was clouded over, and the night densely dark.

Leaping his mare over a hedge, Hugh galloped on across the meadows until he reached the bend in the road, where he halted.

Choosing the deep shadow of some overhanging trees, he waited for the carriage.

He examined his pistols with great care; they were primed and loaded well.

He then searched for a mask with which to hide his face, but to his dismay found that he had in his hurry forgotten it.

"Bah! it is no matter," he cried, "the night is too dark for anyone to see me."

Onward came the carriage wheels, it was close upon him now, and as it turned the corner he put spurs to his horse, and dashing forward, discharged a pistol at the coachman, at the same time thundering the word—

"Stand!"

The coachman dropped the reins instantly, and rolled beneath his seat.

The next moment Hugh Fenton had dashed his pistol through the carriage window, and presenting it at Captain Jennings demanded his money or his life.

"For mercy's sake my good man!" exclaimed the Captain, "do put that pistol down."

"No nonsense," said Hugh sternly, "your money or your life."

"Yes, yes, I understand," said the Captain, apparently very much agitated, "but how is a poor fellow to recover his wits whilst that nasty, dangerous thing is placed so uncomfortably near his brains."

"I have no time to waste, and I shall not remove it until I have your money."

"Dear, dear me, where have I put my purse?" said the captain, feeling about as if in the greatest state of nervous excitement.

"I thought my gallant gentleman," said Hugh laughing, that no highwayman could rob you singly, eh? speaking and doing are different things."

"No, no," replied the captain, as the moon burst from behind a cloud, "neither would you have dared had it not been for that rough looking fellow behind you; the one in the moonlight."

Hugh was taken off his guard, and turned quickly round to see who was there.

At that moment the captain drew a pistol and fired it at the highwayman.

Luckily for Hugh, in turning he had jerked the reins, and his horse sprang on one side, or the contents of the captain's pistol would have undoubtedly passed through his body; as it was they entered the horse's neck.

With a wild neigh of agony the horse dashed down the road till it fell dead.

Poor Hugh gazed at the horse which he dearly loved, and cursed the day he had been so sure of his own cleverness. How his comrades would laugh when they heard how easily he had been duped; and how successful the captain had been.

He dragged the horse into a ditch by the wayside, and walked back wearily to the inn, where he related to the landlord what had occurred, and to avoid suspicion retired to bed.

Worn out with fatigue and anxiety, he soon fell asleep, but had not long been in that blissful state, when he was disturbed by a loud knocking at the door.

"Who is there?" he cried, springing from his bed.

"That is the voice," cried a man outside, "burst in the door."

The next moment the door lay smashed on the ground and Captain Jennings, followed by several constables, the landlord, landlady, and Janet, rushed into the room.

"That is the man who attempted to rob me on the King's highway, seize him."

"Really sir, this must be some mistake," cried the landlord, "this house is a respectable house, and I would'nt have a bad character in it for the world."

"I don't doubt you for an instant," replied Captain Jennings, "a nice respectable party I met here this evening."

"But the gentleman has not left the house all the evening," said Janet, "he went to bed because he was ill."

"If he can prove that," said Captain Jennings, "of course he will not be hurt, but he must do so at the proper place and time."

"But how can you tell he is the man," asked the landlady.

"Because I saw his face in the moonlight," cried the captain, "and knew him to be one of the fellows I saw here. So come along my fine fellow, come quietly, for

escape is impossible. I told you the highwayman who stopped me would regret it."

CHAPTER XLI.

HOW THE GOVERNOR OF NEWGATE FALLS INTO THE TRAP LAID FOR HIM.

WHEN Hugh Fenton had started on his expedition, which the reader will perceive turned out so unfortunate for him, Batswing arose and bade his men prepare to follow him.

The horses were soon brought round to the front of the inn, and the men leaped into their saddles, and then stood ready for their leader's orders.

"Janet," said Batswing to the pretty waiting maid, "if anything should go wrong with that hot-headed fellow, Hugh Fenton, and you hear of it, take care that I am informed of the circumstances directly. He is a good lad though somewhat hot-headed, therefore we must not lose him."

"Trust to me," said Janet, "there never was a likelier girl than Janet to get a smart young fellow out of a scrape."

"Or to get him into one," laughed Batswing, "those eyes of yours are positively dangerous."

"Nevertheless, they are honest."

"That they are not, for they steal away men's hearts. Look to what I have told you, and you shall have a silk gown, and now farewell."

Snatching a kiss from the pouting, but not unwilling girl, Batswing sprang upon his horse, and putting himself at the head of his troop, rode gaily away.

Carefully avoiding the roads, the party of horsemen crossed the meadows and fields, clearing hedges and ditches in the darkness, with a coolness and exactitude that plainly showed they were well used to that part of the country.

At length they arrived at a small dismantled hut at the bottom of a bosky dell, so completely hidden by trees and underwood that a casual passor by would never have noticed it.

Here they pulled up, and each of the men procured some thick rope, some yards of which they coiled up at their saddle-bows.

Batswing entered the cottage, and reappeared in about five minutes dressed in the long black cloak and sable garments in which the reader first made his acquaintance. He then directed the men to change their clothes, which they did, and in a few moments all were dressed in the same sombre manner.

"Are you all ready?" demanded Batswing, when the men had mounted.

"All," was the reply, given in deep stern voices.

"Your pistols well loaded and your swords ready for action?"

"They are."

"Then follow me in silence."

Again they commenced their headlong race till they arrived at a thick plantation, across which it was with difficulty they could make their way on horseback.

However, they managed to scramble through, and arrived on a steep bank that led down to a broad, clear, road.

Halting at the top of the bank, Batswing placed half of his men in such a position that they were entirely hidden by the trees from anyone coming up the road.

He then crossed over to the other side of the road, where there was an embankment exactly similar to the one we have already described, and on that he stationed the rest of the troop

He then dismounted, and going into the roadway, emptied a small keg of gunpowder in a heap, right in the centre of the path, carefully laying a thick train along the ground up to where he was concealed.

He then gave his men special orders not to move until they heard him give the scream of the screech owl, when they were to utter the same weird cry, and charge upon anyone who might be in the road, but not to pursue those who fled unless specially commanded so to do.

Slowly the time seemed to creep along. Not a sound was to be heard, save the rustling of the wind through the trees and the occasional cry of the owl as it flew after its prey—the timid field mouse.

Presently Batswing's quick ears caught the sound of something coming along the road.

He dismounted from his horse, and placing his ear to the ground listened intently.

By this means he was able to tell that there must at least be some half-dozen horses coming along the road at a sharp trot, whilst he could also distinguish the grating of wheels, clearly proving that there was also a carriage.

"It is as I thought," he exclaimed, "Mr. Pitt is sure to be in the carriage, so if all goes well, we shall have a very easy victory."

The sound of horses and wheels drew nearer and nearer.

They were evidently urging on their horses at a good rate.

At length the cavalcade turned a point in the road, coming in full view, for at that moment the moon broke from behind a cloud and shot down her silvery rays, so that for a second the riders were distinctly visible; but the next minute a dark cloud passed over the moon, and all was dark again.

Nevertheless, during the transient light, Batswing was enabled to tell the strength of the enemy.

Six men, well armed, rode in advance of a large coach, which was drawn by two heavy Flemish horses; two men, both armed, were seated on the box, and Batswing had but little doubt that the coach was also full of men.

"So this is what Mr. Pitt calls half a dozen men, not more," he muttered. "Well, if he break his word, why should I not do the same?"

The clouds had now so covered the moon that it was with the greatest difficulty Batswing could ascertain how near the troop of horsemen was.

Just as the noses of the foremost horses were within a foot of where the gunpowder had been placed, Batswing fired the train.

There was no explosion, but a loud hissing noise, and the next moment a bright yellow mass of flame flew up towards the sky.

With a scream of terror, the horses on which the six men were mounted reared on their haunches; then, mad with fear, dashed down the road at a terrific pace.

Batswing at that moment uttered the wild cry, which was repeated by his men. Two of his followers sprang forward and seized the horses which were in the coach, whilst two others mounted the box, and seized the men who were seated thereon, and bound them with the cords before they could recover from their surprise.

Batswing then advanced to the carriage, in which he found Mr. Pitt, and his faithful follower, Mr. Grummidge.

"You have come to take Batswing?" demanded the Bat."

"Ye-e-ees, sir," stammered Mr. Pitt.

"He is here," said Batswing, in deep tones. "Where is the reward?"

"I—I did not bring it," faltered Mr. Pitt.

"So you would have cheated us?" cried Batswing. "This must be looked to."

"I—I meant to have paid the money in a day or two —I did indeed."

"Take all the arms from these men," cried Batswing.

In a moment both pistols and swords were removed from Mr. Pitt and his companion, who stared in amazement at the grim band that surrounded them.

"I must trouble you to alight, gentlemen," said Batswing.

With trembling steps the two men did so.

"Now take those two men from the box, and place them in the carriage."

This was also soon done.

"Unharness the horses in the carriage," said Batswing "and strap these two men on them."

In vain Mr. Pitt and Grummidge begged and prayed to be excused. They were hustled up, and strapped to the horses much in the same way as Mazeppa was said to have been.

Batswing then ordered two of his men to lead the horses on which the luckless governor and his companion were bound. Then, turning to the two men who were in the carriage, he said,

"Gentlemen, you may now perceive how hopeless it is for you to attempt to arrest Batswing. He defies all mortal power. Should your companions return, bid them not endeavour to follow me—they cannot find me. I intend taking this luckless governor to my abode, which is *not on earth*."

"Oh! mercy! mercy!" roared Mr. Pitt.

"Put cloths over those men's faces," said Batswing; and then continued—"There, he will see how men who punish others for their own greed will be punished. Farewell : be warned, and make no further attempts to arrest Batswing or his band."

Uttering a wild yell, which was echoed by the band, Batswing wheeled his horse round, and the next moment the trembling constables were alone.

CHAPTER XLII.

WHAT BECAME OF THE GOVERNOR OF NEWGATE, AND HOW HE PASSED HIS EVENING.

THE kerchiefs that had been placed over Mr. Pitt's and his assistants' faces were certainly not of the ordinary sort, for they had not been there long before both the gentlemen became insensible.

Perhaps the reason of the narcotic being used was to save those gentlemen from pain, which, otherwise, they would have undoubtedly suffered to no slight degree; for the wild weird band held on their course at a rattling pace, clearing hedges and ditches, reckless how the governor and Mr. Grummidge were shaken about; although it must be confessed that the position in which they were riding was not the most conducive to comfort.

At length they reached the old Abbey and passed through the secret passage to the vaults.

The two men were unstrapped from the horses and laid upon the floor.

Two empty coffins were then procured, into which the hapless governor and his lieutenant were placed whilst still insensible.

They then proceeded to light a fire in the middle of the chamber; and as the flames shot upwards, they cast some powder on them so that they burnt with a livid light.

Batswing seated himself on a raised seat, and his companions sat around him.

Huge bowls of steaming punch were brought in, and the robbers commenced drinking freely, whilst waiting for Mr. Pitt's return to consciousness.

It was not long before the two persons began to revive.

Both uttered deep groans and sighs; then Mr. Pitt slowly arose in a sitting posture.

Casting his eyes around him he beheld the grim troop of his tormentors, their faces made quite livid by the ghastly light thrown out by the fire.

"Lord have mercy upon us," he exclaimed, "we are dead and in h—l."

And closing his eyes sank back into his coffin with a groan.

This exclamation so startled Grummidge, that he, in his turn, sprang up, but no sooner did he behold the ghastly group than he uttered one long yell and fell back, screaming, into the coffin.

Batswing and his followers could scarcely repress their laughter at this, but as it was Batswing's determination to punish the governor as much as possible, they controlled their mirth, well knowing that mysterious silence would be more dreadful than screams of demoniacal merriment.

"Pray for us, sir, pray for us," entreated Grummidge.

"I can't," whined Mr. Pitt, "I can't remember a prayer; they stick in my throat."

Whereupon they both fell to work sighing and sobbing in a tremendous manner.

After this had continued some time, Batswing, in deep sepulchral tones, commanded that they should be brought before him.

Four men advanced to the coffins, two of whom dragged Mr. Pitt on to his feet, whilst the others performed the same kind office for Grummidge, and led them up to the place where Batswing was seated.

"So," cried Batswing, "the governor of Newgate has come at last, ho, ho, ho, how well he looks; we welcome you to the nether regions. A cup of our best for the worthy Mr. Pitt."

At this a man stepped forward and thrust a goblet of boiling punch into Mr. Pitt's hand, at the same time commanding him to drink.

The unhappy man put his lips to the cup but quickly withdrew them.

"It's too hot, if you please, sir," he grasped.

"Drink!" was the stern reply.

"But really—" commenced Mr. Pitt, but before he could say another word he was seized by the two men, and the boiling liquor poured down his throat.

"Mercy, mercy," he grasped, "Oh! the skin has come off the roof of my mouth."

So comical were the faces that Mr. Pitt made that all the men were obliged to burst out into a hearty roar of laughter.

"We have yet another visitor, cried Batswing, "he also must drink our health."

Another goblet of boiling punch was handed to Grummidge, who, seeing how his master had been treated, made no bones about it at all, but drank it off at once.

No sooner had he swallowed it than he commenced dancing about with the pain.

"Bravely done," cried Batswing, "gentlemen, be seated."

The two luckless wretches were placed upon two iron seats, which were so contrived, that they held a small lamp in each of them, which caused them to become so hot, that Mr. Pitt and Mr. Grummidge fidgetted about most uncomfortably, although they sat quite on the edge of their seats.

More hot grog was supplied to them, but they were not forced to drink it as they had done the first, still their mouths were so burnt that everything seemed boiling to them.

"How like you your new abode?" demanded Batswing.

"Oh, its—its very comfortable, sir," replied Mr. Pitt, "it's rather warm."

"Ah! that's the beauty of it," said Batswing, "no catching cold here. It will be much better presently, the fires are rather low at present."

"It's quite warm enough for me thank you," stammered Mr. Pitt.

"Oh you're new to it at present," said Batswing, "in a hundred years or two you will be more used to it."

"A hundred years or two," gasped Grummidge, "but I-I can't stop here all that time, I must get back if you please sir."

"Back! who talks of going back? No, no, you must remain here," replied Batswing.

"But my wife?" emplored Mr. Pitt.

"Is far happier without you."

"But I won't stop here," cried Mr. Pitt springing up, "I would sooner die first."

"You are dead," said Batswing solemnly.

"With a heavy groan Mr. Pitt sank back again.

"Have you forgotten that a few days ago you broke your necks falling off two horses to which you had been strapped."

Neither of the men spoke, but both sobbed aloud.

"You have been sent to me for judgment," said Batswing.

"What have I done?" demanded Mr. Pitt.

"What have you done?" exclaimed Batswing passionately, "have you not tormented the poor wretches of prisoners who have been unfortunate enough to be placed under your charge. Have you not treated poor debtors worse than rich criminals. What shall be his punishment for that?"

"The lash, the lash," shouted the men.

"Have you not ground down the prisoners, wringing every penny from them, making their miserable lives even more miserable, depriving them even of their right to use the Press Yard unless they could pay you?"

"Oh have mercy, have mercy," said Mr. Pitt.

"As for you," said Batswing turning to Grummidge, "you are but a bad copy of your master. Whilst such men are permitted to rule over a place, men like yourself, dull to all feelings of honour and humanity, are sure to be plentiful. Therefore your punishment will not be so great."

"Thanks, oh! thanks," exclaimed Grummidge.

"As one has been the cause of the other's sin, so shall one be the cause of the other's punishment. Bring in the instruments of torture," said Batswing.

In a minute two cat-o'-nine-tails were produced.

These were most formidable instruments, each tail being studded with sharp pieces of metal inserted in the thong. The handles were not more than a foot-and-a-half long whilst the lashes exceeded two feet.

"Prisoners stand up," said Batswing.

The two prisoners were made to stand facing each other but about three feet apart.

"Give each one a whip," commanded Batswing in a cold hard voice.

This command was soon carried out, and Mr. Pitt and Grummidge grasped their whips convulsively, and eyed each other with looks askance.

"Now," continued Batswing, "you must each thrash the other until I tell you to stop; and mind, if I see either of you trying to avoid striking the other as hard as you can, I shall at once order my tormentors to use the whips in your place."

The two men stood trembling, their eyes fixed on each other, but neither moved.

"Come! no hesitation, but commence at once," cried Batswing.

After one or two preparatory swings of their whips each brought down his lash upon the other.

Both screamed with pain, and losing their tempers, commenced flogging each other without mercy. What with their howls of pain, and the vigour with which they used the cat-o'-nine-tails, the scene became irresistably comic to the spectators who roared with laughter.

Grummidge was a much stronger man than Mr. Pitt, and consequently soon got the best of the struggle. So much indeed was he the conqueror, that Mr. Pitt fairly turned tail and fled.

But Grummidge was smarting under the punishment he had received, and was determined to have revenge.

Yelling out as if he were still under the lash, he belaboured the governor with all his might until the unfortunate man fell down on the ground in agony.

Even then the vengeful Grummidge would have continued his attacks upon his master, but at Batswing's command the cat-o'-nine-tails was taken from him.

"You have now received your daily punishment," said Batswing, "and can make up your mind for enjoyment. Let the banquet be spread."

In a few moments a beautiful banquet was spread on a large table and the prisoners were forced to join the others at the feast.

When they had finished the repast, during which many a joke was cut at the unfortunate governor's expense, the viands were cleared away and the drink again resorted to.

The prisoners had with difficulty been able to force a few mouthfuls of food down their throats to oblige their captors, the pain they had suffered having taken away their appetites; but now that they were allowed to drink cold wines, they began to drink so fast that they soon forgot their pains in a great measure.

"Come," cried Batswing, "a song, a good comic song."

Mr. Pitt looked round at his grim captors, and wondered that these grim creatures, whom he fully believed to be supernatural, should really give way to singing, especially songs of a jovial character. Indeed, he greatly wondered at their having any mirth at all, for although they had laughed so heartily during the castigation of the governor and jailer, yet the pain of the flogging had been so great that neither Mr. Pitt nor Mr. Grummidge had noticed the merriment their contortions had caused.

"A song! a song!" cried the company, as if in rapture, but all keeping without a smile, and speaking in deep tones.

Rising from the table, a most cadaverous-looking man responded to the call in the following song:—

The Two Ghosts.

Two ghosts sat on an old tombstone,
    Clad in their garments white;
They were playing at dice, and to see the sport
    A raven croaked with delight.
The box was made of a baby's skull,
    The dice of dead men's bones.
And ever and anon as they shook them up,
    The echoes answered dull.
Ho! ho! croaked the raven, this is rare sport,
    To see these dead men brave,
As they rattle their bones on the cold tombstones,
    On top of a mouldy grave.

A round of applause followed this lively song, and then Batswing called upon Mr. Pitt to oblige the company.

"I—I never sing," stammered the unfortunate governor.

"Well, then, you must do something to amuse us," replied Batswing. "If you will not sing you must dance. Come, no hesitation, or I shall have to order in the cat-o'-nine-tails again."

In spite of his groans and entreaties, Mr. Pitt was dragged from his seat, and placed in the centre of the room.

Then there came a wild strain of demoniacal music, so weird and unearthly that Mr. Pitt nearly sunk to the ground with terror. But at that moment the long lash of a whip fell heavily round his legs, making him perform a most wonderful caper.

Again and again the lash twisted round the governor's legs, which being only protected by thin stockings, suffered fearfully. As the blows fell the governor rose. He leaped, he capered, he twirled and twisted, doing such strange contortions that the company fairly roared

with laughter. At last he was so worn out that he fell exhausted on the floor.

"What!" exclaimed Batswing, "do you dare to give up dancing until I give you permission? Up at once, or fear the consequences."

"Oh! most gracious sir," exclaimed Mr. Pitt, "have mercy on me, I beseech you. I tremble now with horror and fear of the punishment I have already received, and pray that you will spare me all further torture."

"Did you ever show mercy to one of your prisoners?" demanded Batswing.

"Yes, sir, truly I have, when Lord——"

"Oh!" cried Batswing, "a lord! Of course you showed him mercy; firstly, because he had power to injure you, and secondly, because he had money to pay you."

"Oh! spare me, spare me!" cried Mr. Pitt, who could not deny this statement.

"Have you ever shown mercy to the weak and the poor? Never. Have you ever lent a kindly ear to a plea for pity? Never. Gold has been your god, you have lived for that, and that alone. Therefore by that, and that alone, shall you purchase commiseration from us, and by no other means."

"I am a poor man, sir, really a poor man," pleaded the governor.

"Poor!—you are rich from the wretched money pressed from the miserable prisoners, and only by disgorging that shall you preserve yourself from pain."

"But I have no money with me," urged Mr. Pitt.

"We have a cheque-book on your bankers," said Batswing. "You can sign one of those cheques. We know your account is good."

"Well, well," said Mr. Pitt, "I will sign a cheque for fifty pounds."

"Fifty pounds! You will sign a cheque for one thousand pounds."

"I have not so much to my account."

"You lie; you have just twelve hundred."

Mr. Pitt stared, for he knew that that was just the amount that he really did hold on his banker's account. Little did he dream that the robbers had taken the precaution to ascertain that fact the day previously.

With many a sigh and groan the cheque was signed and handed over to Batswing, who secretly dispatched a messenger with it at once to London, so as to be able to get it cashed the first thing in the morning.

"It is now time to retire," said Batswing, "to bed, gentlemen, and I trust you may sleep well; to-morrow we will resume our sports."

The two prisoners groaned when they thought of the kind of sports they had enjoyed.

"Conduct these men to their beds," cried Batswing, "to your beds, gentlemen, at once."

The men were seized instantly and once more placed in the coffins.

Then followed a tremendous clashing of gongs and cymbals, and in an instant all was darkness.

Hour after hour passed away, neither Mr. Pitt nor his companion in misfortune daring to speak, although minutes seemed ages to them.

At last, just about the break of day, each felt an icy cold hand placed upon his throat, and a cloth, saturated with some spirit, placed over his mouth.

For a moment their pulsations seemed too violent to bear, and then they became unconscious.

In this state they were lifted from the coffins and deprived of their coats, shoes, stockings, and everything of value.

Their arms were then pinioned behind them, and labels bound round their necks in such a manner that they could not get them off.

On Mr. Pitt's label was inscribed, THIS IS MR. PITT, GOVERNOR OF NEWGATE; and on that of Mr. Grummidge was written, "This is one of the worst jailers in Newgate, show him no mercy."

They were then hoisted on to the shoulders of some men, who bore them out into the forest, where they left them in a ditch, taking great care that they were so far apart that they were not likely to meet each other.

It was broad daylight when Mr. Pitt awoke, and miserably cold, crawled out of the ditch.

He scarcely could walk for the pains in his limbs caused by his horse-riding and by the flogging.

His garments were covered with blood that had flowed from the wounds inflicted by the cat-o'-nine-tails.

Moaning and groaning, he wandered about until he came to some labourers, but so terrible was the spectacle he presented, that the simple people ran away in terror, and it was not without much difficulty that he could persuade them to render him some assistance.

At length, by promising them a good reward he managed to get them to unbind him. A thing they did with great fear and trembling, as they fully believed him to be an escaped lunatic; they then threw some old coats about him, but refused to let him go until they had taken him to Newgate, "for," argued they, "if he be Mr. Pitt, we shall then get the reward he has promised us, and if he is not Mr. Pitt, we shall, doubtless get the reward from his friends, or from the lunatic asylum whence he has escaped."

Bruised as he was, he was hurried into a heavy cart and driven at a jog-trot into London, moaning with agony at every jolt of the cart.

At length he arrived at the jail and was recognised by his wife, but the countrymen would not depart until they had received the reward.

A messenger was at once dispatched to the bank to stop the cheque, but found that it had already been paid. So Mr. Pitt took to his bed, after ordering that double the severity was to be shown to the prisoners, and mentally repeating an oath not to attempt to arrest Batswing again.

CHAPTER XLIII.

JERRY AND FLICKER BECOME KNIGHT ERRANTS, AND START ON AN EXPEDITION TO RELEASE IMPRISONED DAMSELS.—THE DOUBLE COMBAT IN THE CELLAR.— THE HEROES HAVE A BANQUET IN HONOUR OF THEIR VICTORY, AND TAKE MORE DRINK AND VOWS THAN ARE GOOD FOR THEM.

ABOUT the same time at night as Batswing and his companions had been refreshing themselves at the Load of Hay, Jerry Blinker was on his way to Drury Lane, accompanied by little Flicker, who, although he had not recovered from his wound, yet had acquired that love for adventure so common amongst lads of his kind.

As the reader already knows, the night was far from a pleasant one; indeed a perfect storm would have been almost preferable to the intermittent rain and fitful glimmer of the moon.

Nevertheless the two lads pressed on their way, neither of them uttering a word, Jerry being evidently too much occupied with his own thoughts, and whistling, to pay much attention to his companion.

At length Jerry paused suddenly, both in his walking and whistling.

For a moment he stood still, and then, giving a regular caper in the air, exclaimed,

"Blest if that wouldn't be a joke. I'll do it, by Jingo!"

"What will be a joke?" asked Flicker. "What are you going to do?"

"Why, you see this, Master Flicker," said Jerry, pompously, "it has pleased the Captain to select me to perform a very difficult duty; that is, to discover two beauteous damsels in distress. Now it strikes me I can improve on this occasion by not only discovering the two beautiful maidens, but saving them. Eh, Mr. Flicker, what do you think of that, my young buck?"

"Prime," was Flicker's laconic reply.

"Now, nothing is done without discipline," continued Jerry. "One must command, the other obey."

"I 'spose you want me to obey?" said Flicker, quietly.

"You've hit the right nail on the head for once,' said Jerry.

"Very well," said Flicker. "I don't mind obeying, if you show pluck."

"Good," cried Jerry; "I like your sentiments, they do you honour, and I nominate you my lieutenant."

Seeing that the newly-constructed band consisted only of two, it was difficult to see what else Flicker could have been but the second in command.

"And what are your plans?" demanded Flicker.

"Well, I ain't decided yet," replied Jerry. "I must wait and see what turns up. One should never work in a hurry—it ain't good enough. We must see what old Toby Crick says about it first."

Having come to this conclusion, they resumed their journey, and soon arrived at Toby Crick's snug tavern.

"Well, and what do you want?" demanded Toby, looking in surprise at the lads.

"Some refreshment," replied Jerry. "I'm as hungry as a hunter, and dry as a bone."

"Bless my heart alive!" cried Toby, opening his eyes in astonishment. "Why, who are you?"

"I have come from Mrs. Wapshaw, of the Bird Cage Inn, at Stamford Hill, with a letter to you," replied Jerry. "You know Widow Wapshaw?"

"Bless my soul alive, yes. Wapshaw and I were quite old friends once."

"Well, here's the letter, so let's have the grog."

Toby Crick took the letter, and read it; but he had no sooner done so than his face turned blue, and hurriedly telling Jerry and Flicker to follow him, led the way into the small parlour.

No sooner had he seen them safe in than he closed the door, and putting his back against it, waved the letter in their faces, and gasped out,

"This letter ain't from the widow at all, you young scamps."

"I know that," replied Jerry, winking. "It's from the Cappen."

"And what on earth has he sent you here for?" demanded Toby.

"To see into the matter about them there girls?"

"But I can't assist you in committing a robbery," cried Toby.

"Who asked you to?" retorted Jerry. "You might wait till you are asked!"

"If you don't want me to help you, why do you come to me?"

"For the last thing I should expect to get from you —information," said Jerry.

"Information about what?" demanded the landlord, not wholly reassured.

"Why, about some old woman as lives a few doors up this street, and has some girls."

"Oh; I know whom you mean," said Toby. "It's Mother Jenkins, the milliner."

"Milliner, is she?" said Jerry.

"That is, she says she is; but it's deuced little work either goes in or comes out of the place—ay, or victuals either. I do fear the poor creatures are badly treated."

"That's the very thing we want to know," said Jerry, "for me and my lieutenant intend liberating them this very night. What do you think of that, eh?"

A broad smile illumined Mr. Toby Crick's face as he looked at the two lads.

"Bless my soul alive, but you are a pair of mummies!" he said.

"Ha! we're the right sort, the reg'ler tip-top breed, that's what we are," said Jerry.

"There's no mistake about us," answered Flicker, "so let us have something to eat and drink."

The landlord, who was evidently pleased with the boys, soon placed a substantial meal before them, to which they did the most ample justice.

Jerry then regaled himself with a pipe of tobacco, much to Toby Crick's delight.

Having finished his smoke and drank a stiff glass of grog, Jerry declared himself ready for the expedition.

In the first place he looked to his pistols, and having ascertained that they were all right, he placed them in his pockets, so as to be ready to his grasp.

He then stuck a long knife in his belt, and his arrangements were completed.

In all these particulars he was carefully followed by Mr. Flicker, the two lads evidently considering themselves of the greatest importance.

Being now perfectly ready for their undertaking, Jerry in a haughty tone commanded Toby to "lead the way," which that gentleman did, by leading them up to the top of the house, nearly suffocating with suppressed laughter as he did so.

"This is the window," he said, "I'll give you a leg up."

With Crick's assistance the two lads were soon safely lodged on the top of the house. Looking over the parapet, Jerry called to the worthy landlord.

"I say landlord; if I send for any drink or grub let the person have it at once, and without asking questions, I'll settle afterwards."

"All right yer honour," said Toby laughing, and the next moment the lads crept slowly along the roof of the houses, while Mr. Crick returned to his parlour.

The boys had not advanced far when they recognised the window Batswing had described to them as the one by which he had entered.

Here Jerry looked about cautiously to see if he could find a letter.

He searched every hole and corner but no such thing could he find.

"Well, I'm blest if I can understand this," said Jerry, "the cappen said it was sure to be here. Well, I shall act on my own responsibility."

As he spoke he drew his knife, and passing it through the crack in the window, managed to force the casement open, and the next moment the two lads crept stealthily into the bedroom.

All was dark and silent in that desolate chamber.

The lads drew closer together as they passed into the darkness.

"I think we must have got into the wrong house," whispered Flicker.

"No;" replied Jerry "I know we are right. Hush! what is that?"

A low wailing sound seemed to come from the bed, making both the lads start in horror.

"What can it be?" said Jerry trembling, for like most people at that time he was superstitious.

"It sounds like some of those queer noises I used to hear down in the Fleet," said Flicker, "they used to go on exactly like that."

"Who used to go on like that?" demanded Jerry.

"Them as was thrown down the ditch before they were quite dead," replied Flicker.

"Let us see who or what it is," said Jerry.

Grasping each other by the sleeve, they slowly advanced to the corner from whence the mournful sounds proceeded.

Stretched on a rude pallet, lay a poor girl, her hands and feet tightly bound to the four posts of the bed in such a manner that she was quite unable to move.

"Well I'm blest if this 'ere aint a rum go," said Jerry.

"In mercy release my hands," implored the poor girl, "I will do anything you want."

"What is the matter my dear?" demanded Jerry.

"I am dying with thirst; these ropes cut me to the bone. Oh! have mercy I pray."

"We'll soon set you free," said Flicker, and in an instant he cut the ropes with his sharp knife, and then assisted the girl to rise.

"There's no doubt now about our being in the right house," said Jerry.

"In the right house; what do you mean?" asked the girl.

"Do you remember saving two gentlemen from the constables?" asked Jerry.

"Perfectly," replied the girl, "it is for doing that and losing the reward, that I have been treated in this manner."

"But I thought there were two girls?" said Jerry looking round.

"My sister is punished in the cellar far more than I am, because she refused to state which way the men had gone, but tried to let the constables know how we and our companions are treated by Mrs. Jenkins."

"Who is this Mrs. Jenkins?" demanded one of the lads.

"She calls herself a milliner, and we poor girls become her apprentices, of course our friends paying a premium with us. But she never teaches us the trade, but nearly starves us and treats us as her slaves."

"But why do not your friends interfere?" asked Flicker.

"Alas! we have no true friends; those who put us here never wish to know more about us; and when they hear of our deaths, which generally happens through torture and starvation, they very willingly pay the slight funeral expenses that are charged; being only too glad never to see us again."

"Well. we have come to release you," said Jerry valiantly, "we come as the substitutes of the two gentlemen you saved. You saved them and we will save you."

"Oh may heaven bless you, sir, for those kind words," said the girl.

Jerry seemed an inch taller for being called 'sir,' and cocking his hat on one side, said—

"And how many poor creatures are there in this house, in the same position as yourself?"

"Some nine or ten sir," replied the girl sorrowfully.

"And who keeps guard over them?" continued Jerry.

"Only Mrs. Jenkins and her cat," replied the girl.

"Her cat!" exclaimed the boys.

"Yes; she has a terrible wild cat that flies at and scratches everyone but her."

"Amiable animal," said Flicker. "I should like her very much."

"I suppose all you girls would gladly escape if you could?"

"Oh! most gladly," said the girl.

"Well, Miss—Miss What's-your-name?"

"Louisa Jackson," replied the girl.

"Well, I suppose then that all these girls will help us if we set them free."

"Oh, yes, gladly!" cried Louisa, clasping her hands.

"Very well; where does the old witch sleep?"

"On the ground floor, by herself; but you must be careful of the cat."

"Never fear; we will be *very* careful of that lovely animal," replied Jerry.

"But hadn't we better get the girls all loose first?" asked Flicker.

"Perhaps we had,' said Jerry; "where are they, my dear Louisa?"

"Some of them sleep in the rooms beneath this, but there are others, among st them my sister, who are confined downstairs in the cellars."

"They must be left to the last. Now this is my plan: first of all every one must be armed, so give me a hand here, Flick, and don't make a row."

"AT HER TOM, AT HER," CRIED THE OLD CRONE,

In a minute the boys had wrenched the old bedstead to pieces—for it was of the slightest make—and the old-fashioned thin legs made formidable bludgeons.

"Now, my dear," said Jerry, "you must creep down and wake your companions: they won't scream at seeing you, but the sight of *men* would frighten them."

"Take this 'ere knife," said Flicker, "you may need it; only don't use it unless you're forced to. I hate blood. I have seen too much of it lately."

"Now lead on," said Jerry, in as martial a tone as could be conveyed in a whisper.

"Don't you think we had better take off our shoes first?" said Flicker; "not to make a noise, you know. If we disturb the old woman she will get assistance, perhaps."

"True," said Jerry, "so off with our trotter-cases."

The two boys quickly removed their boots, but the poor girl had none to remove.

Creeping slowly downstairs, they entered a long room wherein were some dozen wretched little beds, all of a row.

Some of them were empty, but the greater number were occupied by poor emaciated girls, whose hands were tied to the bed so that they could not rise.

Louisa had quickly liberated these poor creatures and communicated to them the good news that a deliverer was near; so that Jerry and Flicker found themselves the centre of admiration of some eight or nine interesting damsels.

"Now lead us to the old woman's room," said Jerry; "that is, if you are quite dressed."

This enquiry was a very natural one on Jerry's part, inasmuch as the young ladies' toilets were of the scantiest; but they assured him that Mrs. Jenkins never allowed them any more clothes, and that therefore it was out of their power to dress more.

" I say," said Flicker to one of the girls, " haven't you got a sheet or a table cloth ?"

" What for ?" demanded the astonished girl.

" For the cat; if I can get that I don't mind the animal."

" Yes ; I can get you that," said Louisa. " There is a thick counterpane, that I washed to-day, hanging up in this room. I will get it for you."

This was soon procured, and Flicker threw it carefully over his arm.

" You and the girl pitch into the old one," said Flicker to Jerry. " Leave the cat to me."

" This is the room," whispered Louisa.

They turned the handle of the door gently, and entered a nice, comfortably-furnished room, in which blazed a good fire.

On the top a bright copper kettle sung cheerfully, whilst supper was laid on the table, on which was also placed a case-bottle of spirits.

" My eye, don't the old girl like herself though ?" ejaculated Jerry.

" Yes, but where is she ?" demanded Flicker, who held his counterpane like a matador at a bull fight. " Where's the blessed cat ?"

With the exception of Louisa and another girl, the poor apprentices had drawn back in alarm, for the old hag had so crushed their spirits by cruelty that they feared even to enter her presence, protected as they were by Jerry and Flicker.

" She must be in the cellar torturing some one—most likely my sister," said Louisa.

" The old brute," said Jerry. " We will go and catch her in the act."

" It's no good our taking those frightened creatures with us," said Flicker, " they'll only scream."

" True," replied Jerry, " and that sort of thing won't suit us at all. We must do it quietly,"

Turning to the girls, he commanded those who were afraid to fight the old hag to go into the room, and await the result of the combat, at the same time warning them that if they screamed, or caused a disturbance, they would ruin all.

Jerry then fastened the street door, putting the key in his pocket, to cut off all escape.

All the girls except Louisa and another entered the sitting room, trembling with fear.

" Bravo, my plucky ones," said Jerry. " Blest if you shan't be my sweetheart, Loo, that you shall; for when you've had a little more beef and pudding you'll be a regular beauty, you see if you wont."

Directed by the girls, Jerry and Flicker descended to the cellars.

" Take care," said Louisa, as they reached the kitchen, " you will have to descend to the cellars by a trap. If she hears us coming, she will certainly attack us."

" Is she armed ?" enquired Flicker.

" Not that I know," replied the girl, " but she has plenty of instruments of torture laying about; and if you do not take her by surprise she will fight like her wild cat."

" Never mind," replied Jerry boldly, " we must make the attempt."

The girl led them to the trap, which they found open, showing the old woman was there.

" Now keep quiet," whispered Jerry, " don't speak whatever may happen."

Softly they crept down the cellar steps, so that they did not make the slightest sound.

At the foot of the ladder they paused in horror and amazement.

The sight was almost too terrible for them to trust their own eyes.

They were standing in a vaulted chamber lit only by a torch stuck upon the wall.

The roof and walls were dripping with moisture, and huge fungi sprouted between the stones.

The floor was unpaved, and pools of stagnant water were plentiful.

In the centre of the ceiling was a large pulley, through which was passed a thick rope.

One end of this rope was tied tightly round a young girl's wrist, in such a manner that she was suspended at a distance of one foot from the ground.

Her other wrist was bound to one of her feet, so that the foot was pulled up.

Her other foot was allowed to hang down, but under it was placed a spike, so that when the poor creature sought rest she wounded the sole of her foot.

The moans and sighs of the poor girl were perfectly heartrending.

In front of her stood Mother Jenkins, an old hag, withered and blear-eyed, but whose thin bony figure showed considerable strength.

She was warmly and comfortably dressed, forming a great contrast to her victim.

In one hand she grasped a heavy cat-o'-nine-tails, which she had evidently been using upon the delicate frame of the poor creature whom she was watching.

Round about the feet of this ugly old wretch walked an enormous black cat.

As it rubbed itself against its mistress's legs it arched up its back and purred loudly, but ever and anon it cast fiery, vindictive glances from its green eyes at the poor girl, and spit in anger at her.

" At her, Tom, at her," cried the old crone to the cat, in great glee.

In a moment Tom flew at the girl, and buried its talons into her quivering flesh.

" Now's our time," whispered Jerry, and springing forward he struck the old woman a violent blow with the bed staff, over her head.

Violent as the blow had been, it did not have the desired effect upon the old witch, who seemed to be endowed with superhuman strength.

She reeled back a few paces, but quickly recovering from the blow, rushed furiously at Jerry, who with great difficulty escaped the blow she aimed at him.

Not to be daunted, Jerry returned to the charge, and, bending down his head, rushed like a mad bull at the old woman, butting her so violently in the stomach that she was sent flying into a corner, where she fell prone on the ground ; but, unluckily for Jerry, so violent had been the charge he made that he too followed and fell on the top of the screaming old hag, knocking her breath out for the second time by the force with which he came down upon her.

Then commenced the tug of war in real earnest. At it they went, tooth and nail.

Jerry—keeping his face as well as he could against the old woman's breast, so as to avoid her scratches— pummelled into her like a true Briton; whilst she tore, bit, and scratched as violently as she could.

Tufts of Jerry's red hair flew out, looking as if the old woman was plucking a flamingo.

Deep were the curses Jerry swore, shrill were the screams the hag uttered.

Over and over they rolled on the soft oosy floor, covering each other with mud and blows at the same time, both seeming determined never to give in.

How the combat would have terminated it is hard to say, had it not been for the two girls, who seeing how boldly their tyrant had been attacked, overcame their terror of her.

In a moment they rushed to Jerry's rescue, and each seizing an arm of their fallen foe, held her down, whilst Jerry—who was far from being above taking such an advantage—to use his own term, " let her have it to rights," so that the old woman was forced at last, not only to surrender at discretion, but also to plead hard for mercy.

Nor was this, by any means, the fiercest battle that was raging within the narrow limits of that under ground torture chamber.

When Jerry had attacked the old woman, Flicker, spreading out the counterpane, had rushed to attack the wild cat, hoping to envelop it in the cloth.

But "there is many a slip 'twixt the cup and the lip," and so Flicker found to his cost.

Swiftly he sprang at the cat, but, unfortunately, not swiftly enough, for the cat, uttering a fierce howl, sprang on one side, and the next moment was on top of Flicker, who, in hopes of catching her, had thrown himself on the floor, her long sharp claws plunged into the most fleshy part of her would be captor's back.

Flicker had borne too much in his lifetime to call out for pain; he therefore endeavoured to defend himself from this rear attack to the best of their ability with his hands, but he soon became convinced that all efforts made in that manner would be worse than useless, for besides clinging more desparately, plunging her claws into fresh places as if to get better hold, the cat bit his hands fearfully until the blood ran again.

For a moment Flicker paused as if thoroughly beaten, but in truth only to consider what would be the best means of crushing his enemy.

Crush his enemy? it was the very thing to do, in fact the only thing he could do.

No sooner did the idea strike him, than picking out the hardest piece of ground in the place, he suddenly threw up his legs, and fell in a sitting posture on the floor, the wild cat forming a soft, but by no means comfortable cushion.

Flicker groaned at the pain he was suffering, for although the cat was greatly injured by its fall and the lad's weight, it still bit and scratched tremendously.

At length Flicker managed to get the animal's head securely fastened up in a corner of the counterpane; he then seized the two first paws and bound them together. Having done this, he managed to lay hold of the tail, round which he knotted a long bit of string, one end of which he tied to the ladder. With a tremendous effort he shook off the animal and kicked it into the corner, where it lay vainly endeavouring to get rid of the counterpane and to free its fore paws.

The two combats came to an end about the same time, and our young conquerors having secured their prisoners, rose up and gazed proudly in each others' faces.

Having congratulated each other on having gained so complete a victory, they commenced staunching the blood which flowed freely from their wounds. But to far different parts did they apply their handkerchiefs, for as Jerry dabbed his face Flicker did the same to the antipodes of his head.

"You don't seem much hurt," said Jerry, looking at Flicker rather contempuously.

"You don't see *where* I am hurt," replied Flicker, gravely.

"Heugh! the old hag nearly scratched my eyes out," cried Jerry.

"The old cat did not touch mine," said Flicker, "but I sha'nt sit down with ease for a month to come I assure you, not to mention the clothes that are spoiled."

Turning round, he showed Jerry the tattered state of his garments, which now were scarcely decent.

Poor Jerry could not suppress his laughter, and forgetting his own condition, roared aloud.

But this merriment was soon stopped by the yells from the old woman, the girls having taken it into their heads to bring her to by a sound application of the cat-o'-nine-tails.

"Hold hard my beauties," cried Jerry, "all in good time, but a little of that goes a long way, as the woman said to the judge what sentenced her to be hung, I want to make that old woman useful before I have done with her. Trust me she shall be punished enough. Besides in our hurry we've forgotten this poor creature here."

It was indeed true; in the thick of the combat everyone had forgotten the poor girl who had fainted with terror and pain. They now, however, quickly released her, and the two girls bore her upstairs, leaving the two lads to do what they would with old Mrs. Jenkins; all agreeing that nothing could be too bad for her.

"Now to begin with the old lady," said Jerry, "we'll leave the cat in case we want it. Just help me to pinion this old woman's arms, old Flick. There, that will do. they are bound rather tightly, but she's used to rope like that."

The boys then fastened a rope securely round the old woman's ankle, and taking hold of one end of it, gave her one or two heavy cuts with the whip at the same time telling her to rise.

"Oh, my good gentlemen, what can you want with a poor old woman," she cried.

"Poor old woman!" cried Jerry; "a wretched old hag you mean. Come, get up; and to start with, I may as well tell you not to expect any sympathy, for you won't get any."

With a dreadful imprecation the old woman rose to her feet, and stood scowling viciously at her young captors.

"Now don't cast your evil eyes on me," cried Jerry, "or I'll knock them out of your head. Now, right about face and creep up those stairs. Don't try to run, because if you do I shall pull you back by the rope round your ankle, and don't be too slow, or I shall enliven you with my whip. Now then, be off, old lady."

With many a fierce oath the hag mounted upstairs, and at Jerry's command entered her own parlour, where she found all the girls dancing with delight at the thoughts of gaining their freedom, and rejoicing at the punishment that had been inflicted on their cruel torturer.

"Now, Mother Jenkins," said Jerry, giving a jerk to the cord so that the old woman made an involuntary kick out behind, "you have made all these poor creatures your slaves, and now I intend you to be theirs. So look alive and see you obey me directly, for I have no time to lose, and shall have to enliven you up, if you don't mind, a great deal more than you will like, I fancy"

"What do you want with me?" demanded the old woman.

"First of all your keys. Come, make haste, or—— you know what you'll get."

The old hag looked at the whip, and at once handed over the keys.

"That's right. Now, Mr. Flicker, if you will be so kind as to take these keys I should feel much obliged; Mother Shipton here will walk round the room and open the trunks, drawers, and boxes, or rather tell you which key will open them; you will unlock them, and we will examine the contents together."

Vainly the old woman protested and grumbled; the terrible lash whistled in the air, now and then coming so unpleasantly near her shoulders that she thought it much better to hobble away and comply with her captors' commands. Box after box, drawer after drawer was opened, and the lads stood in amazement at the wealth thus revealed to them.

Not only jewels and plate were in these boxes, but superb dresses for ladies and gentlemen, the former trimmed with valuable lace and the latter with gold.

"My eyes!" cried Jerry, as these riches were heaped on the floor, "here's a go! Blow me if I don't think the old gal is a fence. How did you come by these riches, eh?"

"I—I—deal in them," faltered the old woman, glancing sharply at the girls.

"Is that true, Louisa?" asked Jerry of the girl.

"I don't know, but I know that a load of men and women servants bring them here at different times, and she buys them."

"It's false, you jade," screamed the hag, springing at Louisa.

Had she been at liberty there is no doubt that she would have done the girl some great harm, but as the cord happened to be held rather tightly by Jerry, she nearly jerked herself upon her nose.

"It is true," replied the girl, "for I have often crept downstairs and listened, and have heard you wrangling with them about the price. They always called you a stingy old cat, and declared you never gave a tenth of the value."

"So, so, mistress," cried Jerry, "a receiver of stolen goods, eh? Very well, very well indeed: I think this ought to be looked into. Now we will go all over the rest of the house and see what we can find. Mind you don't deceive me; for I won't stand it. While we are gone, ladies, select what garments you want, and dress yourselves out, for I intends giving a party at this lady's expense."

The old woman was obliged to conduct the boys all over the house.

One room she would gladly have passed, but the lads' quick eyes discovered it, and they insisted upon her going in.

In it they found a strong box, which they opened and discovered to be filled with gold, silver, and notes.

These they immediately transferred to their own pockets, and discovering, concealed in a desk, a book in which the numbers of the notes had been entered, they carefully destroyed it, so that no trace could be left.

Having completely searched the house, they returned to the room where they had left the girls, whom they now found not only well dressed, but also decked with jewels.

Jerry and Flicker then selected two handsome suits that would fit them, and retiring to another room, soon returned dressed superbly.

"Business first, pleasure afterwards, as the heir said when he buried his father. Now, old lady, please to sit at this desk."

Sullenly the old woman sat at the desk, and Jerry made her cancel the indentures of the poor girls; writing across each a full confession of the cruelties and deceptions she had used, and giving to them certain articles of jewellery, wearing apparel, and some money, as compensation.

In this manner he made the old woman distribute all her property, only reserving a good suit of clothes, some rings, &c. and a good amount of cash for Flicker and himself.

This having been done, he made the girls pack up their separate bundles, so as to be ready for instant removal.

"Now, then, clear the tables," cried Jerry, "and let us have a good supper."

Mrs. Jenkins was immediately forced into the service, and under the invigorating stimulant of the lash, became one of the most active in clearing the tables and preparing for supper, although inwardly she was swearing vengeance against one and all of them, and endeavouring to make some plan to overthrow Jerry and his companion.

One of the girls was despatched to a shop close by, from whence she quickly returned laden with steaks, chops, sausages, tripe, and many other good things, all of which Mrs. Jenkins was compelled to prepare and cook.

Then two more of the girls were despatched to Toby Crick's, and speedily they returned with sundry bottles, all of which were uncorked by Jerry and Flicker, and placed upon the table.

Whilst supper was preparing Jerry brewed a good bowl of punch, while Flicker reclined upon a sofa, smoking a long clay pipe, which he held with one hand, whilst the other encircled the slender waist of Maria Jackson, who had wonderfully revived from her torture, her spirits having been kept up by a glass of good old port, a bottle of which had been specially provided for her benefit.

At length supper was laid by Mrs. Jenkins, who had to wait on all.

Jerry took the head of the table, and Flicker the foot, whilst the girls sat round, eyeing the food with hungry eager eyes.

Jerry gave the signal to "fall to," and in an instant nothing was to be heard but the clatter of knives and forks, and the clinking of glasses.

But even the hungriest were at last satisfied, and then Jerry, lighting his long clay pipe, and cocking his leg over the arm of the chair, called for a song, at the same time making such a clatter with his glass as to deafen the modest refusals of the ladies.

At last one was sung, and then followed another and another.

Jerry and Flicker, greatly amused and delighted as they were, did not neglect the bowl, but drank deeply thereof, in spite of the remonstrances of both Louisa and Maria Jackson, who began to dread that Mrs. Jenkins might take advantage of their protectors' inebriety to make an attack on them.

"Hang the witch!" cried Jerry, hic-cupping. "What do I care for that old hag? Hasn't she tormented my dear Louisa, the queen of my heart, the ap-ap-apple of my eye? Curse the old Beldame!—what's she to me? I'm a gentleman! I've been on the road, and don't care for anybody or anything—'cept lovely woman and rosy wine! They are the things I swear by, and she's the thing I swear at!"

"Oh! don't drink any more," said Louisa. "I do hate a man who drinks too much."

"Drink too much!" shouted Jerry. "I—I never drinks too much—(hiccup)! Show me the man that ever did drink too much! I don't believe in the existence of a man who drinks too much! I know there are many men who don't drink enough—white-livered, cowardly hounds, who can't say boo! to a goose. But I'm a regular toper, that's what I am! Did you ever hear 'The Toper's Excuse,' eh?"

"'The Toper's Excuse,' what's that?" asked Flicker, who was a little, but only a very little, more sober than his companion.

"Why, 'The Toper's Excuse' is a song," said Jerry, "a song, ladies and gentlemen, that I am about to sing to you, so please be all attention."

Casting up his eyes to the ceiling, and looking as much like a dying duck in a thunder-storm—if ever such a thing was seen—in rather a melancholy tone of voice Jerry trolled out the following song:—

The Toper's Excuse,

The baby whose mother is laid in the grave,
    Will roar till he hurts his young throttle,
To find him relief there is but one way,
    He must have recourse to the bottle—the bottle,
        He must have recourse to the bottle.
The poets may tell of poor dear Philomel,
    Whose heart was upset by love's tug,
To give her relief, and soothe her deep grief,
    She spends ev'ry night at her jug, jug, jug,
        She spends ev'ry night at her jug.
When death comes at last, and deprives us of life,
    Our friends may perchance shed a tear,
But little we'll care, if they let us sleep on,
    And leave us alone to our bier, bier, bier,
        And leave us alone to our bier.

As Jerry finished his song the pipe dropped from his nerveless hand, and the tears mounted up to his eyes, filling them with water—a needless trouble, for they were already swimming—and turning to Louisa, he threw his arms round her neck, and swore that he would never leave her, that she, and she alone, should be his bride; that they would fly or die together.

No sooner did Flicker perceive how far his companion

had gone than he threw his arms around Maria's neck and took the same vows.

Drawing the lads from the room the two girls shook them somewhat roughly, and, having brought back a little sense to them, Louisa said—

"Would you undo all you have done? Would you return us to captivity?"

"I? I would return you to nobody. You are mine" stammered Jerry.

"If you have no thought for us think for yourselves," continued the girl.

"I think for both of us—all of us"—said Jerry, thickly.

"In an hour it will be break of day, and we shall not be able to leave here."

"Eh!" said Jerry; "then we must be off now. Look here; you two girls must make your way to the Bird Cage Inn, Stamford-hill, as fast as you can. There you must ask for a Mrs. Wapshaw, and tell her you come from me; she will tell you where to go. The other girls must follow at a distance—not all together—and must go a little past the inn and turn down the lane next it on the left. Down that they will find a sort of hut or shed; the widow will send them some one who will let them in. Now, be off."

Jerry and Flicker amused themselves, whilst the girls were going, by pouring cold water over their heads in order to sober themselves, being totally regardless of Mrs. Jenkins' carpet.

When all the girls had gone, they seized Mrs. Jenkins, and, taking her down into the cellar, bound her hand and foot in a chair. They then gagged her, and Jerry wrote out a large placard, which he hung round her neck, on which was written, "*This is the work of Jonathan Wild the thief-taker.*"

They then seized the wild cat by the tail, and Flicker was about to dash its brains out, when Jerry began to doubt its ferocity.

"If you don't believe it try it," said Flicker, warmly.

"No, thank you," said Jerry; "let us see the old woman have a turn."

No sooner said than done. The counterpane was removed, and the wild cat, suspended by the tail, over its mistress' head.

Setting up an awful yell the cat dashed its claws into its mistress, who writhed and groaned with agony.

"Dash it all, I can't stand that," cried Flicker, who knew what the pain was too well. "I know the old beast deserves all that we can give her, but I can't stand that nohow."

Saying which the young fellow drew his knife and instantly killed the vicious animal.

"Well, good bye, Mrs. Jenkins," said Jerry; "I hope you will enjoy yourself down here as much as the poor creatures you have placed here so often. I think we ought to have hung you up the same as you hung them up, but we'll spare you this time. Only, mind this: if you attempt to repeat any of these games we will visit you again, and pay off both old and new scores together, so be careful."

Leaving the trembling old woman to her meditations, Jerry and Flicker ascended the ladder. They filled their pockets with the valuables they had set aside for themselves and then stole quietly out into the street, carefully locking the street door and taking the key away with them, so as to delay the robbery being discovered.

CHAPTER XLIV.

MAUD ATTACKS LADY HAMILTON'S CARRIAGE.—ARRIVAL OF LADY HAMILTON'S ESCORT.—MAUD'S STRATAGEM.—THE INVISIBLE PURSUER.

WHILST Batswing was enjoying himself at the expense of the governor of Newgate, and Jerry Blinker was rescuing the distressed females, Maud was not idle.

According to the plan already proposed Maud had mounted her horse, and, turning its head southwards, rode through Abridge on to Woodford.

As we have already stated, the night was anything but a pleasant one.

The uncertain light of the moon, as it shot down its rays between the fast-flying clouds, made everything partake of a ghastly aspect.

Hedges and bushes, in the gloaming light, seemed to grow double their size, and to assume strange, gaunt, and ghastly shapes.

Having reached the common, Maud drew in her bridle and slackened her pace, allowing her horse to proceed at a gentle walk, whilst she gazed up at the heavy clouds that flew rapidly over the sky.

In this manner she proceeded across the common until she came to the road, then, choosing a large tree, she pulled up underneath it, so that she might be hidden by its shadow.

It must not be considered that highwaymen, as a rule, started out on their expeditions without knowing whether they might meet any people. They were generally well informed as to who would be on the road, in most cases knowing almost the exact time the travellers would be passing a certain spot.

For this information they were mostly indebted to the servants and postboys, who were generally in the pay of the knights of the road.

In the present case intelligence had been brought to Batswing that old Lady Hamilton would cross the common after dark, and that she would be without any escort.

Under these circumstances, it was considered that this would be a very easy case, and it was therefore entrusted to Maud, who had refused any assistance, preferring to take all the risk upon herself.

Maud had been on her station for a little more than half-an-hour when the distant sound of wheels smote upon her ear.

Reining her horse back, so as to be ready to spring out upon the carriage, she drew and cocked one of her pistols.

Up rolled the carriage, and with one bound Maud was at the coachman's side, and, presenting a pistol at his head, called upon him to stop.

So sudden was the action that the coachman involuntarily pulled up the horses, and then crouched down under his seat, begging for mercy.

Commanding the coachman not to stir at his peril, Maud rode up to the carriage, dismounted from her horse, and opened the door.

The occupants of the coach was an elderly female, wrapped up in large fur cloaks, and Cashmere shawls, over which her long hooked nose projected like the handle of an old-fashioned umbrella.

By the side of this elderly female, who was no other than Lady Hamilton, was a young girl of about twenty.

The girl was very beautiful, the paleness of her complexion caused by the fright making her look almost too ethereal for this world.

Her dress was of the simplest, forming a strange contrast to that of the old lady.

"What do you want, fellow?" screamed the old woman, in shrill tones.

"A thousand pardons for interrupting you," said Maud, raising her hat politely. "I am very sorry I am sure to disturb you, but I will not detain you a moment."

"Do you know, fellow, to whom you are speaking?" shouted the old lady.

"Undoubtedly," replied Maud: "I have the honour of addressing Lady Hamilton."

"Knowing that, how dare you presume to thrust your presence upon me?"

"I presume upon the right of might," said Maud, quietly.

"Begone, vulgar fellow!" screamed Lady Hamilton, "relieve me of your presence."

"Decidedly when I have relieved you of your jewels," was the cool reply.

"Would you dare to rob a peeress of the realm?" cried Lady Hamilton.

"Ay, that would I," replied Maud. "I would rob his most gracious Majesty King George, if I could only get the chance, with the greatest pleasure."

"Oh, the brute, the disloyal vagabond," screamed the lady; "I'll have you hanged."

"For heaven's sake, my lady, do not anger him," cried the young girl.

"How dare you speak to me, Miss Chetwynd," cried the lady; "learn that it is the place of a poor companion never to speak unless she is spoken to."

"Silence!" cried Maud fiercely; "have you forgotten that after death there is no distinction of rank; that in the grave all are equal? Surely you, a tottering old woman, should never forget that, seeing that your days must soon be merged in night, that the solemn portals of the grave are close at your feet, and that in a few more steps you must pass the grim threshold!"

For a moment the old woman seemed unable to speak.

She clenched her withered lips and turned livid with passion.

At length she overcame her paroxysm, and, seizing a heavy volume that was placed by her side, she hurled it with all her might at Maud.

Fortunately for Maud the book passed over her head, but unfortunately it struck her horse a violent blow on the neck.

In a moment the noble animal sprang round, dragging her bridle away from Maud's grasp whereon it had been slung, and the next moment dashed down the road, and in a few minutes was lost to sight.

Here was a nice predicament for Maud! how was she to manage without a horse?

Unable to govern her temper Maud shook the old woman violently.

"You wretched old harridan," cried Maud, "you mass of worldliness and vanity, had you treated me properly I should merely have taken away your jewels; but now I must take away your horses and leave you on the common."

"Dare to touch my horses?" screamed the old lady; "where can be my escort?"

"Escort!" cried Maud, "what do you mean by that?"

"Ha, ha, ha!" laughed the old woman; "did you not know that I had an escort? They had not arrived at Epping when I did, and, as I never stop for any one, I came on and ordered them to follow."

"Is this true?" asked Maud of Miss Chetwynd.

"It is indeed, sir, and therefore I beseech you to fly while there is still time."

"Fly!" shrieked Lady Hamilton; "how can he fly? His horse is gone."

For a moment Maud paused as if uncertain what to do.

"You see there is no escape for you," cried the old woman; "you'll be hanged."

"I think not," replied Maud quietly; "anyway, I will have your jewels first."

In spite of her resistance Lady Hamilton had to surrender up all her valuables.

Scarcely had Maud done this than her quick ears caught the sound of approaching horses, and she had no doubt it was Lady Hamilton's escort.

Calling to the coachman not to move if he valued his life, Maud sprang into the carriage, and seizing Lady Hamilton stripped her of all her cloaks and shawls. She then took a kerchief with which she gagged the old woman, and, having tied her legs and feet, thrust her most unceremoniously beneath the carriage seat.

Having accomplished this Maud wrapped herself up in the shawls and furs so that she might be taken for Lady Hamilton, and seating herself by Miss Chetwynd's side, she closed the coach door and lowered one of the front windows.

"Hark'ee, coachman," she said, sternly, "do you value your life?"

"Oh, sir, do have mercy," groaned the terrified man.

"I do not intend to hurt any one if you will obey me; but if you attempt to betray me I shall certainly blow your brains out, and place a bullet in the noble body of Lady Hamilton; so I give you fair warning. I am a desperate man, and will keep my word. Now drive on slowly, and let the escort overtake us, and remember, one hint to them of my presence here will be the signal of your death."

Groaning in abject fear the coachman gathered up his reins and drove off.

"Miss Chetwynd," said Maud, "I believe that is what the old Lady called you—I am extremely sorry to have had to interfere with you; but as you see it is with me a case of life or death. If I had not treated Lady Hamilton as I have done she certainly would not have allowed me to escape."

"But why did you stop us?" faltered Miss Chetwynd.

"I stopped you because you are rich, or rather Lady Hamilton is so, and I am poor. You, my dear Miss Chetwynd, must know how unfairly property is divided in England. The so-called aristocracy, who rob and trample the poor, have the best of them sprung from assassins, and the worst of them trace their noble descent back to ladies of easy virtue who have been loyal enough to forget their duty to heaven to please a king. Whilst such things are allowed; when ducal bastards and regal harlots are permitted to rob the people, you must not be surprised that the people retaliate. But hark: your escort is arriving. Now remember, I for the present am Lady Hamilton, you are my companion, and must obey me in all I wish. Your refusal will be the signal for Lady Hamilton's instant death."

"We are in your power, sir, you must do with us what you will," said the girl.

The beat of horses' hoofs was now plainly heard coming along the road, and in a few moments some half dozen men rode up to the carriage.

"So you have come at last, have you?" cried Maud, in shrill tones, imitating Lady Hamilton's voice. "A pretty set of people, indeed. I might have been robbed and murdered on the common, and no one near to help me."

"Really, my lady," commenced one of the men, riding up to the carriage window.

"Don't dare to speak to me, fellow," cried Maud. "Miss Chetwynd, desire these people to ride on in front, so as to see the road clear. If we sink into the ruts, as we did before, I feel certain I shall never recover myself, that I do."

Miss Chetwynd, trembling with fright, gave the necessary order, and the men rode on.

During this conversation Lady Hamilton had been making furious efforts to release herself, but Maud, in the quietest way possible, had made her ladyship a footstool for the time being, and had so managed to keep her down.

"How far are we from Romford?" said Maud to the coachman.

"About two miles, sir," replied the man, trembling in fright.

"That will do. Summon the leader of the escort."

"Here, Paul," shouted the man, "the gentleman——"

"Silence, you fool," said Maud. "You mean Lady Hamilton."

"Oh! yes, sir, to be sure I do," replied the coachman. "Paul, her ladyship wants you."

"Miss Chetwynd, you must tell the man to hurry on

with the escort to Romford, and see that beds are prepared at the inn there, as Lady Hamilton will not proceed further to-night, as she does not feel very well. You must also make the coachman drive slowly, to prevent jolting."

When Paul arrived at the carriage window, Miss Chetwynd delivered her message, whilst Maud, wrapped up to the eyes, groaned as if in acute pain.

"But had I not better leave part of the escort?" demanded Paul.

Miss Chetwynd would gladly have accepted this offer, but the glitter of a pistol-barrel pointed towards the floor of the carriage made her alter her mind, and hastily bidding Paul to obey her ladyship's commands, she sunk back in the coach, overcome with fear.

Rising up in her seat, Maud looked through the window in front, and watched the escort out of sight. Then, placing a pistol to the coachman's head, she said,

"Turn your horses round, and drive back on to the common."

"On to the common?" gasped the frightened coachman.

"Yes, back on to the common, and that as fast as you can."

The trembling coachman turned his horses round, and drove as he was commanded.

After they had proceeded about four miles, Maud ordered the man to stop, and getting out of the carriage, allowed Lady Hamilton to rise.

"You see, madam," said Maud, "I am not likely to hang just yet. Had you suppressed your passion you would most likely have been now in Romford, whilst your escort would have been pursuing me."

"I'll see you hanged yet," screamed the old lady. "Drive on, John."

"Don't do anything of the kind, John," said Maud. "I have not done yet."

"Not done yet!" cried Lady Hamilton. "Why, what more do you want?"

"A horse, in the place of the one you frightened away."

"You would not leave us here without horses?" she cried, alarmed.

"No; I will leave you one, and take one myself."

"But I shan't arrive in town to-night," cried Lady Hamilton.

"So much the better," replied Maud. "There will be less chance of my being pursued. This horse will suit me admirably. Coachman, unharness him."

This was soon done, and cutting down the reins, Maud converted them into a bridle; then, springing lightly on the horse's back, she raised her hat politely, and galloped back towards Epping.

She had not proceeded far on her way, when she plainly heard the beat of horses' hoofs on the road.

She paused and listened. Could she be pursued.

Whoever it was, she could not doubt but what the horse was coming towards her. Turning her horse's head, she urged him on in the opposite direction.

Still the horse's hoofs could be heard gaining on her rapidly.

For some time the chase was kept up, until it became evident to Maud that her pursuer—and she could not doubt that such it was, for she had doubled over and over again, and yet the sound of the horse followed her—was gaining on her fast, and that further flight was useless.

Her steed, which was a heavy carriage horse, was covered with foam.

Drawing up close to the road-side, Maud cocked her pistols, and determined to fight to the last, sooner than surrender.

On, on came the ring of the horse's hoofs, but nothing could be seen.

Maud peered into the darkness, but could not see anything.

She was able now to tell by the sound that there was only one horse approaching. Nearer and nearer came the sound, when Maud, judging that the horse must be close upon her, called out "Halt," in a firm voice.

In a moment the sounds ceased, but, to Maud's surprise, no answer was returned.

For some minutes Maud remained silent, hoping to hear some one speak.

All was silent and still as the grave.

"This is strange," she muttered. "What can it be?"

Maud was no coward, but the mysterious sound startled her.

Turning her horse round, she rode slowly from the spot.

She had not proceeded a dozen yards when she distinctly heard the sound of the horse's hoofs again, plainly showing her that she was followed.

Facing in the direction from which the sounds came, Maud drew her pistol.

"Whoever you are," she cried, "and what ever your meaning may be in thus tracking me, I warn you that I am armed, and am in no mood to be played with."

She paused for an answer, but no answer came.

"I command you to answer, or I will fire."

Still all remained silent, no answer being made.

The night was now pitch dark, so that not a thing could be seen.

Keeping her pistols ready for action, Maud rode gently back towards the sound.

She had proceeded some way down the road, when she paused in horror. The sound of the horse's hoofs was again behind her.

A cold shiver ran through her frame, and putting spurs to her horse, she dashed away, as well as she could make out, in the direction of Epping Forest, but the night was so dark, and she had ridden about so much, that she had really lost her way.

But whatever turning she took her invisible pursuer still followed. If she galloped he galloped, if she trotted he trotted, so that they remained at exactly the same distance from each other.

This puzzled Maud greatly, for she knew that the pursuer must be better mounted than herself, by the ease with which he kept close to her.

At length the grey light in the east told Maud that morn was breaking. Wheeling her horse round, she again gazed back for her pursuer, and this time with better success.

Bursting into a merry laugh, she exclaimed,

"Why, if it is not my own poor old horse!"

And so indeed it was. There stood the faithful animal gazing at its mistress.

Springing from the coach horse, Maud quickly mounted her own animal, and then made her way towards a cottage she saw in the distance, where she proposed to seek shelter for the night.

As she approached the house she did not much like the appearance. It was a mean, miserable-looking shed, built mostly of wood. At the back of it was a thick plantation, which Maud guessed was part of Epping Forest, and therefore determined to venture to ask for shelter in this wretched place, uninviting as it was, as it must be close to Batswing's retreat

CHAPTER XLV.

MAUD FALLS INTO THE HANDS OF JONATHAN WILD'S
FRIENDS. THE DRUGGED WINE AND ITS UNEX-
PECTED RESULT.

AFTER Maud had knocked at the door for some time, it was thrown violently open, and a rough-looking farmer man presented himself.

"What do you want here at this time of the morning?" demanded the man.

"I wish for a little rest, if you will kindly afford me some."

"Rest! why, it is time for all honest folk to be rising," said the man.

"Not if they have been out all night," replied Maud, smiling.

"Honest folk don't stop out all night," said the man, suspiciously.

"They do if they have lost their way," said Maud.

"And had you lost your way?" enquired the man, staring at Maud.

"Of course I had, or I should not be here. Is that Epping Forest?"

"Ay; that be Epping Forest sure enough," said the fellow. "If you're coming in you had better come. I've no time to spare. Take your horse round to the shed first."

Maud led her horse round to the shed as desired.

At first she felt inclined to mount her horse and be off, for she did not like the looks of the man; but a love of adventure made her come to the conclusion to stop, in order that she might see if her suspicions were correct.

Having seen to her horse she entered the house, where she found the man seated by the fire, eating some cold meat and bread with a huge clasped knife.

"Sit down there," said the man, pointing to a chair with his knife.

Maud did as she was bidden, and drew the chair closer to the fire.

"So you've been out all night, have you?" said the man.

"Unfortunately I have been compelled to be," said Maud.

"And on what business?" asked the man, suspiciously.

"I have business at Epping; very particular business," said Maud.

"It's rather strange you should have come to the wrong side of the forest," said the man.

"Did I not tell you I lost my way a few miles this side Romford?"

"No, you didn't; and what's more, coming from London you should not have come to Romford at all. I fancy you haven't been up to much good."

"Nonsense! what harm could I be up to?"

"What harm indeed? as if it aint well known that Epping Forest is full of thieves and highwaymen. I suppose you haven't heard of Batswing?"

"Indeed I have though," replied Maud, pretending to be frightened at the name.

"Ah! I thought you would, now," said the man, winking furiously.

"Yes, I have certainly heard about him, but I understand he was killed by the soldiers a few nights ago in Epping Forest: that's why I ventured alone."

"Bah! he's not killed," said the man; "he's no more dead than you or I."

"Indeed! you surprise me. How is it such a fellow can escape the law?"

"The law!" cried the man; "ho, ho, ho, ho. Come, I like that. What does such fellows as Batswing care about the law? Nothing! He's no respect for the old blind girl nor her scales, not he. All he cares about is a merry life, that's all."

"You seem somewhat inclined to side with him," said Maud.

"Why shouldn't I?" replied the fellow. "I am a poor man who has to work hard for a living, that's what I am. I don't care for the rich folk, for they never care for me. Me and mine might starve before they would do a thing to save us."

"Can this man be one of the band?" thought Maud. "He may be, but I won't trust him: his looks are anything but prepossessing, to my fancy."

"If I had a horse like yours," continued the man, "I wouldn't be as poor as I am now; no, and what's more, some people would not be as rich."

"This man is endeavouring to draw me out," thought Maud. "I don't believe one word he says, except that he is an arrant rogue. I'll be on my guard."

"I suppose you are hungry?" said the man, after a pause.

"No," replied Maud, "I supped late last night."

"At least you must be thirsty," said the fellow; "all true men drink."

"I have no objection to a glass of something, certainly," said Maud.

With a sharp glance of delight the man rose and went to a cupboard.

Having unlocked the door, he took out a bottle and poured out a glass of wine.

He then replaced the bottle, but purposely upset it so as to have an excuse for staying by the cupboard, and Maud saw him pour some red fluid out of a small vial into her glass.

"There, that will do you good," he said as he handed her the glass; "you must be tired, so drink that off and then throw yourself down on yonder rug. You'll sleep like a top after you have drunk that. It's the right sort."

The fellow said this with such a diabolic grin that Maud felt instinctively for her pistols, but discovered to her horror she had left them in her holsters.

Raising the glass to her lips, she exclaimed in a cheerful voice,—

"Here's to our better acquaintance, friend, and thanks for your hospitality."

Just as she had placed the glass to her lips she paused, and starting violently, exclaimed,—

"Merciful heaven! what was that?"

"Which?" demanded the man, uneasily, as he glanced sharply at her face.

"That peculiar cry," said Maud, "it sounded to me like a cry for help."

"Where from?" demanded the man. "You must be mistaken."

"I am not mistaken," said Maud; "it was a cry for help, and came from the direction of the forest."

Muttering an oath, the man rushed to the door and looked out.

Whilst he was so engaged Maud emptied her glass on the floor, taking care to preserve enough to wet her lips, so that the man might think she had drunk the whole of the drug.

"There is no one there," said the man, "I told you you were mistaken."

"I suppose I must have been," said Maud, as she smacked her lips and placed the glass upon the table. "You must excuse me; I am rather nervous."

The man gave her a sharp glance, but did not say anything.

"By the way, that wine of yours has a strange, dull flavour."

"Your mouth is out of order," grumbled the man; "the wine is good enough."

"Perhaps you're right," said Maud, yawning; "I really am so sleepy that I don't exactly know what I am doing. Everything seems in a mist—a whirl."

Remembering what the man had said about the wine making her sleep, she staggered towards the rug he had pointed out, and throwing herself upon it, pretended to fall fast asleep almost immediately.

The man leant upon the table and watched her with fiendish delight.

"So!" he whispered. "He did drink it, after all. I was doubtful at first."

Softly approaching Maud, he felt in her pockets from which he drew the jewels.

"Jewels! diamonds!" he exclaimed; "a knight of the road, as I thought."

"KEEP OFF!" CRIED ALICE, "BY YCUR HANDS MY FATHER DIED."

Having been so fortunate in making this discovery, he proceeded in his search.

Pocket after pocket he emptied, little dreaming that Maud was conscious of all that he was doing. At length he undid her coat to feel if she had anything concealed in her breast or some secret pocket.

Uttering a cry of astonishment, he sprang quickly to his feet.

"By heavens!" he exclaimed, "it is not a man! There is some mystery here."

For a moment he paused, as if in deep thought, then again kneeling down by the side of Maud, he gently replaced a part of the least valuable jewels, and re-arranged her dress.

Having done this he gathered up the rest of the jewels and took them into another room.

No sooner had he disappeared than Maud sprang to her feet, and creeping to the door peeped through the

crack into the second room, where she beheld the man kneeling on the floor just under a large oaken table.

Taking out his clasped knife he raised one of the boards, underneath which was a large cavity containing some beautiful jewels, and in this hole he placed those he had just taken from Maud; who, having seen so much, crept back to the rug, and throwing herself into the same position she had assumed when robbed, pretended to be fast asleep, in order that the man might not suspect her.

Of course she was now doubly convinced that she was in great danger, but what puzzled her most was why the man had left her any jewels.

Presently the man returned, but this time not alone.

He was accompanied by a tall, muscular, heavy-browed fellow, attired much after the style of a common farm-labourer. There was a peculiar, stolid, animal look about this man's face that was more awful than the most vicious expression.

With his hands thrust deeply into his breeches pockets, his shoulders rounded, he slouched along until he stood looking down at Maud.

"Have you ever seen her before, Darrell?" asked the first man.

"No, Farmer Croft, I haven't," replied Darrell.

Maud trembled when she heard the name of Farmer Croft, for she knew well that she had fallen into the hands of a friend of Jonathan Wild.

"I have seen her somewhere," continued Farmer Croft, "but I cannot say where; but I feel certain that at one time of my life she crossed my path."

"Then why don't you settle her at once?" asked Darrell.

"What do you mean? I do not understand you?"

Darrell made no reply, but drawing out a clasped knife, opened it with an ominous click.

"Tut, man," said Farmer Croft, "you must be mad to think of such a thing."

"And why? One gash and she won't interfere with you again."

"She won't interfere with me," replied Croft, "I rather think she is valuable."

"Valuable! Curse me if I ever saw a woman who was worth anything yet."

"There you are mistaken, Darrell; women are sometimes valuable."

"Each one according to his taste; I wouldn't give a sixpence for the best of them."

"Do you remember the night we gave Wild the tip that Batswing was at the Fleet?"

"Rather: and nicely we were done by that young ragged devil Jack-o'-Lantern."

"Just so; the rascals escaped by the Fleet."

"Yes, and through Jonathan Wild's house, from whence they removed a woman."

"Yes, I heard something about it," said Darrell.

"This is the same woman," said Farmer Croft; "she has taken to the road."

"Then what are we to do with her?" asked Darrell.

"Why, keep her a prisoner until we can give her up to Jonathan and get the reward."

"Reward! Is there any reward to be had?"

"Of course there is. Now you must keep watch over her until I return."

"Why, where are you going?" asked Darrell. "I thought we were to stay here for Wild."

"So we were to, but Wild must know that we have caught this fair unwary at once, so that he may send people to carry her back to his tender keeping."

Poor Maud's blood ran cold as she heard the two men laugh.

"You must watch her carefully," continued Farmer Croft, "if she attempts to escape, knock her down. I don't think she will, as I have drugged her heavily."

"I hope she will sleep until you come back," said Darrell, "I hate women's talk."

Farmer Croft put on a heavy riding coat, and taking down a huge whip strode to the door, followed by Darrell.

"Saddle my horse, Darrell," said Croft, "I shall soon be back."

"What, and leave her alone?" asked Darrell.

"Tush! did I not tell you that I had drugged her, and that she would not wake for at least three or four hours. Come, look alive, for I have no time to lose."

The two men hurried out of the hut, carefully closing the door behind them.

At first Maud thought of attempting flight, and a little consideration showed her that that was almost impossible.

The thought of once more being in Jonathan Wild's clutches seemed to paralyse her.

Suddenly a thought flashed across her brain, it was a poor chance, but her only one.

Springing up, she hurried to the cupboard, and took therefrom the bottle of wine.

This she ascertained was nearly half-full, and into it she emptied the whole of the contents of the vial that held the opiate.

This bottle of drugged wine she placed conspicuously on the mantlepiece in such a position that Darrell could not help seeing it.

She had scarcely succeeded in doing this than she heard Farmer Croft ride away.

Hurrying back to her rug, she had just resumed her former position when Darrell entered the room.

Seating himself at a table, Darrell drew forth a short pipe and commenced smoking.

"I can't tell what there is about women," he commenced, moralizing, "that people should make such a fuss about them. I had a wife once; she became troublesome; she created disturbances; she was found dead; that was an end of it."

For a moment the brute continued smoking, when his eye caught sight of the bottle.

"Hillo!" he cried, "why the captain has left out his wine. Hang me if I don't have a glass. It will do me good; cheer up my spirits."

Drawing the cork, he placed the neck of the bottle to his lips and took a deep draught."

"By Jove, this is not bad tope at all," he exclaimed, "here's the Captain's health."

Again and again he drank, until the drug commenced its work.

"What's this," he exclaimed, "my brain is dizzy, I—I see it all, I've drunk the drugged wine. May be I'm poisoned. I—I can't stand. Help, help."

He dropped the bottle on to the ground, and gazed stupidly at it as it lay smashed at his feet; the few drops of wine that remained in it trickling slowly like blood.

Suddenly he raised his head and gazed fixedly at Maud, who was now sitting up watching the effect the drug was taking on her jailer.

"Curse me, I see it all!" cried the man, seeming to pull himself together for a few seconds, "this is the work of that hell-cat yonder, But I'll have revenge, revenge."

Drawing his clasped knife he staggered towards Maud.

In an instant she sprang to her feet, and managing to avoid him placed the table between herself and her pursuer, who stood in delirious frenzy, gazing with rolling eyes upon her, the knife clasped tightly in his hand.

"You—you have done this," he gasped.

"I know I have," replied Maud, "you are in my power. Put down that knife or I will kill you; remember you cannot conquer the effects of that drug."

For a moment the man seemed to hesitate as if in doubt.

The next instant he raised the knife, staggered forward a few paces, then uttering a fearful yell, fell heavily to the ground.

Having satisfied herself that he was really asleep, Maud hastened into the next room, where lifting up the loose board, she not only took back all the jewels which Farmer Croft had taken from her, but also appropriated all the others.

She then returned to the other room, and having found some strong rope, bound Darrell both hand and foot, after which she smashed the bottles in the cupboard, in order that if there had been any more drugged wine, it should be wasted.

Having performed all this she prepared to leave the house, when her eye fell upon a letter, which had evidently been left by accident on the mantelpiece.

She did not hesitate to open it, and read as follows:—

"Be at the hut by the forest. There is work on hand. I shall want you to go with me and Lord R. to Tillingham. Have Darrell with you.—"Yours,

"JONATHAN WILD."

"So, so," she exclaimed, "Lord R. must mean Redfern. Anyway, I will cross Wild's purpose, and should I be able to ruin Redfern at the same time, my revenge will be doubly sweet. This must be put at once into Batswing's hands. He may know more about the matter, and will direct me what is best to be done."

Hurrying to the stable, she was overjoyed to see her horse still there, and having saddled it, she rode rapidly through the forest towards the Abbey, which she soon reached, and at once hastened to Batswing, whom she found talking with Janet, who had brought him the news of Hugh Fenton's arrest.

"This is indeed bad news," cried Batswing, when he had heard all the story, "and all the worse that so many things come together, that I know not what to do."

"Had we not better start at once for Tillingham?" asked Maud.

"Not yet, for if the danger in that quarter was as imminent as you appear to think it, Jonathan Wild would not still be in town. No, I must see poor Hugh Fenton before I start for Tillingham, come what may."

"But Lor bless you, sir," cried Janet, "he is in Newgate, you would not go there?"

"Indeed I shall," replied Batswing, laughing, "I may one day have to go there against my will; surely, then, I may go to please myself if I like."

"But this Lord Redfern," said Maud, "I must, I will cross him."

"So you shall if you have patience, you must obey my commands."

"With pleasure, what are they?" said Maud.

"In the first place you may start for Tillingham this afternoon. Take plenty of money with you, and the handsomest clothes you can find in my wardrobe. Growling Teddy must go with you as your servant. Should you come across Bob Blow-the-Bellows on the road, tell him to hurry on to Tillingham at once. Some half-dozen of your men must also start for that place, but don't all go together, but rather travel in ones and twos, so as to avoid notice. Remember, we all put up at the 'Three Cutters,' and I shall be there to meet you. Now all is arranged, and see that my plans are thoroughly well carried out."

CHAPTER XLVI.

THE VISIT TO NEWGATE.

Mr. Grummidge was seated in his little lodge by the gate of Newgate, smoking a pipe and conversing with a friend and brother turnkey, Mr. Zachariah Blood.

Mr. Grummidge was paler and thinner since the evening he had passed with Batswing, and the tone of his voice was not quite so gruff as it used to be.

A settled gloom seemed stamped upon his features, and ever and anon gusty sighs heaved his chest.

"So Mr. Wild's off again after Batswing," said Zac.

"So I hear," sighed Grummidge, "he was just coming round here to see our prisoner when he was fetched away all of a sudden like."

"Why didn't he come to see the prisoner afore?" asked Zac.

"Well you see, the governor don't exactly hit it with Mr. Wild; they are jealous."

"But the governor aint got a chance against Mr. Wild," said Zac.

"No," returned the other, "I should like to know who has."

"Oh! so would I," said Zac. "It's my belief that Mr. Wild's more governor of Newgate nor Mr. Pitt is. I know which I'd sooner please."

"I know which I'd sooner not offend," replied Grummidge meaningly.

"Ay, and so do I. I wouldn't offend Mr. Wild for fifty guineas."

"I wouldn't offend him for anything," replied Grummidge, "he'd hang yer as sure as a gun."

"Is the governor still abed?" asked Zachariah.

"Of course he is," replied Grummidge. "Look here Zachariah Blood, if you'd agone through half what I and Mr. Pitt did t'other night, you'd awished to have been in bed too. But you see I'm only a turnkey and he's the governor, and so he can keep in his bed while I am forced to attend to my duty."

"Oh! but they do say he was a deal worse than you."

A sly smile of delight played over Mr. Grummidge's features when he thought of the severe beating he had administered to Mr. Pitt. He felt a wondrous kind of inward satisfaction at having been able to inflict such injuries on his master.

"I never heard the whole truth of the matter," said Zac, "how did it occur?"

"Don't ask: don't ask," said Grummidge solemnly, "such things aint to be talked of lightly I can tell you. It's my firm conviction that that there Batswing aint mortal; he's unnatural, that's what he is. If you'd aseen the awful sights he showed us, you'd scarce dare breathe his name. I don't think even Mr. Wild will ever take him, that I don't; and as for myself, I'll never try it again."

At this point the conversation was interrupted by a sharp knock at the door.

Shaking his head ruefully, Grummidge opened it, and admitted an elderly man dressed in livery, who, touching his hat respectfully, asked to see the governor.

"The governor's ill abed," growled Grummidge, "and can't see nobody."

"I'm sorry for that," said the footman, "as I come on special business."

"And what may that business be?" demanded Grummidge.

"I dare say you will do as well," said the footman, "you have a prisoner here."

"We've got more nor one," put in Zac with a broad grin.

"Yes, yes, I know that of course; but I mean a highwayman as was taken up for attempting to rob Captain Jennings down somewhere by Epping."

"Yes we have; but what of that?" demanded Grummidge impatiently.

"Well sir; only that I want to see the prisoner," replied the footman.

"Can't be done," cried Grummidge. "It's against all orders."

"But I want to see if I can recognise the man," pleaded the footman.

"What do you know about highwaymen?" asked Grummidge.

"I've been stopped twice when driving my master's coach," answered the man.

"And who may your master be?" demanded the turnkey.

"Alderman Turner of East Cheap."

"Did he send you?" asked Grummidge, who knew the Alderman had been robbed.

"Of course he did," replied the footman, opening his eyes in astonishment at the question.

"Then the worthy alderman ought to have known that he must give you a pass."

"And so he did, or rather he gave me this," replied the footman, producing an open letter.

The turnkey took it, and read the contents, which was merely a request that John Green, Alderman Turner's footman, should be permitted to see the man now in custody for having attempted to rob Captain Jennings.

The document seemed in good form, and the signature of the worthy alderman was affixed to it in regular form.

"Why didn't you show this to me before?" demanded Grummidge.

"Because you didn't ask," replied the footman with a vacant grin.

"Here Zac," cried Grummidge, "take charge of the lodge whilst I show the prisoner."

Taking a huge bunch of keys from the wall, Grummidge led the way, muttering to himself as he went "John Green indeed! Green enough, heaven knows."

"And is this a prison?" cried the footman, "Lord, what a dreadful place, and what are those things up there? Fetters! dear me, I wonder how the men can bear them."

To all these questions Grummidge vouchsafed short answers, wondering at the ignorance of the questioner, but at the same time not deeming it wise to offend an alderman's coachman.

At length they arrived at a low, narrow corridor, the walls on each side of which were pierced with small but massive doors; at one of which Grummidge paused, and having selected a key from one of the bunches, unlocked and opened the door, admitting John Green to the cell in which was confined Hugh Fenton.

It was a miserable, dirty place, the only light to which was admitted through a small grating placed close to the ceiling, and through which snow, rain, or hail found easy access.

Beneath this grating was a low truckle-bed, on which was seated Hugh Fenton, heavily fettered.

The rest of the furniture consisted of a small deal table and a rickety stool.

"There," said Mr. Grummidge, "that's the man you want; is it the one as robbed you?"

John Green gazed at Fenton, who returned his look with a defiant stare.

The coachman hesitated as if undecided, and lifting his hand, scratched his head slowly.

In a moment Hugh Fenton's look changed, and springing from the bed he exclaimed—

"Am I to be treated like a wild beast Master Jailer, that all the boobies in the town are to be brought to gape and stare at me. Take that ass away or he may get into trouble."

"Softly, softly, my fine fellow," replied Grummidge, "this person's come to identify you."

"Oh!" exclaimed Hugh with a laugh, "he has come with his mind made up to do so, has he? Then I think he might as well have perjured himself without putting me to the inconvenience of this interview. If you are determined to hang me, at least let me choose my companions whilst I am on this earth. It may be a privilege denied me in the other world."

"But I don't 'dentify the gentleman," said John Green, "he's not the man at all."

"Are you certain of that?" demanded Grummidge.

"Positive!"

"You see Master Jailer," cried Hugh, "there is some honesty in the world. The fellow won't perjure himself for the pleasure of seeing a fellow creature hanged. I like the fellow for it, and with your permission will drink a bottle of wine with him. Of course you'll join us in despatching the bottle."

"Ay, but who's to fetch the wine?" demanded Grummidge.

"You of course," replied Hugh, throwing down a guinea, "there is the money, and you can keep the change; only make haste, and let us have the liquor of the best."

"Not so fast sir, not so fast. What am I to do with Alderman Turner's footman whilst I go to fetch the wine; eh?"

"Why you may leave him here. I dare say he will not be frightened to pass ten minutes under lock and key, although in the company of a supposed highwayman."

"Eh!" exclaimed Grummidge suspiciously, "if he doesn't object I do."

"But I *do* object," exclaimed John Green, "the gentleman may be a very honest man, and as far as I know he is; but still he may be a highwayman, although not the one I've met; and to be left alone with a highwayman, oh Lord! I should never survive it."

Hugh Fenton glanced in astonishment at the coachman, and then said—

"Well, well, as you like. You had better take the nervous gentleman with you. Perhaps under your escort he would not mind seeing a little more of Newgate; only please make haste; for not only am I thirsty, but sitting here alone is dull work."

"I should like to see some of the prison," said Green quickly.

"Very well; then come along with me," said Grummidge, "as long as I have my eyes on you I don't mind; and curse me if I mean to take 'em off you."

Mr. Grummidge first led his new-found friend to the prison tap, where the footman paid his footing most cheerfully and liberally, a circumstance which greatly raised him in the eyes of the turnkey; who afterwards led him through the prison.

They visited the Stone Hall, and saw the heavy fetters and handcuffs; they even ventured into Bluebeard's Room, or Jack Ketch's Kitchen, that terrible place where the quarters of persons who had been executed to satisfy the blood-thirsty tastes of the highly christian house of Hanover were boiled in pitch before being exposed on the city gates for the gratification of a loyal populace.

From thence they passed to the different wards and to the Condemned Cells, all of which were wretched to an excess, and filthy in the extreme; a fact which seemed to give John Green's highly moral mind an immense satisfaction. "For," said he, "such horrid creatures as thieves and such like, can't be too badly treated."

In the Condemned Cells, which seemed the part of the building that interested John Green more than any other; he asked, and obtained permission, to copy some of the inscriptions engraved on the walls by those poor wretches who had passed the last few hours of their miserable existences in those dreary holes.

Mr. Grummidge read them out to the footman, who wrote them down on a piece of paper, which he afterwards folded carefully and placed in his pocket.

They then went back to the tap, and having procured a bottle of wine, returned to the prisoner.

The bottle of wine was soon broached, and taking their glasses the trio were about to pledge each other, when John Green discovered that there was a piece of cork in his glass. This he fished out with a small piece of paper that he had twisted up for the purpose, and which he afterwards threw under the truckle-bed, seeming to have quite forgotten that it was the same paper on which he had written in the Condemned Cells.

"Well master what's your name," said Hugh, "what do you think of Newgate?"

"Oh! it's an awful place, it makes one feel all of a shiver," replied the man.

"It's nothing when you're used to it," said Grummidge with a grin.

"That's a matter of opinion," replied Hugh Fenton, "I don't think I shall ever get used to it."

"I don't think you're very likely to leave it," replied Grummidge, "at least you won't live long anywhere else. I fear the case is too good against you."

"You're mighty good to be sure," laughed Hugh, "but I hope you're mistaken."

"Is the case so very bad against the gentleman?" demanded John Green.

"Undoubtedly! Captain Jennings swears he saw his face in the moonlight as plain as he could possibly have seen it at daylight."

"Is that the only evidence against him? Is there no other?"

"Yes, that is all, and enough too I should think, least-wise it's a scragging matter."

"But the gentleman may have been mistaken?" said the footman.

"Not he! But come, I must not waste more time. Now Mr. Pitt is ill I have all my work to do to keep things in order. So I must trouble you to move."

John Green wished Hugh good-bye and shook hands with him in a timid, respectful manner that greatly pleased Mr. Grummidge, who declared him a "regular softy," and avowed that "he'd never seen such a nincompoop in all his born days," and "that anybody could do what they liked with him," an assertion he put to the proof by taking Mr. Green down to the tap and making him pay his footing the second time before he was allowed to depart.

No sooner had the turnkey and coachman left the cell, than Hugh knelt down and picked up the piece of paper from under the bed, and read what had been written in the Condemned Cells with avidity. The writing was as follows—

"You nearly spoiled all by wishing to be left alone with me. I have been round the prison, but see no means for your escape, at least, not before your trial. I will have counsel ready for you. Plead 'Not Guilty.' Don't know anything or anybody connected with the case. I feel certain I shall get you acquitted. Eat this when you have read it.—Yours, B. W."

CHAPTER XLVII.

BOB BLOW-THE-BELLOWS ON THE TRAMP.—HE HAS A FIGHT AND MAKES A FRIEND.—THE MESSAGE DELIVERED.

IT was a fine, warm afternoon, the sun was sinking down rapidly in the west, shooting up its bright red rays across the heavens and gilding the broad estuary of the River Blackwater.

It was in a deep secluded vale leading down to the river that Bob Blow-the-Bellows threw himself down beneath some thick shrubs to watch the setting sun and rest himself.

Now it so happened that Bob Blow-the-Bellows was for once in his life in a very bad temper. During his journey from Stamford he had scarcely met a soul, with whom he could be on good terms. All seemed—or at least so he thought—to look on him with suspicion and mistrust, and therefore he had been doomed to silence in spite of his immense love of loquacity.

Added to this, Bob had thought deeply over his engagement with Mrs. Wapshaw, and although he by no means repented it, yet he did not like the way he had been entrapped into proposing by "that young vagabond, Jerry," as he called him.

Altogether, anyone looking at the merry smith as he lay with his hat drawn over his eyes, gazing out at the shining waters, would have considered his sobriquet as decidedly a misnomer, for he looked one of the most miserable creatures in existence.

With a deep sigh he drew some cold meat and bread from his wallet, uncorked a keg that he carried slung across his shoulder by a strap, and commenced his evening meal.

In the midst of this he was disturbed by hearing footsteps coming down the path, and a cheery voice singing a very old song, which the smith remembered to have heard many years before at Bartholomew Fair. It ran thus—

"Of all the occupations
A beggar's is the best,
For when he is aweary
He lays him down to rest.

Then a begging we will go,
A begging we will go,
And a begging we will go—o—o,
And a begging we will go."*

As the last part of the chorus—which by the way was given with much gusto and force—finished, the stranger arrived at the spot where lay Bob.

The new comer was a man about the middle height, broad shouldered and well made. His eyes were a clear, bright, blue, with a merry twinkle that matched well with the good humoured smile which played round his rather voluptuous mouth. He was evidently considerably over forty, yet not a wrinkle appeared on his broad forehead, neither were there any lines about his eyes.

His hair, which was long and curly, had a few lines of silver in it, but save on his temples there was no sign of baldness. His walk was easy, with a lithesomeness that would have done justice to a youth; whilst his gestures, although at times somewhat exaggerated, were never without grace.

He wore a broad-brimmed hat, which had evidently seen a great deal of wear, as had all his garments, from his brown square-cut coat to his loose, broad-toed shoes. A loose bag was slung on his back, and in his hand was a long thick staff of oak sapling, which he seemed to carry more for amusement than anything else, for big as it was, he swung it about as though it were but a switch.

Catching sight of Bob Blow-the-Bellows, the singer ceased his song, halted, leant on his staff, and raising his hat gracefully, addressed him.

"Good morning, brother, how wags the world with you? Merrily, I trust."

"I'm none the better for seeing you," growled the smith.

"And none the worse, I hope," cried the other, gaily. "'Good wine needs no bush,' and your face, overcast though it be, needs no words to prove you a jolly fellow; therefore I'll sit by you and bear you company; nay, more, I'll eat of your bread, and drink of your wine."

As he spoke he threw his wallet away, and cast himself by the smith's side.

"I tell you I do not want your company," cried the smith, who besides being in a bad humour, looked upon his new-found acquaintance's familiarity with a great deal of suspicion.

"As you will, friend," replied the other. "This world is large enough for all, therefore go your way, and leave me in peace."

"But I was sitting here before you came," argued the smith.

"That's true. 'And he who doth gainsay it breathes a lie.' Therefore remain there, friend."

"Then get you gone," replied Bob Blow-the-Bellows, angrily.

"Nay, friend, there you are wrong," said the other. "You were not sitting *here* on this spot where I am, therefore in this spot I am the new-comer. Therefore go thy ways, and trouble me not, 'I'm not i' the vein.'"

"Why come so near me?" cried the smith, angrily.

"Because I choose," replied the other. "Did you not hear my song, how a beggar may 'lay him down and rest' wherever he pleases? Listen to the next verse.

'In a hollow tree
I live, and pay no rent;
Providence provides for me,
And I am well content."

"Silence!" cried the smith. "If you do not stop

* The songs sung by this character are taken from old English Ballads; those sung by other characters are original.

that yelling, by heavens I'll make you cry on the other side of your mouth—ay, and to another tune."

"Singing, not yelling," replied the other, coolly. "If there is one thing I pride myself on, it is my singing. I belong to the honourable society of beggars, which might take for their motto the words Will Shakespeare puts in Master Shallow's mouth, 'Barren, barren, barren; beggars all.' Yet am I lighthearted, for I never forget Autolycus' song :—

> 'Jog on, jog on the footpath way,
>   And merrily bent the stile-a
> A merry heart tires in a day,
>   Your sad tires in a milo-a.'

So you see I will never be dull. I am ready to oblige you in any way you like. I will sing you a snatch, recite you a poem, or break your head with the greatest of pleasure, but dull I will not be."

"Come on then," cried the smith, springing up, "we will see if you will break my head."

"'By cock and pie,' I'm with you" cried the other.

They both seized their staves, and in a few minutes were knocking splinters out of the hard wood, but neither of them seemed able to hit the other.

"Bravely fought," cried the beggar, as they both drew back to gain breath.

"If you only sang half so well as you fight," said the smith, smiling in spite of himself, "you would not be so bad, after all."

"Say you so," cried the other. "I never knew anything yet like a fight to melt a man's coolness. Why, you're half thawed already. Let's have another turn, and you will become my best friend on earth. So, 'on guard.'"

Once more they set to work striking and parrying with a rapidity that was really astonishing, it being marvellous how the men escaped.

Suddenly the beggar's staff descended on the smith's head, but at the same moment Bob's fell with great violence on his opponent's right arm.

"By Jove! you've the best of it after all," cried the beggar; "'see what a rent the envious Casca made;' no, I don't mean a rent, but bruise."

"I hope I have not hurt you much," said the smith, now all good humour, although he was rubbing his forehead, on which was a large bump.

"No, such little matters will soon be set right. Now let us be friends. My name is Richard Ray, commonly known as Roaring Ric the Ranter, from a bad habit I have of spouting. I am by profession an actor, but by choice a beggar. Nature made me strong but idle, and therefore I never work unless compelled."

"I am, as you see, a tinker," returned Bob, "and my name is Stevens."

"You don't seem to have chosen the best paths to gain work, Mr. Stevens," said Ric the Ranter dryly.

"Neither have you chosen the best for begging purposes," rejoined the smith.

Roaring Ric burst out into a loud laugh, and winking violently said—

"Singing songs is not the only thing I have copied from Autolycus; I freely confess that, like him, I am 'a picker up of unconsidered trifles;' you understand."

"Perfectly."

"And are we still to be friends?"

"If you will pledge me your faith to be true; for I like your spirit."

"There's my hand on't," replied Ric; "I will help you in all your undertakings."

"Well then, I may soon make you useful; but mind, if you are false you are certain to be killed. I have many friends to avenge a wrong."

"That have not I; but doubt me not, I will be true as steel."

"Then let us be trudging on our way," said the smith, gathering up his wallet and keg.

They walked on for some distance without conversing, both seeming lost in thought.

At last Roaring Ric commenced by suddenly asking why Bob was so dull.

"Dull!" exclaimed Bob; "I am not dull, I am merry."

"You don't look so. Come, who is the woman? for a woman I know it is. Nothing else could make your jolly old phiz look so sombre.

> Prithee, why so pale, fond lover?
>   Prithee, why so pale?
> If looking well won't please her
>   Will looking ill prevail?
>   Then prithee why so pale?"

"A truce to all this nonsense," said the smith, "if we should become firm friends, as we shall soon see if that is likely, you shall know all; till then ask no questions, and I will tell you no lies."

"As you will," replied the other, "but in the name of all the heathen gods and godesses don't be dull. Give me a drink out of that keg of yours and tip me a stave."

"Here is the keg," said the smith, throwing it to him, "but as to staves, I should have thought you had had enough of them already for to-day."

"Not so," cried Ric, "I love a song; it shortens our journey through life, so begin."

Thus pressed, the merry smith threw out his chest, and in a deep clear voice sung—

"To Horse and let us away."

> When poverty wrings the heart of a man,
>   And his stomach cries out for a meal,
> To find relief there is but one plan—
>   And that is to steal, to steal, to steal,
>   And that is to steal, to steal.
>   Then to horse, and let us away,
>   The travellers' carriage to stay,
>   I'll warrant my lads you'll find it is
>   A game that's sure to pay.
>
> The son of labour tries by toil
>   Some hard earned pence to save,
> But ah! he finds his native soil,
>   Will yield him but a grave.
>   Then to horse, and let us away,
>   The travellers' carriage to stay,
>   I'll warrant my lads you'll find it is,
>   A trade that's sure to pay.
>
> And if perchance we should be nabbed,
>   And forced to take our trial,
> We'll laugh at them by whom we're grabbed,
>   And meet death with a smile.
>   So, to horse——"

Bob Blow-the-Bellows paused suddenly, for his well practised ear had caught the sound of horses' hoofs on the road.

"Hush!" he whispered, "let us draw on one side and see who it is."

They drew into the hedge, and as the two horsemen came up Bob recognised Maud and Growling Teddy.

"High! my good fellow," cried Maud to the smith, as if he were a stranger, "will you see to my horse's girths."

The smith did as he was commanded, and Maud stooping down whispered, "Who is that man? Be at Tillingham, at the Three Cutters, to-night. Is there any news on the road?"

"The man may become one of us, he is of the right sort," whispered the smith—"I'll be there. Lord Redfern has been up and down the road once or twice lately. That's all."

"Thanks my good friend," said Maud in a loud voice as she threw Bob some money, "there is something to drink my health with, and may you have a speedy journey."

In another moment they rode away, and Bob desiring his friend to make haste, walked rapidly on towards Tillingham.

CHAPTER XLVIII.

JONATHAN WILD AND HIS ASSOCIATES ARRIVE AT TILLINGHAM HALL.—THE TWO INTERVIEWS.—LORD LESLIE'S FLIGHT.

TILLINGHAM HALL was a fine old mansion, built in the Elizabethan style. Its sides were clothed with ivy, which hung in festoons round the windows, creeping over the gables, and twisting itself round the tall, thin chimney-pots.

A splendid avenue of elms led up to the mansion, spreading their huge arms across the path, so as to cause a pleasant twilight there even in mid-day.

For all the beauty of the place, Tillingham Hall was not one to impress one either with the idea of comfort or with the sweet feeling of home.

But one large, rambling wing seemed habitable at all, the rest being merely a ruin, grand and stately it is true, but still merely a ruin.

That the dilapidation was not merely the effect of time was fully proved by the charred beams that were to be seen through the broken windows.

Altogether it was a strangely weird and romantic place, one in which ghosts might lurk, gliding about from one deserted room to the other, sighing mournfully at the desolation reigning in the place that had once been the home of all their joys and sorrows.

But on a night like the one in which this chapter opens, Tillingham Hall appeared even more desolate than usual.

A low wind coming from off the sea, swept through the trees, and moaned around the pointed gables of the house.

No light could be seen in the dreary building, which was occasionally lit up by vivid flashes of lightning. Heavy drops of rain fell slowly on the leaves, whilst the moaning of the sea mingled with the rolling of the distant thunder.

The gloom of this scene seemed to have its full effect on four horsemen as they dashed up the old avenue, for neither of them spoke until they reined in their horses opposite what had once been the grand entrance.

"Bah! what a miserable place," snarled one, "a fitting nest for crime."

"Treason has been hatched in it often enough," replied the other, "You see Mr. Wild, the sea shore being so near, it was a convenient place for the Jesuits to work in. Many and many a plot has been made here, I can assure you."

"I can well believe that," replied Jonathan Wild; "Lord Redfern's house must have treason in it."

"There you wrong me," replied Redfern, "for in those times the place was not in my family."

"No," replied Jonathan, "but your *family was in the place,* hence the treason. Here Darrell, take the horses round to the stable; see that they are well attended to for we may want them to-night. Farmer Croft will follow us."

Taking a key from his pocket, Lord Redfern opened the door, and the three men entered the gloomy building.

Passing down a long passage, Lord Redfern led the way into a small room where there was a cheery fire blazing on the hearth, and a substantial supper placed ready for them on the table.

"I am glad to see that hospitality still has its existence in these dreary walls," said Jonathan, pouring out a large cup of wine, "here's to the success of our project. Come gentlemen and pledge me that."

The three men filled their glasses, clinked them, and then tossed off the contents.

"We must not delay," cried Croft; "the schooner is out in the roads, and we must take care not to miss the tide."

"You are right," said Lord Redfern; "but I have still my prisoners to see. We must make Leslie go quietly if we can; if not, we must use force. But"—

"Tut, tut!" cried Jonathan, sharply; "you know as well as I do that *he* is never to touch land again when once he is on board. Do not fear: the skipper has strict orders how to settle with him. He goes on board as a fugitive from the law, under a false name. When they are half way over to Hellevoetsluys, he *falls* overboard, and no one is the wiser. Don't fear; we shall not be seen in the matter. You tell him that the ship is a smuggling vessel—that will account for their villainy; and, by George! Keel-hauling Jack, the skipper, has no equal in villainy anywhere. *He* won't let the lawyers catch him."

"Well, well," cried Redfern, "you eat some supper, whilst I go to him and prepare him for his flight."

Taking a lamp from the table, Lord Redfern left the room.

Hurrying down one or two passages, he arrived at last before a small door, so constructed that only those persons knowing the house well would know of its existence.

This he opened and entered a small ante-room, where he paused and listened. After a moment, he approached another door and tapped gently.

"Come in," cried a gentle, sorrowful voice.

Bowing low, Lord Redfern entered the room.

It was a beautiful little boudoir, furnished in the style of Louis XIV.

On a sofa, at the further end of this apartment, sat Alice Landon, her beautiful face made more lovely from the bitter grief which she had experienced.

"You here!" she exclaimed, shrinking back as she beheld Redfern. "I am your prisoner; but, at least, you might spare me the pain of your presence."

"A man cannot live without his heart," replied Redfern; "you are my life, my love, my soul. Why are you so cold to me?"

"Keep off!" cried Alice, waving her persecutor back. "You know what cause, what terrible cause, I have to hate you. By your hands my father died."

"For the love of you, my sweet Alice," argued Redfern.

"Hold!" cried Alice; "dare not breathe those words to me."

"Hear me," cried Redfern, passionately; "I swear by heaven—"

"Silence!" exclaimed Alice, drawing herself up to her full height; "have you no reverence for aught that is pure and holy that you swear by the heaven you have so grievously wronged and offended?"

"'Tis false," cried Redfern; "heaven is full of love, and he who loves most is nearer heaven. I tell you, Alice, that my passion is beyond control. Say that you will be mine, and wealth, rank, and power shall be yours. You shall be the gayest of the gay, and I your humble slave. Should you refuse me, I swear that you shall not leave this room alive."

"I heed not your threats," exclaimed Alice; "neither do I wish for wealth nor power. You think to frighten me by death. I long for it. It is my only wish; life has no more charms for me; death no terrors."

"This is madness," cried Redfern, "if my love for you were not so great I would kill myself to please you; but I cannot, will not, permit you to be another's. You shall be my wife. I give you till to-morrow; if after that you still refuse me, I must employ other means."

With ill-disguised rage he strode from the room, slamming the door after him.

As he did so he thought he heard the sound of retreating footsteps.

He hastened to the door of the ante-room. It was as he had left it.

"Bah!" he exclaimed, "it is only my imagination, nothing more."

Walking rapidly down the corridor he entered another room, where, stretched on a low couch, pale and thin, lay Lord Henry Leslie.

"Who is there?" demanded Lord Henry, faintly.

"It is I, my lord," replied Lord Redfern in a quick manner, "I have but just this moment arrived from London, the bloodhounds are after you."

"Let them come," replied Leslie, "I have done no wrong, and therefore will not fly."

"This is madness my lord," cried Redfern, "not only do you risk your own life, but mine for concealing you."

"How so? it was a duel!"

"No one believes it so. All agree in calling it murder."

"Then it is my duty to clear my character from so false an aspersion. If Sir Arthur were alive he would clear me of so foul a charge."

"True, my lord, but Sir Arthur is *not* alive, and therefore cannot clear you, so the charge lies just the same, and unless you escape until the time comes when you can clear yourself, trust me, you will die branded as a murderer."

"My God, this is fearful," cried Lord Henry Leslie.

"It is doubtlessly the work of some foul plot," said Redfern.

"It must be," said Lord Henry.

"Time alone can show how, and by whose means this has arisen, therefore I beseech you to fly at once. A schooner is now riding in the roads. I will see you placed safely on board, and she will convey you to Hellevoetsluys, where you need not fear the consequences of this deplorable duel."

"I suppose you are right," said Lord Leslie, "I must wait until I have discovered who has wrought this plot against me. I will no longer be the idle creature that I have been, but will work with energy to discover who has thus wronged me, and I swear that when I have discovered him he shall answer to the full."

"Hum!" thought Lord Redfern, "he *must* die." Then he added aloud—

"Come my lord, there is no time to lose. I have some gentlemen downstairs who will protect you with their lives, should any attempt be made to prevent your going on board the schooner. So we have nothing to fear."

"Is there so much danger then?" said Lord Henry.

"There is indeed, we must start at once. Quick, wrap this cloak around you."

Wrapping a cloak round Lord Henry, and placing a large slouch hat on his head, Lord Redfern hurried him down the stairs out into the open air, where he blew a shrill whistle which was immediately answered by the appearance of three men, all closely cloaked and masked.

"These are our friends," he whispered to Lord Henry, "they are good and true, therefore you must reward them well. We will walk a little in advance, and they will follow us. Don't speak, but keep close to me as we shall have to make our way down a narrow path in the cliff where one slip might be fatal."

CHAPTER XLIX.

BATSWING TO THE RESCUE.—THE FIGHT ON THE BEACH.
—THE FIGHT AT SEA.—CAPTURE OF THE SCHOONER.

THE "Three Cutters" was a snug little public-house, perched on the top of a cliff, from which elevated position it looked out seawards. It was a low, rambling place, with small gable ends, round which the fierce wind blowing from the German Ocean howled mournfully. Cheerless as the hostelry looked outside, the interior was the very reverse. The long room where the general company assembled was fitted up to represent a ship's cabin with wondrous exactitude.

Quantities of brasswork, beautifully polished, were fixed on the doors. A large telescope hung over the fire, in company with a long duck gun, and a huge pair of cutlasses.

The company assembled in this room were mostly all seafaring men, deep-chested, strong-built fellows, whose faces were the colour of mahogany, from exposure to the weather, and whose laughter was as boisterous as the waves on which they made their living.

Close by the chimney-corner sat Bob Blow-the-Bellows, and his new acquaintance, Roaring Ric the Ranter.

Each had a jug of steaming liquor before him, to which they applied themselves with wondrous regularity.

Groups of sailors were seated round, smoking and drinking at the tables, whilst the landlord, a rough, burly-looking fellow of about forty, was passing round, serving out the drink.

"By the Lord Harry!" cried Roaring Ric, "this place is wondrous comfortable!"

"Trust Will Watch for that," replied Bob, winking knowingly.

"And who may Will Watch be?" demanded Ric.

"He is our worthy host," said the smith.

"Certainly a most worthy one," exclaimed Ric, "for I notice that though he stints no one in their liquor, he don't seem to take a penny from any one."

"Probably they are old customers, and have credit."

"Nay, that cannot be, for I am no old customer, and much I doubt if anyone would give me credit, not even if they knew me. In fact, that would be a reason for their not doing so. Yet, for all that, this is the third jug of punch I have had without having shown him the colour of my money."

"Doubtless he gives you credit because you are a friend of mine."

"Hem!" said Ric, suspiciously, "then you are an old friend of his."

"Yes; I have known Will ever since I was a boy," replied the smith.

"So, so," cried Ric. "I thought you were a stranger in these parts?"

"And so I am," cried Bob Blow-the-Bellows, hastily; "but I have nevertheless known Will for many years. You see, he has been a sailor, and therefore travelled a good deal, and——"

"Enough of your excuses, good master tinker," cried Ric. "I will not ask you any more questions, for while I am well treated I have but little curiosity. It matters not to me if the spirit I drink has paid duty or not, so long as it is good, and there is plenty of it."

At this moment Will Watch approached the fire, and nodding carelessly to Bob, said, in a rough voice,

"It's a nasty night at sea, messmates. It'll be blowing big guns before the morning, you may depend. I can hear the surf rolling out yonder already."

"There's nothing strange in hearing the surf, is there?" demanded Bob.

"Not as *you* mean it," replied Will Watch; "but when the sound from across the bar comes like the low wail of a woman in pain, why then you may be certain that many a good ship's crew will have struck to King Death and gone to Davey Jones's locker before morning."

"Bah! you make me feel quite uncomfortable," cried Bob.

"Nevertheless, it's true; I only trust that the Black Hawk won't make a run to-night, that is all I can say. Come messmates, don't let the grog stand, as on such a night as this, one can't drink too much."

"THE RAGE OF THE CREATURE SEEMED TO REDOUBLE!"

The smith was about to drink off the remains of his grog, in order that his jug might be replenished when Growling Teddy entered the room and whispered a few words in the smith's ear, who at once arose, and, bidding Ric await his return, hastily left the room.

Crossing through the bar, Bob Blow-the-Bellows entered a small room in which he found Batswing and Maud in deep conference.

Batswing's appearance had again altered, his dress being now that of a handsomely-dressed captain in the merchant service.

Thick, heavy boots, reaching up to the middle of his thigh, encased his legs; whilst a stout jacket, made of some strong blue material, was closely buttoned round him.

How is this?" he said sternly, as Bob entered the room; "are our lives to be played with so lightly that you dare to bring a stranger amongst us, and at such

a time too, when we are about to perform a most hazardous attack. Who and what is this man?"

"Trust me, captain, the man is all right," replied the smith; "he is one of those careless fellows who may be trusted with anything but money and drink. He is willing to join us, and will, I am sure, be useful."

"How know you that?" demanded Batswing, sharply.

"Because he can fight well. This bump which you see on my head was part of his work. He handles the quarter-staff like an angel."

A smile passed over Batswing's countenance as he demanded of the smith—

"Do angels, then, use quarter-staves? I should have thought otherwise. But go, bring hither this man; we will question him. If he be true he can join us; if not, means must be taken to prevent his baulking our plans."

"I'll answer for him with my life," replied the smith; "he is too jolly to be a traitor."

16

The smith soon returned with Roaring Ric, whom he introduced to Batswing.

"Hark ye, friend," said Batswing, "do you know what kind of people you are amongst? Have you any suspicion as to their trade or profession?"

"Faith, I have more than suspicion," said Ric; "I am certain."

"And what may your certainty be?" demanded Batswing, sternly.

"Why, that I am among as pretty a set of cut-throats as can be."

"Such being the case, what do you intend doing?"

"I intend being as polite as possible; shutting my eyes to all little short-comings, my ears to any little secrets, and only opening my mouth to eat and drink."

"Friend," said Batswing, "you have spoken wisely. By your looks I should think the world has not treated you too well. Am I right?"

"For the matter of that I don't complain," said Ric. "The world is not such a bad one as folks make out; it is like a woman, and treats others according to how it is treated."

"How so?" demanded Batswing, amused at the fellow's philosophy.

"Why, you see, those that are too fond of the world, and will do anything to please her, are just like doting husbands and get deceived; but he who treats the world as a goodly pleasant place, is like an honest, well-meaning husband who is master in his own house, and therefore is beloved by his wife; who treats him with respect and is dutiful. You see the world, sir, is pretty much what we like to make it. When we are jolly it is jolly, when we mope and are miserable, then this world is a dull place."

"I see you are a philosopher; will you take service with me?"

"That all depends on two things," replied Ric.

"And what are they?"

"In the first place, is there much work to do?"

"No, you can still lead your idle life."

"In the second, are the wages good and the provisions plentiful?"

"Your pay is good, and you may eat and drink as much as you like."

"Then am I with you," cried Ric, "such places are not often met with."

"Good," replied Batswing, "you must take the oath of allegiance."

"I will take any oath you like," said Ric, "they are all one to me."

"Remember, if you break your word, you will be doomed to death."

"Which I shall not mind, as I shall have deserved it."

"Do not flatter yourself that you can escape; I have emissaries all over England, and if you escaped me some, others would kill you."

The oath was soon taken, and Roaring Ric the Ranter became one of the band.

The ceremony was scarcely completed when Will Watch entered the room.

"How now Will?" cried Batswing, "what has happened to disturb you."

"The Black Hawk, is making signals out in the offing."

"It is well," said Batswing, "I ordered her to be here."

"But a gale is springing up and a strange sloop has been cruising off here all day. It will be impossible to run a cargo to-night."

"We shall not attempt to run a cargo to-night," replied Batswing.

"Then what do you want the Black Hawk here for?"

"That must for the present remain a secret. Who have you in the house?"

"None but friends," replied Will, "all good men and true."

"Well, see that the house is closed, and let no one enter but our men."

Will Watch departed on his errand, whilst Batswing looked to the priming of his pistols and buckled a huge cutlass round his waist.

He then directed Bob Blow-the-Bellows, Maud, and Roaring Ric to remain at the Inn, unless they heard sounds of a combat, when he ordered them to make their way at once to Tillingham Hall, force an entrance, and if they discovered Alice to bear her away to Epping.

This done, he ascended to a small room above the long parlour, and tapping gently at the door, waited patiently until he was bidden to enter.

In this room was seated Sir Arthur Burdon, his face pale and thin from the anxiety he felt about Alice Landon.

"All is prepared, Sir Arthur," said Batswing, calmly, "but before attacking Tillingham Hall, it is my intention to see that the boat is ready to bear you away to my sloop, the Black Hawk, we will then rescue Alice and you can fly with her to France. Once there, make her Lady Burdon, and you will be safe."

"But this accusation of murder that is made against me?" cried Sir Arthur.

"Must be left until we have a fit occasion to disprove it."

"But should Alice not be at the Hall," argued Sir Arthur.

"She must be. If not, why should Lord Redfern and Jonathan Wild be there."

"True," replied Sir Arthur, "there is some mystery here."

"Yes, and one that I will unravel come what may."

"Are you all prepared to start?" asked Sir Arthur eagerly.

"Yes, everything is ready, so let us be off."

In a few moments Sir Arthur had placed his pistols in his belt and buckled on his sword.

They then descended to the large room, where they found some dozen men, all fully armed, waiting impatiently to start.

No sooner had they appeared than Will Watch pulled up a trapdoor that was in the middle of the room, but so well constructed that none would have known it was there.

This trap door led to a flight of stairs cut out in the solid rock.

Down these they descended until they reached a large cave.

The roaring of the wind and the dash of the waves told them they were close on the sea shore.

This was indeed a fact, for a few moments afterwards they were standing on the sands, the fierce waves breaking in anger at their feet as they walked.

"By Jove," muttered Will Watch to Batswing, "there's that strange schooner."

"What can she be?" demanded Batswing in an under tone.

"I can't make her out," replied Will, "she's not a government ship, that's evident."

"How near she stands in," said Batswing, "her captain must know the coast well."

"Yes and she must draw very little water," said Will.

"See what is that!" cried Batswing, seizing his companion's arm and holding him back.

Down close by the foot of the cliff a small blue flame seemed to flit.

Backwards and forwards it went, making the superstitious sailors tremble.

"Gracious powers," murmured Will Watch, "it is a corpse candle."

"It is no such thing," cried Batswing, "it is a signal."

Scarcely had the words passed his lips, than a similar light appeared on board the schooner. The two lights then became stationary and seemed to become larger and more intensely bright until they both suddenly disappeared.

Instantaneous as the light had been, Batswing had by its aid seen a band of armed men. amongst whom was a figure wrapped in a huge cloak and evidently being supported by the others.

By the side of this cloaked figure stood two men whom Batswing knew at once.

One was the burly form of Jonathan Wild, the other, Lord Redfern.

"Quick," shouted Batswing as the sound of oars came plainly on their ears, "quick to the rescue; it is that villain Jonathan Wild, and they are bearing off Alice Landon. Now lads, show the rascals what English sailors are."

With a wild shout, Batswing's party dashed forward, pressing on the other.

With a loud cry of defiance the others met them, boldly standing their ground.

Swords clashed, spreading sparks around, whilst the sharp report of the pistols rent the air, mingled with the curses and oaths of the combatants.

Long and fierce was the struggle without either side gaining the advantage.

Jonathan Wild's harsh, cruel voice was heard distinctly above the rest giving directions to the men whilst he led them on against the enemy.

Desperately as Sir Arthur Burdon and Batswing fought, they could not approach the cloaked figure so closely was he hemmed round by his conductors.

Calling to his men to make one desperate charge, Batswing waved his cutlass and at the head of his men rushed upon Lord Redfern and his party.

To his surprise Jonathan Wild's usual cry of defiance was not given in return.

Could it be possible that some lucky blow had stretched him lifeless on th ground?

With a hasty prayer that such was the case, Batswing redoubled his efforts and drove his enemies down to the very edge of the sea.

"Forward my lads," he cried, "they must yield, they cannot retreat."

But he was mistaken, for at that moment a boat shot to the shore.

In less time than it takes us to tell, the cloaked figure was thrust into the boat by two men who sprang after it, and the next minute pushed off to sea.

So unexpected and sudden was this movement, that Batswing and his companions stood still with amazement, a circumstance of which their adversaries left on shore took advantage by running away as fast as they could.

"By all that is horrible!" exclaimed Sir Arthur, "they have borne her off.

"We will follow them still," cried Batswing.

"How can we do that?" demanded Sir Arthur, "we have no boat."

Without waiting to reply, Batswing turned to Will Watch and cried—

"Give the signal for the Black Hawk to stand close in shore and to intercept."

Will drew from his pocket a small square cardboard box with a fuse at one end.

This he lighted, and immediately a bright flame shot up into the air.

He then drew from his pocket a paper, containing some powder, which he shook now and then on the flame, which, as the drug fell upon it, changed to a bright purple, so that the light changed at intervals from white to purple.

Whilst this was being done, Batswing had led his men back into the cave, where they discovered a large rowing boat.

By his command the men seized hold of her gunwale, and with a merry cheer rushed with her towards the sea, her keel scraping along the shingle at a tremendous rate, and the next minute she was launched, and all the men safely on board, including Will Watch, who had received the return signal from the Black Hawk, and therefore knew his message was understood.

"Give way, my lads," cried Batswing; "a hundred guineas to you if we overtake them."

With a hearty cheer the men dashed on, their oars cutting the water with that wondrous regularity only obtained by long practice.

Will Watch took the helm and steered the boat, whilst Batswing cheered on his men.

Heavier and heavier grew the sea, and the wind, chopping round from the east to the south-west, drove the boat with great rapidity.

Taking advantage of the change of the wind Batswing ordered the men to rig up a mast and set a sail. This was soon done, and the next moment a large lateen sail was hoisted, and after shivering a few moments filled out, heeling the boat over so that its lee gunwale was level with the water, and away sped the boat like lightning.

"Hurrah, my lads!" cried Batswing, "we are coming up to them hand-over-hand."

At that moment a bullet whistled close past his ear.

"So, so," he cried; "we are within musket-shot, are we. Try your aim, Will."

Taking a long gun from the bottom of the boat, where it had been concealed by some tarpawlings, Will took aim and fired.

A sharp scream from the pursued boat followed the explosion.

"For mercy's sake do not fire," cried Sir Arthur. "You may kill her."

"True," said Batswing. "We shall soon overtake them, so it does not matter."

At that moment the shot was returned with good effect, the bullet cutting away the sheet, and the next moment the severed rope flew through the ring-bolt, and the sail fell over the bow of the boat, stopping her further progress, and nearly filling her with water by the suddeness with which she righted.

"Cut away the gear," cried Batswing. "Unship the mast and take to your oars."

These orders were obeyed with a rapidity that was astonishing, but the delay that the loss of sail had caused, enabled the pursued boat to reach the strange ship. With a ringing cheer the men sprang on board. The next moment the schooner's helm was put up, and she was flying through the water away from the pursuers.

"Come back, come back, you cowards," cried Sir Arthur, in impotent rage.

Just then the sharp report of a cannon was heard in the distance.

"Hurrah! my brave boys," cried Batswing, "the day may still be ours. Give way, the Black Hawk has seen her prey, and they must sail fast to outsail my ship. Give way, lads, and we will overhaul them yet. By Jove! if we take the schooner, the prize will indeed be worth the having."

Each man bent to his oar until the boat groaned again.

"Easy all," cried Batswing. "Back water. Now seize that rope. Steady, lads, steady."

A low grating noise was heard, as the boat ran against the side of the Black Hawk, and in a few moments they stood upon the deck of the smuggling vessel.

"Now, Will," cried Batswing, "spread every stitch of canvas she will bear. A stern chase is a long one they say, but we will make this as short as possible. Jackson, run out the bow chaser and give yonder schooner a salvo as the ship dips; now, boys, clear the decks for action, for I warrant me we will have as pretty a war dance to-night as any of you can remember."

In a moment the decks were cleared, the little brass cannons were run out, and the men, each armed with a boarding cutlass and a brace of pistols, stood ready at their posts.

It was a grim sight to see those stern looking individuals stripped to the waist, their chests covered with hair, their brawny arms tattooed, their firm mouths clenched and their fierce eyes turned towards the flying enemy.

By this time Jackson had got his gun right, the helm was put down to port, and as the Black Hawk leaped over the curl of a wave, a light wreath of smoke flew from her bows, followed by a loud report.

Unfortunately the shot flew wide, whilst the firing of the gun threw the Black Hawk several points off the wind.

"Confusion," cried Batswing, "has Will Watch brought the vessel up to the wind again; have you lost your skill Master gunner that you can only impede instead of aid us? Load her again and let me try."

Whilst the gun was being loaded, the pursued vessel returned the fire from her stern chaser, and although she did no more damage than knocking a few splinters out of the gunwale of the Black Hawk and severely wounding two of the crew, still she gained this advantage over her pursuers, the recoil of the stern chasers aided her flight, whilst the recoil of the bow chaser greatly hindered the pursuers.

Still the firing was kept up and great damage was done to the rigging of both ships, but still they held on their course, the sailors repairing the damage done as well as they could as the ships cleaved through the waters.

It was evidently the endeavour of the enemy to cripple the masts and rigging of the Black Hawk, but fortunately most of the shots flew wide of the mark.

The action now became very warm, the men serving the cannons like devils.

A shout of triumph rose from the fugitives as a shot carried away the top mast of the Black Hawk; but a moment afterwards it was changed into one of dismay as a chance shot tore away the main mast of the flying vessel, leaving her rigging a perfect wreck.

The Black Hawk now ceased firing and steered up to the enemy to board. With a tremendous thud, which shook them both, the ships struck together.

A terrific yell arose from the Black Hawk crew as they leapt on board their adversary, and a short but most terrible hand to hand encounter took place, wherein many a gallant fellow met his fate.

A few minutes afterwards Batswing stood in the after deck triumphant.

But where was Alice?

They sought for her in vain, but to their astonishment, found Lord Leslie.

"Leslie!" cried Sir Arthur, "Lord Henry Leslie, and alive."

"Can it be possible?" exclaimed Lord Leslie, as he grasped Sir Arthur's hand, "they told me you were dead, and bitterly, oh! bitterly have I regretted that duel; in which you behaved so nobly, and I, alas, so foolishly."

"Do not mention it, my Lord," said Sir Arthur, "but where is Alice?"

"That I know not," replied Lord Leslie, "I have never seen her."

"How then did you come here?" enquired Batswing.

"Lord Redfern told me that Sir Arthur was dead," replied Lord Harry, "and that a reward was out for my apprehension; hence my flight."

"I see it all," cried Batswing, "we have been duped by Jonathan Wild and Lord Redfern. Where are those treacherous knaves."

The ship was searched in every part, but neither of them could be discovered. The dead were examined but without either the bodies of Wild or Lord Redfern being found, so that it became evident they were either killed on shore or had taken flight.

"Let part of the crew be put on board this vessel," said Batswing, "we will return to the Black Hawk and speed back to England. Trust me there is more villainy about, but we may stop them yet."

"We had better keep out to sea," said Will Watch, "the night is too dark and wild to be able to steer well, and both the wind and waves are rising. We shall have a terrible night of it, I fear."

"Be the night as it will," cried Batswing, "I am determined to return."

"As you like, Captain," said Will, "but to my thinking it is better to be safe and sound in a good ship than at the bottom of the sea."

"Fear not," replied Batswing, "we will make to the Devil's Crag, when we have approached the shore as near as we can without danger, I will go on shore in a boat. You will take the Black Hawk to France."

"As you will," said Will Watch, as he prepared to give the orders to 'bout ship, but to my thinking the Devils Crag will be your tomb."

CHAPTER L.

JONATHAN RETURNS TO TILLINGHAM HALL AND CARRIES OFF ALICE.—REDFERN MEETS MAUD.— THE INTERVIEW.—THE EXHORTATION.—THE PISTOL SHOT.

THE sudden disappearance of Jonathan Wild that so startled Batswing was very easily accounted for.

He had no sooner discovered that Batswing's followers were likely to be successful, or at the least to cause such a serious opposition to Lord Leslie's embarking, that all good to be gained by it would be overthrown, than he quietly withdrew from the fight and made his way to the cliff tops, where he found his horse all ready saddled waiting for him.

"They can't follow me," laughed Jonathan, as he threw himself into the saddle, "the fools did not take the precaution to have *their* horses brought down to the beach. How the devil did Batswing find out the plot? He seems mad about this girl, Alice Landon. There must be some cause for this, and I will find it out. She must have money, or Redfern would not wish to marry her; that being the case, his schemes must be thwarted, and she must be mine."

Communing with himself in this pleasant manner, Jonathan dashed along the pale flashes of distant lightning aiding him to keep the road.

"That fool, Redfern!" he muttered, "to think that he could out-wit me. Me! Jonathan Wild, the thief-taker; he who cheats the thieves and the government too, ho, ho, ho! a likely tale. Little did Redfern think, when he went to see the pretty Alice, that I was close by and heard the conversation. They must get up early, indeed, who would take in Jonathan Wild."

By this time he had reached the side entrance to Tillingham Hall.

Fastening his horse to a tree, he approached the house and whistled softly.

In an instant the sound of withdrawing bolts was heard and the gate oppened.

The next moment Farmer Croft demanded softly who was there.

"It's all right, Croft," replied Jonathan Wild, has any one been here?"

"No; all is as still as possible. Did I not hear firing just now?"

"Aye, and had you been nearer you would have heard the ring of steel also."

"What! were you attacked by a number of men?"

"Yes, by more than we could match. They fought like devils."

"That is unfortunate? where is Lord Redfern?"

"I know not; neither do I much care what has become of him."

"Then our party has been put to flight; the game lost?"

"Yes, and no; I saw some of them escape in a boat; the rest were beaten."

"And then you came away as no more good could be done."

"Just so, but there is no time to be lost; how about the servants here?"

"There are only two, an old man and an old woman, both in their dotage."

"And you told them that Lord Redfern commanded them not to come into this wing."

"I did; not even if they should hear cries of murder and shrieks for help."

"Good, now keep watch in the plantation; but mark, under no consideration attack anyone, only watch, and to-morrow let me know what has happened."

"And you; what are your plans? do you remain here?"

"Ask no questions, but do as I command, *Squire*, fear not, you shall be well rewarded with *golden* showers."

Farmer Croft shrank back as Jonathan emphasised the two words "Squire" and "golden;" then putting on a low chuckle, meant for a laugh, strode away.

Such was the power of this singular man, Jonathan Wild, that every one feared him. All secrets seemed known to him, and like a spider he wove a web round his victims, until they became completely in his power.

"There goes a man more after my own heart than any other," said Jonathan as he watched Farmer Croft's retreating figure, "his only weakness is his love of show, of pomp, and his family. Well, well, he is deeply in my power and will serve me faithfully for his own sake, for he knows I brook no flinching or disobedience."

Closing the gate after him he stole along the passage until he came to the secret door leading to Alice Landon's department.

To open it was the work of an instant, and a few steps brought him into the presence of the beautiful girl.

Alice overcome with excitement and grief had fallen fast asleep.

"She is indeed beautiful," said Jonathan, as he gazed at her face, "yet for all her beauty I do not believe Redfern would make her his wife without she had wealth. His mistress I could understand, but not his wife."

Placing his hand gently on her head, he said in as soft a tone as he could assume.

"Awake maiden the time has come for you to escape."

With a frightened cry Alice sprang from the sofa and retreated from Jonathan.

"Why do you fear me?" demanded Jonathan, "I am your friend."

"Friend?" repeated Alice incredulously, as she pushed back her long hair which in her agitation had fallen over her brow, "friend! I have no friends, I am alone in the world, an orphan and friendless, at the mercy of villains."

"Tut, tut, you wrong me," said Jonathan, "why should I be here if I were your foe?"

"Are you not a friend of Lord Redfern?" demanded Alice scornfully.

"No!" replied Jonathan fiercely, "I was, but am not now. He deceived me."

"Can I trust you?" demanded Alice hopefully, "will you assist me to escape?"

"For what other purpose am I here?" replied Jonathan.

"But how are we to escape?" demanded Alice quickly.

"You must trust to me. My horse is in the park ready saddled; in an hour we shall be at Maldon and from thence a post-chaise shall take you to London."

"Alas!" exclaimed the poor girl, "I have no friends there; where can I go for safety?"

"Trust to me, all will be well," cried Jonathan, "but we must not lose an instant."

Fearing that Alice might alter her determination, Jonathan rushed forward to seize her by the arm, but in doing so his cap, which he had worn pulled close down over his face was thrown off, whilst he came close under the rays of the lamp so that his diabolical face was fully lit up.

In a moment Alice recognised him, and with a scream of horror.

"Back, back," she exclaimed, "I know you now, approach another step and I will call for help."

"You know me, do you?" muttered Jonathan between his teeth, "then be warned and do my bidding; for mark this, no one crosses Jonathan Wild with impunity."

"Do your bidding?" cried Alice proudly, "sooner would I meet death than bow to you. You are the lowest of mankind, the very wolf has a kinder heart than you. Begone, I cannot fear you, my scorn is so great."

"Fool!" cried Jonathan, mad with passion, "be warned in time. You are in my power and nothing can save you. I am no trifler like Redfern, and never lose an opportunity for want of determination so come."

"Help! help! help!!" screamed Alice.

"Silence!" cried Jonathan. "who is there to help you? Your lover Sir Arthur Burdon is dead. You are my prisoner, remember I have the power of delivering you over to justice for your father's murder. Come, come, my pretty Alice, you cannot escape. You are mine body and soul."

Without pausing for further parley, Jonathan rushed on the trembling girl.

She turned to fly, but her strength failed her and she fell lifeless on the floor.

"Ah!" said Jonathan with a sigh of relief, "that is much better, there is no trouble when they go off in this manner. I think they do it to save trouble."

Quietly taking his cravat from round his neck, he bound it round Alice's mouth so as to completely gag her.

He then took off his cloak in which he tightly enveloped the fainting girl.

All this was done in less time than it takes to tell, for Wild was used to such work.

He had just raised the girl in his arms, when he was startled by hearing footsteps coming rapidly down the passage.

He listened for a moment, he knew the step too well, it was Redfern's.

Hastily snatching a mask from his breast, he placed it over his face, and then lowered the lamp to a mere glimmer.

Snatching the girl up in his arms, he stood close by the door, waiting Redfern's approach.

"Villain," screamed Lord Redfern hurrying through the ante-room, "I have discovered your plans you cannot fly me now. Too long have I been your dupe."

As he rushed into the room Jonathan struck him a violent blow which stretched him senseless on the ground before he had time to see his adversary.

Throwing Alice lightly over his shoulder Jonathan sprang over Redfern's body, rushed to the side entrance and in a few moments had mounted his horse, placing Alice in front of him. Putting spurs to his horse, he dashed off in the direction of Maldon where he had taken the precaution to have some of his emissaries stationed.

Severe as the blow had been, Lord Redfern quickly recovered himself, and springing to his feet, prepared to pursue Jonathan Wild, but as he approached the door he was met by Maud and her companions, who stood with their pistols presented at his breast.

"What is the meaning of this?" cried Redfern, "dare you break into my house and——"

"Enough Lord Redfern," replied Maud, "we are not here to rob you."

"What then is your purpose? It cannot be of good or you would not need those arms which you now hold so closely to my heart."

"Heart!" exclaimed Maud contemptuously, "it would be a difficult matter to find yours. We have not come I repeat, to rob you, but to rescue an innocent girl from your clutches. Where is Alice Landon?"

"Alice Landon?" said Lord Redfern in a tone of astonishment, then suddenly changing his manner, he said in a kindly voice, "you are right gentlemen, only a few minutes before you arrived Mistress Alice Landon *was* here, but she has fled with one Jonathan Wild, whom gentlemen, from your looks—pardon the insinuation—I should imagine you were better acquainted with than I am."

"Fled with Jonathan Wild!" exclaimed Maud and Bob Blow-the-Bellows.

"Yes gentleman, with Jonathan Wild, who I find has during my absence been employing these old ruins for his nefarious practices. I merely keep an old man and woman down here, so that doubtlessly he has not been disturbed or perchance my servants have been bribed. I heard screams issuing from this chamber and at once hurried here, where I found the lady in Jonathan's arms and before I could expostulate he struck me to the earth."

"I cannot believe this," said Maud, "search this room well."

The men searched the room thoroughly but of course with no success.

When they had examined everything, Maud said.

"Now go and search the house, but leave one man at the door in case I should need assistance; but mind, unless you hear me call do not interrupt us."

"Will it be safe to leave you with this man?" whispered Bob.

"And why not?" demanded Maud, "*I* have no fear of him now."

"Nay, I said not that you had fear, but the bravest may be overthrown by treachery."

"Do you see any cause to dread treachery here?" asked Maud.

"Not especially; but I always dread treachery when near Jonathan Wild or his friends."

"But this man is an arrant coward," said Maud contemptuously.

"The more reason he should be treacherous, cowards always are. See he is armed."

"Still I have no fear that he will harm me; if he were to, he could not escape."

"At least let me take his pistols?" urged the Smith.

"Do as you will," said Maud, "but delay not for we must return to tell Batswing the news."

During this conversation which had been carried on in a low voice, Redfern had been pacing the further end of the room in the greatest agitation.

There was something in Maud's manner alarmed him, although owing to her disguise he could not tell who she was, indeed so well did she play her part that he took her for a man, one of Batswing's lieutenants.

"Deliver up your pistols," said the smith in no gentle tones.

"There they are, take them," said Redfern throwing them on a table.

The smith took them up and placed them in his belt.

"Now go," said Maud, "I would speak to this man alone."

Slowly the men left the room closing the door after them.

"Now sir," said Maud sternly. "I need scarcely inform you that your life is at my mercy. I have but to give the word and your blood will stain the floor."

"And may I ask what good *that* will do?" demanded Redfern.

"The good of relieving the world from a scoundrel," replied Maud.

"If the world were released of *all* the scoundrels, it would be but thinly populated," said Redfern coolly, "come, come my good fellow, I see what all this is done for, you want me to ransom myself; I am willing to pay you anything in moderation. Now, how much do you think my life is worth?"

"I want not your money," cried Maud, "I want not your worthless life."

"Then what can you require of me?" demanded Redfern in astonishment.

"You must answer me three or four questions, and mind truly, or you shall not live."

"Speak on," said Redfern, "I have no secrets, therefore will answer you freely."

"In the first place I would know how you became friends with that fiend, Jonathan Wild?"

Lord Redfern changed colour and bit his lip, but answered calmly.

"Some time ago I was robbed, and wishing to detect the thief, sent for Mr. Wild."

"Is that *all* you ever had to do with him?" demanded Maud.

"Yes; what more should I, a nobleman, have to do with such a fellow?"

"Nothing more; are you quite certain of that?"

"Positive; you would not compel me to tell a lie?"

"You know that you lie now," exclaimed Maud, "you know 'twas with his knowledge you last carried off Alice Landon. Tell me now, or else beware my vengeance, why this girl is so persecuted by you. Who is she? What is she?"

"A farmer's daughter," replied Lord Redfern pettishly, "a base born peasant. As to her persecution, there are but few in her station look upon a nobleman's attention in that light. Neither does Mistress Alice, I can assure you. She is but little pleased at the meddling busy-bodies who watch her actions so closely."

"It is false," cried Maud; "false as your own black heart. I know your lying tongue too well: you who betrayed your father, who betrayed his master to make your fortune. Ah! you see I know you well, your history and your family."

"Silence," gasped Redfern, "breathe not a word of this and you shall be well rewarded."

"Rewarded! Think you that money can hide a murdered father's body?"

"Silence, I say," cried Redfern. "'Tis false, I did *not* do it."

"You did not do it?" exclaimed Maud contemptuously, "I have heard you confess the crime. Oh! it is well, William Redfern, to look so scared now. I once thought you had a conscience, but I was mistaken; for one night, when your evil passions slept, your conscience woke, and then you cried aloud for mercy, declaring how you poisoned your father's wine to gain his lands."

"It is false," cried Redfern, livid with fear and passion.

"It is true: alas, too true. I can prove it to the world."

"Listen!" cried Redfern in a hoarse whisper; "I am not rich, not very rich, but I will purchase your silence with half my estate. You would not ask for more?"

"I touch your estate, that estate which was torn from others."

"But legally so, legally so." urged Redfern.

"Legally so? Can an unjust law make a bad deed a good one?"

"Say then you will not betray me," pleaded Lord Redfern.

"I will not betray you until the proper time comes."

"How can I bribe you to be silent," said Redfern, wiping the large drops of perspiration from his brow, "you will not touch my gold or lands, what am I to do?"

"Repent," said Maud earnestly; "repent while there is yet time, and before your many crimes are brought fully against you."

"Repent!" exclaimed Redfern; "are you mad to talk thus?"

"No," cried Maud in the same impassioned tones, "I give you the only chance left you: make peace with God, for you will find none here."

"Would you murder me?" exclaimed Redfern slinking back.

"No, but I feel, I know that your days are numbered, and that your death will be a violent and terrible one. I therefore beseech you, by the love you once professed to bear for her whom afterwards you so cruelly deceived, by your baby son long since departed from this weary world, by all these do I pray you to repent in time, and pray for forgiveness."

For a moment Lord Redfern seemed speechless with fear.

He fixed his eyes steadily upon Maud, and his lips quivered with emotion.

Her features, although greatly concealed by the slouch hat she wore, seemed known to him. Where could he have met this strange creature before.

"Who and what are you?" he exclaimed at last in a low voice. "Have we met before?"

"Alas! yes," cried Maud. "Oh, would to heaven we never had."

"And you are——?"

"Maud! your victim—the mother of your murdered son."

As Maud spoke she threw open her cloak, and cast her hat upon the floor.

With a suppressed cry of rage, Lord Redfern staggered back a few paces.

"Yes," cried Maud, "I have escaped from the prison where you had confined me. I bore for years the cruel treatment of Wild and his vile tortures, for I knew that we should meet again, that vengeance was near. Therefore I say to you again, repent, for your days are numbered."

For a moment Redfern seemed overcome with rage and astonishment.

Quick as lightning he drew a pistol that he had had concealed in his breast, and presenting it at Maud, exclaimed,

"What! you hell-cat, have you again crossed my path? This, then, shall finish all."

With terrible precision the pistol was levelled, the hammer fell, a sharp explosion, and uttering a loud shriek, Maud fell upon the ground.

In an instant the men, headed by Bob Blow-the-Bellows, rushed into the room.

"Where is the treacherous knave?" cried the merry smith, "have you killed him?"

The next minute his eyes rested on Maud prone on the ground.

"Good heavens," he cried, "he has killed her."

"Hush!" whispered Maud as he knelt beside her, "bind up my wounds."

With hands tender and gentle as those of a woman, the smith performed this office.

"Thanks, thanks," said Maud squeezing Bob's hand, "now, where is he?"

They looked round the room, and to their amazement found Lord Redfern had gone.

Vainly they sought all over the room; no where could he be found.

They ran their swords through the hangings, sounded the panels without success. The windows were not only fastened, but thick iron bars protected them.

How then could he have escaped? was the question asked all round.

Many shook their heads solemnly, for in those superstitious times, numbers of people believed that some folk were in league with the devil, and the quaint, dismal old Hall of Tillingham was just the sort of place for such things to happen.

Their search being fruitless, they raised Maud on their shoulders and bore her firstly to the Three Cutters, and afterwards to a large comfortable chamber, cut out of the cliff beneath that hostelry, a place where she would be safe from detection.

CHAPTER LI.

A NIGHT AT THE DEVIL'S CRAG.—BATSWING AND HIS FRIENDS GO DOWN THE DEVIL'S GULLET.—WHAT THEY MEET THERE.—THE FIGHT WITH THE SEA MONSTER.—DISCOVERY OF THE OLD DEVIL'S STAIRS.

THE Black Hawk rolled heavily as she altered her course to steer landward. Quickly the sails were taken in one after the other, until she had only just enough to carry her on, for the current was setting in shore, and they dared not approach the land at too rapid a rate.

Rougher and heavier grew the sea, the waves breaking over the schooner's brow as she sped along, now plunging forward into the trough of the sea, now rising upon the crest of a wave, shaking out her wet sails as a war horse its mane.

Deep and loud rolled the thunder, whilst the lightning was every instant more vivid.

"Bother the lightning," said an old sailor, "it nearly blinds one."

"You leave the lightning alone," said Will Watch gruffly, "or mayhap it won't leave you alone; and it's a case of touch and go with that, and no mistake."

"It's a dreadful night," said Sir Arthur to Batswing.

"Yes," replied the other, "yet, perhaps it's the best kind for us."

"How so; surely a calm moonlight night would be better to steer in."

"Undoubtedly," replied Batswing, "and so would it be for his Majesty's cutters."

"Are there any about here?" demanded Sir Arthur.

"The noise of our firing will sure to bring them down about here. They are like the vultures, and snuff war from afar and flock to it."

"What was that huge white thing down out yonder during the last flash, is it a ship?" cried Lord Leslie pointing towards the land, "see, there it is again."

"By Jove, it is the Devil's Crag, "cried Batswing; "how plain the lightning brings it out to-night. Look out, Will, we must soon lower the boat."

Again they shortened sail, and soon after prepared to lower the boat.

"Lord Leslie," said Batswing, "you had better go to France, from whence you can return under more favourable circumstances. At present your delicate state of health would render it impossible for you to land in this weather. You also, Sir Arthur, had better not attempt so dangerous a task. Under the care of my old comrade, Will Watch, you will be quite safe."

"Pardon me, cap'n," said Will Watch, "if you land, so do I. I'll follow you through fair or foul weather, and Davy Jones himself shall not prevent me."

"And so will I," cried Sir Arthur, "I will never rest until Alice is found."

"Cannot I be of any good?" asked Lord Leslie, "I have done so much harm that I am anxious to do all in my power to make up for it."

"In your present state you would only hinder us," said Batswing, "therefore I must insist upon your remaining here."

"As you will," said Lord Leslie, sighing, "but I shall not rest until you return."

The boat was now launched and in a few moments those who were about to attempt the landing tumbled into her. The ropes were cast off and away she went.

"This will be awkward landing shipmates," said Will, "but come what may we must try."

Rapidly they approached the shore and could plainly here the heavy surf running on the beach.

At a word from Will the men commenced backing with their oars against the surf to prevent it dashing them on the beach until the fitting moment arrived. Waiting for the third wave, which is always the greatest, Will shouted loudly, "give way," and the next moment they were thrown with terrific force on the beach. Naturally the boat was shivered to pieces by the force of the shock, but the men luckily made good their escape, and bruised and drenched crept up into the cave, known by the smugglers as the Devil's Mouth.

The opening to this cavern was not more than ten feet wide and four high, so that they had to creep to enter it.

The passage narrowed as it went on until it was not more than three feet broad, and then suddenly it expanded into a large and lofty chamber, with narrow dark gloomy passages extending far on each side.

Will Watch, who seemed thoroughly up to the place, clambered up a few rough stairs, cut in the side of the cave, and from a niche cunningly concealed took a box which was found to contain flint and steel and all the necessaries requisite to produce a light.

Some sticks were then placed in a corner and a fire made, round which the men clustered to warm themselves and dry their dripping clothes.

"This is an awful place," said Sir Arthur, "how did it gain its present name?"

"That is a long story," said Will Watch, "and an awful one."

"Well, we have a dreary night before us," said Batswing, "so let us hear it. It will help to beguile the time, and take our attention from other thoughts."

"Well, you must know that this cave thirty years ago was known by the name of the Brandy Tunnel, because of the shape of the entrance, and the number of runs made by the smugglers of good strong old brandy.

"You see the king's men never knew about this cave, and for the matter of that neither do they now, but about that time a very fearful accident happened.

"But I must tell you that in those days this cave had another entrance.

"That dark low opening to the left leads down a very rough flight of steps into a pool of water which seems very deep but won't reach over a man's waist.

"Now when you have waded through this water, you come to another set of stairs which leads to a long passage that opens out on the left side of the Devil's Crag. There is an iron rod fastened safely in the cliff, at the mouth of this passage, and round this the men used to pass a double rope and lower themselves down like the samphire gatherers.

"This lowered them on to a place high and dry from the sea, from whence they could get comfortably to the cliff tops, and be safe.

"Of course the fellows always carried their ropes away so that the king's men never could make out how so many cargo's of brandy were run.

"This went on for a long time and all seemed right till one day a chap named Parker went down the stairs and was never seen afterwards.

"This threw a gloom over all the fellows, but the same work went on, but after a couple a days or so two more men were missing.

"We all became alarmed at this, and for some time no one went down that way until one night poor Bill Sanders had been taking too much and would venture it."

"And what became of him?" demanded the others eagerly.

"Nobody ever knew," replied Will, shaking his head mournfully, and puffing out his smoke. After a short silence he continued in a most funeral tone.

"One night we all determined to see what was the cause, and taking lights we descended the stairs, taking good care to have a sharp watch all round.

"We had scarce reached the pool when suddenly it commenced to foam.

"We gazed in horror at the water which seethed like that in a cauldron.

"Suddenly it became still, and the next moment a horrible, huge, white corpse-like face, with great dead eyes rose to the surface of the pool.

"Not a word was spoken but we all turned and fled.

"When we arrived here we gazed in each others horror-striken faces, and then, as if by mutual consent, took to our boats and rowed home.

"From that moment that place has been known as the Gullet, and we smugglers never venture here unless driven to do so by the king's men."

"And do you believe this?" asked Batswing incredulously.

"I saw the creature myself," said Will, "it was a most awful sight."

"Why did I not hear of this before?" asked Batswing.

"It's ill talking of these things, at least so we seamen think."

"Doubtless the foam was caused by some large fish in the pool, and your excited imaginations turned it into the portrait of the Old Gentleman."

"You may laugh cap'n, but there is one thing I am firm about : the men *did disappear*, and that being the case, where did they go unless eaten by the Devil."

"Doubtlessly they fell down some deep hole," replied Batswing.

"Not a bit of it, for most of them could swim well," replied Will Watch.

"Be it as it may," cried Batswing, "I am determined to try to escape by the Devil's Gullet, as you call it, to-night. Anything is better than stopping here."

"For mercy's sake, cap'pen, don't," exclaimed the sailors in alarm.

"Why not? Believe me, there is nothing to fear; besides those who do not care to follow me can remain here. Come what may, alone or not, I go to explore the terrible cavern whose horrible history you have just so admirably related."

"Alone you shall not go," cried Sir Arthur, "I will accompany you."

"As you will gentlemen," said Will, "I see you are determined to kill yourselves."

"If we die, Will," laughed Batswing, "you can add our names to the list of victims you have already: it will increase the interest of the story."

"If you die I shan't escape," said the old man solemnly.

"What do you mean?" demanded Batswing in surprise.

"Why that I shall go with you. Devil or man never made Will Watch leave his leader."

Silently the sailors all rose and prepared to follow, although evidently disliking the task.

"Stay a moment," said Will Watch, as Batswing seizing a brand turned towards the cavity, "we have better torches than that for this kind of work."

Again mounting to the niche he, with the assistance of some of the sailors, drew therefrom a large chest in which were thick torches, ropes and hatchets.

The torches were soon alight, and two ropes selected as the strongest.

Each of them then seized a hatchet which they carried ready for use in their right hands, whilst in the left they held a flaming torch.

ASTOUNDING EFFECT OF AN ALMANACK.

They then loosened the swords in their sheath's and examined their pistols. These having been found all right they commenced their march, Batswing leading them on.

It was indeed a terrible passage, from the walls and roof long snake-like weeds of emerald green hung in profusion.

The roughly carved steps were covered with the same slimy weeds.

Drip, drip, drip, fell the water in the cavern, down which there seemed to be a hollow whispering noise, as if the elves and gnomes of the place were telling each other of the approach of human creatures in their domain.

In spite of all these weird sounds, onward advanced the men.

As the stairs approached the place where they could see the reflection of the torches shine like blood on the black pool, the cavern widened out considerably.

At length they stood by the waters edge and paused to look into its depths.

Smooth and tranquil was the dark lake, save where now and then a drop of water fell from the caves roof on to its sullen bosom.

For a few minutes they stood gazing at this strange pool, when suddenly their looks of awe were changed into glances of surprise.

The waters of the lake, as if imbued with sudden emotion, commenced to rise and fall against its banks.

The motion became stronger and stronger, until the water, as Will had described it, appeared like that seething in a cauldron.

Each man grasped his weapon with more firmness, and awaited the result of this curious phenomenon, which struck terror into the hearts of the boldest.

After the commotion had continued a few seconds, a huge monster became visible.

It looked like an immense bag of jelly, from the

17

mouth of which came eight long arms, that wreathed rapidly about, causing the motion in the lake,

Each of these arms had numerous spots down their sides, looking like ulcers.

But the most terrible part of this dreadful creature was the eyes.

They were immensely large, with a look of evil that is indescribable, but the horror consisted in their appearing *glazed and dead*.

From the midst of these eight arms protruded a sharp bill, much resembling that of the macaw.

The men all stood spell bound, watching this hideous creature.

Waving its ulcered arms as if weaving some charm the terrible creature rose slowly further and further from the water and advanced upon the rash invaders.

With a quick movement it threw forth one arm, and encircling Batswing with it, drew him towards the lake.

In a moment Batswing had seized hold of a projection in the rock, and swinging his axe on high, brought it down on the horrible monster.

But the flesh seemed like india-rubber, and although cut deeply, it closed immediately.

One good effect of the blow was to revive the courage of the men, who at once rushed to their leader's assistance, for they saw that the creature was no devil.

A terrible and terrific combat commenced.

The creature clutched the men around the waists with his terrible arms, the marks on which proved these limbs to be suckers, that served not only to hold the men firmly, but by some mysterious manner to paralyze their limbs.

Batswing with another blow cleft the monster's beak in half, just as it was about to tear with its fearful teeth Sir Arthur Bowring, whom it now had firmly in its grasp.

The rage of the creature now appeared to redouble, and the dreadful arms seemed endowed with renewed life.

Man after man it seized and hurled into the water, so that many of the torches were extinguished.

A new terror now was that they would soon have to fight in complete darkness.

"Back all men who have torches," shouted Batswing, "back to the steps."

The order was but just given in time, for only one torch bearer had escaped.

The dark fluid the creature emitted had now stained the water a bright purple.

"Aim at its face," cried Batswing who had discovered that the only blows which had any effect were those dealt upon that part of the creature's body.

By this time Batswing had managed to get free from the terrible arms, and drawing a pistol, he discharged it close in the monster's face, with wondrous effect.

For a moment the creature paused as if stunned, but quickly returned to the fight.

But from that moment the victory was sure to the sailors, who redoubled their efforts. Pistol after pistol was discharged, and sword after sword plunged into those dreadful eyes, until the whole face was completely destroyed, and then, but not till then the huge creature ceased to struggle.

With the united assistance of all the men it was dragged into the cave, and there cut to pieces.

"There," said Batswing, to Will Watch, "your devil is laid for ever."

"It is a terrible monster," said Sir Arthur.

"It is indeed," replied Batswing. "They are very common in the West Indies, but are rarely found anywhere of such gigantic proportions as this one. It is known as the octopus. But come, we must make our way once more down the Devil's Gullet, and escape that way."

Once more they crossed the dreary lake, but this time in perfect peace, although not without great fear on the part of the sailors, in case another octopus should be lurking there.

The Devil's Stairs were found, and the whole party reached the second cave in safety, where they found the iron bar as Will Watch had described.

A rope was fastened to this, and the whole of the party except Will lowered themselves on to the beach. Will then drew up the rope, unfastened it from the bar, and tying one end round his waist, passed the rope round the bar, and slowly paying out the slack line, lowered himself down to the ground. By this means he was able to remove the rope, so that the King's men should not know of the cave's existence.

CHAPTER LII.

ROARING RIC HITS OUT A NEW PLOT.—BATSWING'S RETURN TO LONDON.

BATSWING and Sir Arthur made their way back to the Three Cutters, whilst the rest of the party separated so as not to create suspicion.

By the lights flashing through the night, down by the shore, they knew that the noise of the combat had reached the ears of the King's men, and therefore the smugglers made their course inland.

Although the preventive men were so near, yet there was but little danger to the smugglers, for no one could guess how they could land save on the open beach. Will Watch went on to the Three Cutters, to see all clear, for, as he was the landlord, the preventive men were least likely to suspect him.

Having made sure all was safe, he returned to Batswing and Sir Arthur, whom he conducted to the chamber beneath the Three Cutters, where he found Maud being carefully attended on by Bob Blow-the-Bellows and Roaring Ric.

"How did this happen?" exclaimed Batswing.

"Lord Redfern shot her," replied Bob Blow-the-Bellows.

"And Redfern, what has become of him?" demanded Batswing.

"He has escaped," replied the smith.

"Escaped!" cried Batswing, furious with rage. "And you dare tell me so."

"How could I prevent it?" replied Bob.

In a few minutes everything was explained to Batswing, who sat by Maud's side in silence, watching her pale face, and listening to her heavy breathing.

At length he rose quietly, and beckoning the men to follow him, held a council in the further end of the room.

They spoke in low whispers, not to disturb Maud, who was in a deep sleep.

"It is unlucky that Redfern should have escaped," said Batswing.

"It is indeed," said Bob. "I cannot tell where he could have gone."

"Tillingham Hall," said Batswing, "is full of strange places: secret doors, double walls, traps and springs, are all over the place. No doubt it was by the aid of one of these that he managed to escape after his cowardly deed."

"It must be a queer old place," said Roaring Ric; "I should like to go over it very much. I was always fond of these mysterious buildings."

"Well, they are useful certainly," said Bob, "but I can't think them agreeable."

"Somehow or another we must discover what has become of Alice, and also what Lord Redfern intends to do. He is not the man to be still long."

"Pardon me, captain," said Roaring Ric, "I may not be up to so many moves as you are, and consequently may be mistaken; but nevertheless, it seems to me that you go the wrong way to fight these men."

"How so: what way would you set about it?" demanded Batswing.

"In the simplest manner in the world," replied Ric.

"To fight a knave one must have recourse to knavery. Now you and all your band have shown these men that you are their enemies, and consequently they are on their guard. Now if you had pretended to have been their friends you would have known most of their secrets and could have soon been equal with them."

"There is some truth in that," replied Batswing, "but he knows us all too well now; besides, if he did not Jonathan Wild would, and that is just the same."

"Pardon me captain, but there is one person in your band whom you seem entirely to overlook; a person whom I consider worth any two others,"

"And who may this remarkably valuable person be?" asked Batswing."

"Your humble servant," replied Roaring Ric, placing his hand on his heart and bowing."

"You!" exclaimed Batswing laughing at the fellows coolness.

"Yes me; there is nothing very surprising in the fact as far as I can see."

"Perhaps not, still I should like you to prove the assertion."

"With pleasure; in the first place my value is double that of any member of your band as I am not under the ban of the law. I do not mean to say that I have not deserved to be, only I have most fortunately escaped being placed under the particular attention of the Bow Street Runners. Such being the case, I can go about freely and without fear, where no other of your band would care to trust themselves, therefore it strikes me that *I* am the one to watch these men."

"You are right, but can I trust you?" enquired Batswing thoughtfully.

"You may trust me with anything but women, wine, and money."

"Since you have shown your talent for plotting so far, perhaps you can suggest a plan whereby we can catch these men."

"I think I have a plan that will succeed; but I should like to know something of this same Lord Redfern, for all depends upon his character."

"I will answer all your questions as far as it is my power; so speak on."

"In the first place has he courage."

"Yes and no; If he once gets into a fight he will fight, but—"

"He would rather keep out of it; I understand," interrupted Ric, "but that is not quite the courage I mean. Is he superstitious?"

"Very!"

"Do you think he could be easily duped?" inquired Roaring Ric.

"That greatly depends upon the person who tried to dupe him."

"Well: if anybody can do it I am sure I shall be able to. Now in the second place which of you knows the most about Tillingham Hall?"

"I know its history," said Batswing.

"Yes, yes;" replied the other, "that is all very well, but I mean, can you tell me the secret passages, the spring doors, and sliding panels?"

"I can tell them all to you," said Batswing, "nay more; I can give you a plan of the house, with full instructions how to open or close these different secret places."

"Then I am all right," cried Roaring Ric, "you see I am a bit of an actor, and in my time I have played many parts. The part I now mean to play, if all goes well, will be a pleasant one. All I wish you to do is to let me know all you can about Redfern's past history and also that of Tillingham Hall."

Batswing drew him on one side, and for about half-an-hour they were in deep and earnest consultation. At length they appeared to have settled everything, and rejoined the others.

"My men," said Batswing, "our new comrade has undertaken to find out what plots are set on foot by Lord Redfern and Jonathan Wild. To do this is no easy matter, therefore I command you all to obey him, should he require your services. If he should meet you, do not recognise him unless he first recognises you. That is all you require, is it not?" continued Batswing turning round to Ric.

"I beg your pardon," replied Ric, "I want money and disguises."

"You shall have both and in plenty," said Batswing. "Maud, poor thing, must remain here, and if she recovers will assist you. She knows more of Redfern than anyone."

As he spoke he approached the bed and leaning over Maud gazed into her face.

She was deadly pale and breathed heavily.

Suddenly a smile wreathed her white lips, and she murmured softly the name of the poor link-boy who had brought consciousness to her when she was a captive in the vaults of Jonathan Wild.

"Poor creature," murmured Batswing, "how she loves that boy. Well, he shall be near to attend to her."

"A boy," said Roaring Ric, quickly; "is he a good sharp lad?"

"Yes."

"Up to any mischief; do anything 'for the fun of the thing,' as the lads say?"

"Yes; he is not so sly as Jerry Blinker, but mischievous enough."

"He will do: send him down here by all manner of means."

"He shall be here as soon as possible," replied Batswing.

At this moment Will Watch came into the apartment and informed Batswing that morning was beginning to break, so, wishing all good-bye, he returned with Will to a private room in the Three Cutters, where he changed his dress for a handsome riding one, and once more appeared as the elegant Percy Marvel.

Mounting his horse, which stood ready for him at the door of the hostelry, he shook hands with Will and bade him good-bye.

"You'll have a nasty, rough ride of it, sir," said Will.

"Possibly," replied Batswing, "but I have no choice. To-day Hugh Fenton is to be tried, and I must be there."

"You!" exclaimed Will; "why, you surely won't venture into the lion's den."

"I must," replied Batswing, laughing; "I have no choice."

"No choice! why, what on earth do you mean?"

"Why, I am summoned to attend as a witness."

"You!"

"Yes; is there anything astonishing in that, eh?"

"You will only risk your own life and not save Hugh's," growled Will.

"Save Hugh," laughed Batswing; "I am not a witness for, but against him. I am summoned for the prosecution."

For a moment Will looked in amazement, then slowly a broad grin spread over his face, and he winked his eyes furiously.

"Curse me if you aint a good one!" he cried; "we'll have a glass over that to drink you success, though its almost too much to expect."

He disappeared into the door of the public-house, and soon returned with two large tankards containing some strong waters.

"Here's wishing you all success," cried he.

"May you have the same, and a speedy return of the Black Hawk."

The two men tossed off their liquor, and the next moment Batswing was riding swiftly down the road in the direction of London, taking care, however, to give Tillingham as wide a berth as he possibly could.

The storm had given over, and the morn gave every promise of being fine.

Swiftly, swiftly he dashed along, hoping to place a good distance between him and Tillingham before daylight.

As he passed St. Mary's the cold grey light of morning was hanging over all.

Still he kept on his headlong pace.

He passed many large tilted waggons. The waggoners glanced at him suspiciously, but with bent down head, he dashed on, nor did he draw rein until the stones of London were rattling under his horse's feet. At length he arrived at his own lodging having performed the distance in less than three hours.

CHAPTER LIII.

HUGH FENTON'S TRIAL.   THE ALMANAC.   THE GAOL FEVER.

THE prisons in the present day have become as well conducted and healthy as perhaps it is possible to make places of punishment. Indeed, many people complain that they have been made *too* comfortable; that the prisoners don't mind the punishment, but rather enjoy it.

This may sound very well in a book or a newspaper but those who have been over our modern prisons know how false it is.

The men look clean and healthy, and beyond a doubt they are so in body, but the torment is mostly in the mind. They are prisoners—*that* is alone enough to make them miserable; the "heaven-born blessing, liberty," is wanting, and they cannot be happy in their confinement.

Again, that terrible "silent system;" forbidden to communicate with their fellow-men, the convicts become miserable, the brain feeds upon itself; not producing remorse, as is supposed, but mostly generating that hot desire for revenge which but too often terminates in crimes of the most terrible character.

But we have already described the filthy state of the prisons and the lax discipline that was conducted in them at the time in which our story is placed.

A fierce and terrible fever, known as the "gaol fever," always lurked within those gloomy walls, ready to seize its unhappy victims and hurry them to the grave.

But illnesses, like death, are no respectors of persons. The prison officials often were seized in the same way as the persons in their charge; nay, more, the prisoners often carried the infection into the close court where they were tried, and imparted it to the judge and jury.

Hugh Fenton was glad to hear that his trial was about to take place, for his gaoler had brought him the news that several cases of the terrible malady had shown itself, with fatal consequences, in the prison.

He was up betimes, and had dressed himself with the most scrupulous care, so that his personal appearance might act favourably on the jury.

"Well, you do look a swell," said Mr. Grummidge, as he brought in the breakfast things; "one would think you were going to a party instead of your trial."

"And where is the difference?" said Hugh, assuming a light and airy manner, although his heart was heavy enough. "At both places I shall meet gentlemen, and, I trust, ladies. My dear Mr. Grummidge; you do not understand these sort of things. There is more occasion to be dressed well on a trial than at a ball. In the former case you are the observed of all observers, the chief actor, as it were, in the small drama proceeding in the court, whilst in the latter case there may be fifty men who attract as much attention as yourself. So you see one must, at such a time as this, be most careful."

"Perhaps you're right," replied Grummidge; "but for myself, if I were so near my end as you are, I should not be so blessed particular."

"But how do you know I am so near my 'end,' as you so plainly put it?"

"Oh, everybody knows you are," replied Grummidge; the lawyers and all say there is no help for you but to swing. I wouldn't wish to hurt your feelings, for you've behaved like a real gentleman whilst you have been here, but I *know* you're booked for Tyburn, so don't trust in vain hopes. Keep up your spirits, and die like a man. If you want a bottle of wine to make you more jolly, I don't mind getting you one and helping to drink it afterwards."

"There can be no objection to that, my kind friend," said Hugh Fenton, throwing the money, on the table, "fly and bring some of the best wine you can procure."

The turnkey required no further orders, but took the money, tossed it into the air, and at once departed to fetch the wine.

Poor Hugh, for all his gaiety of manner, was very down hearted.

What had become of Batswing; had he deserted him at the last moments?

He drank deeply of the wine when it came, but spoke little, for his thoughts were far away, wondering if his friends would help him.

He knew that counsel had been provided for him, for he had had several consultations with the legal gentleman who had held out but very little hope of his escape; but Batswing had neither sent nor been near him since the day he came as a footman.

"Well," said Grummidge, when the bottle was finished, "I must go now, but I shall be back in half-an-hour to fetch you."

"Does my case come on early then?" asked Hugh Fenton.

"No, I don't suppose yours will come on until midday," replied Grummidge, "but we always have the prisoners ready in the passage so as no time is lost."

Drearily did the time pass until Grummidge returned, and telling Hugh to follow, conducted him into a low stone passage, leading into the court, where he placed him under the guard of some soldiers.

There were a queer haggard, rugged set seated on the benches. Hugh Fenton's handsome dress formed a terrible contrast to them, and they all looked at him with admiration and envied the "Knight of the Road."

At length he was called, and walking between two of the prison officials, was placed in the dock.

It was a miserable, dirty little hole, that court, with queer little arched windows, the tops of one or two of which were opened to let in the air, for the atmosphere was very close and unpleasant.

Hugh gazed round the court, and seeing several gaily dressed ladies seated at one side, bowed to them in a most elegant style.

A little further on, in deep conversation with the prosecutor, Captain Jennings, was a gentleman with his back turned towards the prisoner.

He was most richly dressed, and seemed to know a good many of the fashionable ladies, for he shook hands with some and bowed to many.

Suddenly the gentleman turned, and a ray of hope rose in Hugh's breast.

It was Batswing, disguised as Percy Marvel.

Coldly, nay, almost scornfully did Batswing examine the prisoner.

Hugh then saw him turn to Captain Jennings and speak to him earnestly.

The next minute the charge was given, the counsel opened the case, stating how Captain Jennings had been waylaid, and giving all the particulars, which the reader already knows.

They then proceeded to call witnesses.

The landlord of the Load of Hay swore positively that Hugh Fenton was in bed at the time of the attempted robbery, and, therefore, could not have been the man.

Janet went further: she not only declared that Fenton was in bed, but also that another man, very much like Fenton had left the company and ridden away just after Captain Jenning's carriage had driven from the inn.

Things began to look brighter for Hugh when the counsel called Percy Marvel into the witness box.

Batswing stepped into the box with an air of grace, and faced the counsel.

"Mr. Marvel," said the counsel, "I believe you were robbed on the same night and near the same place as that upon which Lord Clumbers plate was carried off."

"I had that honour, sir," replied Batswing.

"You, I believe, were attacked by two or three men."

"I was."

"You saw their faces, I believe?" continued the counsel.

"I did, and I shall never forget them till the longest day I live."

"Look at the prisoner, Mr. Marvel," said the counsel.

"I *have* been looking at him ever since he stood in that box."

"Is he one of the men who stopped you?"

"On my oath he is not," said Batswing, with emphasis, "the men who stopped me were like this."

He then coolly proceeded to give an exact description of Lord Redfern and Jonathan Wild, until he was stopped by the counsel and told to stand down.

The next witness was Captain Jennings, who, in a clear, calm voice, related all that had happened. In vain they cross-examined him, his evidence was not to be shaken.

"Are you sure you can remember this man's face," asked the counsel, for Hugh Fenton.

"Positive," replied Captain Jennings.

"You can swear then that he is the man. Remember his life is at stake, and through a mistake you may condemn an innocent man to death."

"I am perfectly ready to swear that he is the man."

An awful silence was in the court after this answer.

The counsel paused as if rather taken aback, and then continued—

"You must excuse me, Captain Jennings, asking you this question: Have you never made a mistake, that you are so positive?"

"To the best of my belief, no. Certainly not in such a case as this."

"How were you, on a dark night, able to see the man's face?"

"Because the moon burst forth suddenly, and I saw him as plain as by daylight."

"Then if there had been no moon you could not have sworn to him?"

"Certainly not."

"And you positively swear there was a moon?"

"Of course I do," exclaimed the witness. How else could I have seen him?"

"Very well, sir," replied the counsel, with a bland smile. "Of course you could not be mistaken in this case, any more than in the other points."

"Most certainly not. I could stake my life on the fact," replied the captain.

"I don't think I need ask you any more questions, sir," said the counsel; "you may stand down."

Captain Jennings bowed, and with a glance of triumph at Hugh, left the box.

"My lud," exclaimed the counsel, turning round to the judge and extending his left hand, in which he held a small open book so that the judge might see it, whilst he pointed with the index finder of his right hand to a certain line in the page; "my lud! I hold in my hand, as your ludship may perceive, one of the Admiralty Almanacs. Now, my lud, you have heard Captain Jennings swear that he recognised my client by the light of the moon; whilst he freely admits that without it he would not have been able to do so. Gentlemen of the jury, you have heard the honourable captain declare that he is so much above the ordinary run of human creatures that he never makes a mistake—he is perfection—but if so, gentlemen, his Majesty's Astronomers are very faulty, for in their almanac I find that on the night when Captain Jennings was attacked there *was no moon visible*."

Judge, jury, and Captain Jennings were struck with amazement.

At last the judge asked for the book, and it was handed to him and afterwards to the jury, and closely examined by all.

"I now, gentlemen of the jury, leave the entire matter in your hands," continued the counsel; "merely stating that Captain Jennings, perfect as he is, may have made one or two other mistakes as well as the one about the moon. In a word, may not the entire story be *moonshine*."

The judge summed up in a very short speech. The jury retired for a few moments, and then returned with their verdict.

"Now, gentlemen," said the clerk of the court, "are you all agreed?"

"We are," replied the foreman of the jury.

"What say you? Guilty or not guilty?"

An awful silence fell upon the court as the jury replied—

"Not guilty."

A slight applause ran round the court as the verdict was delivered.

Captain Jennings could scarcely be held back by Percy Marvel, or rather Batswing, from rushing forward and expostulating with the judge, counsel, and jury.

Hugh Fenton bowed politely to the court, made a special bow to the captain, kissed his hand to the ladies, and left the court.

With a suppressed oath Captain Jennings broke from Batswing, and dashed from the court into the street.

"Shall I follow him, or shall I not?" thought Batswing. "No, I think I had better remain here for a little while. It will look less suspicious."

He waited about and heard one or two small cases, and then was about to leave the court when he perceived Captain Jennings making his way towards the counsel who had been employed to prosecute Hugh Fenton.

Quickly placing himself in such a position that he could see without being seen, Batswing, almost bursting with laughter, awaited the result.

After a few moments consultation with the captain, the counsel arose.

"My lud!" he cried, growing crimson with passion as he spoke, "I rise to point out that this court has been cruelly and basely deceived. Never yet was there such a case of gross imposture or of contempt of court. How and by what means, and by whose connivance it has been done, I cannot say, but I am here ready to show that it has been perpetrated in this court not an hour ago."

"I do not understand you, my learned brother," said the judge; "come to the point at once, if you please."

"In the case, my lud, of the Crown v. Fenton, just tried, the prisoner was acquitted and a gentleman's honour impugned in consequence of an almanac. I now hold in my hand an almanac just procured from the printers, and it states that there *was* a moon on the night in question."

A murmur of surprise ran round the court as the almanac was handed in.

"Where is the other almanac?" demanded the judge.

"Here my Lord," said the counsel who had defended Hugh.

The judge compared the two almanacs with the greatest care.

He examined the covers, the printers name in fact everything.

At length he pulled the leaf wherein it was stated there was no moon.

It yielded to his touch, and came out of the book.

As it did so something very much like an oath came from the judge's lips.

"We have indeed been deceived," he cried, "this sheet has been printed specially and inserted in place of the right sheet in a true almanac. It has been done to deceive the court in order to gain the release of the prisoner. Where is the prisoner?"

"Gone my lord," said the turnkey, "he left the court directly he was acquitted."

A slight titter ran round the court at this announcement.

"Silence!" cried the judge, purple with rage; then turning to the counsel for the defence he demanded if he knew anything of the matter.

"Not I my lord," replied the astonished counsel, "the almanac was brought me by the prisoner's friends, and I used it in good faith.

"All I can say is there has been a base defeat of justice," cried the judge.

"I can assure you I put the almanac in, in good faith," replied the young counsel.

"Perhaps you did—"commenced the judge, but before he could finish he put his hand to his head as if he had forgotten what he was speaking about, his face turned deadly pale and he fell back in his chair.

"The judge is ill!" cried many of the people.

"Look, look, at the jury box," cried others.

Two of the jury had also been taken in the same sudden manner.

A horrid whisper ran round the crowded court spreading dismay everywhere.

"It is the gaol fever."

In a moment those who were not actually compelled to remain in the court fled, whilst the judge and the two jurymen were borne away.

Batswing no sooner saw that no more business would be done, for the counsel were making their best way from the tainted court, than he resolved to depart at once, and set off for Toby Crick's, where he found Fenton enjoying his dinner.

"What, Batswing!" cried Hugh Fenton springing up, "give me your hand."

"Are you a fool to stop here?" asked Batswing sharply, "do you think they will not soon discover the hoax?"

"What hoax?" demanded Hugh Fenton in the greatest surprise possible.

"Why the false leaf in the almanac that I had printed."

"Bless my soul alive," exclaimed Toby in astonishment, "and was it you as had the leaf put in the almanac? Well I never; did you ever? Lor bless my heart and eyes. I shouldn't have thought of such a thing for a thousand pounds in a thousand years. Bless my soul no, that I shouldn't."

"Probably not," said Batswing, "but there is one thing evident, and that is Hugh must not stop here. It is true he has been acquitted, but they will easily get up another case against him and nothing will then save him. So you must set off at once to Tillingham. There you will find Maud; mind you obey her, and also our new found comrade. But you will hear all from Maud. if, as I trust, she is able to meet you. Now be off instantly or it will be too late."

CHAPTER LIV.

LORD REDFERN MEETS A MYSTERIOUS STRANGER. THE BLUE ROOM.

LORD Redfern watched anxiously till day broke in his secret hiding place, between the walls of Tillingham Hall.

At length the grey light of dawn crept slowly through the narrow slits in the outer walls, telling him that dawn was approaching.

Uncomfortable as his position was, still he determined to wait until people were astir, for he feared falling into the hands of the smugglers.

At last the strong yellow rays of the sun and the merry chirping of the birds, told him that the day was well advanced, and he ventured to leave his hiding-place.

He passed through the deserted rooms, pausing every now and then to listen if the robbers still remained.

All was quiet, so he ventured on until he reached that part of the hall that was still inhabited, here he found his two old servants almost dead with alarm at the noises they had heard in the night.

He quickly dispatched the old man to the nearest magistrate, stating that the Hall had been attacked by thieves, and requesting that some assistance should be sent immediately in case of a renewal of the attack.

Afterwards he ordered the old woman to prepare him some breakfast, and whilst this was being done, strolled out into the grounds.

Lost in thought, he had walked further from the house than he intended, when he was startled by hearing the weak, trembling voice of an old man.

Looking over a hedge he beheld a man bent double with age, busily searching for something in the hedge-side.

He was a robust old man, dressed in a long coat that hung down to his heels.

A long grey beard flowed to his waist, and lank white locks came from under his velvet skull cap.

There was a peculiar look about the old man that struck Lord Redfern.

The old man's eyes were bright, and in spite of his age his step was firm.

In his hand he grasped a long oaken staff on which he leant, as he stooped to gather the herbs for which he was evidently searching.

"Good morning father," said Lord Redfern, who was glad of any society.

The old man started as if surprised to find anyone near him.

"I hope I do not trespass, sir," he exclaimed, in humble tones, "I only come to gather some few poor simples that have a wonderous charm in cases of illness"

"And what may those you have be good for?" demanded Redfern.

"For colds and pains in the joints, and many other ills that flesh is heir to."

"Are you then a doctor?" demanded Lord Redfern, with a smile.

"Yes, and no, good sir," answered the old man, "that I do cure some complaints it is true, but the healing power is, in my mind, of but little consequence."

"Indeed! may I ask what science it is you follow?"

"That is a secret," replied the old man, gravely; there be sciences which people who do not understand them deem unlawful. Mark me, I do not say that I study these sciences, yet, still he who has knowledge in these dark times had better not impart the secret rashly."

Lord Redfern drew back from the old man, for like most people in those days, he had a full belief in sorcery.

He took a pace or two from the old man, and then paused in thought.

In the year 1716, only a year and a few months past, he remembered being in Huntingdon and witnessing the execution of Mrs. Hicks and her daughter,* and he almost feared to have any communication with the old man.

* This is perfectly true, they were condemned to death for witchcraft, and were executed April, 17, 1716.

But curiosity and lust for gold overcame all his scruples, and once more he returned to the spot and commenced cross-questioning the herb gatherer.

"So you have dabbled a little in the black art," he said.

"Pardon me, good sir, I said not so: I did but say that some did."

"Come, be candid!" exclaimed Lord Redfern, "trust me, I will not betray you."

"Betray me?" cried the old man, "I have done nothing to fear betrayal. If having taken these few poor and common herbs be treason, I will give you back their value."

"Tut, tut man," cried Redfern, "I want not your money; I wished but to gain knowledge."

"To do that one must study, my lord," replied the old man.

How know you I am a lord?" demanded Redfern, suspiciously.

"By your overbearing manner, and your wishing to command where you should obey."

Lord Redfern stared in amazement at the old man.

"You speak proudly," said Redfern, after a short pause.

"But truly," replied the old man, gravely.

"Surely then there is no harm in telling me if there be such a thing as witchcraft?"

"Your judges say so, and punish people for it; therefore, there must be."

"But is alchemy true?"

"Why do you ask?" demanded the old man, sternly.

"Because I could almost fancy that you are an alchymist."

"Perhaps you are right, replied the old man, slowly."

"Are there such things as the philosophers stone and the elixir of life?"

"There are more things in Heaven and earth than are dreamed of in your philosophy," replied the old man earnestly, yet with a sly twinkle in his eye.

"Then you are a magician, can read fortunes, cast nativities."

"My son," interrupted the old man, "you are anxious to learn; why not acknowledge it."

"I am," said Lord Redfern slowly and in a low voice."

"Have you courage to pass through the ordeal.

For a moment Lord Redfern paused as if in alarm, then answered—

"I have. Teach me what I wish to know and I will shower gold upon you."

"Gold!" exclaimed the old man in a passion, "what need have I of gold who holds the secrets of the earth, the air, nay, of that beyond the grave. Gold! I need it not."

"How then can I repay you?" urged Lord Redfern.

"By your duty!" exclaimed the old man, "by obedience to my will."

"I will be obedient; you shall command me."

"I want but a home wherein to study and prepare my plans."

"This hall is mine!" said Lord Redfern, "choose which room you will, it is at your service."

"I see that you are willing my son," said the old man, "but I must not decide in haste."

"But surely no spot could suit you better;" cried Redfern anxiously.

"It is a suitable spot," said the old man as if talking to himself, "the herbs grow plentifully and of good quality; the sea is near to yield up its treasures and the house wrapt in silence and free from interruption and noise."

"Then why not come?" demanded Lord Redfern, "my two old servants shall tend upon you, and all that you require shall be fitted up in your room."

"I will think over it; but now I need refreshment so leave me."

"Not so!" cried Redfern, as the old man brought forth some coarse viands out of his havresack and commenced eating, "my breakfast is ready, come and join me, in that time I may persuade you."

"Son your earnestness nearly tempts me," said the old man."

"Come then, you will study none the worse for a good breakfast, so come."

Half reluctantly the old man permitted himself to be led away, and soon he and Lord Redfern were seated at a substantial breakfast in the Hall.

All the time the old man was eating, which he did with great appetite and gusto, Lord Redfern kept asking him questions as to his magical powers, the possibility of the transmutation of metals and such like; unto all of which the sage made evasive answers, as one who was not willing to part with his secret too readily, or without testing the truthfulness of his confidant.

"I have now offered you all that is in my power, seeing that gold is no use to you," said Lord Redfern, "all I must say is, that my protection is not worthless, and that in this old Hall you might practice those arts, which if known would be dangerous."

"Softly my son," cried the old man, "I said not that I might not want gold. my experiments are expensive, but I want it not now. All I should want at present is a chamber of oblong shape running from east to west, this must be fitted up according to my orders, and no one must enter there without my permission.

"That you shall readily have, and if you but succeed in making—"

Lord Redfern stopped, for at that moment a strange alteration came over the old man.

His eyes became fixed and glaring as if some terrible object met their view.

His hands, which trembled as if in awe, were extended in supplication.

A strange gurgling noise came from his lips as if he were seized with a fit.

Rising suddenly from his chair, he exclaimed in hollow tones—

"Wondrous Hermes Trismaegistus, thou the friend of Osiris, father of the Maji to whom all the secrets of earth, air, and water were laid bare, and by whom nature's book was profoundly studied; what would'st thou with thy slave?"

Lord Redfern gazed in terror at this strange scene, watching the old man closely.

"Can the old man be mad?" he asked himself, "he must be."

For a moment the old man stood as if listening intently.

"If 'tis thy will," he murmured at last, "oh! Hermes Trismaegistus, I will obey.'

"What folly is this!" exclaimed Lord Redfern in a frightened voice.

"Hush!" exclaimed the old man seizing him by the arm, "silence or your life may answer for it. Look in yonder corner—can you not see his garments of clouds fade slowly away—there—there—now he is gone and we are safe."

Lord Redfern strained his eyes at the spot indicated, but could see nothing.

"I see nothing," said his lordship, "surely you must be crazed."

"Alas! my son I had forgotten that you are still in darkness;" said the old man.

"Darkness!" exclaimed Lord Redfern, "the room is light and—"

"You mistake my meaning. I mean that you are not initiated into the mysteries of our order. Nevertheless I have good comfort for thee.

"How so?" demanded Lord Redfern anxiously.

"It has pleased our grand Master Hermes Trismaegistus, more often known as Hermes of the Fiery Bill, to appear to me and order me to accept your offer and to stay here, and he will bless our endeavours and crown them with success."

"This is indeed good news," cried Redfern on whom the sages manner had made a deep impression.

"Stay, my son, there are certain conditions that must be complied with."

"Name them," cried Lord Redfern, "they shall be obeyed."

"In the first place, the furniture must be beautiful."

"You may select from any room in the house, I care not what."

"Good! Secondly, you must not let anyone disturb me. Whatever noise you may hear, no one must approach me. Nay, they must not enter the anteroom, or even the passage leading thereunto."

"No one shall interrupt you, I swear," said Lord Redfern. "Besides, *that* is the haunted chamber, and you will be clever indeed if you get any people into that room after dark. No one will venture near it after nightfall."

This news did not seem to disconcert the sage at all, who at once set to work ordering the servants to carry mirrors, tables, chairs, hangings, and all sorts of furniture to his room, making the servants work hard, but scarcely speaking a word himself; giving all his commands in dumb show.

"My son," he said, when the servants had completed their work, "I must now be left alone for three days, for this room must be prepared for the wonders to be performed therein by fasting and by prayer. If I am disturbed all will have to be commenced again, and thereby much time will be wasted. Therefore be cautio...."

"But, father, shall not the servants bring you some viands?"

"Tempt me not to break my fast, or the spell will be broken. They may place a bottle or so of wine here, in case I faint; that alone may I touch, but it must be of the best, lest it should make me ill."

The wine was soon brought, and with a low bow Lord Redfern left his new-found friend.

No sooner had he gone than the magician's manner altered considerably.

He first locked and bolted the door of the anteroom, then listened to see if either Lord Redfern or one of the servants might return.

Having ascertained that they had left him alone, he drew out from his wallet a gimlet, with which he made two large holes in the flooring, close to the door, but some distance apart. Into these holes he forced two stout iron pegs, so that no one could open the door without using the greatest violence imaginable.

He then hurried to the windows, and, closing the shutters, securely barred and bolted them, using screws and iron pegs as he had done with the door.

Having done this, he lighted a small lamp that was placed on a side table.

He then quietly removed his skullcap, at the same time taking off his grey hair and beard, leaving the jolly face of Roaring Ric the Ranter exposed to view.

Drawing the plan he had received from Batswing from his breast, he began examining the walls, and by the aid of the chart soon discovered numerous secret doors leading to strange winding passages and cunning little recesses.

The same examination of the floor led to the same result.

"A nice old gentleman the man who built this house must have been," said Ric; "he must have been more timid and had as many enemies as a rat."

He then set to work arranging the furniture as he desired it, putting up the hangings and fixing the mirrors in a most peculiar manner.

This done, he laid himself down on a sofa and fell fast asleep, for the work of the previous night had tired him out.

The time flew past, and still Roaring Ric slept soundly.

At last he awoke with a start, wondering how long he could have been asleep.

Removing one of the pegs, he unbolted the shutters and looked out.

It was night; a glorious night, still and silent as a sleeping babe.

The large, broad moon rose up above the dark trees in the park, and scattered her silver rays in broken fragments on the verdant grass beneath.

Far out in the distance gleamed the sea, shining like a band of silver.

CHAPTER LV.

JONATHAN WILD COMMENCES SPINNING A WEB FOR BATSWING. ALICE IN PRISON. FLICKER'S NEWS.

JONATHAN WILD sat in his office lost in deep thought.

His heavy brow rested on his large bony hand, whilst he beat the floor with his foot.

"Is it possible," he muttered at last, "that this Batswing is leagued with the devil? No, it cannot be; and yet he crosses me at every turn, as if guided by some unearthly power. Who can he be? I, who have found out secrets that seemed lost in the past, have been baffled by this highwayman. This must end."

Touching the bell, he summoned his henchman, Rough Ralph.

"Ralph!" he exclaimed, "have you ever forgotten your treatment in the cellar?"

"Do you think I ever shall?" growled Ralph, between his teeth.

"Judging from your usual temper, I should think not," replied Jonathan.

"Then why did you ask?" Ralph demanded, in a sharp manner.

"You need not be angry with me, Ralph," said Jonathan; it was not my fault."

"No; but you need not remind me of the matter: the thought aint pleasant."

"Perhaps not; still, to forget it would be cowardly," said Jonathan, quietly.

"I aint likely to forget it, Mr. Wild; you know that well enough."

"I suppose not; but have you any plan of revenge?" enquired Jonathan.

"None as yet; but once let me get my hands round his throat, and you'll see."

"Good. When you do get the chance; but how will you get it?"

"I don't know as yet; but it will come, I know that."

"If I promise you that it shall come, and that quickly, will you promise to obey?"

"I will."

"Then it will be necessary for you to change your dress and manner."

"The one's easy, the other aint," replied Rough Ralph.

"Nevertheless it must be done," said Jonathan Wild firmly.

"If it must, it must," said Ralph sulkily. "What am I to become now?"

"You understand horses, I suppose," said Jonathan.

"I ought to; I was head stable man in Sir George Gresham's stables in York, for five years."

"And left there in consequence of a burglary being committed at Gresham Hall."

"You know all about it, Martin; so that is enough," replied Ralph sulkily.

"I was employed to find out the burglar, and——"

"You found him," said Ralph hastily; "that is enough, so let the matter drop."

"Pardon me, my dear fellow, I can't let the matter drop at present."

"WHERE DID YOU GET THIS BRACELET FROM?" "I—I, BOUGHT IT, THIS NIGHT, STAMMERED THE JEW."

"You and I know all about it, so what more do you want?" cried Ralph.

"I found out who was the thief; his name was——"

"Austin," cried Ralph eagerly; "He was tried and hanged at York."

"Truly Austin was hanged, but he was *innocent*; the true criminal escaped."

"Don't be too hard on a fellow," said Ralph.

"You, Ralph, were the thief. I had, nay still have the proofs, but I spared you."

"But you had the plunder," snarled Ralph showing his teeth.

"I had; that is quite true, and on condition that you gave it to me at a certain price."

"Certain price!" growled Ralph, "oh Lord, oh Lord, only a few pounds."

"At a certain *price*," continued Jonathan without noticing the interruption. "I gave you your liberty, and took you into my service. You must not forget that although I had honest old Austin hanged; I threw such suspicion on you, that by a word from me you could be arrested, tried, and condemned as his accomplice."

"And what would become of the receiver of the stolen property?" asked Ralph.

"I presume you allude to me," said Jonathan quietly, "oh, I should be all safe you know. The plate was all melted down long ago, no one could recognise it now. But you need not be alarmed as it is not my purpose to betray you, all I want you to understand is that you are in my power, and that I mean to exert that power to the utmost. If you serve me well you shall be well paid for your services, but if on the other hand, you will not serve me well, or indeed falter in the least in obeying my orders, you shall swing at York as old Austin did."

"You have but to command," growled Rough Ralph; "I must obey."

"Then to commence; you must dress yourself up in livery and I will get you a place."

"Another burglary on I suppose?" enquired Rough Ralph.

"Then you suppose wrongly," replied Jonathan, "and what is more if you attempt to steal one thing from the person who is to be your master, you will suffer death."

"Who is to be my master then?" demanded Ralph, "speak out and have done with it."

"Your master will be no less a personage than Lord Redfern," said Jonathan.

"Phew! why what game is up now master?" enquired Ralph opening his eyes.

"You will have to watch him and let me know his plans."

"But how will that give me my revenge on that Devil Batswing?"

"Leave it to me, and trust me your hands *shall* soon be round his throat."

"If once *that* happens," cried Ralph clawing the air, "he will not trouble us any more."

"Lord Redfern is sure to be here soon," said Jonathan, "show him in here and then summon me by the private bell; you understand. I shall now go and see our new prisoner. Have you seen her this morning?"

"I have, she is quiet, but firm as a rock. *She'll* take some taming."

"Now go," said Jonathan, and Rough Ralph left the room

For a few moments Jonathan Wild paced up and down his room, then taking up a small lamp lit it and descending to the dungeons that were beneath his house proceeded to open one of the doors.

This prison, unlike the rest, was not so uncomfortable as most places of the sort.

It was plainly but neatly furnished as a sitting-room and bedroom.

Being under ground all light was excluded, but a small bronze lamp which swung from the ceiling shed a mild light all over the room.

On the small truckle bed, absorbed in grief, was Alice Landon.

Jonathan placed the lamp on the table and stood watching her.

After a few moments, perceiving that she had not noticed his presence, he spoke to her.

"Mistress Alice Landon," he said in as gentle tones as he could assume, "I have come to confer with you on business of the utmost importance. Can you answer me?"

As his voice fell on her ear Alice sprang to her feet and faced him proudly.

"What would you with me?" she exclaimed haughtily, "I am your prisoner; at least let me have my prison in quietude."

"Alice Landon!" cried Jonathan, "you *must* hear me. Nay, start not; I intend you no violence. In my life I have had to mix with good and bad; the most virtuous and the most vicious, and with those extremes I have always found it best to play my game openly; for the vicious are pretty sure to know your game, whilst the virtuous too often foil you by their ignorance of knavery."

"Go on sir," replied Alice, "I cannot help but hear you, since I am in your power."

"It is well you know that you are in my power, as doubtless you will be more tractable."

"Trust me sir," said Alice proudly, "I know your power. My body you may scourge and torture, but my will is free, and that shall never bend to such as you."

"I like your courage," said Jonathan, "but think it ill advised just now."

"True courage is never ill advised," cried Alice, "it is but a love of good."

"That being the case," laughed Jonathan, "I fear I never had true courage. Unless my love for your fair self be a love of good: for you are good."

"Your love for me!" cried Alice contemptuously, "are you come to mock me?"

"Indeed not I," replied Jonathan, "but rather to teach you to be a sensible girl. Sit down and listen patiently to me for I have much to say."

Almost mechanically Alice Landon seated herself on her bed.

"You have, Mistress Landon," said Jonathan, "been persecuted by Lord Redfern."

"I have," replied Alice, "and by his vile associate Jonathan Wild."

Jonathan bit his lips savagely but said not a word.

"Lord Redfern has always spoken to me of his love. Does he love you?"

"You say that he professes to," replied Alice scornfully, "I know no more."

"Come, come, Mistress Alice," said Jonathan, "you are not the woman to be deceived. You know whether this man loves you or no. Is it a real love?"

"Dare you, his associate, ask me such a question?" cried Alice.

"I ask for information or I should not ask at all," said Wild quietly.

"How can he who slew the father love the daughter?" demanded Alice.

"True my pretty Alice," said Jonathan, "but yet he wishes to wed you."

Alice made no reply but by a movement of disgust.

"Would you not like to be Lady Redfern, eh? The title is good."

"I would rather die," exclaimed Alice passionately.

"This is strange," muttered Jonathan; then turning to Alice he continued. "See here Alice, I will be open with you. Redfern does not love you; he never loved anything but himself, therefore I am convinced there is some grave reason why he should so desire this wedding. Have you no idea what are his reasons?"

"I have told you that I have not," replied Alice Landon firmly.

"You will not believe me, but I am your friend," said Jonathan.

"I do *not* believe you," said Alice calmly, "you cannot think I should."

"Possibly not, and yet for all that I am willing to help you, and more so as I am Redfern's enemy."

"You his enemy: you who have followed him as a dog?"

"Tut, tut, if I have followed him like a dog, trust me 'twas but to bite his heels. He is in my power, and I can do with him what I wish. But before I bring him to justice, as I most assuredly shall, I would know the cause of this love to you. Was there any mystery about your birth?"

"None!" replied Alice in wonder and surprise.

"Have you ever heard that your father had property; that he was a miser who hoarded wealth and lived, for the sake of making money?"

"Never," cried Alice indignantly," my father was liberal and good."

"Redfern would not wish to marry you for those qualities," said Jonathan grimly, "those are the last things he would like to inherit. You know that he has spread the report that you with Batswing slew your father, and that there is a warrant out for your arrest."

"I do."

"So well has he laid the plot that if you are taken your death is certain."

Alice shuddered but did not answer.

"I alone can save you, aye and others too. For you must know that Sir Arthur Bowring and Batswing are all in my power. They attempted to carry you off at Tillingham and were arrested. Now Lord Redfern is the only man to appear against them. He is now at Tillingham, and through you alone can I save them."

"My friends in danger," cried Alice clasping her hands, "how can I help them?"

"By writing a note which I will deliver to Lord Redfern, appointing to meet him on the cliff two miles north of the Three Cutters, tell him that you are imprisoned, do not say by whom, but that the night after tomorrow you will make your escape and join him there. Tell him he must come alone."

"This is some trick," cried Alice, "how will that letter save my friends?"

"He will keep the appointment; I will have some men in readiness who will seize and bind him, ship him on board a vessel and carry him to France."

"If you hesitate, all will be lost," said Jonathan after a pause.

"And will you give me my liberty?" asked Alice.

"That I cannot at present. You forget that you are safer here than anywhere else. No constables would think of seeking for you here, whilst if you were once seen in the streets your arrest would be certain. You must be contented to remain in captivity a little longer; when once Redfern is a prisoner, you will be free. Come do not hesitate. Remember your friends' lives depend upon your complying."

Moved by this threat, Alice took the pen and ink and paper with which Jonathan had taken care to be well supplied, and wrote the letter as desired

With a fiendish chuckle Jonathan folded the note and placed it in his pocket-book, at the same time leering horribly at Alice.

"There!" he said, "that will soon put matters right. Fear not my pretty Alice, Lord Redfern shall not marry you: sooner than that I would make you Mrs. Wild. Ho, ho, ho, ho, good-bye for the present. Don't fret for me, I shall be back soon."

"Monster," cried Alice, "you have deceived me. Oh! what have I done."

"What have you done?" retorted Jonathan, "why played into my hands beautifully, that is what you have done. How beautiful you look when you're in a passion. I must have a kiss, really I must. 'Pon my word I think I love you after all, and if it does prove you have money, you shall be Mrs. Wild; if not—why you shall remain my prisoner. Come one kiss, only one."

Screaming with terror the frightened girl retreated to the further corner of the room, whilst Jonathan, with out-stretched arms and fiendish grin, advanced upon her.

Suddenly he paused and listened. Yes it was the ringing of a bell.

"Business," he muttered, "business first and pleasure afterwards. Farewell my little pet, I shall return soon, and then we will be more friendly."

With a horrid grin he took up the lamp and left the room.

Having carefully locked the door he returned to his office, where he found Rough Ralph and Lord Redfern awaiting him.

"So sir!" cried Redfern, but Wild stopped him with a gesture.

"Patience my lord, if you please. Ralph, leave the room," said Wild calmly.

No sooner had Ralph gone than Lord Redfern's passion burst forth again.

"So sir, you have deceived me?" he cried, "broken your compact, lied—"

"Have a care, my lord," said Jonathan sternly, "those are hard words, and I never forgive or forget. Please explain wherein I have deceived or offended your lordship."

"In this way," cried Lord Redfern, "when we were attacked by the smugglers on the shore, you turned and fled, leaving us to be cut to pieces by them."

"You are right, I turned and fled, but not before I saw they must win."

"But they did not win," cried Lord Redfern, "the boats arrived in time and carried off Lord Leslie."

"That was well done," said Jonathan, "what happened afterwards?"

"Of course we no sooner saw our man safe than we turned and fled also. My men spread along the shore to avoid pursuit, whilst I returned to the Hall dreading it would be attacked and Alice carried off."

"And you found she had been," said Jonathan coolly.

"No: but I found you in the act of carrying her off," cried Lord Redfern.

"Was it you my lord whom I struck to the ground?" said Jonathan as if surprised.

"You know it was," cried Redfern, "and by Heaven I'll be revenged."

"I know it my lord!" exclaimed Jonathan as if struck with astonishment, "do you think when I had hastened up to save your prisoner from the attack of those lawless bands, that I should have struck you down? What good could I have done by that? Believe me I imagined that you were one of the enemy, and therefore struck you to the earth in order to carry off your prisoner in safety."

For a moment Redfern paused as if in doubt, and then said—

"So you carried her off in safety for me. If so where is she?"

"I did not say that I did carry her off in safety, I attempted to but as I reached the door I was struck down myself, the girl torn from me, and I only escaped by a miracle."

"Then it must have been by the party headed by Maud that threatened me."

"Doubtless my lord it was. I stopped not to look but fled."

"And Alice?"

"Is in their power my lord. It will be unpleasant should she and Maud meet."

"Curses on it!" exclaimed Lord Redfern passionately, "what is to be done?"

"We must fight these men with their own weapons. You must take my man Ralph into your service. I think I have a plan whereby the Bat will make his last flight. Look over the cliff at Tillingham in a couple of days' time, and you will see a sight there that will warm your heart and satisfy your revenge."

"Do you swear this," cried Lord Redfern.

"I do, the bait is ready and I know that it is one that will not be refused."

"Then I will do all in my power to aid you," said Redfern.

"So Maud is still with Batswing," said Jonathan Wild.

"I doubt whether she is alive," said Redfern with a grim smile, "I shot her."

"You shot her?" said Jonathan in surprise, "where, and how?"

"She headed the band that attacked the Hall, I shot her and escaped."

"And the body?" demanded Jonathan.

"Oh, they carried that away with them," said Lord Redfern.

"Then she is not dead. But come we must have Ralph disguised and—"

At that moment Ralph knocked at the door and entered.

"Well!" demanded Jonathan Wild, "what is the matter now?"

"There's a messenger downstairs waiting for you," said Ralph, "there were two, but one's gone, just leaving the message with me as you were engaged."

"And what was the message?" demanded Jonathan, "make haste man."

"The gaol fever is in the prison, the judge was took this morning."

"Is that all?" said Jonathan coolly, "what is that to me?"

"That aint all," said Ralph, "the highwayman, Hugh Fenton, has escaped."

"Confusion!" cried Jonathan, "I meant to have bribed him with his life to trace out the other robbers of Epping. Send up the other messenger."

In a few minutes a ragged sailor lad appeared in the room.

His face was begrimed with dirt and plastered over as if he had been wounded.

One eye was covered over with a patch, whilst the other was quite black.

A more deplorable object could scarcely be imagined.

"Well my lad," cried Jonathan, "what may you want with me?"

"Please sir, I'se the boy what escaped from the Seagull."

"Escaped from the Seagull?" cried Jonathan and Redfern together.

"Why yes yer honours," replied the boy, "you know the night we had the skummige."

"Yes, yes," replied Lord Redfern, "go on, go on, don't stop."

"Well yer honour, we'd got up alongside the boat and our men had tumbled up the side of the ship, and we had given a cheer at having escaped the other boat—"

"The other boat; what other boat?" demanded the listeners.

"Why the boat as came from the shore yer honours, and fired on us. Well we had just as I said got 'em on deck, when, whiz, came a shot right through the mainsel, and we saw that ugly old privateer, the Black Hawk, making all sail to overhaul us. She stopped to take up the crew of the other boat, and so we forged ahead, but she soon came up to us and we had to strike."

"Who was the captain of the Black Hawk?" cried Jonathan.

"A chap called Batswing I think, and there was another fellow they called Sir Arthur, along with him."

"Confusion! all is lost," cried Redfern, "Batswing has gone to France."

"Begging your honours pardon, he put in shore in a small boat, and made me go too, the boat capsized and all on 'em save Batswing and myself were lost, so I came here to tell you the news. Hoping as how you won't forget a shipwrecked sailor lad."

"Take that and be gone," cried Redfern throwing the lad a guinea.

"Well," said the lad as he walked down the street, "it's my idea that I've paid my way to Tillingham, or my name's not Flicker."

CHAPTER LVI.

BATSWING GOES TO A FANCY BALL WHERE HE TAKES A FANCY TO ONE OR TWO THINGS.—THE TWIN SISTERS.—THE SNUFF BOX.—THE DUEL.

BUCKLERSBURY was all in a blaze of light.

Queer old lumbersome coaches rattled along over the rough stones.

Chairmen shouted and swore at each other as they trotted along with their swinging burdens of powdered and perfumed gentlemen.

Link boys dashed about, making the air murky from the smoke of their links.

Footmen hustled footmen into the dusty road: all was confusion.

And what was the cause of all this hub-bub and noise?

Nothing more nor less than Sir Jacob Hide, Alderman for the ward of Portsoaken, and chief warden of the Skinners Company had given a fancy ball.

What on earth had induced this worthy civic dignitary to have perpetrated this folly would indeed be hard to state. He had never disguised himself in anything before but good old wine, whilst his round figure made it rather difficult to assume any character but that of Falstaff; nevertheless he was determined to give the party, and of course as he was a rich man his invitations were readily accepted.

Onward came the crowds pushing, leering, and, shame to tell, swearing, for our grand mammas as well as our grand papas delighted not a little in strong language and liquors.

Here was a fierce-looking demon handing a charming angel from her sedan. Behold how yonder Jew smiles and smirks at the pretty Saint Catherine, whilst that ferocious Turk, who by the way is the mildest of hen-pecked husbands, follows quietly in the wake of the Circassian slave, his wife.

Bowing and scraping at the other end of the saloon stands the worthy alderman and his better half to receive their guests.

Sir Jacob, throwing to the winds all such trifles as stature and figure, has dressed his funny little podgy person up as that 'blessed martyr,' Charles the first, whilst his lady, who is as dried and thin as a sand eel, is dressed as Catherine Parr.

Onward comes the crowd, pushing, struggling, shaking hands with their worthy host and hostess, and then hurrying away to laugh at them unobserved.

"By Jove, this is hot work," said Captain Jennings, who was dressed as a monk, to another gentleman who wore a large black domino.

"Pardon me, father," replied the other, "but has your reverence a dispensation from the pope that you swear by a heathen deity?"

"Bother the Pope and all the heathen deities too," laughed the captain, "I am a soldier."

"Truly, I thought you men of war swore by three of those same deities."

"Indeed, which?" demanded the captain, "though by my faith I believe we swear by anything."

"Need you ask which," replied the other, "why Venus the goddess of beauty, her son, the boy-god of love, and rosy Bacchus god of wine."

"Well said," cried the captain, "I believe in those Gods firmly."

"So firmly," laughed the domino, "that the latter oft makes you unsteady."

"Curse me, but you are merry, friend," said the captain "let us crack a bottle together now. I warrant you old Hide's wine is good. Good wine, they say, needs no bush, but his nose carries the true sign of the grape."

"Stay, Master Captain," cried the domino, who are these fine lasses dressed as shepherdesses? By heavens they are very lovely; the arched neck, the pencilled eyebrows, rose buds for mouths, skin-like—"

"By the Lord Harry, Master Domino, you too are a votary of Venus," cried the captain.

"And who would not be at such a sight. Do you know them?"

"No, they must be some people of distinction; see how Sir Jacob bows and my lady courtesies—there's a cheese,* we must find out who they are."

Pushing their way through the crowd, they at length came to a small crowd, who, like themselves, had evidently been discussing the appearance of the new arrivals.

* Old fashioned term for a low courtesy.

"Rich!" cried one of the men, "he rolls in riches, positively swims in them."

"And how many children has he?" enquired another, languidly.

"Only those two beauties; aye, and they are as proud as they are beautiful."

"But how does he make his money?" enquired another.

"By farming, everything he touches turns to gold, hence his name of the Golden Farmer."

"Curse me if I don't give the 'view-halloo' and run one of them down," cried a young fellow, dressed in hunting costume.

"Better leave it alone, Harry," replied the first speaker, "you don't know those girls. I do."

"Why, what do you know against them?" asked one young fellow.

"Much, yet nothing. To look at, they are angels, but their lovers find them—well different."

"How so? I do not understand you. Perhaps they flirt."

"Yes and no; the whole thing appears to be a mystery. Certain it is that those who love them are sure to be ruined, whilst many of them disappear."

"Tut, tut, Cavendish." cried one young man, "you go too far."

"Perhaps so, but if you observe, those men who know them best, avoid them most."

"Is there any case that can be proved against them?" asked Captain Jennings.

"Nothing can be proved against them," replied the other, "beyond that they drive their lovers to despair and ruin. The poor fellows then put themselves out of the way, and the fair shepherdesses like Circe, seek new victims."

"Of a certainty they are not asked to dance," whispered Captain Jennings.

"Let us ask them then, Captain," returned the Domino; then speaking to a gentleman called Cavendish, he enquired if the Golden Farmer would be at the ball.

"Yes, he is pretty certain to be here," replied the young man, "but he never keeps near his daughters. He is a good, honest, rough sort of fellow enough, there is no doubt of that, and lets his fair daughters do what they like. He either cannot or will not see any harm in them; in fact he believes them angels, incapable of doing wrong."

"You speak harshly of the young ladies, sir," continued the Domino, "have you suffered?"

"No, sir; but three friends of mine have; I surely need no more."

"Well," laughed the Domino, "though the fruit is poisonous, it is so lovely I cannot resist it."

"You had better be warned," cried Mr. Cavendish, "do not act rashly, sir."

"At least I'll tread one measure with them," cried the Domino, gaily.

"I' faith and I'll follow your example," said Captain Jennings.

The group of young men watched the Domino and his companion approach the girls.

A few compliments seemed to pass, and the next moment each had selected his partner.

To dance in those days was dancing. There was none of the "walking through" as we have now-a-days. No, every step had to be made, each bow was a study, and to walk a minuet properly was only to be gained by long study and much practice.

The domino—whom doubtless the reader has already recognised as Batswing acquitted himself to the general admiration of the company.

After the dance was concluded, he led his partner to a sofa and seated himself by her side.

For a few moments they remained gazing into each others eyes.

Batswing took particular notice of the lady whose beauty no one could doubt.

Her form was exquisitely rounded and slender, her movements lithe and graceful.

Her complexion was almost too delicate, making one dread consumption.

Her hair was a pale auburn, and hung in sweet waves upon her ivory shoulders.

Her eyebrows were thin and well pencilled, being arched over two beautifully formed and bright eyes, whose only defect was their colour, they were *green*.

Her delicately carved nose came in a straight line from her forehead which rather slanted. Her mouth was small with very thin red lips, which scarcely showed when she spoke, her small white teeth, although they were of matchless beauty.

Such was Zarah Saunders, the eldest daughter of the Golden Farmer.

"Are you fond of dancing?" enquired Batswing, in a tender tone.

"Oh, I dote on it," exclaimed the lady, gushingly, then lowering her voice she added, "that is when I have a partner whom I like."

"I sincerely trust that you will reckon me amongst that number," said Batswing.

The lady raised her soft green eyes and shot a glance at him.

A glance! yes, but such a glance, it only made Batswing shudder, why he knew not.

"I suppose you frequent these parties so much that they almost weary you?"

"Oh, no," replied the young lady, frankly, "I cannot admit that; you know my father is only a farmer, and although he is rich—folks *do* say very rich, still he is not able to place us in the highest society. High ho; it must be very charming to go to court."

"To court you, would be very charming," replied Batswing, with a bow.

Again the lady shot one of those quick glances at him from beneath her fringed eyebrows.

Batswing could not tell what it was in those glances that made him shudder so.

There was a cruel, hungry cat-like look which was terrible.

The smile on those rosy lips was not kindly. The lips drew back almost giving the expression of a wild animal snarling. A terrible tigerish look that made one's blood run cold.

"Ah!" she sighed, who can believe you gentlemen of the Court? You are such flatterers."

"Flatterers we may be to some ladies, but it would be impossible to flatter beauty so rare as yours."

Again the same glance fell upon Batswing.

"It must be very pleasant to live amongst the aristocracy," she sighed; "these city people are so rough. They have no ideas beyond their shops and warehouses; their only talk is about the money-market, the price of shares, and wheat, and such like things."

"That is true," laughed Batswing; "their whole heart and soul is in their business."

"True; they have no idea of poetry and beauty; and as for love—"

"That is too ethereal for their dull comprehension; and yet I should have thought—"

He paused and gazed tenderly at the fair creature before him.

"You would have thought what?" she enquired encouragingly.

"Why, I should have thought that you would have inspired love in the most icy heart."

"Ah, you flatter. I scarce dare trust myself to speak to you."

"And why not? Surely it must be delightful to be admired—and loved."

"Yes, it must be so," replied the lady, sorrowfully; "but I fear I shall never be so.'

"Any why not? Surely many have knelt at those feet and poured forth their tale of love."

"Love! Do you think that love is known to all?" asked the girl.

"Who could be in your presence an hour and not know it," replied Batswing.

"Oh, you are good to say so," replied the girl; "but that is not what I call love."

"Indeed! will you, then, teach me the lesson. I promise I will be a willing pupil."

"Not now," replied the girl, hurriedly, as a tall muffled figure passed them; "we are observed. See the dancing is about to commence, and—"

She stopped suddenly, cast down her eyes, and blushed deeply.

"And we are not in our places," said Batswing, bowing; "come, let us take them."

With easy grace he led Zarah to the quadrille and walked a measure.

"See! there is our friend the Domino dancing again," said young Cavendish.

"Do you know him, Captain Jennings?" asked another, as that gentleman came up.

"No; he keeps the hood of his domino drawn so over his face, no one can know him."

"He evidently is a thorough gentleman. See how well he dances," said Cavendish.

"His conversation and manners prove him that," said the captain.

"Doubtless he is some noble come here for the fun," laughed Cavendish.

"He is evidently caught in the snares of the fair Zarah," said another gentleman.

"Without a doubt: see, the dance is ended; look how he leads her into the conservatory."

"There among the leaves and flowers,
Like sweet minutes fly the hours,
Time and troubles quickly fly,
Wafted by a lover's sigh."

"Yes, gentlemen, I am afraid the Domino, whoever he may be, is deeply smitten."

Such, indeed, would appear to have been the case, for Batswing, the charming Zarah leaning on his arm, had entered the conservatory, and, walking gently through it, stood on a large balcony that overlooked—start not reader, but remember this house was in the city—a narrow court that ran behind the building. Here Batswing renewed the conversation.

"Now we are alone will you not tell me what is love," he whispered.

"Surely you must know," replied the blushing maiden, timidly.

"Since I have seen you I have, but until then I knew not the passion."

"Alas! I wish we had never met," exclaimed the girl, sorrowfully.

"And why? Do you, then, love and love another?" demanded Batswing.

"No, no, oh no," replied the girl. "I—I never loved till"—she paused suddenly.

"Till when?" demanded Batswing quickly; "why not tell me?"

"Oh, I'm foolish, very foolish," cried Zarah, pressing her pocket handkerchief to her eyes.

"And why are you foolish?" said Batswing: "Zarah, have I offended you?"

"No, no, oh no; but you are a stranger. Do not press me to answer now."

"Hem!" thought Batswing; "it strikes me that madam flirt don't want much pressing."

His arm stole gently round her waist and he whispered gently, "Zarah."

She dropped her head upon his shoulder, and we silently and sweetly.

Softly he raised her head and imprinted a kiss upon those ruby lips.

"Hush!" he exclaimed suddenly; "some one is coming. You must not be found here."

"No, no," exclaimed the girl; "if my father knew this he would kill me."

"Quick, then, pass behind these curtains; you can then reach the other end of the conservatory, and from thence into the ball-room; don't pause, I will follow you."

The girl gave him a pressure of the hand and the next moment was gone.

No sooner had she departed than Batswing quickly slipped off his domino.

He bound it round with a cord so that it formed a light bundle.

Having done this, he gave a low whistle, which was repeated from the lane.

He threw the bundle into the lane. A footboy darted from the shadow of the wall, seized it, and with a scarcely perceptible sign disappeared.

Having accomplished this feat, Batswing now appeared in a handsome dress, made of Genoa velvet richly braided with gold.

Quickly re-arranging his hair, and pulling down his ruffs, he made such a change in his personal appearance that no one would have known him as the Domino.

"What is that girl's game?" he muttered as he completed these arrangements." She has no heart. Her jewels were worth a queen's ransom, yet she would inveigle every man she meets. What cruel eyes she has, but bright as her diamonds, of which, by the way, I think I have the finest specimens."

With a quiet laugh he drew forth a handsome diamond bracelet, which had but a few minutes before glanced on the rounded arm of the beautiful Zarah, and after looking at it for a few moments, placed it carefully in his bosom.

"'Pon my word it is a shame," he laughed; "but needs must when the Devil drives: it cost me all my ready money to get that fool, Hugh Fenton off, and I have work in hand that must not be neglected, and to do which it will be necessary to have money. Besides, after all, I believe I have only robbed an enemy: that girl means mischief to mankind at large: I believe all that that young fellow said of her; I will try her in my new character, and if I am deceived I will return her the bracelet, if not, old Ichabod Joel shall have it; at all events, he will lend me money on it until I make up my mind."

Thrusting the bracelet into his breast Batswing crept behind the curtains, and keeping close to the wall made his way towards the ball-room.

He had not proceeded half way when the sound of voices fell upon his ears. One was that of a man, the other that of a woman.

Both seemed strangely familiar to him, but he could not tell where he had heard them.

Drawing a knife from his pocket he made a small slit in the curtains.

Through the hole thus made he was able to see the speakers.

One was Zarah, the other was the tall cloaked figure she seemed so anxious to avoid.

They were evidently deeply interested in the conversation, for they spoke low but earnestly.

"Do you not know his name?" asked the man quickly.

"No, but I know he is a gentleman," replied Zarah; "of that I am certain."

"How are you certain?" replied the man sharply; "did he tell you so?"

"No; had he done so I should not have believed him," replied the girl.

"Well, you know best," replied the man; "but be careful, be careful."

"I tell you farther," replied Zarah, "that I cannot succeed if you watch me so."

"You see, Zarah, I am frightened that harm may come to you," replied the man.

"Harm! what harm can come to me?" replied the girl, contemptuously.

"If you should fall in love?" urged the father; "only fancy that."

"Love! Is it likely that I should do that?" replied the young girl, with scorn.

"No, not very," replied the father; "but women are so strange that——"

"Yes, women are strange," replied Zarah, "but I am not as other women."

"No, Zarah, that indeed you're not. Now if Kate—"

"Silence!" replied the girl, her green eyes shooting forth a horrid light; "I have told you that I will not have her know the secret. She would spoil all."

"She might do more business if she did," grumbled the man, under his breath.

"Her innocence is the best lure," replied Zarah. "Trust me; I know best. If she were to know the fate of her lovers she might refuse to work; now she does all we want, and is happy."

"And so are you, I hope," said the man, in a softer tone.

"Happy! yes, as the devils are in hell. Happy! there, let it pass. We have our work to do, let us not lose time. The black domino will be an easy victim. I have but to make an assignation with him, and he will come at once. Young Mervin is to be here to-night; he shall follow, and I will now get a new victim."

"Good!" said the man, in a delighted tone; "Kate has got a captain in tow. Ha, ha, ha, ha; we shall soon have our hands full. More work, more money."

"Go now, there is no time to be lost," said Zarah; "you go that way, I will go this."

With a mysterious sign the father and daughter separated, each seeking the ball-room.

"Phew!" said Batswing, as he came from his hiding place, "what a couple of ogres."

For a moment he stood as if unable to realise the dreadful conversation he had heard.

"'Pon my word, this is dreadful!" he said at last. "Fee fo fum, I smell the blood of an Englishman. Surely I must be dreaming, or I have been making love to Mrs. Blunderbore, the ogress, all this time. What shall I do? I must not tell Captain Jennings, or in fact anyone else, for they would make me divulge the secret to the magistrates, who in their turn would make me state who and what I am. No; I must try to fight this game by myself. One comfort, I can sell the bracelet without any compunction now. But, before I go, I will let Miss Zarah try her charms on the wondrously soft and susceptible heart of Percy Marvel."

With a light laugh he strolled into the ball-room, as if only just arrived.

They had queer old manners, those grandfathers of ours, with their silk stockings with clocks at the sides, their high heels (painted red) and diamond shoe and knee buckles. Look how their large stiff coat-tails stick out behind them, whilst their slim but deadly rapiers, ever ready to their hands, swing on their left sides. How rich and white are their lace falls and dainty ruffles of point lace.

With what a magnificent air they open their gold snuff-boxes, and with tapering fingers, delicate and white as any lady's, take out a pinch, which they airily place to their well-chiselled noses, taking care that the gems in their rings shall catch the rays of light.

Rays of light! Not much of that at this period. Candles, nothing but candles and a few oil lamps make their dismal presence felt by their unpleasant odour. Gas and the many other charming inventions to give us light were unknown to our grandfathers.

Nevertheless they were a hearty, jovial race, and danced their minuets beneath the flaring tallow candles with as much pleasure and more grace than their grandchildren dance the *valse a deux temps* underneath the cut-glass chandeliers of Willis's Rooms.

Gently waving his pocket-handkerchief and pointing out his toes, Batswing entered the ballroom with the consummate ease and grace of a Chesterfield.

Taking his position at the door, he cast his glances round in search of Zarah.

Yes, there she was, dancing and flirting with a young man, who did not seem too amiable.

"Is that the Mervin who is to be the victim after myself?" thought Batswing.

He was interrupted in his meditation by a hearty slap on his shoulder.

Turning round, he beheld Captain Jennings standing by his side.

"Why, Mr. Marvel!" exclaimed the captain, "I am glad to see thee. What makes you so late?"

"I was detained at White's," replied Batswing, carelessly. "Sir George Armitage would play."

"Indeed, I hope he lost," said the captain; he always will be at the cards."

"He did not lose much," replied Batswing, who was delighted to see that his acting was so good that even his friend did not know him; "only a cool hundred or two."

"By the way, I owe you a hundred," said the captain.

"Indeed; 'pon my honour I had forgotten it," said Batswing, offering his snuff-box.

"Don't you remember that you bet me that that confounded highwayman would get off, although I told you I could swear to the man as safely as I could to you?"

"Oh yes, I remember," replied Batswing, with a queer smile, "but you were mistaken."

"Mistaken! the fellow got off by a trick. But let us not talk now. We have better work to do."

"Indeed! may I ask what is this pleasant work?" said Batswing.

"To dance, to make love, after which we will crack a bottle."

"You are merry to-night, captain," said Batswing; "what is the cause of your mirth?"

"My dear boy," exclaimed the captain, enthusiastically; "I have found an angel."

"Then in heaven's name leave her alone," said Batswing.

"What do you mean? I do not understand you," said the captain.

"You think her an angel now, yet she is but a woman. Marry her, she will be a woman still, but you will soon think her a —— very different sort of angel."

"Tush, man, you do not know her, or you would not speak thus."

"As you will," replied Batswing, with a shrug; "where is the beauty?"

"Over yonder; she has a sister almost as lovely as she is."

"Indeed, and where is this sister who is so near perfection, eh?"

"I don't know; she was dancing with a fellow in a black domino just now."

Batswing could scarcely refrain from laughing when he heard this announcement.

"Well, you must introduce me to these ladies. Who knows? we may become brothers-in-law."

"So I will; but see, the dance is about to begin again. I must not lose her."

"Then you had better make haste, for that young fellow is evidently making up to her."

"So he is, by Jove; stay here and I will come to you after the dance."

Percy Marvel strolled through the room, talking to the different people he met.

Sir Jacob met him, and producing a massive gold snuff-box set with brilliants, offered to exchange a pinch of snuff with him, which our hero at once did.

"This box," cried the worthy knight, "was presented to me by the Prince of Wales, for having managed a small loan for him in the city. He's a wild fellow, that same prince, a very wild fellow; but I like him for it. Egad, sir, but I do."

"I am sure, Sir Jacob," replied Batswing, "his royal highness must appreciate your love."

"Egad, sir, he does; I know he does. But there's my Lord Todhunter over there. I must see him."

And so the worthy knight hastened away, but not before Batswing, with astounding celerity, had removed the snuff-box that had been the donation of the "greatest gentleman in Europe" from the alderman's pocket to his own.

By this time the dance was over, and Captain Jennings introduced Kate to Batswing.

She was indeed better-looking than her sister, and her eyes had not that terrible look.

"There can be no doubt they are sisters," thought Batswing. "But this girl can love, the other never could. Still, I must watch the noble captain."

As a matter of course, Kate introduced her sister Zarah to Batswing.

A dance followed, in which our hero, by his graceful movements and fine figure, shone out wonderfully, becoming the admiration of the whole room.

Again he was alone with Zarah, and again he flattered her, but in such a manner that she should not notice any likeness to the black domino.

Eagerly the girl seemed to listen to his addresses and high-flown compliments.

Sometimes she appeared so simple that Batswing almost doubted himself.

Then there was that dreadful conversation, and that cruel, hungry glance.

Again he led her to the conservatory and poured out a tale of love.

"Madam," he cried, "until this moment I have not known what it was to live."

"Pardon me, sir," replied the blushing Zarah; "I do not understand you."

"Oh! sweetest and gentlest of your sex," exclaimed Batswing, "until I beheld your face I knew not the pleasures of life. All things seemed dead to me; but your beauty has illumined the darkness of my life, and heaven seems opening on me. Tell me that you love me. Say that I must not despair—that I may hope."

With downcast eyes Zarah allowed Batswing to press her hand to his lips.

"Oh, the cat!" he thought; "she accepts all who offer. She *must* be an ogress."

Again he urged his suit, and the beauty was about to sink on his shoulder and confess her love, when they were disturbed by a strange hubbub which arose in the ballroom.

Both started back and listened intently to the sound of extraordinary confusion.

People seemed rushing to and fro, and all talking at once.

Suddenly a man's voice was heard, exclaiming, in loud tones, so that all might hear—

"Ladies and gentlemen, please keep your places; please keep your places."

"What is the matter? What is the matter?" shouted several voices.

"By some mischance a thief has entered the room, and has stolen several articles."

A general scream was heard from the ladies as this announcement was made.

"Amongst which is a diamond snuff-box presented by the Prince of Wales to Sir Jacob."

Another shriek of horror arose, followed by great confusion and stamping.

"I'm in a pretty fix," thought Batswing; "I wish I had not this girl with me."

For a short time they both remained listening to the confused sounds in the ballroom.

"How the deuce can I get rid of the girl?" thought Batswing; "if she were gone I could escape."

At this moment Zarah saved him all further trouble by hurrying into the ballroom.

She had no sooner disappeared than Batswing drew forth his pocket-book, and tearing a leaf from it, wrote he put with the bracelet and snuff-box first into a thick pair of gloves that happened to be in his pocket, and then tied them altogether in a pocket-handkerchief.

He then gave the same soft whistle as he had used before.

Again the boy advanced from the shadow of the wall into the light.

The handkerchief containing the gems was thrown to him by Batswing.

The lad dexterously caught them, and the next instant disappeared.

"There," said Batswing, "I am safe now," and he sauntered back into the ball room.

The scene here was if not awful, at least comic in the extreme.

Ladies stood with their dresses gathered round them, eyeing even their friends with suspicion.

"By Jove this is too bad," exclaimed Captain Jennings to Batswing.

"What is too bad?" demanded that gentleman taking a pinch of snuff.

"My dear fellow do you not know that there is a thief in the room?"

"I should be surprised if there was not," replied Batswing coolly, "seeing the number of people."

"But you do not understand me, Sir Jacob's snuff box has been stolen."

"So I heard," replied Batswing, "but is that any reason he should disturb his guests?"

"'Pon my word you are one of the coolest fellows I ever met in my life."

"Why should I not be; where is Sir Jacob? Let us go to him."

Taking his friend's arm, Batswing strolled up to the Alderman and said—

"Really my dear Sir Jacob, I am extremely sorry to think that you should have lost—"

"Lost!" exclaimed the Alderman, "it is not lost sir. it is stolen."

"Dear me: but now you have lost your snuff box, why lose your temper?"

"Temper sir; the box was given me by the Prince of Wales," cried the Alderman.

"I have no doubt about that, but would it not be better to set about clearing up the mystery instead of raving about it? The thief must still be in the room."

"Doubtless he is," said the Alderman, "but how am I to know him?"

"Let everyone be searched before they leave," replied Batswing.

"But I should insult all my guests," cried the poor alderman.

"Not a bit; those who are innocent will be glad to clear themselves, whilst the guilty person, whoever that may be, will be no loss to you. Come I will be searched first."

With an easy air Batswing slipped into a side room and was searched.

As may well be imagined, nothing was found upon him.

With a profusion of apologies the alderman shook hands and bowed both Batswing and the captain who also was searched, to the door.

"'Pon my word I can scarcely keep from laughing," cried Batswing.

"How so?" demanded the captain, "had it not been for you I would not have been searched."

"Tut man, what harm has it done you? Bah! you are too particular."

"But consider the disgrace," cried the captain sharply.

"Disgrace; what disgrace? It would have been more disgraceful had you refused."

"How so?" demanded the captain, cocking his hat and looking fierce.

"Do you not see? the first one who refuses to be searched will be looked upon as guilty."

"But had we all refused, what then?" cried the captain.

THE FATE OF ROUGH RALPH.

"What then? why then we should all have been suspected: each one by—his friends."

"But if the box is *not* found?" argued the captain, who was in a bad humour.

"Then the alderman has mislaid it. It becomes his mistake, and we are innocent. For my own part I don't believe it will be found."

"To be searched," muttered the captain, "such a disgrace."

They had just turned round a corner when a man darted out of a dark doorway.

He raised a bright blade, and the next moment would have plunged it in Batswing's heart.

Fortunately for our hero, at that very moment Captain Jennings seized the man's arm.

"Murderous scoundrel," cried the captain, "what would you do?"

"Thanks Captain," said Batswing quietly, "I owe

you my life. Trust me I will not forget the favour. Young man, give me that dagger," continued Batswing.

The young fellow threw the dagger on to the ground.

Batswing removed the would-be assassin's hat, and gazed in his face.

"So my young friend," cried Batswing laughing, "this is caused by jealousy."

"It is," cried the young fellow bitterly. "I saw you speaking to her in the balcony."

"The devil you did," cried Batswing hastily, "and what more did you see?"

"You kissed her, and then I fled or I should have killed you in her arms."

"Bah!" said Batswing greatly relieved to think the young fellow had seen no more, "you are mad. Besides my dear fellow, don't you see the girl don't care a fig for you."

"She does," cried the young fellow, "she has sworn it; promised to be mine."

"But my good lad does it not strike you that what you saw proves that she does not care for you?"

"I will not believe it," cried the youth, striking his forehead.

"If you will *not* believe it of course I cannot make you," replied Batswing.

"I demand satisfaction," cried the young man in a loud voice.

"Satisfaction!" cried Batswing, "I like your asking that after trying to murder me."

"My birth is equal to yours," cried the young fellow, "you cannot refuse me."

"What is your name then?" said Batswing good temperedly.

"My name is Walter Mervin," said the young fellow proudly.

"Then Walter Mervin thou art a very foolish fellow. Still I will oblige thee."

The two men put themselves in position, and the next moment Mervin was disarmed.

"Get thee gone lad," said Batswing, "and thank thy stars thou canst depart with a whole skin. Many a man has forfeited his life for a far less offence. And hark thee lad. Have nought to do with Mistress Marsh. She will not spare thee as I have done. Now go thy way and say no more."

The young man hung down his head and departed in silence.

When they were alone they walked on in silence until Captain Jennings said—

"Master Marvel, I cannot comprehend you at all."

"And why not, my good Captain?" asked Batswing.

"Of a surety you are a gentleman, your language and manners show us that."

"I thank you for your good opinion Captain," replied Batswing.

"You have money in plenty, fight like a man of honour, and yet—"

"And yet what?" demanded Batswing in a light airy tone.

"And yet you speak against a lady, you yourself keeping your life a secret."

"Captain Jennings," replied Batswing, "you have to-night saved my life, therefore I pardon you much; but remember, curiosity is a dangerous sin."

"But why speak against that lady just now? She is as fair as—"

"Sin," exclaimed Batswing, "mark me Captain Jennings, fly whilst there is yet time."

"Fly! why should I fly? Her sister Kate is lovely. I would die to save her."

"You *will* die to please her if you do not take my advice."

"You speak in riddles. If you know ought against her, speak plainly."

"I have spoken plainly," said Batswing, "you saw that boy, you heard what he said. This girl Zarah has sworn to love him. To-night she swore to love me, as also I am told she did a gentleman in a black domino. Can she be honest?"

For a moment Captain Jennings paused in amazement, and then said—

"Still I will not believe her sister is so. She may be a flirt, but Kate—"

"Is an angel of course," laughed Batswing, "although angels and flirts don't often mix together. However, I see you are determined to pursue your game. Do so, but you never did a luckier thing than saving my life to-night. Trust me I will return the debt in full. I only ask you to be cautious. And now good night, your way is over there; whilst yonder are my rooms."

"Good night," said the captain, "I thank you for your advice. We shall meet soon again."

CHAPTER LVII.

THE FENCE—THE TWO CLIENTS—THE BRACELET—THE JEW IN DIFFICULTIES.

WHEN Batswing left his friend, he turned as if going home, but quickly seemed to alter his determination; for, passing his own door, he entered a small court which ran down the side of his house.

Here he found a lad waiting for him with a small bundle.

"Is that you, Jerry?" he asked sharply.

"That's me, sir, sure enough," replied Jerry; "I've a note for you."

"Indeed! where is it?" said Batswing, as he took from the bundle a large cloak, a rough riding coat, and a slouched hat, on which he rapidly changed his own handsome garments, putting them back into the bundle.

"Here's the note, sir," said Jerry, holding out a small letter.

"How did it come?" demanded Batswing. "I see it is addressed to 'The Bat.'"

"No one knows how it come," said Jerry; "it was flung into the window of the Three Cutters."

Batswing completed his toilet, which gave him the appearance of a roystering blade.

Having done this, he stood under a lamp and managed to read the note.

"By heavens, it is from Alice," he exclaimed; "meet her at Tillingham: then she must still be there! Stay, is this not some trick to ensnare me? Why should she wish me to come alone? Well, let what will happen I will be there."

"Is it good news, cap'pen?" asked Jerry, touching his hat.

"I cannot say," replied Batswing; "you must haste at once to Toby Crick and see that my horse is well groomed and fed; have her well looked to: much may depend upon that.

You must have her ready saddled the first thing in the morning: for I must leave London by day-break. Now go. Stay, where is the bundle I threw you from the window?"

"Here you are, cap'pen; they are all right and tight."

"Now go, and mind my orders are thoroughly obeyed."

Jerry Blinker touched his forelock and hurried quickly away.

Pulling his hat well over his eyes Batswing turned his face eastward, and crossing Holborn Bars turned up Gray's Inn Lane, along which he proceeded at a rapid rate until he came to a dirty ruinous wooden house.

He cast one rapid glance up to the windows, but not a light was to be seen.

Knocking gently three times at the door, he placed his ear to the panel and listened.

Presently he heard the shuffling, as of some one in slippers, walking in the house.

Again he knocked gently, and this time his knocks were repeated inside the door.

"The old rascal knows the tap," he muttered; "why can't he let me in?"

Again he knocked, and the knocks were answered in such a manner that it was evident that the person inside was capable of conversing with our hero by raps.

"Confound the old brute, he is up to some of his games," said the Bat; "he signals danger."

He stood for some time looking sharply up and down the street.

"This is a trick," he exclaimed at last; "no one is near, I *will* go in."

He gave one or two sharp raps, and the door was opened a little way, the chain being kept up.

"What is the meaning of this, Ikey?" he demanded. "You know I will not be played with."

"Play vith you, my tear," exclaimed the Jew, who was a blear-eyed dirty little man.

"S'elp me, vy should I play vid you now. Now go avay, there's a tear, there's danger."

"There will be danger for you if you do not do as I wish," cried Batswing.

"Oh, you vill ruin us all, you vill ruin us all," cried Ikey.

"Ruin you? I have come to make your fortune. So open the door at once."

The Jew, seeing that Batswing was determined, opened the door slowly.

"There," said Batswing, as he entered, "why could you not do that at once?"

"You see the runners have begun to get suspicious," said the Jew.

"Begun!" laughed Batswing; "they ought to have done that when you were born."

"But they are very suspicious now, really: do go avay as soon as you can."

"Well, show me to your office, Ikey; I won't detain you very long."

Taking a wretched candle that was fixed in a lump of clay the old man led the way up the creaking stairs, shuffling along in his slippers, which were down at heel and showed his toes through the points.

He was dressed in a greasy dressing-gown that hung down to his heels.

A greasy skull cap was on his head, but so ragged was it that his hair came through many a hole, looking like tufts of silver.

Sniffing and snuffling as if he had a cronic cold the old man mounted the stairs.

It was a miserably dirty house, with a damp musty smell about it.

Large lumps of the plaster were broken from the wall, and showed the laths beneath.

At length they reached a miserable apartment, where, putting the candle on the table, Ikey turned round and, facing Batswing, demanded what he wanted.

"Money, to be sure," replied Batswing, as he threw himself into a chair.

"Holy Moses, be careful," called out Ikey, "you'll smash the chair to pieces."

"Never mind your chair, Ikey, look at this," cried Batswing, showing the bracelet.

"Holy Moses, this is very beautiful," cried Ikey in rapture.

"Yes, they are of the right water, and make your mouth water too."

"Oh, they are splendid," cried the Jew; "they are beautiful."

"Well, and what will you give me for that?" demanded Batswing.

"I'm a poor man," said the Jew sorrowfully, but I'll give you fifty pounds."

"Fifty pounds!" cried Batswing, "are you mad to offer such an amount."

"But look here, captain," cried the Jew, "I am so short of monish."

"Ikey: you are an abominable liar; hand me over two hundred pounds for it."

"I can't, indeed, I can't," cried Ikey, looking about uneasily.

"What the deuce is the matter with you?" demanded Batswing, "can't you sit still."

"Yes, yes, my good Captain," said Ikey, "but you want too much monish."

"Too much, why the diamonds are worth twice as much."

"Yes, yes, but I am poor, very, very poor, indeed," groaned the Jew.

"I have had enough of that, Ikey," replied Batswing, "I must have the money."

The old Jew did not appear to hear the last sentence, but started violently, and listened.

"Why, what's up now, Ikey," demanded Batswing, sharply, "I don't like your looks."

"Nothing, oh! nothing," returned the man, turning deadly pale, "I thought I heard—"

Again the Jew paused and listened intently, the cold sweat breaking out on his brow, and his lean, bony hands trembling with emotion.

"Look here, Ikey," said Batswing, firmly, "there is something wrong here; what is it?"

"Nothing, on my vord," replied the Jew, "only the Robbins have been watching me, and I am afraid they suspect my business. Ah, and its a poor one too."

"Cannot you speak for once without lying, you old Fence," said Batswing.

"Well, well, don't be hard upon me, Captain, don't be hard upon me; I'll give you the two 'undred pounds, only go at once. Promise me that you will go at once."

"Give me the money, Ikey, and I will soon relieve myself of your presence."

Unlocking a chest that stood in one corner, the Jew drew forth a bag of gold. With many a bitter groan and trembling hands he counted out the pieces.

"There, there," he cried, "there is your money, now go, now go."

The Jew's agitation and hurry to get rid of our hero was so evident, that Batswing felt but little inclined obey the old man, and, therefore, counted the money as slowly as he possibly could, at the same time keeping an eye on the Jew's anxious face.

He had scarcely pocketed the money, when he heard the street door open.

The Jew started to his feet and clasped his hands as if in deepest anguish.

"What is the meaning of this," demanded Batswing, sharply, "have you betrayed me?"

"No, by Abraham's beard I have not," moaned the Jew, "but he will."

"He, whom do you mean?" whispered Batswing, hurriedly.

"The man who has just entered this house. Oh! you are lost."

Batswing could hear the footsteps as the new comer crept up stairs.

"If I am betrayed," he muttered, "I will at all events sell my life as dear as possible."

The footsteps were close upon the door, when Batswing, perceiving an old cabinet, sprang into it, and pulling the door after him, held it so that he could see into the room and hear all that was passing without being seen, whilst at the same time he could take deadly aim at the Jew with a pistol which he had drawn from his belt.

"Hark thee my Hebrew friend," cried Batswing, "if you betray me I will blow your brains out. If you make one sign to warn the stranger of my presence, or if he attempt to raise an alarm I will kill you, not him. Remember that, and be careful."

The Jew looked in horror at the glittering pistol barrel, but did not move.

The next moment the door opened and the stranger strode into the room.

He was a big burly man, closely wrapped in a large cloak.

A huge flap hat was pulled down so as to conceal his features.

"How now, Ikey," he cried, "what ails thee, man? did you not hear the signal?"

"I—I was fast asleep, my master," stammered Ikey Joel.

"Fast asleep? I would I could have caught you at that moment. It would to my thinking be as difficult to catch a Jew asleep as a weasel."

"You are pleased to be merry," grinned Ikey Joel, trying to look at ease.

"There you are wrong, you patriarchial scare-crow. I am infernally dull."

"Dull!" cried the Jew shrugging his shoulders; "you the rich, the brave, dull?"

"Aye, tremendously so," cried the man flinging himself into a chair, so that his back was towards the cupboard in which Batswing was concealed, "dull as ditch water; so get me a bumper of your best canary to try to drown these megrims."

The Jew glanced uneasily at the cupboard, for he feared to move; but seeing that the pistol barrel was pointed towards the stranger, he rightly judged that it was a sign that he might get the wine, leaving the stranger as a hostage.

The wine was soon put upon the board, and the stranger drank bumper after bumper.

The Jew watched his wine going with a sorrowful face, but did not utter a word.

In vain did Batswing try to see the stranger's face. He fancied he knew his voice, or at least he was certain he had heard it before, but he could not tell where.

"Well, Ikey, I feel better now," cried the man, "much better."

Ikey groaned as he beheld the almost empty flask of wine.

"I went to the fancy ball at Sir Jacob Hide's this 'ening," said the stranger.

"Indeed," replied the Jew; "I trust you enjoyed yourself. What character did you go in?"

"Not in my *own*, you may swear," laughed the other. "I went there on business."

"Were you successful?" demanded the Jew glancing uneasily towards the cupboard.

"Hang it, no," replied the man; "luck seems dead against me."

"May I enquire what your business was?" asked the Jew, who seemed in such a state of nervousness that he scarcely knew what he was saying; but he added quickly, "but what does that matter, seeing that you were unfortunate. It's best not to talk of these things."

"And why not, between old friends?" demanded the man, who evidently had been drinking. "We have no spies here, I suppose? If there were, I'd stop their peaching."

"Surely, surely you would," cried the trembling Jew. "Sit down and tell me your business."

"I went to the ball to steal Sir Jacob's presentation diamond snuff box."

"Well!" enquired the Jew, "and you did so; of course you could not fail."

"I beg your pardon, I would not have failed, but unfortunately some d——d thief had been before me. The robbery was discovered, the company searched, but not a thing found."

Batswing could scarcely refrain from laughing when he heard this story told in such doleful tones.

"I am sorry, very sorry you have been so unsuccessful," said the Jew.

"I'd be sworn you are," laughed the other, "you wanted your share, of course."

"But you wrote to me on some business that you wished to see me about."

"Ah! yes. Have you ever had any dealings with one Batswing?"

Had the Jew seen a ghost, he could not have looked more scared than he did.

What could he say? If he admitted anything against Batswing, there was little doubt that his life would answer for it; whilst if his companion happened to discover that their conversation had been overheard, it was more than probable all his fury would fall on the unlucky Jew.

"What is the matter with you, Ikey?" demanded the stranger.

"I—I don't feel well," groaned the Jew.

"I don't wonder at it, stived up in this horrible home," said the stranger.

"Yes, it is very close in here," gasped the old man wiping his forehead.

"Take a glass of wine," cried the stranger, "and answer me that question. Do you know Batswing? Have you had any dealings with him?"

"I have seen him once or twice," stammered the Jew.

"I need not ask you on what business he came," said the stranger. "Look here, Ikey; you and I are old friends, and you must stick tight to me."

"I always do, don't I?" pleaded Ikey. "I always serve you faithfully."

"Up to the present time you have, and you must now do me a service of some danger; but it will also be of good profit. I know that this same Batswing has had dealings with you, and that you can find him at any time. I should'nt wonder but that you could put your finger on him at once."

"Me?" screamed the Jew. "Holy Moses, how could I do that?"

"Don't look so startled, Ikey," laughed the man; "I don't suppose he is here."

"No, no," cried Ikey greatly relieved, "of course he is not here, how could he be?"

"For all that, a letter from you would bring him here in twenty-four hours."

"But what do you want him for?" demanded Ikey.

"I want him to be delivered up to justice. The full price is on his head now, so Mr. Wild and myself have determined to put a stop to his games. Beside, we have other reasons for determining to crush the gentleman."

"But he is not so easily caught," cried the Jew, "and his vengeance is awful."

"Tut, tut, you shall be all safe. You must write to him, and state that you have private intelligence to give him. Tell him that he must be here by twelve o'clock to-morrow night, and—"

"Not to-morrow, not to-morrow," gasped the Jew, "the night after will be better, or—"

"Well, the night after, if you like; but mind, not later. I will have some men ready to receive the gentleman, and before morning he shall sleep in Newgate, and you will pocket a cool couple of hundred."

The Jew's feelings when he heard that statement can be better imagined than described.

He watched the pistol barrel, and every moment expected to hear the click of the lock.

"I must go now," said the stranger rising. "See that you have everything prepared as I have said."

As he spoke he removed his gloves from the table on which he had thrown them.

In doing so, his eye happened to fall upon the diamond bracelet which Ikey in his confusion had not quite hidden.

With a muttered imprecation, he snatched up the jewel and examined it closely.

"By heavens, it *is* the same. Where did you get this from?"

"I—I bought it this night," stammered the Jew.

"To night? Ay, I'll be sworn you did, for this evening I saw it on a lady's arm."

"Indeed," muttered the Jew, who began to think all escape was hopeless.

"Yes, sir; and that lady was no other than my daughter," continued the stranger.

"Your daughter?"

"Yes, my daughter. Look here, Ikey Joel; you and you only know my secret. I know you will not betray me, for if you were to, you would swing as well as I. My daughter Zarah, as you know, was at Sir Hide's ball—"

"Stop, stop, for mercy stop," cried Ikey, "you should not speak of these thinks. Secrets should not even be breathed. Who knows who might hear you."

"Hear me? Who can hear me in this place? Why, what's up now, Ikey?"

"I—I'm not well; I'm nervous, very nervous. Living alone makes me so."

For a moment the man watched Ikey closely, and then

tarned quickly away, pushing his hat from his face as he wiped his forehead.

In that moment Batswing recognised the man——it was *Farmer Croft*.

"May be it is dull here," he said. "From whom did you buy this bracelet?"

"I bought it."

"Indeed! who from?"

"A boy was sent with it—a boy as used to be down at the Fleet."

"Phew! then my friend Batswing must be the man?" cried the other.

"I don't know," said the Jew, doggedly; "the boy's a link-boy, and may have found it."

"That may be so," muttered Croft, "how much did you give for it?"

"Two hundred pounds," grumbled the Jew.

"What! you gave two hundred pounds for this bracelet?"

"Yes, and its worth it too," replied the Jew.

"Worth it! its worth three times as much; but you would not give that sum to a boy? No, no, Ikey, you would make him take less."

"Make him take less! You don't know those boys," grumbled the Jew; "they know the value of things just as well as we do; they ain't to be done, I can assure you. That's why our business ain't as good as it used to be."

"Well, Ikey, I won't rob you of this two hundred; I'll take the bracelet and you shall have the money. Remember, the word must be carried to Batswing as soon as possible. If you fail me in this, beware!"

"Oh, I will not fail, he shall have what you say: but if he won't come, how am I to help that? He is very obstinate, and may refuse."

"Bah! word your letter rightly and he will come. Make the bait tempting and never fear that that he will bite. And now, good night. Show me a light down your stairs; they're so ricketty that I wonder you have not broken your neck long ago."

Farmer Croft walked to the door as he spoke, and throwing wide open gazed out into the dark passage down the old tumble-down stairs.

Ikey Joel seized the candle, and, shading it with his hand, hurried towards the door.

The Jew gave one glance behind him and saw that Batswing had opened the cupboard door and was still pointing the pistol at him.

Farmer Croft passed down the stairs, Ikey following with the candle.

Once the Jew felt inclined to whisper to Croft that the conversation had been overheard, but, happening to glance behind him, he discovered that Batswing was gliding after them.

The next moment the farmer had opened the door, and, wishing the Jew a surly good night, was gone.

More dead than alive Ikey returned with Batswing to the room.

"So Mr. Joel," cried Batswing, when they were alone; "this is the way you treat friends."

"I could not help it; indeed I could not. You don't know that man's power."

"I know this: if you dare to try and deceive me, you will not last a moment after. I have a chance of putting a couple of bullets into you. You can't escape."

Ikey groaned audibly, but returned no answer.

"If, on the other hand," continued Batswing, "you serve me all will be well for you."

"But the farmer," gasped Ikey, who evidently feared that between the two men he should come to the ground. "How am I to pacify him?"

"By doing all that was asked of you to do. You need not send me the message, as I have heard that already; but you may tell Mr. Croft that at twelve o'clock the night after to-morrow he may be here, for I am certain to come soon after that time. By doing this you will satisfy him, but be careful that you do not hint that I have been here, or your life will answer it. Now, good night."

Without deigning any further conversation, Batswing strode away.

CHAPTER LVIII.

THE MEETING ON THE CLIFF—THE FIGHT.—END OF ROUGH RALPH.

A DARK night, with a driving wind bearing rain in its black bosom.

The hoarse roar of the sea could be heard miles inland, and its spray made the chill air salt and dank.

Far over the cliffs could be seen the blinking lights from the cottages scattered; whilst, far down in the hollow, was the little village where the fishermen lived, and its snug little port, where their smacks were safely moored out of the raging storm.

It was not a cheerful night to be out in, especially on the cliff-tops, for it was so dark, and the grass was so slippery from the wet, that there was great danger of falling over.

Batswing, however, had determined to keep the appointment made in Alice's letter. He knew that it was her writing, but doubted if she had written it of her own will. Still he was determined to keep the appointment, in case she should wish it.

Having arrived at the spot mentioned some half-hour before the time, Batswing crouched down in a hollow and waited patiently to see if Alice came.

To wait for any one is never pleasant; but, on a dark night, with a fair share of rain falling, to have to wait for a person who may be a foe in disguise, is most uncomfortable.

Batswing turned uneasily round in his cramped position and listened carefully.

Not a sound could he hear but the sighing of the storm as it passed away.

Suddenly the clouds broke assunder and the full moonlight came streaming down, showing the white crests of the waves silvered by her light.

It was now past the appointed time, and Batswing was about giving up all hopes of seeing Alice, when he was startled by a sound close by him.

A few paces from him was a bush, which in the darkness he had not perceived.

Forcing his way stealthily through the bush was a man.

The fellow paused and looked round him carefully as if waiting for some one.

"It's no use," he growled, "he won't come; he's not such a fool.

Batswing examined the man carefully, but so good was the disguise that even our hero, clever as he was at detecting such practices, failed to recognise Rough Ralph. He however knew Lord Redfern's livery, and that put him on his guard.

The man crouched down behind the bush again, evidently to conceal himself.

"I wonder whether that fellow is alone?" thought Batswing; "if so I would not mind him."

It was in vain however that he strove to catch a glimpse behind the bush, so as to gain the information he required, his only satisfaction was to know that the bush was too small to conceal more than two men.

Taking the advantage of the moon being overclouded for a few seconds, he stole from his hiding-place, and, making a slight detour, walked rapidly towards the bush, so that it might appear that he had only just arrived.

When he had approached within some half-dozen yards of the spot Rough Ralph sprang from the place of his concealment, and, touching his hat respectfully, asked, in a feigned voice, "whether he was the gentleman as had come to meet Mistress Alice Landon?"

"I am," replied Batswing, stepping back a pace or two and placing his hand upon his sword, so as to be ready to stand on the defensive should circumstances require it.

"Then, yer honour, she has sent me to say that she can't come."

"Indeed! may I ask you where she found so trusty a messenger?"

"Why, you see, she is at Lord Redfern's, and I'm his coachman."

This last information made Batswing still more cautious than ever.

"You must excuse me," he replied, quickly, "but unless you have some proof that you are sent by that unfortunate lady, I shall refuse all conversation with you. You must know that your master is the chief cause of all that lady's misery, and therefore one bearing his livery is scarcely the man to be trusted."

"There you are right, sir," replied Ralph, in a soft tone, "and sorry am I that I do bear his livery, for there's little to get in his service but blows. He seems to think that poor people don't feel like rich folk. Maybe he's right, but if so, I'll make him suffer in a few moments all that he has made me bear for years."

"You hate him, then?" enquired Batswing.

"I do, with all my heart and soul," growled Ralph, with such vehemence that Batswing could not help trusting him. He little knew that Rough Ralph by nature hated all mankind, and took pleasure in tormenting them.

"And what message has the fair Alice sent me?" demanded our hero.

"She says that Lord Redfern holds her a prisoner, and wishes to compel her to marry him. This, he owns, is not for love, but for some reason he won't explain. She therefore wishes you to tell her if you know the cause, and if not to find it out for her, so that she may know how to baffle him."

For a moment Batswing paused. Could this story be true? It was possible; indeed he could not doubt but that there was some mystery about Alice, or such a man as Lord Redfern would not be anxious to marry her.

He was about to step up close to Rough Ralph when he fancied he heard a strange rattling noise in the hedge. Could there be another man there listening?

It was so slight a sound that he fancied he must be mistaken.

However, he determined to act with the greatest caution.

"And where does Lord Redfern keep his prisoner?" asked Batswing.

"She is imprisoned at Tillingham Hall," replied Rough Ralph.

Now this was the most unfortunate mistake Ralph could make, for Roaring Ric had played his cards so well that Batswing knew that Alice was certainly not at the Hall; and therefore this answer at once aroused his suspicions.

"Is she so strictly guarded that she could not escape?" he asked.

"That she is, poor creature," replied the man; "my heart aches for her."

"There is some money for your sympathy, honest fellow," said Batswing. "Meet me here to-morrow and I will bring you an answer for Mistress Alice."

As he spoke he gave Ralph a guinea, and, turning on his heel, walked away, being determined to consider how he should answer these questions; for, although he could not prove them false, yet the last answers caused him to be very doubtful as to the messenger's veracity.

He had scarcely made two steps when he received a violent blow on the shoulder.

Placing his hand on the part, he found he had been wounded.

Luckily, the thick coat and cloak he wore had turned the dagger on one side, so that the wound was of the slightest.

Quickly turning round, he grappled with his powerful antagonist before he could repeat the blow.

At that moment the moon beamed forth, and Batswing, glancing at the hedge, beheld Jonathan Wild grinning demoniacally as he beheld the struggle. Both were powerful men, and the fight was a fierce one.

Batswing, although a much lighter man than his antagonist, possessed a greater amount of skill, and was dragging Rough Ralph towards the edge of the cliff, for he plainly saw the struggle must be one of life or death.

No sooner did Ralph perceive what was Batswing's design than his courage forsook him, and consequently he became an easy conquest.

Vainly he struggled and cried for help; he was now on the brink of the precipice.

Still Batswing could not throw him over, for fear, which had deprived him of the power to continue the struggle, had endowed him with wonderful strength to grasp his opponent in an embrace of iron.

"Save me, save me, master," screamed the wretch, in mortal terror.

Batswing knew that if Jonathan Wild came to the man's rescue all chance of his escaping would be gone. He therefore redoubled his efforts to throw the man.

Planting his right foot firmly on the ground, he swung himself round on it.

At the same time Jonathan Wild discharged a pistol at him.

A wild shriek rang through the night, and Rough Ralph relaxed his grasp.

He had received the bullet intended for Batswing.

The next moment our hero had hurled the man from him.

The unhappy man clutched at the grass as he fell.

For a few seconds it kept him hanging over the precipice.

Then slowly it gave way, and with a deep groan he disappeared.

Batswing paused in horror as he heard the heavy thud as the man fell against the cliff, followed by the splash as the sea received him. He then turned to seek for Jonathan Wild, but he had fled on witnessing Rough Ralph's fate.

CHAPTER LIX.

FARMER CROFT SETS HIS TRAP. THE RESULT.

FARMER CROFT did not fail to keep his appointment with old Ikey.

The clock had scarcely tolled out midnight when he drove up to the old Jew's house.

He gave the usual signal; the door opened, and he entered.

"Well," he demanded sharply of the Jew, "he has not cried off?"

"No," said the Jew, shaking his head sorrowfully; "but, Mishter Croft, do be careful."

"Careful! what have I got to be careful about?" demanded Croft, with a laugh.

"Don't be too venturesome with this Batswing; he's not to be trusted."

"Not to be trusted!" laughed Croft; "ha, ha, ha, I should rather think he was not."

"But I don't mean that, Mishter Croft. I really think this Batswing aint mortal."

"We shall see that to-night," said the farmer. I have a good force of constables at the corner of the street, who at a whistle will surround the house."

"But you won't call them in here?" demanded the terrified Jew.

"Indeed I shall, old Joel," replied Croft. "Come, no flinching. You shall be safe enough."

"Holy Moses," groaned the Jew; "only to think of constables in my house."

"It's better that they should be in your house than you in their's."

The old Jew groaned audibly, but made no answer.

"Well old Ikey, I will take care that no harm shall befall you," said Croft, "only obey me. Now, these are my plans. Batswing must be admitted in here, you must tell him that you have reason to know that my Lord Russell will be on the North road to-morrow, having with him property to a vast amount, and but badly guarded. You understand me? Well, while you are doing this, I will, from the window in the room above, whistle twice. The house will be surrounded, Batswing secured, and handed over to the constables and the tender mercies of his friend Mr. Pitt."

"Yes, I understand, I understand," said the Jew hurridly.

"Hush! what is that?" demanded the farmer.

"That is his signal. Don't let him see you here, for he would escape."

"Oh! then you are anxious to have him arrested now, are you?"

"Of course I am. Do you think he would let me live if he thought I betrayed him?"

"Perhaps not," said Croft; "so you had better see that you make no mistake."

"I suppose I had better let him in?" demanded the Jew.

"Yes, or he may grow suspicious; therefore, go and admit him. I will take up my post."

Farmer Croft crept stealthily upstairs, and placed himself in the room above that in which the Jew was to receive Batswing.

After he had lighted Croft upstairs, Joel made his way slowly to the street door.

The usual form of blows was gone through, and Ikey opened the door.

Placing his finger on his lip, Batswing whispered softly, "Has he come yet?"

"Yes," replied the Jew, "he's upstairs, and he has given me these directions."

In a low voice the Jew rapidly recounted all that Farmer Croft had told him.

"It is well," said Batswing, "we will catch him in his own trap. Drop your light."

The Jew with many a curse dropped his light upon the floor.

Whilst the old man was making loud lamentations and apoligies, so that Croft could hear them, Batswing stepped to the door, and hastily whispered a few words to a man who was stationed outside.

He then returned to the Jew, and uttering many imprecations, bade him get a light.

He then proceeded upstairs, stumbling and cursing as he went.

They entered the room, and Ikey Joel soon relit his candle.

"Look here, Ikey," cried Batswing passionately, "I don't like this sort of thing."

Ikey gave a quick glance towards our hero, and catching his meaning, said,

"Vot is it ash you don't like, my tear? Don't you like good business?"

"Good business," retorted Batswing, "yes, I do like that, but I don't like those fellows."

"Those fellows? vot fellows?" asked the Jew innocently, at the same time grinning silly.

"You know well enough; the fellows lurking in this street."

"Fellows in the street! I know no fellows in the street," said the Jew.

All this conversation had been carried on in so loud a voice that Croft could hear it.

"Dash the fellows," he muttered, "he evidently suspects something is wrong."

"Don't be frightened, my tear," continued the Jew; "you're not well to-night. Have some wine."

"Bravo Joel," grinned Croft to himself: "the Jew is safe enough."

"Yes, let me have wine, my old patriarch. Wine is a glorious thing; wine, wine!"

Croft could hear the glasses clink, and was delighted to think how tipsy Batswing was getting, and what an easy victim he would be.

He heard the Jew relate how Lord Russell would soon be on the road, and that there was an immense amount of jewels to be had; to all of which Batswing replied by oaths that the booty should be his, and that Joel should have his share.

He then roared out snatches of songs, and commenced giving health after health with such rapidity that Croft felt certain that all would be ready in a very short time.

Gently raising the window, he made ready to give the signal.

At that moment he heard the Jew calling him in a low whisper.

"What the devil is it now?" demanded Croft savagely. "Why do you risk doing this?"

"There is no risk about it at all, my tear," said the Jew, "he's fast asleep."

"Fast asleep, is he? Well, I will only just give the signal and creep down to you."

He crept back to the window, gave the signal, and soon had the satisfaction of hearing it repeated.

He then descended the stairs, and found the Jew trembling with fear in a corner.

"What's the matter with you?" demanded Croft, "what are you trembling at?"

"Him," replied the Jew, pointing at Batswing; "he's frightened me so."

Farmer Croft glanced at Batswing, who appeared to be sound asleep, his head resting on his folded arms, which were placed on the table.

"Don't go near him," cried Ikey, "look what he has got in his hands."

Farmer Croft did look, and started back at what he saw.

Grasped firmly in each hand was a pistol, the index finger placed carelssly on the triggers, and the barrels pointed severally in the direction of Croft and the Jew.

"How the devil is this?" cried Croft springing back, "you said he was asleep."

"So he is, but he fell asleep in that position. I think he always sleeps so."

"Confound it; why don't you open the door and call in the fellows?" muttered Croft between his teeth.

"I have opened the door by this spring," said the Jew showing one in the wall. "Why don't they come?"

Croft looked uneasily round, and muttering something between his teeth, hastened to the door.

He had just placed his hand on the handle when it was thrown open.

With a cry of terror he staggered back. *They were not his men.*

He turned round towards the Jew to seek for some explanation.

There, transfixed as if with terror, sat the old man, his hands tightly clasped.

Opposite to him stood Batswing, no longer asleep, but with one pistol presented straight at the Jew and the other at Croft.

"Come in, gentlemen," said Batswing with a merry laugh; "don't stand on ceremony, come in."

"What is the meaning of this?" gasped Croft turning pale as death.

"Meaning?" replied Batswing, "why, that a trap was laid for me and you have fallen into it."

"Mercy, mercy," groaned Ikey, who, as the reader will perceive, was only acting a part, but who deemed it advisable not to offend Farmer Croft.

"Mercy!" laughed Batswing; "yes, I'll have mercy on you, you rascals,"

"What have I done to injure you?" demanded Croft of Batswing.

"Rather let me ask you that question since you have been so anxious for my capture."

"How so? I never saw you in my life before," cried Farmer Croft.

"Indeed!" laughed Batswing; "have you ever heard this song before?"

In a mellow voice he commenced chanting—

"You cracksmen and footpads who want a good treat,
Why just pad your hoofs and be off to the Fleet;
There's 'baccy and spirits, and lots of good beer,
And never a dubsman or robin to fear."

"By jingo, you're one of us," cried Croft; "tip us your daddle."

"Pardon me," replied Batswing; "but, before we come to such friendly terms, I must trouble you to explain one or two little things; trifles in themselves, perhaps, but all put together, of the utmost consequence to me."

"Why, you cannot have forgotten that night in the Fleet?" said Croft.

"I certainly have not forgotten it, neither do I think it likely I shall."

"Well, we are in the same swim you know and—"

"Pardon me for a moment," said Batswing; "if we are in the same swim, why have you been so treacherous as to try to betray me? On the night down at the Fleet you sent for Jonathan Wild: it was you who forced this poor old Jew to send for me. Think you that I cannot tell *all* that has happened? Do you think I should have escaped so often if I had not more than mortal power? No; I saw you on the beach at Tillingham. I saw you in the hut by the forest when you would have arrested one whom I guard from the evil fangs of Jonathan Wild and Lord Redfern. I will spare your life, but you must not escape unpunished."

Springing back Farmer Croft placed himself against the wall and presented a pistol at Batswing.

"Keep back," he exclaimed, "or I fire; I am not one to be taken in by such stories."

"Are you mad that you would tempt me to do you more harm?" said Batswing.

"I will not surrender," cried Croft; "how can I trust you?"

How much further the dispute might have gone is hard to say, for at that moment one of Batswing's followers drawing forth a snuff-box discharged all the contents in Croft's eyes, causing him to drop the pistol in his pain.

In a moment he was seized and bound tightly.

By Batswing's orders he was then stripped of his clothing, and a suit of clothes which they had brought for the purpose were substituted for the others.

He was then not only gagged but a large cloak was bound tightly over his head. Inside this cloak Batswing placed a letter addressed to Jonathan Wild.

"Now, my lads," cried Batswing, "bear him along, but be cautious."

Batswing, wrapped up in the large cloak that Croft had used, led the way down the stairs into the street. He took the first turning leading to Gray's Inn Gardens, and close by those then charming grounds he found some constables with a hackney coach waiting to receive him,

"Here's your man," said Batswing, imitating Croft's voice; "we have had no end of trouble to take him."

"Shall we put him in the coach?" asked one of the constables.

"To be sure," replied Batswing; "one of you had better go in with him. I will go on before to the gaol to see all is ready for him. We shall need heavy irons for him."

He had scarcely spoken when Croft somehow succeeded in getting the gag from his mouth and commenced shouting loudly for help.

In a minute Batswing had grasped him by the throat and struck him a blow over the head with a pistol that stunned him.

"I say comrade," said one of the men, "aint that agoing it a little too far?"

"If you had had the trouble we have had with him you would not be so particular," replied Batswing. "Come, don't waste more time, but be off at once."

The men sprung in their places, and in a minute all was ready.

"I will follow," cried Batswing; "I shall be there as soon as you are."

"Aint your honour going to take your horse?" asked one of the men.

"Curse me, the fellow has given us so much trouble that I nearly forgot my horse."

Perceiving that the men glanced suspiciously at each other, Batswing swung himself on the horse that he had not noticed as it was standing behind the coach, and bidding the men to follow dashed quickly away.

"I say Bill," said one of the men, "did you notice that?"

"Yes, I did; I'm blest if he seemed to know where his horse was."

"I'm bles't if I think its him at all," replied the other.

"Nonsense, whom else could it be?" asked Bill; "besides, he's gone the right way."

"Well, don't let us loose time, but hurry after him as quickly as we can, that's all."

Acting on this advice, they drove off, and soon arrived at the entrance to Newgate, where they found Mr. Pitt all anxiety for their return.

The cloaked figure was dragged into the lodge and the cloak removed.

The men all gave a cry of amazement as they recognised the features of Farmer Croft.

"Why, what is this?" shouted Mr. Pitt; "this aint Batswing."

"I'm blest if I don't think that fellow is the devil himself," said one of the men.

"Here is a letter, sir," said one, picking up that which Batswing had put in the cloak, and which had fallen unobserved to the ground.

Mr. Pitt seized the letter, and tore it open without looking to whom it was addressed.

The contents were as follows:—

"MY DEAR JONATHAN,—

The old saying of 'set a thief to catch a thief' has in this case succeeded remarkably well, but not quite as well as you wished. I send you back your lieutenant, Croft, and trust you will make much of him, for he has suffered much for your sake. I warn you to beware how far you proceed with your worthless companions. Redfern will soon be in my power, for Lord Leslie will return to England to expose him. W shall meet again, when I hope to return your kind attention of the other night, but with better success.

I remain.
Yours at liberty,
THE BAT."

By this time Farmer Croft had revived, and, starting from his chair, he commenced abusing the constables for having permitted such a trick to have been played upon them, and also for their allowing Batswing to give them the slip.

"How are we to know?" retorted the men. "We should have been all right if you had not altered your orders. You first tell us to do one thing and then the other, so that I'm blest if one knows what to do at all."

"I alter my orders!" shouted Croft; "when did I alter my orders?"

"SLOWLY THE LADY TURNED ROUND AND GAZED TOWARDS REDFERN. IT WAS MAUD!"

"Why, directly almost after you left us, you sent a man back with the watchword, to tell us to wait near the Gardens, and not to come unless you sent the fellow for us, as Batswing was alone and could be easily captured."

"I never sent anyone to you," roared Croft, stamping with rage.

"But how did the fellow know the password then?" asked one.

Two of the men felt inwardly that they could have answered that question, for, while lighting their pipes at a link which a boy carried, they had casually remarked that "the word, *diamond bracelet*, was a queer one. They had no doubt but that the link-boy was one of Batswing's numerous agents, but they thought it much better to remain silent on that point.

"I see it all!" screamed Croft; "it is that wretched old Jew who has done this."

20

"A Jew!" asked Mr. Pitt; "do you mean the man in whose house the arrest was to be made?"

"Yes; he is the one who has betrayed us. He has betrayed us all."

"Do you know anything about him?" asked Mr. Pitt, suspiciously.

"No; that is, he had a reward from Mr. Wild to give up Batswing."

A gleam of delight shot over the governor's face as he asked, anxiously—

"Did Mr. Jonathan Wild pay for the reward before he had his man?"

"No, curse it, no," growled Farmer Croft; "but I did. I made so sure of him."

"He, he, he," laughed Mr. Pitt, delighted to see others done as well as himself; "he, he, he. Only to think of that now. You made sure of him, and he made sure of you."

"It may be very funny to you, sir," cried Croft. "I

think it would be much better if you were to try what can be done, instead of standing there giggling like a—like a—"

"Like a what, sir?" demanded Mr. Pitt, in a rage. "I won't be called names in my own prison, by you or by anyone else."

"Your own prison," retorted Croft; "I think it ought to be your prison indeed!"

"What do you mean by that base insinuation;" cried the governor.

"I think, sir, you ought to be imprisoned for neglect of duty, sir."

"What neglect of duty do you mean, sir?" cried Mr. Pitt."

"Why, sir, this prison is getting quite a disgrace, sir; quite a disgrace. Why, the prisoners have more liberty here than they have when they are free. Free! if it were not that they are so comfortable here, they soon would be free."

"What do you mean by that?" cried the governor, red with passion.

"Can you deny it, sir?" retorted Croft. "Has not that notorious scamp, Jack Sheppard, broken out of this 'stronghold?'"—this word was said very contemptuously. "Yes, sir, you may look red, but it is a fact; he broke out of this *stronghold* with ease, and yet, sir, he is only a lad—a mere lad."

"Jack Sheppard, sir!" cried the governor; "who can hold him? Why, the devil himself could not hold that young vagabond."

"Perhaps that is the reason you can't succeed," sneered Croft.

"Since you are so clever," said Mr. Pitt, "perhaps you'll advise what shall be done."

"I should advise you not to read Mr. Wild's letters," cried Croft, who had just seen the address on the one the governor held in his hand; "he does not like such freedom."

In a moment Mr. Pitt threw the letter on the ground in fright.

"Secondly, I should advise you to send some men with me to search the Jew's house."

"Take what men you like," sneered Mr. Pitt, as he turned on his heel, "but I hope they will be better employed this time than in serving as your footmen and coach driver. Ha, ha, ha, a nice night's work indeed for his Majesty's servants."

Mr. Croft did not pause to attend to these sneers—indeed, he felt that he had already lost too much time—but, selecting several of the strongest and best armed men, he returned to the Jew's house; but, to his great disappointment, he found it quite deserted. Search as they would, not one thing of value could they find.

CHAPTER LX.

THE BLUE CHAMBER.—ROARING RIC AND BOB BLOW-THE-BELLOWS AT WORK.—THE GHOST AT TILLINGHAM HALL.

WHILST these various adventures were taking place, Roaring Ric the Ranter had not been idle, but had been hard at work preparing to deceive Lord Redfern.

We left him, as the reader will remember, gazing out at the beautiful night.

"I wonder whether I have overslept myself and the merry smith has gone," he muttered, "if so I shall stand a better chance of fasting than I intended. Well, here goes for a trial."

Nearly closing the shutters so that no one might see they were opened, he whistled gently through the small aperture he had left.

He paused for a moment, and then heard the cry of the white owl.

"He is still there thank Heaven," he muttered as he opened the window softly.

He gazed out at the open lawn that stretched out between the house and a plantation, and perceived a man creeping from bush to bush nearer the house.

At length the man reached the window where Ric was, and handed him up a large basket.

This Ric placed on the floor, and then helped the man, who was no other than the merry smith, to enter the room.

This done, they once more closed and barred the window and shutters.

"Well?" demanded Bob, "how goes the work? Bravely I hope."

"Could not be better," cried Ric, "the old fool believes anything and everything."

"So much the better," said Bob, "and now let us to work."

"Begging your pardon," interrupted Ric, "my motto is pleasure first and business after, I have had nothing to eat since breakfast, and therefore will examine the contents of your basket."

"As you will," replied Bob, "and as you have kept me so long waiting I don't mind joining you."

The two men sat down and made a jolly meal off the viands from the basket, washing them down with Lord Redfern's wine.

Whilst they were at this meal Roaring Ric related how he had duped Lord Redfern, and they both laughed loudly at his lordship's credulity.

"Now our repast is over, I am ready to work," said Ric, "you must follow my directions and don't mind what noise you make, only when you hammer you must utter the most unearthly yells, so as to frighten the people in the house."

In a minute both men were hard at work hanging up curtains, placing mirrors, building up altars, indeed so much was done in so little time, that they were surprised themselves at the progress they had made before daybreak.

All day long they rested themselves, and at night they returned to their work, after having regaled themselves on the provisions which were supplied to them by their emissaries outside, along with many other things that Roaring Ric required to complete his 'show' as he called it.

So hard had they toiled that they had completed their entire work by nine o'clock on the second night.

Chemicals, skulls, thigh bones, tripods, and all the paraphernalia of the magi, were placed round the room, and Ric examined his work with a look of great complaicency.

"And what is to be done now?" demanded Bob Blow-the-Bellows.

"Done now? well I suppose it will be time to explore these secret passages."

They at once started on their exploration down those mysterious hiding-places.

One that they traversed they discovered led them up to an old ruined tower on the roof of the hall; they found many others leading to all parts of the house, for all of which they soon discovered what springs were necessary to touch to open the farther doors.

They had proceeded some way down one of them when they were stopped by a thin panel that was evidently a door.

They paused a moment and listened.

There was no doubt about it; the room on the other side of the panel was inhabited.

They could plainly hear people in conversation, and the speakers were evidently both old. One voice was that of a man, the other that of a woman.

Ric at once recognised the voices as those belonging to the old man and woman who had charge of the Hall during Lord Redfern's absence.

"Many a year have I lived here," said the old man, "but never heard such fearful sounds."

"It's ever since that horrid old man came here," continued the woman.

"I doubt me much that they are working some evil deed."

"They? why who in the name of reason do you mean?" demanded the woman.

"My Lord and that mysterious stranger. Even the ghosts dread them."

"Aye! and such a ghost too," said the old crone.

"I never heard the story of the ghost?" asked the man. "what is it?"

"You have often heard the ghost though," said the woman.

"Aye, that I have," replied the man, "and have asked his Lordship about it."

"But he won't answer. No, of course he won't. But the people down in the village yonder aint so particular; *they* talk about it pretty much."

"Tell us all about it Bridget tell us all about it," asked the old man tremulously.

"Well snuff the candle and pull the embers together and I will begin."

"There," said the old man raking the embers together, "now begin."

Ric and Bob could hear them drawing their chairs together, and the old woman commenced the history of the ghost of Tillingham hall.

HISTORY OF THE GHOST OF TILLINGHAM HALL.

"It's many and many a year ago that the lord of this hall—I don't remember his name—it wasn't Redfern, that's certain, for they are new people, had a very beautiful daughter named Alice.

"Now Mistress Alice was her father's great love and joy, and was reckoned one of the most beautiful girls in the country. But she had strange ways with her that no one could make out.

"She used to wander over the hills and groves picking up herbs, and many a night it was said she was seen flitting amongst the tombs in that old churchyard by the ruined Abbey, and the gossips did say that she gathered other things besides herbs there.

"Be it as it may, the Lady Alice was wondrously fair, and suitors came far and near to look upon her charms and kneel at her feet.

"She was kind to all; so that they all flattered themselves that they were favoured more than the rest, and consequently each made certain of carrying off the prize from under their rival's nose.

"Lady Alice seemed to take a mischievous delight in making these gentlemen quarrel and fight, so that many and many a duel was fought behind the old Abbey, and the meadow then got to be called the Fatal Field, and none of the people will go past it even now after dark.

"By these means the Lady Alice thinned the number of her suitors very considerably, and even the most attached to her became alarmed as they saw the fate of their friends. So vexed at her coolness did they become, that they determined to meet all together in the hall of the chapel and consult what they should do.

"'What say you, gentlemen,' cried the boldest, 'have we not suffered enough at this beautiful, but cruel lady's hand? We do all we can to please her and our only reward is that she fools us.'

"'Nay, say not so,' cried a younger man, 'no fairer creature or kinder lady lives.'

"'She is most kind to me,' cried out another.

"'She gave me this knot of ribands this morning,' said the first young fellow.

"'And me this bow this afternoon,' said the other youth.

"'By heavens! you—'

"'Pause, gentlemen, pause,' cried the first speaker, 'do you not see now how false is this fair lady? Who can trust her; who can rely upon her promises?'

"A good deal was said of the same sort, until the elder, and more discreet knights determined to ride away that night without so much as wishing their mistress farewell.

"But the younger fellows were so enamoured that they determined to stay and try their fortune again, hoping that their friends' departure would increase their chances of success.

"Away went the gallant gentlemen, and merrily they rode along, their love seeming to grow less and their hearts lighter as they went further and further away from their mistress.

"But it was not so with the Lady Alice; no sooner did she hear that they had left, than she flew into a most fearful passion, her eyes flashed fire and her bosom heaved with the fierceness of her passion.

"The servants fled in fright, that is, all those who were not bound to remain.

"'What,' she cried, 'have these creatures dared to escape me; do they think that I have not the power to reach them outside my mansion as well as in? Begone, slaves! Tell the gallant gentlemen who have chosen to remain true to me, that I will meet them at a banquet directly, and he who proves the bravest shall win my hand.'

"'But my dear lady,' cried the housekeeper, 'the banquet cannot be spread.'

"'The banquet *must* be spread,' cried the lady, in full wrath, 'begone, and see 'tis done.'

"The trembling servants hastened to do their mistress' bidding in silence.

"The young men received the message with the greatest glee, congratulating each other on having determined to remain.

"The banquet was spread, but how, not one servant could tell.

"They all declared that there were dishes placed on the board, no one in the hall had cooked, and strange wines the butler had never decanted.

"All this happened in the very same room the mysterious stranger now inhabits.

"Well, the Lady Alice soon appeared amongst her guests, and taking the youngest by the hand led him into the hall, and placed him by her side at the head of the table.

"This at first made the others all jealous, but the lady was so kind to all that they soon became good humoured and drank deeply to the health of their mistress.

"Presently the lady rose, and taking up a quaint goblet of crystal, filled with a deep red liquid, called upon the gentlemen to fill their glasses and respond to a toast she was about to propose.

"They, being all flushed with wine, quickly accepted the challenge.

"'Gentlemen,' she cried, 'you who have remained true to me, are you determined to remain by me, come weal, come woe?'

"'We are,' cried the young men, in chorus.

"'Will you swear it?' she demanded.

"'We will,' cried the young fellows.

"Scarcely had the words fallen from their lips when a terrific peal of thunder seemed to burst over the building.

"The young men turned pale at this strange coincidence, but not so the Lady Alice; she lifted up her cup, and cried aloud in her demoniac glee—

"'Pledge me then, you who are faithful, and drink a wet journey to those who have fled.'

"All the young fellows drank the toast except the one whom the Lady Alice had placed by her side, and he had been seized by such a strange chillness that his tongue could not move, so that he had not been able even to swear to be true to his lady.

"Scarcely had the words been spoken than the thunder storm burst in all its fury. Swords of fire seemed flashing over the guests' heads, whilst shrieks of devilish laughter rang through the air. The servants fled in fear, but the young men remained immoveable.

"What happened after this, no one can safely say; all that is known was that an old servant, who, on seeing the flames rush round the room, had fled into the ante-room and there fell down and broke her leg, swore that she heard a terrible voice in the thunder cry—

"'YOUR TIME HAS COME!'

"To which Lady Alice was heard to cry out—

"'I have given thee victims enough, and have a husband; this youth is mine, whom I have preserved alive. He gives me more years to live.'

"'Fool,' cried the voice, 'he never took the oath. Therefore you are lost.'

"Immediately there followed a fearful scream, that seemed as if it would never cease. So terrific was it that the servant fainted dead off."

"Is that all?" asked the old man, in a very shaky voice.

"No; the next morning when they—I mean the servants—had summoned the villagers, they ventured into the blue room and there found all the young men, except the one who sat by the lady, were dead, as was also the Lady Alice.

"They were all charred up to a cinder, so that you could not tell one from the other.

"A large gap was made in the wall, through which no doubt the devil pulled the poor creatures' souls when he flew away with them.

"Large burned places were seen on the cloth, especially where the knives had been, and they do say, right opposite where the lady sat was the print of a hoof.

"Strange to say, even those gentlemen who rode away did not escape. The next morning, which was the most beautifully calm you ever saw, the noble gentlemen were found all drowned in the Blackwater, close by that dangerous ford."

"And what became of the youth who was still alive?" demanded the old man.

"He was never happy afterwards," replied the old woman. "Some folks say he lost his wits. Be that as it may, he gave up all his lands to the church, and died in the Abbey yonder under the care of the monks, who swore that the Lady Alice had sold herself to the devil, and had entrapped the young men and sold them also. But doubtless the young man saved himself by going into the abbey."

"And the Lady Alice; does she haunt this place?" asked the old man.

"Of course she does. On stormy nights you always hear her. She comes with low moans and groans, and then, as the storm breaks, her shrieks are heard, even as we heard them in the Blue Room during the last two nights. I wouldn't go near that place after dark; nay, nor in the daylight if I can help it, for a thousand pounds, that I wouldn't."

"Neither would I," replied the old man. "Oh! Bridget, such things make one think of their latter end. I swear I can't sit easily for fear of it."

Ric and his companion could hear the old people draw their chairs together.

It must be confessed that Bob Blow-the-Bellows did not like the story, and a strange sensation, known as "creeping" seemed to pass all over him; but Ric could not forego the pleasure of a practical joke.

Placing his mouth close to the partition he first sighed heavily, and then groaned in such a lugubrious manner that even Bob started in fear.

They could hear the old people clinging to each other in mortal fear.

Catching Bob by the arm Ric led him away as fast as he could.

"Phew! that is a terrible story," said Bob, when they were once more in the Blue Room.

"Not bad," replied Ric; "but what a lot time and old women make of a little."

"What do you mean?" enquired Bob; "do you not believe it, then?"

"What do you mean? my worthy fellow," replied Ric; "if you ask me if I believe all that this old crone has said, I answer plainly, no. But parts of it I do."

"If you believe part, why not all?" demanded the smith.

"For the best of all reasons," replied Ric; "part is true and part is not, A story is like a little water spilt upon the floor: the further it goes the more it spreads. Now, it so happens that I know the truth of this story. The lady who was honoured by having the same reputation for magic as I was was a highly virtuous and accomplished woman, who had studied simples so as to do good to her fellow-creatures. It is true many suitors came to woo her, and she certainly selected one of them.

"One evening the disappointed suitors and their friends rode away, and the lady had a quiet supper with her affianced husband and some two or three of his cousins. During the meal a violent thunder and lightning storm swept over the country, scattering death and desolation around.

"Now, it so happened, that Tillingham Hall was struck by a thunder-bolt, and the Lady Alice and all her guests, saving her affianced husband, who escaped by a miracle, were killed. The hole in the wall, through which the old lady says the devil went, was likewise caused by the lightning, as was also the marks on the tablecloth, which you will observe occurred chiefly where there was steel, which attracted the lightning. No doubt the sword, daggers, and steel buckles caused the death of the gentlemen, whilst the young fellow who escaped may probably have worn no sword or dagger."

"But how about the mark of the hoof?" said Bob Blow-the-Bellows.

"Probably caused by some vessel of iron on the table; perhaps it was not there at all."

"But the gentlemen who were drowned—"

"Very stupidly tried to ford a river, always dangerous, after dark and when the storm had swollen it. Any one who have seen how a river swells during a thunder-storm will not wonder that they were drowned."

"But the voices in the air?"

"Were not in the air, but in the imaginations of the idle people who have since related the story. But come, let us have some wine, and then to sleep; we have all our work to do, though it is easy enough now we have discovered that one of these passages leads out into the park close by the cliffs."

CHAPTER LXI.

ROARING RIC ACTS THE MAGICIAN—LORD REDFERN SEES THE MAGIC MIRROR.

IT was about ten o'clock of the third night when Roaring Ric left the Blue Room.

He soon found that he had no difficulty in keeping the servants away from his apartments; indeed, his greatest trouble was to get them to approach him at all.

However, he managed to sieze upon the old woman Bridget, and sent her with a message to her master, stating that he wished to see Lord Redfern.

His lordship, who had been waiting impatiently for the interview, at once hastened to Ric, whom he found waiting at the door of the anteroom.

"Is all prepared, father?" demanded Redfern, eagerly.

"All is prepared, my son," replied Ric, imitating the voice of an old man with the greatest exactness; "all is prepared, my son, by me; but art thou prepared?"

"I am," replied Redfern; "that is, I trust I am, father."

"Thou hast answered well, my son," replied the

mock magician. "Modesty on the lips of the uninitiated is as pure gold, for it is most valuable. Still, my son, I have sent for thee thus early, so that I may still further prepare thee for the ordeal through which all must pass who wish to learn the secrets of nature and gaze into the future. Come then, my son, there shall no harm approach thee if you obey my commands; but be warned that thou must do all I bid thee, or else there will be no help for thee. Trismegistus will not be played with, and I, by my long fasting and prayer, have obtained from him the power of showing thee much which thou would'st, in the usual course of things, have had to study years to know."

Having said this, Roaring Ric led the credulous Lord Redfern into the anteroom.

A cold shiver passed over Lord Redfern when he entered this room.

It was hung all round with black curtains, looped up at certain places as if to show some door leading into another apartment, but which, like the walls, was covered with black cloth.

At one corner of the room was a long black object, which Lord Redfern had no difficulty in recognising as a coffin, although it was covered with a deep velvet pall.

The only light in this ghastly room was produced by some half-dozen large wax candles, that emitted a lurid blue light, their wicks having been soaked in some chemical by Roaring Ric.

"This, my son," said Ric, "is the room of the tomb. In studying these wondrous secrets all must be learned by symbols; thus, as we all know that after we have passed through the portals of the tomb, all, or at least much, that is now hidden to us will be opened to our view. That which is concealed shall be revealed, and many mysteries shall be made manifest. Thus you see that death is but the beginning of life, even as life is but the beginning of death."

In this strain Roaring Ric continued to talk to Lord Redfern, until his lordship actually trembled with fear, and half repented that he had ventured so far.

Roaring Ric, who larded his conversation with scraps from old plays and books, had gone on without noticing his companion's looks, but when he did turn towards him he found his lordship in such a state of perturbation that he began to fear that he had gone too far, and therefore hastened at once to tender his dupe some consolation in the shape of encouragement—showing him the rewards he would have.

"Be not downcast, my son," he cried; "am I not near to protect thee; and if we once gain the wondrous philosopher's stone, the mines of Potosi will not contain as much wealth as we shall have; besides which, the future will be an open book unto our eyes."

"Shall we then be able to learn the future?" enquired Lord Redfern.

"Is not the book of fate for all men?" enquired Ric, sternly.

"Of a truth it is, father. But shall we be permitted to read therein."

"My son," replied Ric, "the book of fate was written at the creation of the world. Remember that that which has passed was once the future; yesterday was the to-morrow of the day before, and the moment we are speaking was a second ago in the future, and ere the echoes of our voices cease it is buried in the past. It then follows that as the past may be known, so the future can be studied, and all generations that have existed can be called from the grave of the past, so all generations to come can be summoned from the cradle of the future."

"Can you commune with the departed?" enquired Redfern, with great agitation.

"It is by them and through them that we gaze into the future," replied Ric.

"Surely such science is unlawful," cried Redfern.

"Unlawful!" cried Ric, "behold how near you would bring danger on your own head."

"What do you mean?" demanded Redfern, in great alarm.

"I mean that our great master, Hermes Trismegistus, is hovering near, calling upon the spirits of Fire, Water, Air, and Earth, to do our bidding; therefore think you that he would be pleased to hear his wondrous works called unlawful?"

"I crave pardon humbly," said Lord Redfern, looking round him as if he expected to see the great Hermes floating about the chamber.

"It is granted, my son," said Roaring Ric, with a slight twitching at the corners of his mouth, which he could scarcely conceal, "but I see that the weight of the burthen put upon you is more than you can bear. And what wonder? you have only just crossed the threshold. Come, I will give you a prepared drink that will strengthen you."

Passing to one of the places where the curtains were looped up, Ric drew therefrom a curiously-shaped decanter and glass.

Pouring from the former a deep red liquid into the glass, he muttered some magical words.

He then carefully replaced the decanter, and handed the glass to Lord Redfern.

Redfern seized the goblet with trembling hands, and drank off the contents.

It tasted to him very much like a very powerful Burgundy, and certainly there was little wonder that it did, for it had been abstracted from the cellars of Tillingham only half an hour before, whilst the only addition that had been made to it was a simple drug, the effects of which was like that celebrated herb used in the East, which makes men's imagination overcome their better judgment, and leaves them a helpless prey in the hands of those who would dupe them.

No sooner had this draught been administered than the clock of the Hall struck twelve.

"The hour is arrived," cried Ric; "wait here, my son, until I return. I will not keep you long."

Redfern remained standing in the middle of the room, gazing at the door leading to the Blue Room, through which Roaring Ric had disappeared.

Strange, unearthly noises of chatting rose up in the air, mingled with fiendish laughter.

Then for a moment all was still—still as the grave.

Anon there came deep groans and sobs, as if women were weeping.

Then came a wild strain of rich music, which seemed to float from the earth up to the sky, and die away amidst the stars in a solemn manner.

No sooner had the music ceased than the black curtains covering the door leading to the Blue Room rolled on one side, and Roaring Ric stood on the threshold.

Yes, there was no mistaking him, although his dress was completely changed.

A high-crowned hat rising to a peak was placed on his head.

A long robe of black velvet, with loose hanging sleeves, clothed his body, and nearly touched the floor. On the dress were strange cabalistic characters wrought in gold.

His long grey hair and beard hung over this handsome garment, giving Ric a wondrously venerable appearance.

In one hand he held a long white wand, whilst with the other he beckoned Lord Redfern to enter the Blue Room. Thrice he beckoned him and then disappeared.

For a moment Redfern stood undecided whether to fly or advance.

At last his resolution was taken, and, with a firm step, he entered the Blue Room.

He started back with horror at the gloomy sight presented to him.

This room, like the others, was all hung round with black velvet.

In the centre was an altar, on which stood a small brasier, holding some burning charcoal.

Roaring Ric, wand in hand, stood by the side of the altar, the lurid light from the charcoal throwing a death-like hue upon his face.

Round the altar and the magician was a circle of human skulls and cross-bones.

At the back of the altar was a deep crimson curtain, covered with hieroglyphics.

Summoning courage, Redfern attempted to cross the circle of skulls.

Although Ric did not move, something seemed to strike him a sharp blow and hurl him back.

"Back, rash man!" cried Ric sternly; "tempt not the demon's wrath."

Lord Redfern recoiled to the further corner of the room, and waited there patiently.

"The charm works well," cried Ric, at the same time throwing some powder on to the brasier, which made the flames leap up, and changed their colour to a deep red.

"Father, may I not approach?" demanded Redfern meekly.

"Not for thy life. Hark! the spirits come; I hear their wings."

Strange discordant sounds did seem to fill the air, making Redfern tremble.

"Speak, my Lord," cried Ric, after a pause," and say what you wish to know. Would you search in the future, or would you have the mirror turned back and know the past?"

"Why should I seek to know the past?" cried Redfern; show me the future."

"Be it so," cried Ric; "but whatever you see, venture not to speak."

Mumbling a strange jargon, Ric cast some powder on the fire, which filled the room with smoke, at the same time causing bright corruscations of fire to flash out.

As the smoke cleared away, the curtain at the back of the altar was drawn aside as if by invisible hands, and strains of soft music floated on the air.

As the curtains separated, a huge mirror was seen, the surface of which reflected nothing but the smoke that still curled up from the fire on the altar.

"What wouldst thou know?" demanded Ric.

"I would know if the outlaw, Batswing, is arrested?" said Redfern.

"He is free, he is free, he is free," shouted a shrill voice close by Lord Redfern's ear.

He turned round, but all was still, and no one seemed near him.

"You have your answer," said Ric; "what more would you ask?"

"I would know where is my Lord Leslie? and what he is doing?"

"He is in France," shouted the same shrill voice, which was no other than Flicker's, who was concealed behind the curtains.

"Will he return to England soon?" cried Redfern, eagerly.

"In three days, if he is alive, he will be on English ground," replied the voice.

"Shall I be successful in my schemes?" demanded Redfern.

"Yes and no," was the answer.

"What will be my fate; canst thou show me that?" cried Redfern, who was now utterly careless as to the demoniacal cries and groans that seemed to come from the walls and ceilings of the chambers

"Be not rash," cried Roaring Ric; "remember, you have learned much to-day."

"I have no fear," cried Redfern, "and would learn my fate."

"Rash man, you shall have your will," said Ric; "Spirits of Earth, show this mortal what must be his fate."

As he spoke he cast some more powder on the fire, changing its colour to green.

Slowly the mists seemed to separate, and a bright light came from the mirror.

In it Redfern beheld a man on the ground struggling with a boy.

The man's face was from him. Suddenly the boy raised a dagger and plunged it into the man's breast; at the moment the man turned, and Redfern saw it was himself.

Instantaneously a terrific noise as of an explosion took place, and the next moment the curtains fell over the mirror, and all was darkness again.

"Hast thou seen enough?" demanded Ric, in a solemn voice.

"Cannot this fate be avoided?" demanded Redfern?

"Have I not said the book of fate was written at the creation? Who, then, can alter it?"

"Must I then die by violence?" cried Redfern, in despair.

"You must," replied Ric; "but in all these things, although the fate cannot be averted, yet the time of their happening may be postponed."

"How so?" demanded Redfern, eagerly.

"Dost thou not know, my son, that in the spirit-world time is unknown? It is only mortals who have a finite existence that are bound by time. So, you see, you may put off the fate you so much dread by employing care and prudence. If it were not for that, there would be but little good in the wondrous art we possess."

"True, father," replied Redfern; "with your counsels I will endeavour to avoid this fate."

"I will do all to assist you, my son," replied Ric; "live honestly and steadily is the best way."

"What would you have me do?" demanded Redfern; "I have but certain schemes to work; they once accomplished, then I shall be content, and will re-build this old hall and live on the estate."

"A worthy resolve, my son, but why not do so now at once?"

"Father, it is necessary that I should wed a young lady whom I know."

"Do you love her so much, then, that it is necessary to your peace of mind?"

"Not so, father, but she is worth everything to me. With her, titles and lands are mine; without her, I know not how soon I may be reduced to penury."

"Indeed!" cried Ric, scarcely able to hide his curiosity; and this lady is?"

"A mere country wench, who seems to have taken a hatred to me."

"That is indeed strange," said Ric; "what is her name?"

"That can concern thee but little," said Redfern, eying Ric suspiciously.

"Of a truth you are right," replied Ric; "though a country wench refusing a lord is enough to make one curious. Such cases are not often met with in this selfish world."

"Could you show me the portrait of the lady who will share my title?" demanded Redfern, who had evidently noticed Ric's anxiety to learn Alice's name.

"I could show you what you wish," replied Ric; "but before I attempt it, you must answer me one or two questions. They are of little importance, but as what we are about to do is fraught with danger, I must ask them."

"Proceed," said Lord Redfern, coolly; "so that they trespass not too far I will answer them."

"Tell me, then, has any crime been committed in this house lately. A crime that would pollute its sanctity, such, for instance as blood?"

Lord Redfern looked uneasy at this, for he remembered how he had shot Maud.

"A few days ago," he muttered, "some thieves broke in and one was wounded,"

"That is no pollution, my son," said Ric, "they come on an unlawful errand."

"Beyond that I know of no other crime,' replied Redfern.

"The other question is, if there is a young woman in this house?"

"Why should you ask that question?" demanded Redfern, sternly, "have I not shown you all my people; do you dare to doubt my word? Or is there some other reason for these strange and idle queries?"

"Strange they may be, idle they are not," replied Ric, haughtily, "I care not whether you answer me or not; but till I have had that question answered, I will show you no more. What have I made by you? Nothing—I have fasted in your house, not feasted: I have served without wages, and have received incredulity for my pains."

"Nay, good father, be not impatient," cried Redfern, "I will answer you."

"I require not your answer," said Ric, "I have but to cross this circle of skulls and the charm is lost. What, ingrate, have I gained by serving thee."

"My good father, do not cross the barrier, I will answer you. There is no maiden in this house; she was borne away on the night the thieves attacked the Hall."

"She, who?" demanded Ric.

"The—the—the maid you spoke about," faltered Lord Redfern.

"I spoke of no maid," said Ric, "I suppose you mean the one you would wed?"

"I do," replied Redfern.

"Do you not know where she is?" demanded Ric, who, as the reader will perceive, was endeavouring to make Lord Redfern tell him all his secrets.

"No, I do not," replied Lord Redfern, "can you not, with all your art, let me know that?"

"I might, if the spirits are propitious," replied Ric, musingly, "but you must tell me her name."

For a moment Redfern paused, and then said in a clear voice,

"Alice Landon."

Now this last question considerably puzzled Roaring Ric, for he was not at all certain that Lord Redfern might not be merely trying his powers. Besides, although it was more than probable that Redfern knew where Alice was concealed; it was certain that Ric was quite ignorant of the fact. Added to this, his confederates, who were hidden away in the secret passages and behind the curtains, had not prepared any answer to such a question, never having dreamed it would have been asked.

However, there was nothing to be done but to make the endeavour.

Roaring Ric again cast powders into the fire and muttered all sorts of gibberish.

He continued doing this for some time, so that he might gain time.

But it was all in vain; he knew nothing much about the matter, and knew not what to do.

"The spirits reply not," he said, "still, we will try them further."

He had scarcely finished speaking, when sighs and groans, and dismal sounds came all round them.

By this, Ric knew that his confederates knew, or had determined to give, an answer.

"Spirit of the mist," he cried, "tell me where is this Alice Landon."

"Ask Jonathan Wild," said a plaintive female voice.

"Is she imprisoned by him?" continued Ric.

"Ask no more; dismiss me," replied the voice in solemn tones.

"Go then and seek thy home amongst the mountains," said Ric.

"It is then as I thought," exclaimed Redfern, "so Master Jonathan plays fast and loose with me; but I will be equal with him yet, trust me I will."

"Stay my lord," said Ric as Lord Redfern was about to hurry from the room. "All is prepared for you to see the lady who will share your title."

"Say you so," cried Redfern, "that will indeed test your power."

Again Ric had recourse to imitating the actions usually ascribed to magicians and astrologers. The smoke which he had caused cleared away, and once more the magic mirror was uncovered.

There, in the centre, stood a tall and graceful lady, but her back was towards the room.

"How is this," muttered Ric, as if in alarm, "the lady is already married."

"Married!" exclaimed Redfern, "it cannot be possible."

"Hush," whispered Ric, "see she turns round."

Slowly the lady turned round and gazed towards Redfern.

It was Maud!

With a yell of anger Lord Redfern sprang forward as if he would have clutched the mysterious figure, but, again, some invisible obstacle seemed to cross him, and he reeled back as if struck across the breast with a sword.

He had scarcely sprang forward when the light and fire were extinguished, so that everything was enveloped in darkness.

At the same time discordant howls were heard, and the beating of gongs became terrific.

At that moment, Redfern felt himself seized by the arm and dragged violently from the room.

In the ante-room, by the aid of the dim light from the candles, he beheld Ric.

"Fool," exclaimed Ric, as if overcome with anger, "thou little knowest what thou hast done. I have, with difficulty, saved you, but I must return. If in three days you do not hear from me, then enter this room, for I shall be no more. Now, begone, and leave me to my fate. Be warned, and do not attempt to enter here before."

Without waiting to hear what Redfern might reply, Ric hurried him to the door, and having pushed him into the passage, closed and bolted the door after him.

He then hastened back to the Blue Room, where he found Bob Blow-the-Bellows, Maud, and Flicker waiting his arrival.

For some minutes they could not speak for laughing.

"Come," said Ric, "there is no time to be lost, we most clear these things away."

They all set to work with a good will, taking down the gloomy fittings.

All the candles, skulls, bones, and such things were thrust in a secret cupboard.

The smith, meanwhile, commenced unscrewing a thin iron band, which had been stretched across the room, at about the height of a man's chest, the edge being turned outwards, so that it was invisible in the gloom. This was the mysterious power which had forced Lord Redfern back when he had attempted to enter the circle.

The mirror had been managed in the simplest manner possible.

It was a large glass that had formed at one time a panel in a boudoir.

They had cleared the back from the silver so that it remained like a pure piece of glass.

They had then fitted it in the entrance of the secret passage, so that when the passage was dark any one could stand close behind the glass without being seen, but no sooner was the passage illuminated than the person seemed to be in the mirror.

"There," said Ric, when they had all finished, "I think that will do."

"I don't think we have discovered much for all that," said Bob.

"Well, I don't know that, we have learned that Redfern suspects Wild."

"And more than that," said Maud, "we know that Alice Landon has wealth; nay, that in some mysterious way she is connected with Redfern, whose property seems under her control. Come what may, she must and shall be saved."

———

CHAPTER LXII.

JONATHAN CONDOLES WITH FARMER CROFT. REDFERN
AND WILD HAVE A STORMY INTERVIEW. THE
MURDERS PLANNED.

JONATHAN WILD had ridden as fast as he could, on the night that Rough Ralph met his fate, from Tillingham to London.

A tremendous passion burned in his breast, and bitter were the oaths he took against Batswing.

On reaching his home, he had shut himself in his own room, refusing to see anyone until he had recovered himself enough to appear unruffled, for Jonathan Wild, like all bad men, dreaded to be taken in unguarded moments.

He had not arrived home until nearly mid-day, and, tired as he was, he sat brooding over his misfortune, or pacing up and down the room, giving vent to oaths and curses.

At last, as night approached, he threw himself on his bed and fell fast asleep.

So tired was he that he did not wake until the sun was well up in the sky.

Hastily washing his face and hands, he changed his travel-stained garments for new ones.

This done, he descended to his office, and touching a bell, signified his willingness to see any one that might call on special business.

He had not been long reading his letters, when Farmer Croft entered.

"Well!" said Jonathan, abruptly, "what is up now?"

"Up!" cried the farmer, "all I know, we are pretty considerably knocked down."

"How so?" demanded Jonathan.

"In the first place," cried the farmer, "do you know a man called Ikey Joel?"

"What! Old Ikey of Gray's Inn Lane? I should think I did. But what of him?"

"He has robbed and swindled us," cried Croft, in a rage.

He then, without further preamble, told Wild how he had attempted to arrest Batswing and failed.

Unlike his usual temper, which would have been to enjoy his companions misfortune, Wild raved and stormed at this ill-fortune, not even blaming Croft.

"It is no use our trying these plans," he said, "we must have recourse to other measures."

"Curse me if I don't think we shall have to have a silver bullet to shoot him," cried Farmer Croft; "they do say that leaden ones won't hurt those who are leagued with Old Nick. Is that not so, Mr. Wild?"

"How should I know?" said Wild; "I have been wounded once or twice. Have you?"

"No, not yet," said the farmer, who did not seem to like the turn the joke took.

"This man," cried Jonathan, "is no more than an ordinary man. He is a clever one, whilst we are fools. But it is a long road that has no turning, and, trust me, we will have him yet. Look here, Croft, I know I can trust you."

"If you cannot, nobody can," said the man, with a leer.

"That don't say much," said Jonathan; "but as I know your secrets, you will serve me."

"And as I know you pay well, and can always put the robins on the wrong track, I shall always be willing to serve so old a friend in any way in my power."

"Good; you have two daughters?" said Wild, enquiringly.

"I have; and although I say it myself, as pretty girls as there are in England."

"Sweet angels!" sneered Wild, "doubtless they have taken example from their father, eh?"

"Zarah has, as you know, but Kate don't know anything about our business."

"The very thing," cried Wild; "you must know that I have here a young lady whom I am extremely anxious to put out of the way. You must take her to your house, and keep her so that no one will find her."

"I see; make her silent for life, eh?" chuckled Croft.

"No! that is not my purpose," cried Wild; "the girl must be well looked after and kindly treated, until you have further orders from me."

"Oh, I see!" grinned Croft; "caught at last, Mr. Wild. Ho, ho, ho!"

"Cease this foolery; when you get the girl to your house, tell her that it was I who had her sent away to avoid her being seized by the police or Lord Redfern."

"Ah! I understand; you want to work upon her gratitude, eh?"

"That is right; you must lead her from here directly," said Jonathan.

"But supposing she won't go, what then?" demanded the other.

"Bah! did you ever know a prisoner that would not go willingly out of my house?"

"By Jove! that is true enough at all events," laughed Croft.

Jonathan Wild touched a bell, and when his man appeared he ordered him to take Farmer Croft to Alice's prison, and then to procure a hackney coach, in which the farmer and Miss Landon were to be allowed to depart unmolested.

"Now go," said Wild, "and mind that you see my orders well obeyed."

The farmer, giving a knowing wink and a nod of intelligence, left the room.

Jonathan Wild paced slowly up and down turning over in his mind what value it was that Lord Redfern saw in Alice Landon.

He had tried to fathom this mystery in every way but without success.

"Bah!" he exclaimed, "had there been anything of real importance about this wench I should have found it out. No: I suppose it is Redfern's evil passions or love of revenge that causes all his anxiety about her. After all with such an ass as Redfern is—"

He had not time to finish the sentence before the door was flung open and Lord Redfern, red with passion, strode into the room.

"So," he commenced, "I have found out your treachery, how you have cheated me."

"Indeed!" replied Jonathan quietly, "will you inform me what I have done?"

"What you have done," screamed Redfern, "have you not deceived me in everything. You who promised me to arrest Batswing: you who declared that Sir Arthur Bowring should not escape and—"

"Have failed in all," replied Jonathan coolly, "have you ought else to urge against me."

"Yes, far more. Alice whom I had carried off you stole from me."

"My lord, my lord," cried Wild, "surely you must be mad to accuse me thus a second time of the same fault which I explained to you before. Did I not tell you that I was struck down and Alice carried away."

So great was Lord Redfern's passion that he could not speak.

THE NEXT INSTANT CROFT DREW FORTH A KNIFE AND PLUNGED IT INTO HIS DAUGHTER'S BOSOM.

During the pause Wild walked to the window and saw a coach drive away.

He knew that it held Alice Landon and Farmer Croft.

In a moment his resolve was taken and turning to Redfern he said blandly,

"It has pleased you, my lord, to accuse me of working against you, while if you had waited I should have been able to prove that I have been working for you."

"Working for me!" cried Redfern contemptuously. "it seems so."

"That it is so I can prove, my lord," replied Wild, "the night before last I was at Tillingham, and there had a terrible encounter with Batswing."

"Indeed," cred Redfern in the greatest astonishment, "how did it end."

"As you may see, I escaped unhurt, but my follower Rough Ralph was killed."

"What, Rough Ralph whom I have seen here?"

No. 21.

"Yes, Batswing shot him, and flung him over the cliffs," cried Jonathan.

"And you: how did you escape?" asked Redfern anxiously.

"It was covering my flight that my brave follower fell," said Wild.

"Then you fled?" cried Redfern, "fled from this Batswing you swore to kill."

"I did," replied Wild calmly, "but—*not alone!*"

"Not alone? I do not understand you," exclaimed Lord Redfern.

"Mistress Alice Landon lay fainting across my saddle bow."

"What! you have her here then?" cried Redfern. "The magician was right."

"The magician?" asked Wild; "what magician?"

"A man, a wonderous fellow," said Redfern impatiently; "but where is Alice?"

"I told you, my lord, that Alice *was* here; but she is not now."

"Why do you torment me thus?" cried Redfern; "where is she?"

"I cannot say," replied Wild. "Some one has helped her to escape from prison."

"Can I believe you?" said Redfern, "or are you deceiving me again?"

"My lord, I never deceived you; what I tell you is a fact. Doubtless by this time the body of Rough Ralph has been found at sea, dressed in your livery. Alice by some means has escaped. How, I know not; but I have already set men upon her track."

"I will give you five hundred pounds if you find her," cried Redfern.

"Look here, my lord," said Wild calmly; there is some mystery in all this. Why are you so anxious to have this fair Alice? Has she much wealth?"

"Wealth! no; I do not think old Landon could have left more than a few pounds."

"Perhaps not; but *was he her father?*" demanded Jonathan.

"Good gracious, Mr. Wild!" exclaimed Redfern starting; "what do you mean?"

"I know not, my lord," replied Jonathan, "but I am sure there is a mystery."

"Bah!" laughed Redfern, "she is a beautiful woman, you know."

"Which counts for nothing with my Lord Redfern against five hundred pounds."

For a moment Redfern seemed unable to answer this question.

At length he looked up, and with a cruel laugh replied,

"You are right, Mr. Wild; I do not value a woman's beauty a straw. But there are other reasons that I should make Alice Landon my wife."

"And they are?" enquired Jonathan coolly.

"Well, her father was murdered, and—and—a wife cannot bear witness against her husband."

"True," said Jonathan calmly; "but dead people tell no tales."

"Well, I care not about more blood," said Redfern doggedly, "but at her death you can have the reward; but mind, I *must* see the body. I take no one's word."

This answer seemed to puzzle Jonathan for a moment; he paused, and then said,

"Well then, I am on her track; but I do not think it will be easy to capture her."

"Indeed, and may I ask your reason for thinking so?"

"She is doubtlessly under Batswing's protection; that is why I think so."

"Then it will be as difficult to——"

"Murder her?" put in Jonathan; "no, that is much easier done."

"It is a terrible thing," said Redfern wiping his forehead.

"It is; but in two days all will be over. The reward will be ready?"

"Yes, yes. Have you heard Lord Leslie is about to return to England?"

"Yes, and have drawn on your lordship for a couple of hundred pounds."

"What for?" enquired Redfern. "I do not owe you any money."

"No; but the amount was needed to stop Lord Leslie's return."

"But you cannot bribe him; he is immensely rich."

"We cannot bribe him, but we can *silence* him," said Jonathan, "Now go, and trust to me, I will save you, and Alice will soon cease to trouble us."

"Are you sure he will never return?"

"As sure as a man can be : two of my men are on his track. He will never return."

"I must trust to you," said Redfern; "would that it were all over."

"It soon will be. Had it not been for Batswing, all would have been well long ago."

"Is there not another way to secure this man?"

"That I know not: these men seem to have a charmed life; they escape from the most terrible dangers with the greatest impunity, but the time always *does* come when they are caught, and most often they fall into the simplest trap. Leave him to me, my Lord. I have sworn to have him in my power, and I will, and you may be sure if once he is in my power he won't escape with life. Now go."

Lord Redfern, who was little more than a puppet in the hands of Jonathan Wild, made no further attempt to cross-examine that gentleman as to his designs, but with a heavy sigh, turned to leave the room. Suddenly he turned on his heel and walked back to Wild, and placing his hand on his arm, exclaimed—

"Maud has escaped me. She is still alive; she must be re-captured."

"She shall be," replied Wild, "I don't think it will be easy to take her alive."

"Kill her, then; it were better she were dead," cried Redfern.

"Let me see," mused Jonathan, "Alice, Maud and Leslie, all to die, 'pon my word, my Lord, you—"

"Hush!" cried Redfern, "remember walls have ears. Do what I ask you, and your reward shall be large. By the way, where did you say Leslie was?"

"Rue de Chatelet, Boulogne," said Wild, surprised by the suddenness of the question.

"Good," said Redfern, "do not fail me, and your reward shall be great."

"He is about some new plot," said Wild, as Redfern left the room, "I was a fool to tell him that address. It must be seen to."

He rang a small bell, which was quickly answered by one of his men.

"Take this money," cried Jonathan, "follow that man who has just left me until you know what crime he is meditating. No words, but go."

The man bowed silently, took the purse and left the room.

CHAPTER LXIII.

DRURY LANE THEATRE.—THE COUNTESS AND THE CHEVALIER.—THE COUNTESS' DIAMONDS.

"Hi! hi! hi! room for my Lord Powderpuff's carriage."

"Clear the road there for my Lady Farthingale's chair."

"Keep those orange-girls back whilst the Countess of Sourkroutzenberg, that stout—not to say grossly fat—painted, middle-aged lady passes into the saloon."

It is true had Charles II. been on the throne one of the pretty English lasses might have held the countess' place as royal favourite, but those days have passed; wit is out of fashion, and stolidity is the rage.

Carriage after carriage came rolling up to the front entrance of Drury Lane Theatre, for a new piece had just been produced by Mr. Cibber, entitled the 'Nonjuror,' which had taken the fashionable world by storm.

The interior of a theatre in those days was indeed a grand sight.

The boxes were filled with gaily-dressed ladies and gentlemen, dressed in silks and satins, glittering with gold and gems, odours and perfumes, painted, powdered and patched, and with morals as frail as their lace ruffles.

The pit was supposed to hold the "wits;" gentlemen who strolled up and down making doubtful jokes, quizzing the piece, performers, and audience, with an impertinence that would not be tolerated in the present day, and passing scandal round as freely as they did their snuff-boxes.

Most of these gentlemen's only claim to wit was that

they possessed an income large enough to prevent the necessity of having to work, that they frequented White's or the Cocoa Tree coffee-houses, and had sufficient courage to back their impertinence with their rapiers, which they always kept ready to their hands.

"For Gad," cried one, "why, there is the Countess of Sourkroutzenberg. How is it she is alone?"

"Have you not heard the last news?" demanded another gentleman, with a sneer.

"Fore George, no," replied the other, turning somewhat paler, "the countess has not—"

"Turned virtuous?" put in the other, "no my dear Tom, quite the contrary."

"What on earth do you mean?" exclaimed the one, called Tom, anxiously.

"I much fear, my dear Tom, that your chance of a post has gone."

"Stab my vitals, Jack; why do you play with me?" cried the other.

"Hast thou not, oh, most sapient Tom, heard the great scandal at the Cocoa?"

"Confound it, Jack, quit thy jeering, and let me know the news at once."

"Lud! how impatient thou art, but still to please you, I will relate my history."

"Do so, I pray thee, without further preface," continued the other.

"Well, then, my dear Tom, you must know that the Countess Sourkroutzenberg, has for some time exerted a strange influence over his Majesty, with whom she came from Hanover to England, and that she has had many grants of lands, money, and titles given her."

"Yes, yes, I know," said his friend, "the brown Hanoverian rat has already began to eat up the black little English ones,* we all know that well enough. But what has that to do with the Countess?"

"You know scandal does say that the Count Sourkroutzenberg married her ladyship, who was of no good birth, to please the king; be that as it may, the Count has always some mission to do abroad, whilst his lady attends the court, and has pretty much her own way with the king."

"Well: and has she not promised to use her influence to procure me a post?"

"Just so, but it seems her influence is somewhat on the wain. The Countess Grogrossagen, who has come to court, is even fatter and more coarse than Sourkroutzenberg, and of course his Majesty has noticed her greatly. Still the Sourkroutzenberg might pull through, but she appears to have gone mad over a young Frenchman, who has come from no one knows where, and whose family is known by no one. The King has heard of this, and wherever his faults are, he is not one to share his mistress with anyone, much as there is of her, and naturally the Countess is slightly under a cloud. I would thou had'st thy post, Tom, for I would fain see the Countess disgraced."

"If I once had it I would not mind," muttered the other, between his teeth.

"It is not that I complain of her pride, it is her avarice."

"Faith, let disgrace come when it may, she will have wealth enough, look at her diamonds.

"Worth a king's ransom," said Tom, "yet she never gave a penny in charity."

"But has taken money from people as bribes to get them posts."

"Hush, Tom, hush," laughed the other, "you should not tell your private affairs."

"Curse her," muttered Tom, "I wish I had my money back."

"Look!" cried Jack, "what imprudence! why the young Frenchman has entered her box."

* This is true, the now common brown rat came from Hanover with George I., and has destroyed the English black rat.

Leaving these gentlemen to console each other, we will enter the box of the Countess.

The Countess of Sourkroutzenberg was a fat, vulgar woman of forty, one of the number of that class who did us the honour of crossing to England with George the first.

It is not our intention to enter into particulars of her life; it is sufficient to say that the character the young gentlemen in the pit had given of her was not a bit too bad, for her name was known all over England for meanness and rapacity.

At the moment we speak of, she was leaning back in her chair, talking to a handsome young man, who, from his dress and the cut of his beard appeared to be a foreigner.

The conversation was carried on in pure French by the young man, and a vile mixture of that language and German by the fat Countess.

"Ah, Chevalier," she sighed, putting her fan before her eyes, to hide a blush that might have appeared, had it not been for the thick coating of rouge, "you are a terrible man."

"A terrible man, Madam?" replied the Chevalier, "I do not understand you."

"You Frenchmen have such a way of winning the ladies."

"Say, rather madam, that the ladies have such a way of captivating the Frenchmen, every French gentleman is only too proud to be the slave of some beautiful woman."

"Ha, Chevalier, you are so different from these English."

"Par Dieu! Madam, I trust so," replied the Chevalier, "these Islanders are a strange people; rough, rude, and slow in anger. They insult one another and call it wit. They spend their money recklessly, yet begrudge their wives the slightest liberty, and their king the right to bestow away his property; for every loyal gentleman knows that what is the subject's is the king's."

"Very true, indeed, Chevalier, I have often told his Majesty so," cried the Countess.

"Now, in France, our king is a king, and we nobles do rule the land. If I wish for anything—no matter what—on my estates in Provence, think you I would allow my peasants to stay me? And if my gracious sovereign desired my life, or aught that I possess, do you suppose I would or could stay him? Your king should do the same."

"Ah, in this wretched land the people are the rulers."

"The people!" cried the Chevalier, "why, they are only made to wait upon us."

"Just my opinion, Chevalier," cried the lady, "they ought to be our slaves."

"Assuredly, Madam," cried the Chevalier; "but surely all persons must be your slaves."

"There you go again, Chevalier," cried the Countess, "always flattering. But would you believe it; these English actually grumble at the few small presents the king has given me; declaring that they are oppressed and such nonsense."

"Oh! abominable!" cried the Chevalier, "the idea of daring to question a King's Acts. There is only one thing in the world, in my opinion, wherein a subject is equal to a king."

"And that is—?" enquired the Countess.

"Love!" replied the Chevalier, gazing into her eyes with a passionate look.

For some moments the old woman sat ogling the handsome young fellow.

Sigh was answered by sigh, and pressure of hand met pressure of hand.

"And do you love?" whispered the Countess, after a little while.

"Can you ask?" demanded the Chevalier, "look in your glass and see if I could help it."

"But the King will be so jealous," said the Countess, behind her fan.

"Heaven help him," replied the Chevalier, "but it is not my fault."

"Oh, Chevalier," cried the Countess, "I have been too rash to come here already."

"Say not so, charming Countess; I have prepared all so that no suspicion shall attach to you. I will take a note to your coachman, ordering him to be here an hour earlier, you can be taken ill, leave the theatre alone, and I will meet you at the end of Drury Lane. I spring into your carriage, we drive to your house, and no one knows that the Countess Sourkroutzenberg has met the Chevalier de Clervaux."

The Countess, who needed no more pressing, at once handed the Chevalier the slip of paper containing the order. He bowed low and at once left the box.

An hour had scarcely past when the Countess arose and quitted the box.

Her footman was waiting for her, but she almost screamed when she looked into his face.

It was the Chevalier de Clervaux in disguise.

"Hush, Madam," he whispered, all is prepared, "I borrowed this livery from one of your men. Do not falter and no one can suspect us."

The Countess leant upon the Chevalier, who led her respectfully to the carriage.

The people drew round, and groaned as she entered the lumbering guilded coach. The Chevalier sprang up behind by the side of another footman, and the coach drove off.

Onward they rattled through the ill-paved and worse-lighted streets.

At length the coach stopped and the Chevalier entered the coach.

We will not pause over the love scene that ensued between the Countess and the Chevalier.

The Countess knew the Chevalier was rich; had he not lost large sums at cards at her own house, sums of which she had had a good share? Therefore she was determined to win him. Start not, reader: such harpies not only lived, but were in favour at Court. Women of such a tender nature that they had lost their hearts whilst children, and never troubled to find them again; but considered a heavy balance at their bankers a good equivalent for honour, modesty and reputation.

To make love when one is not in love, requires a considerable amount of tact, and will keep one's attention fully employed; and doubtlessly that was the reason that the Countess did not perceive that the carriage had got considerably out of its way until they were nearly upset by the wheel going into a rut.

"Great heavens, where are we?" she demanded, in terrible alarm.

"You are perfectly safe, madam," replied the Chevalier; "your men are close by."

"Close by!" cried the terrified Countess; "of course they are driving the coach?"

"Pardon me, madam," replied the chevalier; "those are my servants, not yours."

"Villain!" she cried; "would you dare to carry me off?"

"On the contrary," replied the Chevalier, coolly; "that is the last thing I would do."

The Countess fell back in alarm and despair, unable to understand what all this meant.

One glance out of the windows of the carriage showed her that she was being driven over the open country.

Presently the carriage stopped, the door was opened, and the Chevalier leaped out.

"Madam," he said, quietly raising his hat in the most graceful manner; "I will not trouble you to alight. If you will hand me over your jewels and money that will suffice."

"What!" screamed the Countess, "you a thief, a common thief?"

"Not exactly, madam," replied the Chevalier; "I flatter myself I am an uncommon thief."

"I am the Countess Sourkroutzenberg," she cried with dignity; "I will not give up my jewels."

"Pardon me, then, madam, but I must order one of my men to take them."

"Would you dare to use violence?" screamed the lady.

"I certainly would not, for none is necessary. Hark ye, Madam; you have stolen those jewels from the English people, and I intend stealing them from you. You think that the poor were only made for the rich; I think that the rich were only made for the poor. Perhaps we may be both wrong; but I have might on my side, and mean to exercise it."

"Where are my men?" screamed the Countess.

"All of them but one are very tipsy at a public-house near Bow-street. The one who is sober I kept so specially to drive you home. So madam, you see, I was thoughtful for your comfort, after all. Now madam, if you please, I have no time to lose; your jewels."

By this time the Countess found resistance useless, and therefore handed over all her property.

"The King shall hear of this," she exclaimed, "you shall be hanged."

"As you will, madam," replied the Chevalier; "I should advise his Majesty not to repeat it, even if he does hear it, and also to order the Countess never to go to a theatre alone again."

Having completely stripped the Countess of all her jewels, Batswing—for need we say he was the Chevalier—gave a low whistle, which was instantly answered by some two or three men on horseback, each leading a loose horse with him. The chief of the party also conducted the Countess' coachman, whom they placed on the box and directed to drive home at once.

"Farewell, madam," cried Batswing, "and remember, when you rob the people another time that there are those amongst them who are not only willing but able to retaliate upon you." And, with a merry laugh, he and his men rode away.

CHAPTER LXIV.

HOW ALICE ESCAPED FROM JONATHAN WILD'S.—FARMER CROFT'S HOME AND DAUGHTERS.—THE SLEEPING DRAUGHT.—THE WARNING VOICE.—THE MURDER PLANNED.—THE CONSEQUENCES.

FARMER CROFT had found it no very difficult matter to remove Alice Landon.

The poor girl had such a horror of Jonathan Wild, whom she now no longer doubted was in league with Lord Redfern, that she would have trusted herself anywhere sooner than in his power.

Croft, who had received a better education than common, could, when he liked, assume a kind, fatherly air, and he did it with perfection in this case.

No sooner had the gaoler opened the prison door than he stole into the room, and, placing his finger on his lip, motioned Alice to remain silent.

"Hush!" he whispered; "I have come to save you from a dreadful danger."

Alice rose up haughtily from her couch, and facing him demanded—

"Who are you? Am I never to be left in peace?"

"Speak not so loudly," whispered Croft; "I tell you I have come to save you."

"Why should you, a stranger, interest yourself in my fate?" asked Alice, incredulously.

"Because I am bidden to do so," replied Croft; "now, do you understand?"

"No," replied Alice, calmly: "if you have been sent tell me who sent you."

"Batswing, the great outlaw, sent me," replied Croft; "he sent me to save you."

"I have already been cheated into writing a letter that may entrap those who would help me," replied Alice. "I will not yield again."

"Maiden, I have heard of that; and although your letter was used to entrap Batswing, as you rightly suspect, our brave captain escaped, having cast one of his antagonists over the cliffs."

This last speech had a great effect on Alice, for it proved her conjectures as to how her letter would be used was perfectly correct; whilst the pride with which Croft spoke of Wild's overthrow made her believe that he must be a friend of Batswing.

"I trust that you speak truly," she said; "but if you speak falsely, am not I in your power, and therefore must needs go wherever you will; therefore, sir, I obey."

"Trust me, madam, you will not repent doing so," replied Croft.

"Whither would you conduct me?" enquired Alice, listlessly.

"To my own house, where my daughters, Zarah and Kate will attend to you."

"You mistake, sir, I am but a poor girl," said Alice, "and need no attendance."

"Poor now, but when Sir Arthur wills you will be a lady."

A swift blush passed over Alice's cheek, but she made no reply.

"Wrap this cloak well round you," said Croft, pretending alarm; "I have bribed the gaoler to let us pass, but should we be discovered by Wild, then all were lost indeed."

Alice obeyed his commands almost mechanically, and permitted herself to be led out of the house and placed inside the coach.

After a few words to the coachman, Croft jumped in after her, and they drove rapidly away.

Bearing down Snow Hill, they mounted Holborn, and at length reached the road leading to Tottenham Court, up which they rolled at a good rate.

They soon passed that old building—long since pulled down—and taking a road that led a little towards the left, made their way towards the west side of Hampstead.

It was a bright cheery day, and the fresh air did Alice good after her imprisonment.

Farmer Croft wisely thought it would be much better not to talk too much to Alice, but to allow her to enjoy her own meditations and the relief of the country air.

However, he answered any questions she put to him in a quiet fatherly way, so that at last poor little Alice became trustful in him and talked to him about her troubles.

At length they arrived at Croft's house.

Alice was quite delighted with this building: it was so picturesque.

It was one of those dear old cosy houses, half wood half red brick, nearly covered with ivy that hung round its laticed windows.

It stood upon a fine old knoll, which trees that had stood there for hundreds of years, encircled, stretching forth their mighty arms to shelter the paths from the storm or sun.

Pigeons cooed on the stables and outhouses, whilst the rooks cawed on the trees, or, flapping their large black wings, flew over the shining country.

Not a house was to be seen for miles round, save in the distance a large farm and windmill, which Croft told Alice were his, and that only his people lived there.

The gardens round this comfortable place were luxurious in flowers, and showed that no expense had been spared in their cultivation.

"Do you think you could be happy here?" asked Croft

"Oh! this is splendid," cried Alice; "how beautiful the flowers smell."

"Ah!" cried the farmer, with a burst of heartiness; "here come my two most charming roses."

As he spoke Zarah and Kate came tripping down the walk to meet their father.

"Here, girls," cried Farmer Croft, "come here and give your warmest welcome to this lady."

Alice thought Zarah looked rather haughtily at her, but Kate embraced her at once.

"This young lady has had a quantity of trouble," continued Croft, "so be kind to her."

"Fear not, dear father, but that we shall do all to pleasure her," said Kate.

Croft led Alice a little on one side and whispered to her kindly—

"I would not tell those young creatures your troubles: they are not used to the world, and I would not have them know that maidens are liable to such persecutions. It will do you no good, and may do them harm. Besides, girls talk, and if your sad history was spread about how could I defend you?"

Alice, who could not deny the wisdom of this remark, had to acquiesce, although she wished in her heart to tell her young friends everything.

How swiftly the day passed to Alice, wandering in the open air amongst the flowers!

Only those who have been imprisoned for some time know the full pleasures of liberty.

So Alice thought, as in the cool of the evening she walked with Kate round the garden and watched the sun sink slowly down into the west.

"Oh, I am so glad you have come," cried Kate; "I have been so dull alone."

"Dull!" said Alice, astonished; "but your father and sister are always with you, are they not? How, then, can you be dull?"

"Oh, papa is very often away for weeks together," said Kate; "and as for Zarah"—

The young girl stopped and cast down her eyes, as if afraid to proceed.

"Well," enquired Alice, "does she not make you a good companion?"

"Oh, she is very good, too good," cried Kate, "and I am very wicked, I fear."

"Wicked! you surely jest," cried Alice; "how can you be wicked?"

"I don't mind telling you, Alice," whispered Kate; "but you promise you won't tell?"

"No, I will not tell," laughed Alice; "but had you not better keep your secret?"

"No, no," said the girl, hurriedly glancing round her as if frightened she should be heard.

"I would sooner tell you: I feel that if I had this horrid fear, this secret, off my breast it would be a relief."

"If that be so," said Alice, astonished at the young girl's manner, "I will gladly hear you."

"Oh, Alice, I know that I am not only very wicked," said Kate, "but very stupid. I have such horrible fancies at times. I suppose that is why no one loves me."

"No one loves you: surely, with your beauty and fortune, you cannot want for suitors."

"No, I have had plenty; but—but, Alice—they all leave me or disappear."

"I fear you are too cruel to them," laughed Alice.

"No, Alice, I cannot tell why it is; but all Zarah's lovers do the same."

"That is, indeed, strange, but may not some of this be fancy?"

"It may be; but the other is no fancy," said the young girl, shuddering.

"What is no fancy?" enquired Alice, catching the young girl's horror.

"Whenever I approach Zarah," whispered the young girl, "I shudder."

Alice looked at Kate's pale face and stood still with amazement.

A strange horror seemed to creep over her as she listened to the words.

"This is some foolish fancy," she said at last hurriedly; "you must break yourself of it."

"I know it is," said the girl; "but I cannot help it. Zarah is all kindness to me, to every one, and I am to blame. I told you I was wicked, but you will cure me. Teach me to be good and get over these—these fancies. Will you not?"

"That will I, my dear," replied Alice, in a cheery voice.

"But you have not seen my beautiful horse, Beda. Stay, I will call him."

With a laugh, which struck Alice as being somewhat forced, Kate drew a whistle from her pocket.

"Now you will see the prettiest thing in the world," she laughed.

Putting the whistle to her lips she blew two soft notes thereon, which were immediately answered by a beautiful little Arab horse, who trotted up and commenced fondling his mistress.

"There," cried Kate, "is it not a beauty? She is so quiet: see, he has put his nose to your cheek. He has taken a fancy to you already. You take the whistle and make him follow you."

The young girls were amusing themselves in this way, when they were interrupted by Farmer Croft and his eldest daughter, Zarah.

So suddenly did these two come that both Kate and Alice felt like school girls who had been caught romping, and hung down their heads, Alice putting the whistle that she had been blowing hastily into her pocket.

"Well, lasses, what is the matter now?" cried Farmer Croft, somewhat sharply.

"Oh, papa," said Kate, running to him and putting her arms round his neck; "we have been having such a game with Beda. I believe he likes Alice as well as he does me."

The father gazed fondly at his daughter and kissed her.

Alice was watching this scene when a shudder passed over her.

She turned round as if she expected to see an evil spirit near her.

There, not a foot from her, stood Zarah, her green eyes fixed on Alice.

Slipping quickly up to our heroine, Zarah took her hand, and smiling said—

"I see the cold has affected you. Come with me and I will show you your bed-room. I have chosen it next to my sister's, as you seem to be such friends. Really, I shall grow quite jealous. But, then, where is the use of that? Every one loves Kate."

"And every one who loves Kate *disappears*," a strange voice whispered in Alice's ear.

In vain she tried to banish the thought, still that warning was whispered to her.

Chatting merrily as she went, Zarah showed Alice a beautiful little bed-room on the ground floor, the windows of which opened out on to the gardens.

"You need not be frightened to be alone," said Zarah, opening a side door, "for in this room my sister sleeps, so that you will have company. Poor Kate, she walks in her sleep, so we are obliged to lock her in." She added rather hurriedly, "Still, she will hear you if you want anything."

Having shown Alice her sleeping apartment, they returned to the sitting-room, where they found supper already laid for them.

"Come, lasses," cried Farmer Croft, "you must make yourselves useful. Miss Landon, I never permit my girls to be idle. I made my money by hard work, and they must help to keep it together in the same way. Besides, labour keeps one in health, and health is happiness. So, you see, we have no ceremony here. This is Liberty Hall; every one does what they like, and in helping themselves they help each other."

For all the farmer's boisterous mirth, the supper was somewhat of the quietest.

The warning voice kept whispering in Alice's ear, and she could not eat.

Added to this, Zarah's green eyes were constantly fixed upon her like a serpent's.

At last the supper was cleared away by the girls, and Farmer Croft mixed himself a good stiff glass of grog, and filled himself a pipe.

"I hope you don't object to smoking, Miss Landon? No! Ah, that's a sensible girl. I often think what we should have done without this weed. Smoking makes a man think and moralize. Do you remember what the old song says?—

'This Indian weed, now withered quite,
    Green at noon, cut down at night,
    Shows thy decay;
    All flesh is hay.
        Thus think, and smoke tobacco.'

"There's philosophy for you, fancy that. 'Green at noon, cut down at night.' Ah! it is too true: 'All flesh is hay.'"

"I really think you might select a more amusing song for Miss Landon's edification," said Zarah, darting one of her sharp glances at her father.

"A more amusing song!" exclaimed Croft; "impossible. Listen to this, young ladies, and think of your laces and flounces—

'And as the smoke ascends on high,
    Thus you behold the vanity
    Of worldly stuff,
    Gone with a puff:
        Thus think, and smoke tobacco.'"

"Miss Landon is tired," said Zarah, sharply; "so we will retire to bed, and leave you to enjoy your tobacco alone, or rather together with your philosophy."

"And grog, my dear; don't forget the grog. Come, girls, have a little drop before you go."

In vain Alice protested that she would rather not, the farmer insisted.

"Come, Zarah, you mix them some and carry it up in their bed-rooms. Don't be squeamish, it will do you good."

As the farmer would take no refusal, Alice and Kate went up to bed, whilst Zarah remained below to mix what Farmer Croft termed a "night cap."

Poor Alice could not shake off the gloom which Kate's fancies, as she called them, had thrown over her.

She threw herself into a large old-fashioned armchair, and was soon lost in thought, until aroused by Zarah who brought her the liquid.

"What! not in bed yet?" exclaimed Zarah; "I see I must act lady's maid."

"Pardon me, I pray," said Alice; "I would sooner rest here a little while."

"But you must be tired, the fatigues of the day have been so much."

"Yes, I am tired, and will retire shortly. The day has been so full of strange events that I would fain calm my thoughts in solitude before I sink to rest."

"Well, as you will," laughed Zarah; "you are our guest, and must be humoured; but do not sit up too long; we must bring roses back to those thin pale cheeks."

Kissing Alice affectionately, Zarah bade her good night, and was about hurrying from the room when she perceived that she had left the key in Kate's door.

With a sharp exclamation of anger she walked hastily up to the door of her sister's bed-room, and was about to remove the key therefrom when Alice stopped her.

"Do not remove that key," she exclaimed; "I shall feel safer with it here."

"Have I not told you that my sister walks in her sleep?" said Zarah, impatiently.

"But she cannot enter my room if I have locked the door on this side."

This was so self evident a fact, that Zarah could not refute it, so with a short laugh, she said—

"Do as you will then, we all have our fancies, and that is one of yours. I don't suppose Kate will walk to-night, she is too tired for that. So drink up that horrid grog, as papa calls it—and which, by the way, will do you good, and hurry into bed."

With a light laugh, Zarah hurried away, rather annoyed as Alice fancied.

"There," exclaimed Alice, when she was alone, "there is another fancy of mine. I believe that silly girl, Kate, must have imbued me with her fancies."

Fancies! were they fancies? If so, what had made Alice shudder when by Zarah?

Why had that voice of warning always been whispering in her ear?

Hastily determining not to give way to such thoughts, she sipped the brandy and water.

Was it fancy, or was there really a queer dull taste about it?

She held it up to the light, and felt certain she could see small particles of something floating in it. She tasted it again. There was no fancy, it did taste peculiar.

At that moment she was startled by a slight tapping at Katey's bedroom door.

Putting down the glass, and concealing her doubts as well as she could, she turned the key.

The door opened quietly and admitted Katey.

"Oh, I am so glad you would have the key," whispered the girl, "they say I walk in my sleep, but I don't believe I do. I was so afraid they would remove it, I mean the key, as they have always done before, and I did so want to sleep with you, dear. You will let me?"

"Yes, there can be no harm in that," said Alice, who somehow seemed to gather strength in this weak girl's presence. "You are undressed, jump into bed."

"But you have not drank your brandy," said the girl, laughingly.

"I—I never touch spirits," faltered Alice, not liking to breathe her suspicions.

"Oh you foolish old thing," cried Kate, "I like doing those sort of little things, like tasting spirits, just because people say you mustn't. Do you know I once smoked a cigar—that is, part of one. Oh! it made me so ill."

Poor Alice could not believe that there could be harm where this little creature was, and turning her head, wiped away a tear that had gathered in her eye.

Taking advantage of Alice's not looking, Miss Kate seized the glass and drank off the contents.

"What have you done?" exclaimed Alice, in alarm.

But Kate could not answer her for laughing. She buried her head in the bed clothes—for she was frightened that her sister might hear that she had escaped from her own room, and laughed until she was nearly suffocated.

This last act fairly upset Alice's suspicions, and she caressed the young girl's head, admiring the golden curls that hung down about her fair shoulders.

"Oh! you don't know what fun it is to do something naughty like that," whispered Kate,

"There surely is no very dreadful sin in what you have done."

"Isn't there?" enquired Kate, innocently. "Zarah has always told me never to touch our guests drink if I valued my life. That is why I did it."

A horrible suspicion flashed across Alice's mind, but she quickly banished it.

"But why should Zarah tell you that?" she asked.

"I don't know," replied Kate, "I suppose she thinks it is rude, that is all."

"Have many people stopped here then?" demanded Alice.

"Oh, yes," yawned Kate, who now seemed unable to keep her eyes open, "several, but—they all—they all —" here her voice died away as in sleep.

"They all what?" demanded Alice, anxiously, "they all what, dear Kate?"

"They all—they all—go away," said the girl, who was evidently fast asleep.

"But Kate, dear Kate—where do they go?" urged Alice.

"Oh, don't bother—let me sleep—*they disappear*."

Again that word! Alice recoiled in horror, as it fell upon her ears.

Could it then be true, that she was indeed in a place where murders were committed.

Hastily seizing her candle, she examined the face of the sleeping girl.

The eyes were half open; the muscles of the jaw were firm and rigid.

There was no longer room for doubt, the brandy and water had been drugged.

In her alarm, Alice dropped the candle, and in a moment it was extinguished.

First, in deep despair, she threw herself in the arm chair and prepared to wait the worst.

Then she would vainly try to rouse the sleeper, but her endeavours were useless.

Nothing could be heard but the deep and heavy breathing of the sleeper.

Yes; Alice could hear something more—there were *footsteps on the gravel path by the window.*

Cautiously approaching the window, she drew one of the long curtains over her and listened.

At first the sounds came indistinctly to her, but at length she heard the conversation.

The voices were those of Farmer Croft and his terrible daughter, Zarah.

"I do not like this business," muttered Croft, "Ill will come of it."

"And why? Have you not Jonathan Wild's order?" answered Zarah.

"Aye, nice orders too. He always manages to shove the dangerous work on others."

"The work is no more dangerous than many we have done before."

"True! but why should Jonathan Wild have changed his orders? I was to have treated her kindly."

"Well, those were your first orders, your second was to see that by to-morrow she *is dead*.

A cold perspiration broke out on Alice's forehead when she heard this.

"I tell you," continued Croft, "that I do not like this sort of thing. Kate has taken to her so."

"Kate takes to everything," said Zarah, contemptuously, "why, have you not spared her lovers?"

"Well, I suppose it must be done," muttered Croft, "is Kate all safe?"

"Yes, I locked her in; besides, I drugged her drink as well as the girl's."

"And the window?" enquired the man.

"The bolts are all shot, but they don't catch, so come, do not let us waste time."

Alice drew back and beheld with horror the shadows of the father and daughter appear on the blind.

The window opened *outward*, by which Alice plainly saw they had been made on purpose for such diabolical deeds as that about to be enacted.

The blind, in some mysterious way, which Alice could not discover, rolled silently up.

The next moment Farmer Croft and Zarah stole softly into the room.

Stealthily they moved towards the bed, neither of them speaking a word.

Zarah drew back her hanging sleeves, and quickly placed her hand on her sisters mouth.

The next instant Croft drew forth a knife and plunged it into his daughter's bosom.

Alice, who had watched these proceedings as if spell bound, could bear no more.

Uttering a fearful shriek, she sprang through the window and rushed down the garden.

"Confusion," cried Croft, "what was that."

Zarah, quick as lightning, turned the head of the murdered woman towards the light.

Both uttered a scream of horror as they beheld the features of Kate Croft.

"Miserable wretch that I am," cried Croft, I have killed my child."

But Zarah was made of sterner stuff than her father, and much as she loved her sister—and strange as it may sound, this fiend, in human shape, really did love her—she at once set to work to repair, as far as might be, the evil that was already done.

Quickly tearing up one of the sheets to staunch the wound, she cried to her father:—

"Follow the girl, if she escape us all is lost. Kill her openly sooner than she should escape. Your excuse is *that she murdered Kate.*"

This advice was too good to be lost, and much as the farmer loved his daughter, he was not a man of such refined feelings as to miss the opportunity of escaping the consequences of his crimes.

He, therefore, did not hesitate a moment, but at once hastened after Alice.

Terror had lent wings to the poor girl, and she sped away towards the open country.

The moon kept glancing from between the clouds down on the earth, lending its pale light in fitful rays to guide her on her way.

As she rushed along she fancied she heard footsteps behind her.

She turned, and to her horror she beheld Farmer Croft in full pursuit.

For a moment Alice felt inclined to turn and face her pursuer, to grapple with him, for the very horror of the dreadful tragedy she had just witnessed gave her courage.

"Stop," yelled Croft, "stop, or I fire upon you, you she devil."

The sound of Croft's voice planted a new terror in her breast, and she bounded on.

Poor Alice found that although she strained every nerve to outstrip her pursuer, he gained upon her.

With that strange impulse, which fear so often causes, she kept gazing behind her, to see how much nearer Farmer Croft was, although she lost ground each time she did so.

Croft was now within twenty or thirty feet of her, and she felt that her strength was giving way rapidly.

She gazed rapidly round to see if she could discover any help at hand.

At a little distance she saw poor Kate's little Arab horse.

Quickly she drew the whistle from her pocket, for luckily she had forgotten to return it to its owner, owing to the sudden appearance of Croft and Zarah.

The horse pricked up its ears at the sound, and then dashed up to Alice.

With a cry of joy, the young girl seized the horse's mane and sprang safely on its back.

As if conscious of the precious charge he carried, and fully aware of the danger that followed them, the gallant little horse stretched forth its neck, and with extended nostrils, as if snuffing the wind, darted away across the country.

With a dreadful oath Farmer Croft saw the young girl disappear over a hedge, and turning round he hastened to where his own horse was quietly grazing.

Leaping on its back he urged it on in pursuit, trying to guide it with his hands, in lieu of a bridle.

The intelligent creature seemed to understand its master, and galloped off in the direction he required, clearing hedge and ditch with wondrous ease.

The farmer, knowing the country well, had made a cut across it so as to reach the high road at a bend, in order to overtake Alice, who, he rightly conjectured, would take the first road she came to, as more likely to lead her to habitations, and being better for riding.

He, however, reached the road a moment too late, for as he leapt the hedge Alice dashed passed.

"Stop, stop, or I'll kill you," shouted the farmer.

The rattle of hoofs evidently startled Beda, for placing her ears back on her neck, and giving a snort of defiance, she flew forward like an arrow, distancing her pursuer.

Turning sharply to the left, the Arab, who seemed enjoying the chase, turned into a wild heath or common, across which it flew like the wind.

Although he was distanced, Farmer Croft still kept up the pursuit, in hopes that Alice might be thrown, or meet with some accident that would prevent her continuing her flight.

He had just dashed to the summit of a knoll, when he beheld a sight which made him check his steed. It was a party of horsemen, into whose midst the gallant little Arab had borne Alice.

Quickly turning his horse, he rode back home as fast as he could.

Meanwhile, Alice, overcome with the excitement she had suffered, had sunk fainting on the ground, from which she was raised by one of the horsemen.

CHAPTER LXV.

HUE AND CRY AFTER JACK SHEPPARD. JERRY BLINKER SAVES HIS FRIEND.

ALTHOUGH Maud, as the reader may remember, had robbed Lady Hamilton in a very clever manner, yet it must not be imagined for a moment that that lady was at all inclined to put up with her loss.

She had at once communicated with the Bow Street authorities, who had sent out their runners far and near with orders to arrest the daring highwayman at all risks. She had also paid Jonathan Wild a visit, and requested his co-operation in the matter, a request he at once complied with, as the pay was good.

Consequently, the roads about Epping were as unsafe for Batswing and his followers as could well be imagined.

But one person was left to play spy on the robins, and that was no less a person than Jerry Blinker, to whom our story now returns.

Jerry was tired in the extreme of the life he was leading. He longed for excitement, and even his usual solaces—whistling, tobacco, and beer—brought not comfort to his weary soul.

One evening towards dusk he was leaning, as usual, against the horse-trough, whistling.

A pipe was held tenderly between the fingers of his left hand, whilst his right held a pewter pot, which he was moving round slowly so as to give the contents a head, at the same time gazing into it wistfully.

"No, I can't stand this," he murmured; "blowed if I can. Stagnation to a chap is as bad as stagnation to water; it *kivers* both over with green. 'My soul's in harms and heager for the fray,' as the chap says in the play. I'm growing rusty, that's what I am. I shouldn't wonder but what I shall grow to this 'ere trough; stick to it like a limpet. Ah! it's a fearful thing for a fellow like me to be left to rot, when he feels he's made for great things, that's what it is."

Sighing deeply, Jerry took a pull at his beer, and then fell to whistling again.

"THE STRANGER WAS A POWERFUL, BROAD-BUILT FELLOW, AND HAD A DAGGER!"

"It is odd," he continued at length, "how things is a-going. Now there's the cap'en coming the respectable caper. He's always a-rushing about getting into all sorts of scrapes for somebody else's good, and not for his own. I think I must have a cut in myself, that I do."

Once more Jerry fell-to whistling in his usual doleful style.

"Hilloa!" he cried, looking up, "what's the row now? Blest if there aint a hue and a cry on. They're running some poor devil to ground that's certain." There could be little doubt of that, for over the fields, leaping hedges and ditches, came a crowd of men and boys pursuing one unfortunate wretch, who, straining every nerve, rushed blindly on, striving to out-run his pursuers, for he knew his life depended upon it.

No. 22.

"Stop thief! stop thief!! stop!!!" roared the crowd.

The panting man was so close now, that Jerry knew his features.

"Blow'd if it aint Jack Shepherd," he cried, "It's luck there aint nobody but Mrs. Wapshaw in the house. I must save my pal: well here's something to do at all events. Here goes my wit against the robins, and we'll see whose best."

Opening the stable door Jerry stood behind it in such a manner that he could not be seen.

He had not long to wait, for in two minutes Jack rushed into the stable yard. He was covered with dirt, and the perspiration poured down his face.

"Jack, Jack! quick, quick this way," whispered Jerry.

Jack heard the sound and dashed into the stable.

"Jump in here," said Jerry, opening the corn bin, "I'll save you yet."

Jack had no time to hesitate for the fall of his pursuers feet could be plainly heard. He sprang into the bin; Jerry closed the lid! locked it, and having put the key in his pocket, stretched himself on the top of the box, pretending to be in a sound sleep.

"He must have hidden in these stables," Jerry heard one of the constables cry.

"I rather think he is," thought Jerry.

"Search everywhere; we've got him at last," cried the constable as he entered the stable where Jerry was pretending to sleep.

"Hilloa! my lad," he cried, "Wake up, have you seen a man pass in here, eh? Come wake up," he continued, shaking Jerry.

"What's the matter?" demanded Jerry, vacantly, as he rubbed his eyes with his knuckles, "It aint time to get up yet: what do you want?"

"Not time to get up, you sleepy rascal! why it's past two o'clock."

"Why, what's the matter?" asked Jerry, as if he had just realized the fact that the stables were filled with men, "the 'ouse beant on fire, be it?'

"No; but Jack Shepherd, the famos house breaker, has hidden here."

"Hidden here! O Lord! O Lord!" cried Jerry, rolling on the bin as if in the greatest terror, "then we shall all be murdered in our beds; I know we shall."

"The lad's an idiot," said the constable, "leave him alone, and search the stables and the lofts, he must be here."

Away went the men, turning over the straw and hay, climbing into the lofts and examining everything, but as the reader may guess, without success.

As for Jerry, he seemed paralyzed with fear, and remained on the bin merely ejaculating now and then "O Lord! O Lord! we shall be murdered alive."

"We've searched every where," said one of the men to the chief constable, "he must have escaped."

"Impossible, he must be here, some of you go and search the house."

"Jerry could not help grinning when he heard the order, for he knew that the widow Wapshaw would deeply resent the intrusion. That he was right, was soon proved by the sound of the hostess's voice in loud altercation with the men.

"Search my house will you," cried the widow, "where's your warrant? Do you think that I, an honest woman, would shelter house breakers? Not likely indeed. Yah! come down stairs I say: you shall not go into my bedroom, you nasty impudent fellow, come down I say."

The widow's voice died away in the distance, so Jerry concluded that the officers were carrying out their search in spite of the widow.

"He's not there sir," said the men, returning to the stable where the chief constable had lingered, as if still convinced that Jack was there.

"Then I suppose he must have escaped, as we have searched everywhere."

"Everywhere except in that corn bin," said one of the men.

"Ah! let us look in the corn bin?" said the constable.

Jerry jumped off the bin with alacrity. They tried it, but found it was locked.

"It's locked sir," said one of the men.

"'A course it is," said Jerry, catch the Missus a-leaving the corn unlocked."

"Well it's evident he can't be there," said the constable," but how he could have got through this yard I don't know."

"He could have climbed over the wall at the back, just behind the stable, it's only two feet high," said Jerry.

"Why did you not tell me that before?" cried the constable, angrily.

"'Cause you didn't ask," said Jerry.

"Bah! the lad's an idiot," said the constable, "come lads, we may have him yet."

In another minute Jerry had the extreme pleasure of seeing the constables move out of the yard.

He watched them until they were two fields off, and then returned to the stable muttering, "not quite such a fool after all, master constable."

"It's all right Jack," he said as he let Shepherd out of the bin, "the robins have cleared off. Just follow me and I'll make you comfortable."

He led the way up into one of the lofts and placed Shepherd behind some hay, so that should the constables return they might not find him. He then procured a pot of foaming porter and some cold meat pie, which he handed to Jack.

"My heye! how he does eat," said Jerry in admiration of the quick manner in which Jack put away the food, "there's a reduction in taking a quantity there at all events, your living don't cost nothing."

"There," said Jack when he had finished, "and now my kind young friend let me have an hour or two's sleep, for I ache for want of rest."

"All right, I'm fly. I'll lock the stable door so that you shan't be disturbed."

"Thanks: I will not forget your kindness."

"Look here," said Jerry, "Will you grant me one request?"

"If it is in my power I will," replied Jack.

"Oh! it's in your power right enough if you'll do it."

"Well then I give you my promise."

"Honour bright?"

"Honour bright."

"It is that you take me on your next Cracksman's lay."

"My young friend—"

"Come no crying off—you know you promised me."

"Well then I'll keep my word; only for mercy's sake leave me alone just now, for I am dying for sleep."

Jerry shook Jack by the hand and then left him to his slumbers.

CHAPTER LXVI.

THE ASSASSINATION OF LORD HENRY LESLIE—THE PAVED YARD AND THE LETTER—THE MYSTERIOUS STRANGER—LORD REDFERN'S ESCAPE.

SOME few nights after the sea fight between the "Black Hawk" and the "Sea Gull," Lord Henry was seated in the Rue de Chatelet. His lordship was dressed in a loose dressing-gown, and had the appearance of being a great invalid, as indeed he was, for the wound inflicted by Sir Arthur, in the unfortunate duel, had burst forth again, owing to the excitement caused by the combat at sea.

Lord Henry was busy writing letters, but such was his state of weakness, that every now and then he had to pause from his task and pass his hands over his eyes to clear away the mists that seemed to gather before them. Still he resumed his task with wonderful determination, although, from the sighs that escaped his lips it proved that it was by no means a pleasant or easy one.

Having finished a letter, he leant back in his chair, oppressed with a strange faintness.

"It is strange," he muttered. "I have to day felt nearer death than when first I received this wound. What base treachery have I been subject to. Lord Redfern, to whom I have shown the greatest kindness, would ruin and kill me. For what reason I know not. Well, well; these letters which I shall despatch to-morrow, will expose his guilt and save the innocent."

Rising from his chair, he approached the open window and gazed out at the night. Far up in the heavens sailed the moon, casting her silver light over the quaint old city, with its tall houses and narrow streets.

Glancing to the right, his eyes fell upon the old ramparts, whilst to the left there were the extinguisher-capped turrets of the chatelet, from which the street took its name.

Beneath him was a small courtyard, now perfectly disused, and therefore after the manner of the French, perfectly neglected. Long tufts of grass grew up between the flag-stones with which the yard was paved, and the whole place had a look of desolation.

"Thank heaven! I shall soon leave this place," said Lord Henry. "My heart seems to tremble with a vague terror that I cannot overcome. A sense of danger hangs over me. I wish that I had made some one sit up with me. Pshaw! this is cowardice; and yet I cannot shake off the feeling."

For some moments he paced up and down the room, evidently endeavouring to overcome the unpleasant sensation that was creeping over him.

The dim light of the lamp cast a dull ray over the room, making the place more lonely and desolate.

"It is no use," said his lordship, suddenly, "I cannot stand it. I will call up my host, tell him I am ill, and cannot bear to be alone in this wing of a building, where I should not be heard were I to call for help as loudly as possible. Francois is an honest fellow, and will cheer my spirits with his talk."

As he spoke, he moved towards the door, but suddenly paused in horror. He knew that he had locked the door before seating himself at his writing-table. To his amazement he saw the key turn, and heard the bolt of the lock fly back.

The next moment the door opened gently and without noise, admitting a man dressed in a long cloak that reached to his heels, so as to totally disguise his person, whilst a crape mask covered his face.

The stranger, whoever he was, had evidently not expected to find Lord Henry sitting up, for he started as violently at seeing his lordship, as his lordship had done at seeing him.

Nevertheless, he seemed quickly to have made up his mind how to proceed, for he closed the door behind him, and locking it, placed the key in his pocket.

"Who are you, and what do you want here?" demanded Lord Henry.

"Silence!" said the man, in a low, stern voice. "If you speak a word you die."

"Great heavens!" exclaimed Lord Henry. "What have I done to deserve this fate?"

"That I know not," replied the man. "All I know is that I have had my orders."

"Your orders?' said Lord Harry, who, weak and ill as he was, felt it would be useless to make any defence. "And what may your orders be?"

"To kill you," replied the man, in the same muffled tones.

"Indeed!" said his lordship, and may I ask who gave you these orders?"

"Well, I don't know that I ought to answer that question.'

"Surely, as I am to die, it can do no harm to tell me. Doubtless you know that I have no chance of help coming to me here, and that in my weak state I shall be able to make but small resistance. In a few minutes my life will be closed for ever in this world. I shall not plead for revenge to human judges, but unto one who reads the hearts of men, and to whom all secrets are known. Come, tell me who sent you."

"Well, perhaps there is no harm in that," replied the man, "but I have no time to waste. You have offended a certain gentleman by falling in love with a certain lady. He tried to kill you in a duel. Failing to do so, he put the matter into my hands, for he knows I never Miss my man."

"You cannot mean Sir Arthur Bowring," cried Lord Henry.

"Aye! he's your friend," replied the man. "But come, we've had enough of this. Are you prepared? You see it is useless to struggle, so it will be much better for you to submit quietly."

"Stay!" said Lord Henry, coolly. "I have been writing letters here; they are on private business. Will you allow me to destroy some of them?"

"No!" replied the man. "I intend going through your papers for you, and will destroy them—that is if I don't want them myself."

"At all events you will let me write a few lines to an old friend."

"Yes, you may do that if you like; but make haste, and be careful what you write, as I shall read it when you're dead, and if it don't please me I shall burn it."

The man threw himself carelessly on a chair, and producing a pistol, presented it at Lord Henry, as much as to give him notice that if he attempted to escape he would shoot him on the spot.

Lord Henry seated himself at the writing-table, and wrote a short note, which he carefully folded and placed in an envelope. This done, he directed and sealed it, rose from his chair, and approached the window, as if in deep thought.

"Well, have you finished?" demanded the stranger, in a coarse voice?

"I have," replied Lord Henry, throwing the letter out of the window.

"What have you done?" cried the stranger, springing from his chair.

"Come and see," replied Lord Henry, calmly."

The stranger approached the window, and gazed out into the paved yard.

"You see that small courtyard below?" said Lord Henry Leslie.

"I do," what of that?" demanded the stranger. It is not very pretty.

"No; but there is only one way of entering it, and that is by passing through the front of this house where the landlord and his family sleep. Were you to attempt to do that, your arrest would be certain."

"Probably," said the stranger dryly." but I shall not attempt it."

"Well, into that yard I have thrown a letter stating that I have been murdered; also giving the names of my murderers, and their reasons for committing so base and cowardly a crime. Now, cried Lord Henry, defiantly, do your worst, I will sell my life as dearly as I can."

He had scarcely finished speaking when the stranger flew at his throat.

The struggle was a short and fierce one, but most unequal.

Lord Henry was weak from his recent wound, and was unarmed.

The stranger was a powerful, broad-built fellow, and had a dagger.

For a moment they clutched each other in a tight embrace.

Suddenly the stranger shook off Lord Henry's grip, by which means his right hand was liberated.

Grasping his dagger firmly, he raised it in the air, and then brought it down with all his might on Lord Henry's neck.

With one deep groan Lord Henry relaxed his grasp, staggered back a few paces, and then fell backwards on the floor.

"Fool!" exclaimed the stranger, as he spurned his prostrate foe, "had you but obeyed me you might have been alive."

Walking to the table the stranger commenced opening and reading the letters.

"Hum," he muttered, "so the authorities declaring that the duel was a fair one. Exonerating Sir Arthur Bowring, eh? Well, it is fortunate I came so soon. Another declaring Mistress Alice, virtuous. Well, well, the game is mine now, thanks to my own courage and skill. It's a nice custom the French porters have of pulling a string at night to let in anyone who likes to ring. No one has seen me enter; no one will see me leave, so I shall be free. Stay, I must take these letters with me; any papers destroyed here would look suspicious."

He gathered up the letters and placed them in his pocket.

"Now just to make certain he is dead," said the stranger, turning over the body.

As he turned it over, to his horror Lord Harry clutched him once more by the throat.

The livid eye-lids opened—in a hoarse whisper Lord Harry said,—

"The letter, thrown out—out of window."

"Well; what of that?" asked the stranger, trying to release himself.

"It has the names of my murderers written therein," gasped Lord Harry.

"I can't help that; Sir Arthur must look to himself," said the other.

"You lie!" said the dying man, "you must look to yourself. Do you think I could mistake your voice? You have been my ruin; my evil genius through life; and now have caused my death. I know you Redfern, in spite of your disguise. Reform: I am dying, and I forgive you, but I warn you to repent. I have in that letter shown your base dealings with that fiend, Jonathan Wild; his and your own downfall must ensue. Therefore with my last breath I warn you to fly. I would not carry hatred with me to the grave; I wish not for revenge, but only to save the innocent; not to punish the guilty. Fly at once; save your life that you may have time to repent!"

With a bitter imprecation, Lord Redfern struck the dying man full in the face.

"Curse you!" he cried, "if I am to die I will have the satisfaction of seeing you go first. I have hated you all along. Now I have my revenge!"

Seizing the dagger, he plunged it over and over again into Lord Harry's heart.

The young nobleman uttered no groan, but sank back, never to rise again.

The dreadful crime committed, Lord Redfern rose to his feet.

It was not the first time his hands had been dipped in blood, but yet he shuddered when he saw the colour.

Entering the bedroom he quickly washed off what stains he could.

The next thing he did was to ransack the drawers for money and papers.

This being done, he was about to leave the place, when he suddenly thought of the letter Lord Henry had cast into the little paved yard.

He dared not leave it there; and yet how was he to obtain it.

He walked to the window and glanced down to see if he could see it.

He drew back in horror, and trembling with terror. *The letter was gone!!*

Gone! He had marked the spot where it had fallen, for the white paper had glittered like a piece of silver in the moon light.

Who could have taken it. Could it be possible that the avenging angel was already on his track. He gasped for breath, and the cold sweat burst out on his forehead.

Then came the wild hope that he had not looked in the proper place, and again he leant out of the window and peered down into the yard.

"It is all right, my lord," cried a voice. "*I* have the letter quite safe."

Lord Redfern staggered back from the window in surprise.

There, at an open window opposite, stood a man waving the letter.

"I saw you complete your task," continued the man,

"and very well you did it at the price; but don't another time leave the window open when you have such business on hand."

"Who are you," said Lord Redfern. "Give me that letter and you shall be well paid for it."

"Perhaps I may if we both are safe back in England. Return there at once, or the French authorities will be on you. I'm off directly."

The fellow waved the letter again, and then closed the window.

"Who can the fellow be?" was the question that Lord Redfern asked himself.

The man had spoken in English, and had evidently been on the watch, expecting the crime to be committed. How had he managed to reach the yard? Redfern knew that the house, at the window of which the man had appeared, was one that stood in a little dirty street running behind the Rue de Chatelet, and he was certain that there was no communication between it and the yard.

"He must have lowered himself down by a rope," muttered Redfern; "one thing is certain, I must escape from here. Stop! if I am pursued how to throw them off the scent? I have it; I must borrow some of my Lord Leslie's clothes; he won't need them in future, and they may be of the greatest use to me."

With a coolness that positively surprised himself, he once more proceeded to the bed-room, stripped off his own clothes, folded them up carefully, after having emptied the pockets, and placed them away in the drawers.

He then took the best suit he could find, dressed himself in it rapidly, and selecting a hat and sword, was preparing to leave the room, when his eye fell upon his cloak, hat, and mask.

"A good thought," he cried, as he picked them up, "these will help to mislead the police, should they be placed on the scent by that fellow."

Going to the window, he dropped the hat into the yard.

He then threw the cloak so that it might alight on the side wall.

"Capitally done," he said with a chuckle, "they will now think that I lost my cloak in trying to escape that way. And now to make my way to the beach. Once there I am tolerably safe; for no one knows that I am out of England, except the smugglers who have brought me. They dare not turn against me, for their lives have been forfeit to the law over and over again."

With this cheering thought, Lord Redfern unlocked the door; removed a pair of spring pliers,—by the aid of which he had opened the lock in the first instance from the outside—then closing the door, stole gently down stairs, and into the street.

Managing to avoid the sentinels who were stationed about the ramparts, he gained the lower town, and was about to make his way towards the river Loire, when he heard a wild cry and the rush of many feet.

His first idea was flight, for he made certain he was pursued.

Turning down a narrow street, he hurried rapidly along.

The sounds of pursuit grew louder and louder behind him.

They were evidently close behind him, yet he paused, for he could hear the same cries coming down the lane to meet him.

Was he surrounded? Had the alarm been given by the man, the body discovered, and the police in pursuit? He tottered into a doorway, hoping to conceal himself, and that in the confusion of the crowds meeting he might manage to escape.

Redfern, as the reader already knows, was a coward. He had no remorse for the murders he had committed, but he writhed in agony when he thought he might be detected, and receive the punishment he deserved.

The cries came nearer, and he listened in agony as they approached.

Hark! what was that? Yes, he could not be mistaken, he was safe.

His crime had not been detected; the cry was that of "Fire!"

Fire! fire!! fire!!! The terrible cry awoke the echoes of the night.

Loudly the bells from the church steeples poured out their deep notes from their brazen throats, calling on the people to arise and help to extinguish the devouring element, and to aid the sufferers in saving their property.

A broad red glare shot athwart the sky, giving a strange flickering light.

Up in the air flew the burning wood, scattering sparks right and left.

The crowd now surrounded Lord Redfern, but he cared not for it.

He joined with them and yelled "Fire; fire!!" until he was perfectly hoarse.

They were close by the burning house, and Redfern could not escape.

The crowd carried him right up before it, and commenced yelling furiously, stamping and gesticulating at the blazing mass, as though that would quench it.

Presently the regular tramp of men showed that the soldiers were near.

"Back! stand back," cried the soldiers, pressing the mob back with their muskets.

"Form line!" cried the officer in command. "Form line, to pass the buckets."

In a minute the crowd was driven back into a line, Redfern amongst them.

Then from the surrounding houses, pumps. and wells, little buckets of water were quickly passed from hand to hand, until they reached some fireman, who cast them into the burning fire, without, as one may think, extinguishing it.

For some time Redfern worked in this manner with pleasure, for he knew that during the confusion he should pass unnoticed.

At length the fire had burned itself nearly out, and the buckets were passed down the line with less rapidity.

Redfern was thinking about making his escape, when his attention was arrested by the conversation of two men who stood behind him.

"Ventre gris!" exclaimed one, "this is a night of terror."

"Yes," replied the other, "it has been a good fire."

"Ah! but that is not the worst of it; there is a young English *Milord* who has been assassinated in the Rue de Chatelet.

"Sapriste," it is indeed terrible. Have they succeeded in catching the murderer.

"No; the affair is a mystery altogether. The authorities received notice in the strangest manner imaginable. I was at the *Gen-d'armerie* at the time."

"How was it done, Pierre?" enquired the other, anxiously.

"Why, a boy was sent in with a note telling how the murder was done. It was written in English, and described the murderer as being dressed in a long black cloak. We went to the house, found the body as described, but the assassin must have escaped over the wall, for his hat and cloak were found in the paved yard. But come, Adolphe, let us have a small glass of brandy, and I'll tell you more; for I know what plans are being taken to ensure the murderer's escape becoming impossible. The two men moved slowly away, leaving Lord Redfern in anything but a pleasant state of mind.

What plans would be taken to prevent the murderer's escape? was the anxious question he asked himself. He would have given anything to follow the two men so as to gain information, but dared not.

With bent down head he crept along the road, and keeping to all the back streets, made for the sands, where he expected to find a boat waiting for him.

As he passed down the low pier, he fancied he heard the sound of men's voices.

He paused and listened, fancying they might be constables.

"I'll not go till just before the break of day," said one.

Lord Redfern's heart beat with delight, for the man spoke in English.

"It's madness for us to stop here," replied the other; "I tell you there's a regular noise up the town about a man being murdered; they do say by an Englishman; at all events I know that they were seeking after a man just answering your lordships description, and most likely they have him by now."

"It's no good your arguing with me," replied the other. "I've nothing to do with what goes on ashore. I'm only engaged by his lordship to manage the cutter, and that I'll do."

"And quite right too," said Lord Redfern, stepping forwards, "what is the meaning of this fellow's daring to advise you to sail without me."

"I beg your honour's pardon," said the man, "but when I went up town I heard such nasty rumours that I thought we'd better stand out in the offing until we were certain you would come."

"You're a fool," said Redfern; "I enquired about the rumour of the murder, and find it is not true. Quick, my lads, shove off the boats, we must reach the Essex coast as soon as possible."

As he spoke, Lord Redfern threw himself into the stern sheets of the boat. The two men shoved her off, and pulled silently to a cutter which lay at anchor in the roads.

"Saunders," said Lord Redfern, when they were on board, "who was that fellow who was speaking to you on the beach?"

"He's a man I only engaged for this run, your honour. You came down without giving us any warning, and I couldn't get the crew together, and as he had been hanging about the yacht and seemed to be a very good fellow, I engaged him. He's not much of a sailor, I find, in spite of his having pitched me a yarn of having been in the coasting trade."

"Never engage him again," said Lord Redfern, "get rid of him as soon as you can. Now make all sail, for I must be in London to-morrow."

Having given these orders to the captain, Lord Redfern locked himself in his cabin.

"I say skipper, what was the governor saying to you?" asked the new man.

"Why, mate, he says as how he didn't like the cut of your jib, and that the sooner we can part company the better he shall like it," replied Saunders.

"Well, I'm sure I don't care how soon that comes to pass either," said the man.

"Do you know matey, that I don't think you've had much to do with the sea."

"I've had more than I like," replied the man, "but don't let's quarrel; you and I have no cause to fall out; so let us have a good glass of grog."

"With all my heart," replied the good-hearted sailor, "you run down and mix it, while I look after the wheel; the skipper wants a quick run, and I shall have to be up all night, so make the grog stiff."

"I say," said the man, stopping at the hatchway, "did you notice anything strange about the skipper when he came on board?"

"No; only he was in a bad temper, and that's no rarity."

"I noticed he had changed all his clothes. It's rather strange, that's all."

CHAPTER LXVII.

HOW BATSWING MEETS ALICE LANDON—ALICE TELLS
HER STORY—BATSWING PROMISES TO PROTECT ALICE.

WE left Alice Landon fainting on the ground surrounded by a party of horsemen.

"Why what the deuce does this mean?" cried one
swinging himself out of the saddle, "is this some run-
away fair one: if so where is her pursuer?"

"I saw some one ride away over yonder," said another
of the party.

"Shall we pursue him captain?" demanded a third.

"No, we have no time for that. Let us see what the
girl is like."

As he spoke he raised the girl in his arms, and, putting back her hair, gazed into her face; but he had
scarcely done so when his manner changed.

"By heavens," he cried, "it is Alice Landon."

"Alice Landon!" cried the men in surprise.

"Providence has indeed guided us here. Pray heaven
that I have not come too late to save her from violence.
Alice: Alice, my own sweet Alice: speak to me. Do
you not know me; you are safe now, I am Batswing,
who will die to save you. Look up and speak to me
Alice. Tell me you are unhurt."

"Blest if I ever heard the cap'en speak like that
'afore," muttered Growling Teddy, "blame me if I know
what is the matter with women; they're always getting
into scrapes, and making other people pay for 'em."

But Teddy the Growler's remarks found no willing
ear: for all the men were too deeply interested in the
case before them to attend to him. But the terrible
scene which Alice had witnessed had been too much for
her and she remained insensible.

"We must bear her away from here," said Batswing,
"we must procure help."

"But where can we take her?" demanded one of the
men.

"I scarcely know," replied Batswing, "would that we
had come earlier."

"We might have missed her altogether then," said
Growling Teddy.

"Aye! and we should have lost all the Countess
Sourkroutzenberg's jewels." said another, and I guess
they are of some value."

"True! cried Batswing," the jewels are of the greatest value."

"They are worth *millions* to me; for with their aid I
will obtain my revenge on my enemies and protect those
I love."

"But what are we to do now," said one.

"Make to the French Horn at Mill Hill. We will
there lay out some plan whereby we will discover the
cause of all these plots against this poor girl. My men,
you know who and what I am, and can trust me."

"We can, we can," replied the men with earnestness.

"Then listen to me: not one word about the Countess's jewels must be breathed to any one of our men.
How we shall manage I know not; but it is evident
that Jonathan Wild and other powerful men are working their hardest against us. We have lost many of our
brave fellows by the attack upon our cave, and therefore
have less chance of meeting them. If we have to dis-
perse, I have enough for all of you: if we are arrested,
I must do my best to save you. Trust me, I will never
deceive or desert one who has been faithful to me."

"We do trust you: we do trust you," cried the men.

"Then swear to keep my secret," said Batswing.

"We swear!" said the men solemnly.

"Enough," cried Batswing, as he placed Alice gently
on the saddle, "now follow me to the French Horn, we
shall there find a hearty welcome and time to deliberate."

The cavalcade set off at a gentle pace so that Alice
should not be inconvenienced. Keeping across the

fields; making through gates so as to avoid the hedges,
they at length reached their destination.

They found the inn closed for the night, and it was
not without repeated knocking that they gained ad-
mission.

"You sleep soundly," said Batswing to the landlord,
who opened the door.

"We are seldom called at this time of night," replied
the landlord.

"Quick, bring a light here," continued Batswing, not
noticing the man.

"Hilloa! what's up now: a gal? well I never," cried
the landlord.

"Don't stand gaping there, but bring some cordial to
revive her."

The cordial was brought and administered to Alice,
who in a few moments opened her eyes and gazed
around.

"Where am I?" she exclaimed.

Then passing her hands over her eyes, she shuddered
violently, as she remembered the terrible scene she had
witnessed.

"Fear not, Alice," said Batswing, "you are with
friends now."

"Oh! thank heaven, I am saved!" cried Alice, bursting into tears.

It was some time before she was sufficiently composed
to relate her story.

Batswing listened to it with attention, but could not
help making some exclamations of horror and disgust,
as he heard of Croft's cruelty.

When the story was concluded, he paced up and down
the room in deep thought.

"Alice!" he exclaimed, "there is some deep mystery
in this."

"Oh! why should they persecute me so," sobbed
Alice, "I never injured them."

"Compose yourself, Alice," said Batswing, "this is a
time for work, not for tears."

"But what can I do?" asked the girl, "I am poor; I
have not the means to escape their treachery; I cannot
even fly from them."

"The time has past for that," said Batswing; "we
must meet them boldly now."

"Tell me what to do, and I will obey you," said
Alice.

"In the first place, Alice, tell me whether there was
any mystery about your father? Had he many friends,
or did he live in perfect seclusion?"

"I scarcely understand how to reply," said Alice,
"my earliest remembrance dates back to our little farm,
I was always treated with the greatest indulgence by
both father and mother."

"Your mother! Do you remember much about her?"
asked Batswing.

"Not much," said Alice, "she died when I was very
young."

"Can you not remember whether she hinted at any
change of fortune?"

"No—unless sometimes it was that she spoke about
living at some hall where she had been housekeeper.
She used to weep frequently, and pray. I think she
was a Roman Catholic."

"And your father, did he profess the same faith?"
demanded Batswing.

"No, never," said Alice, "he was always vexed when
my mother told her beads.

"Indeed!—that is strange—most men allow their
wives freedom of religion."

"I remember once I had the beads playing with, and
my father seeing them flew in a dreadful passion, exclaiming: 'Have we not seen misery enough, caused by
these Popish plots, without causing more; was not this
girl's brother murdered by them, and our good master
and mistress destroyed.'"

"That is strange language, indeed," said Batswing;

"did not either your father or mother mention any name. The name, for instance, of their unfortunate master, or of one of their old fellow servants?"

"No, not that I could remember—yet stay, once and once only I saw her kissing a likeness, she called it Lady Constance. But I was so young, that I have but a faint recollection of all this."

Batswing made no answer, but paced the room up and down, muttering,—

"Lady Constance! Lady Constance!! I see it all now. Yes. it must be so."

"Surely you cannot have discovered the reason of my persecution?" said Alice.

"I fear I have not discovered all Alice, but I have some clue. But fear not, to-morrow I shall place you in safety; till then you must stay here."

With a low bow, Batswing raised the fair girl's hand to his lips, and left the room.

"My lads," he said, when he once more stood with his followers, "I can but give you but short time for rest to-night. We must be up and away before sunrise Two of you must get a close coach and drive that lady we discovered on the heath to my house in St. James's; there you will wait upon her as though you were her servants; but in reality you must guard her; for, mark me, I shall hold you answerable for any harm that may befal her. Now go; and remember we must be up with the lark."

Of course, Teddy the Growler made some remark about the bother of women, but not one of Batswing's followers even questioned his orders, for they all loved and trusted in him. So drinking one more cup each to their captain's health, they bade him good night, and retired to snatch a few hours' sleep.

CHAPTER LXVIII.

LORD REDFERN'S RETURN—THE MERRY SMITH AND JONATHAN WILD'S TURNKEY — FLICKER FORMS A PLOT—REDFERN SOLD.

LORD REDFERN had a very bad passage back to Tillingham, for they had scarcely left the coast of France when the winds became contrary and the sea dreadfully rough, pitching the little cutter about like a rowing-boat.

It was, therefore, late at night when he reached Tillingham, and carefully avoiding observation, made his way back to the old Hall, where the old servants were so accustomed to his sudden appearance and disappearance, that he felt certain his present return would not be noticed.

Saunders, the captain of the cutter, had discharged the new sailor directly he arrived in port, according to Lord Redfern's order.

"Well, I've made a good thing of it and no mistake," said the man to Saunders. "I've got my death of cold, and am wet through to the skin, and all for a few shillings. I'm blest if I'll go to sea any more."

"Don't be too sure of that, mate," replied Saunders, "I should think the odds were in favour of your being transported."

"Thank you for nothing," said the fellow. "Perhaps after that you'll tell me where I can get a night's lodging cheap?"

"Newgate," replied the other. "Look'ee here, mate. I don't quite understand you curse me if I do. I find you hanging about this place, and you tells me you belongs to it. Now, that must be a lie, seeing as how you don't know where to bring yourself to an anchor. You then says you've been brought up to the sea, and looking at your togs I took your word as true; but when I saw you turn coward at a puff of wind, and white at a little bit of sea-running, why, curse me, I think you have been sailing under false colours; so I warn you to sheer off, before I fall foul of you."

"I suppose there's no harm in giving a fellow-cre'tur the way to get a bed?" said the other. "And that poor fellow-cre'tur wet to the skin with salt water."

"Aye, and nearly full up to the skin with grog. Oh! you may look, but I saw you pulling away at the bottle; and had I not been too much engaged, I would have squared up matters with you before this. Curse me if I don't think the skipper's right, and you're a queer lot."

"Did he say that?" demanded the other. "Then he shall pay for it."

"Stow that!" cried Saunders, "when I sail with a man no one shall speak against him."

"What reason had he to speak against me, then?" demanded the other.

"I've told you, ; you prig the grog and tells lies, and then asks that. I'm ashamed of you. Come, sheer off, or I shall make things worse for you."

Grumbling some hearty curses against the sea and all belonging to it, the man walked away; but he had not gone far, before he heard some merry fellows roaring out a jolly song as they marched along the road.

The song ran as follows:—

Song.

"The sea is running bright and clear,
    The wind blows from the land—
Then hoist the sail, boys, with a cheer,
    Let each one lend a hand.

Hurrah! we leave the shore behind
    And fly across the sea;
We bound away before the wind
    So merry and so free."

"Merry and free!" exclaimed a jovial voice. "How can you be merry and free when you're shut up in a ship? Not a bit of it; a sailor is the man who suffers most in the world. He is ruled by the captain, he is not his own master at all. Now, the lads of the forest are free. Now list to my song—

Song.

"Freedom grows in forests deep,
    In the glades and dells
Where the fur facied conies sleep,
    'Neath the heather bells.

From each bough the birds will sing
    Blithely at the dawning,
Grateful hearts come hither, bring
    Welcome in the morning."

"Good gentlemen, I pray you not hurry on so fast," cried the man who had just left the cutter, "but pause and lend a poor fellow your assistance. I am a stranger in these parts, and would willingly pay for a night's lodging somewhere."

"Say you so," cried out the man who had sung the first song, "then come up alongside, and I will take you to the snuggest inn in the county. A stranger indeed you must be not to know the 'Three Cutters.'"

"The 'Three Cutters?" said the man, starting back at the name.

"Aye! the 'Three Cutters,'" replied the other, "you don't know anything against the house, I suppose. If so, I'll trouble you to let me know it, as I'm the landlord."

This invitation was given in such a tone and manner that the man hastened to assure the Merry Smith and Will Watch—for the singers were no others—that he had not heard one word against the "Three Cutters," and pointed out to them that it was impossible he could have done so, seeing that he had not been in the neighbourhood half an hour.

"Well, that being the case, come along with us," said Will, sharply.

"And as you're tired, perhaps you'll walk between us and give us your arm. It will help you along the road," said the Smith.

The man saw in an instant that their offers were simply made so as to prevent his escaping, but he looked at the men and dared not refuse.

"And so you have only just arrived here?" said Bob Blow-the-Bellows.

"That is all, Sir," faltered the man, "I am a poor sailor."

"A sailor!" cried Will, smacking the man on his back, thereby jerking all the breath out of his body; "A sailor! I love them all. What ship do you belong to, and what port do you hail from?"

"I—I don't belong to any ship now," gasped the man; "I have only just left her."

"Just left her?" cried the Smith, "then you must have come in that little cutter yacht we saw come in just now. A nice craft, eh?"

"Yes sir, very, but she pitches a good deal in rough weather."

"Pitches a good deal in rough weather," growled Will Watch, "I should think she did; most ships do. That's old Saunders's boat; a good man, and true. I hope you left the vessel with a good clean bill of health?"

"Oh yes; Mr. Saunders and I parted the best of friends, I assure you."

"And may I ask your name?" said the Smith, "we're all friends here."

"My name is Jacob Becker," said the man, taken off his guard.

"Well, Jacob, you see that light yonder? That house is the 'Three Cutters,' and we mean to have a carouse there to-night; you will join us?"

"If it's all the same to you, I'd sooner get on with my journey, Sir."

"Journey! why what journey can you have to do to-night?" cried Will.

"I have some important business up in London, Sir, and—that is, it is not very important, only I ought to have been up there by now."

"Oh, nonsense," cried the Smith, "the business has waited, and so can wait a little longer. I know you can sing a good song, and, therefore, have made up my mind that you shall stop. There, that's all settled."

Jacob Becker found it not the slightest use to object, and, therefore, yielded in the best fashion he could.

The kitchen of the "Three Cutters" was filled by a number of men, all drinking and smoking.

Jacob Becker was placed close to the fire, so that his clothes might dry; a hot tumbler of punch was given to him, under the influence of which he began to soften, and he soon was laughing with the rest of the company.

Songs flew about, glasses were replenished as soon as emptied.

As for Bob Blow-the-Bellows and Jacob Becker, they swore eternal friendship, for Jacob sang a good song, and the Smith loved a man who could sing.

Jacob was hard at work pouring forth a love ditty, when Bob felt some one pull his coat-tail, and on looking round beheld Flicker.

The boy put his finger to his lips and warned the Smith to silence.

He then pointed to Jacob Becker, and stealing from the room, signed for the merry Smith to follow him.

When the song was done, Bob Blow-the-Bellows went out into the passage.

"Hush!" said Flicker, taking him by the arm, "follow me in silence."

The lad led the Smith out of the house, and then said—

"Do you know who that fellow is that you and Will brought in?"

"No, young Bell-the-Cat, how should I?" said the Smith; "all I knows is that he drinks his grog in a proper manner, and sings a good song."

"Perhaps he does, Bob; but he'll make you sing to another tune."

"What do you mean? you young Wild-Cat; he's a jolly companion."

"So may Jack Ketch be, for all I knows: but I don't wish to meet him."

"Now look here, young goggle eyes, don't go playing any jokes on me."

"I don't think you'll find this 'ere much o' a joke," replied Flicker.

"What do you mean?" cried the Smith, losing patience, "spit it out, can't yer?"

"I mean that that fellow, Jack Becker, is a robin."

"No! It's impossible!" cried the Smith, starting back.

"It ain't though," replied Flicker, "I know his mug too well."

"Where have you seen him before!" demanded the Smith, eagerly.

"At the Fleet, along o' Mr. Wild; he's one o' his men."

"Is he?" said the Smith, "then I'm very sorry for him, that's all."

"Why, what do you intend doing?" asked Flicker, anxiously.

The smith made no answer, but opened a large clasp knife.

"Don't do nothing of the kind," said the boy. "I know a lay worth two of that. You only do what I tell you, and we'll have him nicely."

"Fire away, my hinfunt progeny," said the smith, who doubtlessly meant infant phenomenon. "You'll equal Jerry Blinker soon."

"I should hope so," said Flicker, proudly. "Look here, I no sooner seed him than I walks off to the Sol's Arms lower down by the port, you know, and who should I see but old Saunders, and he was talking about the weather he had been having at sea. He's been on the coast of France with Redfern. You see, my being a boy, they didn't notice me a bit, and talked free and easy like. This fellow Jacob went with them, but Redfern did not know it, and told Saunders to sack him at once."

"Well, but Lord Redfern is in with Wild, ain't he?" said the Smith.

"No, of course not. Did you ever know Wild well in with anyone?"

"Well, there is some truth in that, certainly," replied the Smith.

"Of course there is," said Flicker, "Now, listen to what I've got to say."

Flicker pulled the Smith's head down and whispered for a minute or two in his ear. What he said must at present remain a secret; all I can say is that the Smith's mouth drew back until the corners of it seemed as if they would reach his ears.

"Bravo!" he exclaimed, "you'll do Just you tip Will, and he will see the other fellows, and make all right."

"That's it," said Flicker, "you go and pile it on with the dubsman, and I'll get all ready for the go. Oh! won't we have a lark, that's all."

Bob Blow-the-Bellows winked and nodded violently and then went back to the room, where he found Jacob Becker rapidly approaching a high state of intoxication. There sat the unfortunate dubsman, smiling on all, for the wine had made him unsuspicious.

"Come, another bowl," cried the merry Smith, "and another song from our new friend, Jacob Becker. Come, lads, fill up your glasses, and then attention for the song."

"I—I could sing you a rare song," said Jacob, "if I knew you true men."

"JONATHAN TOUCHED A SPRING IN THE WALL, WHEN A TRAP OPENED UNDER BECKER'S FEET—"

"True men! can you doubt us?" cried the Smith.

"No, no; I don't mean that—but true to the laws of your country."

"Of course we are!" cried the men in a chorus.

"And you won't betray me to my master?" cried Jacob, who was so far gone that he was oblivious about the danger he ran.

"Your master, Jonathan Wild? Of course not," said the Smith.

"How—how do you know that he is my master?" asked Jacob, suspiciously.

"Why, you told us so a little time since. Come—come, give us the song, we won't betray you, never fear," said the merry Smith.

"The song! the song!" shouted the men, in voices loud enough to drown all further arguments, "No more speechifying, but give us the song."

No. 23.

Holding his pipe in his hand, much as an officer does his sword when on parade, Jacob Becker leant back in his chair—under which he drew his feet, until only the toes touched the ground—gazed at the ceiling, and then commenced :—

Tom Sheppard and Jonathan Wild.
A LEGEND OF THE GALLOWS.

I.

When Tom Sheppard was hung on old Tyburn tree—
A rare goodly sight all declared it to be—
But his spirit, they say, from earth would not go,
But put on the shape of a carrion crow.
　　A carrion crow, an old carrion crow,
　　That round, round the gibbet, would constantly go.
　　A proper old bird, as you must all agree,
　　To take up its perch on an old gallows tree.

II.

A deep, deadly black, is the hue of his coat,
And terribly harsh is the sound of his note;
Oh! he caws with delight, and welcomes with glee,
Each blossom, fresh borne, by that old tripple tree.
   That carrion crow; oh! that jolly old crow,
  Which round, round the gibbet does constantly
   go;
  With the clapping of wings, and deepest of caws,
  He welcomes each sacrifice, paid to the laws.

III.

To drive that old crow from the spot, they have tried,
But all their endeavours he seems to deride;
They say, from that tree, he will ne'er be beguil'd,
Till it bears for its fruit, cruel Jonathan Wild.
   Then off on swift wings, that old carrion crow,
  Wild's spirit will bear, to a place, full of woe;
  And Sheppard and Wild, so the people all say,
  Will dine with old Nick, on the very same day.

"Hurrah! hurrah!! hurrah!!!" shouted the men, as the song came to a conclusion; and so great was the applause, that the last verse had to be repeated over and over again, before the company was satisfied, and each time the chorus was shouted louder and louder.

The pride of success, and the din and confusion made by the people, caused the drink to rise rapidly to Jacob Becker's head.

The merry Smith perceived this, and immediately struck up the,—

Song of the Merry Smith.

I.

Bob Blow-the-Bellows is my name,
 A Smith by occupation;
No home have I, but constantly
 I roam about the nation.

"Chorus, gentlemen!" shouted the Smith, and immediately all sang:—

  I like a glass,
  I love a lass,
   And gaily blow the bellows;
  And by Saint George
  When at my forge,
   I'm the happiest of fellows.

II.

The sparks that from the iron are flung,
 Are like my Polly's eyes;
The hammer rings just like her tongue,
 The bellows mock her sighs.

  Tho' she may cry,
  I ne'er reply,
   But gaily blow the bellows;
  I let all pass,
  And quaff my glass
   The happiest of fellows.

"Th-th-th-ats not a good song," hicoughed Jacob, "not even the cl-cl-ang of a hammer—drown womanish tongue—I-I-I've a wife—tongues never still— drive fellow mad—blow the bellows—blow my wife—blow Redfern, Wild, and everybody. I'se go to sleep."

Suiting the action to the word, he put his arms on the table, leant his head upon them, and in a few moments was snoring violently.

"Poor fellow," said Bob Blow-the-Bellows, "he's fast asleep—fast."

"Ah!" he's had a good deal too much," said Will, "we'll put him to bed."

With a significant grin to the other men, Will and Bob Blow-the-Bellows carried the intoxicated Jacob Becker from the room, leaving the rest of the company to enjoy their pipes and grog in quietude.

Jacob was soon put to bed, and left to his pleasant dreams.

"There, it's all settled," said the Smith to Will Watch; "that boy, Flicker, ought to make his fortune. He's sharp as a needle."

"Aye, that he is," replied Will," but how that woman—Maud, I think yon call her—helps him."

"Yes," replied the Smith, " we couldn't have done it without her help."

As they reached the passage, they heard the trample of horses, and the next minute Lord Redfern entered the house.

"You have a man here," he began, " a sailor. I would see him."

"We've several here, your honour," replied Will, "What may be the name of the one as you wants?"

"What was his name, Saunders?" demanded Redfern, turning to the captain of his yacht, who was following him, " don't hesitate—his name?"

"Blest if I know," replied Saunders; "I've forgotten it."

"Do you mean the one as sailed with you from France?" asked Will.

"Yes, yes; that is the man," exclaimed Redfern and Saunders together.

"Why, he went away more than two hours ago," replied Will.

"D—n!" cried Redfern, "we have missed him."

"That, indeed, you have," said Will; I hope he ain't robbed your houour?"

"What does it matter, if the man be gone?" said Redfern. "Come, Saunders, we must see if we can overtake him."

They flung themselves on their horses, and galloped away.

"By jove! Flicker's right!" cried the Smith, "the captain will thank us for this."

"Yes," replied Will, "just see how they're tearing after a man who is asleep in bed; ho! ho! ho! ho!

Both laughed heartily, and then went back to join their comrades.

CHAPTER LXIX.

JONATHAN WILD GIVES AUDIENCE TO HIS SEVERAL AGENTS—AND LEARNS NEWS THAT DOES, AND SOME THAT DOES NOT, PLEASE HIM.

JONATHAN WILD sat in his office, in no pleasant humonr.

Everything he had attempted lately had gone wrong entirely.

He had gone far away into the north, to arrest a famous thief, and also to be out of the way of several crimes that he knew were to be committed—for he himself had given the orders—but which he was particularly anxious that it should in no way come out that he was connected with.

He had returned home sorely vexed, for the thief had slipped through his clutches.

But he had hoped that he should find that all the crimes he had planned would have been committed during his absence.

But no news had been brought him, that such was the case.

So Jonathan Wild sat in his office, ready to quarrel with everyone and everything.

At length he touched a bell, and one of his men appeared.

"Has anything, or anyone, come yet?" demanded Jonathan, sharpely.

"There's a Farmer Croft, down stairs, and here are some letters for your honour."

"Show Croft up," replied Wild, savagely, as he threw the letters carelessly on the table.

The man disappeared, as if glad to get from the room, and in a few minutes Croft, all pale and trembling, entered it.

"So you are to be seen at last?" cried Croft, furiously.

"It seems so," replied Wild, in amaze at his follower's wild looks and passion; "most of my friends agree with my enemies, in saying I am plain enough."

"You have ruined me! you have caused my heart to break!" cried Croft.

"Your heart! bah!" said Jonathan, "you never had any."

"Mark me, Jonathan Wild," cried Croft, "Mark me, you shall repent this."

"Repent *what*?" said Wild, impatiently, "if you don't take care, I *will* mark you; and when I do that, folk don't soon forget it. Come, cease this wretched attempt at acting; life's too full of romance and adventure, for me to care for the imitation—especially when it is such a very bad one."

So great was the power this extraordinary man had over his companions in crime, that even when their feelings were most injured, and their passions at the strongest, he could rule them with the greatest ease.

In the present instance, Farmer Croft became calmer, and took the chair that Jonathan Wild indicated he wanted him to take.

"Well, now to business," said Jonathan, "what have you done with Alice?"

"She has gone!" cried Croft, "gone! gone! Oh that I had her here!"

"Gone! and you dare tell me so?" screamed Jonathan, springing to his feet.

"Stay, and listen to me," cried Croft, "hear me before you blame."

He then related the whole of the murder—how it was planned—how executed.

"But," he screamed, in agony, "when the deed was done, I found that I had been betrayed. I had killed my daughter! my favorite, darling, child!"

For a moment Wild stared in amazement, and then burst into a loud laugh.

"Fiend!" cried Croft, "this is your fault, and you shall answer for it!"

The next moment he had sprang at Wild, and had clutched him by the throat, but Jonathan's quick eye had perceived his intention in time, and snatching up an oak bludgeon from the table, he felled Croft to the ground with a blow.

"Dog, would you turn and rend your master?" growled Jonathan. "Rise and take that seat, and listen to me. Move one inch, and I'll shoot you."

Croft rose up slowly, like a cur fearing the lash, and crept to the chair.

"Now listen to me," said Jonathan, "you have killed your child. I can't see how one murder more or less can matter to you. However, that is a matter of opinion; all I know is, I can hang you at any moment I like; aye, and could have done so years ago. You asked me to *mark* you. I will, and if I see any cowardice or repentance in you—you go to Tyburn."

Farmer Croft shrank from Jonathan's gaze, but made no answer.

"Where did Alice go, when she escaped?" asked Jonathan.

"She escaped on horse back," replied Croft, "I followed after her, but she was met by a party of horsemen; so I had to turn and fly."

"Have you heard anything about Batswing," demanded Wild.

"Yes," replied Croft, "he has shown that he is at liberty, pretty plainly."

"How so?" demanded Jonathan.

"The night I made that fatal mistake, he robbed the Countess of Sourkroutzenberg."

"Impossible!"

"That is what I have heard, only this morning," replied Croft, sulkily.

"But the Countess Sourkroutzenberg would have come to me," cried Wild.

"She is more likely to keep silent," said Croft, "for they do say that she was robbed in a very peculiar way, and would not like the king to know how,"

"How then did you get the information?" asked Jonathan, suspiciously.

"I merely heard a rumour; how it got about, I know not."

"Go now, and find out where is Alice," said Jonathan, sternly, "and remember, one word, one hint, one look, about me, and you swing."

Croft made no reply, but left the room, in a rough, surly, manner.

"I mistrust that fellow," muttered Wild, when the door was closed, "I must have him looked after."

Again he touched the bell, and the man appeared.

"Here," said Jonathan, "take this letter to Alderman Turner; it is for a warrant to arrest that man who has just left. Follow the fellow with the warrant for his apprehension, and should you see the slightest sign of his 'peaching,' seize and bring him here at once."

"All right, your honour," said the man, "Jacob Becker has just come in."

"Send him here directly," said Jonathan.

The man nodded, and hurried away to perform his task.

"Well!" said Wild, as Jacob Becker entered the room, "what news do you bring; good or bad?"

"Good, replied Becker. "When I arrived at Tillingham I found that Lord Redfern had engaged a private yacht to go to France, and at once set to work to get myself employed on board of her: I succeeded."

"Excellent," said Wild, rubbing his hadds, "and about Lord Leslie."

"He is murdered," replied Becker. "Murdered by Lord Redfern."

"Are you sure of that?" asked Wild. "Quite sure?"

"I saw it done with my own eyes," said Becker, who then commenced relating how he had taken a room at the back of Lord Leslie's house, and had seen the murder, as we have already described it.

"Changed his clothes before he came on board, eh?' said Wild.

"Yes," replied Becker. "How he managed it I don't know."

"That letter Leslie threw into the yard. We ought to have that."

"I have it," replied Becker, in triumph. "I saw it fall, and lowered myself into the yard by the aid of a rope. Here is the letter."

Bravo!!" cried Jonathan Wild, as he seized the letter and tore it open. "He is now so firmly in my grasp that nothing can save him.".

As he spoke he ran his eyes over the letter; his colour changed, and in a voice of thunder he demanded—

"What is the meaning of this? Are you mad that you dare show me this letter. Do you think I am to be bearded in this manner?"

"I don't understand your Honour," cried Becker. I have done my best. I picked the letter up and brought it to you as I found it. I have not the slightest knowledge of its contents."

"Listen then, and you shall hear them," cried Jonathan, and then read—

"Jonathan Wild,—Let this be a warning to you that your plots are being all discovered. We know Lord Redfern murdered Lord Leslie in the Rue de Chatelet at your instigation; your man, Jacob Becker, witnessed the deed, and stole the letter thrown in the yard. Wishful that justice should be done we regained the letter, and when the time comes will use it."—THE BAT.

Jacob Becker turned deadly pale as he heard the contents of the letter.

"Where and how could you have lost that letter," cried Jonathan.

"On my word I cannot tell," said Jacob. "This Batswing must be the devil."

"Idiot—dolt—fool," roared Wild. You have been duped by one of his followers, and to save your own vile neck would make out that it was done by supernatural agency. Think not that you shall thus escape my revenge. If by your folly aught should go wrong, you die for it; and now begone," said Jonathan, opening a side door. "Let no one see you go from here. Leave the house by the back gate, so that it may not be known that I have seen you. Discover who stole that letter, or in a week you bid this world farewell."

One glance at Jonathan told the unhappy wretch that he had no hope of mercy.

So, with a cringing bow, he left the room, feeling that danger was near.

He had scarcely proceeded a dozen steps down the passage when Jonathan touched a spring in the wall. Instantly a trap opened beneath Jacob Becker's feet, and he was precipitated into a dungeon.

The trap closed before he could cry for mercy, and the last sound his ears caught was Jonathan's fiendish laughter.

"There goes one witness," said Jonathan. "Ho, ho, ho, ho. He has his reward."

And with a diabolical chuckle he returned to his room, where he had not been long seated before Lord Redfern entered, pale as a ghost.

"Hullo!" said Jonathan, "what the devil's up now. Have you seen a ghost, or have you *committed a murder?* The latter most likely."

"Wild," cried Redfern, "have you played me falsely. Answer me truly."

"Don't be a fool, my lord," replied Jonathan. "If I had I should not tell you so. Come, tell me what you want."

"Have you settled about Alice?" demanded Redfern, trying to assume calmness.

"No, she has fled. She is in the power of Batswing."

"Great powers! How have you managed that?" cried Redfern.

"I did not manage it, it was your fault. You deceived me."

"How so?"

"You asked me to prevent Lord Leslie's return to England."

"Well, have you not done so?" said Redfern, glancing nervously round.

"No; you did it yourself. You murdered him so clumsily, that you not only had a witness to your crime, but also allowed your victim to leave unquestionable evidence of your guilt."

Lord Redfern groaned, and buried his face in his hands.

"You see, my lord, your life is in my hands. Take care, lest I crush you."

"Spare me! spare me!" cried the miserable wretch.

"On one condition, I will."

"Name it?"

"You must write out a full confession of your crime. Come, there is the paper."

At first Redfern wavered, but at length complied with the command.

"And now write out a full statement of the birth of Alice Landon."

"Never!" cried Redfern, "I will die first!"

"As you will," said Jonathan, stretching out his hand towards the bell. "I will oblige you directly. I know part of her history, and can get the proofs with you on a scaffold, better than with you alive."

"Stop!" cried Redfern, in agony, the cold sweat on his brow, "have you no mercy?"

"None—do as I command you, or I arrest you at once."

Lord Redfern took the pen, and wrote rapidly.

"Mind, I know most of the secret," said Jonathan, "therefore write the truth, or beware."

With a trembling hand, Lord Redfern continued writing the document.

It was a terrible sight to see these two men.

Jonathan's evil face, shaded by his huge hand; his elbows placed on the table, and his eyes fixed on the livid countenance of Lord Redfern, who, pale and trembling, wrote what he had been commanded.

"There," he said, at last, as he threw the pen down, and passed the paper over to Wild, "now you know all; will that content you?"

Jonathan read the paper over rapidly, and then, stamping with rage, exclaimed,—

"Fool!—madman!—cowardly knave!—why did you not tell me this before!"

"I did not wish to be more in your power than I already was."

"More in my power!" cried Jonathan, "How could you be more so than you are now? Oh! if I had but known of this before; I would have played a better game."

"What is to be done now?" demanded Redfern, in a low voice.

Jonathan paused, and cast a sharp, shrewd glance, at his companion.

Quickly changing his tone to one of friendship, he said,—

"Cheer up, my lord; all shall yet be well. Never try to deceive me again. You must get me the proofs —mark me—proofs of what you have written here. I will save you, in spite of yourself. No more double dealing; you *must* trust to me, or you will be lost. This paper has decided me to crush Batswing and his gang, for they protect this girl. I will lock these papers up," he continued, suiting the action to the word. "You must fetch me the proofs instantly."

Before Redfern could answer, a sharp knocking was heard at the door, and on Jonathan ordering the person to come in, a man entered to state that Jack Sheppard was taken.

"What!" shouted Jonathan, "taken at last. Quick, quick; where is my hat. Come, my lord, we will visit this fellow."

"I care not about seeing such creatures," said Redfern.

"Perhaps not," whispered Wild. "Remember he is one of the fellows who assist Batswing. Come at once, we may learn something."

Hastily putting on his hat and coat, he hurried away, shouting—

"Ho, ho, ho. Jack Sheppard taken. The game of death has begun. Old Tyburn tree will bear rich fruit this year."

CHAPTER LXX.

JACK SHEPPARD AND JERRY SET OUT ON THEIR EX-
PEDITION——JACK FALLS INTO A TRAP.

As the reader already knows, Jerry Blinker and Jack Sheppard had determined to commit a burglary together.

All things were prepared by Jack, and Jerry looked on with admiration at the quick and business-like way in which the notorious housebreaker arranged the tools, saw to the priming of the pistols, and placed all in order.

"Now, Jerry, see what sort of a night it is," said Jack.

"Jerry, who was all excitement, hurried out into the yard, and quickly returned.

"It's dark as pitch, there ain't no moon, and the clouds is spitting with rain."

"That's the ticket," cried Jack; "couldn't have had a better night had we made it ourselves. Now then, Jerry, you take these things and shove them into your pocket. I'll look after these. We'll just have one pull of brandy, and then we'll be off."

"All right," cried Jerry. "Here's the swig. Let's drink to those that we love."

"You love," laughed Jack. "Why, how many sweethearts have you, Jerry?"

"Can't say. You see the gals won't speak, 'cause they don't think it proper, and I don't like to, 'cause I don't wish to commit myself. I don't want to become a breach of promise and be stuck in all the newspapers."

"You're very considerate," said Jack, laughing merrily.

"Werry. I've a 'art like a summer cabbage, large, soft, and tender."

"Well, come along, and I'll show you some of my art," replied Jack Sheppard.

They were soon upon the road, and for some time walked on in silence.

It was indeed an unpleasant night, the wind came in sharp, heavy gusts, and the rain began to pour steadily down, so that Jerry and Sheppard were soon both wet to the skin.

Poor Jerry had, by Jack's advice, changed his stable clothes for the disguise of a field labourer, so that he felt the cold even more than his companion. His teeth chattered dreadfully, still he pushed on manfully by the side of Jack Sheppard.

"Jerry, my poor lad," said Jack, "you seem very cold, how you shiver."

"A icicle is nothing to me," said Jerry. "You might skate down my back."

"You see that light over yonder," said Sheppard, pointing down a lane,

"Rather," said Jerry. "I should think I does. Its a pub."

"Just so. Now, we must not be seen together, only one of us can go in."

"Very well," cried Jerry, interrupting, "I don't mind sacrificing myself for the good of the cause; I'll go in and get something—Oh! you can stop here."

"But Master Jerry Blinker, I happen to be the captain."

"A distinction of which you ought to be proud—the captain's post is that of danger," urged Jerry, who did not seem to fancy standing out in the cold.

"True," replied Sheppard, "he is the leader, therefore I shall go into the inn."

"And it's my duty to follow the cap'in," said Jerry, "so go ahead."

"I shall never teach you anything," said Sheppard, laughing.

"Not if you treat me in this manner," replied Jerry, "why, I'm numbed with cold."

"Well, then, Jerry, listen to me; I was going to say, when you interrupted me, that I could go into that inn, and call for some grog, passing myself off as a gentleman. Do you understand me?"

"Yes, I understand," replied Jerry, doing a double shuffle, to keep his feet warm.

"Well; after I have been there some five or six minutes, you must come in as a tramp, and beg for assistance. This I will give you, and ask you several questions. You must ask your way to Hampstead, I will direct you, then I will leave, and you can follow me."

"All right," said Jerry, "only make haste, or I shall freeze to the spot."

Jack hurried down to the little way-side public house, and entered the bar, where he found—much to his annoyance—a great many men assembled.

None of them, however, seemed to notice him; so taking up a position opposite the door, he ordered some hot brandy and water, and waited for Jerry.

He had not long to wait, for that hopeful youth longed for something to warm him, and, therefore, made the five minutes as short as he could.

The first notice of his approach, was the sound of the following verse, sung in a drawling, snivelling manner, to a mournful tune, each word that ended a line being drawn on as long as possible.

The Song of the Beggar.

I.

Footsore and we-ary,
    I travel on my ro-o-oad;
The night is dre-ary,
    And heavy is my lo-o-oad
Of sorrows I car-ar-ry;
    The rain is falling fa-a-st,
Oh! pray let me tar-ar-ry,
    For bitter is the bla-a-ast.

"Well, that's a pretty song, anyhow," said one of the men.

"It's enough to give one the agey to hear him shake," said another.

Jerry was now close on the door, but fearing he might arrive too soon, and to give Jack Sheppard warning, he commenced again.

II.

Oh! yes, I am star-ar-ving,
    Don't turn me from your doo-or-or;
I'm good and desar-ar-ving,
    Though so ragged and poo-or-or.
My boots, they have van-an-ished,
    My feet, they are fro-roo-rooze;
With hunger, I'm fam-am-ished,
    So listen to my wo-wo-woes.

Jerry finished with such a mournful howl, that Jack nearly burst out laughing; however, he controlled his mirth, and Jerry came to the door.

Jerry! but how changed! Changed even since Jack had left him.

He shuffled along, with his body bent forward, his arms crossed over his breast, and his hands tucked under his armpits to keep them warm.

Shiver! an aspen leaf was nothing to him; he shook until his bones rattled again, and the people who looked at him, actually shivered out of sympathy; his very rags trembled.

In a tremulous, whining voice, he commenced,—

"Kind christian friends, have pity on a poor lad as has no father or mother. Help the horphan, and you shall be rewarded. My father died a year afore I was born, and my mother soon afterwards, so I was cast on this 'ere cold world to perwide for myself at a hearly hage, like the seed by the wayside. I've not had anything for the last three days, but the agey, which, as you will perceive, gentlemen, is a rattling and shaking my life out on me. So I beg of you, kind friends, to help the horphan as ain't got nobody to care for him."

"A horphan, eh?" cried a huge, sinister-looking man, who sat smoking in a corner, "well, seeing as how you say the old man and woman pegged out so soon, I should think you were pretty used to find for yourself."

The words were not said unkindly, yet there was a peculiar tone about them, which made the whole of the company turn and look at the speaker.

He was a tall, square-built fellow, dressed as a well-to-do farmer.

His coat was made of coarse, brown cloth, his breeches of the same, whilst his boots were huge riding ones, coming above the knee.

A thick woollen scarf was wrapped round his neck, and his three-cornered hat was pulled low down over his brow, so as to hide as much of his face as he possibly could.

Over his left eye he wore a large black patch, which matched beautifully with a large slip of plaster of the same colour, which ran across his nose.

But the absence of his left eye was fully made up for by the brilliancy of the right one—it perfectly glittered from its deep socket, sending forth sharp, piercing rays, that were perfectly dazzling.

"Yes, my young coney, I should think by this time you might be able to find for yourself, pretty well," said the man, shaking his head, and puffing out his smoke.

"And so I should, sir," said Jerry, whining, "I've tried everything to get a living, but I've allus failed. I'm unfortunate, that's what I am."

"Have you ever tried honesty and hard work?" demanded the man.

"All the days of my life I've stuck up for them two things," said Jerry.

"You'll be *strung* up for the want of them, one day," said the man.

"Come, come; " perhaps you're too hard on the poor fellow," said Jack.

"Perhaps I am," grunted the man. "But if he don't take care there are others as will be harder on him nor I've been. It ain't always those as speaks the softest as is the kindest, not by long chalks."

"Any way, actions are better than words," said Jack Sheppard, as he flung a piece of money on the counter. "Here, landlord, give this poor shivering piece of humanity a pint of purl.

"Thank you, oh! thank you, honoured sir," said Jerry. "May the —"

"Tut, man, I need no thanks," said Jack. "Drink up the purl and get warm."

"He don't shiver as much as he did," said one of the men.

"Thanks to this kind gentleman," said Jerry, "I'm much warmer."

"I've no doubt about it," said the one-eyed man "Have you come far?"

"All the way from Enfield," said Jerry.

"And where are you going to?" demanded the one-eyed man.

"Hampstead; and please your honour I am told there are a great many of my ralations out that way"

"True enough, there be a great many donkeys there," said another.

"Are you going to Hampstead too, sir?" demanded the one-eyed man, suddenly, fixing his flaming little optic on Jack.

"Certainly not, I have just come from there," replied Jack, "although why I should answer such impertinent questions, I don't know."

"I ask pardon," said the man. "I mean no offence. Only as you seem to have taken such a fancy to this lad, I thought you might have shown him the way; that's all."

"Had I been going that way I should only have been too happy to do so," replied Jack Sheppard, "for in my thinking all men are equal whether rich or poor, and churlishness does not become anyone."

"Maybe you're right," said the man, getting up and laying down his pipe, "for my own self I don't think you're right; but I don't want to argue the matter. Each one can do what he likes, that's what I say. As for myself, I'm rather particular what company I keep, so I'll wish you a very good evening."

"So saying, with a careless nod the stranger left the house.

"Who be that man, Gaffer?" asked one of the men of the landlord.

That was the very question that Jack had longed to put, but had not dared to do it. He therefore listened anxiously for the answer.

"I'm sure I don't know," said the landlord. I never saw him afore. He comed in here a little more nor a hour ago, and put his horse up for a rest."

"Put his horse up for a rest? could it be possible that he was on the road?"

Jack devoutly hoped so, but did not like to ask any question.

Somehow the man had made a strange effect on Jack Sheppard.

He had never seen him before, and therefore had no cause for his suspicions.

For all that he was uneasy, and would have been glad to speak to Jerry on the subject, but dared not do so.

Meanwhile, Jerry had been making the best use of his time.

He had had his glass replenished three times by the kind-hearted countryman, and was now busily engaged eating some bread and meat the landlord had given him. Jerry, as the reader knows, had as much as he could eat at home, and therefore one would have thought that to eat the great hunk of bread and meat would be the most difficult part of the acting. But Jerry was a young man capable of going through a large quantity of eating, and therefore he played the part of the hungry beggar-lad to perfection.

One by one the countrymen commenced leaving the public-house, and Jack knew that it was time they were making a start for Hampstead.

But how was he to get Jerry away from his kind patrons?

At first he hoped that all the men would go, and that he and Jerry would be alone.

But two or three of the fellows who made Jerry drink would not leave.

They seemed to take a huge affection for the lad, and pressed him for a song.

Seeing that matters were becoming serious, Jack wrote on a piece of paper the following words, taking care that no one saw him do so:—

"Get rid of these men as soon as you can; meet me at the house, West Hampstead."

Wrapping some coppers up in this paper, he threw it to Jerry, saying,

"Here my lad, take these. I must be getting on my way, and I should advise you to be doing the same, for the night grows stormier every moment."

Jerry caught the coppers, pulled his forelock, and gave Jack a knowing look.

Jack bade the rest of the company good night, and left the house.

At first he turned, as if he did not intend going to Hampstead; but, after walking some hundred paces down the road, he sprang the hedge, and made his way in the direction of Highgate, intending to cross from there

The night had indeed grown more stormy. The rain fell in torrents, and the wind blew violently, causing the trees to sigh and groan, as they tossed their giant arms towards the inky sky.

But Jack pushed boldly on, neither looking to the right or left.

Once, and once only he paused, and then it was to listen, for he fancied he heard the sound of footsteps following him.

All was still, so he resumed his journey over the fields.

Whatever the cause, Jack could not be gay. He tried once or twice to think of pleasant subjects, but to no purpose. Back on his mind the foreboding of evil came sailing, and his heart grew heavy in the extreme.

"I wish I had not left the lad, Jerry Blinker," he muttered. "I hope he will not get into danger. I am a good mind to give up this expedition, and go back to see if I can find him. Bah! if he does not turn up, I can manage it myself, and who ever knew Jack Sheppard turn back. No; I'll go on.'"

There is something terrible in being alone on a stormy night in the open country.

The thoughts of past years come back to us with terrible force

Jack, in spite of himself, began pondering over his past career, which, full of adventure as it had been, had also been one of anxiety, misery, and crime.

He bitterly regretted what he had done, and thought how different all things would have been, had he applied the same energy he had shown in crime, to some honest calling.

Dashing a tear from his eye, he burst out into a wild laugh, and quickening his pace, exclaimed,—

"It's no good snivelling now—it was all my own fault, 'as you make your bed, so you must lie on it,' says the proverb. Well, I've made mine full of brambles, so I must not complain about the thorns. I wish that lad had not come with me—I'd sooner do this deed alone, then bring him into it. Well, perhaps, if I get there in time, I may do so. At all events, I'll try, so here goes for a good quick run; it will keep my blood warm."

As he finished speaking, he set off in a good quick trot, but somehow his thoughts were still overcast with gloomy forebodings; and as a heavy heart is about the most difficult burden to carry, he soon slackened his pace.

He was passing through a low copse, when he heard the rustle of someone creeping through the hedges, as if making their way towards him.

In a moment he halted, and placing his hand on his pistol, tried to see who it was; but the night was so dark, that he could not see anything.

"Who goes there?" he demanded, in stern tones, "answer, or I'll shoot."

"Hist! don't you know me, Jack," said a voice, close by him.

"Is that you, Jerry?" enquired Jack, in the same low tones.

"Yes; wait a moment, whilst I get through the hedges," replied the voice.

"Well, I'm glad he has come at last," thought Jack, as he replaced his pistol.

He had scarcely done so, than he was felled to the ground by a heavy blow.

Before he could recover himself, a man threw himself upon him, and grasped his throat with both hands, and placed his knee upon his chest.

"It's no good, Jack," you'd better give in quietly, you're my prisoner now."

"Not till I've had a good fight for it," said Jack, striking at the man.

"So ho! that's the game, is it," said the man, "here Jack, Tom, Harry."

The call was soon answered by two or three men, who leaped over the hedge.

"Here one of you fellows, tie up his legs. D—n! how he kicks and struggles."

Jack was certainly making the best use of his limbs that were at liberty.

With one vigirous kick he had sent one of the men sprawling, whilst with the other leg which the other man had seized, he pushed the fellow backwards and forwards, so that he could not assist in securing the prisoner.

"It's no good, Jack, expostulated the man, who was kneeling on his chest, "I have you now, and I mean to stick to you. Come now, don't be a fool, Jack. I don't want to hurt you, but I really must if you go on in that way."

But Jack had no idea of submitting quietly, for he had tasted the hospitality of Newgate before, and had no desire to enjoy again.

He, therefore, renewed his struggle for liberty, and managed so well, that he struck the man who held him down, full in the face.

"Dash my wig, you've given me a blow in my off peeper," cried the man, "I really can't stand that, so here goes." So saying, he drew his pistol, and taking it by the barrel, struck Sheppard a heavy blow on the forehead.

With a deep groan Sheppard ceased his struggles.

"There," said the man, getting up, and wiping his forehead, "I knew that it would be so."

Quick as lightning the fellow's followers bound Jack Sheppard hand and foot, then dragged him to the bank, where they sat him down.

"Where am I?" muttered Jack, "What's up now?—who are you?"

"My name's Gribble, that's what it is. I daresay you know me."

"No I don't," said Jack, "but I can guess what you want."

"I should think you could. So come along, Jack, for we must be moving."

"How can I move with my legs tied?" demanded Jack.

"Well, that's true, anyway," replied the man, "now look here, Jack, if you will promise to go quiet, I don't mind undoing your legs. Will you?"

"No, I won't," replied Jack; "if I must go, I will be carried—there."

"Very well," said Gribble "anything to accomodate you, as the boa-constrictor said to the rabbit, when he swallowed it; so come along."

Poor Jack was hoisted up on the men's shoulders and carried as far as the turnpike road, where they came to a closed carriage.

"You see I had all prepared for you," said Gribble, "I swore to have you, and I've kept my oath."

"Yes—and having kept that, you can surely dispense with me," said Jack.

"A wery good joke, Master Sheppard," said the man, "but it won't do."

They had now reached the carriage, and by the lamp Jack saw Gribble's face.

He was the one-eyed man he had met at the public-house.

"Ah! you know me now," said Gribble. "I knew you all the time."

"Why did you not arrest me, then?" said Jack Sheppard.

"Because I wanted to take you red handed, as it were; and as I guessed you had some little game on hand, I thought it better to give you time."

"But you see you are mistaken," said Jack

"Well, so I thought; that is why I made down on you at last."

"What have you done with the boy?" asked Jack, anxiously.

"Boy! exclaimed Gribble. What boy? You don't mean to say that that beggar-boy we saw at the public-house what sung the song was one of your pals? Blest if I didn't think so at first, but when you and he played the game so cool like, I'm danged if I didn't think as how he was some poor softy as you would perhaps take in."

This was good news for Jack, as he knew that Jerry had escaped.

"I did not know the lad," said Jack, "only I know you constables are so suspicious, and I thought you might have taken him up."

"I almost wish I had now," muttered Gribble, as the carriage drove along.

Jack fell into a deep, thoughtful mood, for he knew that there was but little chance of his escape from Newgate now, he having done so so often, that extra precautions were sure to be taken against him.

At length they rattled up the Old Bailey to the prison.

The streets, owing to the late hour, were dark and gloomy, but as the heavy doors of the prison rolled back and the carriage drove in, the very air seemed shut out.

CHAPTER LXXI.

WHAT BECAME OF JERRY BLINKER—HE MISSES HIS FRIEND, BUT VENTURES ALONE—HE WITNESSES A STRANGE FUNERAL—JERRY BLINKER CONVERTED.

JERRY BLINKER sat in the little public-house drinking his purl and amusing the company, little thinking of the sad fate of his friend.

By the kind invitation of some friend he had mounted a pipe.

"Well, he do look jolly," cried one of the men, as he gazed on Jerry

"'Cause why?" cried Jerry, "the time of my agey fit has passed.

"Ah! and you are nice and warm now, ain't you?" cried another.

"As a baked potatoe," said Jerry. "Done to my wery coat."

"Well, then, tip us another stave," said one of the follows.

"No," said Jerry. "I must be going now. I'm in a hurry."

"What about," said the man. "You can't have any pertickler engagement, as I can see, unless it be with the parish beadle and the stocks."

"You may take your oath it ain't the parson as I wants," said Jerry.

"Well, thin, fill up another can, and give us a love ditty."

Thus pressed, the soft hearted Jerry yielded. The glasses were filled with the steaming liquid. He took one good pull, and leaning back, commenced—

My Fine Marigold.

"You may talk of your lasses of beauty most rare,
But there ain't ne'er a one which to mine can compare;
For her colour is blooming as that of the rose,
And she is perfection from her head to her toes.

"Chorus, gentlemen," shouted Jerry.

Singing Oh! my sweet mar-i-golds,
All fine March Marigolds,
    All a growing and a blowing!
Oh! my fine marigolds.

II.

"Her hair it is red as the cabbage they pickle,
She sticks to her *oaths*, so she can't be called fickle ;
She's as strong as a 'orse, and brave as a lion,
So jokes on my Polly you had better not try on.

Singing, Oh! my fine mar-i-golds,
All fine March Marigolds,
    All a growing and a blowing!
Oh! my fine marigolds.

III.

"When I makes enough money my Polly I'll marry,
For I loves my Polly, and she loves her Harry,
Our children in dozens shall play in the gutter,
And these are the first words I'll teach them to utter,

Oh! buy my sweet mar-i-golds,
All fine March Marigolds.
    All a growing and a blowing,
Oh! my fine marigolds.

This song received such applause, that Jerry found it very difficult to refuse an encore; but he knew that he had no time to waste, and, therefore, managed to slip out during the confusion.

Jerry had stayed so long, that he knew he should have to run to make up for lost time, and, therefore, set off at a rapid rate at once.

The quantity of purl he had drunk, had made his blood flow softly through his veins, and he sped over the fields like a gay lap-wing.

He reached the place of rendezvous, and waited impatiently for the coming of Jack Sheppard.

"Bother it! I must have run too fast," said Jerry to himself, "I wonder he don't come."

Patiently Jerry waited for the coming of his captain, but, as the reader knows, Jack about that time, was rolling rapidly towards Newgate,

The distant church clocks tolled out the hours, and Jerry grew alarmed.

"Something has happened to keep him away," muttered Jerry. "What's to be done?"

"I know," he added, after a moment's meditation, "I'll crack the crib myself."

No sooner did he take the idea into his head, than he determined to carry it out.

He managed to climb to the top of the wall that surrounded the garden.

Along this he crept until he was close to the side of the house.

Here he paused, for the unexpected sound of voices struck upon his ear.

"Whew!" whistled Jerry, "there's something wrong here."

He listened attentively—the voices were those of a man and woman.

It was evident that they were disputing violently.

Jerry crept on to a sort of verandah that sheltered the window leading into the room where the speakers were engaged in earnest conversation.

The window was open, and through a crack in the verandah, Jerry could see the people, and overhear all that passed between them.

The first speaker was a tall, rough man—the second a handsome young woman.

Both seemed deeply moved, the man with grief, and the girl with vindictive passion.

Drawn to her full height, she stood proudly before the man.

Her face was pale as death, her white, thin lips compressed, her eyes lit with a lurid light, her hands clenched, and her frame shaking with emotion.

The man, seated on a chair beside a small table, leant his head upon his hands, and was evidently finishing some story, as Jerry saw them.

"That is all," said the man, "you know the best and the worst of it."

"So!" cried the girl, in a burst of passion, "he laughed, did he?"

"Yes—laughed at my grief first, and then threatened me."

"Let him look to himself," exclaimed the girl, "I am not one to be played with."

Jerry looked at the girl, and thought he'd sooner play with a tiger.

"Hush!" cried the man hurriedly, "do not speak so loudly. Who knows who may hear."

"And what do I care who may hear," cried the girl, stamping her foot on the ground, "think you that I am one of the base, crawling slaves, to bow and cringe before that monster. Look, father, look at me; wherein is that fellow our superior. Is he more virtuous? Virtue! ha! ha! ha! can either of us boast *that* quality. Is he more wicked; has he committed more crimes? No, no, a thousand times no. If he is a devil incarnate, as some men believe, so are we also. Then why tremble before him?"

"He has power," muttered the man, "terrible power."

"And are we children? The sword, the pistol, the dagger, are equally free to our grasp as his. Nay more —*we* know how to use that more terrible weapon, which, coming in a pleasant shape, creeps into their blood, and

"QUICK!" SAID THE GIRL, "FILL IN THE EARTH AT ONCE."

Steals away their lives. Ha! ha! ha! anyone can wield a dagger, or draw a trigger. These are but clumsy things, but the poisoner must know his drugs, and, if he use them skilfully, can do his work, leaving no trace behind!"

"The female monster," thought Jerry, "I'll take care she never becomes Mrs. Blinker."

"What would you have me do?" demanded the man.

"Ask him to dine here; I'll see that the dinner is prepared."

"It would be useless; he would not come," said the man.

"Then I will go to him," replied the girl, "I have sworn to have revenge, and I will. Come what may, I will bring that man to ruin."

"I fear that even now his men are after me," said the man.

The girl paused for a moment, as if in deep thought, then said.

"Father, you may be in danger, but I am not—fly."

"And leave you, my child?" said the man, looking up in wonder.

"Child!" cried the girl, pushing back his extended arms, indignantly.

"But how am I to leave you here? his men may come to-night."

"Then let them; and may he be at their head. Fear not; I'll meet him."

"But surely not alone?" cried the man, in horrified amazement.

"Alone! and why not? Do you think you could help me? Go look in the mirror at your livid face, and read there the answer I spare you!"

"But remember, you are my child, and should any mishap—"

"Silence!" cried the girl, "talk not to me of affection. You are my father; of that there can be no doubt. We have the same cruel nature, the same love of gold and revenge, the same hate and had (here the girl lowered her voice), the same love, but that has gone. I have more will, more courage, but still you are my father. Beyond that we have no affection for each other; we never can have, never shall have. Go, save yourself, when I have carried out my plot, I will join you, if we are both alive."

The man shrank back in his chair, as if overpowered by his daughter.

At length he looked with a side-long glance at her face, and said,—

"But if he comes, he must not find it here—that must not be."

"No," said the girl, "it must go now. Did you do what I told you?"

"Yes: the—the place is dug," said the man, gasping.

"Come," said the girl, "we have no time to grieve, we must work."

The two people moved so far back, that Jerry could not see them.

"Well, I'm blest," he muttered, "this 'ere's a pretty go, I don't think."

He heard footsteps approaching, and presently the man and girl came out into the garden.

The girl carried a lantern, and the man bore a long bale, wrapped up in a white sheet.

Jerry knew instantly that it was a dead body, and shuddered at the marks of blood which stained the sheet.

He knew it was a murdered person.

Silently they walked down the path, until they came to a sort of copse, beneath which Jerry, by the light of the lantern, discovered a grave.

No prayer was uttered, no last look taken of the dead.

The man placed the body gently in the grave, and kneeling down, gazed at it.

"Quick!" said the girl, "fill in the earth at once—why do you pause?"

"I cant't, I cant!" cried the man. "Oh God! my daughter!"

"Silence!" said the girl, in a deep voice, "are you mad?"

"My fair, my trustful Kate; my hand struck the fatal blow."

"And whose directed it?" demanded Zarah, for it was she, "Jonathan Wild."

"My child! my trustful, pretty child," cried the wretched man,

"Father," said Zarah, sternly, as she pointed into the grave, "there lies all we loved on earth. We dare not pray. Prayers from such creatures as we are, would beat against the heavens, and falling from thence in curses crush us. We have but one thing left us to do. Revenge! Swear with me, that from this moment we devote our lives and wealth to the ruin of that man! Now, on your knees, over our dear Kate, swear death to Jonathan Wild!"

The man knelt down and took the oath dictated to him.

So horrified was poor Jerry at the scene, that he really did not know what to do.

He was a kind-hearted lad, and could not help weeping at the scene, and pitying the unhappy wretches; cruel and wicked as they were.

Taking advantage of Zarah and Croft's back being turned to him, he crawled to the wall. and dropping from thence into the field, walked mournfully away.

"There!" said he, taking the house-breaking instruments from his pocket, and throwing them away, "I'll never do another sin, if I can help it, as long as I live."

From this moment I'll make a turn; work hard to get an honest living, and pray to heaven to help me to do so. Innocent pleasure is one thing, but there's no knowing where crime may end!"

CHAPTER LXXII.

COURT SCANDAL.—BATSWING APPEARS AGAIN AS PERCY MARVEL.—HE BECOMES A POLITICIAN, AND SAVES TWO FRIENDS BY PLAYING A GAME OF SEE-SAW.

THE rooms of the Duchess of Kendal were all in a blaze of light.

The Duchess had a grand reception that evening, and her royal keeper, George the First, had promised to attend in private.

But there was even a greater wonder than that; for everybody knew that George I. never had any decency, any more than his mistresses; the last great wonder was, that there was a rumour that the Countess of Sourkroutzenberg had been asked by her rival, and what was even still more wonderful, that that old creature had accepted the invitation.

So there was to be a meeting between the king's two most famous—or infamous, mistresses.

"What could it portend?" was the question asked by the courtiers.

A question which Walpole answered thus,—

"Mischief of course—are they not women?"

The fat old Sourkroutzenberg sailed into the room, looking about as graceful as a Dutch galiot amongst a squadron of neat little yachts.

Yet all the the ladies bowed low, for had not the woman had the honour of being dishonoured by the king.

But where was the king?

In the Duchess of Kendal's private apartments, to be sure, round the door of which were gathered a group of sycophantic courtiers, who would have worshiped the scandal woman of Bablylon, if they had lived in her time; nay, most of them would have gladly sacrificed their own female relations to the same fate, and deemed themselves honoured—such is the true feeling of loyalty.

Poor Sourkroutzenberg was not much noticed, for some strange rumours had got about, that certain handsome jewels presented to her by the king, her royal master, had disappeared.

Therefore, Sourkroutzenberg received but cold recognition from many, to whom she had been kind. and who, a few days ago, would have only been too happy to place their neck beneath her feet.

Whilst she was fanning her fat face and bosom—the latter swelling to twice the usual size, with suppressed passion—a young man, beautifully dressed, glided behind her, and whispered in her ear,—

"How fair and blooming the Countess looks to-night."

The old woman started, and glanced quickly round at the speaker.

"Ah! Mr. Marvel!" she exclaimed, glad to have some one to speak to at last, "you were always a flatterer. I wonder you do not attend the court now?"

"Faith, Madam, it would only be to court you more, if I did," replied Percy.

"It is strange," said the Countess, looking him full in the face, "but you always set me in mind of a gentleman I once knew, a Frenchman, the Chevalier de Clervane."

"It would be strange if I did not," thought Percy, otherwise Batswing, otherwise Chevalier de Clervane; but he merely bowed.

"Oh! he spoke such charming French," continued the Countess, pointedly.

"And I do not know a word of that musical language," said Percy.

"Just what the Chevalier said of English," replied the Countess.

"He was unfortunate, madam; but why talk about him, when we might pass our time with so much greater advantage."

"How so?" replied the Countess, for all her suspicions that the Chevalier and the handsome Percy Marvel were one, vanished at once, "I do not understand you."

"Could we not talk of you, madam?" said Percy, in a low, sweet voice.

"Beware Mr. Marvel," said the Countess, shaking her finger, "the king—"

"Is enjoying the society of the Duchess of Kendal," said Percy, pointedly.

The Countess with great difficulty prevented herself from uttering an oath.

"'Put not your trust in princes,' Countess; it is an old and true saying."

"What do you mean, sir?" demanded the Countess, passionately.

"I mean this. To-night His Majesty will be most gracious to you—"

"Indeed!" cried the Countess, delighted, "how do you know that?"

"Do you not know that I am an astrologer?" laughed Percy.

"Ah! I see you would laugh because His Majesty has turned against me."

"Not I, I can assure you," replied Percy, "I am perfectly serious."

The Countess looked sternly in his face, to see if he were in earnest.

Percy never smiled, but returned her gaze with an undaunted look.

"Are you really in earnest?" she asked, in a low voice.

"I am—grant me a favour, and I will tell you more"

"So you are a true fortune teller," said the Countess, "and must be paid in advance."

"No—you have but to *promise* me the payment conditionally."

"How so? I begin to be interested, and long to test your powers."

"In this manner. Some time ago, a young friend of mine, Sir Arthur Bowring, had the misfortune to be mixed up in a duel. His antagonist *fell*, but *not* mortally wounded. However, for some vile purpose, the wounded man was declared dead, and a charge of murder instituted against my friend. There is also some sort of a charge of my friend having become highwayman. As if Sir Arthur Bowring, of Staveley Hall, Devon, would do such a thing."

"Well; and to what does all this tend?" demanded the Countess.

"To this. Here is a free pardon granted to Sir Arthur, on all charges made against him up to the present time. Believe me, he is innocent of them, or I would not ask you to assist him. This paper the king must sign to-night. In return I will tell you what will happen in the next twenty-four hours.

"But how am I to ask him? He looks cold on me now."

"He will shortly enter that door; advance to him, he will receive you warmly."

"Ah!" it cannot be true!" exclaimed the Countess, in raptures.

"It will be true. After you have spoken to him a few minutes, request that he will sign this pardon. I will be near, should the demand any explanation,"

"But should he refuse, how then will you tell my fortune?"

"He will not refuse," said Percy. "Do as I tell you, and you must succeed."

"This is most strange," said the Countess. "It cannot be possible?"

"Do you agree to my terms?" demanded Percy. "Remember it costs you nothing."

"Well, then, I agree," said the Countess. "Now commence."

"Give me your hand, then; I must read the lines."

Percy took the Countess' hand and scanned it attentively.

"This is strange," he muttered, "very strange. This shows me that now you are in distress. A cloud hangs over you—that must mean the King's disfavour—but here the clouds smile again, but it seems only for a short time. Countess, in twenty-four hours you will have regained and relost the King's favour. Trouble is all around; more I cannot see beyond this; with care you will be saved. Do what I ask you, and I will be your friend. Trust to me. Hush! here comes the King."

A movement at the other end of the room plainly showed that the King approached.

The door was thrown open, and the King entered the room.

Something had evidently ruffled his Majesty, for he had very much the appearance of an apoplectic turkey-cock. He glanced around with an air that would have been terrible, had it not been rendered ludicrous by the man's utter want of intellectual refinement.

He rapidly passed through the ceremony of receiving several people of distinction; and then, to the utter astonishment of old Sourkroutzenberg, motioned for her to approach him, which it was needless to say she did in all haste.

It would neither be edifying nor proper to listen to all that passed between the King and his mistress. Love-making at any time is slow work, and when two such ponderous people as George I. and his mistress were engaged, it must have been terrible. It is sufficient for our history to relate that in a few minutes Percy Marvel had the pleasure of seeing the pardon produced and shown to the King. He glanced at it, signed it at a side table, and handed it back to the Countess, who managed soon after to slip it into the hands of our hero.

"That point is gained any way," said Percy, as he buttoned up the pardon in his pocket. She shall have a few more hours to bask in the royal sunshine, and then she must suffer—for a time at least—an eclipse.

With a shrug of the shoulders he turned away, and walked through the rooms.

He had not proceeded far, when he heard two men in loud dispute in an ante-chamber.

The men were evidently fast losing their tempers, so Percy drew behind a curtain to see if he knew either of them; so that, should such be the case, he could stop the quarrel before it grew dangerous.

"I tell you captain," cried one, in a voice that showed he was both old and fat, "I tell you that I will never forgive you. Your conduct, to my thinking, admits of no excuse."

"Pardon me, my lord, but I would first put one or two points before you."

"If I were a young man, sir, I would soon put a *point* before you—the point of a sword; and I would tell if your's could guard your person better than it did my plate. If it did not, one great cause of my complaint would be removed."

"If you will not listen to reason, I cannot help it," replied the young man.

"Reason! I'll listen to reason, but not to you. Do you think the loss of my plate of no consequence? But I'll have revenge, ha, ha, ha. You don't know how soon, too."

"Really, my lord, I shall be very glad when you succeed in having your revenge," replied the young man, proudly, "for I am tired of listening to your threats. Were you indeed a younger man, I should have silenced them long ago."

"You, you young Jack-a-napes! Now listen to me. Sir Robert Walpole has taken up the matter at last,

Ha! ha! ha! my young friend, do you tremble now, eh?"

"No, sir, I do not. I know Sir Robert has need of his friends to retain him in office, and therefore wonder not that he should stoop to use such as you for a tool. But I do wonder, when I see a man of birth and education stooping to be used. Enough, sir, let me pass."

"You shall be broken, sir," screamed the old lord. "Broken and disgraced."

"Gentlemen, gentlemen," said Batswing, entering the room. "What means this disturbance?"

"Ah! my dear Percy," cried Captain Jennings, who was the younger speaker. "I am glad to see you. For heaven only knows what I might have been made to do by the gibes, threats, and sneers of this old—"

"Hush! Captain, for heaven's sake," said Percy.

"Oh, let him go on, said Lord Clumber," the elder speaker. "He's bold now that there's no one to meet but an old man. How do I know who stole—"

"Silence, my lord, or else the King will hear you." cried Percy.

In a minute all were silent, for they knew that to be found quarrelling there would be to cause the disgrace of both.

"Now you are both calm, what is all this about?" demanded Percy.

"The loss of the plate belonging to Lord Clumber," said Captain Jennings.

"But that was not *his* fault, my lord," said Percy.

"I know not that; I know not that. He and Sir Arthur Bowring had charge of it, and I'll have revenge. I have had it on Sir Arthur."

"You!" exclaimed Batswing, in surprise.

"Yes; me. I had the duel called murder.; ha, ha, ha, ha! I had some power then, but lost it soon after. But I have it again now."

"I have the pleasure, then, to inform you, my lord, that Sir Arthur Bowring has received a free pardon from the King, on that and all other charges."

"Thank God!" exclaimed Captain Jennings. "He was quite innocent."

"Oh! you're pleased he has escaped, are you? Your punishment shall be double for it. Mark me, just double. The Countess Sourkroutzenberg reigns again, and she is Walpole's friend. Ha, ha, ha. I have you now."

With a shout of laughter that was demoniac, the old man hurried from the room.

"I'm afraid things don't look pleasant, Captain," said Percy.

The Captain shook his head, and sighed deeply.

"If it be true that old Sourkroutzenberg is again in favour, I am indeed done," he added, after a pause. She and old Clumber are friends with Sir Robert Walpole. Well, if the worst comes to the worst, I must go back to the country, and lead a quiet life."

"It is quite true Sourkroutzenberg is in favour again," said Percy.

"Are you sure of that?," demanded Captain Jennings,

"Positive; she is now deeply engaged with the King. But cheer up, Captain. I think I shall soon be able to bring you good news."

"You! I do not understand you?" cried Captain Jennings.

"Indeed! Well I'm not surprised. All I ask is that you will follow my advice, without asking me the why and the wherefore."

"That I can easily promise, my dear fellow, for I have no one else to ask."

"All I ask is that you will remain quietly in yonder little room until I come for you. When I come I shall bring you your fate; so do not be impatient should I be some time. Do you agree to that?"

"Willingly;" but if you love me, be not long.

The two young men shook hands and separated, Captain Jennings to the little private room indicated, and Percy to stroll through the rooms.

One quick, sharp glance around, showed Batswing that the fat Countess still held sway.

The king was laughing with her : Sir Robert Walpole —the cleverest statesman of the day—was making them both laugh with his wit, and the courtiers fluttered around, ready to bow to any one of the three.

"A pretty sight," muttered Batswing, bitterly, " it is hard to tell whether there is more vice in royal court, or in a beggar's alley. The Duchess of Kendal is not here. Then I have no time to lose; the Countess must not think me a false prophet. 'Pon my word, I think I was born to be a statesman. Thank heaven, all this will soon be over, and I shall be in peace."

Carefully avoiding the company, Batswing, (or Percy Marvel, as he called himself on this occasion), passed through a side door into a small boudoir.

The room was dimly lighted, but he could see that a lady was reclining on a sofa in the middle of the room.

She was beautifully dressed, but had thrown herself on the couch, regardless of her dress, and was weeping bitterly from vexation.

Percy knew directly that he was in the presence of the Duchess of Kendal.

"A thousand pardons, madam, for thus interrupting you," said Percy.

"Who is there?" said the Duchess, springing to her feet.

"It is your friend, madam," said Percy, in a humble voice

"How dare you, sir, [intrude into my private apartments?" cried the Duchess.

"It was by mistake, your grace," said Percy, advancing, "although had I known where the door led, I certainly should have passed it,"

"Master Marvel," said the Duchess, "I have given you too much liberty."

"And have had no reason to repent it," replied Batswing.

"That I confess," replied the Duchess, "you have done me much service."

"Had you followed my advice, you would not have been alone here now."

"True!" exclaimed the Duchess, "but I thought myself so sure of his favour."

"I advised you not to interfere with Sir Robert Walpole."

"But I thought myself so sure of the kings' favour," she cried.

"A kings' favour is like quicksilver, madam—hard to hold."

"Who and what are you, Master Marvel?" demanded the Duchess. "Sometimes I think you are a Jacobite, a spy, and hate the house of Hanover."

"I neither hate nor love it. King George, or king James I care not which."

"This is treason!"

"It is the truth. Listen; I am a traveller. I have seen many countries and many governments, and have found lust, tyranny, and cruelty at the head of all of them. It so chanced I did you a slight service; since then you have introduced me into society. I am grateful, and would save you."

"You! how can you save me?" demanded the Duchess.

"By bringing the king back to you!" replied Batswing, calmly.

"And how is this wonder to be performed?—and how soon?"

"He shall return to-night, if you will follow my advice."

"Speak! you need not fear but that I will obey."

"Madam, sometime ago His Majesty gave the Countess a handsome ring, set with large diamonds. Do you remember it? I should think you must."

"I do, indeed," said the Duchess, bitterly, " It was

once his mothers. I had asked him for it a thousand times, and been refused on that plea "

"And still he gave it to her. I think when you told me the story, you said that he had made her promise never to part with it, as she valued his royal favour."

"Yes, yes," said the Duchess, breathless with impatience.

"*She has lost that ring!*"

"Great heavens! I am saved!" exclaimed the Duchess, clasping her hands.

"Exactly so, Madam," replied Batswing, in the same measured tones, "you are saved; you have only to whisper into the king's ear, ' your mother's ring; why does not the Countess wear it?' and you are saved."

"Saved! saved!" cried the Duchess, as she walked quickly up and down the room. " Oh! I see it all, how clever you are Mr. Marvel—*Sir Percy Marvel* you shall be 'ere long. What can I do for you? Why do you not enter into politics, you would make a capital statesman. Tell me what to do, ask what you will, and it shall be yours."

"I have nothing much to ask, madam," replied Batswing, carlessly,—"yet stay, I could help you to crush an enemy, and at the same time help an old friend of mine. It would be done in one word; gained with a smile."

"Name it—I am at your service. Do not hesitate."

"You know old Lord Clumber, madam."

"Ah! the old wretch, perfectly. He is a friend of Sir Robert."

"Just so, madam. I saw him just now triumphing at your fall."

"Indeed!" said the Duchess, her brow darkening, "he shall answer for that."

"And declared his intention of ruining an officer, one Captain Jennings, who happened to be unfortunate enough to lose some of the old misers plate."

"And you would have me save this young man? That is what you mean."

"It is—by doing so you repay me and punish Clumber."

"It shall be done; bring your friend up as near to the king as possible."

"Stay, madam, you forget our contract. I am not to be known as the one who gives you these wonderful pieces of information."

"True! you are a wise man, Mr. Marvel, and fear enemies."

"I avoid having them, madam—*that* is better."

"Take this white rose," said the Duchess, "give it to your friend to wear in his coat, and tell him to stand where I can easily see him. Lose not a moment, or it will be too late. Remember, I am your debtor."

The Duchess presented her hand.

Percy Marvel raised it to his lips, bowed low, and left the room.

"Cheer up, Captain," cried Percy, as he met his friend, "the day is yours."

"Mine! verily Percy Marvel, you must be the devil!"

"I have heard people say that before," laughed Percy, "come stick this rose into your coat. Place yourself where the Duchess of Kendal can see you, and trust me, all will be well. Don't mention my name. Now don't lose a moment, but go, or you will undo all that I have done."

In the meantime the Duchess of Kendal, smiling on all she met, as though still basking in the king's favour, had left her boudoir, and drawn near to the chair on which was seated the king, having the Countess on his right hand.

The king's brow grew even heavier than nature had already made it, but still the Duchess moved steadily on, until she had taken the vacant place on his majesty's left hand.

"Your Majesty looks weary," she said with a smile,

"I fear the company I have selected must trouble you."

"I like the company very much," replied the king, in a tone and manner that in a gentleman would have been called rude. but in a king was dignified.

"I am delighted that I have pleased your majesty. I always endeavour to do so. See," she added, in a low tone, "*I* wear the rings you gave me."

The king looked first at her rings, and then at her, with astonishment.

"What could she mean?" he thought, " of course she wears the rings I gave her."

Not only was the king too slow of comprehension, but too quick of temper, and he was about making another reply, even more dignified than the last, when the unfortunate Countess, conscious that she had lost the king's present, tried to draw her hand from the grasp in which he held it.

The movement caused the king to look down, and he noticed the absence of the ring.

"Where is the ring?" he cried, in kingly wrath, squeezing the Countess' fingers, until she nearly screamed with pain. "Where is that ring?"

"I—I left it at home, your Majesty," faltered the Countess.

"Perhaps you have lost it, madam," said the Duchess.

One glance at the Countess convinced the King that such was the case.

An oath—yes, an oath—fell from the royal lips. The King arose, and taking the Duchess by the arm, walked away from the Countess.

Once more the courtiers bowed to the Duchess, neglecting the Countess.

Oh! what terrible weathercocks people are. Even kings are the same.

Captain Jennings was not the least surprised at what he saw.

There he stood, with the white rose in his coat, almost too astonished to advance towards the King, when the Duchess, with a move of her fan, beckoned him to do so. At last, however, he gained courage, and advancing, fell on one knee.

"What is this I hear?" said the King. "You lost Clumber's plate?"

"I had that honour—misfortune, I mean—your Highness.

"Clumber, let me see, Clumber; he was for the Stuarts until he found them losing, then he came over. Was a staunch Roman Catholic when it payed, but changed when it did'nt. Serve him right to lose his plate—fortunate for him he did not lose his head. He won't forgive you, eh? Well, we do. Rise Major Jennings.

"*Captain* Jennings," corrected the Captain.

"No, no," interrupted the Duchess, "the King grants you the rank of Major. You shall have your commission to-morrow."

"Oh! your Majesty, a thousand thanks," cried Jennings, with a low bow.

He withdrew before the amazed King, who had never intended to grant him the rank, could explain himself. Thus, through the thick-headedness of a monarch and a woman's wit, Captain Jennings gained his promotion in the British army.

He was neither the first nor last who has done the same.

"That fellow Percy, is a wondrous fellow," said Major Jennings, as he forced his way through the crowd. "I wonder where he has gone."

But Batswing had no sooner seen his friend righted, than he left the house, for he had received a package from Tillingham, informing him that Lord Leslie had been murdered.

"This must be seen to," he muttered. "I will cross to France myself."

In vain did Jennings inquire for Percy; so, coming

to the conclusion he had gone, the gallant Major took his departure also.

That Percy Marvel is my good angel," he cried. "I can never repay him."

"That Percy Marvel is a devil, I *will* repay him." said a voice close by him.

The Major turned," but as no one was near him, he came to the conclusion that he must have fancied the speech, so hurried home.

Had he waited a moment he might have seen Lord Clumber come from the shadow of a house, with three men in his company.

CHAPTER LXXIII.

JACK SHEPPARD IN THE CONDEMNED CELL—HE RE-CEIVES SOME VISITORS—HIS FIGHT WITH WILD—JONATHAN LEARNS SOME STRANGE NEWS FROM LORD REDFERN.

JACK SHEPPARD was seated, broken-hearted, in the con-demned cell.

He had broken out of prison so often, that no one was allowed to visit him; that is, he was only allowed to be seen by respectable—well-known people—who could be trusted.

There was no want of that kind of visitor. Ladies beautifully dressed, and delicate creatures, actually dared the prison fever, to take a glance at the doomed man. Men of high talent came and glared at the poor wretch, as though he were a wild animal placed there for their especial amusement.

Jonathan Wild attended to nothing else; he hovered about the prison like a bird of evil omen, and snuffed up the air, as though he already smelt his victim's blood.

It would be useless to attempt to describe the nume-rous escapes Jack Sheppard made from Newgate; they are too well known. Sufficient to say that Jack was now so heavily ironed, and so well guarded, that hope of escape there was none.

Terrible, indeed, it must be when the iron gates of the prison close on the condemned man, never to open again until the day of execution.

Jack had been pestered to death all day by visitors, so that it was with a hearty curse he heard the key turn in the lock to admit some others.

The door opened slowly, and a lady accompanied by a lad of about fifteen years of age, entered the room.

The lady and the youth were dressed in deep black, as if in mourning—the lady for her husband—the boy for his father.

"Hullo!" said Jack, "how many more admirers have I got?"

"Come, come," said Mr. Grummidge, who was the turnkey in charge, "don't turn cross, Jack. You've had many a good pull in your time, let me have a go-in now I've a chance. I can assure you, mam, that some o' these devil-may-care fellows is a fortune to us," he continued, turning to the lady, 'some gents and ladies gives us a guinea—well that we look on as mean—but the swells —the reg'lar ones, not your show lot, they drops us five, as cool as if money wasn't of no value at all.'"

The lady, without saying a word, placed five guineas into the fellows hand.

"Well now, you *are* a lady," said the man, "and if anyone dared to say that you wasn't, I'd see him turned off with the greatest pleasure.''

"Well, if I am to be made an exhibition of," said Jack, "I think I ought to be allowed to have a share of the money. Any way you might get me a bottle of wine."

"Well, Jack, I don't mind doing that lot; only you must let the lady have her five guineas worth out first. Would you like to speak to him, mam? You needn't be frightened, he won't hurt you, mam."

"No, no," said the lady, hurriedly, "I merely wished to show my son what is the consequence of leading an evil life, so that he may resist temptation."

"A very good idea, mam, very," said Jack, "look here, my young fellow. You see before you an unfortunate fellow creature, doomed to die. A highly pleasant and edifying sight it must be for a young christian. Now go away and be a good boy ever after—not for fear of God, but to avoid the gallows—be a coward and hypo-crite, and you may not only rob with impunity, but receive high praise from respectable people for so doing. There, learn your lessons well—take out your five guineas worth of staring at me, and don't be afraid."

"I am not afraid," replied the lad, stoutly, "and al-though I know you deserve your fate, yet I pity you."

"Pity me!" cried Jack, in an altered tone, "well, thank you for that, young master. Bah!" he continued, as he passed his hand over his eyes, "to think that Jack Sheppard should be thankful for a boy's pity."

"And why not?" said the lad, "it shows that your heart is in the right place."

"It soon will be," replied Jack, with a bitter laugh, "'dust to dust; ashes to ashes."

"This is dreadful," said the lady, "let us leave—I feel faint."

"Get the lady some wine, jailor; see, she faints," said the lad.

It was but too true; the lady fell into the lad's arms, insensible.

"Quick, quick," cried the lad, "some wine! some wine! Do you not see how ill she is. Great heavens! perhaps it is the terrible jail fever."

"Yes, but how am I to leave the prisoner?" said the jailer.

"Lock us in with him, he will not hurt us. Quick, fetch the wine, and you shall be well paid. My mother may die for want of restoratives. If you have the heart of a man, go at once."

Carried away by the boy's impetuosity, the man hurried from the cell, taking great care, however, to lock the door, so as to prevent all chance of escape.

No sooner had he gone than the lad sprang to his feet, and the lady also arose from the ground, on which the lad had placed her.

"Good heavens! What is this?" cried Jack.

"Hush!" whispered the lad, "speak softly. Do you not know us, Jack?"

"Why, it's Flicker!" exclaimed Jack, "and this is Maud."

"Now, we have not a minute to spare, so let us pro-ceed to business."

"Business," said Jack, looking at his fetters. "There's no hope for me. Look here."

"They are indeed heavy," said Maud, "but you must not despair."

"That's easier said than done, Mistress Maud," said Jack.

"Look here, Jack," replied Maud, "when I was chained in that horrible dungeon in which you found me, I never despaired. One thing alone kept me from that. It was the hope of revenge. Already I have tasted part of my desire, and before long I shall succeed in all."

"Ah!" cried Jack." if I could accomplish the ruin of Jonathan Wild, I should die happily. But my game is up; I am in his power."

"Rest assured that if the worst comes to the worst, there are those who will see that Jonathan Wild re-ceives his reward."

"Were I well convinced of that, I should not care so much as to death."

"You may rely on that. But now to yourself, can you manage to get from this cell?"

Jack looked round at the grim walls and shook his head.

"Here is a spring saw to cut through your fetters," said Flicker.

"Well, that is something," said Jack. "I'll soon have these off."

"I wish Batswing was in London," said Maud, thoughtfully.

"Where is Batswing?" demanded Jack Sheppard, eagerly.

"He has disappeared suddenly. We believe he has gone to France. Lord Leslie was murdered there by Redfern."

"Hush!" whispered Flicker, "here comes the jailer; can we do anything else for you, Jack? Ask what you like, and if it be in our power we'll do it."

"There is nothing to be done more than you have done," said Jack.

"Then you will make another attempt to escape?" asked Maud.

"Yes, to-morrow night. That is the night before the morning named for my death"

"Good; we will have people outside ready to receive you," said Flicker.

"If you fail, we will attempt a rescue, so be prepared," added Maud.

"Quick, quick! he is here," cried Flicker.

In a moment Maud threw herself on the ground. Flicker knelt by her side, rubbing her hands, and Jack Sheppard stretched himself at full length on the stone settle, humming a tune, as if wishing he was rid of his visitors.

The door opened, and the jailer entered with the wine

"Thank heaven, you're come at last," said Jack, "these people will drive me mad soon. It's jolly hard a fellow can't spend the few hours he has of life in peace. Give me some wine—this snivelling makes me feel quite down in the mouth too."

"Ladies first, Jack," said the jailer, "gents arterwards."

Maud took some of the wine the jailer offered her, and just put it to her lips.

"There, you'll be better now, mam—much better," said the man.

"Thank you, kindly," said Maud, in a weak voice, "let me leave this horrible place. Oh, how ill I feel—why, why, did I ever come here?"

"If you are asking me riddles," said Jack, "I give 'em up, for I don't think this either the place or time to be up to such games. There, good bye old girl: hope you'll be happy. Take her away, jailer, and leave me alone to enjoy my wine."

Maud, who acted her part admirably, was led away by Flicker and the jailer, seemingly scarcely able to walk.

They took her to the prison lodge, and there let her remain for some time, so that she might recover herself.

Of course the men knew that they had no right to do this; but Maud was profuse with gold, and, therefore, they treated her with due defference.

Had the jailer attended to his strict orders, Maud would not have been allowed to see Jack Sheppard at all; but prison discipline in those days was thoroughly rotten, and gold not only purchased the freedom of visiting a prisoner, but the freedom of the prisoner himself.

Maud would willingly have purchased Jack Sheppard's liberty, but she knew that it would be impossible to do so for two reasons.

Firstly, he was far too noted for the jailers to dare to allow him to escape, and, secondly, Jonathan Wild haunted the prison night and day, for he had sworn to have Jack's life, and he never broke such oaths.

A couple of hours passed, and still Maud declared herself too ill to leave the lodge, and the jailers began to grow frightened, for they well knew that Jonathan Wild would soon be going his round of the prison.

"You really must go now, missus," said one, "Mr. Wild will be here soon."

"Well, I will try to walk," replied Maud, rising, for she had gained all the news she could from the men's talk. "Dear me, I will never enter a prison again. Come, my dear boy, and let this terrible sight be a lesson to you."

She drew down her veil, and leaning on Flicker, staggered from the lodge.

She had just reached the gate, when the wicket was opened, and Jonathan Wild stood before her.

Luckily for Maud her veil was so thick that it hid her features.

"Who is this woman?" demanded Jonathan sternly.

"It's a woman who came to see her husband who's in for debt," answered the man.

"Look here, master Grummidge," said Jonathan, sternly, "this is after hours. How dare you allow strangers in here, when you have such a terrible charge as Jack Sheppard under your care. Mark me, if he escapes again, I hold you answerable."

"I beg your pardon, Mr. Wild, I'm sure I do all I can to oblige, and—"

"Enough!" cried Jonathan, "You have heard what I have said. Now turn the woman out into the streets. I am going the round of the prison."

Grummidge hurried Maud away, and felt greatly relieved when she was gone.

Jonathan Wild knew every turn and passage in Newgate.

It was his boast, that if he was locked up at any time, in any part of the building, he could escape from it with ease—a boast he did not carry out.

He passed round the different wards, examined the fastenings of all the doors, and at length being perfectly contented that all was safe, ordered the jailer who accompanied him, to conduct him to the cell in which Jack Sheppard was imprisoned.

Jonathan had no reason for going there, but he wished to gloat over Jack.

"How does he take his imprisonment and sentence to death?" he asked.

"Pretty well, sir, he don't seem to mind much, but sometimes he's dull."

"Dull! ah! that is when he thinks of his ride to Tyburn. Come, open the door, and let me see him. Oh, how I long to see him in the cart!"

The man threw the door open, and Jonathan entered.

Jack Sheppard appeared to be sound asleep on his truckle bed.

"You can leave me, Grummidge," said Jonathan, "he is too heavily ironed to attempt to do me any mischief. Besides, I am armed, and he is not."

The jailer withdrew, only too glad to get away from Jonathan Wild.

"Well, Jack," said Jonathan, "how are you? Wake up, man; I wish to speak to you."

Jack stretched himself and yawned, as if only just awakening, and made no reply.

"Don't you hear me speak to you?" demanded Jonathan, fiercely.

"Oh! you're there, old devil's-heart," replied Jack quietly.

"Yes, I've come to tell you of all the nice preparations I've made for you."

"You're very kind, I'm sure," said Jack, "but I don't care about lecturing."

"But it's right you should know," laughed Jonathan, "ho, ho, ho, it's glorious."

"Well, go on, old viper," said Jack carelessly. "You make me so sick of the world that I shall be glad to die!"

"Then you will be glad enough the day after to-morrow," rejoined Jonathan, "for then you swing; there's no chance of escape, not the slightest."

"I do not intend trying to escape," said Jack quietly.

"We have the foot-guards and the horse-guards to protect the road."

"You do me too much honour," said Jack bowing.

"Then the sheriffs will have their javelin men, and we are going to double the number of constables. Oh! it will be a splendid sight."

"Doubtlessly it will," replied Jack, "one I shall take care not to miss, as I shall never see another like it."

"That I'll swear to," laughed Jonathan, "I mean to ride close by the cart, and if you make an attempt to save yourself, I'll cut you down."

"Take care you are not cut down," replied Jack, "I have good friends and true."

"So, so, cried Jonathan, "then there is a plot for a rescue, eh?"

Of course, it was very foolish of Jack to give this hint, but he was so annoyed at Jonathan's taunts that he could not help replying as he had.

"Well, send your friends," said Jonathan, after waiting a few moments for a reply, "the more the merrier; we shall be ready for them, and send a few of the infernal rascals to their last account. Oh! I'll make it hot work for them." Jonathan was so tickled at the prospect of bloodshed that he roared with laughter. "Look here, Jack," he said, suddenly becoming serious, "I can still save you."

"You lie," retorted Jack, "you couldn't if you would, and you wouldn't if you could."

"Don't be too sure of that, Jack, I can if I like," replied Wild.

"And as you do not like, I cannot see what it matters to me," said Jack.

"I can and will save you on certain conditions," said Wild, earnestly.

"And what may those conditions be?" asked Jack Sheppard.

"You know Batswing: you know the secrets of his gang.

"I do!" replied Jack Sheppard, "What then?"

"Why this; if you will give me the means of arresting them, the moment they are safely in prison you shall go out of it. Now, what say you?"

"That I would sooner die a thousand deaths than betray a friend," replied Jack. "It is true that I do know where to find the people that you want, but I would be torn limb from limb rather than breathe a word to hurt them."

"Death and furies!" cried Jonathan in a rage, "have you forgotten that you are in my power; that you are already under the shadow of the gallows?"

"Forgotten it! how could I, with such a gallows-bird near me as you?"

"Remember Jack, I hanged your father because he crossed me."

Jack made no reply, but bit his lips till the blood came.

"I brought him to the gibbet as I will you, because he would not yield to me. I broke your mother's heart because she would not obey me."

Unable to suppress his rage, Jonathan Wild, so taking him by surprise that he threw him to the ground with the greatest ease. He knew that Jack was so heavily ironed that he moved with difficulty. How then had he accomplished this marvellous feat?

The clank of Jack's fetters as they fell to the ground explained all.

He had cut through the iron with the watch-spring saw Flicker gave him.

A most terrible struggle took place. Each man knew he was fighting for life. Jack was not so strong as Wild, but he was more supple; besides this, he had the advantage of having his opponent under him.

With deadly hatred he gripped Wild by the throat and beat his head against the stone pavement of the cell.

Wild fought desperately, but to little purpose, for Sheppard kept so close down on the body that Jonathan's blows lost more than half their force.

At length Wild began to feel his senses going rapidly.

A heavy mist fell before his eyes; a dreadful singing sounded in his ears; his tongue protruded from his mouth, and foam flecked with blood covered his lips. Summoning all his strength for a final effort, he managed to draw a pistol and discharged it at Jack Sheppard.

Luckily for Jack, Wild was unable to aim, and the bullet flew wide.

However the report saved Wild's life.

Footsteps were heard hurrying along the stone passage.

The door was thrown open, and Grummidge, followed by Lord Redfern and several under turnkeys rushed into the cell.

With deadliest hate, Jack struck Wild a fierce blow in the face.

The next minute they had seized him, and raised Jonathan Wild.

"I have had some revenge," cried Jack "and am happy now."

For some minutes Jonathan remained silently wiping the blood from his face.

At length he turned to Grummidge and said, in a hard, cold voice.

"Bring the heaviest set of irons you have, and fix them on him."

"I have made a discovery," commenced Redfern in Jonathan's ear.

"Silence!" roared Jonathan, "I'll attend to nothing until I have this fellow chained down. Oh! that I might use torture! Oh! that I might put him on the rack! tear his body with red-hot pinchers! brand him with hot irons! pour boiling oil down his throat! Oh! for the dear, good old days, when we were allowed to have the pleasure of torturing our prisoners.

Mr. Wild certainly had an inventive genius, as far as torture was concerned; for, when Grummidge returned with several sets of irons, he selected from amongst them, a very small, but immensely heavy and thick set.

"I don't think you will be able to get them on him, sir," said Grummidge.

"No!" exclaimed Jonathan, "and why should I not be able?"

"Why, sir, they're not large enough. I don't know who they were made for, indeed, no one here does, but there is a legend that they were made some hundred years ago, to suit a deformed man of small stature, but gigantic strength. You'll find it very difficult to get them on."

"All the more difficult to get them off, then. Down with him. He shall wear these fetters if they crush his bones. Ha! ha! Jack whose revenge now?"

The turnkeys reluctantly commenced fixing on the irons, which were so small that the rings that encircled the wrists and ankles, sank deep into the flesh before they could be forced to meet.

At length the thing was done, and Jack was thrown on the floor.

So short were the the irons that it was impossible for him to straighten his body.

Although Jack had suffered so tremendously, not one cry of pain escaped him.

This naturally enraged Jonathan, who loved to hear his victims implore mercy, he, therefore, determined to increase Jack's torture by having him fastened to a ring-bolt that happened to be in the floor.

A large padlock having been found for this purpose, Jonathan Wild locked it, put the key into his own pocket, and then, bestowing a kick on his prostrate foe, led the way out of the cell.

"Well," he demanded of Redfern, "and what have you discovered?"

"That Maud is in London—that she is now plotting against us."

THE BURNING OF JONATHAN WILD'S HOUSE.

"Indeed! that is news—but how did you come to discover so much?"

"I called at your house for you, and heard that you were here, so followed at once. Just as I was coming near the gates, a woman and a lad came out."

"Ha!" exclaimed Jonathan, stopping suddenly, "came from this prison?"

"Yes, I followed them unperceived. At last, thinking they were alone, the woman raised her veil. It was Maud!"

Why did you not arrest her?" cried Wild, impatiently.

"Just at the time she was joined by two or three men, who conducted her to a carriage. She got in, accompanied by the lad, and the next moment they drove away."

No. 25.

"How were they dressed?" screamed Jonathan, livid with rage.

"Both the woman and the boy were in deep mourning," replied Redfern.

"I see it all," cried Jonathan, turning, on Grummidge, you have let these people in against orders. That is how that fellow's irons were cut. By heaven! I am tempted to kill you on the spot. Speak villain; tell the truth, or your life shall answer for it."

"I merely gave them one glimpse at the prisoner," said Grummidge, trembling.

"Follow me," said Wild, and he at once returned to Sheppard's cell.

"Search, and search carefully for the saw," he exclaimed.

They did so, and in a few moments the little spring saw was found.

"You see, Jack" cried Wild, "I know all your secrets."

"What a pity you did not know them sooner," replied Jack, "you might have saved your beauty—that is, not have been made so ugly.

"Laugh away," said Wild, bitterly. "I'll leave you this bit of news to comfort you. Maud is taken, and has confessed those secrets you refused to tell."

"You lie," replied Jack, "taken she may be, but round on her friends she never would."

"Bah! she is a woman, and fears death," said Jonathan.

"That is false. She bore the torture in yon dungeon firmly, and with but one hope, that was to be revenged on you. Mark me, Jonathan Wild, before many hours are over that woman will have punished you severely. Jonathan Wild sprung forward and would probably have killed Jack, so mad was he with passion, but the jailers held him back. Muttering many deep curses Jonathan ordered one of the jailers to stop and watch Jack Sheppard all night so that he should not escape. "As for you, he cried, turning to Grummidge, "I shall consider whether I shall report your conduct or not. If Jack Sheppard hangs the day after to-morrow, I will forgive you; if not, you shall take his place. So look to it, you have been a jailer and therefore, I should not think, too anxious to be a prisoner. Come my lord," he continued, turning to Redfern, "we must look to this woman. The cat means mischief, but it shall go hard with me if I do not bell her yet. If once I get her in my power, she shall tell me the secrets of this Batswing, or I will wring them from her by such cruel tortures as have not been dreamed of in the darkest days. Come, we have no time to lose.

So saying, he seized Lord Redfern by the arm, and led him from the prison to his own house, where they passed the night in debate.

CHAPTER LXXIV.

MAUD AND FLICKER GO TO THE FLEET—MEETING OF THE RATS—FARMER CROFT AND ZARAH JOIN THEM —"VENGEANCE AGAINST JONATHAN WILD"—THE PLAN OF ATTACK.

ON November the 14th, in the year 1724 a thick fog wrapped all London in its damp, choking folds. A fog in the present time is far from pleasant, although we have all the advantages of gas and well-paved streets. But a hundred and fifty years ago fogs were more dangerous than storms. The dim, flickering oil lamps could not pierce the thick cloud; the streets were broken and rough, whilst in some places the sewers were open, so that unwary pedestrians who lost their way fell headlong into them and were suffocated.

As the drainage at the time we speak about was very defective, fogs were of much more frequent occurrence than at the present time, and crimes were frequently perpetrated under cover of the darkness of the fog. The fog was always thickest by the banks of the Thames and over the rank waters of the Fleet Ditch, rendering those localities more than usually dangerous, and therefore, much to be avoided, as indeed they were even in the brightest weather, for both places were the favourite resort of the worst kind of thieves.

In spite of the weather on the night we speak of, two persons were making their way as rapidly as they could down Holborn Hill in the direction of the Fleet. They both were enveloped in long cloaks, and felt their way by clinging to the houses and walls.

The youngest evidently acted as guide, for he walked first, and now and then he stopped and stretched out his hand to see if his companion had not missed him.

"Ah! you're there all right," he said, "I was frightened you might have turned the wrong way. You must take care here or it will be all up with you."

"What do you mean?" asked the other, "where is the danger?"

"Only that, if you go down a court that is here on our left, you come to some old houses that they're pulling down, and they commenced by uncovering the drain; that's all. One or two people have either fallen, or been put down there."

"This is a terrible place," muttered Maud, for it was she.

"That it is," replied her companion, who was no other but our young friend Flicker.

"Are you sure that you will not lose your way?" demanded Maud.

"Trust to me; I know every turn about here; but it is jolly dark I must own."

"Dark! why it is impossible to see an inch before you."

"All the better, for no one will be able to see us."

For some moments they walked on in silence; at last Flicker stopped.

"Give me your hand," he said, "I hear the rush of the ditch."

A low, gurgling sound struck upon the ear, showing that they were near running water.

"For heavens sake take care" said Maud, "to me it seems that no death would be so horrible as that of being suffocated in that terrible ditch."

"Never fear, keep tight hold of me and I will guide you rightly."

With great caution Flicker led the way over the rotten bridge.

Scarcely had they passed it, when a deep voice demanded, "Who goes there?"

"Rats," replied Flicker, promptly.

"Pass rats," replied the voice, and Maud and Flicker hurried on their way, being occasionally stopped by the same question.

"You seem to be well guarded here," said Maud.

"Rather," replied Flicker, "it would be a bad look out for anyone who attempted to come this way without knowing the pass word. He would find the ditch fast enough, and no mistake. But here we are."

As he spoke he drew Maud into a door-way.

He paused for a moment, then stooping down, whistled softly into the key hole.

"Whose dare?" demanded a voice from inside of the door.

"Rats, Moses," replied Flicker, through the keyhole; true rats of the Fleet, that have followed Jack-o'-Lantern, and have come to aid in the good cause."

"Vate a moment, and I'll let you in," replied the Jew.

In a few seconds the pushing back of bolts, the dropping of bars, and the rattle of chains were heard, and then the door opened wide enough to admit Flicker and his companion.

"Dey all down stairs," said the Jew, in a hoarse whisper; "Blueskin is nearly mad about the cap'en. None of the fellows dare to speak to him; they ain't done nothing yet, but drink and smoke; and, holy Moses, how they do drink, it's something terrible; but it makes them ready for anything."

Talking all the way, the Jew led them down to the cellar, where they found some fifty or sixty men seated in groups, conversing in whispers, as they smoked their pipes and drank their grog.

In one corner of the room sat Blueskin, silent and gloomy.

He had no one near him, neither did he seem interested in what was going on.

A broken pipe lay by his side—he was too sad to smoke—but he applied himself constantly to a bottle of spirits that stood before him.

As Maud and Flicker entered the room, he raised his blood-shot eyes, and fixed them upon them.

Then with a deep curse, he arose, and striding across

the room, seized Moses by the collar, and shook him violently.

"Holy Moses! vat is de matter, Mishter Blueskin, vat have I done?"

"Do you know what you are doing, you old hater of swines' flesh!" cried Blueskin.

"Vat have I done, kind shentleman? Do let me go."

"Who are these people you have just brought in here?" cried Blueskin.

"What, Blueskin! don't you know me?" cried Flicker, throwing off his cloak.

"Blow me if it ain't little Jack-o'-Lantern," cried Blueskin.

"The same article," replied the boy, "come back like a bad halfpenny."

"And now you have come back, what do you want?" asked Blueskin.

"To help to save Jack Sheppard," cried Flicker, "come, don't look so glum, Blueskin, all will go well yet. You see if it don't."

"And what can you do towards saving the cap'en?" said Blueskin, contemptuously, "it'll take all men's work to get him out, let alone boys."

"We'll have plenty of men, Blueskin, besides women and boys," said Flicker.

"Women!" said Blueskin, in disgust; "they're more likely to put a fellow into quod, than to take him out. I don't believe in them at all."

"Be polite, old boy," said Flicker, for there is a lady present."

"Where?" demanded Blueskin, looking round in amazement.

"Here!" replied Maud, standing up, and throwing off her cloak and hat.

Blueskin stood in utter amazement.

Maud had so improved since she had gained her liberty, that no one would have recognised in the fine, handsome woman, the emaciated female who had once been prisoner to Jonathan Wild.

"And who the devil are you?" demanded Blueskin, surlily; "I know you not."

"I am lieutenant to Batswing, and as he is abroad, I have come to take his place and help you in your counsels."

A general murmur of applause ran round the room at this speech.

"And what do you propose doing, Mistress Lieutenant?" asked Blueskin.

"In the first place, I intend standing punch all round; in the second, I do not intend standing any impertinence from any one," replied Maud, touching the but-ends of her pistols. "I came here to try and save Jack Sheppard, and the one who refuses assistance is Jack's enemy. Moses fetch the punch, and you, Blueskin, resume your seat and silence at the same time."

Blueskin looked in amazement at Maud, and then muttering a deep oath, resumed his seat, and was silent.

The punch was brought in, and at Maud's request the men drew round the table. The glasses were filled, and business commenced.

"My men!" said Maud, rising from her seat, "you all know that Jonathan Wild has sworn to hang Jack Sheppard. Now, it becomes our duty to prevent this being done. How we are to do this is not quite clear, and it is to discuss ways and means that we have met to-night; but before we commence doing so, it will be well that we see there are no traitors in the room, none of Wild's spies."

"If there is," said Blueskin, jumping up, and opening his clasp knife, "if there is, I'll slit his weasand."

"Try them, Blueskin," said Maud, "if you find a spy, have no mercy."

Blueskin did as he was commanded. He passed down the room, and whispered some mysterious words to each of the men, who replied in the same tone. They then shook hands with a peculiar grip, and the examiner was satisfied.

They are all true and staunch men," said Blueskin. "I have proved them."

"Good!" said Maud. "We will now proceed to take the oath of secrecy,"

"Silently each man rose to his feet, prepared to listen and repeat the oath, as dictated to them by Maud.

But each paused and gazed in silence in the wonder-stricken face of his neighbour.

His grey hair standing almost erect, his long, greasy gaberdine floating out behind him, Moses rushed into the room, and stood trembling before them.

"What is the meaning of this intrusion?" demanded Maud, sternly.

"Holy Father Abraham!" cried the Jew, "there is some people at the door."

"Well, have they given you the password?" asked Blueskin.

"They have given me a password," said the Jew, "but not the right one."

A movement of alarm passed through the assembly.

"What is to be done, we are betrayed," said Blueskin, with a deep oath.

"Done?" cried Maud." "Let each one see to his weapons; then we will creep up to the passage, and if there is need, meet violence by violence."

"But what will become of me?" cried the Jew, wringing his hands.

"That I neither know nor care," said Blueskin. "But this I tell you at once, if you do not do all we tell you, I'll blow your brains out myself."

"Flicker." said Maud, "is there no way that you can leave this place unobserved, so as to find out who and how many are at the door."

"That I can do with ease," cried the lad, springing up.

"If you find they are of us, but have not had the word, give it to them."

"You, Moses, go to some upper window and inquire who they are, so that we shall see if they tell the truth."

Flicker shot away on his errand, and the Jew crept upstairs, followed cautiously by the men, with Maud at their head as leader.

They waited a few moments in silence, and then heard Moses open an upper window, and demand, "Who knocked?" in a tremulous voice.

"I knocked," replied a man. "I have given you the word, why don't you open the door?"

"The word!" said the Jew, "I do not understand you. You have made some mistake; I am but a poor man, so go and leave me in peace."

"Come, come, Moses, you know me," replied the man, "so open the door."

At that moment Flicker's voice was heard outside, asking if the gentleman and lady wanted to find their way anywhere.

"What is that to you?" demanded the man.

"'Cause as 'ow I was born and bred here, that's all," replied Flicker, in the whining tones he used to use.

"Why, hang me if it ain't Flicker!" replied the man. "Did'nt you know me, Flicker?"

"How should I in the fog?" replied the lad.

"Well, I'm Farmer Croft," said the man. "You know me now, at any rate.

"Yes, I know you; but there's somebody else. Who is it?"

"Only my daughter," replied the farmer.

"And what do you want?" asked Flicker "Have you come to betray any one to Jonathan Wild, as you did before, eh?"

"Betray men to Jonathan Wild?" cried the farmer. "No! that was the worst night's work I ever did. I have come to ask them to protect me and my daughter from the villain; to ask them to assist me in having revenge upon him, and then they may take their revenge upon me as they like, for I'm tired of life."

"Hillo! guv'nor, that's a new game," cried Flicker, in surprise. "Still, as it sounds honest, I don't mind trusting you. Only mark this, if you only attempt to breathe one word of what you hear in this place, you die."

"Fear not," replied Croft, "when you hear my story you will trust me."

Thus encouraged, Flicker gave the required password; the door was opened, and the farmer and his daughter were conducted, under a strong guard, into the cellar, where, in a few words, he told his story, only stating that Wild had caused his daughter's death and threatened to arrest him.

"Is this story true?" asked Maud.

"It is," replied Zarah, "I was present when the deed was done."

"Enough," said Maud, "You shall join us in this search for revenge. With your other crimes I have nothing to do. Now prepare to take the oath."

They all stood up, and the oath was duly administered.

"Now," cried Blueskin, "I propose we attack the procession as it passes along by Holborn Bridge. The place there is narrow, and the soldiers will not be able to charge us so well as they would be able to do in the broad streets. We can keep our men back in the side streets until the time comes, and at a certain signal rush forward and carry off Jack. We can soon overpower the soldiery; some of them will be for us; and so will a great number of the people. Now there is my plan; what do you think of it?"

"But that does not give us our revenge on Wild!" cried Zarah.

"Why not?" cried Blueskin, "Jonathan will fight like a lion to keep Jack, and I will fight like a tiger to save him. Trust me, either Jonathan or myself will die before the day is out."

"But he may escape," said Zarah, "And we must not let him have a chance."

"You're mighty spiteful against Jonathan," said one of the men. "I thought we had come here to save Jack Sheppard, and for no other purpose."

"You have come to do what the general number decide, cried Maud.

"And he who draws back dies," said Blueskin, with a nasty wave of the knife.

"I'm not drawing back," said the man, "only Mr. Wild never hurt me, and—"

"Fool!" cried Maud, "are you so blind as not to perceive that Jonathan Wild is an enemy to all of us? He treats us as a farmer does his sheep, letting us go about until we are fat enough to kill, and then showing us no mercy. Think you that he has pity for you? Mark me! if you spare him, the day will come when he will have your life. He never spares. I have felt his cruelty for years; I was his prisoner, and suffered daily torture at his hands. No: Wild must be removed. Year after year has he tempted others to commit crimes out of which he alone has received the profit, and when his victims have grown restive, or government has offered a large reward for their lives, his hands have conducted them to the gallows: he has not only taken them there, but, with fiendish taunts and gibes increased their misery. Yes, the greater the agony of his victims, the greater has been his pleasure. I ask you all to look round and reckon up how many of your friends, who twelve months ago were seated with you, have died by Jonathan Wild's hands since then. He who has brought hundreds to the gallows has been the only one to escape. What then is to be his doom? Pause ere you answer, but when you do, let that answer be irrevocable."

For a few seconds the men remained silent, and then, as if with one voice, proclaimed Wild's fate.

"Death!!!"

"Then," continued Maud, "this is my plan. If we attack the procession on the way to Tyburn, Wild may escape and Jack Sheppard may be hanged, for we may be beaten back by the troops, as double the usual number have been ordered to attend the execution. If we fail there, we have no further chance. Now, I propose that we should attack Wild's house to-morrow night, burn it to the ground, rob it of all its valuables, Should he escape us, the loss of his gold will be a terrible punishment to him. Beneath Wild's house is a secret passage leading to Newgate. We will force this and rescue Jack Sheppard, who will not be so well guarded."

"But should we fail to rescue the captain," growled Blueskin, "what then?"

"Why, then your plan shall be carried out, and we attack the procession."

"Good," said Blueskin, "I'm in for a slap at Jonathan at all events."

"Now to prepare for the plan of attack," said Maud, "we must assemble by threes and fours, so as not to call forth suspicion."

"First let us select our leaders," said Blueskin, "then they can lay their plan of attack, whilst the rest look to our arms and beat up our forces."

This plan was agreed upon, and some half dozen people were selected as captains of the various bands; amongst them Maud and Blueskin. They then selected some five or six men who could be trusted, and despatched them to the various houses in the Fleet, to give warning to the inhabitants that the "Rats," as they called themselves, were to make a night attack, and where and when to meet their captains.

Flicker was mounted on horseback, and started for Epping with orders to bring as many of Batswing's band as he could.

The rest of the people remained in the Fleet, cleaning their pistols and sharpening their swords, whilst the leaders laid the plans for the attack.

CHAPTER LXXV.

STORMING OF JONATHAN WILD'S HOUSE—REDFERN AND FLICKER MEET—THE FATAL FIGHT—JERRY BLINKER'S SCHEME—ZARAH'S HORRIBLE DEATH—WILD'S ESCAPE.

LORD REDFERN sat in Jonathan Wild's room, looking at the various horrible and gastly trophies therein contained, now and then shuddering when one more than usually horrible met his eye.

Jonathan with his head bent down, and his hands clenched behind him, was pacing up and down, evidently in deep thought.

Things had not gone well with Jonathan lately All his plans had failed.

It is true that he had made sure of Jack Sheppard, but his face still smarted from the heavy punishment he had received from Jack, whilst a large plaster on the back of his head, showed that his head had suffered severely from the beating against the stone pavement of the cell.

Jonathan, at the best of times, had always been ugly, but now he was frightful.

Amongst other things that annoyed him, was that he could not discover for certain where Batswing had gone; whilst Maud's visit to Newgate made him feel doubtful whether Jack would not attempt another escape.

Now and then he cast an angry glance at Redfern, for, somehow or another, he could not help connecting all his recent failures with that nobleman.

He not only hated Redfern, but he had an immense contempt for his cowardice.

"Well!" he said, suddenly stopping before Redfern; "what are you thinking about?"

"I—well I must confess I was wondering at your

taste in collecting these things," replied Redfern, pointing at the several articles about the room.

"Ha! ha! ha!" laughed Jonathan, "that is my museum, why should I not please my taste as well as other people? Mine may be a strange one; I don't say that it is not, but then it *is* my taste, and, therefore I do it."

"Oh, certainly, of course; still I don't think another person in the world would do the same; I'm sure I should not," said Redfern, with a shudder.

"Perhaps not. Here is the rope that hung Tom Sheppard; to-morrow I mean to have the one that will send his son after him. This razor was the one used by Bradleigh, when he cut his wife's throat. See, the blood is still upon the blade, and—"

"In mercy be quiet," cried Redfern, covering his face with his hands, "you make me feel sick. Give me some brandy, I am faint—very faint."

Wild gave a short, dry laugh, and walking to the cupboard, brought out a bottle of brandy and some glasses, which he put before his guest.

"There," he said, "drink that, perhaps it may put blood and courage into your craven heart. Drink well; such mean spirits as yours need it."

Redfern required no further invitation, but drank off one or two bumpers.

"That is good," said Redfern, as he set down the glass.

"It ought to be," said Wild, filling his tumbler, and holding it up to the light, "I have many a time drank this until I was mad, and then, ho! ho! ho! I've visited my prisoners. They know when I've tasted this, for then they taste what my temper is like, ho! ho! ho! Here's a quick ride for Jack Sheppard, to-morrow."

With another fiendish laugh, he winked at Redfern, then drank up his brandy at a draught.

"What sort of a night is it?" he asked curtly.

"Bad," replied Redfern, "the fog has cleared greatly since yesterday, but it is still very thick over the city."

"Hark!" said Wild, pausing, as he was about to pour out some brandy, "what was that strange noise, just now?"

"The wind is getting up, nothing more," replied Redfern, "it will clear the fog."

"Look here, my lord," said Wild, after he had tossed off his brandy, "I think that it is time that we settled up accounts. I am tired of this life, and mean soon to retire from business. Therefore I shall call in my money."

"Call in your money!" said Redfern, in astonishment; "I owe you nothing."

"Perhaps you do not *owe* me any, but I have certain secrets for sale—that it would be well for your safety to purchase. You understand me, eh?"

"You cannot, dare not, demand so dastardly a thing," cried Redfern.

"As for the 'cannot,' I will soon prove that to you; the 'dare not,' I have already answered by doing it. Now, I must and will have half your estates. At least I must have the value of them in money."

"You surely cannot mean what you say," said Redfern.

"If you do not comply with my terms, I expose you; and then, my lord, I think it will not be long before you follow Jack Sheppard to Tyburn. I should rather like to have a rope that had hanged a lord. It would be worth something, and—"

He paused as the strange murmur again smote upon his ear.

"That noise is *not* the wind," he cried, suddenly, "it is the sound of a crowd."

"Probably some fire," said Redfern, glad to change the conversation.

"Here come my men to tell me," said Jonathan, as the sound of hurrying feet sounded along the stone passage. "There *is* something wrong."

The door was thrown open, and one of his men hurried into the room.

"Well, what is the matter now?" demanded Jonathan, coolly."

"The Rats of the Fleet have assembled," gasped the man, "and are armed."

"Well, what of that?" said Jonathan, whilst a nervous twitching at the corner of his mouth, showed that the news had affected him more than he cared to show.

"They have been assembling, it seems, for some hours," gasped the man.

"Why did you not let me know that before?" cried Jonathan, "we must send for the aid of the military, to drive these vermin back to their holes."

"I did not know they were coming," replied the man, "they assembled without noise, and the fog prevented my seeing them. There are thousands of them."

"The fools will attack Newgate in hopes of rescuing Jack Sheppard," said Jonathan, "I must go and give Mr. Pitt warning at once. They shall repent this."

"Stop, sir, stop!" cried the man, "the house is surrounded, they will attack here first, Darrell, farmer Croft's man, sneaked away from them under cover of the fog to give you warning. He says that Croft and his daughter are with them, and they have all sworn to have your life."

Uttering a cry like a wild animal mad with rage, Wild threw up his arms and paced rapidly up and down the room. He stamped, swore and laughed in the same breath, making even his companion shudder. "Have my life, will they?" he exclaimed. "Fools, I will hang them all. Not one shall escape. Ha, ha, ha! They would venture into the lion's den, would they? well, they shall have their reward. What preparations have you made?"

"I have bolted and barred every window and door," said the man.

"And the men, where are they?" asked Jonathan, "this will be a rare night."

"You surely do not mean to stop and fight them," cried Lord Redfern.

"And why not?" replied Jonathan coolly, for he had gained his self-possession.

"But there are thousands to your half-dozen," urged Lord Redfern.

"The more to kill," replied Jonathan, "then we shall have your lordship's help."

"Mine!"

"You surely would not run away, my lord," said Jonathan, mockingly.

"I—no—of course not—but—that is—the people do not want me."

"Well then, go," said Jonathan grinning, "go at once. Remember the house is surrounded, and they will let no one pass without questioning."

"Surely they will not stop a nobleman?" cried Redfern.

"Try them!" shrieked Jonathan, in fiendish delight, "just try them. Ask Maud to let you pass, or Batswing, ho! ho! ho! Do you think these rats would have the courage to face *me* without a leader? No, Batswing is at the bottom of all this, and Maud—your darling Maud—is with him! Now will you go, my lord; or will you fight! Ho! ho! ho! how white his lordship is, even his nose has changed colour. Fight, my lord, fight! you must; you can't help yourself, ho! ho! ho! how the blood of the false steward shows in the noble lord!"

Jonathan seemed quite oblivious to the increasing sounds of the mob, as they gathered round his house; his whole thought seemed wrapped up in the enjoyment of seeing the cowardly Redfern compelled to fight. But soon a cry arose, that made him cease his merriment, and gnash his teeth.

"DEATH TO JONATHAN WILD! DOWN WITH JONATHAN WILD!!" shouted the mob.

In a moment Wild became perfectly calm and collected.

He walked across the room, and took from the wall a tremendous cutlass.

This he strapped round his waist by a thick belt, in which he stuck several pistols.

He then opened a chest, and took therefrom a number of guns and pistols.

These he handed over to the man to load, and place in readiness by the window.

He then handed a cutlass and a pair of pistols to Redfern, bidding him, with a grim smile, to use them well, as he valued his life.

Lord Redfern took them with a sickly smile, and placed them in his belt.

"Now," said Jonathan, turning to his man, "close all the doors and lock them up to the first floor. There, barricade the iron door, so that if they gain an entrance they will have to force that, whilst we can fire through the loop-holes at them in perfect safety. Bring the men up here, and see that they are well armed."

The man, gaining fresh confidence from Jonathan's coolness, departed cheerfully.

Wild filled a large tumbler with brandy drunk off the contents, and said—

"Now, my lord, you shall see some fun. I will show you how to defy a mob."

He walked to a window, undid the fastenings, and threw it open.

Lord Redfern followed him, and looked out, but quickly withdrew, for the sight drove away the little courage which the brandy and despair had lent him.

It was, indeed, a terrible sight, yet not without some touch of grandeur.

The paved court before Jonathan's house was crammed with a rough crowd of men, mostly dressed in loose, coarse fustain; but there were others who were well and showily dressed. These acted as the leaders of the party.

A great many men in the crowd, which extended far down the Old Bailey, carried torches, so that Jonathan could make out and recognise several of the men; but the fog and the thick smoke from the links rendered it difficult to be certain of the identity of any but those who possessed some personal peculiarity by which they might be distinguished.

There was something demoniac in this torch-lit crowd.

For some seconds nothing could be heard but that peculiar hum common to all crowds, but then the terrible cry arose "Down with Jonathan Wild."

"There is Blueskin," muttered Jonathan, "I'd swear to him anywhere."

Taking deliberate aim at Blueskin, Jonathan fired.

An angry yell rose from the crowd, and Jonathan had only time to see that he had missed his aim, before the crowd saw him and fired a volly at the window.

"Hum! they are well armed," said Jonathan, "now to work. Come, my lord, I can have no idlers here. You must fight, or by all the devils in hell, I will shoot you myself. Crouch low and fire; they cannot hit you." So low did Redfern crouch that it was not only impossible for the crowd to hit him, but also impossible for him to hit them unless they were up on the roofs of the neighbouring houses.

Jonathan was now reinforced by his men, who poured down a murderous fire, receiving in return but little hurt from their assailants, owing to the protection of the window.

"Hush!" cried Jonathan suddenly, "they have broken down the door. We must now fight through the grated one on the stairs."

The window was closed, and the fight re-commenced on the staircase.

Jonathan and his men fought desperately. Indeed, all but Jonathan Wild and Redfern sank mortally

wounded before the strong iron door gave way. But the fierce assaults of the beseigers at length succeeded, and the iron door fell crashing from off its hinges.

Jonathan paused to discharge a brace of pistols at his assailants, and had the pleasue of seeing Farmer Croft stagger back, shot through the heart.

With a cry of trimuph, Jonathan sprang up another flight of stairs.

"Save me, save me!" screamed Redfern, rushing after Wild.

"No!" thundered Jonathan, "you have fought like a cur—die like a dog!"

The next minute he slammed the door at the head of the second staircase, leaving Redfern at the mercy of the mob.

Redfern turned in despair, but was instantly seized by the throat by Flicker.

So rapid was the boy's attack, that Redfern fell to the ground.

He saw the lad raise a sharp knife, and heard a voice he knew to be Maud's, crying in imploring accents,—

"Hold! hold! for heaven's sake, do not strike! *He is your father!!*"

The warning came too late, the knife was buried in Redfern's bosom.

High above the roar of the crowd came Jonathan's yell of delight.

"Ho, ho, ho!" he shrieked, "Redfern killed by the son he would have murdered. Ho, ho, ho! this pays me for all!"

Maud commanded some of the men to remove Redfern to a place of safety, and then, for the first time, discovered that Flicker had also been wounded.

A shot—one of Jonathan's last—had passed through the boy's shoulder; and, overcome with pain and loss of blood, he sank insensible in the arms of the men, who bore him out of the house.

The sound of Jonathan's laughter had so exasperated the crowd that they rushed madly at the door. It gave way, and the entire building was in their hands; they searched everywhere, but Wild was gone.

By some means he had managed to make his escape over the housetops.

Yelling, tearing, howling, hooting, the people raced through the house.

They tore up the floors, and discovered the secret passages and dungeons.

In one of these they discovered Jacob Becker in almost a dying state.

"Bring him here, cried Maud. "Give him some brandy to revive him."

The poor wretch clutched eagerly at the brandy, and drank with avidity,

"Who and what are you?" demanded Maud.

"My name is Becker," said the man. "I know all Jonathan Wild's secrets, and therefore he placed me in that horrible place to die. Thank God you have saved me, kind gentlemen; and I shall now be able to hang Jonathan Wild and Lord Redfern. I saw Lord Leslie killed, and—"

"Enough, enough!" cried Maud, bear the fellow away. Keep him safe, for he will be useful. Then pillage the house, whilst I search these papers."

The men were but too glad to have permission to pillage, and set to work at once.

It would be impossible to describe the immense amount of valuables that they found. Rings, watches, chains, and jewellery of all kinds were packed away in boxes; many of these trinkets were of great value, and bore the crests and coats of arms of several well-known noblemen.

Wild had for years been a receiver of stolen goods, and had made an immense fortune by his nefarious trade.

Money, jewels, and all sorts of valuables were quickly removed to the Fleet, where they were afterwards fairly divided amongst those who took part in the fray, thus proving that a certain amount of honour was to be found amongst thieves.

Rich and rare as the plunder was, it soon disappeared under such very nimble-handed and light-fingered management.

Then the people turned them to the cells and dungeons, where they discovered such horrid sights, that, hardened by vice and debased as they were, they shuddered in horror.

Skeletons, dead bodies in different stages of putrifaction, instruments of torture, such as one would have thought no human creature could have dreamed of, bludgeons, and whips clotted with blood; chains, fetters and ropes, all told their tale of suffering and terror.

But hark! there is the tap of the drum and the shrill scream of the fife.

"The soldiers; the soldiers," cry the people. "Fly, fly"

"No!" shouts Blueskin, who, with one or two others, has been trying to find the secret passage leading to Newgate, "no, we will not retreat until we have released Jack Sheppard. Follow me, my lads; we'll have him out yet. He has often broke *out* of Newgate, by all the devils we'll break into it. Some of you stay here and burn down the house. If we can't kill Jonathan Wild, we'll make him as poor and miserable as possible.

"Hurrah! hurrah!! hurrah!!!" shouted the men, and away they dashed.

The upper part of Jonathan's house was now almost deserted.

One person alone remained there, walking quietly through the rooms.

"They've all gone now," he said at last, as he looked over the ballasters, "Yes, there they are down there, a-piling up the furniture as never was. Oh! Jerry Blinker, Jerry Blinker, air these your good resolutions? If you was caught now you would be rewarded by being presented at court, your character examined by twelve of your enlightened countrymen, and finish up with a ride in a cart, on the top of a coffin to Tyburn. And then they'd call that justice. Justice! when I've only come here to do a good action. Jerry Blinker is a altered individual. I haven't fired at anyone; I ain't stole a fraction o' anything, although I've been sorely tempted; but I says to myself, says I, 'Jerry, don't be weak, be wirtuous as you're beautiful; remember that there terrible scene in the garden, and don't go for to fail in your resolutions,' and I ain't. But there's no time to be lost. Which o' these 'ere corpses will suit me best?"

As he spoke he turned over the dead bodies.

"My eye!" he exclaimed, as he came to one, "if this 'ere ain't the cove as buried the gal in the back garden. Well, he'll do as well as another, and there ain't no time for picking and choosing. Now, by your leave, sir, I'll remove your clothes."

Taking out his knife, Jerry deliberately ripped off Farmer Croft's clothes.

He then opened a large knapsack that he carried on his back, and took therefrom a suit of black clothes, in which he encased the body.

After this he buckled a peculiarly shaped black cloak round the dead man's body, and also placed a couple of pistols in his belt.

"There," he said, as he threw the farmer's clothes into a corner, "now you're perfect."

He opened a window that looked out into a back-yard, and placed the body so that it stood as if leaning with its back on the window sill.

He then drew a pistol, cocked it, and deliberately fired in the face of the corpse.

Jerry Blinker could not help shuddering as he saw the body topple out of the window.

"Well," he said, "it's done now, and I hope good may come of it."

He looked down into the yard, but it was too dark to see anything.

"There's one comfort,', he said, as he walked slowly away, "it can do no harm."

He had not descended many stairs, when he was stopped by Zarah.

Her face was flushed with excitement; her hair streamed out wildly, and her eyes were lit up by the fire of madness.

In her right hand she grasped a sword, and in her left a pistol.

"Where is he? where is he?" she exclaimed, "have you found him? have you killed him? Tell me instantly, have you killed him? how did he die?"

"I ain't found nobody, and I ain't killed nobody," said Jerry.

"Not killed him?" cried Zarah, "what did you fire you pistol at then?"

"At?" said Jerry, rather puzzled to answer the question, "at? why, at the ghost!"

"The ghost?" cried Zarah, passionately, "jest not with me, but answer at once."

"Well, if it wasn't a man that was dead," said Jerry, "I never saw one, that's all. In fact I couldn't tell the difference."

"Fool! where did you see it?" cried Zarah stamping.

"Why, just over there by the staircase. I fired, and when the smoke cleared away he was gone."

"It must have been Wild, screamed Zarah, "I will find him yet."

With a cry of triumph she bounded away up the stairs.

"Why, if that there aint the she tiger I saw in the garden along with the cove I've sent into the back yard. Well, I hope she may find Wild, that I does for if she kills he, or he kills she, it will be one bad person the less in this wicked world. And now my business is done, I shall return home quietly to the bosom of my family, by which I means the widow Wapshaw, the fat, fair, and forty hostess of the Bird Cage Inn."

Jerry had only descended the stairs halfway when he was almost suffocated with a thick cloud of smoke that came rolling up from below.

"By Jingo, this is a pretty go!" he cried, "blow me if they haven't been and gone and set the 'ouse a-fire. Well, I'll make a dash at it, for I won't be stewed up here like a stoat in a hole."

Closing his eyes and holding his breath, Jerry made a rush for it, and managed by a great effort to reach the street, where he found but a small portion of the mob, for the main body had rushed off to attack Newgate.

At first he was so dizzy from the smoke that he could not see anything. He, however, soon recovered, and looked at Wild's house.

The devouring element had seized upon it now and wrapped it in its folds. Huge tongues of red flame shot from the windows and shot towards the lurid sky. Up, up, up, into the air were whirled burning pieces of wood, looking like flaming torches carried by invisible hands. The roar of the fire, the screams of the neighbours, were demoniacal.

Jerry felt sick at the sight, and was about turning away, but a cry from the crowd made him stay and gaze once more at the flaming house.

"It is a woman on the roof," cried one, "see! there she is again."

"Look! look!" cried another, "she has a sword in her hand."

Jerry felt faint, for he recognized the figure of Zarah.

Regardless of the thick smoke and the flames that broke through the roof, she rushed backwards and forwards, seeking for Wild.

"Come down, come down!" screamed the crowd, "do you not see that the roof is falling in: spring on to the other house-top: save yourself."

Of course Zarah could not hear the shouts of the crowd distinctly enough to understand what they said, but she turned as if she had done so. The roof of the other house was about two feet higher than the one on which she stood: she could have gained it with ease, but seemed unwilling to leave the burning house until certain that Jonathan Wild was not there. Suddenly she grasped the sword tighter, and with the bound of a tigress, sprang on to the other roof, for there, grinning like a fiend, stood Wild.

With all her might she struck him across the face with her sword, severing his nose in two.

She was about to repeat the blow, when Jonathan caught her in his arms.

He raised her from the ground, and gazed at the mob, breathless, as if about to hurl her down upon them, so that he might have double revenge.

The fire now burst through the roof in hundreds of flames.

The lurid light of the fire showed Wild clutching the girl distinctly.

The crowd below could even see their features, so powerful was the glare.

Suddenly there came an awful crack; the roof was falling in.

With a demoniac yell of delight, Jonathan raised Zarah above his head, and then hurled her into the fiery abyss.

At that moment the roof fell, and a red cloud of fiery smoke, filled with myriads of sparks, rushed up to the sky.

For a moment Jonathan stood in the same position as he had taken when he had hurled the girl into the fire. He gazed after her as if he could still see her writhing in the flames; then, tossing his arms aloft, burst into a fiendish laugh and disappeared.

A cry of rage arose from the mob, and they were about to rush to sack the house into which Wild had escaped, when the roll of musketry was heard, and the mob that had been attacking Newgate came rushing back.

The troops, with bayonets fixed, marched down the street at double quick time, and soon managed to clear the streets.

Jerry waited to see no more, but fairly turned and fled.

So ended the burning and pillage of Jonathan Wild's house.

CHAPTER LXXVI.

JACK SHEPPARD'S EXECUTION — BATSWING RETURNS HOME AND HEARS SOME NEWS — MAUD'S NOTE — LORD REDFERN'S CONFESSION AND DEATH — FLICKER'S FATE.

THE morning after the riot, Jack Sheppard was conducted to Tyburn, and executed.

Several attempts were made to rescue him, both on the road and at the gallows; but all were successfully resisted by the soldiers and police.

Jonathan Wild rode close by the cart that contained Jack Sheppard.

Many people fell in their mad endeavours, and amongst them Blueskin, who was killed by a bullet from Wild's pistol, as he was cutting down the body.

The crowd at length dispersed, and London resumed its usual appearance.

In was not until the evening of the day, in the morning of which the execution took place, that Batswing — under the name of Percy Marvel — returned from France.

Deep and bitter were the regrets, when he heard of Sheppard's death, but he had little time to consider such things, for a servant, dressed in Lord Redfern's livery, brought him a note, the contents of which ran as follows:—

"Dear Friend,—"Come at once; I am here at my husband's house, nursing him, but without hope. He is sinking fast. Come directly, and bring with you a magistrate and a clergyman. Redfern is penitent. If you come as Percy Marvel, no one will know you. I do not say have no fear, for I know you have none. But great things depend on your coming; lose no time. Since that strange report about you is so firmly believed, no one will know you. How that came about, I know not. Still it will be of great service to you.—Yours,

"MAUD REDFERN."

"I guessed as much," said Batswing, when he had read the letter, "then turning to the servant, he added: "tell Lady Redfern I will come at once."

He then wrote off a hasty note, which he gave to his servant to deliver to the Countess Sourkroutzenbeg, with directions that he was to see it given into her own hands.

This done, he dispatched another servant for a clergyman and a magistrate, and ordered his carriage to be ready.

While he was waiting, a servant announced that Major Jennings wished to see him.

After a moment's thought, Batswing ordered the major to be shown up.

"Ah! Marvel," cried the major, "I have found you at home at last."

"Yes," replied Batswing, "but I have only just returned from abroad."

"I have been wishing to return you my thanks for your services the other evening."

"Really Major you owe me none," replied Batswing, bowing, "I did it as a slight return for the many kindnesses and services you have rendered me."

"'Pon my word, you are a wondrous fellow, how can I repay you?"

"Well, there is one service I should like you to grant me."

"You have but to name it and it shall be done."

"It is to accompany me to Redfern's; he is dying—his wife wishes to see me."

"His wife! why he always passed as being unmarried."

"Still, he was married. You may see and hear many strange things to-night, but I wish you to promise me to keep them all secret till I ask you to divulge them. Will you do as I request?" asked Batswing.

"With the greatest of pleasure. So Redfern is dying? I heard that he got that wound in Jonathan Wild's house. He is a bold, bad man, that Redfern: Report says that he had queer dealings with Wild. Inquiries are to be made into all Wild's doings, and it is believed that he will soon ride the same road as Jack Sheppard did this morning."

Batswing had not heard the news, and therefore asked the major all the particulars of the burning of Wild's house. These Jennings gave very fully, for he had had the command of the soldiers who had suppressed the riots.

"Still, it is an ill wind that blows no one any good," said the major in conclusion, "the rioters were evidently led on by an old enemy of mine, a desperate fellow, the terror of the country. The fellow was killed in the fight, so that there is one rascal less in the world."

"Indeed!" said Batswing, "who is the man, or rather who was the the man."

"A fellow called Batswing," said the major, carelessly.

"Batswing!!" cried our hero, "you are joking, major."

"Fact, upon my life. The fellow was found in the back yard of Jonathan's house, his head all blown to pieces."

"If his head be blown to pieces, how do they know it is the man."

"Oh! by his dress; there is no mistaking the Batswing. The country people thought he could not be touched, but Jonathan, or one of his men, has proved the difference."

'Perhaps so," said Batswing, smiling. "Well Major he will not rob you any more. But come, here is my servant. I see by his appearance without being summoned that the magistrate and clergyman have arrived. So we will start at once."

Major Jennings bowed, and Batswing conducted him to the carriage, where they found the magistrate and clergyman waiting for them.

Batswing explained to the gentlemen what he required of them, and in a few moments they were rolling rapidly on their way.

They soon arrived at Lord Redfern's mansion, and were conducted to the room where his lordship lay.

It was a handsomely-furnished room, with every luxury about it. By the side of the bed sat Maud, no longer clothed in male attire, but in a beautiful robe of black velvet, suitable to her station. In one corner of the room there was a smaller bed, on which was poor Flicker, tossing about and talking wildly in delirium.

Maud, her beautiful pale face bathed in tears, beckoned them to the bedside.

They all drew near in solemn silence.

"They have come, Frank," said Maud, gently, "tell them all."

"Thank God!" said Redfern. "Gentlemen, I am dying, and would confess."

"Speak then," said Batswing, "we are all friends, for death destroys enmity."

"You are Mr. Marvel?" enquired Redfern, "and have befriended Maud."

Batswing only answered this question with a bow.

"I am the son of Lord Gaisford's steward," said Redfern, "my father betrayed the old Lord Gaisford, and gave him up as a Jacobite. The hall at Tillingham was seized, and in the affray both Lord and Lady Gaisford were killed. The daughter, Alice, was entrusted to the keeping of an old servant, on condition that he brought her up as his own child. My father had meant to claim the property, when it was forfeited to the crown, as his reward for betraying his master, but as Lord Gaisford was killed, and his son had been carried off by the priests, the attainder did not hold good. However, by forged documents my father managed to gain the estate, and afterwards the title of Baron Redfern. No one enquired into the matter, as most of the Gaisfords had had to fly with King James, so that my father had it all in his hands. But his crimes came heavy on him at last, as they do on me now, and he beseeched me to find out the children, and give them back the estates. I promised to do so, but inwardly determined never to part with them; and for that purpose never enquired who was the farmer that had charge of the girl. The boy I knew had been taken to St. Omer, and kept there by the Jesuit priests, whom my father bribed. I afterwards heard that he escaped, and joined some smugglers, and was either killed in a fight on the French coast, or was drowned. At all events, he only appeared once again, and that was at Tillingham, where he scanned my father's face, and nearly burned down the place. My breath fails me; give me some drink."

They handed him some wine; he drank, and continued.

"During my father's life, I married Maud Rainsford, my present wife. How I treated her, she can tell you, I have no breath to do it. All I can say is that it was base and cruel treatment. I found the

child of Lord Gaisford through an accident, and carried her off, after killing Farmer Landon, who had protected her. Alice Landon is the rightful owner of Tillingham. My time is growing short, I must be brief. One crime brings on another. I slew Lord Leslie, hoping to place the murder on the shoulders of Sir Arthur Bowring. I became the creature of that wretch, Jonathan Wild. I can say no more, gentlemen. Let me sign the deposition. This lady, Maud, is my wife, and there lies my son, whose hand struck the blow by which I die. This is all true, I swear."

Silently they handed him the deposition, to which he placed his signature.

He kissed his wife affectionately, and then fell back, never to speak again.

"This is a terrible history," whispered Major Jennings to Batswing.

"It is, indeed," replied our hero, "but one that must be kept a secret."

"It shall be," replied the Major, "but the boy, let us look at him."

They did so, and found that his spirit had also taken wing.

"God help us all," said Batswing, "this world is one of trouble."

Gently they led Maud from the chamber of death.

Deep was her grief, for, woman-like, she had forgotten all her sufferings, when she saw the man she had once adored, suffering and dying, and all her old love returned.

She then told them how Redfern had met her, wooed, and won her; but she was poor, and so he had declared the marriage false, that he might wed a wealthy bride. When she had come to London to try and claim her rights, he had taken her to Jonathan Wild's, who had imprisoned and treated her as we have already described.

She had discovered Flicker to be her son, through a birth mark, and, as the reader knows, the boy had been found in the Fleet, down which Jonathan Wild had imagined Maud had thrown him, but where really the baby had fallen when his mother had fainted.

"We have now all the proofs," said the magistrate; "but where is this Miss Landon, or, rather, I should say, Lady Gaisford?"

"Fear not, sir," said Batswing. "She shall be forthcoming at the proper time. All I ask you now is to be secret. When all is prepared I will send to you. Till then, gentlemen, receive my best thanks."

"Oh! Mr. Marvel, you may rely upon us," said the magistrate. "I will be as silent as a counsel who has had no fee, and my friend, the clergyman, as a church mouse. Ha, ha, ha! Good day, Mr. Marvel, I trust we shall have the pleasure of meeting soon."

"And what do you intend doing now?" asked the Major, when the others were gone.

"I shall return home," said Batswing, "for I have an appointment. But you must allow me to drop you at your place."

They jumped into the carriage, and drove to the Major's rooms.

"Remember," said Batswing, "silence until I bid you speak."

"On the honour of a gentleman and a soldier," replied the Major.

CHAPTER LXXVII.

ALICE BECOMES AN HEIRESS, A LADY OF TITLE, AND A WIFE.

ON his return home, Batswing retired to his room, and began examining some papers that Maud had given him privately, before he left Redfern's chamber. They were the proofs of Alice being the daughter of Lord Gaisford, Maud having found them amongst Wild's papers.

"Strange!" he muttered, "these proofs are quite sufficient to regain the estates and title of my father. No one can hold them now. Yet, if the King should turn against us. Why should he? Alice is a protestant, and Sir Arthur Bowring a staunch supporter of the government that is. Ah! but the estates are mine, and I was brought up by the Jesuits of St. Omer. George I. will never trust them to me. But I ask them not. They are for Alice, my sister; my own dear sister. Sister! I dare not tell her of our relationship; to her and to Sir Arthur I have had to confess that Percy Marvel and Batswing are one. Well, it must be so. In secret I will love her, and feel pride in knowing that she rules where my dear mother ruled; that her children shall play where I played, and the old Hall shall re-echo with their laughter. Hark! I hear a carriage drive up to the door; it is the Countess."

Hastily removing the papers from the table, he threw himself into a chair and waited patiently the Countess's arrival.

He had not long to wait, for in a minute a servant ushered in a lady so deeply veiled that it was impossible to see her features, but her fat figure showed it was the Countess.

The servant bowed in silence to Batswing, and retired.

"Ah! Countess," said Batswing, rising and taking the lady's hand, "this is indeed kind."

"Hush! for heaven's sake," cried the Countess. "Should some one hear us."

"Do not fear, my dear Countess. I have too many mysterious visitors for me to permit of even the chance of eavesdroppers. Be seated, Countess."

"None of your visitors are so mysterious as yourself," said the Countess.

"You flatter me," replied Batswing. "Can poor Percy Marvel be thought mysterious?"

"No one knows anything about you. You are wealthy, that is evident. You mix in the best society; but no one knows how you got your introductions. That you can tell the future, I have had good proofs. In a word, Mr. Marvel, you are the most mysterious person I ever knew."

"Be it so," laughed Batswing; "I am thankful that I have raised some interest in the fair bosom of the lovely Countess Sourkroutzenberg."

"But where have you been these last few days? I have sent for you constantly."

"I have been on your business," replied Batswing. "I sent for you directly I returned."

"But why did you not come to me?" asked the Countess, petulantly.

"Because I was too busy," replied Batswing, coolly; "besides, Countess, I am doing you a favour, therefore you must come to me."

"You are proud, Master Marvel," said the Countess, drawing herself up.

"I am," replied Batswing; "but now to business. I am, as you say, a mystery. Almost as much to myself as I am to others. I am a restless wanderer on the face of the earth, having but one pleasure, and that is to discover other people's secrets, and by my knowledge to help the distressed, and punish those who would crush them."

"You must have plenty of work to do," sneered the Countess.

"I have," replied Batswing, "and therefore have no time to waste. Now, in my travels I often met one Lord Redfern—a bad man. You knew him, my lady?"

"But slightly; his character was so bad that he was not encouraged at court."

"He must have been bad, indeed," said Batswing.

"Well, madam, I discovered that he wrongfully held an estate which belonged to a lady—one Alice Landon."

"What! the horrible wretch who killed the old farmer, her father," cried the Countess.

"Lord Redfern on his death-bed confessed that he killed Landon and tried to carry off Alice, so that there might be no claimant against him for the estates of Tillingham.

"Here, my lady, is his confession," said Batswing, producing the papers, "here also are the proofs of Alice's title to the estate, so that we can claim all by law. But law is a long and tedious course, I must have all this done quicker."

"How would you have it done?" demanded the Countess.

"The King must recognise Lady Alice, and declare that the estates of Tillingham are hers. Lady Alice must be presented at court and well received by the King."

"And who is to present this country girl?" demanded the Countess.

"You will!"

"Never!" cried the Countess. "I, the Countess of Sourkroutzenberg, introduce a peasant."

"Very well," said Batswing, coolly, "then the Duchess of Kendal will."

"Are you mad?" screamed the Countess; "you shall answer for this, sir."

"The Countess forgets that she is not in the royal favour just yet."

The Countess bit her lips with rage, for she knew too well that this was truth.

"This girl is young and pretty," she began.

"Yes; therefore the King will not notice her; his taste is not that way."

"Sir!"

"Madam, madam, I have had enough of this, and must ask you to speak business, or our interview is at an end. Either you or the Duchess of Kendal will present Lady Alice Gaisford at court, where the King shall publicly acknowledge her. His Majesty shall also grant her the estates wrongfully kept from her. There will be no dispute about it, for Lord Redfern's confession on his death-bed will stay that. I care not who presents the girl and gains the royal sanction, but this I know. The hand that presents Lady Alice shall hold the ring which his Majesty once gave to the Countess Sourkroutzenberg."

"What, you have it?" screamed the Countess. "Where is it?"

"Pardon me, I have it not," said Batswing; "but seeing the disastrous effects of your having lost the ring, I determined to regain it, so as to have you in my power. I knew you would never part with it willingly, and therefore concluded you had been robbed. Who could have robbed you? Batswing, and no other. I determined to see the fellow. I did so, and purchased, for ten thousand pounds, the king's favour. I shall get the ring when I have your written bond, either to pay me that amount, or do as I have asked you."

"And if I refuse?" demanded the Countess.

"Then I present the Duchess of Kendal with the ring, and a short history of how the fascinating Countess went to Drury Lane Theatre with a certain young chevalier, who afterwards robbed her of all her jewels. Now, Countess, what will you do?"

"Mr. Marvel, you are a devil!"

"Countess," replied Batswing, bowing low, "you are an angel."

"Give me the bond, I will sign it. But stay, this Batswing is dead—half the court have gone to Newgate to see the monster's body. How can you get the ring then?"

"The court does the body too much honour," said Batswing smiling, "but that matters not, the ring is in the keeping of a Jew, who will give it to me on payment of the sum mentioned. Now, Countess, will you sign?"

The Countess seized the pen, and signed the paper.

"The ring will be at your house to-morrow before nine," said Batswing, folding up the paper.

"Then I may send to the King to tell him that I will show him the ring."

"Yes; tell him you have got over your sulks, and cannot spare his royal presence any longer," replied Batswing, dryly; "with the ring I shall enclose a document for the King to sign; I shall expect to have that returned in the afternoon, with the requisite signature. I will also enclose you copies of the proofs, and of Redfern's confession. Do what I ask you, and I will purchase back a great part, if not all of your jewels. I am rich, and will not spare money."

"It shall be done," cried the Countess. "I suppose you will wed this fair girl."

"Pardon me, she is already engaged to a gentleman I respect as a brother."

"Indeed! May I ask his name?"

"Certainly—Sir Arthur Bowring, of Stavely Hall, Devonshire."

"What! the Sir Arthur whose pardon you made me procure from the King?"

"The same," replied Batswing, smiling and bowing.

"Master Marvel, you have played a deep game," said the Countess; "still, what you ask seems to be for good, therefore I will help you."

"Thanks for your disinterested kindness," replied Batswing. "One more favour I must ask; that is, that you stir up the King's mind against Jonathan Wild. If I fail to get back all your jewels, it will be *his* fault, for he is bidding for them, in hopes to gain the favour of the Duchess of Kendal."

"The wretch!" cried the Countess, "he shall die. I swear it. I engaged him to help me."

"There will be no want of evidence against him, for there is no crime he has not committed. Besides, public feeling is dead against him. Now, Countess, I will see you to your carriage."

Taking her hand, he led her to her carriage, and bowed to her as she drove away.

"Now for the Duchess," he muttered, as he returned to the room.

Taking some note paper, he wrote the following hasty note:—

"To her Grace the Duchess of Kendal,

"Your Grace,—It has just come to my knowledge that the Countess of Sourkroutzenberg will regain the King's favour—and this through the instrumentality of Jonathan Wild. Fear not, in a few months you will again be in the ascendant. I wish you to use your influence in favour of one Lady Alice Gaisford; for, although the Countess will favour her also, yet I would rely on you. Besides, it will keep you in favour with the King, who will be delighted to see you both asking the same thing. Trust in me, and I will serve you.—Yours,

"PERCY MARVEL."

He addressed the note, touched a bell, and directed the servant who answered the summons, to take the letter at once to the Duchess of Kendal.

"There," he said, closing his writing case, "if all goes well, Alice will be mistress of Tillingham in a week, and I—God knows where I shall be. But I must break the news to her."

With a wearied look and heavy tread he entered Alice's room.

He found the beautiful girl seated at chess with Arthur Bowring.

"At chess?" he laughed, leaning on the back of Alice's chair. "You have been playing a mimic warfare whilst I have been playing a real one."

"You have not been in danger?" cried Alice, starting up in alarm.

"No danger, fair sister," said Batswing, folding her in his arms.

"Sister!" cried Sir Arthur, in amaze.

"Sister—by adoption," sighed Batswing. "I have protected, saved her; therefore, when alone, I claim the title and rights of a brother—that is all. Come, I have much to tell you. Sit one on each side of me and listen."

They did as he bid them, and commenced:

"First of all, Sir Arthur, do you love this lady?"

"With all my heart and soul. You know I love her," cried Sir Arthur.

"And would you marry this poor and penniless country girl?"

"Directly I can clear my character from the stain that has been cast on it, Alice Landon shall become Lady Bowring. Oh! Master Marvel, whilst we have been your prisoners, I have spent such happy hours that I have determined to be a prisoner all my life, with Mistress Alice as my jailer."

"That is well," said Batswing. "Here, Sir Arthur, is your pardon from the King."

"You overwhelm me with gratitude, I—"

"Enough," said Batswing. "This lady is not poor. The estate at Tillingham, wrongfully held by Lord Redfern, is hers, and she is Lady Alice Gaisford. I hold the proofs, and in a few days she will have her property. I need no thanks. When she is mistress of Tillingham, then she shall marry, but not till then."

"We have too much to thank you for, not to obey you," said Alice.

"Adieu for the present, fair sister," said Batswing; "be always as good and true as you have been, and I shall be well rewarded."

He kissed her on the forehead, and then with a stifled sob, rushed from the room.

CHAPTER LXXVIII.
CONCLUSION.

IT was a fine morning in the month of June.

The sun burst through a golden mist, and sent its bright rays dancing along the tips of the wavelets, until they fell in a broad shower on the sands of Tillingham. Up, up, far in the air soared the lark, pouring down his rich music to cheer his mate on the nest.

The thrush and blackbird whistled in the hedgerow, the brown bees hummed drowsily, as they flew from flower to flower; the gaudy dragon-fly shot amidst the hedges.

All nature seemed teeming with happiness.

Tillingham Hall, too, how changed it is!

No longer a ruin, but a beautiful building, green with ivy—the growth of many years—its windows gleaming as if they were on fire as they reflect back the rays of the morning sun.

No longer does the old hall wear a look of sadness; it has a jolly, hospitable, healthy appearance, as all English country houses should have.

Listen to the church bells! what a flood of rich music they are pouring out from the old ivy-clad tower.

Oh! what a clash they make, as if the bells were running a race round the belfry, and now and then rushed together.

Those ringers must be broad-shouldered, jolly, red-faced men—a thin cadaverous man could never make such jovial music.

But see, the churchyard is full of the country people dressed in their Sunday best.

Now they take off their hats, and wave them in the air; and oh! what a shout.

There is a bridal party leaving the church. Who are the bride and bridegroom?

Why, Sir Arthur Bowring and Alice; behind them walk Batswing and Maud, and then come a load of people, all gaily dressed, and all looking happy.

Need we dwell on the wedding breakfast?

No; suffice it to say that it would have made a Lord Mayor's mouth water.

But it is not only in the hall that feasting is going on.

The lawn before the house is covered with a huge tent under which all the tenantry, or, in fact, all who like to come, are sumptuously regaled.

Surely that fellow at the head of the table is our friend the merry Smith, and that stout lady, the widow Wapshaw.

No, they were those persons, but now they are changed into Mr. and Mrs. Steven, host and hostess of the " Three Cutters " Inn, now called the "Tillingham Arms."

Lower down the table is Jerry Blinker with Maria Jackson, the girl he saved from the old hag in Drury Lane.

Oh! Jerry, Jerry, is it necessary that you should marry to reform?

In a word, many were the faces round the table, that had once been in Epping.

These good fellows had followed the fortune of their young master, and now that his sister, Lady Alice, had gained possession of the estates, they had returned to their own homes again.

What a cheer they gave when Percy Marvel—no longer Batswing—proposed Sir Arthur and Lady Bowring! It actually shook the weathercock on the clock tower.

It was drawing near the close of the day when Percy Marvel and Maud were about to say farewell, for they had determined to leave England for some years, if not for ever.

The last words had been said: tears rose to eyes that seldom had been moist before. The two self-exiled people stood at the door, about to depart, when a courier dashed up, and, inquiring for Percy Marvel, placed a dispatch in his hand.

He read it, and replied, " Get some refreshments : then take a fresh horse and gallop back to the Countess. Tell her that I will keep my promise. She shall have the rest of her jewels."

Then stepping out amidst the men on the lawn, who stood with sorrowful faces waiting to say farewell to him, he said in a loud clear voice :

" My men, I have kept my oath. Jonathan Wild was hanged this morning for receiving stolen goods. And now, my lads, farewell. I may see you again, and if I do, let me learn that you have been brave and honest servants to Lady Alice."

A hearty cheer was the response.

Jerry stepped up to Batswing, and touching his forelock, said :

" Can't I go with you, Cap'en? I'll serve you faithfully, that I will."

" No, Jerry, you must remain here and be happy. But tell me, Jerry, was it you who dressed that body up in my clothes in Wild's house?"

" Yes, Cap'en."

" Who was it?"

" That there fellow Croft."

" What made you do it?"

" I saw you were giving up the road, and I thought if the robins thought you were dead they would not trouble you, that's all."

Batswing smiled and slipped a heavy purse into the young fellow's hand.

But why ponder over the grief of separation? In a little time Maud and Batswing were on board the *Black Hawk*. The white sails were shaken out to the wind, and she sped away from old England.

As the ship disappeared the people returned to the Hall, but they cared not for dancing.

Their hearts were heavy, and many a one gazed seaward anxiously, praying a speedy return of their leader, Batswing.

THE END.

www.ingramcontent.com/pod-product-compliance
Lightning Source LLC
Chambersburg PA
CBHW08040250626
47161CB00009B/3130